BOOKS BY
ANTHONY POWELL

THE MUSIC OF TIME

A Question of Upbringing

A Buyer's Market

The Acceptance World

A Dance to the Music of Time

(A COLLECTION OF THE ABOVE THREE NOVELS)

At Lady Molly's

Casanova's Chinese Restaurant

The Kindly Ones

A Dance to the Music of Time: Second Movement

(A COLLECTION OF THE ABOVE THREE NOVELS)

The Valley of Bones

The Soldier's Art

The Military Philosophers

A Dance to the Music of Time: Third Movement

(A COLLECTION OF THE ABOVE THREE NOVELS)

Books Do Furnish a Room

Temporary Kings

Hearing Secret Harmonies

A Dance to the Music of Time: Fourth Movement

(A COLLECTION OF THE ABOVE THREE NOVELS)

OTHER NOVELS

Afternoon Men

Venusberg

From a View to a Death

Agents and Patients

What's Become of Waring

GENERAL

John Aubrey and His Friends

Brief Lives: And Other Selected Writings of John Aubrey

PLAYS

The Garden God and *The Rest I'll Whistle*

A Dance to the Music of Time

Fourth Movement

A Dance
to the Music of Time

Fourth Movement

BOOKS DO FURNISH A ROOM
TEMPORARY KINGS
HEARING SECRET HARMONIES

BY

Anthony Powell

★ ★ ★ ★

LITTLE, BROWN AND COMPANY
Boston *Toronto*

FIRST EDITION

T 04/76

LIBRARY OF CONGRESS CATALOGING IN PUBLICATION DATA

Powell, Anthony, 1905–
   A dance to the music of time, fourth movement.

    CONTENTS: Books do furnish a room.—Temporary kings.—Hearing secret harmonies.
   I. Title.
PZ3.P867Daq3   [PR6031.074]   823'.9'12   75-34418
ISBN 0-316-71548-4

PRINTED IN THE UNITED STATES OF AMERICA

A Dance to the Music of Time

Fourth Movement

Books do Furnish
a Room

for
Rupert

1

REVERTING TO THE UNIVERSITY AT forty, one immediately recaptured all the crushing melancholy of the undergraduate condition. As the train drew up at the platform, before the local climate had time to impair health, academic contacts disturb the spirit, a more imminent gloom was re-established, its sinewy grip in a flash making one young again. Depressive symptoms, menacing in all haunts of youth, were in any case easily aroused at this period, to be accepted as delayed action of the last six years. The odd thing was how distant the recent past had also become, the army now as stylized in the mind—to compare another triumphal frieze—as the legionaries of Trajan's Column, exercising, sacrificing, sweating at their antique fatigues, silent files on eternal parade to soundless military music. Nevertheless, shades from those days still walked abroad. Only a week before, the peak of a French general's khaki képi, breaking rather too abruptly through the winter haze of Piccadilly, had by conditioned reflex jerked my right hand from its overcoat pocket in preparation for a no longer consonant salute, counterfeiting the gesture of a deserter who has all but given himself away. A residuum of the experience was inevitable.

Meanwhile, traditional textures of existence were laboriously patched together in an attempt to reaffirm some sort of personal identity, however blurred. Even if—as some thought—the let-up were merely temporary, it was no less welcome, though the mood after the earlier conflict —summarized by a snatch Ted Jeavons liked to hum when in poor form—was altogether absent:

'Après la guerre,
There'll be a good time everywhere.'

That did not hinder looking forward to engrossment during the next few weeks amongst certain letters and papers deposited in the libraries here. Solitude would be a luxury after the congestions of wartime, archaic folios a soothing drug. War left, on the one hand, a passionate desire to tackle a lot of work: on the other, never to do any work again. It was a state of mind Robert Burton— about whom I was writing a book—would have well understood. Irresolution appealed to him as one of the myriad forms of Melancholy, although he was, of course, concerned in the main with no mere temporary depression or fidgetiness, but a 'chronic or continued disease, a settled humour'. Still, post-war melancholy might have rated a short sub-section in the great work:

THE ANATOMY OF MELANCHOLY
What it is, with all the Kindes, Causes, Symptomes,
Prognostickes, and severall cures of it. Three Maine Partitions
with their severall Sections, Members and Sub-sections,
Philosophically, Medicinally, Historically, Opened and cut up
by Democritus Junior. With a Satyricall Preface, conducing to
the following Discourse. Anno Dom. 1621.

The title page showed not only Burton's own portrait in ruff and skull cap, but also figures illustrative of his theme; love-madness; hypochondriasis; religious melancholy. The emblems of jealousy and solitude were there too, together with those sovereign cures for melancholy and madness, borage and hellebore. Burton had long been a favourite of mine. A study of him would be a change from writing novels. The book was to be called *Borage and Hellebore*.

As the forlorn purlieus of the railway-station end of the town gave place to colleges, reverie, banal if you like, though eminently Burtonesque, turned towards the relatively high proportion of persons known pretty well at an earlier stage of life, both here and elsewhere, now dead, gone off their rocker, withdrawn into states of existence they—or I—had no wish to share. The probability was that even without cosmic upheaval some kind of reshuffle has to take place halfway through life, a proposition borne out by the autobiographies arriving thick and fast —three or four at a time at regular intervals—for review in one of the weeklies. At this very moment my bag was weighed down by several of these volumes, to be dealt with in time off from the seventeenth century: *Purged Not in Lethe . . . A Stockbroker in Sandals . . . Slow on the Feather . . . Moss off a Rolling Stone . . .* chronicles of somebody or other's individual fate, on the whole unenthralling enough, except insomuch as every individual's story has its enthralling aspect, though the essential pivot was usually omitted or obscured by most autobiographers.

However, nearly all revealed, if not explicitly in every case, a similar reorientation towards the sixth climacteric, their narrative supporting, on the whole, evidence already noticeably piling up, that friends, if required at all in the manner of the past, must largely be reassembled at about this milestone. The changeover might improve consistency, even quality, but certainly lost in intimacy; anyway that peculiar kind of intimacy that is consoling when you are young, though probably too vulnerable to withstand the ever increasing self-regard of later years.

Accommodation was in college. The place looked much the same as ever. Only one porter, his face unfamiliar, was

3

on duty at the lodge. After studying a list for a long time, he signified a distant staircase for the rooms allotted. The traditional atmosphere, tenuously poised between a laxly run boarding-school and seedy residential club, now leant more emphatically towards the former type of institution. The rooms, arctic as of old, evidently belonged to a fairly austere young man, whose only picture was an unframed photograph of a hockey team. It stood curling on the mantelpiece. In the bookcase, a lot of works on economics terminated with St John Clarke's *Dust Thou Art*, rather a recondite one about the French Revolution, which might be pleasurable to reassess critically. I pushed on into the bedroom. Here a crisis declared itself. The bed was unmade. Only a sombrely stained blue-grey mattress, folded in three, lay on the rusty wires of the frame. Back at the porter's lodge, the inconceivable difficulties of remedying lack of bedclothes at this hour were radically discussed. Later, in hall, a few zombie-like figures collected together to consume a suitably zombie-sustaining repast.

This was the opening of a routine of days in the library, nights collating notes, the monotony anodyne. One became immediately assimilated with other dim, disembodied, unapproachable entities, each intent on his own enigmatic preoption, who flit through the cobbled lanes and gothic archways of a university in vacation. It was what Burton himself called 'a silent, sedentary, solitary private life', and it well suited me during the middle of the week. For weekends, I returned to London. Once Killick, a hearty rugby-playing philosophy don of my college, now grunting and purple, came bustling up the street, a pile of books under his arm, and I accosted him. There were explanations. Killick issued an abstracted invitation to dinner. The following week, when I turned up, it was to be told Professor Killick had gone to Manchester to give two lectures. This oversight hardly came as a sur-

4

prise. In a city of shadows, appointments were bound to be kept in a shadowy fashion.

At the same time something very different, something perfectly substantial, not shadowy at all, lay ahead as not to be too long postponed, even if a latent unwillingness to face that fact might delay taking the plunge. A moral reckoning had to be discharged. As the days passed, the hypnotic pull to pay a call on Sillery grew increasingly strong, disinclination—that was, of course, far too strong a word, indeed not the right word at all—scarcely lessening, so much as the Sillery magnetism itself gathering force. Pretendedly heedless enquiries revealed that, although retired for some time from all administrative duties in his own college, Sillery still retained his old rooms, receiving visitors willingly, even avidly, it was reported, with so far as possible the traditional elements of welcome.

To enter Sillery's sitting-room after twenty years was to drive a relatively deep fissure through variegated seams of Time. The faintly laundry-cupboard odour, as one came through the door, generated in turn the taste of the rock-buns dispensed at those tea-parties, their gritty indeterminate flavour once more dehydrating the palate. The props round about designed for Sillery's nightly performance remained almost entirely unaltered. Eroded loose-covers of immemorially springless armchairs still precariously endured; wide perforations frayed long since in the stretch of carpet before the door, only a trifle more hazardous to the unwary walker. As might be expected, the framed photographs of jaunty young men had appreciably increased, several of the new arrivals in uniform, one in a turban, two or three American.

In this room, against this background, Sillery's machinations, such as they were, had taken shape for half a century. Here a thousand undergraduate attitudes had been penitentially acted out. Youth, dumb with embarrassment,

5

breathless with exhibitionism, stuttering with nerves, inarticulate with conceit; the socially flamboyant, the robustly brawny, the crudely uninstructed, the palely epicene; one and all had obediently leapt through the hoop at Sillery's ringmaster behest; one and all submitted themselves to the testing flame of this burning fiery furnace of adolescent experience. Such concepts crowded in only after a few minutes spent in the room. At the moment of entry no more was to be absorbed than the fact that another guest had already arrived, to whom Sillery, with much miming and laughter, was narrating an anecdote. Any immediate responses on my own part were cut short at once, for Sillery, as if ever on his guard against possible assassination, sprang from his chair and charged forward, ready to come to grips with any assailant.

'Timothy? . . . Mike? . . . Cedric? . . .'

'Nick—'

'Carteret-Owen? . . . Jelf? . . . Kniveton? . . .'

'Jenkins—how are you, Sillers?'

'So you've come all the way from New South Wales, Nick?'

'I—'

'No—of course— you were appointed to that headmastership after all, Nick?'

'It's—'

'I can see you haven't quite recovered from that head wound . . .'

The question of identification was finally established with the help of the other caller, who turned out to be Short, a member of Sillery's college a year senior to myself. Short had been not only a great supporter of Sillery's tea-parties, but also vigorously promulgated Sillery's reputation as—Short's own phrase— a 'power in the land'. We had known each other as undergraduates, continued to keep up some sort of an acquaintance in early London days, then drifted into different worlds. I had last heard his name, though never run across him, during the war when Short had been working in the Cabinet Office, with which my War Office Section had occasional dealings. He had probably transferred there temporarily from his own Ministry, because he had entered another branch of the civil service on leaving the University.

Short's demeanour, now a shade more portentous, more authoritarian, retained, like the sober suit he wore, the same consciously buttoned-up character. This mild, well-behaved air concealed a good deal of quiet obstinacy, a reasonable amalgam of malice. Always of high caste in his profession, now almost a princeling, he stemmed nevertheless from the same bureaucratic ancestry as a mere tribesman like Blackhead, prototype of all the race of *fonctionnaires*, and, anthropologically speaking, might be expected to revert to the same atavistic obstructionism if roused.

Sillery, moustache a shade more ragged and yellow, blue bow tie with its white spots, more likely than ever to fall undone, was not much changed either. Perhaps illusorily, his body and face had shrunk, physical contraction giving him a more simian look than formerly, though of no ordinary monkey; Brueghel's Antwerp apes (admired by Pennistone) rather than the Douanier's homely denizens of *Tropiques*, which Soper, the Divisional Catering Officer, had resembled. Even the real thing, Maisky, defunct pet of the Jeavonses, could not compare with Sillery's devastating monkeylike shrewdness. So strong was this impression of metempsychosis that he seemed about to bound up on to the bookcases, scattering the photographs of handsome young men, and pile of envelopes (the top one addressed to the Home Secretary) as he landed back on the table. He looked in glowing health. No one had ever pronounced with certainty on the subject of Sillery's age.

7

Year of birth was omitted in all books of reference. He was probably still under eighty.

'Sit down, Nick, sit down. Leonard and I were talking of an old friend—Bill Truscott. Remember Bill? I'm sure you do. Of course he was a wee bit older than you both'— Sillery had now perfectly achieved his chronological bearings—'but not very much. These differences get levelled out in the sands of time. They do indeed. Going to do great things was Bill. Next Prime Minister but three. We all thought so. No use denying it, is there, Leonard?'

Short smiled a temperate personal acquiescence that could not at the same time be interpreted for a moment as in any way committing his Department.

'Wrote some effective verse too,' said Sillery. 'Even if it was a shade derivative. Mark Members always sneered at Bill as a poet, even when he respected him as a coming man. Rupert Brooke at his most babbling, Mark used to say, Housman at his most lad-ish. Mark's always so severe. I told him so when he was here the other day addressing one of the undergraduate societies. You know Mark's hair's gone snow white. Can't think what happened to cause that, he's always taken great care of himself. Rather becoming, all the same. Gives just that air of distinction required by the passing of youth—and nobody got more out of being a professional young man than Mark when the going was good. He was talking of his old friend—*our* old friend— J. G. Quiggin. JG's abandoned the pen, I hear, perhaps wisely. A literary caesarean was all but required for that infant of long gestation *Unburnt Boats*, which I often feared might come to birth prematurely as a puling little magazine article. Now JG's going to promote literary works rather than write them himself. In brief, he's to become a publisher.'

'So I heard,' said Short. 'He's starting a new firm called Quiggin & Craggs.'

8

'To think I used to sit on committees with Howard Craggs discussing arms embargoes for Bolivia and Paraguay,' said Sillery. 'Sounds like an embargo on arms for the Greeks and Trojans now. Still, I read a good letter from Craggs the other day in one of the papers about the need for Socialists and Communists hammering out a common programme of European reconstruction.'

'Craggs was a temporary civil servant during the war,' said Short. 'Rationing paper, was it? Something of the sort.'

'That was when JG made himself useful as caretaker at Boggis & Stone,' said Sillery. 'I expect that explains why JG dresses like a partisan now, a man straight from the *maquis*, check shirts, leather jackets, ankle-boots. "Well, Quiggin's always been in the forefront of the Sales Resistance where clothes were concerned." That was Brightman's comment. "Even if he did live 'reservéd and austere' during hostilities—'reservéd' anyway." We all enjoy Brightman's rather cruel wit. Brightman and I are buddies now, by the way, all forgiven and forgotten. Besides, I expect JG's circumscribed by lack of clothing coupons. All right for such as me, still wearing the suit I bought for luncheon with Mr Asquith at Downing Street before the Flood, but then it was a good piece of cloth to start off with, not like those sad old reach-me-downs of JG's we're all so familiar with. No doubt they disintegrated under the stress of war conditions. Why not ankle-boots, forsooth? I'd be glad of a pair myself in winter here.'

Sillery paused. He seemed to feel he had allowed himself to rattle on rather too disconnectedly, at the same time could not remember what exactly had been the subject in hand. Like a conjuror whose patter for a specific trick has become misplaced, he had to go back to the beginning again.

'We were talking of Bill Truscott and his verse. I expect

9

Bill has abandoned the Muse now, though you never know. It's a hard habit to break. Would you believe it, I produced a slim volume myself when a young man? Did you know that, either of you? Suggested the influence of Coventry Patmore, so the pundits averred. I suppose most of us think of ourselves as poets at that age. No harm done. Well, that shouldn't be such a bad job at the Coal Board for Bill, if things are constituted as you prophesy, Leonard. Once Bill's been well and truly inducted there, he should be safe for a lifetime.'

Again Short allowed polite agreement to be inferred, without prejudice to official discretion, or additional evidence that might be subsequently revealed.

'But what mysterious mission brings you to our academic altars, Nick? We don't even know what you are doing these days. Back writing those novels of yours? I expect so. I used to hear something of your activities when you were a gallant soldier looking after those foreign folk. You know what an interest I take in old friends. Leonard and I were just speaking of poor Prince Theodoric, who was once going to perform all sorts of benefits for us here, endow scholarships and whatnot. Donners-Brebner was to co-operate, Sir Magnus Donners having interests in those parts. Now, alas, the good Prince is in exile, Sir Magnus gathered to his fathers. The University will never see any of those lovely scholarships. But we must march with the times. There's a new spirit abroad in Prince Thedoric's country, and, whatever people may say, there's no doubt about Marshal Stalin's sincerity in desire for a good-neighbour policy, if the West allows it. What I wrote to *The Times*. Those Tolland relations of yours, Nick? That unsatisfactory boy Hugo, how is he?'

I dealt with these personal matters as expeditiously as possible, explaining my purpose in staying at the University.

'Ah, Burton?' said Sillery. 'An interesting old gentleman, I've no doubt. Many years since I looked into the *Anatomy*.'

That was undoubtedly true. Sillery was not a great reader. He was also wholly incurious about the byways of writing, indeed not very approving of writing at all, unless books likely to make a splash beyond mere literary consideration, of which there was no hope here. He abandoned the subject, satisfied apparently that the motive alleged was not designed to conceal some less pedestrian, more controversially viable activity, and the unexciting truth had been told. A pause in his talk, never an opportunity to be missed, offered a chance, the first one, of congratulating him on the peerage conferred in the most recent Honours List. Sillery yelled with laughter at such felicitations.

'Ain't it absurd?' he shouted. 'As you'll have guessed, my dear Nick, I didn't want the dratted thing at all. Not in the least. But it looked unmannerly to refuse. Doesn't do to look unmannerly. Literal case of *noblesse oblige*. So there it is. A Peer of the Realm. Who'd have prophesied that for crude young Sillers, that happy-go-lucky little fellow, in the days of yore? It certainly gave some people here furiously to think. Ah, the envies and inhumanities of the human heart. You wouldn't believe. I keep on telling the college servants to go easy with all that my-lording. Makes me feel as if I was acting in Shakespeare. They will have it, good chaps that they are. Fact is they seem positively to enjoy addressing their old friend in that majestic way, revel in it even. Strange but true. Genuinely glad to see old Sillers a lord. Ah, when you're my age, dear men, you'll know what an empty thing is worldly success and human ambition—but we mustn't say that to an important person like Leonard, must we, Nick? And of course I don't want to seem ungrateful to the staunch movement that ennobled me, of which I remain the most loyal of supporters. Indeed, we've just been talking of some of Labour's young lions, for Leonard has forgone his former Liberal allegiances in favour of Mr Attlee and his merry men.'

'Of course, as a civil servant, I'm strictly speaking neutral,' said Short primly. 'I was merely talking with Sillers of my present Minister's PPS, who happens to live in the same block of flats as myself—one Kenneth Widmerpool. You may have come across him.'

'I have—and saw he got in at a by-election some months ago.'

'This arose from speaking of Bill Truscott and his troubles,' said Sillery. 'I was telling Leonard how I always marvelled at the quietly dextrous way Mr Widmerpool had poor Bill sacked from Donners-Brebner, just at the moment Bill thought himself set for big things. Between you and me, I would myself have doubted whether Bill offered serious rivalry by that time, but, extinct volcano or not, Widmerpool accepted him as a rival, and got rid of him. It was done in the neatest manner imaginable. That was where the rot set in so far as Bill was concerned. Put him on the downward path. He never recovered his status as a coming man. All this arose because I happened to mention to Leonard that Mr Widmerpool had written to me about joining a society—in fact two societies, one political, one cultural—to cement friendship with the People's Republic where Theodoric's family once held sway.'

'I ran across Widmerpool when I was on loan to the Cabinet Office from my own Ministry,' said Short. 'We first met when I was staying in the country one weekend with a person of some import. I won't mention names, but say no more than that the visit was one of work rather than play. Widmerpool came down on Sunday about an official matter, bringing some highly secret papers with him. We played a game of croquet in the afternoon as a slight relaxation. I always remember how Widmerpool kept his briefcase under his arm—he was in uniform, of course—throughout the game. He nearly won it, in spite of that. Our host joked with him about his high regard for security, but Widmerpool would not risk losing his papers, even when he made his stroke.'

Sillery rocked himself backwards and forwards in silent enjoyment.

'A very capable administrator,' said Short. 'Of course one can't foretell what prospects such a man can have on the floor of the House. He may not necessarily be articulate in those very special surroundings. I've heard it suggested Widmerpool is better in committee. His speeches are inclined to alienate sympathy. Nevertheless, I am disposed to predict success.'

Neither of them would listen to assurances that I had known Widmerpool for years, which had indeed no particular relevance to his election to the House of Commons some little time before this. The event had taken place while I was myself still submerged in the country, getting through my army gratuity. At the time, Widmerpool's arrival in Parliament seemed just another of the many odd things taking place roundabout, no concern of mine after reading of it in the paper. Back in London, occupied with sorting out the débris, physical and moral, with which one had to contend, Widmerpool's political fortunes—like his unexpected marriage to Pamela Flitton—had been forgotten in attempts to warm up, as it were, charred fragments left over from the pre-war larder.

'He'd probably have become a brigadier had hostilities continued,' said Short. 'I'm not at all surprised by the course he's taken. At one moment, so he told me, he had ambitions towards a colonial governorship—was interested in those particular problems—but Westminster opens wider fields. The question was getting a seat.'

Sillery dismissed such a doubt as laughable for a man of ability.

'Elderly trade unionists die, or reap the reward of years of toil by elevation to the Upper House—better merited, I add in all humility, than others I could name. The miners can spare a seat from their largesse, those hardy crofters of Scotland show a canny instinct for the right candidate.'

'Between ourselves, I was able to do a little liaison work in the early stages,' said Short. 'That was after return to my old niche. I'd been told there was room for City men who'd be sensibly co-operative, especially if of a Leftward turn to start. Widmerpool's attitude to Cheap Money made him particularly eligible.'

'Cheap Money! Cheap Money!'

The phrase seemed to ravish Sillery by its beauty. He continued to repeat it, like the pirate's parrot screeching 'Pieces of eight', while he clenched his fist in the sign of the old Popular Front.

Then suddenly Sillery's manner changed. He began to rub his hands together, a habit that usually indicated the launching of one of his anti-personnel weapons, some explosive item of information likely to be brought out with damaging effect to whoever had just put forward some given view. Short, still contemplating Widmerpool's chances, showed no awareness that danger threatened.

'I don't think he'll be a back-bencher long,' he said. 'That's my view.'

Sillery released the charge.

'What about his wife?'

After that question Sillery paused in one of his most characteristic attitudes, that of the Chinese executioner who has so expertly severed a human head from the neck that it remains still apparently attached to the victim's shoulders, while the headsman himself flicks an infinitesimal, all but invisible, speck of blood from the razor-sharp blade of his sword. Short coughed. He gave the impression of being surprised by a man of such enlightened intelligence as Sillery asking that.

'His wife, Sillers?'

Short employed a level requisitive tone, suggesting he had indeed some faint notion of what was behind the enquiry, but it was one scarcely worthy of answer. There could be little doubt that, in so treating the matter, Short was playing for time.

'You can't close your ears to gossip in this University, however much you try,' said Sillery. 'It's rampant, I regret to say. Even at High Table in this very college. Besides, it's always wise to know what's being bruited abroad, even if untrue.'

He rubbed his hands over and over again, almost doubling up with laughter.

'I haven't the pleasure of knowing Mrs Widmerpool so well as her husband,' said Short severely. 'We sometimes see each other where we both live, in the hall or in the lift. I understand the Widmerpools are to move from there soon.'

'Comely,' said Sillery. 'That's what I've been told— comely.'

He was more convulsed than ever.

'Certainly, certainly,' allowed Short. 'She is generally agreed to be good looking. I should myself describe her as a little—'

Short's power to define feminine beauty abandoned him at this point. He simply made a gesture with his hand. Unmarried himself, he spoke as if prepared to concede that good looks in a wife, anyway the wife of a public man, might reasonably be regarded as a cause for worry.

'I expect she'll make a good canvasser, an admirable canvasser.'

Sillery rocked.

'Sillers, what are you getting at?'

Short spoke quite irritably. I laughed.

'I see Nick knows what I mean,' said Sillery.

'What does Nick know?'

'I met her during the war, when she was called Pamela Flitton. She was an ATS driver.'

'What's your story, Sillers? I see you must have a story.'

Short spoke in a tone intended to put a stop to frivolous treatment of what had been until then a serious subject, Widmerpool's career. Being in the last resort rather afraid of Sillery, he was clearly not too sure of his ground. No doubt even Short had heard rumours, however muffled, of Pamela's goings-on. Sillery decided to play with him a little longer.

'My information about Mrs Widmerpool brought in a few picturesque details, Leonard. Just a few picturesque details—I say no more than that. I call her young Mrs Widmerpool because I understand she is appreciably junior to her spouse.'

'Yes, she's younger.'

'The name of a certain MP on the Opposition benches has been mentioned as a frequent escort of hers.'

'By whom?'

'I happen to have a friend who knows Mrs W quite well.'

Sillery sniggered. Short pursed his lips.

'A man?'

The question seemed just worth asking.

'No, Nick, not a man. A young lady. You didn't think an old fogey like me knew any young ladies, did you? You were quite wrong. This little friend of mine happens also to be a friend of Mrs Widmerpool—so you see I am in a strong position to hear about her doings.'

Sillery's own sexual tastes had, of course, been endlessly debated by generations of undergraduates and dons. It was generally agreed that their physical expression was never further implemented than by a fair amount of arm-pinching and hair-rumpling of the young men with whom he was brought in contact; not necessarily even the better-looking ones, if others had more substantial assets to offer in the power world. More ardent indiscretions charged against him had either no basis, or were long forgotten in the mists of the past. Certainly he was held never to have taken the smallest physical interest in a woman, although at the same time in no way setting his face against all truck with the opposite sex. Sillery's attitude might in this respect be compared with the late St John Clarke's, both equally appreciative of invitations from ladies of more or less renowned social status and usually mature age; 'hostesses', in short, now an extinct species, though destined to rise again like Venus from a sea of logistic impediment. Accordingly, Sillery was right to suppose his boast would cause surprise. The scandal-mongering female friend would probably turn out to be a young married woman, I thought, the wife of a don. Before Sillery had time further to develop his theme, from which he showed signs of deriving a lot of pleasure in the form of teasing Short, a knock sounded on the door.

'Come in, come in,' cried Sillery indulgently. 'Who is this to be? What a night for visitors. Quite like old times.'

He must have expected another version of Short or myself to enter the room. If so, he made a big mistake. A far more dramatic note was struck; dramatic, that is, for those used to the traditional company to be met in Sillery's rooms, also in the light of his words immediately before. A young woman, decidedly pretty, peeped in. Leaning on the door knob, she smiled apologetically, registering a diffidence not absolutely convincing.

'I'm sorry, Sillers. I see you're engaged. I'll come round in the morning. I'd quite thought you'd be alone.'

This was certainly striking confirmation of Sillery's boast that he had contacts with young women. However, its corroboration in this manner did not seem altogether to please him. For once, a rare thing, he appeared uncertain how best to deal with this visitor: dismiss her, retain her. He grinned, but with a sagging mouth. The intrusion posed a dilemma. Short looked embarrassed too, indeed went quite pink. Then Sillery recovered himself. 'Come in, Ada, come in. You've arrived at just the right moment. We all need the company of youth.'

Irresolution, in any case observable only to those accustomed to the absolute certainty of decision belonging to Sillery's past, had only been momentary. Now he was himself again, establishing by these words that, for all practical purposes, there was no difference between his own age and that of Short and myself, anyway so far as 'Ada' was concerned. He settled down right away to get the last ounce out of this new puppet, if puppet she were. The girl was in her twenties, fair, with a high colour, a shade on the plump side, though only enough to suggest changes in the female figure then pending.

'I didn't want to disturb you, Sillers. I didn't really, but I'm almost sure you gave me the wrong notebook yesterday. There were two years missing at least.'

Her manner, self-possessed, was also forthcoming. She smiled round at all of us, not at all displeased at finding unexpected company in Sillery's rooms. It looked as if some twist of post-war academic administration had committed Sillery to aspects of tutoring that included the women's colleges. In the old days that would have been much against all his known principles, but changed conditions, possibly in the line of post-graduate courses, might have brought about some such revolutionary situation in the University as now constituted.

'Two years missing?' said Sillery. 'That will never do,

Ada, that will never do, but I must introduce you to two old friends of mine. Mr Short, one of our most cultivated and humane of bureaucrats, and Mr Jenkins who is—you just explained to me, Nick, but I can't recall for the minute —no, no, don't tell me, I'll remember in a second—come here to do some research of a very scholarly kind, something he is planning to write—Burton, yes, Burton, melancholy and all that. This is Miss Leintwardine, my—well—my secretary. That's what you are, Ada, ain't you? Sounds rather fast. All sorts of jokes about us, I'm sure. Sit 'ee down, Ada, sit 'ee down. I'll look into your complaints forthwith.'

Miss Leintwardine took a chair. Clearly well used to Sillery's ways and diction, she accepted this presentation of herself as all part of the game. In the role of secretary she was a little more explicable, though why on earth Sillery should require a secretary was by no means apparent. Perhaps a secretary went with being made a peer. Whatever it was, he now retired to a corner of the room, where, lowering himself on to the floor, he squatted on the worn carpet, while he began to rummage about amongst a lot of stuff stored away in the bottom of a cupboard. All the time he kept up a stream of comment.

'What a way to preserve sacred memories. Isn't that just like me? Might be a lot of old boots for all the trouble I've taken. Nineteen-eight . . . nineteen-four . . . here we are, I think, here we are.'

Miss Leintwardine, who had sat down as requested, showed willingness to make herself agreeable by a laudatory reference to a novel I had written before the war. She was about to expand her views on this subject, but, whatever other modifications had taken place in Sillery's approach, tolerance of his guests' books being discussed in front of him was not among them. Sillery's enemies were inclined to imply that aversion to other people writing was the fruit of pure envy, but it was much more probable that talk about 'writing' simply bored him, unless arousing a sense of conflict. He began a loud confused monologue to put a stop to all other conversation, then suddenly found what he sought, closed the cupboard and rose without effort, holding two or three tattered exercise books. He cast these on the table.

'Here they are. I don't know what I can have been thinking about, Ada. Was it the nineteen-twelve volume I gave you? Let me have a look. Ah, no, I think I understand now. This is supplementary. Ada's helping me get my old diaries in order. Not only typing them, but giving me her valuable—I should say invaluable—advice. I'm pleading as a suppliant before the inexorable tribunal of Youth. That's what it comes to. Don't know what I'd do without her. I'd be lost, wouldn't I, Ada?'

'You certainly would, Sillers.'

'Diaries?' said Short. 'I didn't know you kept a diary, Sillers?'

Sillery, laughing heartily, lowered himself again into a vast collapsed armchair in which he lay crouched.

'Nobody did, nobody did. Strict secret. Of course it's possible nothing will appear until old Sillers is dead and gone. That's no reason why the diaries shouldn't be put in proper order. Then perhaps a few selections might be published. Who can tell until Ada has done her work—and who should help make the decision better than Ada?'

'But, Sillers, they'll be absolutely . . .'

Short was again without words. Only an ingrained professional habit of avoiding superlatives, so he implied, prevented him from giving more noisy expression to welcome a Journal kept by Sillery.

'You've met *everybody*, Sillers. They'll be read as the most notable chronicle of our time.'

Sillery made no attempt to deny that judgment. He

screwed up his eyes, laughed a great deal, blew out his moustache. Miss Leintwardine took up the exercise books from the table. She glanced through them with cold professional competence.

'That's better, Sillers. These are the ones. I'd better bear them away with me.'

She rose from the chair, smiling, friendly, about to leave. Sillery held up his right hand, as if to swear a solemn oath.

'Stay, Ada. Stay and talk with us a while. You must meet people younger than myself sometimes, eligible bachelors like Mr Short. By the way, these gentlemen are contemporaries of another friend of ours, Mark Members, whom you talked of when he was up the other day lecturing on whatever it was. He's left the Ministry of Information now.'

'*Kleist, Marx, Sartre, the Existentialist Equilibrium.*'

'Of course,' said Sillery.' One of Vernon Gainsborough's *jeux d'esprit.* I can't remember, Leonard, whether you've met our latest Fellow. He's a German—or rather was—a "good" German, of course, called Werner Guggenbühl, but Gainsborough's better, we all agree. Of patrician background, but turned early to the Left.'

'You're interested in German literature, Miss Leintwardine?' asked Short.

He must have hoped to gloss over Sillery's rather malicious reference to 'eligible bachelors', but notably failed in this attempt to guide conversation into intellectual channels.

'We were talking of old friends like Mark,' said Sillery. 'J. G. Quiggin, Bill Truscott, all names with which you are familiar from my reminiscing, Ada. Conversation led from them to that interesting couple the Widmerpools, about whom you were speaking when we last met. How goes that union? Well, I hope.'

These last sentences put an end to doubt, explaining Sillery's momentary uncertainty at Ada Leintwardine's arrival. He was well satisfied at the surprise she caused, the confirmation by her presence that he numbered 'young ladies' amongst his acquaintance, but at the same time he had been faced with the decision whether or not to reveal her as his source of Widmerpool information. It was in the Sillery tradition to brag of a great spy network, while keeping secret the names of individual agents. At the same time, with an audience like Short and myself, fullest advantage might be derived from Miss Leintwardine by admitting her as fount of that information, now she was on the spot. That at any rate was what happened. Sillery had decided the veil of mystery was not worth sustaining, especially as Miss Leintwardine herself might at any moment give the show away. However, it turned out she was well aware that contacts with the Widmerpool ménage were too profitable to be squandered in casual enquiry. She was giving nothing away that evening. This attitude was probably due also to other matters connected with her relationship with Sillery which only came to light some minutes later.

'They're both all right so far as I know, Sillers.'

'Leonard here lives in the same block of flats.'

'Oh, do you?'

She spoke politely, no more.

'You were saying Mrs W finds the place rather poky,' persisted Sillery.

Miss Leintwardine did not choose to answer that one. Instead, she addressed herself to me.

'I think you know Pam and Kenneth, Mr Jenkins. They spoke of you. Like so many people, Pam's been having rather a painful reaction now the war's over. Tired, I mean, and listless. Always ill. We've been friends since we were in the ATS together.'

'She was a driver in the ATS when I first met her.'

'Then we both went into secret shows, different ones,

22

and always kept in touch—but for God's sake don't let's talk about the war. Such a boring subject.'

Sillery shouted assent to that, showing distinct signs of displeasure at this interchange. What was the good of presenting Ada Leintwardine as a woman of mystery, if she shared a crowd of acquaintances in common with another guest? Besides, long experience of extracting information out of people must have warned him she was not prepared to furnish anything of great interest that evening, unless matters took an unexpected turn. Grasp of the fact was to Sillery's credit, in some degree justifying the respect paid him in such traffickings by Short and others. He rose once more from his chair, again throwing himself to the floor with surprising suppleness of movement, to scrabble further at the stuff in the cupboard.

'You're sure you've got the right notebooks now, Ada? I'm putting away the ones you brought back, ere worse befall. Don't want to lose them, do we?'

Miss Leintwardine chose this moment of Sillery's comparative detachment on the floor to announce something probably intended to take a less abrupt form. Possibly she had even paid the visit for this purpose, the diaries only an excuse. Since she had not found Sillery alone, she had to take the best opportunity available.

'Talking of J. G. Quiggin, you've heard about this new publishing firm of his?'

She spoke rather self-consciously. Sillery, swivelling round where he squatted orientally on a hole in the carpet, was attentive to this.

'Have you any piquant details, Ada? I should like to know more of JG's publishing venture.'

'I'm rather committed myself. Perhaps you heard that too, Sillers?'

Whatever this meant, clearly Sillery had not heard. He sat up sharply. Miss Leintwardine's manner of asking the

23

question strongly suggested he had been given no opportunity to hear anything of the sort.

'How so, Ada?'

'As it happens, I'm joining the firm myself. I've been reading manuscripts for them since they started. I thought I told you.'

'No, Ada, no. You never told me.'

'I thought I had.'

This showed Sillery in the plainest terms he was not the only one to discharge bombshells. He took it pretty well, though there could be no doubt he was shaken. His eyes showed that.

'Craggs brought in the goodwill of Boggis & Stone, together with such Left Wing steadies as survive. Of course the new firm won't be nearly so limited as Boggis & Stone. We're hoping to get the young writers. We've signed up X. Trapnel, for example.'

She spoke all this quickly, more than a little embarrassed, even upset, at having to break the news to Sillery. He did not say anything. She continued in the same hurried tone.

'I was wondering whether the possibility wasn't worth exploring for publication of your own Journal, Sillers. You haven't decided on a publisher yet, have you? There's often something to be said for new and enterprising young firms.'

Sillery did not pledge himself on that point.

'Does this mean you're going to live in London, Ada?'

'I suppose so, Sillers. I can't very well commute from here. Of course it won't make any difference to my work for you. I shall always have time for that. I do think it should be an interesting job, don't you?'

Again Sillery made no pronouncement on such expectations. His face provisionally suggested that the future for those entering publishing offices was anything but optimistic. There could be no doubt the whole matter was intensely displeasing to him. His annoyance, together with Miss

Leintwardine's now very definitely troubled manner, confirmed that in a peculiar way they must have been having some sort of flirtation, an hypothesis scarcely to be guessed by even the most seasoned Sillery experts. The girl's nervousness, now confession had been made, well illustrated that odd contradictory feminine lack of assurance so typical of the moment when victory has been won—for there could be little doubt that progression on to the staff of Quiggin & Craggs represented a kind of victory over Sillery on her part, escape from his domination. It looked as if she had half dreaded telling him, half hoped to cause him to suffer. Sillery had been made the object of a little affectionate feminine sadomasochism. That was the grotesque presumption. She jumped up.

'I must go now, Sillers. I've got an awful lot of work waiting at home. I thought I'd just bring those wrong notebooks along as they were worrying me.'

She laughed, almost as though near tears. This time Sillery made no effort to detain her.

'Goodnight, Ada.'

'Goodnight, Mr Short. Goodnight, Mr Jenkins. Goodnight, Sillers.'

However much put out by her unexpected arrival, refusal to discuss the Widmerpools, final news that she was abandoning him, Sillery's usual resilience, his unyielding capacity for making the best of things, was now displayed, though he could not conceal relief at this withdrawal. He grinned at Short and myself after the door closed, shaking his head whimsically to show he still retained a sense of satisfaction in knowing such a wench. Short, on the other hand, was anxious to forget about Miss Leintwardine as soon as possible.

'Tell us something about your diaries, Sillers. I'm more interested than I can say.'

Sillery, anyway at that moment, did not want to talk

about the diaries. Ada Leintwardine was still his chosen theme. If she had displeased him, all the more reason to get full value out of her as an attendant personality of what remained of the Sillery court.

'Local doctor's daughter. Clever girl. Keen on making a career in—what shall we say?—the world of letters. Writing a novel herself. All that sort of thing. Just the person I was looking for. Does the work splendidly. Absolutely reliable. We mustn't have pre-publication leaks, must we? That would never do. I hope she's aware of Howard Craggs's little failings. Just as bad as ever, even at the age he's reached, so I'm told. All sorts of stories. She must know. Everyone knows that.'

His manner of enunciating the remark about pre-publication leaks made one suspect Sillery meant the opposite to what he said. Pre-publication leaks were what he aimed at, Miss Leintwardine the ideal medium for titbits proffered to stimulate interest. The Diary was to be Sillery's last bid for power, imposing his personality on the public, as an alternative to the real thing. However, he had no wish to talk to Short about this. If the Journal was of interest, it was likely Sillery would have published its contents, at least a selection, before now. Even if the interest were moderate, there would be excitement in preparation and advance publicity, whetting the appetite of the public. When, in due course, Short and I left the rooms—Sillery admitted he went to bed now earlier than formerly—it was only after solemn assurances we would call again. Outside, the night was mild for the time of year.

'I'm staying in college,' said Short. 'Sillers is always talking of my becoming an Honorary Fellow, I don't know how serious he is. I'll walk with you as far as the gate. Sillers is wonderful, isn't he? What did you make of that young woman? I didn't much care for her style. Too florid. Still, Sillers must need a secretary if he has all that diary material to weld into order. Rather inconsiderate of her to give up work for him, as she seems to be doing. Interesting your knowing Widmerpool. I wouldn't have thought you'd much in common. I believe myself he's got a future. You must lunch with me one day at the Athenaeum, Nicholas. I'm rather full of work at the moment, but I'll tell my secretary to make a note.'

'Is she as pretty as Miss Leintwardine?'

Short accepted that pleasantry in good part, leaving the question in the air.

'Brightman calls Sillers the last of the Barons. Pity there'll be no heir to that ancient line, he says. Brightman's wit, as Sillers remarked, can be a shade cruel. Nice to have met in these peaceful surroundings again.'

Traversing obscure byways on the way back to my own college, I had to admit the evening had been enjoyable, although there was a kind of relief in escaping from the company of Sillery and Short, into the silent night. One had to concur, too, in judging Sillery 'wonderful'; wonderful anyway in categorical refusal to allow neither age nor anything else to deflect him from the path along which he had chosen to approach life. That was impressive, to be honoured: at least something the world honoured, capacity for sticking to your point, whatever it might be, through thick and thin.

'There have never been any real salons in England,' Moreland once said. 'Everyone here thinks a salon is a place for a free meal. A true salon is conversation—nothing to eat and less to drink.'

Sillery bore out the definition pretty well. The following day I was to knock off Burton, and go back to London. That was a cheering thought. When I reached my own college there was a telegram at the porter's lodge. It was from Isobel. Erridge, her eldest brother, had died suddenly. This was a contingency altogether unexpected, not only

27

dispersing from the mind further speculation about Sillery and his salon, but necessitating reconsideration of all immediate plans.

Erridge, a subject for Burton if ever there was one, had often complained of his health, in this never taken very seriously by the rest of his family. Lately, little or nothing had been heard of him. He lived in complete seclusion. The inter-service organization, a secret one, which had occupied Thrubworth during the earlier years of the war had been later moved, or disbanded, the place remaining requisitioned, but converted into a camp for German prisoners-of-war. Administrative staff and stores occupied most of the rooms, except the small wing at the back of the building that Erridge, on succeeding his father, had adapted for his own use; quarters where his sister Blanche had later joined him to keep house. This suited Blanche well enough, because she preferred a quiet life. She undertook, when feasible, the many local duties unwelcome to Erridge himself whose dedication to working for the public good never mitigated an unwillingness to burden himself with humdrum obligations. This disinclination to play a part in local affairs owed something to his innate uneasiness in dealing with people, together with an aversion from personal argument and opposition, unless such contentiousness was 'on paper'. What Erridge disliked was having to wrangle with a lot of not very well-informed adversaries face to face. In these attitudes poor health may well have played a part, for even unhampered by 'pacifist' convictions, his physical state would never have allowed any very active participation in the war.

However much recognized as, anyway in his own eyes, living in a more or less chronic convalescence, Erridge was certainly not expected to die in his middle-forties. George Tolland, next brother in point of age, was another matter. George, badly wounded in the Middle East, had long been

28

too ill to be brought home. From the first, it seemed unlikely he would survive. Back in England, he made some sort of recovery, then had a relapse, almost predictable from the manner in which Death had already cast an eye on him. The funeral had been only a few months before. George's wife Veronica, pregnant at the time, had not yet given birth. The question of the baby's sex, in the light of inheritance, added another uncertainty to the present situation.

The following morning I set out for London. The train was late. Waiting for it like myself was a man in a blue-grey mackintosh, who strolled rather furtively up and down the platform. His movements suggested hope to avoid recognition, while a not absolutely respectable undertaking was accomplished. At first the drooping moustache disguised him. It was an adjunct not at all characteristic. Then, a minute or two after, the nervous swinging walk gave this figure away. There could be no doubt. It was Books-do-furnish-a-room Bagshaw.

The cognomen dated back to the old Savoy Hill days of the BBC, though we had not known each other in that very remote period. A year or two older than myself, Bagshaw had been an occasional drinking companion of Moreland's. They shared a taste for white port. Possibly Bagshaw had even served a brief stint as music critic. The memory persisted—at our first encounter—of Bagshaw involved in an all but disastrous incident on top of a bus, when we were going home after Moreland had been conducting a performance of *Pelleas and Melisande*. If Bagshaw, at no moment in his past, had ever written music criticism, that must have been the sole form of journalism he had omitted to tackle. We had never seen much of each other, nor met for seven or eight years. Bagshaw's war turned out to have been waged in the Public Relations branch of the RAF. He had grown the moustache in India. Like a lot of acquaintances encountered at this period, his talk had become noticeably more authoritative in tone, product of the war itself and its demands, or just the ponderous onset of middle age. At the same time he had surrendered none of his old wheedling, self-deprecatory manner, which had procured him a wide variety of jobs, extracted him from equally extensive misadventures. He was in the best of spirits.

'The subcontinent has its moments, Nicholas. It was a superlative experience, in spite of the Wingco's foul temper. I had to tell that officer I was not prepared to be the Gunga Din of Royal Air Force Public Relations in India, even at the price of being universally accepted as the better man. There were a lot of rows, but never mind. There was much to amuse too.'

This clearcut vignette of relations with his Wing-Commander defined an important aspect of Bagshaw's character, one of which he was very proud.

'You're a professional rebel, Bagshaw,' some boss-figure had remarked when sacking him.

That was true in a sense, though not in such an entirely simple sense as might be supposed at first sight. All the same, Bagshaw had obtained more than one subsequent job merely on the strength of repeating that estimate of himself. The label gave potential employers an enjoyable sense of risk. Some of them lived to regret their foolhardiness.

'After all, I warned him at the start,' Bagshaw used to say.

The roots of this revolutionary spirit lay a long way back. Did he not boast that on school holidays he had plastered the public lavatories of Cologne with anti-French stickers at the time of the occupation of the Rhineland? There were all sorts of later insurgent activities, 'chalkings', marchings, making policemen's horses shy at May Day celebrations, exertions which led, logically enough, to association with Gypsy Jones. Bagshaw was even reckoned to have been engaged to Gypsy at one time. His own way of life, the fact that she herself was an avowed Party Member, made it likely he too had been 'CP' in his day, possibly up to the Spanish Civil War. At that period Quiggin used to talk a lot about him, and had probably learnt a good deal from him. Then Bagshaw was employed on some sort of eye-witness reporting assignment in Spain. Things went wrong. No one ever knew quite what happened. There had been one of Bagshaw's rows. He came back. Some people said he was lucky to get home. Politically speaking, life were never the same again. Bagshaw had lost his old enthusiasms. Afterwards, when drunk, he would attempt to expound his changed standpoint, never with great clarity, though he would go on by the hour together to friends like Moreland, who detested talking politics.

'There was a chap called Max Stirner . . . You've probably none of you ever heard of *Der Einzige und sein Eigentum* . . . You know, *The Ego and his Own* . . . Well, I don't really know German either, but Stirner believed it would be all right if only we could get away from the tyranny of abstract ideas . . . He taught in a girls' school. Probably what gave him the notion. Abstract ideas not a bit of use in a girls' school . . .'

Whatever Bagshaw thought about abstract ideas when drunk—he never reached a stage when unable to argue—he was devoted to them when sober. He resembled a man long conversant with racing, familiar with the name of every horse listed in *Ruff's Guide to the Turf*, who has now ceased to lay a bet, even feel the smallest desire to visit a racecourse; yet at the same time never lost his taste for talking about racing. Bagshaw was for ever fascinated by revolutionary techniques, always prepared to explain everybody's standpoint, who was a party-member, fellow-traveller, crypto, trotskyist, anarchist, anarcho-syndicalist, every refinement of marxist theory, every subtle distinction within groups. The ebb and flow of subversive forces wafted the breath of life to him, even if he no longer believed in the beneficial qualities of that tide.

Bagshaw's employment at the BBC lasted only a few years. There were plenty of other professional rebels there, not to mention Party Members, but somehow they were not his sort. All the same, the Corporation left its mark. Even after he found more congenial occupations, he always spoke with a certain nostalgia of his BBC days, never entirely losing touch. After abdicating the air, he plunged into almost every known form of exploiting the printed word, where he always hovered between the sack and a much more promising offer on the horizon. He possessed that opportune facility for turning out several thousand words on any subject whatsoever at the shortest possible notice: politics: sport: books: finance: science: art: fashion—as he himself said, 'War, Famine, Pestilence or Death on a Pale Horse'. All were equal when it came to Bagshaw's typewriter. He would take on anything, and—to be fair—what he produced, even off the cuff, was no worse than what was to be read most of the time. You never wondered how on earth the stuff had ever managed to be printed.

All this suggests Bagshaw had a brilliant journalistic career ahead of him, when, as he described it, he set out 'with the heart of a boy so whole and free'. Somehow it never came off. A long heritage of awkward incidents accounted for much of the furtiveness of Bagshaw's manner. There had been every sort of tribulation. Jobs changed; wives (two at least) came and went; once DT was near at hand; from time to time there were periods 'on the waggon'; all the while legend accumulating round this weaker side, which Bagshaw's nickname celebrated. Its origin was lost in the mists of the past, but the legend emphasized aspects of Bagshaw that could make him a liability.

There were two main elucidations. One asserted that, the worse for drink, trying to abstract a copy of *The Golden*

Treasury from a large glass-fronted bookcase in order to verify a quotation required for a radio programme, Bagshaw overturned on himself this massive piece of furniture. As volume after volume descended on him, it was asserted he made the comment: 'Books do furnish a room.'

Others had a different story. They would have it that Bagshaw, stark naked, had spoken the words conversationally as he approached the sofa on which lay, presumably in the same state, the wife of a well-known dramatic critic (on duty at the theatre that night appraising the First Night of *The Apple Cart*), a clandestine meeting having reached emotional climax in her husband's book-lined study. Bagshaw was alleged to have spoken the words, scarcely more than muttered them—a revolutionary's tribute to bourgeois values—as he rapidly advanced towards his prey: 'Books do furnish a room.'

The lady, it could have been none other, was believed later to have complained to a third party of lack of sensibility on Bagshaw's part in making such an observation at such a juncture. Whichever story were true—probably neither, the second had all the flavour of having been worked over, if not invented, by Moreland—the nickname stuck.

'There'll be a stampede of dons' wives,' said Bagshaw, as we watched the train come in 'Let's be careful. We don't want to be injured for life.'

We found a compartment, crowded enough, but no impediment to Bagshaw's flow of conversation.

'You know, Nicholas, whenever I come away from this place, I'm always rather glad I skipped a novitiate at a university. My university has been life. Many a time I've put that in an article. Tell me, have you read a novel called *Camel Ride to the Tomb*?'

'I thought it good—who is X. Trapnel? Somebody else mentioned him.'

'The best first novel since before the war,' said Bagshaw.

'Not that that's in itself particularly high praise. Trapnel was a clerk in one of our New Delhi outfits—the people who used to hand out those pamphlets about Civics and The Soviet Achievement, all that sort of thing. I was always rapt in admiration at the way the Party arranged to have its propaganda handled at an official level. As a matter of fact Trapnel himself wasn't at all interested in politics, but he was always in trouble with the authorities, and I managed to help him one way and another.'

Although not in the front rank of literary critics—there might have been difficulty in squeezing him into an already overcrowded and grimacing back row—Bagshaw had reason in proclaiming Trapnel's one of the few promising talents thrown up by the war; in contrast with the previous one, followed by no marked luxuriance in the arts.

'Then he got a poisoned foot. Trapnel was a low medical category anyway, that's why he was doing the job at his age. He got shipped back to England. By the end of the war he'd winkled himself into a film unit. He's very keen on films. Wants to get back into them, I believe, writing novels at the same time—but what about your own novels, Nicholas? Have you started up at one again?'

I told him why I was staying at the University, and how work was going to be disrupted during the following week owing to Erridge's funeral. The information about Erridge at once disturbed Bagshaw.

'Lord Warminster is no more?'

'Heard it last night.'

'This is awful.'

'I'd no idea you were a close friend.'

Bagshaw's past activities, especially at the time when he was seeing a good deal of Quiggin, might well have brought him within Erridge's orbit, though I had never connected them in my mind.

'I didn't know Warminster well. Always liked him when we met, and of course sorry to hear the sad news, but why it might be ominous for me was quite apart from personal feelings. The fact was he was putting up the money for a paper I'm supposed to be editing. I was on the point of telling you about it.'

At this period there was constant talk of 'little magazines' coming into being. Professionally speaking, their establishment was of interest as media for placing articles, reviewing books, the various pickings of literary life. Erridge had toyed with some such project for years, although the sort of paper he contemplated was not likely to be of much use to myself. It was no great surprise to hear he had finally decided to back a periodical of some sort. The choice of Bagshaw as editor was an adventurous one, but, if they knew each other already, Bagshaw's recommendation of himself as a 'professional rebel' might well have been sufficient to get a job in Erridge's gift.

'A new publishing firm, Quiggin & Craggs, is going to produce the magazine. Warminster—Erry, as you call him —was friends with both directors. You must know J. G. Quiggin. Doubt if he's ever been CP, but Craggs has been a fellow-traveller for years, and my old friend Gypsy toes the Party line as consistently as anyone could.'

'What's Gypsy got to do with it?'

'As Craggs's wife.'

'Gypsy married to Craggs?'

'Has been for a year or two. Quiggin's an interesting case. He's always had Communist leanings, but afraid to commit himself. JG doesn't like too many risks. He feels he might get into more trouble as a Party Member than outside. He hasn't got Craggs's staying power.'

'But Erry wasn't a Communist at all. In many ways he disapproved, I believe, though he never came out in the open about it.'

35

'No, but he got on all right with JG and Howard Craggs. There was even a suggestion he did more than get on well with Gypsy at one time. He was going to back the publishing firm too, though they are to be run quite separately.'

'What's the magazine to be called?'

'*Fission*. That was thought to strike the right note for the Atomic Age. Something to catch the young writers coming out of the services—Trapnel, for example. That was why I mentioned him. The firm would, of course, be of a somewhat Leftward tendency, given its personnel, but general publishing, not like Boggis & Stone. The magazine was to be Warminster's toy to do more or less what he liked with. I hope his demise is not going to wreck things. It was he who wanted me to edit it. There were one or two others after the job. Gypsy wasn't all that keen for me to get it, in spite of old ties. I know a bit too much.'

Bagshaw's lack of orthodoxy, while at the same time soaked in Left-Wing lore, was something to make immediate appeal to Erridge, once considered. Then another idea occurred to me. It was worth firing a shot at random.

'You've been seeing Miss Ada Leintwardine about all this?'

Bagshaw was not in the least taken aback. He stroked his moustache, an utterly unsuitable appendage to his smooth round somewhat priest-like face, and smiled.

'You know Ada? I thought she was my secret. Where did you run across her?'

He listened to an account of what had taken place in Sillery's rooms; then nodded, as if understanding all.

'Sillery's an interesting case too. I've heard it suggested he's been in the Party himself for years. Myself I think not, though there's no doubt he's given quite a bit of support from time to time in his day. I'd be interested to know where he really stands. So the little witch has ensnared this venerable scholar?'

'She's kept that to herself so far as you were concerned?'

'Absolutely.'

'Is she a Party Member too?'

Bagshaw laughed heartily.

'Ada's ambitions are primarily literary. Within that area she'll take any help she can get, but I doubt if she'd get much from the Party. What did you think of her?'

'All right.'

'She's got a will of her own. Quiggin & Craggs did right to sign her up. JG was much taken.'

'You produced her?'

'We met during the war—all too briefly—but have remained friends. She's to be on the publishing side, not *Fission*. I'd like you to meet Trapnel. I really do think there's promise there. I'll call you up, and we'll have a drink together. I won't be able to arrange anything next week, as I'm getting married on Tuesday—thanks very much, my dear fellow, thanks very much ... yes, of course ... nice of you to put it that way ... I just didn't want to be a bore about a lot of personal matters ...'

2

RATHER UNEXPECTEDLY, ERRIDGE WAS FOUND to have paid quite recent attention to his will. He had replaced George Tolland (former executor with Frederica) by their youngest, now only surviving brother, Hugo. Accordingly, by the time I reached London, Hugo and Frederica had already gone down to Thrubworth. Accommodation in Erridge's wing of the house was limited. The rest of the family, as at George's funeral, had to make up their minds whether to attend as a day's expedition, or stay at The Tolland Arms, a hostelry considerably developed from former times, since the establishment in the neighbourhood of an RAF station. Norah, Susan and her husband Roddy Cutts, with Isobel and myself, chose The Tolland Arms. As it happened Dicky Umfraville had just arrived on leave from Germany, where he was serving as lieutenant-colonel on the staff of the Military Government (a job to which he was well disposed), but he flatly refused to accompany Frederica.

'I never met your brother,' he said. 'Therefore it would be an impertinence on my part to attend his funeral. Besides—in more than one respect the converse of another occasion—there's room at the inn, but none at the stable. Nobody would mind one of the Thrubworth loose-boxes less than myself, but we should be separated, my love, so near and yet so far, something I could not bear. In addition

—far more important—I don't like funerals. They remind me of death, a subject I always try to avoid. You will have to represent me, Frederica, angel that you are, and return to London as soon as possible to make my leave a heaven upon earth.'

Veronica, George Tolland's widow, was not present either. She was likely to give birth any day now.

'Pray God it will be a boy,' Hugo said. 'I used to think I'd like to take it all on, but no longer—even though I'd hardly make a scruffier earl than poor old Erry.'

His general demeanour quietened by the war, Hugo's comments tended to become grimmer. He had remained throughout his service bombardier in an Anti-Aircraft battery, not leaving England, but experiencing a reasonably lively time, for example, one night the only man on the gun not knocked out. Now he had returned to selling antiques, a trade at which he became increasingly proficient, recently opening a shop of his own with a former army friend called Sam—he seemed to possess no surname— not a great talker, but good-natured, of powerful physique, and said to be quick off the mark when a good piece came up at auction.

Like Hugo—although naturally in terms of his own very different temperament and approach to life—Roddy Cutts had also quietened. There was sufficient reason for that. The wartime romance at HQ Persia/Iraq Force, with the cipherine he had at one moment planned to marry, had collapsed not long after disclosure of the situation in a letter to his wife. While on leave in Teheran the cipherine had suddenly decided to abscond with a rich Persian, abandoning Roddy to his own resources. Susan, who had behaved impeccably during this unhappy interlude, now took over. When Roddy came back to England for the 1945 election, she worked exceptionally hard. He retained his seat by a few hundred votes. As a consequence, Susan's ascendancy was now complete, Roddy utterly under her control. She made him toil like a slave. That was no doubt right, what he wanted himself. All the same, these factors were calculated to reduce high spirits, even in one so generally appreciative of his own good qualities as Roddy Cutts. His handsome, rather too large features were now marked with signs of stress, everything about him a shade less strident, even the sandy hair. At the same time he retained the forceful manner, half hectoring, half subservient, common to representatives of all political parties, together with the politician's endemic hallmark of getting hold of the wrong end of the stick. He was almost pathetically thankful to be back in the House of Commons.

When George Tolland had been buried a few months before, Erridge had not been present at the funeral. He had, in fact retired to bed with an attack of gastritis—then very prevalent—but from the start this absence had been assumed almost as a matter of course by his sisters. That was not because any of them accepted too seriously Erridge's own complaint about chronic ailments, but on the general principle that for an eldest son, no matter how progressive his views, it was reasonable to avoid a ceremony where a younger brother must inevitably occupy the limelight; in this case additionally so in the eyes of those—however much Erridge himself might deplore such sentiments—who felt an end such as George's traditionally commendable; as Stringham had commented, 'awfully smart to be killed'. This last factor was likely to be emphasized by the religious service, in itself distasteful to Erridge. There was therefore more than one reason to keep him away, as of late years he had become all but incapable of doing anything he disliked. It was agreed that, even without illness, he would never have attended.

'A psychosomatic attack was a foregone conclusion,' said Norah. 'Anyway all parties go better without Erry.'

Nevertheless George's death had undoubtedly agitated his eldest brother. Blanche, in her sad, willing, never wholly comprehending way of describing things, had been insistent about that. At least Blanche always appeared uncomprehending. Possibly she really grasped a great deal more than her own relations supposed. The local doctor, Erridge's sole confidant in the neighbourhood, had not seen him for a month, a most uncharacteristic omission. Blanche repeated Dr Jodrill's words.

'The coronary thrombosis revealed by the post-mortem could owe something to emotional disturbance. I venture to suggest Lord Warminster was greatly unsettled by Colonel Tolland's death.'

Perhaps Jodrill was right. Long submerged sentiments might all at once have taken charge. Even Erridge's indisposition at the time of the funeral could have had something to do with these. Still, it was hard to contradict Norah in thinking Erridge better absent. Several army friends turned up at the church, Tom Goring, always a crony—'Rifleman notwithstanding', as George used to say—who had commanded a brigade in the sector where George was wounded. Ted Jeavons was there too, punctilious observance on the part of an uncle by marriage, whose own health was notoriously poor. For obscure reasons of his own, Jeavons made the journey by a different railway line from the rest of the family, returning the same night. The church had not been full, fog and rationed petrol keeping people away.

At George's funeral, as so often on such occasions, the sharp contrast between life and death was emphasized by one of those incongruous incidents that seem to bear on the character or habits of the deceased. So far from diminishing the nature of the ceremony, their aptness often increases its intensity, by-passing, so to speak, ingenuities of ritual and music, bridging with some peculiar fitness the gulf presented to the imagination by the fact of death. The sensibilities are brought up with a start to accept what has happened by action or scene, outwardly untimed, inwardly apposite.

George's coffin had been committed to the moss-lined earth, the mourners moving away, when a party of German prisoners-of-war from the camp, their guard equipped with a tommy-gun (carried with the greatest nonchalance), straggled across the churchyard on the way back from a local excursion. They seemed quite unaware of what had been taking place a moment before, mingling, as it were, with the mourners, at whom they sheepishly gazed. During the service there had been, in fact, no music, a minimum of anything that could be called ritual. The POWs seemed in a manner to take the place of whatever had been lacking in the way of external effects, forming a rough-and-ready, unknowing guard-of-honour; final reminder of the course of events that had brought George's remains to that quiet place.

The church, at the end of the village, was a few hundred yards from the gates of the park. On the day of Erridge's interment, though the weather was not cold for the time of year, rain was pouring down in steely diagonals across the gravestones. Within the mediaeval building, large for a country church, the temperature was lower than in the open, the interior like a wintry cave. Isobel and Norah sat on either side of me under the portrait medallion, lilac grey marble against an alabaster background, of the so-called 'Chemist-Earl', depicted in bas relief with sidewhiskers and a high collar, the accompanying inscription in gothic lettering. A scientist of some distinction and FRS, he had died unmarried in the eighteen-eighties.

'My favourite forebear,' Hugo said. 'He did important research into marsh gases, and something called alcohol-radicles. As you may imagine, there were a lot of contemporary witticisms about the latter, also jokes within the family about his work on the deodorization of sewage, which was, I believe, outstanding.'

Heraldry had evidently been considered inappropriate for the Chemist-Earl, but two or three escutcheons in the chancel displayed the Tolland gold bezants—'talents', in the punning connotation of the arms—over the similarly canting motto: *Quid oneris in praesentia tollant*. The family's memorials went back no further than the middle of the eighteenth century, when the Hugford heiress (only child of a Lord Mayor) had inhabited Thrubworth; her husband, the Lord Erridge of the period, migrating there from a property further north. On the other side of the aisle, almost level with where we sat, a tomb in white marble, ornate but elegant, was surmounted with sepulchral urns and trophies of arms.

Sacred to the Memory of
Henry Lucius 1st Earl of Warminster,
Viscount Erridge, Baron Erridge of Mirkbooths,
G.C.B., Lieutenant-General in the Army, etc.

'Be of good courage and let us behave ourselves valiantly
for our people, and for the cities of our God:
and let the Lord do that which is good in his sight.'
I. Chronicles. xix. 13.

Even if Wellington were truly reported in expressing reservations about his abilities as a commander, Henry Lucius had left some sort of a legend behind him. An astute politician, he had voted at the right moment for Reform. 'Lord Erridge made a capital speech,' wrote Creevey, 'causing the damn'dest surprise to the Tory waverers, and as I have heard he is soon to retire with an earldom, he must have decided to present his valedictions with a flourish before devoting the remaining years of his life to his *hobbies*.' Gronow's Memoirs throw light on this

43

last comment, endorsing the caution displayed by the commemorative text in fields other than military. After noting that Brummell paid Henry Lucius the compliment of asking who made his driving-coat, Captain Gronow adds: 'His Lordship was not indifferent to the charms of the fair sex, but the exquisitely beautiful Creole of sixteen, who was under his immediate protection when he breathed his last in lodgings at Brighton, was believed by many people in society to be his daughter.'

It looked as if Erridge, long shut away from everyday life, would bring together an even smaller gathering of mourners than his brother George. Two or three elderly neighbours were there as a matter of form, a couple of Alfords from his mother's side of the family, a few tenants and people from the village. Most of this congregation stole in almost guiltily, as if—like Bagshaw—they hoped to draw the least possible attention to themselves, choosing pews at the back of the church in which they sat hunched and shivering. There was a longish, rather nerve-racking wait, emphasized by much coughing and clearing of throats. Then came manifestations from the porch. At last something was happening. There was a noise, quite a commotion. It sounded as if the coffin-bearers—just enough men of required physique had been found available on the estate for that duty—were encountering difficulties. The voices outside were raised in apparent argument, if not altercation. From among these tones of dissension a female note was perceptible; perhaps the protests of more than one woman. A pause of several minutes followed before whoever was arguing in the porch entered the church. Then the steps of several persons sounded on the uncarpeted flagstones. A general turning of heads took place to ascertain whether the moment had come to stand up.

A party of six persons, four men and two women, were advancing up the aisle in diamond formation. Widmerpool was at the head. Carrying a soft black hat between his hands and in front of his chest, he was peering over it as he proceeded slowly, reverently, rather suspiciously, up the unlighted interior of the church. His appearance at this moment was wholly unexpected. George, in his City days, had done business with Donners-Brebner when Widmerpool worked there, but, so far as I knew, Widmerpool had no contacts with Erridge. There had been no sign of Widmerpool at George's funeral. At first sight, the rest of the group seemed equally unlooked for, even figments of a dream, as faces became recognizable in the gloom. A moment's thought revealed their presence as explicable enough, even if singular in present unison. To limit examination of this cluster of figures to a mere glance over the shoulder was asking too much, even to pretend any longer that the glance was only a requisite precaution for keeping abreast of the progress of the service. In fact most of the congregation settled down to a good stare.

A man in his sixties, tall, haggard, bent, bald, walked behind Widmerpool, his untidy self-satisfied air for some reason suggesting literary or journalistic affiliations. Beside him was a woman about twenty years younger, short, wiry, her head tied up in a red handkerchief, somehow calling to mind old-fashioned Soviet posters celebrating the Five Year Plan. Too stocky and irritable in appearance, in fact, to figure in pictorial propaganda, she had the right sort of aggressiveness. This was Gypsy Jones. Oddly enough, the look of King Lear on the heath attached to Mr Deacon, when, years before, I had seen him selling *War Never Pays!* with Gypsy at Hyde Park Corner, was suddenly recalled. However different his sexual tastes, Howard Craggs had developed much of the same wandering demented appearance. It was almost as if association with Gypsy—they had lived together years before the marriage reported by Bagshaw—brought about this mien.

Behind these two walked another couple unforeseen as proceeding side by side up the aisle of a church One of these was J. G. Quiggin, certainly an old friend of Erridge's, in spite of many ups and downs. It was also natural enough that he should have travelled here with Craggs, co-director of the new publishing firm. Sillery's description of Quiggin's current Partisan-style dress was borne out by the para-military overtones of khaki shirt, laced ankle boots, belted black leather overcoat. To be fair, the last dated back at least to the days when Quiggin was St John Clarke's secretary. Beside Quiggin, contrasted in a totally achieved funereal correctness, smoothing his grey moustache in unmistakable agonies of embarrassment—either at arriving at the church so late, or presenting himself on such an occasion in the company of mourners so unconformist in dress—walked the Tollands' Uncle Alfred.

However, the last figure in the cortège made the rest seem humdrum enough. At the rear of this wedge-shaped phalanx, a long way behind the others, moving at a stroll that suggested she was out by herself on a long lonely country walk, her thoughts far away in her own melancholy daydreams, walked, almost glided, Widmerpool's wife. Her eyes were fixed on the ground as she advanced slowly, with extraordinary grace, up the aisle. As centre of attention she put the rest of the procession utterly in the shade. That was not entirely due, to her slim figure and pent-up sullen beauty. Another beautiful girl could have created no more than the impression that she was a beautiful girl. It was not easy to say what marked out Pamela Widmerpool as something more than that. Perhaps her absolute self-confidence, her manner of expressing without words that to be present at all was a condescension; to have allowed herself to be one of that particular party, an accepted abasement of the most degrading sort. Above all, she seemed an appropriate attendant on Death. This was

46

not an account of her clothes. They were far from sombre. They looked—so Isobel remarked afterwards—as if bought for a cold day's racing. This closeness to Death was carried within herself. Even in his chastened state, Roddy Cutts could not withhold an audible drawing in of breath.

When they were halfway up the aisle, level with a fairly wide area of unoccupied seats, Widmerpool turned sharply, grinding his heel on the stone in a drill-like motion, a man intentionally emphasizing status as military veteran. His back to the altar, he barred the way, almost as if about to stage an anti-liturgical, even anti-clerical demonstration. However, instead of creating any such untoward disturbance, he shot out the hand of a policeman directing traffic, to indicate where each was to sit of the group apparently under his command.

This authority was by no means unquestioned. Discussion immediately arose among the others, no doubt similar in bearing to whatever disagreements had taken place in the porch. Jeavons, from where he was sitting up at the front of the church, beckoned vehemently to Alfred Tolland in an effort to show where a place could be found among the family. The two of them knew each other not only as relations, but also as fellow air-raid wardens, duties during the course of which an inarticulate friendship may have been obscurely cemented. However, Alfred Tolland was at that moment too dazed by the journey, or oppressed by other circumstances in which he found himself, to be capable of reaching a goal so far afield. He stood there patiently awaiting Widmerpool's instructions, scarcely noticing Jeavons's arms swinging up and down at semaphore angles.

These directions of Widmerpool's had not yet been fully implemented, when Pamela, pushing past the others, precipitately entered the pew her husband was allotting to Alfred Tolland. She placed herself at the far end, under the

47

marble fascicles of standards, lances and sabres that en-crusted the Henry Lucius tomb. Whether or not this seating arrangement accorded with Widmerpool's intention could only be guessed; probably not, from the expression his face at once assumed. Nevertheless, now it had hap-pened, he curtly directed Alfred Tolland to follow, without attempting to reclassify this order of precedence. There was a moment of gesturing between them, Alfred Tolland putting forward some contrary suggestion—he may just have grasped the meaning of Jeavons's signals—so that very briefly it looked as if a wrestling match were about to take place in the aisle. Then Widmerpool shoved Alfred Tolland almost bodily into the pew, where, leaving a wide gap be-tween himself and Pamela, Tolland immediately knelt, burying his face in his hands like a man in agonies of remorse. At Widmerpool's orders, Quiggin went in next; Craggs and Gypsy into the pew behind. They were followed by Widmerpool himself.

The last time I had seen Pamela in church had been at Stringham's wedding, child bridesmaid of six or seven, an occasion when, abandoning responsibilities in holding up the bride's train, she had walked away composedly, later, so it was alleged, causing herself to be lifted in order to be sick into the font. 'That little girl's a fiend,' someone had remarked afterwards at the reception. Now she sat, so to speak, between Henry Lucius and his descendant Alfred Tolland. Would Henry Lucius, 'not indifferent to the charms of the fair sex', rise from the dead? She had closed her eyes, either in prayer, or to express the low temperature of the nave, but did not kneel. Neither did Quiggin, Craggs or Gypsy kneel, but Widmerpool leant forward for a few seconds in a noncommittally devotional attitude that did not entirely abandon a sitting posture, and might have been attributable merely to some interior discomfort.

The dead silence that had momentarily fallen was

48

broken by Widmerpool levering himself back on the seat. He removed his spectacles and began to wipe them. He was rather thinner, or civilian clothes gave less impression of bulk than the 'utility' uniform that enclosed him when last seen. The House of Commons had already left its indefinable, irresoluble mark. His thick features, the rotundities of his body, always amenable to caricature, now seemed more than ever simplified in outline, positively demanding treatment in political cartoon. The notion that a few months at Westminster had brought this about was far fetched. Alteration, if alteration there were, was more likely to be accountable to marriage.

Craggs too shared some of this air of a figure from newspaper caricature, a touch of the Mad Hatter mingling with that of King Lear. His shabbiness, almost griminess, was certainly designed to convey to the world that he was a person of sufficient importance to rise above bourgeois convention, whatever its form. Smiling to himself, snuffling, fidgeting, he gazed round the church in a manner to register melodramatic wonder that such places could still exist, even for the purpose that had brought him there. Such views were certainly held by Gypsy too—who had refused to attend her old friend Mr Deacon's funeral on strictly anti-religious grounds—but unmitigated anger now appeared to prevent her from knowing, or caring, where she found herself. Quiggin looked as if his mind were occupied with business problems. On the other hand, he might have been thinking of the time when Erridge had taken Mona, Quiggin's girl, to the Far East. That difference had been long made up, but circumstances could have recalled it, giving Quiggin a strained uneasy expression.

One of the least resolvable problems posed by Widmerpool's presence was his toleration of Gypsy as member of the party. Once—haunted by that dire incident in the past when he had paid for her 'operation'—he would have gone to any lengths to avoid even meeting her. If, as Craggs's wife, she had to come, that would have been sufficient to keep Widmerpool away. Some overriding political consideration must explain this, such as the idea of attaching himself to a kind of unofficial deputation paying last respects to a 'Man of the Left'. In Widmerpool's case that would be a way of establishing publicly his own *bona fides*, sentiments not sufficiently recognized in himself. Acceptance of Gypsy could be regarded as a gesture of friendship to the extremities of Left Wing thought, an olive branch appropriate (or not) to Erridge's memory.

The more one thought about it, the more relevant—to employ one of their own favourite terms—were Quiggin and Craggs, in fact the whole group, to consign Erridge to the tomb; in certain respects more so than his own relations. It was true that Erridge's abnegation of the family as a social unit was capable of exaggeration, by no means so total as he himself liked to pretend, or his cronies, many of those unsympathetic to him too, prepared to accept. The fact remained that it was with Quiggin and Craggs he had lived his life, insomuch as he had lived it with other people at all, sitting on committees, signing manifestoes, collaborating in pamphlets. (Burton—who provided instances for all occasions, it was hard not to become obsessed with him —spoke of those who 'pound out pamphlets on leaves of which a poverty-stricken monkey would not wipe'.) In fact, pondering on these latest arrivals, they might be compared with the squad of German POWs straying across the face of George Tolland's obsequies, each group a visual reminder of seamy realities—as opposed to idealistic aspirations—the former of war, the latter, politics.

The train of thought invited comparison between the two brothers, their characters and fates. Erridge, high-minded, willing to endure discomfort, ridicule, solitude, in a fervent anxiety to set the world right, had at the same time, as a

comfortably situated eldest son, a taste for holding on to his money, except for intermittent doles—no doubt generous ones—to Quiggin and others who represented in his own eyes what Sillery liked to call The Good Life. Erridge was wholly uninterested in individuals; his absorption only in 'causes'.

George, on the other hand, had never shown much concern with righting the world, except that in a sense his death might be regarded as stemming from an effort at least to prevent the place from becoming worse. He had not been at all adept at making money, but never, so to speak, set the glass of port he liked after lunch—if there were any excuse—before, say, educating his step-children in a generous manner. A competent officer (Tom Goring had praised him in that sphere), his target was always the regular soldier's (one thought of Vigny) to do his duty to the fullest extent, without, at the same time seeking supererogatory burdens or looking out for trouble.

With newsprint still in short supply, Erridge's obituaries were briefer than might have been the case in normal times, but he received some little notice: polite reference to life-long Left-Wing convictions, political reorientations in that field, final pacifism; the last contrasted with having 'fought' (the months in Spain having by now taken mythical shape) in the Spanish Civil War. George was, of course, mentioned only in the ordinary death announcements inserted by the family. Musing on the brothers, it looked a bit as if, in an oblique manner, Erridge, at least by implication, had been given the credit for paying the debt that had in fact been irrefutably settled by George. The same was true, if it came to that, of Stringham, Templer, Barnby—to name a few casualties known personally to one—all equally indifferent to putting right the world.

The sound came now, unmistakable, of the opening Sentences of the burial service. Everyone rose. Coughing

51

briefly ceased. The parson, a very old man presented to the living by Erridge's grandfather, moved slowly, rather painfully forward, intoning the words in a high quavering chant. The heavy boots of the coffin-bearers shuffled over the stones. The faces of the bearers were set, almost agonizingly concentrated, on what they were doing, that of Skerrett, the old gamekeeper, of gnarled ivory, like a skull. He was not much younger than the parson. A boy of sixteen supporting one of the back corners of the coffin was probably his grandson. The trembling prayers raised a faint echo throughout the dank air of the church, on which the congregation's breath floated out like steam. Such moments never lose their intensity. A cross-reference had uncovered Herbert's lines a few days before.

The brags of life are but a nine-days wonder:
And after death the fumes that spring
From private bodies, make as big a thunder
As those which rise from a huge king.

One thought of Father Zossima in *The Brothers Karamazov*. Reference to bodily corruption was a natural reaction from 'Whom none should advise, thou hast persuaded'. Ralegh might be grandiloquent, he was also authoritative, even hypnotic, no less resigned than Herbert, as well. I thought about death. It seemed most unlikely Burton had really hanged himself, as rumoured, to corroborate the accuracy of the final hour he had drawn in his own horoscope. The fact was he was only mildly interested in astrology.

By this time the bearers were showing decided strain from the weight of the coffin. They had reached a stage about halfway up the aisle, and were going fairly slowly. Suddenly a commotion began to take place in one of the pews opposite this point. Pamela was attempting to make her way out. Her naturally pale face was the colour of

chalk. She had already thrust past Alfred Tolland and Quiggin, but Widmerpool, an absolutely outraged expression on his face, stepped quickly from the pew behind to delay her.

'I'm feeling faint, you fool. I've got to get out of here.'

She spoke in quite a loud voice. Widmerpool seemed to make a momentary inner effort to decide for himself the degree of his wife's indisposition, whether she were to be humoured or not, but she pushed him aside so violently that he nearly fell. As she hurried into the aisle he recovered himself, for a second made as if to follow her, then decided against any such action. Had he seriously contemplated pursuit, there had been in any case too great delay. Although Pamela herself managed to skirt the procession advancing with the coffin, it was doubtful whether anyone of more considerable bulk could have freely negotiated the available space in the same manner, especially after the disruption caused. She had brushed past the vicar so abruptly that he gasped and lost the thread of his words. A second later the bearers, recovering themselves, were level with Widmerpool, blocking his own egress from the pew. Pamela's heels clattered away down the flags. When she reached the door, there was difficulty in managing the latch. It gave out discordant rattles; then a creak and loud slam.

'My God,' said Norah.

She spoke the words softly. They recalled her own troubles with Pamela. The service continued. I tried to recompose the mind by returning to Ralegh and Herbert. 'Whom none should advise, thou hast persuaded.' Was that true of everyone who died? Of Erridge, eminently true: true too, in its way, of Stringham and Templer: to some extent of Barnby: not at all true of George Tolland: yet, after all, was it true of him too? I thought of the portraits of Ralegh, stylized in ruff, short cloak, pointed

53

beard, fierce look. 'All the pride, cruelty and ambition of men.' Ralegh knew the form. Still, Herbert was good too. I wondered what Herbert had looked like. In the end one got back to Burton's 'vile rock of melancholy, a disease so frequent, as few there are that feel not the smart of it'. Melancholy was so often the explanation, anyway melancholy in Burton's terms. The bearers took up the coffin once more. The recession was slow, though this time uninterrupted.

'I hope old Skerrett will be all right,' whispered Isobel. 'He looked white as a sheet when he passed.'

'Whiter than Mrs Widmerpool?'

'Much whiter.'

Outside, the haze had thickened. The air struck almost warm after the church. Rain still fell in small penetrating drops. The far corner of the churchyard was occupied with an area of Tolland graves: simple headstones: solid oblong blocks of stone with iron railings: crosses, two unaccountably Celtic in design: one obelisk. Norah, who had never got on at all well with her eldest brother, was in convulsions of tears, the other sisters dabbing with their handkerchiefs. There was no sign of Pamela in the porch. The mourners processed to the newly dug grave. The old parson, his damp surplice clinging like a shroud, refused to be hurried by the elements. He took what he was doing at a thoroughly leisurely pace. There seemed no reason why the funeral should ever end. Then, all at once, everything was over. The mourners began to move slowly, rather uncomfortably away.

'I'll just have a word with Skerrett,' said Isobel. 'He's looking better now. Meet you at the gate.'

Before I reached the lychgate, a tall, rather distinguished-looking woman separated herself from other shapes lurking among the tombstones, and came towards me. She must have sat at the back of the church, because I had not seen

her until that moment. She was fortyish, a formal maga-
zine-cover prettiness organized to make her seem not only
younger than that, but at the same time a girl not exactly
of the present, rather of some years back. Her voice too
struck a note at that moment equally out of fashion.

'I thought I *must* say hullo, Nick, though it's *years* since
we met—you remember me, Mona, I used to be married to
Peter Templer—what ages. Yes, poor Peter, wasn't it sad?
So brave of him at his age too. Jeff says you're *never* the
same in war after you're thirty. We're weaving about fairly
close here, and I've got to *scamper* home this minute, because Jeff's quite *insane* about punctuality. We're living in
a *horrible* house over by Gibbet Down, so I thought I
ought to make a pilgrimage for Alf. It's poor Alf now too,
as well as poor Peter, isn't it? Alf didn't have much of a
time, did he, though he *was* kindhearted in his way,
even if he *abominated* spending a farthing on drink—one's
throat got absolutely *arid* travelling with him. I shall
never forget Hong Kong. JG used to get so *angry* in the
old days if I complained about the *drought* when we
dined at Thrubworth with Alf, which wasn't all that
often. Lack of drink was even worse when I was alone
with him, I can assure you. Fancy JG turning up today too.
So unexpected when he does the right thing for once. I
hear he lived for a time with someone called *Lady Anne
Stepney*, and then she went off with one of the Free
French. That did make me laugh—and Gypsy here too.
Do you think she *did* have a walk out with Alf? He
used to talk about seeing her at those *awful* political con-
ferences he loved going to. I sometimes wondered. Well,
we'll never know now. I just *waved* to JG and Gypsy. I
thought that would be *quite enough*.'

Isobel reappeared.

'Your *wife*? How sad it must be to lose a brother, I
never had one, but I'm sure it is. And not at all old either,

except we're all *centuries* old now, I feel a *million*, but, of course—well, I don't know—anyway, I just thought it was my *duty* to come, even in *daunting* weather. I'll have to proceed back now with all possible speed, or Jeff will be having *kittens*. Jeff's an Air Vice-Marshal now. Isn't that grand? *Burdened* with gongs. He was rather worried about my using the car for a funeral, but I said I was going to a POW camp, and if an Air Vice-Marshal's lady can't inspect a POW camp, what in hell can she do? Well, it's been nice seeing you, Nick, *and* your wife, not to mention having a word about those poor dears who are no more. That erk will have to drive like *stink* if I'm not to be late. We've got some personnel coming to *tea* of all things—drink quite impossible to get for love or money these days, anyway to dish out to all and sundry, as well you must know, so I'll just say bye-bye for now . . .'

While talking, she had fallen more than once into what Mr Deacon used to call a 'vigorous pose'. Now, as she walked away, the controlled movement of her long swift strides recalled the artists' model she once had been. In the road stood a large car, a uniformed aircraftman at the wheel. She turned and waved, then disappeared within.

'Who on earth?'

'That's Mona.'

'Not the girl Erry took to China?'

'Of course.'

'Why didn't you indicate that? I could have had a closer look. What a pity the poor old boy didn't hang on. She might have kept him going.'

As the RAF car drove away, the outlines of Alfred Tolland, picking his way between the graves, came into view. He had been waiting for Mona to move on before he approached. It now struck me that he must have met Widmerpool at the Old Boy dinners of Le Bas's house, because Alfred Tolland retained sentiments about his schooldays that age had in no way diminished. Except for Le Bas himself, he had always—in the days long past when I myself attended them—been the eldest present by at least twenty years.

'Uncle Alfred's a sad case in that respect,' Hugo had remarked. 'Personally I applaud that great enemy of the Old School Tie, the Emperor Septimius Severus, who had a man scourged merely for drawing attention to the fact that they had been at school together.'

Le Bas dinners could explain why Widmerpool and Alfred Tolland had travelled down together after seeing each other at the station. Widmerpool was, in fact, now revealed as standing close behind, as if he expected Alfred Tolland to make some statement that concerned himself or his party, the rest of whom were no longer to be seen. They could be concealed by mist, or have left in a body after the committal. To make sure his own presence as a mourner was not overlcoked by Erridge's family would be characteristic of Widmerpool, even though the reason for his attendance remained at present unproclaimed. He was looking even more worried than in the church. If he had merely desired to register attendance and go away, he would certainly have pushed in front of Alfred Tolland, whose hesitant, deferential comportment always caused delays, particularly at a time like this. Neat, sad, geared perfectly in outward appearance to the sombre nature of the occasion, Tolland stood, head slightly bent, gazing at the damp grass beneath his feet. He had once admitted to having travelled as far as Singapore. One wondered how he had ever managed to get there and back again. Unlikely he had taken with him a girl like Mona, though one could never tell. Barnby always used to insist it was misplaced to speak categorically about other people's sexual experiences, whoever they were.

'Uncle Alfred?'

'My dear Isobel, this is very . . .'

He was all but incapable of finishing a sentence, a form of diffidence implying unworthiness to force a personal opinion on others. Even when Alfred Tolland spoke his own views, they were hedged round with every sort of qualification. Erridge's passing, the company in which he found himself on the way down, stirred within him concepts far too unmanageable to be accommodated in a single phrase. Isobel helped him out.

'A very sad occasion, Uncle Alfred. Poor Erry. It was so unexpected.'

'Yes—quite unexpected. These things are unexpected sometimes. Absolutely unexpected, in fact. Of course Erridge always did . . .'

What did Erridge always do? The question was capable of many answers. The wrong thing? Know he was a sick man? Fear the winter? Hope the end would be sudden? Want Alfred Tolland to reveal some special secret after his own demise? Perhaps just 'do the unexpected'. On the whole that termination was the most probable. Alfred Tolland, this time unassisted by Isobel, may have feared that any too direct statement about what Erridge 'did' might sound callous, if spoken straight out. Instead of completing, he altogether abandoned the comment, this time bringing out in its entirety another concept, quite different in range.

'I'm feeling rather ashamed.'

'Ashamed, Uncle Alfred?'

'Never got down here for George's . . . In bed, as a matter of fact.'

'Nothing bad, I hope, Uncle Alfred.'

'Had a bit of—chest. Felt ashamed, all the same. Not absolutely right now, but can get about. Can't be helped. Didn't want to stay away when it came to the head of the family.'

He spoke as if he would have risen from the dead to

reach the funeral of the head of the family. Perhaps he had. The idea was not to be too lightly dismissed. There was something not wholly of this world about him. Time, for example, seemed to mean nothing. One hoped he would come soon to the point of what he had to say. Although the worst of the rain had stopped, a pervasive damp struck up from the ground and into the bones. Obviously something was on his mind. In the background Widmerpool shifted about, stamping his feet and kicking them together.

'We'll give you a lift back to the house, Uncle Alfred, if you want one. That's if any of the cars will start. Some of them are rather ancient. It may be rather a squeeze.'

'Quite forgot, quite forgot . . . These good people I travelled down with . . . shared a taxi from the station . . . Mr—met him at those dinners Nicholas and I . . . and his wife . . . very good looking . . . another couple too, Sir Somebody and Lady Something . . . also another old friend of Erridge's . . . nice people . . . something they wanted to ask . . .'

Alfred Tolland turned towards Widmerpool, in search of help, to give words to a matter not at all easy to summarize in a few broken phrases. At least he found that hard, which was usual enough, even if the situation were not as ticklish as this one appeared. Widmerpool, not happy himself, was prepared at the same time to accept his cue. He began to speak in his least aggressive manner.

'Two things, Nicholas—though I don't expect you're really the person to ask, sure as I am, as an old friend, you'll be prepared to act for us as—well, as what?—intermediary, shall we say? You know already, I think, the other members of the party I came down with. J. G. Quiggin, of course—must know him as a literary bloke like yourself—and as for Sir Howard and Lady Craggs, of course you remember them.'

One had to admit that 'Sir Howard and Lady Craggs'

conjured up a rather different picture from Mr Deacon's birthday party, Gypsy lolling on Craggs's knee, struggling to divert a too exploratory hand back to a wide area of pink thigh. If it came to that, one had one's own reminiscences of Lady Craggs in an easy-going mood.

'We all wanted, of course, to pay last respects to your late brother-in-law, Lord Warminster—much to my regret I never managed to meet him—but there was also something else. This seemed a golden opportunity to have a preliminary word, if possible, with the appropriate member, or members, of the family, now collected together, as to the best means of approaching certain matters arisen in consequence of Lord Warminster's death.'

Widmerpool paused. He was relieved to have made a start on whatever he wanted to say, for clearly this was by no means the end.

'The late Lord Warminster left certain instructions in connexion with the publishing house Sir Howard Craggs —well, we can talk about all that later. As I say, this seemed a good moment to have a tentative word with the— in short with the executors, as I understand, Mr Hugo Tolland and Lady Frederica Umfraville.'

Whatever complications now threatened were beyond conjecture. Within the family it had been generally agreed that for Erridge to leave the world without arranging some testing problem to be settled by his heirs and successors, was altogether unthinkable. The form such a problem, or problems, might take was naturally not to be anticipated. That Widmerpool should be involved in any such matters was unlooked for. His relief at having made the statement about Erridge's dispositions, whatever they were, turned out to be due to anxiety to proceed to a far more troublesome enquiry from his own point of view.

'Another matter, Nicholas. My wife—you know her, of course, I'd forgotten—Pamela, as I say, was overcome with faintness during the service. In fact had to leave the church. I hope no one noticed. She did so as quietly as possible. These attacks come on her at times. Largely nerves, in my opinion. It was arranged between us she should await me in the porch. She no doubt found the stone seat there too cold in her distressed state. I thought she might have taken refuge in our taxi, but the driver said, on the contrary, he saw her walking up the drive in the direction of the house.'

Widmerpool stopped speaking. His efforts to present in terms satisfactory to himself two quite separate problems, so that they merged into coherent shape, seemed to have broken down. The first question was what Craggs and Quiggin wanted from the executors, no doubt something to do with the matters of which Bagshaw had spoken; the second, which Widmerpool, judging by past experience, regarded as more important, the disappearance of his wife.

Frederica and Blanche, saying goodbye to the Alford relations to whom they had been talking, came over to have a word with their uncle. Alfred Tolland, still considerably discomposed by all that was happening round him, managed to effect a mumbled introduction of Widmerpool, who seized his opportunity, settling on Frederica. He began at once to put forward the advantages of having a preliminary talk, 'quite informal', about straightening out Erridge's affairs. Frederica had hardly time to agree this would be a good idea, before he returned to the question of Pamela, certainly worrying him a lot. Frederica, a very competent person when it came to making arrangements, took these problems in her stride. Like Erridge, she was not greatly interested in individuals as such, so that Widmerpool's desire to talk business, coupled with anxiety about his wife, were elements to be accepted at their face value. Neither aroused Frederica's curiosity.

'Where are these friends of yours now, Mr Widmerpool?'

'In the church porch. They wanted to get out of the rain. They're waiting—in fact waiting for me to obtain your permission, Lady Frederica, to come up to the house as I suggest. I really think the house is probably where my wife is too.'

This then was the crux of the matter. They all wanted to come up to the house. While that was arranged, Widmerpool had judged it best to confine them to the porch. Possibly there had been signs of mutiny. Judged as a group, they must have been just what Frederica would expect as representative friends of her brother, even though she could not guess, had no wish to examine, subtleties of their party's composition. In her eyes Widmerpool's conventional clothes, authoritative manner, made him a natural enough delegate of an otherwise fairly unpresentable cluster of Erridge hangers-on, a perfectly acceptable representative. Frederica and Erridge had been next to each other in age. Although living their lives in such different spheres, they were by no means without mutual understanding. The whim to leave complicated instructions after death was one with which Frederica could sympathize. Sorting out her brother's benefactions gratified her taste for tidying up.

An uncertain quantity was whether or not she remembered anything of Widmerpool's wife. There could be little doubt that at one time or another Dicky Umfraville had made some reference to Pamela's gladiatorial sex life during the war. It would have been very unlike him to have let that pass without comment. On the other hand, Frederica not only disapproved of such goings-on, she took little or no interest in them, was capable of shutting her eyes to misbehaviour altogether. Unaccompanied by Umfraville, whose banter kept her always on guard against being ragged about what Molly Jeavons used to call her own 'correctness', Frederica, on such an exceptional family occasion, may have reverted to type; closing her

62

eyes by an act of will to the fact, even if she knew that, for example, her sister Norah had been one of Pamela's victims. In short, for one reason or another, she did not in the least at that moment concern herself with the identity of Widmerpool's wife. While she was talking to him, Blanche and Isobel made arrangements about getting old Skerrett home. Alfred Tolland drew me aside.

'Thought it would be all right—best—not to wear a silk hat. See you haven't either, nor the rest of the men. Quite right. Not in keeping with the way we live nowadays. What Erridge would have preferred too, I expect. I always like to do that. Behave as—well—the deceased would have done himself. Doubt if Erridge owned a silk hat latterly. Anthony Eden hats they call this sort I'm wearing now, don't quite know why. Mustn't lose count of time and miss my train, because when I get back I've got to . . .'

Again one wondered what on earth he had 'got to' do when he returned to London. It was not the season for reunion dinners. Molly Jeavons no longer alive, he could not drop in there to be teased about family matters. To picture him at any other sort of engagement than these was difficult. It was doubtful whether amicable relations with Jeavons included visits to the house now Molly was gone. One returned to the earlier surmise that he had risen from the dead, had to report back to another graveyard by a stated time.

'I haven't seen Frederica's husband.'

He spoke tentatively, like many of his own age-group, prepared always for the worst when it came to news about the marriages of the next generation.

'Dicky couldn't come. He's with the Control Commission.'

There was no point in emphasizing Umfraville's flat refusal to turn up. The fact of his absence seemed to bring relief to Alfred Tolland.

63

'Remember I once told you Umfraville was my fag at school? Not a word of truth in it. My fag was an older man. Not older than Umfraville is now, of course, he was younger than me, and naturally still is, if he's alive, but older than Frederica's husband would have been at that age. Made a mistake. Found there were two Umfravilles. Been on my conscience ever since telling you that. Hope it never got passed on. Didn't want to meet him, and seem to be claiming acquaintance . . .'

'Probably a relation. It's an uncommon name.'

'Never safe to assume people are relations. That's what I've found.'

'Isobel's beckoning us to a car.'

The dilapidated Morris Eight to which we steered him was driven by Blanche and already contained Norah. Accommodation was cramped. As we drove away, Widmerpool was to be seen marshalling his own party outside the porch. They were lost to sight moving in Indian file between the tombstones, making for a large black car, the taxi in which they had all arrived, far more antiquated than our own vehicle.

'Of course, I knew—Mr—Mr Whatever-his-name-is, knew his face when I saw him at the train,' said Alfred Tolland. 'As soon as he spoke I remembered the excellent speech he made that night—what's the man's name?— took over the house from Cordery—your man—Le Bas— that's the one. The night Le Bas had a stroke or something. Always remember that speech. Full of excellent stuff. Good idea to get away from all that—what is it, *Eheu fugaces*, something of the sort, never any good at Latin. All that sentimental stuff, I mean, and talk about business affairs for a change. Sound man. Great admirer of Erridge, he told me—takes rather a different view of him to most—I don't say *most*—anyway some of the family, who were always a bit what you might call lacking in understanding

64

of Erridge—not exactly disapproving but . . . Widmerpool, that's the fellow's name. He's an MP now. Labour, of course. Thinks very highly of Mr Attlee. Sure he's right . . . I was a bit worried about Mrs Widmerpool. So quiet. Very shy, I expect. Rare these days for a young woman to be as quiet as that. Thought she might be upset about something. Daresay funerals upset her. They do some people. Beautiful young woman too. I couldn't help looking at her. She must have thought me quite rude. Hope somebody's seeing to her properly after she had to leave the service . . .'

This was the longest dissertation I had ever heard Alfred Tolland attempt. That he should allow himself such conversational licence showed how much the day had agitated him. He might also be trying to keep his mind from the discomfort suffered where we sat at the back of the small car. A long silence followed, as if he regretted having given voice to so many private opinions.

'True Thrubworth weather,' said Norah.

She had recovered from her tears. Rain was pouring down again. Mist hid the woods on the high ground behind the house, the timber preserved from felling by St John Clarke's fortuitous legacy to Erridge. The camp was visible enough. On either side of the drive Nissen huts were enclosed by barbed wire. The dismal climate kept the POWs indoors. A few drenched guards were the only form of life to be seen. Blanche made a circuit round the back of the house, the car passed under an arch, into the cobbled yard through which Erridge's wing was approached. She stopped in front of a low door studded with large brass nails.

'I'll put the car away. Go on up to the flat.'

The door turned out to be firmly shut.

'Probably no one at home,' said Norah. 'They've all been to the funeral. I hope Blanchie's got the key. It would be just like her to leave the house without bringing the key with her.'

She knocked loudly. We waited in the rain. After a minute the door was opened. I expected an elderly retainer of some sort, if the knocking were answered at all. Instead of that, a squat, broad-shouldered young man, with fair curly hair and a ruddy face, stood on the threshold. He wore a grey woollen sweater and chocolate-coloured trousers patched in many places. I thought he must be some new protégé of Erridge's about whom one had not been warned. He seemed wholly prepared for us.

'Come in, please, come in.'

Blanche appeared at that moment.

'They'll all be along soon, Siegfried. Will you put the kettle on? I'll come and help in a second. I thought we left the door on the latch.'

'Miss must have closed it.'

'Mrs Skerrett did? Well, leave it unlatched now, so the others can get in without bringing you down to open it.'

'Make her tea.'

'You've made tea already, Siegfried?'

'Of course.'

Grinning delightedly about something, apparently his own ingenuity, he bustled off.

'Who the hell?' asked Norah.

'Siegfried? He's one of the German prisoners working on the land. He loves doing jobs about the house so much, there seemed no point in trying to prevent him. It's a great help, as there's too much for Mrs Skerrett singlehanded, especially on a day like this.'

We passed along the passages leading to Erridge's flat, the several rooms of which were situated up a flight of stairs some little way from the door opening on the courtyard. In the dozen years or so since I had last been at Thrubworth more lumber than ever had collected in these back parts of the house, much of it no doubt brought there after requisitioning. There was an overwhelming accumulation: furniture: pictures: rolled-up carpets: packing cases. Erridge's father, an indefatigable wanderer over the face of the earth, had been responsible for much of this hoard, buying everything that took his fancy. There were 'heads' of big game: a suit of Japanese armour: two huge vases standing on plinths: an idol that looked Mexican or South American. Alfred Tolland identified some of these odds and ends as we made our way through them.

'That oil painting on its side's the First Jubilee. Very old-fashioned in style. Nobody paints like that now. Those big pots are supposed to be eighteenth-century Chinese. Walter Huntercombe came to shoot here once, and insisted they were nothing of the sort. Nineteenth-century copies, he said, and my brother had been swindled. Of course Warminster didn't like that at all. Told Walter Huntercombe he was a conceited young ass. Goodness knows where the tricycle came from.'

Erridge's flat, at the top of a flight of narrow stairs at the end of the corridor, in most respects a severely unadorned apartment, with the air of a temple consecrated to the beliefs of a fanatically austere sect, included a few pieces of furniture that suggested quite another sort of life. His disregard for luxury, anything like fastidious selection of objects, allowed shabby chairs and tables that had seen better days in other parts of the house. In the sitting-room someone—probably Frederica—had removed from the wall the pedigree-like chart, on which what appeared to be descending branches of an ancient lineage, had turned out an illustration of the principles of world economic distribution; now, in any case, hopelessly outdated in consequence of the war.

The books on the shelves, most of them published twelve or fifteen years before, gave the impression of having been bought during the same period of eighteen months or two years: *Russia's Productive System* . . . *The Indian Crisis* . . .

Anthology of Soviet Literature . . . Towards the Under-standing of Karl Marx . . . From Peasant to Collective Farmer. There was also a complete set of Dickens in calf, a few standard poets, and—Erridge's vice, furtive, if not absolutely secret—the bound volumes of *Chums* and the *Boy's Own Paper*, the pages of which he would turn un-smiling for hours at times of worry or irritation. Erridge's Russian enthusiasms had died down by the late thirties, but he always retained a muted affection for the Soviet system, even when disapproving. This fascination for an old love was quite different from Bagshaw's. Bagshaw delighted in examining every inconsistency in the Party Line: who was liquidated: who in the ascendant: which heresies persecuted: which new orthodoxies imposed. Such mutations were painful to Erridge. He preferred not to be brought face to face with them. He was like a man who hoped to avoid the distress of hearing of the depravities into which an adored mistress has fallen.

In this room Erridge had written his letters, eaten his meals, transacted political business with Craggs and Quiggin, read, lounged, moped, probably seduced Mona, or *vice versa*; the same, or alternate, process possibly apply-ing also to Gypsy Jones—or rather Lady Craggs. He used rarely to digress into other parts of the house. The 'state apartments' were kept covered in dust sheets. Once in a way he might have need to consult a book in the library, to which few volumes had been added since the days of the Chemist-Earl, who had brought together what was then re-garded as an unexampled collection of works on his own subject. Once in a way a guest—latterly these had become in-creasingly rare—likely to be a new political contact of one kind or another, for example, an unusually persistent refugee, might be shown round. Erridge had never entirely conquered a taste for exhibiting his own belongings, even though rather ashamed of the practice, and of the belongings themselves.

The once wide assortment of journals on a large table set aside for this purpose had been severely reduced—probably by Frederica again—to a couple of daily newspapers, neither of a flavour her brother would have approved. Beyond this table stood a smaller one at which Erridge and his guests, if any, used to eat. The most comfortable piece of furniture in the room was a big sofa facing the fireplace, its back to the door. The room appeared to be empty when entered, the position of this sofa concealing at first the fact that someone was reclining at full length upon it. Walking across the room to gain a view of the park from the window, I saw the recumbent figure was Pamela's. Propped against cushions, a cup of tea beside her on the floor, by the teacup an open book, its pages downward on the carpet, she was looking straight ahead of her, apparently once more lost in thought. I asked if she were feeling better. She turned her large pale eyes on me.

'Why should I be feeling better?'

'I don't know. I just enquired as a formality. Don't feel bound to answer.'

For once she laughed.

'I mean obviously you weren't well in church.'

'Worse than the bloody corpse.'

'Flu?'

'God knows.'

'A virus?'

'It doesn't much matter does it?'

'Diagnosis might suggest a cure.'

'Are Kenneth and those other sods on their way here?'

'So I understand.'

'The kraut got me some tea.'

'That showed enterprise.'

'He's got enterprise all right. Why's he at large?'

'He's working on the land apparently.'

'His activities don't seem particularly agricultural.'

'He winkled himself into the house somehow.'

'He knows his way about all right. He was bloody fresh. Who's that awful woman we travelled down with called Lady Craggs?'

The sudden appearance beside us of Alfred Tolland spared complicated exposition of Gypsy's origins. In any case the question had expressed an opinion rather than request for information. Alfred Tolland gazed down at Pamela. He seemed to be absolutely fascinated by her beauty.

'Do hope you're . . .'

'I'm what?'

'Better.'

He brought the word out sharply. Probably he ought always to be treated in an equally brusque manner, told to get on with it, make a move, show a leg, instead of being allowed to maunder on indefinitely trying to formulate in words his own obscurities of thought; licence that his relations had fallen too long into the habit of granting without check. Siegfried appeared again, this time carrying a tray loaded with cups and saucers. His personality lay somewhere between that of Odo Stevens and Mrs Andriadis's one-time boy-friend, Guggenbühl, now Gainsborough. He made firmly towards Alfred Tolland, who stood between him and the table where he planned to lay the tea things.

'Sir, excuse, you are in the way, please.'

Called to order only a second before by Pamela Alfred Tolland again reacted more quickly than usual. He almost jumped aside. Siegfried pushed adroitly past him, set the tray on a table, then returned to retrieve Pamela's cup from the floor.

'More of tea, Miss, please?'

'No.'

'Not good?'

'Not particularly.'

'Why not so?'

'God knows.'

'Another cup then, please. There is enough. China tea for the ration more easy.'

'I said I don't want any more.'

'No?'

She did not answer this time, merely closed her eyes. Siegfried, not in the least put out, showed no sign of going away. He and Alfred Tolland stood side by side staring at Pamela, expressing in their individual and contrasted ways boundless silent admiration. Her contempt for both of them was absolute. It seemed only to stimulate more fervent worship. After remaining thus entranced for some little time, Siegfried must have decided that after all work came first, because he suddenly hurried away, no less complacent and apparently finding the situation irresistibly funny. He had certainly conceived a more down-to-earth estimate of Pamela's character and possibilities than Alfred Tolland, who was in any case taken over at that moment by Blanche. He allowed himself to be led away, showing signs of being even a little relieved at salvage in this manner. Pamela opened her eyes again, though only to look straight in front of her. When I spoke of a meeting with Ada Leintwardine, she showed a little interest.

'I warned her that old fool Craggs, whose firm she's joining, is as randy as a stoat. I threw a glass of Algerian wine over him once when he was trying to rape me. Christ, his wife's a bore. I thought I'd strangle her on the way here. Look at her now.'

Gypsy, followed by Craggs, Quiggin and Widmerpool, had just arrived, ushered in by Siegfried, to whom Widmerpool was talking loudly in German. Whatever he had been saying must have impressed Siegfried, who stuck out his elbows and clicked his heels before once more leaving the room. Widmerpool missed this mark of respect, because he had already begun to look anxiously round for his wife. Frederica went forward to receive him, and the others, but Widmerpool scarcely took any notice of her, almost at once marking down Pamela's location and hurrying towards her. To run her to earth was obviously an enormous relief. He was quite breathless when he spoke.

'Are you all right?'

'Why should I be all right?'

'I meant no longer feeling faint. How did you find your way here? It was sensible to come and lie down.'

'I didn't fancy dying of exposure, which was the alternative.'

'Is it one of your nervous attacks?'

'I told you I'd feel like bloody hell if I came on this ghastly party—you insisted.'

'I know I did, dear, I didn't want to leave you alone. We'll be back soon.'

'Back where?'

'Home.'

'After another lovely journey with your friends.'

Widmerpool was not at all dismayed by this discouraging reception. What he wanted to know was Pamela's whereabouts. Having settled that, all was well. The physical state she might or might not be in was in his eyes a secondary matter. In any case he was probably pretty used to rough treatment by now, would not otherwise have been able to survive as a husband. Barnby used to describe the similar recurrent anxieties of the husband of some woman with whom he had been once involved, the man's disregard for everything except ignorance on his own part of his wife's localization. Having her under his eye, no matter how ill-humoured or badly-behaved, was all that mattered. Widmerpool seemed to have reached much the same stage in married life. Anything was preferable to lack of information as to what Pamela might be doing. His tone now altered to one of great relief.

'You'd better lie still. Rest while you can. I must go and talk business.'

'Do you ever talk anything else?'

Disregarding the question, he turned to me.

'Why is that Tory MP Cutts here?'

'He's another brother-in-law.'

'Of course, I'd forgotten. Retained his seat very marginally. I must have a word with him. That's Hugo Tolland he's talking to, I believe?'

'I haven't had an opportunity yet to congratulate you on winning your own seat.'

Widmerpool grasped my arm in the chumminess appropriate to a public man to whom all other men are blood brothers.

'Thanks, thanks. It showed the way things are going. A colleague in the House rather amusingly phrased it to me. We are the masters now, he said. The fight itself was a heartening experience. I used to meet Cutts when I was younger, but we have not yet made contact at Westminster. He had a sister called Mercy, I remember from the old days. Rather a plain girl. There are some things I'd like to discuss with him.'

He left the area of the sofa. Now the war was over one constantly found oneself congratulating people. In a mysterious manner almost everyone who had survived seemed also to have had a leg up. For example, books written by myself, long out of print, appeared better known after nearly seven years of literary silence. This was a more acceptable side of growing older. Even Quiggin, Craggs and Bagshaw had the air of added stature. Craggs was talking to Norah. Either to get away from him, or because she had decided that contact with Pamela was unavoidable, better to be faced coolly, she made some excuse, and came towards us. She may also have felt the need to restore her own reputation for disregarding commonplaces of sentiment in relation to such things as love and death. A brisk talk to Pamela offered opportunity to cover both elements with lightness of touch.

'Hullo, Pam.'

Norah's manner was jaunty.

'Hullo.'

'I never expected to see you here today.'

'You wouldn't have done, if I'd had my way.'

'Unlike you not to have your way, Pam.'

'That's good from you. You were always wanting me to do things I hated.'

'But didn't succeed.'

'It didn't look like that to me.'

'How have you been, Pam?'

'Like hell.'

After saying that Pamela picked up the book from the floor—revealed as Hugo's copy of *Camel Ride to the Tomb*, which he had brought down with him—smoothed out the crumpled pages, and began to turn them absently. Conceiving Norah well qualified by past experience to contend with manoeuvring of this particular kind, in which emotional undercurrents were veiled by unpromising mannerisms, I moved away. Their current relationship would be better hammered out unimpeded by male surveillance. Craggs, left on his own by Norah, had joined Quiggin and Frederica, who were talking together. In his elaborately refined vocables, reminiscent of a stage clergyman in spite of his anti-clericalism, he began to speak of Erridge.

'Such satisfying recollections of your brother were brought home to us—JG and myself, I mean—by the letter you are discussing. It revealed the man, the humanity under a perplexed, one might almost say headstrong exterior.'

Quiggin nodded judiciously. He may have felt a follow-

74

up by Craggs would be helpful after whatever he had himself been saying, because he led me away from the other two. He had been looking rather fiercely round the room while engaged with Frederica. Now his manner became jocular.

'Only through me you infiltrated this house.'

Notwithstanding fairly powerful efforts on his own part to prevent any such ingress, that was broadly speaking true. Obstructive tactics at such a distant date could be overlooked in the light of subsequent events. In any case Quiggin seemed to have forgotten this obverse side of his own benevolence. I supposed he was going to explain whatever dispositions Erridge had left which affected the new publishing firm, but something else was on his mind.

'You saw Mona?' he asked.

'I had quite a talk with her.'

'She was looking very prosperous.'

'She's married to an Air Vice-Marshal.'

'Good God.'

'She appears to like it.'

'Rather an intellectual comedown.'

'You never can tell.'

'Did she ask about me?'

'Said she'd sighted you outside the church and waved.'

'Not particularly good taste her coming, I thought. But listen—I understand you met Bagshaw, and he talked about *Fission*?'

'Not in detail. He said Erry had an interest—that to some extent the magazine would propagate his ideas.'

'Unfortunately that will be possible only in retrospect, but the fact Alf is no longer with us does not mean the paper will not be launched. In fact it will be carried forward much as he would have wished, subject to certain modifications. Kenneth Widmerpool is interested in it now. He wants an organ for his own views. There is another potential backer keen on the more literary, less political side. We have no objection to that. We think the magazine should be open to all opinion to be looked upon as progressive, a rather broader basis than Alf envisaged might be advantageous.'

'Why not?'

'Bagshaw was in Alf's eyes editor-designate. He has had a good deal of experience, even if not of actually running a magazine. I think he should make a tolerable job of it. Howard does not altogether approve of his attitude in certain political directions, but then Howard and Alf did not always see eye to eye.'

I could not quite understand why I was being told all this. Quiggin's tone suggested he was leading up to some overture.

'There will be too much for Bagshaw to spare time for books coming in for review. We'd have liked Bernard Shernmaker to do that, but everyone's after him. Then we tried L. O. Salvidge. He'd been snapped up too. Bagshaw suggested you might like to take the job on.'

The current financial situation was not such as to justify turning down out of hand an offer of this sort. Researches at the University would be at an end in a week or two. I made enquiries about hours of work and emoluments. Quiggin mentioned a sum not startling in its generosity, none the less acceptable, bearing in mind that one might ask for a rise later. The duties he outlined could be fitted into existing routines.

'It would be an advantage having you about the place as a means of keeping in touch with Alf's family. Also you've known Kenneth Widmerpool a long time, he tells me. He's going to advise the firm on the business side. The magazine and the publishing house are to be kept quite separate. He will contribute to *Fission* on political and economic subjects.'

'Do Widmerpool's political views resemble Erry's?'

'They have a certain amount in common. What's more important is that Widmerpool is not only an MP, therefore a man who can to some extent convert ideas into action—but also an MP untarnished by years of back-benching, with all the intellectual weariness that is apt to bring—I say, look what that girl's doing now.'

On the other side of the room Widmerpool had been talking for some little time to Roddy Cutts. The two had gravitated together in response to that law of nature which rules that the whole confraternity of politicians prefers to operate within the closed circle of its own initiates, rather than waste time with outsiders; differences of party or opinion having little or no bearing on this preference. Paired off from the rest of the mourners, speaking rather louder than the hushed tones to some extent renewed in the house after seeming befitted to the neighbourhood of the church, they were animatedly arguing the question of interest rates in relation to hire-purchase; a subject, if only in a roundabout way, certainly reconcilable to Erridge's memory. Widmerpool was apparently giving some sort of an outline of the Government's policy. In this he was interrupted by Pamela. For reasons of her own she must have decided to break up this tête-à-tête. Throwing down her book, which, having freed herself from Norah, she had been latterly reading undisturbed, she advanced from behind towards her husband and Roddy Cutts.

'People refer to the suppressed inflationary potential of our present economic situation,' Widmerpool was saying. 'I have, as it happens, my own private panacea for—'

He did not finish the sentence because Pamela, placing herself between them, slipped an arm round the waists of the two men. She did this without at all modifying the fairly unamiable expression on her face. This was the action to which Quiggin now drew attention. Its effect was

77

electric; electric, that is, in the sense of switching on currents of considerable emotional force all round the room. Widmerpool's face turned almost brick red, presumably in unexpected satisfaction that his wife's earlier ill-humour had changed to manifested affection, even if affection shared with Roddy Cutts. Roddy Cutts himself—who, so far as I know, had never set eyes on Pam̌ ı before that afternoon—showed, reasonably enough, every sign of being flattered by this unselfconscious demonstration of attention. Almost at once he slyly twisted his own left arm behind him, no doubt the better to secure Pamela's hold.

This was the first time I had seen her, so to speak, in attack. Hitherto she had always exhibited herself, resisting, at best tolerating, sorties of greater or lesser violence against her own disdain. Now she was to be observed in assault, making the going, preparing the ground for further devastations. The sudden coming into being of this baroque sculptural group, which was what the trio resembled, caused a second's pause in conversation, in any case rather halting and forced in measure, the reverential atmosphere that to some extent had prevailed now utterly subverted. Susan, glancing across at her husband clasped lightly round the middle by Pamela, turned a little pink. Quiggin may have noticed that and judged it a good moment for reintroduction—when they first met he had shown signs of fancying Susan—because he brought our conversation to a close before moving over to speak to her.

'I'll have a further word with Bagshaw,' he said. 'Then he or I will get in touch with you.'

Siegfried entered with a large teapot. He set it on one of the tables, made a sign to Frederica, and, without waiting for further instructions, began to organize those present into some sort of a queue. Frederica, now given opportunity to form a more coherent impression of Widmerpool's wife and her temperament, addressed herself with cold firmness to the three of them.

'Won't you have some tea?'

That broke it up. Siegfried remarshalled the party. Hugo took on Pamela. Widmerpool and Roddy Cutts, left once more together, returned to the principles of hire-purchase. Alfred Tolland, wandering about in the background, seemed unhappy again. I handed him a cup of tea. He embarked once more on one of his new unwonted bursts of talkativeness.

'I'm glad about Mrs Widmerpool . . . glad she found her way . . . the foreign manservant here . . . whoever he is, I mean to say . . . they're lucky to have a . . . footman . . . these days . . . hall-boy, perhaps . . . anyhow he looked after Mrs Widmerpool properly, I was relieved to find . . . Confess I like that quiet sort of girl. Do hope she's better. I'm a bit worried about the train though. We'll have to be pushing off soon.'

'You'll have time for a cup of tea.'

'Please, this way,' said Siegfried.' Please, this way now.'

He managed to break up most of the existing conversations.

'Just like Erry to find that goon,' said Hugo. 'He's worse than Smith, the butler who drank so much, and raised such hell at Aunt Molly's.'

In Siegfried's reorganization of the company, Gypsy was placed next to me, the first opportunity to speak with her. All things considered, she might have been more friendly in manner, though her old directness remained.

'Is this the first time you've been here?'

'No.'

That was at any rate evidence of a sort that she had visited Erridge on his home ground at least once; whether with or without Craggs, or similar escort, was not revealed.

'Who's that Mrs Widmerpool?'

To describe Pamela to Gypsy was no lesser problem than the definition of Gypsy to Pamela. Again no answer was required, Gypsy supplying that herself.

'A first-class little bitch,' she said.

Craggs joined his wife.

'JG and I have completed what arrangements can be made at present. We may as well be going, unless you want another cup of tea, Gypsy?'

The way he spoke was respectful, almost timorous.

'The sooner I get out, the better I'll be pleased.'

'Ought to thank for the cupper, I suppose.'

Craggs looked round the room. Frederica, as it turned out, had gone to fetch some testamentary document for Widmerpool's inspection. While they had been speaking Roddy Cutts took the opportunity of slipping away and standing by Pamela, who was listening to a story Hugo was telling about his antique shop. She ignored Roddy, who, seeing his wife's eye on him, drifted away again. Widmerpool drummed his fingers against the window frame while he waited. Until Roddy's arrival in her neighbourhood, Pamela had given the appearance of being fairly amenable to Hugo's line of talk. Now she put her hand to her forehead and turned away from him. She went quickly over to Widmerpool and spoke. The words, like his answer, were not audible, but she raised her voice angrily at whatever he had said.

'I tell you I'm feeling faint again.'

'All right. We'll go the minute I get this paper—what is that, my dear Tolland?—yes, of course we're taking you in the taxi. I was just saying to my wife that we're leaving the moment I've taken charge of a document Lady Frederica's finding for me.'

He spoke absently, his mind evidently on business matters. Pamela made further protests. Widmerpool turned to Siegfried, who was arranging the cups, most of them odd ones, in order of size at the back of the table.

'Fritz, mein Mann, sagen Sie bitte der Frau Gräfin, dass Wir jetzt abfahren.'

'Sofort, Herr Oberst.'

Pamela was prepared to submit to no such delays. 'I'm going at once—I must. I'm feeling ghastly again.'

'All right, dearest. You go on. I'll follow—the rest of us will. I can't leave without obtaining that paper.'

Widmerpool looked about him desperately. Marriage had greatly reduced his self-assurance. Then a plan suggested itself.

'Nick, do very kindly escort Pam to the door. She's not feeling quite herself, a slight recurrence of what she went through earlier. Those passages are rather complicated, as I remember from arriving. Your sister-in-law's looking for a document I need. I must stay for that, and to thank her for her hospitality.'

Pamela had certainly gone very white again. She looked as if she might be going to faint. Her withdrawal from church, in the light of previous behaviour likely to be prompted by sheer perversity, now took on a more excusable aspect. That she was genuinely feeling ill was confirmed by the way she agreed without argument to the suggested compromise. We at once set off down the stairs together, Pamela bidding no one goodbye.

'Is the taxi outside?'

'Parked in the yard.'

'Your coat?'

'Lying on some of that junk by the door.'

We hurried along. About halfway to the goal of the outside door, amongst the thickest of the bric-à-brac that littered the passage, she stopped.

'I'm feeling sick.'

This was a crisis indeed. If we returned to Erridge's

81

quarters, again negotiating the stairs and passing through the sitting-room, resources existed—in the Erridge manner, unelaborate enough—for accommodating sudden indisposition of this sort, but the sanctuary, such as it was, could not be called near. I lightly sketched in the facilities available, their means of approach. She looked at me without answering. She was a greenish colour by now.

'Shall we go back?'

'Back where?'

'To the bathroom—'

Pamela seemed to consider the suggestion for a second. She glanced round about, her eyes coming to rest on the two tall oriental vessels, which Lord Huntercombe had disparaged as nineteenth-century copies. Standing about five foot high, patterned in blue, boats sailed across their surface on calm sheets of water out of which rose houses on stilts, in the distance a range of jagged mountain peaks. It was a peaceful scene, very different from the emergency in the passage. Pamela came to a decision. Moving rapidly forward, she stepped lightly on one of the plinths where a huge jar rested, in doing so showing a grace I could not help admiring in spite of the circumstances. She turned away and leant forward. All was over in a matter of seconds. On such occasions there is no way in which an onlooker can help. Inasmuch as it were possible to do what Pamela had done with a minimum of fuss or disagreeable concomitant, she achieved that difficult feat. The way she brought it off was remarkable, almost sublime. She stepped down from the plinth with an air of utter unconcern. Colour, never high in her cheeks, slightly returned. I made some altogether inadequate gestures of assistance, which she unsmilingly brushed aside. Now she was totally herself again.

'Give me your handkerchief.'

She put it in her bag, and shook her hair.

'Come on.'

'You wouldn't like to go back just for a moment?'

'Of course not.'

Her firmness was granite. Just as we were proceeding on towards the outside door, the rest of the party, Widmerpool, Alfred Tolland, Quiggin, Craggs, Gypsy, appeared at the far end of the corridor. Hugo was seeing them out. Widmerpool was at the head, explaining some apparently complicated matter to Hugo, so that he did not notice Pamela and myself until a yard or two away.

'Ah, there you are, dear. I thought you'd have reached the car by now. I expect you are better, and Nicholas has been pointing out the *objets d'art* to you. It's the kind of thing he knows about. Rather fine some of the pieces look to me.'

He paused and pointed.

'What are those great vases, for example? Chinese? Japanese? I am woefully ignorant of such matters. I intend to visit Japan when opportunity occurs, see what sort of a job the Americans are doing there. I doubted the wisdom of retaining the Emperor. Feudalism must go whenever and wherever it survives. We must also keep an eye on Uncle Sam's mailed fist—but I am running away with myself. Pam, you must go carefully on the journey home. Rest is what you need.'

She did not utter a word but, turning from them, walked quickly towards the door. Morally speaking, some sort of warning seemed required that all had not been well, yet any such announcement was hard to phrase. Before anything could be said—if, indeed, there were anything apposite to say—Hugo had gently encouraged the group to move on.

'I think a revised seating arrangement might be advisable on the way back to the station,' said Widmerpool.

'I'm going in front,' said Pamela.

The rest were contained somehow at the back. Alfred Tolland looked like a man being put to the torture for conscience sake, but determined to bear the torment with fortitude. Pamela lay back beside the driver with closed eyes. The taxi moved away slowly towards the arch, hooted, disappeared from sight. No one waved or looked back. Hugo and I re-entered the house. I told him what had happened in the passage.

'In one of the big Chinese pots?'

'Yes.'

'You don't mean literally?'

'Quite literally.'

'Couldn't you stop her?'

'Where was there better?'

'You mean otherwise it would have been the floor?'

'I suppose so.'

'Does that mean she's going to have a baby?'

'I hadn't thought of that.'

'It's the only excuse.'

'I think it was just rage.'

'Nothing whatever was said?'

'Not a word.'

'You just looked on?'

'What was there to say? It wasn't my business, if she didn't want the others to sympathize with her.'

Hugo laughed. He thought for a moment.

'I believe if I were given to falling for women, I'd fall for her.'

'Meanwhile, how is the immediate problem to be dealt with?'

'We'll consult Blanche.'

The news of Pamela's conduct was received at the beginning with incredulity, the first reaction, that Hugo and I were projecting a bad-taste joke. When the crude truth was grasped, Roddy Cutts was shocked, Frederica furious,

Norah sent into fits of hysterical laughter. Jeavons only shook his head.

'Knew she was a wrong 'un from the start,' he said. 'Look at the way she behaved to that poor devil Templer. You know I often think of that chap. I liked having him in the house, and listening to all those stories about girls. Kept your mind off the blitz. Turned out we'd met before in that night-club of Umfraville's, though I couldn't remember a word about it.'

Complications worse than at first envisaged were contingent on what had happened. The Chinese vase had to be sluiced out. Blanche, although totally accepting responsibility for putting right this misadventure, like the burden of every other disagreeable responsibility where keeping house was concerned, voiced these problems first.

'I don't think we can very well ask Mrs Skerrett to clean things up.'

'Quite out of the question,' said Frederica.

There was unanimous agreement that it was no job for Mrs Skerrett in the circumstances.

'Why not tell that Jerry to empty it,' said Roddy Cutts. 'He's doubtless done worse things in his time. His whole demeanour suggests the Extermination Squad.'

'Oh, God, no,' said Hugo. 'Can you imagine explaining to Siegfried what has happened? He would either think it funny in that awful gross German way, or priggishly disapprove in an equally German manner. I don't know which would be worse. One would die of embarrassment.'

'No, you couldn't possibly ask a German to do the cleaning up,' said Norah. 'That would be going a bit far— and a POW at that.'

'I can't see why not,' said Roddy Cutts. 'Rather good for him, to my way of thinking. Besides, the Germans are always desperately keen on vomiting. In their cafés or

85

restaurants they have special places in the Gents for doing so after drinking a lot of beer.'

'It's not him,' said Norah. 'It's us.'

'Norah's quite right,' said Frederica.

For Frederica to support a proposition of Norah's was sufficiently rare to tip the scale.

'Well, who's going to do it?' asked Blanche. 'The jar's too big for me to manage alone.'

In the end, Jeavons, Hugo and I, with shrewd advice from Roddy Cutts, bore the enormous vessel up the stairs to Erridge's bathroom. It passed through the door with comparative ease, but, once inside, every kind of difficulty was encountered. Apart from size and weight, the opening at the top of the pot was not designed for the use to which it had been put; not, in short, adapted for cleansing processes. The job took quite a long time. More than once the vase was nearly broken. We returned to the sitting-room with a good deal of relief that the business was at an end.

'It's Erry's shade haunting the place,' said Norah. 'His obsession with ill-health. All the same, we all supposed him a *malade imaginaire*. Now the joke's with him.'

'I was thinking the other day that hypochondria's a step-brother to masochism,' said Hugo.

This sort of conversation grated on Frederica.

'Do you know how Erry occupied his last week?' she asked. 'Writing letters about the memorial window.'

'The old original memorial window?'

'Yes.'

'But Erry was always utterly against it,' said Norah. 'At least refused ever to make a move. It was George who used to say the window had been planned at the time and ought to be put up, no matter what.'

'Erry appears to have started corresponding about stained-glass windows almost immediately after George's funeral. Blanche found the letters, didn't you?'

Blanche smiled vaguely. Norah threw her cigarette into the fireplace in a manner to express despair at all human behaviour, her own family's in particular.

'Apart from going into complete reverse as to his own values, fancy imagining you could get a stained-glass window put up to your grandfather when you can't find a bloody builder to repair the roof of your bloody bombed-out flat. That was Erry all over.'

'Perhaps he meant it as a kind of tribute to George.'

'I don't object to George wanting to stick the window up. That was George's line. It's Erry. It was just like darling George to be nice about that sort of thing—just as he went when he did, and didn't hang about a few months after Erry to make double death duties. George was always the best behaved of the family.'

Frederica did not comment on that opinion. It looked as if a row, no uncommon occurrence when Frederica and Norah were under the same roof, might be about to break out. Hugo, familiar with his sisters' wars and alliances, changed the subject.

'There's always something rather consoling about death,' he said. 'I don't mean Erry, because of course one's very sorry about the old boy and all that. What you must admit is there's a curious pleasure in hearing about someone's death as a rule, even if you've quite liked them.'

'Not George's,' said Susan. 'I cried for days.'

'So did I,' said Norah. 'Weeks.'

She was never to be outdone by Susan.

'That's quite different again,' said Hugo. 'I quite agree I was cut up by George too. Felt awful about him in an odd way—I mean not the obvious way, but treating it objectively. It seemed such bloody bad luck What I'm talking about is that sense of relief about hearing a given death has taken place. One can't explain it to oneself.'

'I think you're all absolutely awful,' said Roddy Cutts.

'I don't like hearing about death or people dying in the least. It upsets me even if I don't know them—some film star you've hardly seen or foreign statesman or scientist you've only read about in the paper. It thoroughly depresses me. I agree with Dicky about that. Let's change the subject.'

I asked whether he had settled with Widmerpool the rights and wrongs of hire-purchase.

'I don't much care for the man. In the margins where we might be reasonably in agreement, he always takes what strikes me as an unnecessarily aggressive line.'

'What's Cheap Money?'

'The idea is to avoid a superfluity of the circulating medium concentrated on an insufficiency of what you swop it for. When Widmerpool and his like have put the poor old *rentier* on the spot they may find he wasn't performing too useless a rôle.'

'But Widmerpool's surely a *rentier* himself?'

'He's a bill-broker, and the bill-brokers are the only companies getting any sympathy from the Government these days. He's in the happy position of being wooed by both sides, the Labour Party—that is to say his own party—and the City, who hope to get concessions.'

'I find politics far more lowering a subject than death,' said Norah. 'Especially if they have to include discussing that man. I can't think how Pam can stand him for five minutes. I'm not surprised she's ill all the time.'

'I was told that one moment she was going to marry John Mountfichet,' said Susan. 'He was prepared to leave his wife for her. Then he was killed. She made this marriage on the rebound. Decided to marry the first man who asked her.'

'Don't you believe it,' said Jeavons. 'That sort of story always gets put round. Who was Mountfichet's wife—the Huntercombes' girl Venetia, wasn't she? I bet they suited each other a treat in their own way. Married couples usually do.'

'What's that got to do with whether he was going off with Pamela Flitton?' asked Norah. 'Or whether she married Widmerpool on the rebound?'

'People get divorced just because they don't know they suit each other,' said Jeavons.

He did not enlarge further on this rebuttal of the theory that people married 'on the rebound', or that the first choice was founded on an instinctive rightness of judgment. Instead, he turned to the question of how he himself was to get back to London. Wandering about the room chain-smoking, he looked more than ever like a plain-clothes man.

'Wish the train didn't arrive back so late. They must be getting familiar with my face on that line. Probably think I'm working the three-card trick. Anything I can do to help sort things out while I'm here? Cleaning up that mess in the jar's whetted my appetite for work. I'd have offered to be a bearer, if I'd thought I could hold up the coffin for more than a minute and a half, but that lump of gunmetal in my guts has been giving trouble again. Never seems to settle down. Sure the army vets left a fuse there, probably a whole shellcap. Can't digest a thing. Becomes a bore after a time. Never know what you may do when you're in that state. Didn't want to be halfway up the aisle, and drop my end of the coffin. Still, that couldn't have disrupted things, or made more row, than that girl did going out. Wish Molly was alive. Nothing Molly didn't know about funerals.'

Frederica, who had just come in, looked not altogether approving of all this. She was never in any case really sure that she liked Jeavons, certainly not when in moods like his present one. That had been Jeavons's standing with her even before she married Umfraville, for whom Jeavons himself had no great affection. Umfraville, on the other hand, liked Jeavons. He used to give rather subtle imitations of him.

'What you could do, Uncle Ted, is to make a list of the wreaths,' said Frederica. 'Would you really do that? It would be a great help.'

'Keep me quiet, I suppose,' said Jeavons.

He often showed an unexpected awareness that he was gettting on the nerves of people round him.

'I'll duly render a return of wreaths,' he said. 'Show the state (a) as to people who ought to have sent them and haven't, (b) those who've properly observed regulations as to the drill on such occasions.'

Never finding it easy to set his mind to things, the process, if Jeavons decided to do so, was immensely thorough. When he married, he had, for example, taken upon himself to memorize the names of all his wife's relations, an enormous horde of persons. Jeavons familiarized himself with these ramifications of kindred as he would have studied the component parts of a piece of machinery or mechanical weapon. He 'made a drill of it', as he himself expressed his method, in the army sense of the phrase, inventing a routine of some sort that enabled him to retain the name of each individual in his mind, together with one small fact, probably quite immaterial, about each one of them. As a consequence, his knowledge in that field was encyclopaedic. No one was better placed to list the wreaths. Hugo stretched himself out on the sofa.

'Mortality breeds odd jobs,' he said.

'And the men to do them,' said Jeavons.

Later, as he worked away, he could be heard singing in his mellow, unexpectedly attractive voice, some music-hall refrain from his younger days:

'When Father went down to Southend,
To spend a happy day,

90

He didn't see much of the water,
But he put some beer away.
When he landed home,
Mother went out of her mind,
When he told her he'd lost the seaweed,
And left the cockles behind.'

A footnote to the events of Erridge's funeral was supplied by Dicky Umfraville after our return to London. It
was to be believed or not, according to taste. Umfraville
produced the imputation, if that were what it was to be
called, when we were alone together. Pamela Widmerpool's name had cropped up again. Umfraville, assuming
the manner he employed when about to give an imitation,
moved closer. Latterly, Umfraville's character-acting had
become largely an impersonation of himself, Dr Jekyll,
even without the use of the transforming drug, slipping
into the skin of the larger-than-life burlesque figure of Mr
Hyde. In these metamorphoses, Umfraville's normal conversation would suddenly take grotesque shape, the bright
bloodshot eyes, neat moustache, perfectly brushed hair—
the formalized army officer of caricature—suddenly twisted
into some alarming or grotesque shape as vehicle for improvisation.

'Remember my confessing in my outspoken way I'd been
pretty close to Flavia Stringham in the old days of the
Happy Valley?'

'You put it more bluntly than that, Dicky—you said
you'd taken her virginity.'

'What a cad I am—well, one sometimes wonders.'

'Whether you're a cad, Dicky, or whether you were the
first?'

'Our little romance was scarcely over before she married
Cosmo Flitton. Now the only reason a woman like Flavia
could want to marry Cosmo was because she needed a

husband in a hurry, and at any price. Unfortunately my own circumstances forbade me aspiring to her hand.'

'Dicky, this is pure fantasy.'

Umfraville looked sad. Even at his most boisterous, there was a touch of melancholy about him. He was a pure Burton type, when one came to think of it. Melancholy as expressed by giving imitations would have made another interesting sub-section in the *Anatomy*.

'All right, old boy, all right. Keep your whip up. Cosmo dropped a hint once in his cups.'

'Not a positive one?'

'There was nothing positive about Cosmo Flitton—barring, of course, his Wassermann Test. Mind you, it could be argued Flavia found an equally God-awful heel in Harrison F. Wisebite, but Harrison came on to the scene too late to have fathered the beautiful Pamela.'

'I'm not prepared to accept this, Dicky. You've just thought it up.'

Umfraville's habit of taking liberties with dates, if a story could thereby be improved, was notorious.

'You can never tell,' he repeated. 'My God, Cosmo was a swine. A real swine. Harrison I liked in his way. He mixed a refreshing cocktail of his own invention called Death Comes for the Archbishop.'

3

In the course of preliminary conclaves with Bagshaw on the subject of *Fission*'s first number, mention was again made of an additional personage, a woman, who was backing the magazine. Bagshaw, adept at setting forth the niceties of political views, if these happened to attach to the doctrinaire Left, was less good at delineating individuals, putting over no more than that she was a widow who had always wanted some hand in running a paper. As it turned out, excuse existed for this lack of precision in grasping her name, in due course revealed in quite unforeseen circumstances. Bagshaw thought she would cause little or no trouble editorially. That was less true of Widmerpool, who certainly harboured doubts as to Bagshaw's competence as editor. Quiggin and Craggs were another matter. They were old acquaintances who differed on all sorts of points, but they were familiar with Bagshaw's habits. Widmerpool had no experience of these. He might take exception to some of them. Bagshaw himself was much too devious to express all this in plain terms, nor would it have been discreet to do so openly. His disquiet showed itself in repeated attempts to pinpoint Widmerpool himself politically.

'From time to time I detect signs of fellow-travelling. Then I think I'm on the wrong tack entirely, he's positively Right Wing Labour. Again, you find him stringing along with the far, but anti-Communist, Left. You can't help admiring the way he conceals his hand. My guess is he's playing ball with the Comrades on the quiet for whatever he can get out of it, but trying to avoid the appearance of doing so. He doesn't want to prejudice his chances of a good job in the Government when the moment comes.'

'Was that the game Hamlet was playing when he said:

> The undiscovered country from whose bourn
> No fellow-traveller returns, puzzles the will?'

'There was something fishy about Hamlet's politics, I agree,' said Bagshaw. 'But the only fellow-travellers we can be certain about were Rosencrantz and Guildenstern.'

Meanwhile I worked away at Burton, and various other jobs. The three months spent in the country after demobilization had endorsed the severance with old army associates, the foreign military attachés with whom I had been employed 'in liaison'. One returned to a different world. Once in a way the commemorative gesture might be made by one or other of them of inviting a former colleague, now relegated to civilian life; once in a way an unrevised list of names might bring one incongruously to the surface again. On the whole, attendance at such gatherings became very infrequent.

When we were asked to drinks by Colonel and Madame Flores, the invitation derived from neither of these two sources. It was sent simply because the hostess wanted to take another look at a former lover who dated back to days long before she had become the wife of a Latin American army officer; or—the latter far more probable, when one came to think of it—was curious, as ladies who have had an inclination for a man so often are, regarding the appearance and demeanour of his wife; with whom, as it happened, the necessity had never arisen to emphasize that particular conjunction of the past.

The Flores's drawing-room presented a contrast with the generally austere appearance almost prescriptive to apartments given over to official entertaining; not least on account of the profusion of flowers set about, appropriate to the host's surname, but at that period formidably expensive. This rare display, together with the abundance and variety of drink on offer—as Mona had remarked, still hard to obtain—suggested that Colonel Flores was fairly rich himself, or his Government determined to make a splash. It struck me all at once, confronted with this luxuriance, that, although never behaving as if that were so, money was after all what Jean really liked. In fact Duport, even apart from his other failings, had not really been rich enough. It looked as if that problem were now resolved, Jean married to a rich man.

Almost every country which had not been at war with us was represented among the guests round about, 'Allies' and 'Neutrals' alike. The 'Iron Curtain' states (a new phrase), from time to time irascible about hospitality offered or accepted, had on this occasion turned up in force. Looking round the room, one noted an increase in darker skins. Aiguillettes were more abundant, their gold lace thicker. Here was gathered together again an order of men with whom I should always feel an odd sense of fellowship, though now, among this crowd of uniformed figures, chattering, laughing, downing their drinks, not one of their forerunners remained with whom I had formerly transacted military business. Only two or three of those present were even familiar by sight.

Jean, rather superb in what was called 'The New Look' (another recent phrase), was dressed in a manner to which hardly any woman in this country, unless she possessed unusually powerful tentacles, could at that time aspire. She greeted us at the door. That she had become so fashionable had to be attributed, one supposed, to her husband. In the old days much of her charm—so it had seemed—had been to look like a well-turned-out schoolgirl, rather than an enchantress on the cover of a fashion magazine. The slight, inexpressibly slight, foreign intonation she had now acquired, or affected, went well with the splendours of *haute couture*.

'How *very* kind of you both to come.'

Colonel Flores had his CBE ribbon up, a decoration complimenting his country rather than rewarding any very tangible achievement of his own since taking up his appointment in London; indeed presented to him on arrival like a gift at a children's party to animate a cosy atmosphere. There was no doubt—as his predecessor and less triumphant husband, Bob Duport, had remarked—Flores did possess a distinct look of Rudolph Valentino. I thought how that comparison dated Duport and myself. Handsome, spruce, genial, the Colonel's English was almost more fluent than his wife's, at least in the sense that his language had that faintly old-world tinge that one associated with someone like Alfred Tolland—though naturally far more coherent in delivery—or multilingual royalties of Prince Theodoric's stamp.

'My dear fellow—don't mind if I call you Nick, just as Jean does when she speaks of you—how marvellous it must be to have left the army behind. I am always meaning to send in my papers, as you call it, get to hell out of it. Then I give the old show another chance—but you must have a drink. Pink gin? My tipple too. Contigo me entierren. But the army? How should I occupy myself if there was no one to order me about? That's what I ask. Jean always tells me also that I should be getting into trouble if I had too little to do. Our wives, our wives, what slaves they make of us. She thinks I should turn to politics. Well, I might one day, but how much I envy you to be free. My time will come at last. I shall then at least be able to look after my horses properly

'... Ah, my dear General ... but of course ... pernod, bourbon—I must tell you I have even got a bottle of tequila hidden away ... Hasta mañana, su Excelencia ... à bientôt, cher Colonel ...'

I wondered whether Jean trompé'd him with the gauchos, or whatever was of the most tempting to ladies in that country. Probably she did; her husband, having plenty of interests of his own, quite indifferent. The fact was Flores showed signs of being a great man. That had to be admitted. They were quite right to give him a CBE as soon as he arrived. His manner of handling his party suggested he well deserved it.

I circulated among the 'Allies', polite majors, affable colonels, the occasional urbane general, all the people who had once made up so much of daily life. Now, for some reason, there seemed little or nothing to talk about. It was no use broaching to these officers the subject of the newly founded publishing house of Quiggin & Craggs, the magazine *Fission* that was to embody the latest literary approach. At the same time the most superficial military topics once mutually exchanged seemed to have altered utterly overnight, everything revised, reorganized, reassembled; while —an awkward point—to approach, as a civilian, even the exterior trimmings of the military machine, when making conversation with the professional who controlled some part of it, was to risk, if not a snub, conveying an impression of curiosity either impertinent, or stemming from personal connexion with the Secret Service. While I wrestled with this problem, Jean reappeared.

'Your wife has so kindly asked us to dine with you. It's very hospitable, because I know how absolutely impossible it is to give dinner parties these days, not only rationing, but all sorts of other things. They are difficult enough even if you have official supplies and staff to draw on like ourselves. Carlos and I would so much have loved to come, but there has been a surprise. We have just received news from our Defence Ministry that we must go home.'

'Already?'

'We have to leave London almost at once. There has been a change of Government and a big reorganization.'

'Promotion, I hope?'

'Carlos has been given a military area in the Northern Province. It is quite unexpected and might lead to big things. There are, well, political implications. It is not just the same as being in the army here. So we have to make immediate arrangements to pack up, you see.'

She smiled.

'I should offer congratulations as well as regrets?'

'Of course Carlos is delighted, though he pretends not to be. He is quite ambitious. He makes very good speeches. We are both pleased really. It shows the new Government is being sensible. To tell the truth we were sent here partly to get Carlos out of the country. Now all that is changed— but the move must be done in such a hurry.'

'How foolish of them not to have wanted such a nice man about the place.'

She laughed at that.

'I was hoping to take Polly round a little in London. However, she is going to stay in England for a time in any case. She has ambitions to go on the stage.'

'I haven't seen her at your party?'

'She's with her father at the moment—I think you've met my first husband, Bob Duport?'

'Several times—during the war among others. He'd been ill in the Middle East, and we ran across each other in Brussels.'

'Gyppy tummy and other things left poor Bob rather a wreck. He ought to marry somebody who'd look after him properly, keep him in order too, which I never managed to do. He's rather a weak man in some ways.'

'Yes, poor Bob. No good being weak.'

She laughed again at this endorsement of her own estimate of Duport's character, but at the same time without giving anything away, or to the smallest degree abandoning the determined formality of her manner. That particular laugh, the way she had of showing she entirely grasped the point of what one had said, once carried with it powerful intoxications; now—a relief to ascertain even after so long—not a split second of emotional tremor.

'What's he doing now?'

'Bob? Oil. Something new for him—produced by an old friend of his called Jimmy Brent. You may have met him with my brother Peter. How I miss Peter, although we never saw much of each other.'

'I came across Jimmy Brent in the war too.'

'Jimmy's a little bit awful really. He's got very fat, and is to marry a widow with two grown-up sons. Still, he's fixed up Bob, which is the great thing.'

To make some comment that showed I knew she had slept with Brent—by his own account, been in love with him—was tempting, but restraint prevailed. Nevertheless, recollecting that sudden hug watching a film, her whisper, 'You make me feel so randy,' I saw no reason why she should go scot free, escape entirely unteased.

'How well you speak English, Madame Flores.'

'People are always asking if I was brought up in this country.'

She laughed again in that formerly intoxicating manner. A small dark woman, wearing an enormous spray of diamonds set in the shape of rose petals trembling on a stalk, came through the crowd.

'Rosie, how lovely to see you again. Do you know each other? Of course you do. I see Carlos is making signs that I must attend to the Moroccan colonel.'

Jean left us together. Rosie Manasch took a handful of stuffed olives from a plate, and offered one.

'I saw you once at a meeting about Polish military hospitals. You were much occupied at the other end of the room, and I had to move on to the Titian halfway through. Besides, I didn't know whether you'd remember me.'

The Red Cross, Allied charities, wartime activities of that sort, explained why she was at this party. It was unlikely that she had known Jean before the war, when Rosie had been married to her first husband, Jock Udall, heir apparent to the newspaper proprietor of that name, archenemy of Sir Magnus Donners. Rosie Manasch's parents, inveterate givers of musical parties and buyers of modern pictures, had been patrons of both Moreland and Barnby in the past. Mark Members had made a bid to involve them in literature too, but without much success, enjoying a certain amount of their hospitality, but never bringing off anything spectacular in the way of plunder. It had been rumoured in those days that Barnby had attempted to start up some sort of a love affair with Rosie. If so, the chances were that nothing came of it. Possessing that agreeable gift of making men feel pleased with themselves by the way she talked, she was in general held to own a less sensual temperament than her appearance suggested. Quite how she accomplished this investiture of male self-satisfaction was hard to analyse, perhaps simply because, unlike some women, she preferred men that way.

Udall was shot by the SS, on recapture, after a mass escape from a prisoner-of-war camp in Germany. The marriage—in the estimation of those always prepared to appraise explicitly other people's intimate relationships—was judged to have been only moderately happy. There were no children. There was also, even the most inquisitorial conceded, no gossip about infidelities on either side, although Udall was always reported to be 'difficult'. Quite soon after her husband's death, Rosie married a Pole called Andrzejewski, a second-lieutenant, though not at all young. I never came across him at the Titian during my period of liaison duty, but his appointment there, Polish GHQ in London, sounded fairly inconsiderable even within terms of the rank. Andrzejewski, as it turned out, was suffering from an incurable disease. He died only a few months after the wedding. Rosie resumed her maiden name.

'I've just been talking to your wife. We'd never met before, though I knew her sister Susan Tolland before she married. I hear you didn't guess that I was the mysterious lady in the background of *Fission*.'

'Was this arranged by Widmerpool?'

'The Frog Footman? Yes, indirectly. He used to do business when he was at Donners-Brebner with my cousin James Klein. Talking of Donners-Brebner, did you go to the Donners picture sale? I can't think why Lady Donners did not keep more of them herself. There must be quite a lot of money left in spite of death duties—though one never knows how a man like Sir Magnus Donners may have left everything.'

'If I'd been Matilda, I'd have kept the Toulouse-Lautrec.'

'Of course you must have known Matilda Donners when she was married to Hugh Moreland. Matilda and I don't much like each other, though we pretend to. Do you realize that a relation of mine—Isadore Manasch—was painted by Lautrec? Isn't that smart? A café scene, in the gallery at Albi. Isadore's slumped on a chair in the background. The Lautrec picture's the only thing that keeps his slim volume of Symbolist verse from complete oblivion. Isadore's branch of the family are still embarrassed if you talk about him. He was very disreputable.'

To emphasize the awful depths of Isadore's habits, Rosie stood on tiptoe, clasping together plump little hands that seemed subtly moulded out of pink icing sugar, then tightly caught in by invisible bands at the wrist. At forty or so, she herself was not unthinkable in terms of Lautrec's brush, more alluring certainly than the ladies awaiting custom on the banquettes of the Rue de Moulins, though with something of their resignation A hint of the seraglio, and its secrets, that attached to her suggested oriental costume in one of the masked ball scenes.

'Do you ever see Hugh Moreland now? Matilda told me he's still living with that strange woman called Maclintick. They've never married. Matilda says Mrs Maclintick makes him work hard.'

'I don't even know his address.'

That was one of the many disruptions caused by the war. Rosie returned to *Fission*.

'What do you think of the Frog Footman's beautiful wife? Did you hear what she said to that horrid girl Peggy Klein—who's a sort of connexion, as she was once married to Charles Stringham? James had adored Peggy for years when he married her—I'll tell you some other time. There's the Frog Footman himself making towards us.'

Widmerpool gave Rosie a slight bow, his manner suggesting the connexion with *Fission* put her in a category of business colleagues to be treated circumspectly.

'I've been having an interesting talk with the military attaché of one of the new Governments in Eastern Europe,' he said. 'He's just arrived in London. As a matter of fact I myself have rather a special relationship with his country, as a member—indeed a founder member—of no less than two societies to cement British relations with the new régime. You remember that ineffective princeling Theodoric, I daresay.'

'I thought him rather attractive years ago,' said Rosie. 'It was at Sir Magnus Donners' castle of all places. Was the military attaché equally nice?'

'A sturdy little fellow. Not much to say for himself, but made a good impression. I told him of my close connexions with his country. These representatives of single-party government are inclined to form a very natural distrust for the West. I flatter myself I got through to him successfully. I expect you've been talking about *Fission*. I hear you have been having sessions with our editor Bagshaw, Nicholas?'

'He's going to produce for me a writer called X. Trapnel, of whom he has great hopes.'

'*Camel Ride to the Tomb*?' said Rosie. 'I thought it so good.'

'I shall have to read it,' said Widmerpool. 'I shall indeed. I must be leaving now to attend to the affairs of the nation.'

Somebody came up at that moment to claim Rosie's attention, so I never heard the story of what Pamela had said to Peggy Klein.

The promised meeting with X. Trapnel came about the following week. Like almost all persons whose life is largely spun out in saloon bars, Bagshaw acknowledged strong ritualistic responses to given pubs. Each drinking house possessed its special, almost magical endowment to give meaning to whatever was said or done within its individual premises. Indeed Bagshaw himself was so wholeheartedly committed to the mystique of The Pub that no night of his life was complete without a final pint of beer in one of them. Accordingly, withdrawal of Bagshaw's company—whether or not that were to be regarded as auspicious —could always be relied upon, wherever he might be, however convivial the gathering, ten minutes before closing time. If—an unlikely contingency—the 'local' were not already known to him, Bagshaw, when invited to dinner, always took the trouble to ascertain its exact situation for the enaction of this last rite. He must have carried in his head the names and addresses of at least two hundred London pubs—heaven knows how many provincial ones—each measured off in delicate gradations in relation to the others, strictly assessed for every movement in Bagshaw's tactical game. The licensed premises he chose for the production of Trapnel were in Great Portland Street, dingy, obscure, altogether lacking in outer 'character', possibly a haunt familiar for years for stealthy BBC negotiations, after Bagshaw himself had, in principle, abandoned the broadcasting world.

'I'm sure you'll like Trapnel,' he said. 'I feel none of the reservations about presenting him sometimes experienced during the war. I don't mean brother officers in the RAF—who could be extraordinarily obtuse in recognizing the good points of a man who happens to be a bit out of the general run—but Trapnel managed to get on the wrong side of several supposedly intelligent people.'

'Where does he fit into your political panorama?'

Bagshaw laughed.

'That's a good question. He has no place there. Doesn't know what politics are about. I'd define him as a Leftish Social-Democrat, if I had to. Born a Roman Catholic, but doesn't practise—a lapsed Catholic, rather as I'm a lapsed Marxist. As a matter of fact I came across him in the first instance through a small ILP group in India, but Trapnel didn't know whether it was arse-holes or Tuesday, so far as all that was concerned. As I say, he's rather odd-man-out.'

Even without Bagshaw's note of caution, I had come prepared for Trapnel to turn out a bore. Pleasure in a book carries little or no guarantee where the author is concerned, and *Camel Ride to the Tomb*, whatever its qualities as a novel, had all the marks of having been written by a man who found difficulty in getting on with the rest of the world. That might well be in his favour; on the other hand, it might equally be a source of anyway local and temporary discomfort, even while one hoped for the best.

'Trapnel's incredibly keen to write well,' said Bagshaw. 'In fact determined. Won't compromise an inch. I admire that, so far as it goes, but writers of that sort can add to an editor's work. Our public may have to be educated up to some of the stuff we're going to offer—I'm thinking of the political articles Kenneth Widmerpool is planning—so Trapnel's good, light, lively pieces, if we can get them out of him, are likely to assist the other end of the mag.'

Trapnel's arrival at that point did not immediately set at rest Bagshaw's rather ominous typification of him. Indeed, Bagshaw himself seemed to lose his nerve slightly when Trapnel entered the bar, though only for a second, and quickly recovered.

'Ah, Trappy, here you are. Take a seat. What's it to be? How are things?'

He introduced us. Trapnel, in a voice both deep and harsh, requested half a pint of bitter, somehow an unexpectedly temperate choice in the light of his appearance and gruffness of manner. He looked about thirty, tall, dark, with a beard. Beards, rarer in those days than they became later, at that period hinted of submarine duty, rather than the arts, social protest or a subsequent fashion simply for much more hair. At the same time, even if the beard, assessed with the clothes and stick he carried, marked him out as an exhibitionist in a reasonably high category, the singularity was more on account of elements within himself than from outward appearance.

Although the spring weather was still decidedly chilly, he was dressed in a pale ochre-coloured tropical suit, almost transparent in texture, on top of which he wore an overcoat, black and belted like Quiggin's Partisan number, but of cloth, for some reason familiarly official in cut. This heavy garment, rather too short for Trapnel's height of well over six feet, was at the same time too full, in view of his spare, almost emaciated body. Its weight emphasized the flimsiness of the tussore trousers below. The greatcoat turned out, much later, to have belonged to Bagshaw during his RAF service, disposed of on terms unspecified, possibly donated, to Trapnel, who had caused it to be dyed black. The pride Trapnel obviously took in the coat was certainly not untainted by an implied, though unjustified, aspiration to ex-officer status.

The walking stick struck a completely different note. Its wood unremarkable, but the knob, ivory, more likely bone, crudely carved in the shape of a skull, was rather like old Skerrett's head at Erridge's funeral. This stick clearly bulked large in Trapnel equipment. It set the tone far more than the RAF greatcoat or tropical suit. For the rest, he was hatless, wore a dark blue sports shirt frayed at the collar, an emerald green tie patterned with naked women, was shod in grey suede brothel-creepers. These last, then relatively new, were destined to survive a long time, indeed until their rubber soles, worn to the thinness of paper, had become all but detached from fibreless uppers, sounding a kind of dismal applause as they flapped rhythmically against the weary pavement trodden beneath.

The general effect, chiefly caused by the stick, was of the Eighteen-Nineties, the *décadence*; putting things at their least eclectic, a contemptuous rejection of currently popular male modes in grey flannel demob suits with pork-pie hats, bowler-crowned British Warms, hooded duffels, or even those varied outfits like Quiggin's, to be seen here and there, that suggested recent service in the *maquis*. All such were rejected. One could not help speculating whether an eyeglass would not be produced—Trapnel was reported to have sported one for a brief period, until broken in a pub brawl—insomuch that the figure he recalled, familiar from some advertisement advocating a brand of chocolates or cigarettes, similarly equipped with beard and cane, wore an eye-glass on a broad ribbon, though additionally rigged out in full evening dress, an order round his neck, opera cloak over his shoulder. In Trapnel's case, the final effect had that touch of surrealism which redeems from complete absurdity, though such redemption was a near thing, only narrowly achieved.

Perhaps this description, factually accurate—as so often when facts are accurately reported—is at the same time morally unfair. 'Facts'—as Trapnel himself, talking about writing, was later to point out—are after all only on the surface, inevitably selective, prejudiced by subjective presentation. What is below, hidden, much more likely to be important, is easily omitted. The effect Trapnel made might indeed be a little absurd; it was not for that reason unimpressive. In spite of much that was all but ludicrous, a kind of inner dignity still somehow clung to him.

Nevertheless, the impression made on myself was in principle an unfavourable one when he first entered the pub. A personal superstructure on human beings that seems exaggerated and disorganized threatens behaviour to match. That was the immediate response. Almost at once this turned out an incorrect as well as priggish judgment. There were no frills about Trapnel's conversation. When he began to talk, beard, clothes, stick, all took shape as necessary parts of him, barely esoteric, as soon as you were brought into relatively close touch with the personality. That personality, it was at once to be grasped, was quite tough. The fact that his demeanour stopped just short of being aggressive was no doubt in the main a form of self-protection, because a look of uncertainty, almost of fear, intermittently showed in his eyes, which were dark brown to black. They gave the clue to Trapnel having been through a hard time at some stage of his life, even when one was still unaware how dangerously—anyway how

107

uncomfortably—he was inclined to live. His way of talking, not at all affected or artificial, had a deliberate roughness, its rasp no doubt regulated for pub interchanges at all levels, to avoid any suggestion of intellectual or social pretension.

'Smart cane, Trappy,' said Bagshaw. 'Who's the type on the knob? Dr Goebbels? Yagoda? There's a look of both of them.'

'I'd like to think it's Boris Karloff in a horror rôle,' said Trapnel. 'As you know, I'm a great Karloff fan. I found it yesterday in a shop off the Portobello Road, and took charge on the strength of the Quiggin & Craggs advance on the short stories. Not exactly cheap, but I had to possess it. My last stick, Shakespeare's head, was pinched. It wasn't in any case as good as this one—look.'

He twisted the knob, which turned out to be the pommel of a sword-stick, the blade released by a spring at the back of the skull. Bagshaw restrained him from drawing it further, seizing Trapnel's arm in feigned terror.

'Don't fix bayonets, I beseech you, Trappy, or we'll be asked to leave this joint. Keep your steel bright for the Social Revolution.'

Trapnel laughed. He clicked the sword back into the shaft of the stick.

'You never know when you may have trouble,' he said. 'I wouldn't have minded using it on my last publisher. Quiggin & Craggs are going to take over his stock of the *Camel*. They'll do a reprint, if they can get the paper.'

I told him I had enjoyed the book. That was well received. The novel's title referred to an incident in Trapnel's childhood there described; one, so he insisted, that had prefigured to him what life—anyway his own life—was to be. In the narrative this episode had taken place in some warm foreign land, the name forgotten, but a good deal of sand, the faint impression of a pyramid, offering a strong presumption that the locale was Egyptian. The words that made such an impression on the young Trapnel —in many subsequent reminiscences always disposed to represent himself as an impressionable little boy—were intoned by an old man whose beard, turban, nightshirt, all the same shade of off-white, manifested the outer habiliments of a prophet; just as the stony ground from which he delivered his tidings to the Trapnel family party seemed the right sort of platform from which to prophesy.

'Camel ride to the Tomb . . . Camel ride to the Tomb . . . Camel ride to the Tomb . . . Camel ride to the Tomb . . .'

Trapnel, according to himself, immediately recognized these words, monotonously repeated over and over again, as a revelation.

'I grasped at once that's what life was. How could the description be bettered? Juddering through the wilderness, on an uncomfortable conveyance you can't properly control, along a rocky, unpremeditated, but indefeasible track, towards the destination crudely, yet truly, stated.'

If Trapnel were really so young as represented by himself at the time of the incident, the story was not entirely credible, though none the worse for that. None the worse, I mean, insomuch as the words had undoubtedly haunted his mind at some stage, even if a later one. The greybeard's unremitting recommendation of his beast as means of local archaeological transport had probably become embedded in the memory as such phrases will, only later earmarked for advantageous literary use: *post hoc, propter hoc*, to invoke a tag hard worked by Sir Gavin Walpole-Wilson in post-retirement letters to *The Times*.

The earlier Trapnel myth, as propagated in the *Camel*, was located in an area roughly speaking between Beirut and Port Said, with occasional forays further afield from that axis. His family, for some professional reason, seemed to have roamed that part of the world nomadically. This fact—if it were a fact—to some extent attested the compatibility of a pleasure trip taken in Egypt, a holiday resort, in the light of other details given in the book, otherwise implying an unwarrantably prosperous interlude in a background of many apparent ups and downs, not to say disasters. Egypt cropped up more than once, perhaps—like the RAF officer's greatcoat—adding a potentially restorative tone. The occupation of Trapnel's father was never precisely defined; obscure, even faintly shady, commercial undertakings hinted. His social life appeared marginally official in style, if not of a very exalted order; possibly tenuous connexions with consular duties, not necessarily our own. One speculated about the Secret Service. Once— much later than this first meeting—a reference slipped out to relations in Smyrna. Trapnel's physical appearance did not exclude the possibility of a grandmother, even a mother, indigenous to Asia Minor. He was, it appeared, an only child.

'I always wondered what your initial stood for?'

Trapnel was pleased by the question.

'I was christened Francis Xavier. Watching an old western starring Francis X. Bushman in a cowboy part, it struck me we'd both been called after the same saint, and, if he could suppress the second name, I could the first.'

'You might do a novel about being a lapsed Catholic,' said Bagshaw. 'It's worth considering. I know JG would like you to tackle something more *engagé* next time. When I think of the things I'd write about if I had your talent. I did write a novel once. Nobody would publish it. They said it was libellous.'

'People like JG are always giving good advice about one's books,' said Trapnel. 'In fact I hardly know anyone who doesn't. "If only I could write like you, etc. etc." They usually outline some utterly banal human situation, or moral issue, ventilated every other day on the Woman's Page.'

'Don't breathe a word against the Woman's Page, Trappy. Many a time I've proffered advice on it myself under a female pseudonym.'

'Still, there's a difference between a novel and a newspaper article. At least there ought to be. A novelist writes what he is. That's equally true of mediaeval romances or journeys to the moon. If he put down on paper the considerations usually suggested, he wouldn't be a novelist—or rather he'd be one of the fifty-thousand tenth-rate ones who crawl the literary scene.'

Trapnel had suddenly become quite excited. This business of being a 'writer'—that is, the status, moral and actual, of a writer—was a matter on which he was inordinately keen. This was one of the facets of Trapnel to emerge later. His outburst gave an early premonition.

'Reviewers like political or moral problems,' said Bagshaw. 'Something they can get their teeth into. You can't blame them. Being committed's all the go now. I was myself until a few years ago, and still enjoy reading about it.'

Trapnel was not at all appeased. In fact he became more heated than ever, striking his stick on the floor.

'How one envies the rich quality of a reviewer's life. All the things to which those Fleet Street Jesuses feel superior. Their universal knowledge, exquisite taste, idyllic loves, happy married life, optimism, scholarship, knowledge of the true meaning of life, freedom from sexual temptation, simplicity of heart, sympathy with the masses, compassion for the unfortunate, generosity—particularly the last, in welcoming with open arms every phoney who appears on the horizon. It's not surprising that in the eyes of most reviewers a mere writer's experiences seem so often trivial, sordid, lacking in meaning.'

Trapnel was thoroughly worked up. It was an odd spectacle. Bagshaw spoke soothingly.

'I know some of the critics are pretty awful, Trappy,

but Nicholas wanted to talk to you about reviewing an occasional book yourself for *Fission*. If you agree to do so, you'll at least have the opportunity of showing how it ought to be done.'

Trapnel saw that he had been caught on the wrong foot, and took this very well, laughing loudly. He may in any case have decided some apology was required for all this vehemence. All the earlier tension disappeared at once.

'For Christ's sake don't let's discuss reviews and reviewers. They're the most boring subject on earth. I expect I'll be writing just the same sort of crap myself after a week or two. It's only they get me down sometimes. Look, I brought a short story with me. Could you let me know about it tomorrow, if I call you up, or send somebody along?'

Trapnel's personality began to take clearer shape after another round of drinks. He was a talker of quite unusual persistence. Bagshaw, notoriously able to hold his own in that field, failed miserably when once or twice he attempted to shout Trapnel down. Even so, the absolutely unstemmable quality of the Trapnel monologue, the impossibility of persuading him, as night wore on, to stop talking and go home, was a menace still to be learnt. He gave a few rather cursory imitations of his favourite film stars, was delighted to hear I had only a few days before met a man who resembled Valentino. Trapnel's mimicry was quite different from Dicky Umfraville's—he belonged, of course, to a younger generation—but showed the same tendency towards stylization of delivery. It turned out in due course that Trapnel impersonations of Boris Karloff were to be taken as a signal that a late evening must be brought remorselessly to a close.

A favourite myth of Trapnel's, worth recording at this early stage because it illustrated his basic view of himself, was how a down-at-heel appearance had at one time or another excited disdain in an outer office, restaurant or bar, this attitude changing to respect when he turned out to be a 'writer'. It might well be thought that most people, if they considered a man unreasonably dirty or otherwise objectionable, would regard the culpability aggravated rather than absolved by the fact that he had published a book, but possibly some such incident had really taken place in Trapnel's experience, simply because private fantasies so often seem to come into being at their owner's behest. This particular notion—that respect should be accorded to a man of letters—again suggested foreign rather than home affiliations.

When I left the pub, where it looked as if Bagshaw contemplated spending the evening, Trapnel stood up rather formally and extended his hand. I asked if he had a telephone number. He at once brushed aside any question of the onus of getting in touch again being allowed to rest with myself, explaining why that should be so.

'People can't very well reach me. I'm always moving about. I hate staying in the same place for long. It has a damaging effect on work. I'll ring you up or send a note. I rather enjoy the old-fashioned method of missive by hand of bearer.'

That sounded another piece of pure fantasy, but increased familiarity with Trapnel, and the way he conducted his life, modified this view. He really did send notes; the habit by no means one of his oddest. That became clear during the next few months, when we met quite often, while preparations went forward for the publication of the first number of *Fission*, which was due at the end of the summer or beginning of autumn. Usually we had a drink together in one of his favourite pubs—as with Bagshaw, these were elaborately graded—and once he dined with us at home, staying till three in the morning, talking about himself, his girls and his writing. That was the first occasion when the Boris Karloff imitation went on record as indication that the best of the evening was over, the curtain should fall.

A passionate interest in writing, or merely his taste for discussing it, set Trapnel aside from many if not most authors, on the whole unwilling to risk disclosure of trade secrets, or regarding such talk as desecration of sacred mysteries. Trapnel's attitude was nearer that of a businessman or scientist, never tired of discussing his job from a professional angle. That inevitably included difficulties with editors and publishers. Many writers find such relationships delicate, even aggravating. Trapnel was particularly prone to discord in that field. He had, for example, managed to get himself caught up in a legal tangle with the publication of a *conte*, before the appearance of the *Camel*. This long short story, to be published on its own by some small press, had not yet seen light owing to a contractual row. The story was left, as it were, in baulk; unproductive, unproduced, unread. There had apparently been trouble enough for Quiggin & Craggs to take over the rights of the *Camel*.

'The next thing's the volume of short stories,' said Trapnel. 'Then the novel I'm already working on. That's really where my hopes are based. It's going to be bigger stuff than the *Camel*. The question is whether Quiggin & Craggs have the sales organization to handle it properly.'

The question was more substantially how well Quiggin & Craggs would handle Trapnel himself. That looked like a tricky problem. Their premises were in Bloomsbury, according to Bagshaw reduced in price on account of bomb damage. An architecturally undistinguished exterior bore out that possibility. The building, reconditioned sufficiently for business to be carried on there, though not on a lavish scale, had housed small publishers for years, changing hands as successive firms went bankrupt or were absorbed by larger ones. There was no waiting room. Once through the door, you were confronted with the bare statement of the sales counter; beyond it the packing department, a grim den looking out on to a narrow yard. On the far side of this yard a kind of outhouse enclosed *Fission*'s editorial staff, that is to say Bagshaw and his secretary. Ada Leintwardine would sometimes cross the yard to lend a hand when the secretary, constantly replaced in the course of time, became too harassed by Bagshaw's frequent absences from the office to carry on unaided. Apart from that, an effort was made to keep the affairs of *Fission* separate so far as possible from the publishing side, although Craggs and Quiggin sat on both boards.

'Ada's the king-pin of the whole organization,' said Bagshaw. 'Maybe I should say queen bee. She provides an oasis of much needed good looks in the office, and a few contacts with writers not sunk in middle age.'

Ada had made herself at home in London. In fact she was soon on the way to becoming an established figure in the 'literary world', such as it was, battered and reduced, but taking some shape again, over and above the heterogeneous elements that had kept a few embers smouldering throughout the war. London suited Ada. She dealt with her directors, especially Quiggin, with all the skill formerly shown in managing Sillery. She had begun to refer to 'Poor old Sillers.' I had not seen Sillery himself again, as it happened, before the period of research at the University came to an end, calling once at his college, but being told he had gone to London for several days to attend the House of Lords.

When he was not present, Bagshaw was also designated by Ada 'Poor old Books'. That did not prevent them from getting on pretty well with each other. Her emotional life had become a subject people argued about. Malcolm Crowding, the poet, not much older than herself, alleged that the novelist Evadne Clapham (niece of the publisher of that name, and by no means bigoted in a taste for her own sex) had boasted of a 'success' with Ada. On the other hand, Nathaniel Sheldon, always on the look out, though advancing in years, spoke of encouragement offered him by Ada, when he was waiting to see Craggs. No doubt she made herself reasonably agreeable to anyone—even Nathaniel Sheldon, as a reviewer—likely to be useful to the firm. The fact that no one could speak definitely of lovers demonstrated an ability to be discreet. Ada herself was reported to be writing a novel, as Sillery had alleged.

In the humdrum surroundings of everyday business life, when, for example, one met them on the doorstep of the office, both Quiggin and Craggs showed themselves more changed than in the hurried, unaccustomed circumstances of Erridge's funeral. For instance, it was now clear Quiggin had settled down to be a publisher, intended to be a successful one, make money. He no longer spoke of himself producing a masterpiece. *Unburnt Boats*, his 'documentary', had been well received, whatever Sillery might say, when the book appeared not long before the war, but there Quiggin's literary career was allowed to rest. He had lost interest in 'writing'. Instead, he now identified himself, body and soul, with his own firm's publications, increasingly convinced—like not a few publishers—that he had written them all himself.

Quiggin also considered that he had a right, even duty, to make such alterations in the books published by the firm as he saw fit; anyway in the case of authors prepared to be so oppressed. Certainly Trapnel would never have allowed anything of the sort. There were others who rebelled. These differences of opinion might have played a part in causing Quiggin—again like many publishers—to develop a detestation of authors as a tribe. On the contrary, nothing of the sort took place. As long as they were his own firm's authors, Quiggin would allow no breath of criticism, either of themselves or their books, to be uttered in his presence, collectively or individually. His old rebellious irritability, which used formerly to break out so violently in literary or political argument, now took the form of rage—at best, extreme sourness—directed against anyone, professional critic or too blunt layman, who wrote an unfavourable notice, dropped an unfriendly remark, calculated to discourage Quiggin & Craggs sales.

Craggs's attitude towards publishing was altogether different. Craggs had been practising the art in one form or another for a long time. That made a difference. He did not care in the smallest degree about rude remarks made on the subject of 'his' authors, or 'his' books. In some respects, so far as the former were concerned, the more people abused them, the better Craggs was pleased. Certainly he had no great affection for authors as men— for that matter, unless easily seducible, as women—but, unlike Quiggin, his policy in this respect was not subjective; at least not entirely so. It cloaked a certain commercial shrewdness. Craggs, off his guard one day with Bagshaw, expressed the view that there were more ways of advertising a book than dwelling on the intellectual and moral qualifications of its author.

'What matters is getting authors talked about,' Craggs said. 'Let people know what they're really like. It whets the appetite. Look at Alaric Kydd's odd tastes, for instance. I drop an occasional hint.'

Craggs was being unusually communicative when he let that out, because in general nowadays he affected the manner of a man distinguished in his own sphere, but vague almost to the point of senility. Such had been his conversation at Thrubworth, though more defensive than real, to be dropped immediately if swift action were required. There was evidence that he was making good use of his wartime contacts in the civil service. Widmerpool, for his part, seemed to be pulling his weight too in a trade that was new to him.

'He's laid hands on some extra paper,' said Bagshaw. 'Found it hidden away and forgotten in some warehouse in his constituency.'

Walking through Bloomsbury one day on the way to the *Fission* office, I ran into Moreland. When I first caught sight of him coming towards me, he was laughing to himself. A shade more purple in the face than formerly, he looked otherwise much the same. We talked about what we had both been doing since that grim night the Café de Madrid was bombed. Moreland had always been fond of *The Anatomy of Melancholy*. I told him how I was now occupied with its author.

'Gone for a Burton, in fact?'

'Books-do-furnish-a-room Bagshaw's already made that joke.'

'How extraordinary you should mention Bagshaw. He got in touch with me recently about a magazine he's editing.'

'I'm on my way there now to sort out the review copies.'

'He wanted an article on Existential Music. The last time I saw Bagshaw was coming home from a party soon after he returned from Spain. He was crawling very slowly on his hands and knees up the emergency exit stairs of a tube station—Russell Square, could it have been?'

'He must have reached the top just in time for the war, because he was in the RAF, and now has a moustache.'

'A fighter-pilot?'

'PR in India.'

'Jane Harrigan's an' Number Nine, The Reddick an' Grant Road? I should think there was a good deal of that. I refused to contribute, although I suspect I've been an existentialist for years without knowing it. Like suffering from an undiagnosed disease. The fact is I now go my own way. I've turned my back on contemporary life—but what brings you to this forsaken garden? You can't know anybody who lives in Bloomsbury these days. Personally, I've been getting a picture framed, and am now trying to outstrip the ghosts that haunt the place and tried to commune with me. Comme le souvenir est voisin du remords.'

'Burton thought that too.'

'I've been reading Ben Jonson lately. He's a sympathetic writer, who reminds one that human life always remains the same. I remember Maclintick being very strong on that when mugging up Renaissance composers. Allowing for murder being then slightly easier, Maclintick believed a musician's life remains all but unchanged. How bored one gets with the assumption that people now are organically different from people in the past—the Lost Generation, the New Poets, the Atomic Age, the last reflected in the name of your new magazine

Fart upon Euclid, he is stale and antick.
Gi'e me the moderns.

It's the Moderns on whom I'm much more inclined to break wind.'

'If not too late, restrain yourself. As you've just pointed out, the Moderns no longer live round here.'

'Forgive my sneering at Youth, but what a lost opportunity within living memory. Every house stuffed with Moderns from cellar to garret. High-pitched voices adumbrating absolute values, rational states of mind, intellectual integrity, civilized personal relationships, significant form . . . the Fitzroy Street Barbera is uncorked. Le Sacre du Printemps turned on, a hand slides up a leg . . . All are at one now, values and lovers. Talking of that sort of thing, you never see Lady Donners these days, I suppose?'

'I read about her doings in the paper sometimes.'

'Like myself. Ah, well. Bagshaw's request made me wonder whether I would not give up music, and take to the pen as a profession. What about *The Popular Song from Lilliburllero to Lili Marlene?* Of course one might extricate oneself from the whole musical turmoil, cut free of it altogether. Turn to autobiography. *A Hundred Disagreeable Sexual Experiences* by the author of *Seated One Day at an Organ*—but I must be moving on. I'm keeping you from earning a living.'

I suggested another meeting, but he made excuses, murmuring something about a series of tiresome sessions with his doctor. Seen closer, he looked in less good health than suggested by the first impression.

'I've sacked Brandreth. My latest physician takes not the slightest interest in music, thank God, nor for that matter in any of the arts. He also has quite different ideas from Brandreth when it comes to assessing what's wrong with me. Life becomes more and more like an examination where you have to guess the questions as well as the answers. I'd long decided there were no answers. I'm beginning to suspect there aren't really any questions either, none at least of any consequence, even the old perennial, whether or not to stay alive.'

'Beyond Good and Evil, in fact?'

'Exactly—one touch of Nietzsche makes the whole world kin.'

On that note (recalling Pennistone) we parted. Moreland went on his way. I continued towards Quiggin & Craggs, through sad streets and squares, classical façades of grimy brick, faded stucco mansions long since converted to flats. Bagshaw had a piece of news that pleased him.

'Rosie Manasch is going to pay for a party to celebrate the First Number. That's scheduled for the last week in September. None of us have had a party for a long time.'

In the end, owing to the usual impediments, *Fission* did

not come to birth before the second week in October. The comparative headway made by then in establishment of the firm's position was reflected in the fact that, when I arrived at the Quiggin & Craggs office, where the party mentioned by Bagshaw was taking place, a member of the Cabinet was making his way up the steps. As he disappeared through the door, a taxi drove up, and someone called my name. Trapnel got out. The fare must have been already in his hand, because he passed the money to the driver with a flourish, turned immediately, and waved his stick in greeting. He was wearing sun spectacles—in which for everyday life he was something of an optical pioneer—and looked rather flustered.

'I thought I'd never get here. I'm temporarily living rather far out. Taxis are hard to find round there. I was lucky to pick up this one.'

The fact of his arriving by taxi at all did not at the time strike me as either remarkable or inevitable. I was still learning only slowly how near the knuckle Trapnel lived. The first few months of his acquaintance had been a period of comparative prosperity. They were not altogether representative. That did not prevent taxis playing a major rôle in his life. Trapnel used them when to the smallest degree in funds, always prepared to spend his last few shillings on this mode of transport, rather than descend to bus or tube. Later, when we were on sufficiently familiar terms to touch on so delicate a subject, he admitted that taxis also provided a security, denied to the man on foot, against bailiffs serving writs for debt. At the same time this undoubtedly represented as well an important factor in the practical expression of the doctrine of 'panache', which played a major part in Trapnel's method of facing the world. I did not yet fully appreciate that. We mounted the steps together.

'I don't think I'll risk leaving my stick down here,' he

said. 'It might be pinched by some detective-story writer hoping to experiment with the perfect crime.'

No one was about by the trade counter. Guests already arrived had left coats and other belongings at the back, among the stacks of cardboard boxes and brown-paper parcels of the equally deserted packing department. A narrow staircase led to the floor above, where several small rooms communicated with each other. The doors were now all open, furniture pushed back against the wall, typewriters in rubber covers standing on steel cabinets, a table covered with stacks of the first number of *Fission*. Apart from these, and a bookcase containing 'file' copies of a few books already published by the firm, other evidences of the publishing trade had been hidden away.

In the furthest room stood another table on which glasses, but no bottles, were to be seen. Ada Leintwardine was pouring drink from a jug. She had just filled a glass for the member of the Government who preceded us up the stairs. This personage, probably unused to parties given by small publishers, tasted what he had been given and smiled grimly. Craggs and Quiggin, one on either side, simultaneously engaged him in conversation. Bagshaw, not absolutely sober, waved. His editorial, perfectly competent, had spoken of the post-war world and its anomalies, making at least one tolerable joke. Trapnel's short story had the place of honour next to the editorial. We moved towards the drinks.

Bagshaw, like the Cabinet Minister, was taking on two at a time, in Bagshaw's case Bernard Shernmaker and Nathaniel Sheldon. This immediately suggested an uncomfortable situation, as these two critics had played on different sides in a recent crop of letters about homosexuality in one of the weeklies. In any case they were likely to be antipathetic to each other as representing opposite ends of their calling. Sheldon, an all-purposes journalist with a professional background comparable with Bagshaw's (Sheldon older and more successful) had probably never read a book for pleasure in his life. This did not at all handicap his laying down the law in a reasonably lively manner, and with brutal topicality, in the literary column of a daily paper. He would have been equally happy—possibly happier, if the epithet could be used of him at all—in almost any other journalistic activity. Chips Lovell, to whom Sheldon had promised a job before the war, then owing to some move in his own game withdrawn support, used often to talk about him.

Shernmaker represented literary criticism in a more eminent form. Indeed one of his goals was to establish finally that the Critic, not the Author, was paramount. He tended to offer guarded encouragement, tempered with veiled threats, to young writers; Trapnel, for example, when the *Camel* had first appeared. There was a piece by him in *Fission* contrasting Rilke with Mayakovsky, two long reviews dovetailed together into a fresh article. Shernmaker's reviews, unlike Sheldon's, would one day be collected together and published in a volume itself to be reviewed—though not by Sheldon. That was quite certain. Yet was it certain? Their present differences could become so polemical that Sheldon might think it worth while lampooning Shernmaker in his column. If Sheldon did decide to attack him, Shernmaker would have no way of getting his own back, however rude Sheldon might be. However, even offensive admission into Sheldon's column was recognition that Shernmaker was worth abusing in the presence of a mass audience. That would to some extent spoil the pleasure for Sheldon, for Shernmaker allay the pain.

Publishers, especially Quiggin, endlessly argued the question whether Sheldon or Shernmaker 'sold' any of the books they discussed. The majority view was that no sales could take place in consequence of Sheldon's notices, because none of his readers read books. Shernmaker's readers, on the other hand, read books, but his scraps of praise were so niggardly to the writers he scrutinized that he was held by some to be an equally ineffective medium. It was almost inconceivable for a writer to bring off the double-event of being mentioned, far less praised, by both of them.

The dangerous juxtaposition of Sheldon and Shernmaker was worrying Quiggin. He continually glanced in their direction, and, when Gypsy joined his group with Craggs and the Cabinet Minister, he allowed husband and wife to guide the statesman to a corner for a more private conversation, while he himself moved across the room. He paused briefly with Trapnel and myself.

'Where's your wife?'

He spoke accusingly, as if he considered a covert effort had been made to undermine the importance of the *Fission* first number, also his own prestige as a director of the magazine.

'Our child's in bed with a cold. She sent many regrets at missing the party.'

Quiggin looked suspicious, but pursued the matter no further, as the Sheldon and Shernmaker situation had become more ominous. Bagshaw was reasonably well equipped to hold the balance between a couple like this, operating expertly on two fronts, provided the other parties did not too far overstep the bounds each felt the other allowed by convention, given the fact they were on bad terms. This rule appeared to have been observed so far, but Sheldon now began to embark on a detailed account of a recent visit to the Nuremberg trials, his report on which had already appeared in print. At this new development Shernmaker's features had taken on the agonized, fractious contours of a baby about to let out a piercing cry. Quiggin stepped quickly forward.

'Bernard, I'm going to take the liberty of sending you a proof copy of Alaric Kydd's new novel *Sweetskin*. It will interest you.'

Shernmaker showed he had heard this statement by swivelling his head almost imperceptibly in Quiggin's direction, at the same time signifying by an unaltered expression that nothing was less likely than that a work of Kydd's would hold his attention for a second. However, he took the opportunity of moving out of the immediate range of Sheldon's trumpeting narrative, giving Quiggin a look to denote rebuke for ever having allowed such an infliction to be visited on a sensitive critic's nerves. Quiggin seemed to expect nothing more welcoming than this reception.

'There may be trouble about certain passages in Kydd's book—two especially. If it has to be toned down through fear of prosecution, I'd like you to have read what the author originally wrote.'

Shernmaker continued his stern silence. If he allowed his face to relax at all, it was only to register deeper suspicion of publishers and all their works. Quiggin was by no means to be put off by such severity. He smiled encouragingly. Although not by nature ingratiating, he could be industrious at the process if worth while.

'Don't tell me you've washed your hands of Kydd's work, Bernard—like Pilate?'

Shernmaker did not return the smile. He thought for a time. Quiggin, unlike Pilate for his part, awaited an answer. Shernmaker brought his own out at last.

'Pilate washed his hands—did he wash his feet?'

It was now Quiggin's turn to withhold a smile. He was as practised a punch-line killer and saboteur of other people's witticisms as Shernmaker himself. This disrespect for one of the firm's new authors must also have annoyed him. A lot was expected from Kydd. Before further exchanges could take place, Quiggin's old friend Mark Members arrived. With him was a young man whose khaki shirt, corduroy trousers, generally buccaneering aspect, suggested guerrilla warfare in the Quiggin manner, though far more effectively. This was appropriate enough in Odo Stevens, an unlikely figure to turn up at a publisher's party, though apparently an already accepted acquaintance of Members. As Sillery had remarked, white locks suited Members. He allowed them to grow fairly long, which gave him the rather dramatic air of a nineteenth-century literary man who had loved and suffered, the mane of hair weighing down his slight, spare body. Stevens made a face expressing recognition, but, before we could speak, was at once buttonholed by Quiggin, with whom he also appeared on the best of terms. Members now introduced Stevens to Shernmaker.

'I don't know whether you've met Odo Stevens, Bernard? You probably read his piece the other day about life with the Army of Occupation. Odo and I have just been discussing the most suitable European centre for cultural congress—you know my organization is trying to get one on foot. Do you hold any views? Your own co-operation would, of course, be valuable.'

Shernmaker was still giving nothing away. Frowning, moving a little closer, he watched Members's face as if trying to detect potential insincerities; allowing at the same time a rapid glance at the door to make sure no one of importance was arriving while his attention was thus occupied. Shernmaker's party personality varied a good deal according to circumstance; this evening a man of iron, on guard against attempts to disturb his own profundities of thought by petty everyday concerns. His duty, this manner implied, was with a wider world than any offered by Quiggin & Craggs and their like; if a trifle sullen, he must be forgiven. He had already shown that, once committed to such inanities, the best defence was epigram. Members, who had known Shernmaker for years—almost as long as he had known Quiggin—evidently wanted to get something out of him, because he showed himself quite prepared to put up, anyway within reason, with the Shernmaker personality as then exercised.

'You'll agree, Bernard, that effective discussion of the Writer's Position in Society is impractical in unsympathetic surroundings. Artists are vulnerable to circumstance, never more so than when compulsorily confined to their native shores.'

Still Shernmaker did not answer. Members became more blunt in exposition.

'We're none of us ever going to get out of England again, except as emissaries of culture. That's painfully clear. We're caught in a trap. Unless something is done, we'll none of us ever see the Mediterranean again.'

Evadne Clapham, L. O. Salvidge and Malcolm Crowding, the last of whom had a poem in *Fission*, had joined the group. All agreed with this deduction. Evadne Clapham went further. She clasped her hands together, and quoted:

'A Robin Redbreast in a Cage
Puts all Heaven in a Rage.'

The lines suddenly brought Shernmaker to life. He stared at Evadne Clapham as if outraged. She smiled invitingly back at him.

'Rubbish.'

'You think Blake rubbish, Mr Shernmaker?'

'I disagree with him in this particular case.'

'How so?'

'A robin redbreast in a rage
Puts all heaven in a cage.'

Evadne Clapham now unclasped her hands, and brought them together several times in silent applause.

'Very good, very good. You are quite right, Mr Shern-maker. I often notice what aggressive birds they are when I'm gardening. Your conclusion is, of course, that writers must not be held in check. Don't you agree, Mark? We must make ourselves heard. Do tell me about the young man you came in with. Isn't it true he's had a very glamorous war career, and is terribly naughty?'

This question was answered by Quiggin introducing Odo Stevens all round as the man who was writing a war book to make all other war books seem thin stuff. It was to be about Partisans in the Balkans. Quiggin was a little put out to find that Stevens and I had already met, but we were again prevented from talking by an incident taking place that was in a small way dramatic. Pamela Widmerpool, followed by her husband, had come into the room. Quiggin turned to greet them. Stevens was obviously as surprised to see Pamela at this party as I had been myself to find him there. As they came past he spoke to her.

'Why, hullo, Pam.'

She looked straight at, and through, him. It was not so much that she ignored what Stevens had said, as that she behaved as if he had never spoken, was not even there. She seemed to be looking at someone or something beyond him, unable to see Stevens himself at all. Stevens, by nature as sure of himself as a man could well be, was not in the least embarrassed, but certainly taken aback. When he grasped what had happened, he turned towards me and grinned. We were not near enough for comment.

'There's someone I'd like you to meet, dear heart,' said Widmerpool. 'We'll talk business later, JG. There are two misprints in my own article, but on the whole Bagshaw must be agreed to have made a creditable job of the first number.'

Apart from her treatment of Stevens—or signalizing it

by that—Pamela gave the impression of being on her best behaviour. She allowed herself to be piloted across to the Cabinet Minister. Cutting Stevens might be explained by the fact that, when last seen with him, she had slapped his face. It was quite possible that night, the first of the flying-bombs, had been also the last she had seen of him. To start again as total strangers was one way of handling such matters. The most recent news of her had been from Hugo Tolland. Pamela had appeared at his antique shop in the company of an unidentified man, who had paid cash for an Empire *bidet*, later delivered to the Widmerpool flat in Victoria Street; a highly decorative piece of furniture, according to Hugo. Inevitably her sickness at Thrubworth had developed into a legend of pregnancy, cut short artificially and not occasioned by her husband, but that was probably myth.

Widmerpool's demeanour gave no impression of having emerged from a trying domestic experience, though it could be argued the truth had been kept from him. Not long before, a speech of his in a parliamentary debate on the reduction of interest rates had been the subject of satirical comment in a *Daily Telegraph* leader, but, at the stage of public life he had reached, no doubt any mention in print was better than none. Certainly he appeared well satisfied with himself, clapping Craggs on the back, and giving an amicable greeting to Gypsy, with whom he must have established some sort of satisfactory adjustment. The article he had written for *Fission* had been called *Affirmative Action and Negative Values*. Stevens came over to talk.

'Did you notice Pam's lack of recognition? Her all over. What the hell's she doing here?'

He laughed heartily.

'Her husband's part of the Quiggin & Craggs set-up. Why did you hit on them for your book?'

'My agent thought they'd be the right sort of firm, as I was operating with the Commies most of the time I was in the Balkans. The publishers have only seen a bit of it. It's not finished yet. Will be soon. I'm spreading culture with Mark Members at the moment, but I hope to get out of an office—if the book sells, and it will.'

'All about being "dropped"?'

'A murder or two. Some rather spicy political revelations. One of the former incidents mucked up my affairs rather— lost me a DSO.'

'What did you haul in finally?'

'MC and bar, also one of the local gongs from the new régime. Don't know yet whether I'll be permitted to put it up. I shall anyway.'

'When did you get out of the army?'

'It was rather premature. I was never much of a hand at regimental life, even though I wasn't sure at one moment I wouldn't take up soldiering as a trade. So many temptations in Germany. The Colonel didn't behave too badly, but in the end he said I'd have to go. I agreed, so far as it went. I scrounged round for a bit selling space and little articles, then got myself fixed up in this culture-toting outfit. At the moment I'm in liaison with Mark Members and his conference project. I hear you're doing the books on this mag. What about some reviewing for Odo?'

'Why not, Odo? Why should you be the only man in England who's not going to review for *Fission*?'

'Who's the small dark lady talking to Sir Howard Craggs?'

'Rosie Manasch. She too has an interest in the mag.'

'Rather attractive. I think I'll meet her.'

The war had washed ashore all sorts of wrack of sea, on all sorts of coasts. In due course, as the waves receded, much of this flotsam was to be refloated, a process to continue for several years, while the winds abated. Among the many individual bodies sprawled at intervals on the shingle, quite a lot resisted the receding tide. Some just carried on life where they were on the shore; others—the more determined—crawled inland. Stevens belonged to the latter category. He knew where his future lay.

'Any books you can spare. Army matters, travel, jewellery —as you know, I'm interested in verse too. HQ, my cultural boys, always finds me.'

He strolled away. Widmerpool appeared.

'I've been having a lot to do with your relations lately. It turned out your late brother-in-law was on bad terms with the family solicitor. I've managed to arrange that some of the work should be transferred to Turnbull, Welford & Puckering—my old firm, you remember I started the struggle for existence in Lincoln's Inn—has the advantage of my being able to keep a weather eye on things from time to time. The Quiggin & Craggs interests will need a certain amount of attention. Hugo Tolland tells me he did not at all mind Mrs George Tolland giving birth to a son—one Jeremy, I understand—told me he was far from anxious to inherit responsibilities, myriad these days, of becoming head of the family. Titles are a survival one must deplore, but they can be a worry, as Howard Craggs was remarking last week. I see Hugo Tolland's point. He is a sensible young man, in spite of what at first appears a foolish manner. I understand that, as mother of the little earl, Mrs George Tolland—who has two children of her own by an earlier marriage—is going to live in the wing of Thrubworth Park formerly occupied by the late Lord Warminster. Modest premises in themselves, and a good idea. Lady Blanche Tolland is to remain there as before. An excellent arrangement for one of her retiring nature. I talked to her, and greatly approved what she had to say for herself.'

Abandoning for a moment the intense pleasure people

find in explaining in detail to someone the characteristics and doings of their own relations, he paused and glanced round the room. This could have been a routine survey to be taken wisely at regular intervals with the object of keeping check on his wife's doings. She was at that particular moment revealed as listening to some sort of a harangue given by a dark bespectacled personage in his thirties, whom I recognized as Werner Guggenbühl, now Vernon Gainsborough. There could be no doubt there was a look of Siegfried. Widmerpool marked them down.

'I see Pam's got caught up with Gainsborough. I don't know whether you've come across him? He's a German— a "good" German—a close friend of Lady Craggs, as a matter of fact. They go about a lot together. I'm giving away no secret. Craggs, very sensibly, takes an understanding view. He is a man of the world, though you might never guess that to look at him. Gainsborough is not a bad fellow. A little pedantic.'

'He used to be a Trotskyist.'

'No longer, I think. In any case I disapprove of witch-hunting. He stands, of course, considerably to the left of centre. I am not sure he is quite the sort of person Pam likes—she is easily bored—so perhaps it would be wise to come to her rescue.'

He gave the impression that Gainsborough's relationship with Gypsy, however little Craggs might resent it, and however 'good' a German he might be, was not one to recommend sustained conversation with a wife like his own. Widmerpool was about to move off and break up the tête-à-tête. However, Trapnel came up at that moment. Rather to my surprise, he addressed himself to Widmerpool with a formal cordiality not at all like his usual manner. It looked as if he were playing one of his rôles, a habit now becoming familiar.

'It's Mr Widmerpool, isn't it? Do forgive my introducing myself. My name's X. Trapnel. I'm a writer. JG was talking about you the other day. He said you were one of the few MPs who are trying to make the Government get a move on. I do hope you'll do something about the laws defining certain kinds of writing as obscene, when it's nothing of the sort. They really ought to be looked into. As a writer I can speak. You won't have heard of me, but I'm published by Quiggin & Craggs. I've a short story in this opening number of *Fission*.'

'Of course, of course.'

It was not possible to judge how far Widmerpool had taken in Trapnel's identity. I was at a loss to understand the meaning of this move. Trapnel continued to speak his piece.

'I don't want to bother you, just to say this. It looks as if there might be a danger of their bringing a case against Alaric Kydd's *Sweetskin*. I haven't read it, of course, because it isn't out yet—but we don't want JG put inside just because some liverish judge happens to take a dislike to Kydd's work.'

Widmerpool, if rather taken aback at being appealed to in this manner, was at the same time not unflattered to be regarded as the natural protector of publishers, now that he was in a sense a publisher himself. The manoeuvre was quite uncharacteristic of Trapnel. Like most writers in favour of abolishing current restrictions, such as they were, he was not so far as I knew specially interested in the question of 'censorship'. Trapnel's writing was not of the sort to be greatly affected by prohibitions of language or subject matter. He was competent to express whatever he wanted in an oblique manner. At the same time, he might well feel that, if obliquity in the context were less concordant than bluntness, it was absurd for bluntness to be forbidden by law. Language was a matter of taste. It looked as if the theme of censorship had been evoked on the spur

133

of the moment as a medium convenient for making himself known to Widmerpool. Although Trapnel's appearance was of a kind to which he was unused, Widmerpool showed himself equal to the challenge.

'I'm happy you mention the matter. It is one that has always been at the back of my mind as of prime importance. As with so many questions of a similar sort, there are two sides. We must consider all the evidence carefully, especially that of those best fitted to judge in such matters. Amongst them I don't doubt you are one, Mr Trapnel, an author yourself and man of experience, well versed in the subject. My own feeling is that we want to do away with the interference of old-fashioned busybodies to the furthest possible extent, while at the same time taking care not to offend the susceptibilities of simple people with a simple point of view, and their livings to earn, people who haven't time to concern themselves too closely with what may easily have the appearance of contradictory arguments put forward by the pundits of the so-called intellectual world, men whom you and I perhaps respect less than they respect themselves. The prejudices of such people may seem unnecessarily complicated to the man in the street, who has been brought up with what could sometimes be justly regarded as a lot of out-of-date notions, but notions that are nevertheless dear to him, if only because they have been dear in the past to someone whose opinion he knew and revered—I mean of course to his mother.'

Widmerpool, who had dropped his voice at the last sentence, paused and smiled. The reply was one with which no politician could have found fault. Surprisingly enough, it seemed equally satisfactory to Trapnel. His acceptance of such an answer was as inexplicable as his reason for asking the question.

'Admirably expressed, Mr Widmerpool. What I envy about an MP like yourself is not the power he wields, it's his constituency. Going round and seeing how all sorts of different people live, what their homes are like, some friendly, some hostile. It must be a fascinating experience—what background stuff for a novelist.'

This was getting so near utter nonsense that I wondered whether Trapnel had managed to get drunk in a comparatively short time on the watery cocktail available, and, for reasons still obscure, wanted to pick a quarrel with Widmerpool; was, in fact, building up to deliver some public insult. Widmerpool himself totally accepted Trapnel's words at their face value.

'It is indeed a privilege to see ordinary folk in their own homes, though I never thought of the professional advantage you put forward. Well, housing conditions need a lot of attention, and I can tell you I am giving them of my best.'

'You should come and try to pull the plug where I am living myself,' said Trapnel. 'I won't enlarge.'

Widmerpool looked rather uneasy at that. Trapnel, seeing he risked prejudicing the good impression he intended to convey, laughed and shook his head, dismissing the matter of plumbing.

'I just wanted to mention the matter. Nice of you to have listened to it—nice also to have met.'

'Just let me make a note of your bad housing, my friend,' said Widmerpool. 'Exact information is always useful.'

Trapnel had spoken his last words in farewell, but Widmerpool led him aside and took out a notebook. At the same moment Pamela abandoned Gainsborough, whose attractions her husband must have overrated. She came towards us. Widmerpool turned to her. She disregarded him, and addressed herself to me in her slow, hypnotic voice.

'Have you been attending any more funerals?'

'No—have you?'

135

'Just awaiting my own.'

'Not imminent, I hope?'

'I rather hope it is.'

'How are you enjoying political life?'

'Like any other form of life—sheer hell.'

She said that in a relatively friendly tone. Craggs intervened and led Widmerpool away. Trapnel returned. I introduced him to Pamela. It was not a success. In fact it was a disaster. From being in quite a good humour, she switched immediately to an exceedingly bad one. As he came up, her face at once assumed an expression of instant dislike. Trapnel himself could not fail to notice this change in her features. He winced slightly, but did not allow himself to be discouraged sufficiently to abandon all hope of making headway. Obviously he was struck by Pamela's appearance. For a moment I wondered whether that had been the real reason for making such a point of introducing himself to Widmerpool. Any such guess turned out wide of the mark. On the contrary, he had not seen them come into the room together, nor taken in who she was. His head appeared still full of whatever he had been talking about to Widmerpool, because he did not listen when I told him her name. It turned out later that he was determined in his own mind that Pamela was a writer of some sort. Having decided that point, he wanted to find out what sort of a writer she might be. This was on general grounds of her looks, rather than any very special attraction he himself found for them.

'Are you doing something for *Fission*?'

Pamela stared at him as if he had gone off his head.

'Me?'

'Yes.'

'Why should I?'

'I just thought you might.'

'Do I look the sort of person who'd write for *Fission*?'

136

'It struck me you did rather.'

She gave him a stare of contempt, but did not answer. Trapnel, seeing he was to be treated with deliberate offensiveness, made no further effort in Pamela's direction. Instead, he began talking of the set-to on the subject of modern poetry that had just taken place between Shernmaker and Malcolm Crowding. Pamela walked away in the direction of Ada Leintwardine. Trapnel looked after her and laughed.

'Who is she?'

'I told you—Mrs Widmerpool.'

'Wife of the MP I was chatting with?'

'She's rather famous.'

'I didn't get the name. I thought you were saying something about Widmerpool. So that's who she is? I'd never have thought he'd have a wife like that. Bagshaw was talking about him, so I thought I'd like to make contact. I can't say I was much taken with Mrs Widmerpool. Is that how she always behaves?'

'Quite often.'

'Girls like that are not in my line. I don't care how smashing they look. I need a decent standard of manners.'

At this stage of our acquaintance I did not know much about Trapnel's girls, beyond his own talk about them, which indicated a fair amount of experience. Some 'big' love affair of his had gone wrong not long before our first meeting. Ada came round with the drink jug. Trapnel filled up and moved away.

'Not much danger of intoxication from this brew,' she said.

'The Editor doesn't seem to have done too badly.'

'Books had an early go at the actual bottle—before this potion was mixed.'

Bagshaw, rather red in the face, was in fact little if at all drunker than he had been at the beginning of the party, reaching a saturation point beyond which he never over-flowed. He was clutching Evadne Clapham affectionately round the waist, while he explained to her—with some supposed reference to her short story in *Fission*—where Marx differed from Feuerbach in aiming not to interpret the world but to change it; and what was the real significance of Lenin's April Theses.

'Evadne Clapham's coiffure always reminds me of that line of Arthur Symons, "And is it seaweed in your hair?"' said Ada. 'There's been some hot negotiation with poor old Sillers, but we've come across with quite a big advance in the end. I hope the book will justify that when it appears.'

'What's Odo Stevens's work to be called?'

'*Sad Majors*, an adaption of—

Let's have one other gaudy night: call to me
All my sad captains . . .

JG doesn't care for the title. We're trying to get Stevens to change it.'

'Why? We all agree it's a gloomy rank.'

'God—Nathaniel Sheldon's helping himself. He must think he's not being appreciated.'

It was true. Sheldon was routing about under the drink table. Ada hurried off. It was time to go home. I sought out Quiggin to say goodbye. He was talking with Shern-maker, whose temper seemed to have improved, because he was teasing Quiggin.

'Gauguin abandoned business for art, JG—you're like Rimbaud, who abandoned art for business.'

'Resemblances undoubtedly exist between publishing and the slave trade,' said Quiggin. 'But it's not only authors who get sold, Bernard.'

Downstairs in the packing department Widmerpool was wandering about looking for something. He no longer retained his earlier geniality, was now despondent.

'I've lost my briefcase. Hid it away somewhere down here. I say, that friend of yours, Trapnel, is an odd fellow, isn't he?'

'In appearance?'

'Among other things.'

'He's a good writer.'

'So I'm told.'

'I mean should be useful on *Fission*.'

'Ah, there's the briefcase—no, I've just been talking to Trapnel, and his behaviour rather surprised me. As a matter of fact he asked me to lend him some money.'

'Following, no doubt, on your recommendations in the House that interest rates should be reduced.'

'Your joke is no doubt very amusing. At the same time you will agree Trapnel's request was unusual on the part of a man whom I had never set eyes on before tonight, when he introduced himself to me?'

'You know what literary life is like.'

'I'm beginning to learn.'

'Did you come across?'

'I handed over a pound. The man assured me he was completely penniless. However, let us speak no more of that. I merely put it on record. I consider the party for *Fission* was a success. It will get off to a good start, even though I do not feel so much confidence in Bagshaw as I could wish.'

'He knows his stuff.'

'So everyone says. He appeared to me rather drunk by the end of the evening, but I must not stay gossiping. I have to get back to Westminster. Pam had to leave early. She had a dinner engagement.'

We went outside. Trapnel was standing on the pavement. He had just hailed a cab. He must have been waiting there for one to pass for some minutes; in fact since he had taken the pound off Widmerpool.

'Dearth of taxis round this neighbourhood's almost as bad as where I'm living. Can I give anyone a lift? I'm heading north.'

We both declined the offer.

4

IN THE NEW YEAR, WITHOUT further compromise, Dickensian winter set in. Snow fell, east winds blew, pipes froze, the water main (located next door in a house bombed out and long deserted) passed beyond insulation or control. The public supply of electricity broke down. Baths became a fabled luxury of the past. Humps and cavities of frozen snow, superimposed on the pavement, formed an almost impassable barrier of sooty heaps at the gutters of every crossing, in the network of arctic trails. Bagshaw sat in his overcoat, the collar turned up round a woollen muffler, from which a small red nose appeared above a gelid moustache. Ada's protuberant layers of clothing travestied pregnancy. Only Trapnel, in his tropical suit and dyed greatcoat, seemed unaware of the cold. He complained about other things: lack of ideas: emotional setbacks: financial worries. Climate did not affect him. The weather showed no sign of changing. It encouraged staying indoors. I worked away at Burton.

On the whole Bagshaw's tortuous, bantering strategy, which had seen him through so many tussles with employers and wives (the latest one kept rigorously in the background), was designed to conceal hard-and-fast lines of opinion—assuming Bagshaw still held anything of the sort—so that, in case of sudden showdown, he could without prejudice give support wherever most convenient to himself. Even so, he allowed certain assessments to let fall touching on the fierce internal polemics that raged under the surface at Quiggin & Craggs; by association, at *Fission* too. Such domestic conflict, common enough in all businesses, took a peculiarly virulent form in this orbit, according to Bagshaw, on account of political undercurrents concerned.

'There are daily rows about what books are taken on. JG's not keen on frank propaganda, especially in translation. The current trouble's about a novel called *The Pistons of Our Locomotives Sing the Songs of Our Workers*. JG thinks the title too long, and that it won't sell anyway. No doubt the Party will see there's no serious deficit, but JG fears that sort of book clogs the wheels—the pistons in this case—of the non-political side of the list. He's nervous in certain other respects too. He doesn't mind inconspicuous fraternal writings inculcating the message in quiet ways. He rather likes that. What he doesn't want is for the firm to get a name for peddling the Party Line.'

'Craggs takes another view?'

'Howard's an old fellow-traveller of long standing. He hardly notices the books are propaganda. It all gives him a nostalgic feeling that he's young again, running the Vox Populi Press, having the girls from the 1917 Club. All the same, he probably wouldn't argue with JG so much if he wasn't being prodded all the time by Gypsy.'

'And Widmerpool?'

'All I'm certain about is he wants to winkle me out of the editorship. As I've said, he behaves at times like a crypto, but I suspect he's still waiting to see which way the cat will jump—and of course he doesn't want to get too far the wrong side of his Labour bosses in the House.'

'You were uncertain at first.'

'He's been repeating pure Communist arguments about

the Civil War in Greece. He may simply believe them. I'm never quite sure Gypsy hasn't a hold on him of some sort. There was a story about them in the old days. That was long before I came on the scene so far as Gypsy was concerned.'

'How does Rosie Manasch take all this?'

'She's only interested in writers and art, all that sort of thing. She doesn't cause any trouble. She holds those mildly progressive views of the sort that are not at all bothered by the Party Line. Incidentally, she seems to have taken rather a fancy to young Odo Stevens. Trappy's becoming rather a worry. We're always shelling out to him. He writes an article or a short story, gets paid on the nail, is back on the doorstep the next afternoon, or one of his stooges is, and he wants some more. I can handle him all right, but I'm not sure they're doing so well on the other side of the yard.'

Trapnel's financial embarrassments had become unambiguous enough during the months that transformed him from a mere acquaintance of Bagshaw's, and professional adjunct of *Fission*, into a recognized figure in one's own life. His personality, built up with thought, deserves a word or two on account of certain elements not restricted to himself. He was a fine specimen of a general type, to which he had added flourishes of his own, making him—it was hardly going too far to say—unique in the field. The essential point was that Trapnel always acted a part; not necessarily the same part, but a part of some kind. Insomuch as most people cling to a rôle in which they particularly fancy themselves, he was no great exception so far as that went. Where he differed from the crowd was in so doggedly sticking to the rôle—or rôles—he had chosen to assume.

Habitual rôle-sustainers fall, on the whole, into two main groups: those who have gauged to a nicety what shows them off to best advantage: others, more romantic if less fortunate in their fate, who hope to reproduce in themselves arbitrary personalities that have won their respect, met in life, read about in papers and books, or seen in films. These self-appointed players of a part often have little or no aptitude, are even notably ill equipped by appearance or demeanour, to wear the costume or speak the lines of the prototype. Indeed, the very unsuitability of the rôle is what fascinates. Even in the cases of individuals showing off a genuine pre-eminence—statesmen, millionaires, poets, to name a few types—the artificial personality can become confused with the passage of time, life itself being a confused and confusing process, but, when the choice of part has been extravagantly incongruous, there are no limits to the craziness of the performance staged. Adopted almost certainly for romantic reasons, the rôle, once put into practice, is subject to all sorts of unavoidable and unforeseen restraints and distortions; not least, in the first place, on account of the essentially rough-and-ready nature of all romantic concepts. Even assuming relative clarity at the outset, the initial principles of the rôle-sustainer can finally reach a climax in which it is all but impossible to guess what on earth the rôle itself was originally intended to denote.

So it was with Trapnel. Aiming at many rôles, he was always playing one or other of them for all he was worth. To do justice to their number requires—in the manner of Burton—an interminable catalogue of types. No brief definition is adequate. Trapnel wanted, among other things, to be a writer, a dandy, a lover, a comrade, an eccentric, a sage, a virtuoso, a good chap, a man of honour, a hard case, a spendthrift, an opportunist, a *raisonneur*; to be very rich, to be very poor, to possess a thousand mistresses, to win the heart of one love to whom he was ever faithful, to be on the best of terms with all men, to avenge savagely the lightest affront, to live to a hundred full of years and honour, to die young and unknown but recognized the following day as the most neglected genius of the age. Each of these ambitions had something to recommend it from one angle or another, with the possible exception of being poor—the only aim Trapnel achieved with unqualified mastery—and even being poor, as Trapnel himself asserted, gave the right to speak categorically when poverty was discussed by people like Evadne Clapham.

'I do so agree with Gissing,' she said. 'When he used to ask of a writer—has he starved?'

The tribute was disinterested, as Evadne Clapham did not in the least look as if she had ever starved herself. The remark ruffled Trapnel.

'Gissing was more of an authority on starvation than on writing.'

'You don't think hunger teaches things?'

'I know as much about starvation as Gissing, probably more.'

'Then you prove his point—though after all it's dedication that counts in the end.'

'Dedication's often the hallmark of inferior performance.'

Trapnel was in a severe mood on that occasion. He was annoyed at Evadne Clapham being brought to his favourite pub The Hero of Acre. The conversation was reproduced in due course, somewhat more elaborately phrased, with the heroine getting the whip-hand, when Evadne Clapham's next novel appeared. However, that is by the way. To return to Trapnel's ambitions, they were—poverty apart—not only hard to achieve individually, but, even in rotation, impossible to combine. That was over and above Trapnel's particular temperament, no great help. Infeasibility did not prevent him from behaving, where ambitions were concerned, like an alpinist who tackles the sheerest, least accessible rock face of the peak he has sworn to ascend.

The rôle of 'writer' was on the whole the one least

damaged when the strain became too severe, a heavy weight of mortal cargo jettisoned. There were times when even that rôle suffered violent stress. All writing demands a fair amount of self-organization, some of the 'worst' writers being among the most highly organized. To be a 'good' writer needs organization too, even if those most capable of organizing their books may be among the least competent at projecting the same skill into their lives. These commonplaces, trite enough in themselves, are restated only because they have bearing on the complexity of Trapnel's existence. There was a growing body of opinion, including, as time went on, Craggs, Quiggin, even Bagshaw himself —though unwillingly—which took the view that Trapnel's shiftlessness was in danger of threatening his status as a 'serious' writer. His books might be what the critics called 'well put together'—Trapnel was rather a master of technical problems—his life most certainly was the reverse. Nevertheless, people have to do things their own way, and the troubles that beset Trapnel were for the most part in what Pennistone used to call 'a higher unity'. So far as coping with down-to-earth emergencies, often seemingly unanswerable ones, Trapnel could show surprising agility.

One point should be cleared up right away. If comparison of his own life with a camel ride to the tomb makes Trapnel sound addicted to self-pity, a wrong impression has been created. Self-pity was a trait from which, for a writer —let alone a novelist—he was unusually free. On the other hand, it would be mistaken to conclude from that fact that he had a keen grasp of objectivity where his own goings-on were concerned. That judgment would be equally wide of the mark. This lack of objectivity made him enemies; that of self-pity limited sales. Whatever Trapnel's essence, the fire that generated him had to see him through difficult days. At the same time he managed to retain in a reasonably flourishing state—flourishing, that is, in his own eyes—what General Conyers would have called his 'personal myth', that imaginary state of being already touched on in Trapnel's case. The General, speaking one felt with authority, always insisted that, if you bring off adequate preservation of your personal myth, nothing much else in life matters. It is not what happens to people that is significant, but what they think happens to them.

Although ultimate anti-climaxes, anyway in their most disastrous form, were still kept at bay at this period, portents were already threatening in the eyes of those—L. O. Salvidge, for example, one of the first to praise the *Camel* —who took a gloomy view. Others—Evadne Clapham led this school of thought—dismissed such brooding with execrations against priggishness, assurances that Trapnel would 'grow up'. When Evadne Clapham expressed the latter presumption, Mark Members observed that he could think of no instance of an individual who, having missed that desirable attainment at the normal stage of human development, successfully achieved it in later life. It was hard to disagree. The fact is that a certain kind of gifted irresponsibility, combined with physical stamina and a fair degree of luck—in some respects Trapnel was incredibly lucky—always holds out an attractive hope that its possessor will prove immune to the ordinary vengeances of life; that at least one human being, in this case X. Trapnel, will beat the book, romp home a winner at a million to one.

Trapnel said he preferred women to have tolerable manners. The taste was borne out by the behaviour of such girls as he produced in public. When things were going reasonably well, he would be living with a rather unusually pretty one, who was also to all appearances bright, good tempered and unambitious. At least that was the impression they gave when on view at The Hero of Acre, or another of Trapnel's chosen haunts. The fairly rapid turnover suggested they might be less amenable when alone with Trapnel, not on their best behaviour; but that, after all, was just as much potential criticism of Trapnel as of the girl. She usually kept herself by typing or secretarial work (employed in concerns other than those coming under the heading of publishing and journalism), her financial contribution tiding over the ménage more or less—on the whole less rather than more—during lean stretches of their life together.

The pair of them, when Trapnel allowed his whereabouts to be known, were likely to be camped out in a bleak hotel in Bloomsbury or Paddington, enduring intermittent persecution from the management for delayed action in payment of the bill. The Ufford, as it used to be in Uncle Giles's day, would have struck too luxurious, too bourgeois a note, but, after wartime accommodation of a semi-secret branch of the Polish army in exile, the Ufford, come down in the world like many such Bayswater or Notting Hill establishments, might well have housed Trapnel and his mistress of the moment; their laundry impounded from time to time, until satisfactory settlement of the weekly account.

Alternatively, during brief periods of relative affluence, Trapnel and his girl might shelter for a few weeks in a 'furnished flat'. This was likely to be a stark unswept apartment in the back streets of Holland Park or Camden Town. The flat might belong to an acquaintance from The Hero of Acre, for example, possibly borrowed, while a holiday was taken, custodians needed to look after the place; if Trapnel and his girl could be so regarded.

When, on the other hand, things were going badly, the girl would have walked out—this happened sooner or later with fair regularity—and, if the season were summer, the situation might not exclude a night or two spent on the Embankment. The Embankment would, of course, represent a very low ebb indeed, though certainly experienced during an unprosperous interlude immediately preceding the outbreak of war. After such disasters Trapnel always somehow righted himself, in a sense seeming to justify the optimism of Evadne Clapham and those of her opinion. Work would once more be established on a passable footing, a new short story produced, contacts revived. The eventual replacement of the previous girl invariably kept up the traditionally high standard of looks.

Like many men rather 'successful' with women, Trapnel always gave the impression of being glad to get away from them from time to time. Not at all a Don Juan—using the label in a technical sense—he was quite happy to remain with a given mistress, once established, until the next upheaval. The question of pursuing every woman he met did not arise. Unlike, say, Odo Stevens, Trapnel was content to be in a room with three or four women without necessarily suffering the obligation to impose his personality on each one of them in turn.

All the same, if they could feel safe with him in that sphere, Trapnel's girls, even apart from shortage of money, had to put up with what was in many respects a hard life, one regulated by social routines often untempting to feminine taste. A gruelling example was duty at The Hero of Acre. They would be expected to sit there for hours while Trapnel held forth on *Portrait of the Artist*, or *The Birth of a Nation*. Incidentally, The Hero of Acre was to be avoided if absolute freedom from parasites was to be assured, even though Trapnel could drastically rebuff them, if they intervened when a more important assignation was in progress. Dismissal might take a minute or two, should they be drunk, and in any case their mere presence in the saloon bar could be inhibiting.

However, this body of auxiliaries was a vital aspect of the Trapnel way of life. When things were bad, they would

come into play, collect books for review, deliver 'copy'—
Trapnel in any case distrusted the post—telephone in his
name about arrangements or disputes, tactfully propound
his case if required, detail his future plans if known, try—
when such action was feasible, sometimes when not—to
raise the bid in his favour. They were to be seen lingering
patiently in waiting rooms or halls of the journal concerned—at Quiggin & Craggs in the packing room, if cold
and wet, the yard, if sunny and dry—usually the end in
view to acquire ready cash for the Trapnel piece they had
handed to the editor a short time before. Where Trapnel
recruited these auxiliaries, how he disciplined them, was
always a mystery.

This need to receive payment on the nail was never
popular with the publishers and editors. Even Bagshaw
used to grouse about it. The money in his hand, Trapnel
could rarely hang on to it. He was always in debt, liked
standing drinks. He could not understand the difficulties
publishers and editors, especially the latter, made about
advancing further sums.

'After all, it's not their own money. It's little or no
trouble to them. As a matter of fact the accountants, the
boys who are put to the ultimate bother, such as it is, of un-
locking the safe and producing the dough, are far easier to
deal with than the editor himself.'

Accountants, as described by Trapnel, would often leave
their offices after the money had been paid out, and join
him in a drink. Perhaps they thought they were living dangerously. It might be argued they were. Trapnel had made
a study of them.

'People who spend their time absorbed with money
always have a bright apologetic look about the eyes. They
crave sympathy. Particularly accountants. I always offer a
drink when specie changes hands. It's rarely refused.'

Bagshaw was unusually skilful in controlling this aspect

of Trapnel as a *Fission* contributor. Not at all inexperienced himself in the exertions of extracting money, he knew all the arguments why Trapnel should not be given any more until he produced the goods. Bagshaw would put on an immensely good-natured act that represented him as a man no less necessitous than Trapnel himself, if not more so. Trapnel did not have to believe that, but it created some sort of protection for Bagshaw. That was when Trapnel appeared in person. As time went on, these personal visits decreased in frequency.

Living as he did, there were naturally times when Trapnel was forced to apply for a loan. Widmerpool was a case in point. One of the principles dearest to Trapnel was that, as a writer himself, he did not care to borrow from another writer; anyway not more than once. At a party consisting predominantly of writers and publishers—publishers naturally unsuitable for rather different reasons—Widmerpool was a tempting expedient. A man of strong principle in his own particular genre, Trapnel appears to have observed this self-imposed limitation to the best of his ability, circumstances from time to time perforce intervening. The fulfilment of this creed must have been strengthened by practical experience of the literary profession's collective deficiencies as medium for floating loans.

However, almost everyone had their story of being approached by Trapnel at one time or another: Mark Members: Alaric Kydd: L. O. Salvidge: Evadne Clapham: Bernard Shernmaker: Nathaniel Sheldon: Malcolm Crowding: even Len Pugsley. All had paid up. Among these Alaric Kydd took it the hardest. The 'touch' had been one afternoon, when Kydd and Trapnel had met at the Quiggin & Craggs office. They were moving northwards together in the direction of Tavistock Square, according to Kydd, who was very bitter about it afterwards. He had been particularly outraged by Trapnel's immediate offer of a drink, a piece of good-fellowship received not at all in the spirit proffered. Quiggin, whose relations with Kydd were not entirely friendly, although proud of him as a capture, told the story after.

'Alaric had my sympathy. The money was at one moment resting frugally and safely in his pocket—the next, scattered broadcast by Trapnel. Alaric wasn't going to stand Trapnel a drink with it, it's therefore logical he should object to Trapnel wasting it on a drink for him.'

Kydd's never wholly appeased rancour implied abstraction of a somewhat larger sum than customary. A tenner was normal. Quiggin, whose judgment on such matters was to be respected, put it as high as twelve or fifteen— possibly even twenty. He may have been right. He had just signed a cheque for Kydd. There must have been a battle of wills. Trapnel did not on the whole prejudice his own market by gleaning the odd five bob or half-a-crown, though there may have been fallings by the wayside in this respect when things were bad; even descent to sixpences and pennies, if it came to that, for his unceasing and interminable telephone calls from the afternoon drinking clubs he liked to frequent. Such dives appealed to him chiefly as social centres, when The Hero and other pubs were closed, because Trapnel, as drinking goes, was not a great consumer, though he chose to speak of himself as if he were. An exceptionally excited or demoralized mood was likely to be the consequence of his 'pills', also apparently taken in moderation, rather than alcohol.

'The habit of words bestows adroitness on men of letters in devising formulae of excuse in evading onerous obligations. More especially when it comes to parting with hard cash.'

St John Clarke had voiced that reflection—chronologically speaking, before the beginning of years—when Mark Members had not yet been ousted by Quiggin as the well-known novelist's secretary; himself to be replaced in turn by Guggenbühl. Members had goodish stories about his former master, particularly on the theme of handling needy acquaintances from the past, who called in search of financial aid. Members insisted that the sheer artistry of St John Clarke' pretexts claiming exemption from lending were so ornate in expression that they sometimes opened fresh avenues of attack for the quicker-witted of his persecutors.

'Many a literary parasite met his Waterloo in that sitting-room,' said Members. 'There were crises when shelling out seemed unavoidable. St J. always held out right up to the time he was himself remaindered by the Great Publisher. I wonder what luck X. Trapnel would have had on that stricken field of borrowers.'

It was an interesting question. Trapnel was just about old enough to have applied for aid before St John Clarke's passing. His panoramic memory for the plots of twentieth-century novels certainly retained all the better known of St John Clarke's works; as of almost every other novelist, good, bad or indifferent, published in Great Britain since the beginning of the century. As to the United States, Trapnel was less reliable, though he could put up a respectable display of familiarity with American novelists too; anyway since the end of the first war. An apt quotation from *Dust Thou Art* (in the College rooms), *Match Me Such Marvel* (Bithel's favourite) or the much more elusive *Mimosa* (brought to my notice by Trapnel himself), might well have done the trick, produced at the right moment by a young, articulate, undeniably handsome fan; the intoxicating sound to St John Clarke of his own prose repeated aloud bringing off the miracle of success, where so many tired old leathery hands at the game had failed. In the face of what might sound damaging, even contradictory evidence, Trapnel was no professional sponge in the manner of characters often depicted in nineteenth-century novels,

153

borrowing compulsively and indiscriminately, while at the same time managing to live in comparative comfort. That was the picture Members painted of the St John Clarke petitioners, spectres from the novelist's younger, more haphazard days, who felt an old acquaintance had been allowed too long to exist in undisturbed affluence. Members had paused for a phrase. 'Somewhere between men of letters and blackmailers, a largely forgotten type.'

No one could say Trapnel resembled these. He neither lived comfortably, nor, once the need to take taxis were recognized, borrowed frivolously. Indeed, when things were going badly, there was nothing frivolous about Trapnel's condition except the manner in which he faced it. He borrowed literally to keep alive, a good example of something often unrecognized outside the world of books, that a writer can have his name spread all over the papers, at the same time net perhaps only a hundred pounds to keep him going until he next writes a book. Finally, the battle against all but overwhelming economic pressures might have been lost without the support of Trapnel's chief weapon—to use the contemporary euphemism 'moral deterrent'—the swordstick. The death's head, the concealed blade, in the last resort gained the day.

I have given a long account of Trapnel and his ways in order to set in perspective what happened later. Not all this description is derived from first-hand knowledge. Part is Trapnel legend, of which there was a good deal. He reviewed fairly regularly for *Fission*, wrote an occasional short story, article or parody—he was an accomplished parodist of his contemporaries—and on the whole, in spite of friction now and then, when he lost his temper with a book or one of his pieces was too long or too short, the magazine suited him, he the magazine. His own volume of collected short stories, *Bin Ends*, was published. Trapnel's reputation increased. At the same time he was clearly no stranger to what Burton called 'those excrementitious humours of the third concoction, blood and tears'.

One day the blow fell. Alaric Kydd's *Sweetskin* appeared on the shelf for review. Even Quiggin was known to have reservations about the novel's merits. Several supposedly outspoken passages made him unwilling to identify himself with the author in his accustomed manner, in case there was a prosecution. In addition to that, a lack of humdrum qualities likely to appeal to critics caused him worry about its reception. These anxieties Quiggin had already transmitted to Bagshaw. *Sweetskin* was a disappointing book. Kydd had been coaxed away from Clapham's firm. Now he seemed to be only a liability. On the one hand, the novel might be suppressed, the firm fined, a director possibly sent to gaol; on the other, the alleged lubricities being in themselves not sufficient to guarantee by any means a large sale, *Sweetskin* might easily not even pay off its considerable advance of royalties. How was the book to be treated in *Fission*? Kydd was too well known to be ignored completely. That would be worse than an offensive review. Who could be found, without too hopelessly letting down the critical reputation of *Fission* itself, to hold some balance between feelings on either side of the backyard at the Quiggin & Craggs office?

Then an opportune thing happened. Trapnel rang up Bagshaw, and asked if he could deal with Kydd, in whose early work he was interested, even though he thought the standard had not been maintained. If he could see *Sweetskin*, he might want to write a longer piece, saying something about Kydd's origins and development, in which the new book would naturally be mentioned. Bagshaw got in touch with me about this. It seemed the answer. Trapnel's representative came round the same afternoon to collect the review copy.

The following week, when I was at *Fission* 'doing' the books, Trapnel rang up. He said he was bringing the *Sweetskin* review along himself late that afternoon, and suggested we should have a drink together. There was something he particularly wanted to talk about. This was a fairly normal thing to happen, though the weather was not the sort to encourage hanging about in pubs. I also wanted to get back to Burton. However, Trapnel was un-usually pressing. When he arrived he was in a jumpy state, hard to say whether pleased or exasperated. Like most great egoists, a bad arriver, he lacked ease until settled down into whatever rôle he was going to play. Something was evidently on his mind.

'Would you object to The Hero? That's the place I'd feel it easiest to tell you about this.'

If the object of the meeting was to disclose some intimate matter that required dissection, even allowing for Trapnel's reasonably competent control of his creatures, few worse places could be thought of, but the venue was clearly de-manded by some quirk of pub mystique. These fears were unjustified. The immoderate cold had kept most of the usual customers away. The place was almost empty. We sat down. Trapnel looked round the saloon bar rather wildly. His dark-lensed spectacles brought to The Hero's draught-swept enclaves a hint of warmer shores, bluer skies, olives, vines, in spite of the fact that the turn-ups of the tussore trousers were soaked from contact with the snow. He at once began a diatribe against *Sweetskin*, his notice of which had been left unread at the office.

'I warned you it wasn't much good.'

This would mean embarrassment for Quiggin, if Trap-nel had been unremittingly scathing. Coming on top of the 'touch', unfavourable comment from such a source would make Kydd more resentful than ever. However, that was primarily Quiggin's worry. So far as I was concerned the juggernaut of critical opinion must be allowed to take its irrefragable course. If too fervent worshippers, like Kydd, were crushed to powder beneath the pitiless wheels of its car, nothing could be done. Only their own adoration of the idol made them so vulnerable. Trapnel was specially contemptuous of Kydd's attempts at eroticism. To be fair, *Sweetskin* was in due course the object of prosecution, so presumably someone found the book erotic, but Trapnel became almost frenzied in his expostulations to the contrary. It was then suddenly revealed that Trapnel was in the middle of a row with Quiggin & Craggs.

'I thought you got on so well with Ada?'

Ada Leintwardine dealt with Trapnel in ordinary contacts with the firm. She did not control disposal of money —there Quiggin was called in—but questions of production, publicity, all such matters passed through her hands. Book production, as it happened, owing to shortage of paper and governmental restrictions of one kind or another, was at the lowest ebb in its history at this period. A subject upon which Trapnel held strong views, this potential area of difference might have led to trouble. Ada always smoothed things over. After the honeymoon following the transfer of *Camel Ride to the Tomb*, Trapnel and Craggs scarcely bothered to conceal the lack of sympathy they felt for one another. It looked as if Quiggin had now been swept into embroilment by Trapnel's tendency to get on bad terms with all publishers and editors.

In this connexion, Ada was an example of Trapnel's exemption from the need to captivate every woman with whom he came in contact. He would not necessarily have captivated Ada had he tried. Nothing was less likely. The point was that he did not try. He always emphasized his amicable relations with her, how much he preferred these to be on a purely business basis. This proved no more than that Ada was not Trapnel's sort of woman, Trapnel not Ada's sort of man, but, for someone who liked running other people's lives so much as Ada, to get on with Trapnel, who liked running his own, was certainly a recommendation for her tact in doing business.

'Ada's all right. She's a grand girl. It isn't Ada who gets me down. She's always on my side. It's Craggs who's impossible. I feel pretty sure of that. He makes trouble in the background.'

'What sort of trouble?'

'Influencing JG.'

'*Bin Ends* went quite well?'

'All right. They've been looking at the first few chapters of *Profiles in String*—provisional title. I want some money while I'm writing it. I can't live on air.'

'Surely they'll advance something on what you've shown them?'

'They've given me a bit already, but I've got to exist while I write the bloody book.'

'You mean they won't unbelt any more?'

'I may have to approach another publisher.'

'You're under contract?'

'They like the new book all right, what there is. Like it very much. If they won't see reason, I may have to put the matter in the hands of my solicitors.'

Trapnel tapped the skull against the table. Talk about his solicitors always meant a highly nervous state. Even at the time of the monumental entanglement of the *conte*, it was doubtful whether legal processes had ever been carried further than consultation with old Tim Clipthorpe, one of the seasoned habitués of The Hero, his face covered with crimson blotches, who had been struck off the roll in the year the *Titanic* went down, as he was always telling any adjacent toper who would listen. In any case, Trapnel gave the impression that, as publishing rows go, this was not a specially serious one. Even if it were, he could hardly have brought a fellow-writer, not a particularly close friend, to shiver in the boreal chills of The Hero's saloon bar merely to confirm the parsimony of publishers; still less to listen to a critical onslaught against the amateurish pornography and slipshod prose of Alaric Kydd. Even Trapnel's egotism was hardly capable of that. He was, in fact, obviously playing for time, talking at random while he tried to screw himself up to making some more or less startling confession. Again he tapped the swordstick against the table.

'Don't let's talk about all this rot anyway. One of the things I wanted to tell you was that Tessa's walked out on me.'

That was much more the sort of thing to be expected. Even so, Tessa seemed a rather slender pretext for bringing about a portentous meeting such as this one. An attractive girl, she had shown early signs of finding the Trapnel way of life too much for her. Her departure was not a staggering surprise. Sympathy seemed best expressed by enquiry, though the answer was not in much doubt.

'How did it happen?'

'Yesterday—just left a note saying she was through.'

'Things had been getting difficult?'

'There was rather a scene last week. I thought it had all blown over. Apparently not. As a matter of fact I'm not sorry. I was fond of Tessa, but things have to have an end —at least most do.'

'Dowson said something of the sort in verse.'

Trapnel brushed aside further condolences, admittedly rather feeble ones, on the subject of the vicissitudes of love. He was, to say the least, bearing Tessa's abdication with fortitude. I was surprised at quite such a show of indifference, thinking some of it perhaps assumed. Trapnel, although resilient, was not at all heartless in such matters.

'Now Tessa's gone I'm faced with a decision.'

'Giving up women altogether?'

Trapnel laughed with rather conscious bitterness.

'I mean Tessa kept me from making an absolute fool of myself. Now I'm left without that support.'

He did not have the appearance of having indulged in a recent drinking bout, nor too many pep-pills, but was in such an unusual state that I began to wonder whether, after all, Ada was at the bottom of all this; that I had been summoned to give advice on the uncommon situation of an author falling in love with his publisher. The suspicion became almost a certainty when Trapnel leant forward and spoke dramatically, almost in a whisper.

'Nick, I'm absolutely mad about somebody.'

'A replacement for Tessa?'

'No—nothing like that. Nothing like Tessa at all. This is love. The genuine thing. I've never known what it was before. Not really. Now I do.'

This was going a little far. He spoke with complete gravity, though he and I were not at all on the terms when revelations of that kind are volunteered. Trapnel's emotional life, if proffered at all, was as a rule dished up with a light dressing of irony or melancholy. He was never brutal; on the other hand, he was never severely stricken. From the outside he appeared a reasonably adoring lover, if not an unduly serious one. The attitude maintained that night in The Hero was different from anything previously handed out. I had made up my mind to leave very soon now, almost at once. If Trapnel wanted to make a statement, he must get on with the job, do it expeditiously. The night was too cold to hang about any longer, while he braced himself to set forth in detail this amatory crisis, whatever it might be.

'Why isn't this one like Tessa?'

Instead of answering the question, Trapnel opened *Sweetskin* again. He removed from its pages the review slip, which notes date of publication, together with the request (never in the history of criticism vouchsafed) that the publisher should be sent a copy of the notice when it appeared in print. This small square of paper had been inserted earlier by Trapnel to mark a passage of notable ineptitude to be read aloud as illustration of Kydd's inability to write with grace, distinction or knowledge of the ways of women. He had recited the paragraph a few minutes before. Now he took one of several pens from the outside breast pocket of the tropical jacket, quickly wrote something on the back of the slip of paper, and passed it across to me. On examination, this enigmatic missive disclosed two words inscribed in Trapnel's small decorative script, of which he was rather proud. I read them without at first understanding why my attention should be drawn to this name.

Pamela Widmerpool

The whole procedure had been so odd, I was so cold and bored, the final flourish so unexpected—although in one sense Trapnel at his most Trapnelesque—that I did not immediately grasp the meaning of this revealment, if revealment it were.

'What about her?'

Trapnel did not speak at once. He looked as if he could not believe he had heard the words correctly. I asked again. He smiled and shook his head.

'That's whom I'm in love with.'

No comment seemed anywhere near adequate. This was beyond all limits. Burton well expressed man's subjection to passion. To recall his words gave some support now. 'The scorching beams under the *Æquinoctial*, or extremity of cold within the circle of the *Arctick*, where the very Seas are frozen, cold or torrid zone cannot avoid, or expel this heat, fury and rage of mortal men.' No doubt that was just how Trapnel felt. His face showed that he saw this climax as the moment of truth, one of those high-spots in the old silent films that he liked to recall, some terrific consummation emphasized by several seconds of monotonous music rising louder and louder, until, almost deafening, the notes suddenly jar out of tune in a frightful discord: the train is derailed: the canoe swept over the rapids: the knife plunged into the naked flesh. All is over. The action is cut: calm music again, perhaps no music at all.

'Of course I know I'm mad. I don't stand a chance. That's one of the reasons why the situation's nothing like Tessa—or any other girl I've ever been mixed up with. I admit it's not sane. I admit that from the start.'

If things had gone so far that Trapnel could not even pronounce the name of the woman he loved, had to write it down on a review slip, the situation must indeed be acute. I laughed. There seemed nothing else to do. That reaction was taken badly by Trapnel. He had some right to be offended after putting on such an act. That could not be helped. He looked half-furious, half-upset. As he was inclined to talk about his girls only after they had left, there was no measure for judging the norm of his feelings when they were first sighted. Possibly he was always as worked up as at that moment, merely that I had never been the confidant. That seemed unlikely. Even if he showed the same initial excitement, the incongruity of making Pamela his aim was something apart.

'You didn't much take to her at the *Fission* party.'

'Of course I didn't. I thought her the most awful girl I'd ever met.'

'What brought about the change?'

'I was in Ada's room looking through my press-cuttings. Mrs Widmerpool suddenly came in. She's an old friend of Ada's. I hadn't known that. She didn't bother to be announced from the downstairs office, just came straight up to Ada's room. She wanted to telephone right away. I was standing there talking to Ada about the cuttings. Mrs Widmerpool didn't take any notice of me. I might just as well not have been there, far less chatted with her at a party. Ada told her my name again, but she absolutely cut me. She went to the telephone, at once began cursing the girl at the switchboard for her slowness. When she got the number, it was to bawl out some man who'd sent her a jar of pickled peaches as a present. She said they were absolutely foul. She'd thrown them down the lavatory. She fairly gave him hell.'

'That stole your heart away?'

'Something did. Nick, I'm not joking. I'm mad about her. I'd do anything to see her again.'

'Did you converse after the telephoning?'

'That's what I'm coming to. We did talk. Ada asked her if she'd read the *Camel*. My God, she had—and liked it. She was—I don't know—almost as if she were shy all at once. Utterly different from what she'd been at the party, or even a moment before in the room. She behaved as if she quite liked me, but felt it would be wrong to show it. That was the moment when the thing hit me. I didn't know what to do. I felt quite ill with excitement. I mean both randy, and sentimentally in love with her too. I was wondering whether I'd ask both her and Ada to have a drink with me before lunch—perhaps borrow ten bob from Ada and pay her back later in the afternoon, because I was absolutely cleaned out at the moment of speaking—then Mrs Widmerpool suddenly remembered she was lunching with some lucky devil, and had told him to be at the restaurant at twelve-thirty, it being then a good bit after one o'clock. She went away, but quite unhurried. She knew he'd wait. What can I do? I'm crazy about her.'

Trapnel paused. The story still remained beyond comment. However, it was apparently not at an end. Something else too was on Trapnel's mind. Now he looked a shade embarrassed, a rare condition for him.

'You remember I talked to her husband at that party? We got on rather well. I can never think of him as her husband, but all the same he is, and something happened which I wish had never taken place.'

'If you mean you borrowed a quid off him, I know—he told me.'

'He did? In that case I feel better about it. The taxi absorbed my last sixpence. I had to get back to West Kilburn that night by hook or crook. I won't go into the reason why, but it was the case. I'd walked there once from Piccadilly, and preferred not to do it again. That was why I did a thing I don't often do, and got a loan from a complete stranger. The fact was it struck me as I was leaving the party that Mr Widmerpool had been so kind in listening to me—expressed such humane views on housing and such things—that he wouldn't mind helping me over a temporary difficulty. I was embarrassed at having to do so. I think Mr Widmerpool was a bit embarrassed too. He didn't know what I meant at first.'

Trapnel laughed rather apologetically. It was possible to recognize a conflict of feelings. As a writer, he could perfectly appreciate the funny side of taking a pound off Widmerpool; the whole operation looked like a little exercise in the art, introducing himself, making a good impression, bringing off the 'touch'. He had probably waited to leave the party until he saw Widmerpool going down the stairs, instinct guiding him as to the dole that would not be considered too excessive to withhold. At the same time, as a borrower, Trapnel had to keep up a serious attitude towards borrowing. He could not admit the whole affair had been a prepared scheme from the start. Finally, as a lover, he had put himself in a rather absurd relation to the husband of the object of his affections. To confess that

164

showed how far Trapnel's defences were down. He returned to the subject of Pamela.

'Ada says they don't get on too well together. She told me that when I dropped in again on the office the following day. A man who looks like that couldn't appreciate such a marvellous creature.'

'Did you tell Ada how you felt?'

'Not on your life. There's a lot of argument going on about the new novel, as I mentioned, quite apart from notices still coming in for *Bin Ends*. It was perfectly natural for me to look in again. As a matter of fact Ada began to speak of Mrs Widmerpool herself as soon as I arrived. I just sat and listened.'

'Ada's pretty smart at guessing.'

'She doesn't guess how I feel. I know she doesn't. She couldn't have said some of the things she did, if she had. I was very careful not to give anything away—you won't either, Nick, will you? I don't want anyone else to know. But how on earth am I to see her again.'

'Go and pay Widmerpool back his quid, I suppose.'

This frivolous, possibly even heartless comment was made as a mild call to order, a suggestion so unlikely to be followed that it would emphasize the absurdity of Trapnel's situation. That was not at all the way he took it. On the contrary, the proposal immediately struck him not only as seriously put forward, but a scheme of daring originality. No doubt the proposal was indeed original in the sense that repayment of a loan had never occurred to Trapnel as a measure to be considered.

'Christ, what a marvellous idea. You mean I'd call at their place and hand back the pound?'

He pondered this extravagant—literally extravagant—possibility.

'But what would Mr Widmerpool say if he happened to be there when I turned up? He'd think it a bit odd.'

'Even if he did, he'd be unlikely to refuse a pound. A very pleasant surprise.'

Even then it never occurred to me that Trapnel would take this unheard-of step.

'God, what a brilliant idea.'

We both laughed at such a flight of fancy. Trapnel's condition of tension slightly relaxed. Sanity seemed now at least within sight. All the same, he continued to play with the idea of seeing Pamela again.

'I'll get on the job right away.'

There seemed more than a possibility that the pound, so improbably required for potential return to Widmerpool, might be requested then and there, whether or not it ever found its way back into Widmerpool's pocket. The fact no such demand was made may have been as much due to Trapnel's disinclination to borrow in an obviously unornamental manner, as his rule that application to another writer was reluctant. His attack on such occasions was apt to be swift, imperative, self-assured, never less than correct in avoiding a precursory period of uneasy anticipation, often unequivocally brilliant in being utterly unexpected until the last second; at the same time never intrusive, even in the eyes of those perfectly conversant with Trapnel's habits. In the nature of things he met with rebuff as well as acquiescence—the parallel of seduction inevitably suggests itself—but there had been many successes. On this occasion probably Quiggin & Craggs, worsted in the current wrangle about advances, would pay up; anyway a pound. Paradoxical as that might seem, getting the money would be the least of Trapnel's problems, if, in the spirit in which he had first accosted Widmerpool, he wanted to add a grotesque end to the story by settling the debt.

'I can't thank you enough.'

He fell into deep thought, adopting now a different, rather dramatically conscious style. Having derived all that was needed from our meeting, his mind was devoted to future plans. I told him circumstances prevented my staying longer at The Hero. Trapnel nodded absently. I left him, his glass of beer still three-quarters full, rested precariously on the copy of *Sweetskin*. On the way home the whole affair struck me as reminiscent of Rowland Gwatkin, my former Company Commander, revealing at Castlemallock Anti-Gas School his love for a barmaid. Gwatkin's military ambition was narrow enough compared with Trapnel's soaring aspirations about being a 'complete man' and more besides. At the amatory level there was no comparison. Nevertheless, something existed in common, some lack of fulfilment, as Pennistone would say, 'in a higher unity'. Besides, if Trapnel's medical category—not to mention a thousand ineligibilities of character—had not precluded him from recommendation for a commission, no doubt he too would have shared Gwatkin's warlike dreams; a dazzling flying career added to the other personal targets.

After that night Trapnel disappeared. His work for *Fission* continued. The stooges came into play, delivering reviews or other pieces, collecting books and cheques, bringing suggestions for further items. Trapnel himself was no longer available. According to Bagshaw, he even ceased to pursue the question of further payment to assist the completion of *Profiles in String*. Use of surrogates did not prevent complicated negotiations taking place in relation to *Fission* contributions. For example, Trapnel suggested withdrawing what he had written about *Sweetskin*, and replacing the review with a parody. Bagshaw liked the idea. It was better for his own relations with Quiggin that Kydd's novel should not be torn to shreds; better, if it came to that, from my own standpoint too. Alaric Kydd himself might not be altogether pleased to be treated in this fashion, but, a prosecution now pending, he had other things to think about. In any case *Sweetskin* would enjoy more space than in a notice of normal length. Trapnel's lightness of touch in showing up Kydd's weak points as a novelist indicated that the hysterical feelings displayed at The Hero had calmed down; at least infatuation with Pamela had left his talent unimpaired. Possibly this hopeless passion had already been apportioned to the extensive storehouse of forgotten Trapnel fantasies.

Sweetskin was not the only book to cause Quiggin & Craggs worry. Bagshaw reported a serious row blowing up about *Sad Majors*. Here the complexities of politics, rather than those of sex, impinged on purely commercial considerations. Bagshaw was very much at home in this atmosphere. He talked a lot about the Odo Stevens manuscript, which he had been allowed to read, and described as 'full of meat'. However, although written in a lively manner, some of the material dealing with the Communist guerillas with whom Stevens had been in contact was at least as outspoken in its field as Kydd on the subject of sex.

'It appears a British officer operating with a rival Resistance group got rather mysteriously liquidated. Accidents will happen even with the best-regulated secret police. Of course a lot of Royalists were shot, and quite a fair number of people who weren't exactly Royalists, not to mention a crowd of heretical Communists too, the whole party ending, as we all know, in wholesale arrests and deportations. This is, of course, rather awkward for a firm of progressive tone. JG thinks it can be hoovered over satisfactorily. He wants to do the book, because it will sell, but Howard's against. He saw at once there'd be a lot of trouble, if the material appeared in its present form.'

'What will happen?'

'Gypsy won't hear of it.'

'What's Gypsy got to do with it?'

'It's her affair, isn't it, if what Stevens has said is damaging to the Party? She's bloody well consulted, apart from anything else, because Howard's afraid of her—actually physically afraid. He knows about one or two things Gypsy's arranged in her day. So do I. I don't blame him.'

'Have they turned the book down?'

'They're arguing it out.'

The weather was still unthawed when, a month or two later, I dined with Roddy Cutts at the House of Commons. Spring should have been on the way by then, but there was no sign. Our respective wives were both to give birth any day now. Roddy had suggested having a night out together to relieve the strain. A night out with Roddy carried no implications of outrageous dissipation. We talked most of the time about family affairs. He had seen Hugo Tolland the day before, who had been staying at Thrubworth, bringing back an account of how Siegfried, the German POW, was every day growing in local stature.

'Siegfried gives regular conjuring displays now in the village hall. There's talk of his getting engaged to one of Skerrett's granddaughters. He'll be nursing the constituency before we know where we are. Well, I suppose it's about time to be getting along. I'll just see how the debate's going before we make for home.'

Roddy Cutts's large handsome face always became drawn with anxiety when, at the close of any party at which he had been host, he glanced at the bill. This time the look indicated the worst; that he was ruined; parliamentary career at an end; he would have to sell up; probably emigrate. An extravagant charge would certainly have been out of place. Whatever the shock, Roddy made no comment. He dejectedly searched through pocket after pocket in apparently vain attempts to find a sum adequate to meet so severe a demand on a man's resources. The second round through, one of the waistcoat pockets yielded a five-pound note. He smoothed out its paper on the table.

'Give my love to Isobel, and hopes that all will be well.'

'And mine to Susie.'

The change arrived. Roddy sorted it lethargically, at the same time giving the impression that the levy might have been less disastrous than at first feared. His manner of picking up coins and examining them used to irritate our brother-in-law George Tolland. We rose from the table, exchanging the claustrophobic pressures of the hall where the meal had been eaten, for a no less viscous density of parliamentary smoking-rooms and lobbies, suffocating, like all such precincts, with the omnipresent and congealed essence of public contentions and private egotisms; breath of life to their frequenters. Roddy's personality always took on a new dimension within these walls.

'If you'll wait for a minute in the central lobby, I'll just hear how Supplementary Benefits are going.'

Callot-like figures pervaded labyrinthine corridors. Cavernous alcoves were littered with paraphernalia of scaffolding and ropes, Piranesian frameworks hinting of torture and execution, but devised only to repair bomb damage to structure and interior ornament. Roddy reappeared.

'Come along.'

We crossed the top of the flight of steps leading down into St Stephen's Hall, the stairs seeming to offer a kind of emergency exit from contemporary affairs into a mysterious submerged world of mediaeval shadows, tempting to explore if one were alone, in spite of icy draughts blowing up from these spectral depths. Suddenly, from the opposite direction to which we were walking, Widmerpool appeared. He was pacing forward slowly, deliberately, solemnly, swinging his arms in a regular motion from the body, as if carefully balancing himself while he trod a restricted bee-line from one point to another. At first he was too deep in thought to notice our advance towards him. Roddy shouted a greeting.

'Widmerpool, just the man I'm looking for.'

He could never resist accosting anyone he knew, and buttonholing them. Now he began a long dissertation about 'pairing'. Surprised out of his own meditations, Widmerpool seemed at first only aware that he was being addressed by a fellow MP. A second later he grasped the linked identities of Roddy and myself, our relationship, the fact that were brothers-in-law evidently striking him at once as a matter of significance to himself. He brushed aside whatever Roddy was talking about—conversation in any case designed to keep alive a contact with a member of the other side, rather than reach a conclusion—beginning to speak of another subject that seemed already on his mind, possibly the question he had been so deeply pondering.

'I'm glad to come on you both. First of all, my dear Cutts, I wanted to approach you regarding a little non-party project I have on hand—no, no, not the Roosevelt statue—it is connected with an Eastern European cultural organization in which I am interested. However, before we come to public concerns, there are things to be settled about the late Lord Warminster's letter of instructions. They are rather complicated—personal rather than legal bearings, though the Law comes in—so that to explain some of the points to you might save a lot of correspondence in the future. You could then pass on the information by word of mouth to your appropriate relatives, decisions thereby reached in a shorter time.'

Roddy showed attention to the phrase 'non-party project', but, with the professional politician's immediate instinct for executing a disengaging movement from responsibilities that promised only unrewarding exertion, he at once began to deny all liability for sorting out the problems of Erridge's bequests.

'Nicholas and I have no status in the matter whatsoever,

my dear Widmerpool, you must address yourself to Hugo or Frederica. They are the people. Either Hugo or Frederica will put you right in a trice.'

Widmerpool must have been prepared for that answer, actually expecting it, because he smiled at the ease with which such objections could be overruled by one of his long experience.

'Of course, of course. I perfectly appreciate that aspect, Cutts, that you and Nicholas are without authority in the matter. You are correct to stress the fact. The point I put forward is that the normal course of action would result in a vast deal of letter-writing between Messrs Turnbull, Welford & Puckering, Messrs Quiggin & Craggs, Messrs Goodness-knows-who-else. I propose to cut across that. I had quite enough of shuffling the bumf round when I was in the army. As a result I've developed a positive mania these days against pushing paper. Man-to-man. That's the way. Cut corners. I fear pomposity is not one of my failings. I can't put up with pompous people, and have often been in trouble on that very account.'

Roddy was determined not to be outdone in detestation of pomposity and superfluous formality. For a moment the two MPs were in sharp competition as to whose passion for direct-ness and simplicity was the more heartfelt, at least could be the more forcibly expressed. At the end of this contest Widmerpool carried his point.

'Therefore I suggest you forget the official executors for the moment, and accompany me back to my flat for the space of half an hour, where we can deal with the War-minster file, also discuss the small non-party committee I propose to form. No, no, Cutts, I brook no refusal. You can both be of inestimable help in confirming the right line is being taken regarding post-mortem wishes, I mean a line acceptable to the family. As a matter of fact you may both be interested to learn more of your late brother-in-law's system of opinion, his intellectual quirks, if I may use the phrase.'

Curiosity on that last point settled the matter. Roddy enjoyed nothing better than having a finger in any pie that happened to be cooking. Here were at least two. It was agreed that we should do as Widmerpool wished.

'Come along then. It's just round the corner. Only a step. We may as well walk—especially as there are likely to be no taxis.'

Along the first stretch of Victoria Street, dimly lighted and slippery, Roddy and Widmerpool discussed $2\frac{1}{2}\%$ Treasury Stock Redeemable after 1975; by the time we reached the flats, they had embarked on the topic of whether or not, as Governor of the Bank of England, Montagu Norman had adequately controlled the 'acceptance houses'. The entrance, rather imposing, was a high archway flanked by gates. This led into a small courtyard, on the far side of which stood several associated masses of heavy Edwardian building. It was a cheerless spot. I asked if Short still lived here.

'You know Leonard Short? He's just below us. Very convenient it should be so. He's a good little fellow, Short. My Minister has a high opinion of him.'

'Who is your Minister?'

Even Roddy was rather appalled by this ignorance, hastening to explain that Widmerpool had been appointed not long before Parliamentary Private Secretary to a member of the Cabinet; the one, in fact, who had attended the Quiggin & Craggs party, the Minister responsible for the branch of the civil service to which Short belonged. Widmerpool himself showed no resentment at this lapse, merely laughing heartily, and enlarging on his own duties.

'As PPS one's expected to take an intelligent interest in the ministry concerned. The presence there of Leonard Short oils the wheels for me. We're quite an intellectual crowd here. I expect you've heard of Clapham, the publisher, who lives in another of the flats. You may even know him. He is a good type of the old-fashioned publishing man. I find his opinions worthy of attention now I have a stake in that business myself. There's nothing flashy about Clapham, neither intellectually nor socially. He was speaking to me about St John Clarke the other night, whom he knew well, and, so he tells me, still enjoys a very respectable sale.'

The hall was in darkness. There was a lift, but Widmerpool guided us past it.

'I must remind you electricity is now in short supply—shedding the load, as we have learnt to call it. The Government has the matter well in hand, but our lift here, an electric one, is for the moment out of action. You will not mind the stairs. Only a few flights. A surprisingly short way in the light of the excellent view we enjoy on a clear day. Pam is always urging a move. We have decided in principle to do so, inspected a great deal of alternative accommodation, but there is convenience in proximity to the House. Besides, I'm used to the flat, with its special characteristics, some good, some less admirable. For the time being, therefore, it seems best to remain where we are. That's what I'm always telling Pam.'

By this time we had accomplished a couple of flights.

'How is Mrs Widmerpool?' asked Roddy. 'I remember she was feeling unwell at the funeral.'

'My wife's health was not good a year ago. It has improved. I can state that with confidence. In fact during the last month I have never known her better—well, one can say in better spirits. She is a person rather subject to moods. She changes from one moment to the next.'

Roddy, probably thinking of the cipherine nodded heartily. Widmerpool took a key from his pocket. He paused before the door. Talk about Pamela had unsettled him.

'I don't expect Pam will have gone to bed yet. She does sometimes turn in early, especially if she has a headache, or it's been an exhausting day for her. At other times she sits up quite late, indeed long after I've retired to rest myself. We shall see.'

He sounded rather nervous about what the possibilities might be. The small hall was at once reminiscent of the flat—only a short way from here—where Widmerpool had formerly lived with his mother. I asked after her. He did not seem over pleased by the enquiry.

'My mother is still living with relations in the Lowlands. There's been some talk lately of her finding a place of her own. I have not seen her recently. She is, of course, not so young as she was. We still have our old jokes about Uncle Joe in our letters, but in certain other aspects she finds it hard to realize things have changed.'

'Uncle Joe?'

'My mother has always been a passionate admirer of Marshal Stalin, a great man, whatever people may say. We had jokes about if he were to become a widower. At the same time, she would probably have preferred me to remain single myself. She is immensely gratified to have a son in the House of Commons—always her ambition to be mother of an MP—but she is inclined to regard a wife as handicap to a career.'

Widmerpool lowered his tone for the last comment. The lights were on all over the flat, the sound of running water audible. No one seemed to be about. Widmerpool listened, his head slightly to one side, with the air of a Red Indian brave seeking, on the tail of the wind, the well-known, but elusive, scent of danger. The splashing away of the water had a calming effect.

'Ah, Pam's having a bath. She was expecting my return rather later than this. I'll just report who's here. Go in and sit down.'

175

He spoke as if relieved to hear nothing more ominous was on foot than his wife having a bath, then disappeared down the passage. Roddy and I entered the sitting-room. The tone of furniture and decoration was anonymous, though some sort of picture rearrangement seemed to be in progress. The central jets of a gas fire were lighted, but the curtains were undrawn, a window open. Roddy closed it. Two used glasses stood on a table. There was no sign of whatever had been drunk from them. From the other end of the passage a loud knocking came, where Widmerpool was announcing our arrival. Apparently no notice was taken, because the taps were not turned off, and, to rise above their sound, he had to shout our names at the top of his voice. Pamela's reactions could not be heard. Widmerpool returned.

'I expect Pam will look in later. Probably in her dressing-gown—which I hope you will excuse.'

'Of course.'

Roddy looked as if he could excuse that easily. Widmerpool glanced round the room and made a gesture of simulated exasperation.

'She's been altering the pictures again. Pam loves doing that—especially shifting round that drawing her uncle Charles Stringham left her. I can never remember the artist's name. An Italian.'

'Modigliani.'

'That's the one—ah, there's been a visitor, I see. I'll fetch the relevant documents.'

The sight of the two glasses seemed to depress him again. He fetched some papers. Kneeling down in front of the gas fire, he tried to ignite the outer bars, but they failed to respond. Widmerpool gave it up. He began to explain the matter in hand. Erridge, among other dispositions, had expressed the wish that certain books which had 'influenced' him should, if out of print, be reissued by the firm of Quiggin & Craggs. To what extent such republication was practicable had to be considered in the light of funds available from the Trust left by Erridge. Nothing was conditional. Widmerpool explained that the copyright situation was being examined. At present adjudication was not yet possible in certain cases; others were already announced as to be reissued elsewhere. Subsequent works on the same subject, political or economic—even more often events—had put Erridge's old favourites out of date. On the whole, as Widmerpool had promised, the answers could be effectively dealt with in this manner, though several required brief consideration and discussion. We had just come to the end of the business, Widmerpool made facetious reference to the propriety of canvassing Parliamentary matters, even non-party ones, in the presence of a member of the public, when the door bell rang. Widmerpool looked irritable at this.

'Who on earth can it be? Not one of Pam's odd friends at this hour of the night, I hope. They are capable of anything.'

He went to open the door.

'We don't need to waste any more time here,' said Roddy. 'The Erry stuff is more or less cleared up. The non-party project can be ventilated when Widmerpool and I next meet in the House. I don't want to freeze to death. Let's make a getaway while he's engaged.'

I was in agreement. Widmerpool continued to talk with whoever had come to the front door of the flat. Although he had left the door of the sitting-room open, the subject of their conversation could not be heard owing to the sound of the bath water, still running, or perhaps turned on again. It occurred to me that Pamela, with her taste for withdrawal from company, might deliberately have taken refuge in the bathroom on hearing the sound of our arrival; then turned on the taps to give the impression that a bath was in progress. Such procedure might even be a matter of routine on her part to avoid guests after a parliamentary sitting. The supposition was strengthened by Widmerpool's own lack of surprise at her continued absence. It was like a mythological story: a nymph for ever running a bath that never filled, while her husband or lover waited for her to emerge. Now Roddy was getting impatient.

'Come on. Don't let's hang about.'

We went out into the passage. The visitor turned out to be Short. He looked worried. Although only come from the floor below, apparently to deliver a message, he had taken the precaution of wearing an overcoat and scarf. Whatever the message was had greatly disturbed Widmerpool. One wondered if the Government had fallen, though scarcely likely within the time that had passed since we had left the House of Commons. Our sudden appearance from the sitting-room made Short even less at ease than he was already. He muttered some sort of a good evening. I introduced Roddy, as Widmerpool seemed scarcely aware that we had joined them. Before more could be said, evidently returning to the subject in hand, Widmerpool broke in again.

'How long ago did you say this was?'

'About an hour or two, as I told you. The message was just as I passed it on.'

Short was infinitely, unspeakably embarrassed. Widmerpool looked at him for a moment, then turned away. He walked hurriedly up the passage, lost to sight at the right-angle of its end. A door opened noisily from the direction of the running water. The sound of the flow ceased a moment later. The taps had been turned off sharply. Another door was opened. There came the noise of things being thrown about. Short blew his nose. Roddy got his overcoat and handed me mine. I asked Short what had happened.

'It was just a message left for Kenneth by his wife. She rang the bell of my flat about an hour ago, and asked me to deliver it.'

Short stopped. Whatever the message was had seriously upset him. That left us none the wiser. Short seemed for a moment uncertain whether or not to reveal his secret. Then it became too much for him. He cleared his throat and lowered his voice.

'As a matter of fact the message was—"I've left". We don't know each other at all well. I thought she must mean she was going to catch a train, or something of that sort. Had been delayed, and wanted her husband to know the time of her departure.'

'You mean left for good?'

Short nodded once or twice, almost to himself, in a panic-stricken manner. There could be no doubt that one side of his being had been immensely excited by becoming so closely involved in such a drama; another, appalled by all the implications of disorganization, wrongdoing and scandal. Before more could be told, Widmerpool returned.

'It was very thoughtless of her to have forgotten to turn the bath tap off. The hot one too. Nobody in the place will get any hot water for weeks. You know, Leonard, she must have made this arrangement to go away on the spur of the moment.'

'That's just what it looked like.'

Short spoke as if he saw a gleam of hope.

'She often acts like that. I deprecate it, but what can I do? I see she has taken both her suitcases. They must have been quite heavy, as most of her clothes have gone too. Did you help carry them down?'

'The man was carrying them.'

'Do you mean the porter? I thought he was having flu?'

'Not the regular porter. It might have been the taxi-driver or someone driving a hired car. Perhaps they have a temporary man downstairs.'

'I mean it was not just a friend?'

'He hardly looked like a friend.'

'What was he like?'

'He had a beard. He was carrying the two bags. Your wife had a stick or umbrella under her arm, and two or three pictures.'

This piece of information agitated Widmerpool more than anything that had gone before. Short appeared unable to know what to think. Before Widmerpool's return his words certainly suggested that he himself supposed Pamela had left for good; then Widmerpool's demeanour seemed almost to convince him that this was no more than a whim of the moment to go off and visit friends. Now he was back where he started.

'Repeat to me again exactly what she said.'

' "Tell him I'm leaving, and taking the Modigliani and the photographs of myself. He can do what he likes with the rest of my junk." '

'Nothing more?'

'Of course I supposed she was referring to some domestic arrangement you knew about already, that she wanted to inform you of the precise minute she had vacated the flat. I wondered if you had even taken another one. You have always talked of that. It looked as if she might be starting to move into it.'

Short sounded desperate. He must have been to talk like that. Roddy was desperate too, but only to get away. He was taking no interest whatever in the matter discussed. Now he could stand it no longer.

'Look, my dear Widmerpool, it's really awfully cold tonight. I think I'll have to be getting back, as I want to know how my wife is faring. She's expecting a baby, you know. Not quite yet, but you never can be certain with these little beggars. They sometimes decide to be early. We can have a word about your project in the smoking-room some time—over a drink perhaps.'

Widmerpool behaved very creditably. He accepted, probably with relief, that Roddy was not in the least interested in his affairs.

'Most grateful to you both for having looked in, and run over those points. All I want you to do now is to pass on the proposed decisions informally to the executors. If they have any objections, they can let me know. Then we can get the items sorted out. I'm sorry the evening has been interrupted in this way. We'll discuss the non-party matter on another occasion, Cutts. I must offer my apologies. There is nothing Pam enjoys more than mystifying people—especially her unfortunate husband. Goodnight, goodnight. Come into the flat for a moment, Leonard.'

What he was thinking was not revealed. Control of himself showed how far married life had inured him to sudden discomposing circumstances. If he believed that Pamela had deserted him without intention of return—it was hard to think anything else had happened—he kept his head. Perhaps her departure was after all a relief. It was impossible to guess; nor whether Trapnel was by now a figure known to him in his wife's entourage. Short did not look at all willing to enter the flat for yet another rehash of his encounter with Pamela, but Widmerpool was insistent. He would not accept a denial on account of work with which Short was engaged. Roddy and I took leave of them, and set off down the stairs. Neither of us spoke until we reached the street. Roddy then showed some faint curiosity as to what had been happening.

'What was it? I was too cold to take it in.'

'It looks as if his wife's gone off with a man called X. Trapnel.'

'Never heard of him.'

'He writes novels.'

'Like you?'

'Yes.'

'Is he one of her lovers?'

'So it appears.'

'I gather they abound.'

'All the same, this is a bit of a surprise.'

'God—there's a taxi.'

Not so very long after that evening, Isobel gave birth to a son; Susan Cutts, to a daughter. These events within the family, together with other comings and goings, not to mention the ever-pervading Burton, distracted attention from exterior events. Even allowing for such personal preoccupations, the whole Widmerpool affair, that is to say his wife's abandonment of him, made far less stir than might be expected. There were several reasons for this. In the first place, that Widmerpool should marry a girl like Pamela Flitton had been altogether unexpected; that she should leave him was another matter. Nothing could be more predictable, the only question—with whom? A certain amount of gossip went round when it became known they were no longer under the same roof, but, the awaited climax having taken place, the question of the lover's identity was not an altogether easy one to answer; nor particularly interesting when answered, for those kept alive by such nourishment. Few people who knew Widmerpool also knew Trapnel, the reverse equally true. Besides, could it be stated with certainty that Pamela was living with Trapnel?

Everyone agreed that, even if Pamela had embarked on a romance with Trapnel, however unlikely that might be, nothing was, on the other hand, more probable than that she had left him immediately after. All that could be said for certain was that both had utterly disappeared from sight. That at least was definite. Accordingly, the physical presence of two lovers did not, by public appearance, draw attention to open adultery. In the circumstances, interest waned. The question of 'taking sides', in general so much adding to public concern with such predicaments, here scarcely arose, husband and lover inhabiting such widely separated worlds. There was some parallel to the time, years before, when Mona had left Peter Templer for J. G. Quiggin.

A further reason for the story to develop a strangely muffled character, almost as if leaked through a kind of censorship, was the hard work Widmerpool himself put in to lower the outside temperature. However he might inwardly regard the situation, as an MP he was understandably anxious to play down such a blemish on the life of a public man. Just as he had done to Short on the night of Pamela's departure, he emphasized through all possible channels his wife's undoubted eccentricity, circulating anecdotes about her to suggest that she was doing no more than taking a brief holiday from married life. She would return when she thought fit. That was Widmerpool's line. Her husband, knowing her strange ways, paid little attention. In the end more people than might be expected pretty well accepted that explanation. It was a trump card. At first that was not so apparent as it became later.

Of course a friend of Pamela's like Ada Leintwardine— a position in which Ada was, as a woman, probably unique —was thrown into a great state of commotion when the news, such as it was, broke. It was confirmed by L. O. Salvidge to the extent that two or three weeks before he had seen Trapnel in The Hero, accompanied by a very beautiful girl with a pale face and dark hair. They had stayed in the saloon bar only a few seconds, not even ordering drinks. Trapnel wanted to make some arrangement with one of the auxiliaries. Salvidge's information predated the night at Widmerpool's. Ada conceded not only that she had now lost all touch with Pamela, but—an unexampled admission on Ada's part—could claim no suspicion whatever as to what must have been going on. This amounted to confession that, however profound her own powers of intuition, they had fallen short of paramountcy in probing this particular sequence of emotional development. All she had supposed was that Trapnel had been 'rather intrigued' by Pamela; the notion that he should sufficiently flatter himself as to allow dreams of her mastery was something quite beyond credibility. Ada's alliance with Pamela had, in fact, never taken the form of frequentation of the Widmerpool household. They had just been 'girls together' outside Pamela's married life. Ada continually repeated her disbelief.

'It can't really be Trapnel.'

Not only did Trapnel himself no longer appear at the *Fission* office, his representatives now dropped off too. Bagshaw had recently retired to bed with flu. For once the new number was fully made up, left to be seen through the press by the latest secretary, a red-haired, freckled girl called Judy, whom Bagshaw himself had produced from somewhere or other, alleging that she was not at all stupid, but unreliable at spelling. Judy had just brought in a stack of advance copies of the magazine when in due course I arrived to carry out the normal stint with the books. These were being examined by Quiggin and Ada, who were both on the *Fission* side of the backyard.

Quiggin, possibly under the influence of Ada, had now for the most part abandoned his immediately post-war trappings suggesting he had just come in from skirmishing with a sten-gun in the undergrowth, though traces remained in a thick grey shirt. On the whole he had settled for a no-nonsense middle-aged intellectual's style of dress, a new suit in dark check and bow tie, turn-out better suited to his station as an aspiring publisher. Ada was laughing at what they were reading, Quiggin less certain that he was finding the contribution funny. He had taken his hands from the jacket pockets of the check suit, and was straightening the lapels rather uneasily.

'There's going to be a row,' said Ada.

She was pleased rather than the reverse by that prospect. Quiggin himself seemed not wholly displeased, though his amusement was combined with anxiety, which the *Sweet-skin* case was sufficient to explain. An extract from Ada's own novel was to be included in this current number. Her work in progress had not yet been given a title, but it was billed as 'daring', so that in the cold light of print Quiggin might fear the police would now step in where *Fission* too was concerned.

'Are you going to be prosecuted, Ada?'

'I was laughing at X's piece. Read this.'

She handed me a copy of the magazine. It was open at Widmerpool's article *Assumptions of Autarchy v. Dynamics of Adjustment*. Since she had indicated Trapnel's piece as the focus of interest, I turned back to the list of contents to find the page. Ada snatched it from me.

'No, no. Where I gave it you.'

Another glance at the typeface showed what she meant. The page that at first appeared to be the opening of Wid-merpool's routine article on politics or economics—usually a mixture of both—was in fact a parody of Widmerpool's writing by Trapnel. I sat down the better to appreciate the pastiche. It was a little masterpiece in its way. Trap-nel's ignorance of matters political or economic, his total lack of interest in them, had not handicapped the manner in which he caught Widmerpool's characteristic style. If anything that ignorance had been an advantage. The gibberish, interspersed with *double ententes*, was entirely convincing.

'I do not assert . . . a convincing lead . . . cyclical monopoly resistance . . . the optimum factor . . .'

This was Bagshaw taking the bit between his teeth. However one looked at it, that much was clear. In the course of arranging subjects for Trapnel's parodies he had certainly included contributors to *Fission* before now. Alaric Kydd was not, as it happened, one of these, being somewhat detached from the *Fission* genre of writer, but Evadne Clapham, represented by a short story in the first number, had been one of Trapnel's victims. Always excitable, she had at first talked of a libel action. Bagshaw had convinced her finally that only the most talented of writers were amenable to parody, and she had forgiven both himself and Trapnel. All this was in line with Bagshaw's taste for sailing near the wind, whatever he did, but he had never spoken of setting Trapnel to work on Widmerpool. That was certainly to expose himself to danger. The temptation to do so, once the idea had occurred to an editor of Bagshaw's temperament, would, on the other hand, be a hard one to resist.

If, in the light of his business connexions with the publishing firm and the magazine, it were risky to parody Widmerpool, Widmerpool's lack of respect for Bagshaw's abilities as an editor did not make the experiment any less hazardous. For the parody to appear in print at this moment would certainly liven the mixture with new unforeseen fermentations. It was equally characteristic of Bagshaw to be away from the office at such a juncture. Quiggin himself certainly grasped that, at a moment when lurid theories about the elopement were giving place to acceptance of the Widmerpool version, there was a danger of a severe setback for such an interpretation of the story. He saw that circumstances were so ominous that the only thing to do was to claim the parody as a victory rather than a defeat.

'You have to look at things all ways. Kenneth Widmerpool is taking the line that no catastrophic break in his married life is threatened. Whether or not that is true, we

have no reliable evidence how far, if at all, Trapnel is involved. In a sense, therefore, a good-natured burlesque by
X of Kenneth's literary mannerisms suggests friendly,
rather than unfriendly, relations.'

'Good-natured?'

Quiggin looked at Ada severely, but not without a suggestion of desire.

'Parodies are intended to raise a laugh. Perhaps you did
not know that, Ada. If someone had taken the trouble to
show me the piece before it was printed, I might have
done a little sub-editing here and there. I don't promise it
would have improved the whole, so perhaps it was better
not.'

This speech indicated that Widmerpool might not have
it all his own way, if he made too much fuss. It also confirmed indirectly the resentment of Widmerpool's domination that, according to Bagshaw, Quiggin had begun
increasingly to show. Judy, the secretary, feeling that some
of these recriminations were directed against herself, or,
more probably envious of the attention Quiggin was devoting to Ada, now began to protest.

'How on earth was I to know one man had run away
with the other man's wife? Books just handed the copy
over to me, saying he had a temperature of a hundred-and-
two, and told me to get on with the job.'

'Grown-up people always check on that particular point,
my girl,' said Quiggin. 'Don't worry. We're not blaming
you. Calm down. Take an aspirin. Isn't it time for coffee?
I admit I could have done without Bagshaw arranging this
just at the moment the *Sweetskin* case is coming on, and
all the to-do about *Sad Majors*.'

I enquired as to Quiggin's version of the Stevens trouble.

'Odo's written an excellent account of his time with the
Partisans. Adventurous, personal, but a lot of controversial
matter. Readers don't want controversy. Why should

they? Besides, it would be awkward for the firm to publish a book hinting some of the things Odo's does, with Kenneth Widmerpool on the board. All his support for societies trying to promote good relations with that very country. You want to keep politics out of a book like that.'

'Odo isn't very interested in politics, is he?'

'Not in a way, but he's very obstinate.'

I left them still in a flutter about the parody. There was not much Widmerpool could do. It would increase his opposition to Bagshaw, but Bagshaw probably had a contract of some sort. At the end of that, if the magazine survived, Widmerpool was likely to try and get him sacked anyway. It was a typical Bagshaw situation. Meanwhile, he showed no sign of returning to the office. The message came that his flu was no better. Some evenings later there was a telephone call at home. A female voice asked for me.

'Speaking.'

'It's Pamela Widmerpool.'

'Oh, yes?'

She must have known I was answering, but for some reason of her own preferred to go through the process of making absolutely sure.

'X is not well.'

'I'm very sorry—'

'I want you to come and see him. He needs some books and things.'

'But—'

'It's really the only way—for you to come yourself.'

She spoke the last sentence irritably, as if the question of my bringing Trapnel aid in person had already arisen in the past, and, rather contemptibly, I had raised objections to making myself available. Now, it seemed, I was looking for a similar excuse again. She offered no explanation or apology for thus emerging as representative of the Trapnel, rather than Widmerpool, ménage. In taking on the former

position there was not the smallest trace of self-consciousness.

'This man Bagshaw has flu still. I can't get any sense out
of the half-witted girl left in charge at the *Fission* office.
That's why you must come.'

'I was only going to say that I don't know where you—
where X is living.'

'Of course you don't. No one does. I'm about to tell you.
Do you know the Canal at Maida Vale?'

'Yes.'

'We're a bit north of there.'

She gave the name of a street and number of the house.
I wrote them down.

'The ground-floor flat. Don't be put off by the look of the
place outside. It's inhabited all right, though you might not
think so. When can you come? Tonight?'

She added further instructions about getting there.

'What's wrong with X?'

'He's just feeling like hell.'

'Has he seen a doctor?'

'He won't.'

'Wouldn't it be wiser to make him?'

'He'll be all right in a day or two. He's got quite a store
of his pills. He just wants to talk to somebody. We don't
see anybody as a rule. You just happen to know both of us.
That's why you must come. Have you got a book to bring?
Something for him to review?'

I had taken some review copies from the *Fission* shelves
to look through at home. L. O. Salvidge's collection of
essays, *Paper Wine*, might do for Trapnel. I told Pamela I
would produce something. She rang off without comment.

'Don't get robbed and murdered,' said Isobel.

To visit Trapnel in one of his lairs was a rare experience
at the best of times. Once we had both been allowed to
have a drink with him at a flat in Notting Hill, within

range of the Portobello Road, where he liked to wander among the second-hand stalls. He was then living with a girl called Sally. The invitation had been quite exceptional, possibly intended to establish some sort of an alibi for reasons never revealed. The present expedition was more adventurous. The Paddington area, and north of it, supplied one of the traditional Trapnel areas of bivouac. It was surprising that he and Pamela were to be found no farther afield. Their total disappearance suggested withdrawal from such ground to less established streets. It was of course true to say that, even when not specifically retired to the outer suburbs, one rarely knew for certain where Trapnel was living. The absence of news about him from pub sources indicated experiment with hitherto unfrequented taverns. Such investigation would not be unwelcome; by no means out of character. A fresh round of saloon bars would hold out promise of new disciples, new eccentrics, new bores, new near-criminals. Pamela herself might well have objected to a really radical retreat from the approaches to central London. The part she played was hard to imagine.

At this period the environs of the Canal had not yet developed into something of a *quartier chic*, as later incarnated. Before the war, the indigenous population, time-honoured landladies, inveterate lodgers, immemorial whores, long undisturbed in surrounding premises, had already begun to give place to young married couples, but buildings already tumbledown had now been further reduced by bombing. The neighbourhood looked anything but flourishing. Leaving Edgware Road, I walked along the north bank of the Canal. On either side of the water gaps among the houses marked where direct hits had reduced Regency villas to rubble. The street Pamela had described was beyond this stucco colony. It was not at all easy to find. When traced, the exterior bore out the description of looking uninhabited.

The architecture here had little pretension to elegance. Several steps led up to the front door. No name was quoted above the bell of the ground floor flat. I rang, and waited. The door was opened by Pamela. She was in slacks. I said good-evening. She did not smile.

'Come in.'

Lighted only by a ray from the flat doorway left open, the hall, so far as could be seen in the gloom, accorded with the derelict exterior of the house; peeling wallpaper, bare boards, a smell of damp, cigarette smoke, stale food. The atmosphere recalled Maclintick's place in Pimlico, when Moreland and I had visited him not long before his suicide. By contrast, the fairly large room into which I followed Pamela conveyed, chiefly on account of the appalling mess of things that filled it, an impression of rough comfort, almost of plenty. There were only a few sticks of furniture, a table, two kitchen chairs, a vast and hideous wardrobe, but several pieces of luggage lay about—including two newish suitcases evidently belonging to Pamela—clothes, books, cups, glasses, empty Algerian wine bottles. The pictures consisted of a couple of large photographs of Pamela herself, taken by well-known photographers, and, over the mantelpiece, the Modigliani drawing. Trapnel lay on a divan under some brown army blankets.

'Look here, it's awfully good of you to come, Nick.'

One wondered, at this austere period for acquiring any sort of clothing to be regarded as of unusual design, where he had bought the dirty white pyjamas patterned with large red spots. The circumstances were in general a shade more sordid than pictured. Trapnel had been reading a detective story, which he now threw on the floor. A lot of other books lay about over the bedclothes, among them *Oblomov*, *The Thin Man*, *Adolphe*, in a French edition, all copies worn to shreds. Trapnel looked pale, rather dazed, otherwise no worse than usual. Before I could speak, Pamela made a request.

'Have you a shilling? The fire's going out.'

She took the coin and slipped it into the slot, reviving the dying flame, just going blue. As the gas flared up again, its hiss for some inexplicable reason suggested an explanation of why Pamela had married Widmerpool. She had done it, so to speak, in order to run away with Trapnel. I do not mean she had thought that out in precise terms—a vivid imagination would be required to predict the advent of Trapnel into Widmerpool's life—but the violent antithesis presented by their contrasted forms of existence, two unique specimens as it were brought into collision, promised anarchic extremities of feeling of the kind at which she aimed; in which she was principally at home. She liked—to borrow a phrase from St. John Clarke—to 'try conclusions with the maelstrom'. One of the consequences of her presence was to displace Trapnel's tendency to play a part during the first few minutes of any meeting. That could well have been knocked out of him by ill health, as much as by Pamela. He spoke now as if he were merely a little embarrassed.

'There were one or two things I wanted to talk about. You know I don't much like having to explain things on the telephone, though I often have to do that. Anyway, it's cut off here, the instrument was removed bodily yesterday, and I'm not supposed to go outside for the moment, owing to this malaise I've got. You and I haven't seen each other for some time, Nick. Such a lot's happened. As I'm a bit off colour I thought you wouldn't mind coming to our flat. It seemed easier. Pam was sure you'd come.'

He gave her one of those 'adoring looks', which Lermontov says mean so little to women. Pamela stared back at him with an expression of complete detachment. I thought of King Cophetua and the Beggar Maid, though Pamela was far from a pre-raphaelite type or a maid, and, socially speaking, the boot was, if anything, on the other foot. No doubt it was Trapnel's beard. He had also allowed his hair to grow longer than usual. All the same, he sitting up on the divan, she standing above him, they somehow called up the picture.

'I brought some essays by L. O. Salvidge.'

'*Paper Wine?*'

Trapnel, by some mysterious agency, always knew about all books before they were published. It was as if the information came to him instinctively. He laughed. The thought of reviewing Salvidge's essays must have made him feel better. One had the impression that he had been locked up with Pamela for weeks, like the Spanish honeymoon couples Borrit used to describe, when we were in the War Office together. To get back to the world of reviewing seemed to offer a magical cure for whatever Trapnel suffered. It really cheered him up.

'Just what I need—have we got anything to drink, darling?'

'A bottle of Algerian's open. Some dregs left, I think.'

'I don't want anything at the moment, thanks very much.'

Trapnel lay back on the divan.

'To begin with, that bloody parody of mine.'

'I mistook it at first for the real thing.'

That amused Trapnel. Pamela continued to stand by without comment or change of expression.

'I'm glad you did that. What's happened about it? Any reactions?'

'None I've heard about. There was some trepidation at the *Fission* office that trouble might arise from the obvious quarter. Books is away with flu.'

'What a bloody fool he is. I wrote the thing quite a long time ago at his suggestion. He said he'd have to talk to the others about it. I hadn't contemplated present circumstances then.'

'Nor did anyone else.'

'What about Books?'

'The evidence is that he didn't know.'

'Will Widmerpool believe that?'

'What can he do?' asked Pamela. 'He ought to be flattered.'

Even when she made this comment the tone suggested she was no more on Trapnel's side than Widmerpool's. She was assessing the situation objectively.

'That's what Books told Evadne Clapham,' said Trapnel. 'On that occasion I hadn't also run away with her husband. I suppose everything combined means I won't be able to write for *Fission* any longer. That's a blow, because it was one of my main sources of income, and I liked the magazine.'

'JG didn't seem unduly worried. He's got the *Sweetskin* prosecution on hand, and there's some trouble about Odo Stevens's book.'

'I don't want my publishing connexions messed up too. Quiggin & Craggs have their failings, but they aren't doing too badly with *Bin Ends*. I'm not under contract for the next novel. I'm getting near the end now. I don't want to have to hawk it round.'

At one moment Trapnel would give the impression that he was under contract with Quiggin & Craggs, and wanted to get rid of them; at the next, that he was not under contract, and wanted to stay. That was like him. He pointed to a respectably thick pile of foolscap covered with cuneiform handwriting. Although able to type, to use a typewriter was against Trapnel's principles. The books had to be written by his own hand. This talk about the novel seemed to displease Pamela. She began to frown.

'How's my husband?' she asked.

'I've not seen him lately—not since the night you left.'

'You saw him then?'

194

'I'd been dining with another MP. We came back to the Victoria Street flat to discuss some things.'

'Which MP?'

'Roddy Cutts—my brother-in-law.'

'That tall sandy-haired Tory?'

'Yes.'

'Were you there when Short delivered the message?'

'Yes.'

'How was it taken?'

'What do you mean?'

'Well or badly?'

'There was no scene.'

A slight flush had come over her face when she asked these questions. There could be no doubt she derived some sort of sensual satisfaction from dwelling on what had happened. Trapnel, acute enough to recognize, and resent, this process of exciting herself by such means, looked uneasy. The manner in which she managed to maintain a wholly unchanged demeanour in these very changed surroundings was notable; yet after all why should she become different just because she had decided to spend a season with Trapnel? With him, with Odo Stevens, with Allied officers, for that matter with Widmerpool, she remained the same, as individuals mostly do within a more intimate orbit; at home; with a lover; under unaccustomed stress. To suppose otherwise is naïve. At the same time, some require action, others are paralysed by action. That dissimilarity recognized, people stay themselves. Pamela did not give an inch. She was not rattled. She did the rattling.

The same could not be said of Widmerpool. He was obstinate, not easily deflected from his purpose, but circumstances might rattle him badly. He was not, like Pamela, consistent in never adapting his behaviour to others. Her constant search for new lovers made the world see her as existing solely in the field of sex, but the Furies that had

driven her into the arms of Widmerpool by their torments
—no doubt his too—at the same time invested her with the
magnetic power that mesmerized Trapnel, operated in a
manner to transcend love or sex, as both are commonly
regarded. Did she and Widmerpool in some manner supplement each other, she supplying a condition he lacked—one
that Burton would have called Melancholy? Now she
showed her powers at work.

'I'm not satisfied with X's book.'

That was the first aesthetic judgment I had ever heard
her make. When she had earlier changed the subject from
Trapnel's writing, I thought she found, as some women do,
concentration on a husband's or lover's work in some manner vexing. That she should return to his writing of her
own volition was unexpected. It looked as if this were another manner of keeping Trapnel on his toes, because he
reacted strongly to the comment.

'I'm going to alter the bits you don't like. You know,
Nick, Pam's got a marvellous instinct for a sequence that
has gone a shade wrong technically. I can't put it all right in
five minutes, darling. These things take time and hard
work. It'll all be done in due course, when I've thrown off
this bloody thing that's playing such hell with work.'

'This is *Profiles in String*?'

'I can't get the *feel* of the end chapters. Most of the bad
criticism you read is lack of understanding of what it feels
like to get the wheels working internally when you're
writing a novel. Not one reviewer in a thousand grasps
that.'

Pamela showed no interest in subtleties of literary feeling.

'I'd rather you burnt it than published it as it stands. In
fact you're not going to.'

Trapnel sighed. It was unlike him to accept criticism
so humbly. On the face of it, there seemed no more reason
to suppose Pamela knew how a novel should be written—

from Trapnel's point of view—than did the reviewers. In general, if he allowed himself to seek another opinion about how to deal with some matter in what he was writing—a short story, for example— he was accustomed to argue hard all the way in favour of whatever treatment he himself had in mind. Pamela showed contempt for the abject manner in which her objections had been received. Once more she switched the subject to her own situation.

'What are people saying about us?'

'No one knows quite what has happened.'

'How do you mean?'

She pouted. At that moment the bell rang. Trapnel groaned.

'God, it's the man trying to collect the money for the newspapers. He's come back.'

Pamela made a face.

'Take no notice. He'll go away after a while.'

'He'll see the light. It was daytime when he came before, and he thought we weren't in.'

Pamela turned to me.

'You answer the door. Tell him we're away—that we've lent you the flat.'

I showed unwillingness to undertake this commission. Trapnel was apologetic.

'We're being dunned. It always happens if you allow people to know your address. It's like hotels insisting on cleaning the room out from time to time. There's always some inconvenience, wherever you live. I couldn't help giving the address this time, otherwise we wouldn't have had any papers delivered.'

'Perhaps it's for the other people in the house.'

'They've gone away—decamped, I think. Do deal with it.'

'But what can I say to the man, if he is the newspaper man?'

'Tell him—'

The bell rang again. Pamela showed signs of getting cross.

'Look, X can't get up in his present state. Do go. If you had ten bob—twelve at the most—that would keep him quiet.'

There seemed no way of avoiding the assignment. I took ten shillings from my notecase, in so far as possible to cut short discussion, and went into the hall. To see the way, it was necessary to leave the flat door ajar. Even so, the place was inconveniently dark, and the front door required a certain amount of negotiating to open. It gave at last. The figure waiting on the the doorstep was not the newspaper-man, but Widmerpool. He did not seem in the least sur-prised that I should be the person to admit him.

'I expect you're here on business about the magazine, Nicholas?'

'Delivering a book to be reviewed, as a matter of fact.'

'I'm rather glad to find you on the premises. Don't go away from a mistaken sense of delicacy. Matters of a rather personal nature are likely to be discussed. I am quite glad to have a witness, especially one conversant with the circumstances, connected, I mean, by ties of business, albeit literary business. Where is Trapnel? This way, I take it?'

The light shining through the sitting-room door showed Widmerpool where to go. He took off his hat, crossed the boards of the hall, and over the threshold of the flat. It had at least been unnecessary to announce him. In fact he announced himself.

'Good evening. I have come to talk about some things.'

Pamela, hands stuck in the pockets of her trousers, was still standing, with her peculiar stillness of poise, in front of the gas fire. If Widmerpool had shown lack of surprise at my opening the door to him, he had at least expressed what seemed to him an adequate explanation as to why I should be with Trapnel. I arranged reviewing at *Fission*; Trapnel reviewed books. That was sufficient reason for my presence. The fact that Trapnel had run away with Widmerpool's wife had nothing to do with the business relationship between Trapnel and myself. To disregard it was almost something to approve. That view was no doubt more especially acceptable in the light of propaganda put about by Widmerpool himself.

Pamela, on the other hand, except insomuch as having left her husband, he might, in one sense, be expected to come and look for her, in another, could scarcely have been prepared for his arrival. So far from showing any wonder, she made no sign whatever of being even aware that an additional person had entered the room. She did not permit herself so much as a glance in Widmerpool's direction. Her expression, one of slight, though not severe displeasure, did not alter in the smallest degree. She seemed to be concentrating on a tear in the wallpaper opposite that ran in a great jagged parabola through a pattern of red parrots and blue storks, freak birds of the same size.

Widmerpool did not speak immediately after his first announcement. He went rather red. He put his hat on top of Trapnel's manuscript, where it lay on the table. Trapnel himself was now sitting bolt upright on the divan. This must, in a way, have been the moment he had been awaiting all his life: a truly dramatic occasion. That he was determined to rise to it was shown at once by the tone of his voice when he spoke.

'Would you oblige me by removing your hat from off my book?'

Widmerpool, whatever else he had taken in his stride, was astonished by this request. No doubt it presupposed an altogether unforeseen, alien area of sensibility. Picking up the hat again, he replaced it on one of the suitcases.

Trapnel maintained a tone of dramatically cold politeness. His voice trembled a little when he spoke again.

'I'm sorry. I must have sounded rude. I did not mean to be that. I have a special thing about my manuscripts—that is, I hate them being treated like any old pile of waste paper. Please take your coat off and sit down.'

'Thank you, I prefer to stand. I shall not be staying long, so that it is not worth my taking off my coat.'

Widmerpool gazed round the room. It was clearly worse, far worse, than he had ever dreamed; if he had thought at all about what he was likely to run to earth. His face showed that, considered in the light of housing insufficiencies inspected in his own constituency, the flat was horrific. Trapnel, possibly remembering the talk they had exchanged on such deplorable conditions, noticed this survey. He almost grinned. Then his manner changed.

'How did you find the house?'

This time Trapnel spoke with the hollow faraway voice of a horror film. He was determined to remain master of the situation. Widmerpool was quite equal to the manoeuvring.

'I came by taxi.'

'I mean how did you discover where I was living?'

'There are such aids as private detectives.'

Widmerpool said that with disdain. Trapnel laughed. The laughter too was of the kind associated with a horror film.

'I always wanted to meet someone who employed a private detective.'

Widmerpool did not answer at once. He appeared to be jockeying for position, taking up action stations before the contest really broke into flame. He cleared his throat.

'I have come here to clarify the situation. By arrival in person, some people might judge that I have put myself in a false position. Such is not my own opinion. A person of your kind, Trapnel, has neither the opportunity to observe, nor capacity to understand, the demands laid on a man who takes up the burden of public life. It is therefore necessary that certain facts should be plainly stated. The best person to state them is myself.'

Trapnel listened to this with the air of an accomplished actor. His 'hollow' laughter was now followed by a 'grim' smile. It was still a performance. Widmerpool had not got him, so to speak, out in the open yet.

'First,' said Widmerpool, 'you borrow money from me.'

Trapnel's defiance had not been geared to that particular form of attack at that moment. He dropped his acting and looked very angry, quite unsimulated rage.

'Then you lampoon me in a magazine of which I am one of the chief supporters.'

Trapnel began to smile again at that. If the first accusation put him in a weak position, the second to some extent restored equilibrium.

'Finally, my wife comes to live with you.'

Widmerpool paused. He too was being melodramatic now. Trapnel had ceased to smile. He was very white. He had lost command of his rôle as actor. Pamela watched them, still showing no change of expression. Widmerpool must have been to some extent aware that by making Trapnel angry, dislodging him from playing a part, he was moving towards ascendancy.

'You can keep my pound. Do not bother, when you are next paid for some paltry piece of journalism, to make another attempt to return it—which was, so I understand, your subterfuge for insinuating yourself into my house. The pound does not matter. Forget about it. I make you a present of it.'

Trapnel did not speak.

'Secondly, I want to express quite clearly my own indifference to your efforts to ridicule my economic theories.

Some people might have thought that an act of ungrateful-
ness on your part. Your own ignorance of the elementary
principles of economics makes it not even that. Your so-
called parody is a failure. Not funny. Several people have
told me so. And at the same time I recognize it as a deliberate insult. That is a matter between the board and Bagshaw—'

Trapnel burst out.

'You're trying to get Books sacked—'

'Don't interrupt me,' said Widmerpool. 'Bagshaw has a
contract.'

He made a half turn about in order, more unmistakably,
to include Pamela in whatever he was now about to announce. She went so far as to raise her eyebrows slightly.
Widmerpool still primarily addressed himself to Trapnel.

'You may fear that I am going to institute divorce proceedings. Such is not my intention. Pamela will return in
her own good time. I think we understand each other.'

Widmerpool paused.

'That is what I came to tell you,' he said. 'That—and to
express my contempt for the way you live and the way you
have behaved.'

Trapnel threw back the army blankets. He rose quite
slowly from the divan. His body, seen through the spotted
pyjamas, was desperately thin. He retied their cord; then,
in his bare feet, walked very deliberately to where the huge
wardrobe stood in the corner of the room. Against it was
propped the death's-head sword-stick. Trapnel picked up
the stick, and pressed the spring at the back of the skull.
The blade was released. He threw the sheath on top of
Oblomov, *The Thin Man*, *Adolphe*, and the several other
books lying on the bedclothes.

'Get out.'

Trapnel did not actually threaten Widmerpool with the
sword. He held the point to the ground, as if about to raise

the weapon in formal salute before joining combat in a duel. It was hard to estimate where exactly his actions hovered between play-acting and loss of control. Widmerpool stood firm.

'No dramatics, please.'

This calmness was to his credit. He knew little of Trapnel, but what he knew certainly gave no guarantee that a man of Trapnel's sort would not be capable of eccentric violence. If it came to that, I felt no absolute assurance on that matter myself. Whatever his merits as a writer, Trapnel could not be regarded as a well-balanced personality. Anything might be looked for from him. Besides, there were his 'pills'. One had the impression that, as such stimulants go, they were fairly mild. At the same time, he could easily have moved on to stronger stuff. Pamela might have encouraged that course; living with her almost necessitated it. Even the pills in their accustomed form might be sufficient to induce indiscreet conduct, especially when the question posed was evicting from a lover's flat the husband of his mistress.

'Are you going?'

'I have no wish to stay.'

Widmerpool picked up his hat from the suitcase. He brushed the felt with his elbow. Then he turned once more towards Pamela.

'I shall be abroad for some weeks in Eastern Europe. As a Member of Parliament I have been invited to enjoy the hospitality of one of the new Governments.'

'I said get out.'

Trapnel raised the sword slightly. Widmerpool took no notice. He continued raspingly to brush the surface of the hat. This time he addressed himself to me.

'The visit should make an interesting *Fission* article. Some apologists for the Liberal and Peasant leaders have suggested that concessions to the Soviet point of view have been too all-embracing. What I always tell people, who are not themselves in the know, is that our own brand of social-democracy, for better or worse, is not always exportable.'

He reorientated himself towards Pamela.

'When I return I shall not be surprised to find that you have reconsidered matters.'

She looked straight at him. Otherwise she gave no sign that she had heard what he said. Widmerpool went very red again. He passed through the door into the hall. The front door slammed, but did not shut. Trapnel in his bare feet ran out of the flat. He could be heard to pull the front door violently open again. From the steps he shouted into the night.

'Coprolite! Faecal débris! Fossil of dung!'

A minute later he returned to the sitting-room. He took the sheath-half of the swordstick from the bed, replaced the blade and returned it to the corner by the wardrobe. Then he climbed under the blankets again, and lay back. He looked quite exhausted. Pamela, on the other hand, now showed signs of life. A faint colour had come into her face, a look of excitement I had never before seen there. She smiled. Something unexpected was afoot. She came across the room, and sat down on the bed. Trapnel took one of her hands. He did not speak. Comment came from Pamela this time.

'I'm glad you were here, Nicholas. I'm glad it all happened in front of someone. I wish there had been a lot more people. Hundreds more. Now you know what my life was like.'

Trapnel patted her hand. He was much shaken. Not well in any case, he was likely to be dissatisfied with the scene that had taken place. He could scarcely be said to have dominated it in the manner of one of his own screen heroes, even if it were better not to have run Widmerpool through, or whatever was in his mind.

'I do apologize for getting you mixed up with all this, Nick. It wasn't my fault. How the hell could I guess he was going to turn up here? I thought there wasn't a living soul knew the address, except one or two shops round here. Private detectives? It makes you think.'

The idea of private detectives obviously fascinated Trapnel's *roman policier* leanings, which were highly developed. He was also worried.

'Will you be awfully good, and keep quiet about all this, Nick? Don't say a word, for obvious reasons.'

Pamela shook back her hair.

'Thank you so much for coming, and for bringing the book. I expect we shall see you again here, as we aren't going out much, as long as X isn't well. I'll ring you up, and you can bring another book some time.'

She spoke formally, like a hostess saying goodbye to a visitor she barely knows, who has paid a social call, and now explains that he must leave. A complete change had come over her after the impassivity she had shown until now. Before I could reply, she spoke again, this time abandoning formality.

'Bugger off—I want to be alone with X.'

5

I LEFT LONDON ONE SATURDAY afternoon in the autumn to make some arrangement about a son going to school. Owing to the anomalies of the timetable, the train arrived an hour or so early for the appointment. There was an interval to kill. After a hot summer the weather still remained warm, but, not uncommon in that watery region, drizzle descended steadily, while a feeble sun shone through clouds that hung low over stretches of claret-coloured brick. It was too wet to wander about in the open. For a time I kicked my heels under a colonnade. A bomb had fallen close by. One corner was still enclosed by scaffolding and a tarpaulin. Above the arch, the long upper storey with its row of oblong corniced windows had escaped damage. The period of the architecture—half a century later, but it took little nowadays to recall him—brought Burton to mind; Burton, by implication the art of writing in general. On this subject he knew what he was talking about:

''Tis not my study or intent to compose neatly . . . but to express myself readily & plainly as it happens. So that as a River runs sometimes precipitate and swift, then dull and slow; now direct, then winding; now deep, then shallow, now muddy, then clear; now broad, then narrow; doth my style flow; now serious, then light; now comical, then satirical; now more elaborate, then remiss, as the present subject required, or as at the time I was affected.'

Even for those with a prejudice in favour of symmetry, worse rules might be laid down. The antithesis between satire and comedy was especially worth emphasis; also to write as the subject required, or the author thought fit at the moment. One often, when writing, felt a desire to be 'remiss'. It was good to have that recommended. An important aspect of writing unmentioned by Burton was 'priority'; what to tell first. That always seemed one of the basic problems. Trapnel used to talk about its complexities. For example, even to arrange in the mind, much less on paper, the events leading up to the demise of *Fission* after a two-year run, the swallowing up (by the larger publishing house of which Clapham was chairman) of the firm of Quiggin & Craggs, demanded an effective grasp of narrative 'priorities'.

Looking out between the pillars at the raindrops glinting on the cobbles of a broad open space, turning the whole thing over in the mind, much seemed to me inevitable, as always contemplating the past. At the same time, although many things had gone wrong, several difficulties had been successfully surmounted. For instance, the prosecution of *Sweetskin* had been parried; the verdict, 'Not Guilty'. Nevertheless, the case had cost money, caused a lot of worry to the directors. Alaric Kydd himself had been so certain that he would be sent to prison for uttering an obscene work that he let his flat on rather good terms for eighteen months; later finding difficulty in obtaining satisfactory alternative accommodation. He was also wounded by the tone of voice—certainly a very silly one—in which prosecuting counsel read aloud in court certain passages from his novel.

More damaging to the firm in a way, though morally rather than financially, was the *Sad Majors* affair. Bagshaw leaked an account of that. He had come back to the office in a restless, resentful mood after his bout of flu, according to Ada, spending the first forty-eight hours of convalescence drinking, then retiring to bed again for a further day before settling down. Whether or not he had deliberately kept the Trapnel parody 'on the spike' for use at the most appropriate occasion was never cleared up. Most probably, as in previous episodes of Bagshaw's history, an infallible instinct for causing trouble had brought guidance without need of exact knowledge. Widmerpool appeared to have made no complaint to the board. He remained out of touch with Quiggin & Craggs long after the Court Circular announced his return from the People's Republic, where he had been paying his visit. No doubt he was busy with parliamentary affairs. There was in any case not much he could do. If *Fission* had not ceased publication, Bagshaw's contract would in any case have run out. He had dropped hints that he himself wanted to move. No one was going to stand in his way. The fact was that Bagshaw was by now attracted by the promise of helping to open up the still mainly unexplored eldorado of television.

Bagshaw took pleasure in elaborating the Odo Stevens story. He did not like Stevens as a man, but admired him as an adventurer. They used to meet when Stevens from time to time looked into the *Fission* office to see if there were a book to review. Stevens had developed an additional contact with the magazine on account of his association with Rosie Manasch. Never backward at publicizing his successes, he did not at present convey more than that he had an ally in that quarter. If Rosie had decided she needed relaxation with a man considerably younger than herself, she was agreed to have had a distressing time in many ways, and Stevens, whatever his failings, had the advantage of being a figure not to be taken too seriously. Both parties were judged well able to look after themselves. That was how it seemed at the time. However, even at an early stage the relationship was sufficiently strong to play a part in the

Quiggin & Craggs upheaval. This came about when the *Sad Majors* controversy, simmering for some little while, took aggressive shape. Bagshaw, always interested in a row of this sort, was ravished by a move now made.

'You can't help admiring the way Gypsy does things. Good old hard-core stuff. You know the trouble about the Stevens book—thought to bring discredit on the Party. Gypsy's performed one of those feats that most people don't think of on account of their ruthless simplicity. She has quite simply liquidated the manuscript. Both copies.'

'Aren't there more than two copies?'

'Apparently not.'

'How did she get hold of them?'

'After much argument, the original MS had been sent to the printer to be cast off. It was to be allowed to go ahead anyway as far as proof. Then Howard said he'd like to re-read the book in peaceful surroundings, so he borrowed the carbon, and took it home with him. A day or two later, Gypsy, that's her story, thought it was another manuscript Howard had asked her to post to Len Pugsley—who sometimes does reading for the firm, he poked Gypsy briefly—and Len says the parcel never arrived. He was moving house at the time. Stevens's carbon seems to have gone astray between the Oval and Chalk Farm. Meanwhile, the printers got a telephone message, the origins of which no one can trace, to send back the MS they were to cast off. There was some question about it to be settled editorially. Now that copy can't be found either.'

'Stevens will have to write it again?'

'That's where the neatness of the sabotage comes in. Re-writing will take a longish time. By the time it's finished the poor impression Stevens gives of the Comrades and their behaviour will, with any luck, be out of date—anyway in the eyes of the reading public. At worst, all ancient history.'

'How's Stevens taking the loss?'

'He's pretty cross. Can you blame him? The more interesting point is that Rosie Manasch is very cross too. In fact she's withdrawn her support from the mag in consequence of her crossness with Quiggin & Craggs as a firm. That's awkward, because—though personally I think a lot of unnecessary fuss was made about the Trapnel parody—the rest of the board don't feel it a good moment to stir up Widmerpool.'

'Is Stevens getting compensation?'

'You haven't studied the writing paper. The greatest care is taken of manuscripts, but no responsibility. However, they've allowed the contract to be cancelled.'

'That was handsome.'

Compared with the Stevens row, the disappointment caused by Sillery's Diary, after all the haggling about terms, and high advance, was a minor blow, though again there were repercussions. The extracts were called *Garnered at Sunset: Leaves from an Edwardian Journal*.

'A masterpiece of dullness,' said Bagshaw. 'JG read it. Howard read it. For once they were in complete agreement. The only thing to do will be to publish, and hope for the best. I'm surprised at Ada. She's strung them along over Sillery.'

Ada's policy in the matter, as not seldom, was enigmatic, probably dictated by a mixture of antagonistic considerations. The Diary, seen as one of the paths to a career, had not been truly subjected to her usually sharp judgment. Its lack of interest had been obscured by inner workings of the curious kind of flirtation she and Sillery had shared. Those elements might be put forward as excuse for the recommendation. It was also possible, knowing Sillery as she did, that Ada had genuinely found *Garnered at Sunset* absorbing. Publishers' readers, as Quiggin remarked, are no less subjective than other animals. It might be thought that this critical lapse on Ada's part would have prejudiced her position in the firm. On the contrary, nothing more retributive was visited on her than that Quiggin proposed marriage.

Bagshaw suggested that an emotional scene contingent on some sort of reprimand on the subject of the Sillery Journal, had brought things to a head, but there can be no doubt an offer of marriage was already at the back of Quiggin's mind. The fact that the firm was moving towards a close had nothing to do with it. He was accepted. As a married man, the place he had found on the board of Clapham's firm would be advantageous; on the whole a step forward in a publishing career. The two of them were quietly married one August afternoon before the Registrar; Mark Members and L. O. Salvidge, witnesses. Craggs and Gypsy were not asked. Craggs had announced he was going into semi-retirement when the firm closed down, but it seemed likely that he would continue his activities, at least in an inconspicuous manner, with many little interests of a political sort that had always engrossed him. All these things played a part, others too, in the winding up of Quiggin & Craggs, representative of common enough impediments to running a publishing house; exceptional, in as much as they were exceptional, only on account of the individuals concerned. The climax, in an odd way, seemed to be the night spent with Trapnel and Bagshaw. That had been rather different. By then, in any case, both magazine and publishing business had received the death sentence. All the same that night—the symbolic awfulness of its events—was something to put a seal on the whole affair. It confirmed several other things too.

Matters had begun with a telephone call from Bagshaw at about half-past nine one evening four or five weeks before. From the opening sentences it was clear he was drunk, less clear what he wanted. At first the object seemed no more than a chat about the sadness of life, perhaps a long one, but entailing merely a sympathetic hearing. That was too good to be true. It soon grew plain some request was going to be made. Even then, what the demand would be became only gradually apparent.

'As the mag's closing down, I thought a small celebration would be justified.'

'So you said, Books. You've said that twice.'

'Sorry, sorry. The fact is everything always comes at once. Look, Nicholas, I want your help. I'd already decided on this small celebration, when Trappy got in touch with me at the office. He rang up himself, which, as you know, he doesn't often do. He's in a lot of trouble. This girl, I mean.'

'Pamela Widmerpool?'

It was as well to make sure.

'That's the one.'

The fact that Pamela might be Widmerpool's wife had made, from his tone of voice, little or no serious impact on Bagshaw. He clearly thought of her as one, among many, of Trapnel's girls . . . Tessa . . . Pat . . . Sally . . . Pauline . . . any of the Trapnel girls Bagshaw himself had known in the course of their acquaintance.

'What's happened?'

'They've had some row about his novel—you know the one—what—can't quite—'

He made a tremendous effort, but I had to intervene.

'*Profiles in String?*'

'That's the book. He's tremendously pleased with it, but can't decide about an ending. He wants one, she wants another.'

'Trapnel's writing the bloody book, isn't he?'

Bagshaw feigned shock at this disregard for authority conferred by a love attachment.

'Trappy was upset. They had a row. Now he doesn't want to go back and find she's left. She may have done. He wants someone to go back with him. Soften the blow. I said I'd do that.'

'Look, Books, why are you telling me all this?'

'I was quite willing to do that. See him home, I mean. Trappy and I went to the pub to talk things over. You know how it is. I'm not quite sure I can get him back unaided.'

'Do you mean he's passed out?'

Bagshaw was insulted at the suggestion that such a fate might have overtaken any friend of his.

'Not in the least. It's just he's in a bit of a state. Sort of nervous condition. That's what I'm coming to. It's really an awful lot to ask. Would it be too great an infliction for you to come along and lend a hand?'

'Is it those pills?'

'Might be.'

'Where are you?'

'Not far from Trappy's flat. Once we've got him under way there'll be nothing to it.'

Bagshaw named a pub I had never heard of, but, from the description of its locality, evidently not far from Trapnel's base, assuming that unchanged from the night I had visited him. Since that night I had heard nothing of him or Pamela. She had not rung up to ask for further books to review. The L. O. Salvidge notice had never been sent in. Salvidge was aggrieved. Trapnel ceased altogether to be a contributor to *Fission* in its latter days.

'Can he walk?'

'Of course he can walk—at least I think so. It's not walking I'm worried about, just I don't know how he'll behave when he gets into the open. After all, which of us does? You'd be a great support, Nicholas, if you could manage to come along. You always get on all right with Trappy, which is more than some do. I'm full of apologies for asking this.'

Although in most respects quite different, the situation

213

seemed to present certain points in common with conducting Bithel, collapsed on the pavement, back to G Mess; restoring Stringham to his flat after the Old Boy dinner. In some sense history was repeating itself, though incapacity to walk seemed not Trapnel's disability.

'All right, I'll be along as soon as I can.'

Isobel was unimpressed by this call for help. There was much to be said for her view of it. Now that Bagshaw was off the line, compliance took the shape of moral weakness, rather than altruism or benevolence.

'Looking after Trapnel's becoming monotonous. Is Mrs Widmerpool still his true-love?'

'She's what the trouble's about.'

The pub turned out to be another of Bagshaw's obscure, characterless drinking places, this time off the Edgware Road. It was fairly empty. Bagshaw and Trapnel were at a table in the corner, both perfectly well behaved. Closer investigation showed Bagshaw as drunk in his own very personal manner, that is to say he would become no drunker however much consumed. There was never any question of going under completely, or being unable to find his way home. Trapnel, on the other hand, did not at first show any sign of being drunk at all. He had abandoned his dark lenses. Possibly he only wore them in hard winters. He was sitting, quietly smiling to himself, hunched over the death's-head stick.

'Hullo, Nick. I've just been talking to Books about a critical work I'm planning. It's to be called *The Heresy of Naturalism*. People can't get it right about Naturalism. They think if a writer like me writes the sort of books I do, it's because that's easier, or necessary nowadays. You just look round at what's happening and shove it all down. They can't understand that's not in the least the case. It's just as selective, just as artificial, as if the characters were kings and queens speaking in blank verse.'

214

'Some of them are queens,' said Bagshaw.

'Do listen, Books. You'll profit by it. What I'm getting at is that if you took a tape-recording of two people having a grind it might truly be called Naturalism, it might be funny, it might be sexually exciting, it might even be beautiful, it wouldn't be art. It would just be two people having a grind.'

'But, look here, Trappy—'

'All right, they don't have to be revelling in bed. Suppose you took a tape-recording of the most passionate, most moving love scene, a couple who'd—oh, God, I don't know—something very moving about their love and its circumstances. The incident, their words, the whole thing, it gets accidentally taped. Unknown to them the machine's been left on by mistake. Anything you like. Some wonderful *objet trouvé* of that sort. Do you suppose it would come out as it should? Of course it wouldn't. There are certain forms of human behaviour no actor can really play, no matter how good he is. It's the same in life. Human beings aren't subtle enough to play their part. That's where art comes in.'

'All I said was that Tolstoy—'

'Do keep quiet, Books. You've missed the point. What I mean is that if, as a novelist, you put over something that hasn't been put over before, you've done the trick. A novelist's like a fortune-teller, who can impart certain information, but not necessarily what the reader wants to hear. It may be disagreeable or extraneous. The novelist just has to dispense it. He can't choose.'

'All I said was, Trappy, that personally I preferred Realism—Naturalism, if you wish—just as I've a taste for political content. That's how Tolstoy came in. It's like life.'

'But Naturalism's only "like" life, if the novelist himself is any good. If he isn't any good, it doesn't matter whether he writes naturalistically or any other way. What could be less "like" life than most of the naturalistic novels that appear? If he's any good, it doesn't matter if his characters talk like Disraeli's, or incidents occur like Vautrin, smoking a cigar and dressed up as a Spanish abbé, persuades Lucien de Rubempré not to drown himself. Is *Oliver Twist* a failure as a novel because Oliver, a workhouse boy, always speaks with exquisite refinement? As for politics, who cares which way Trimalchio voted, or that he was a bit temperamental towards his slaves?'

'Trappy—no, wait, let me speak—all this started by my saying that, just as masochism's only sadism towards yourself, revolutions only reconcentrate the centre of gravity of authority, and, if you wish, of oppression. The people who feel they suffer from authority and oppression want to be authoritative and oppressive. I was just illustrating that by something or other I thought came in Tolstoy.'

'But, Books, you said Tolstoy wrote "like" life, because he was naturalistic. I contend that his characters aren't any more "like"—in fact aren't as "like"—as, say, Dostoevsky's at their craziest. Of course Tolstoy's inordinately brilliant. In spite of all the sentimentality and moralizing, he's never boring—at least never in one sense. The material's inconceivably well arranged as a rule, the dialogue's never less than convincing. The fact remains, *Anna Karenin*'s a glorified magazine story, a magazine story of the highest genius, but still a magazine story in that it tells the reader what he wants to hear, never what he doesn't want to hear.'

'Trappy, I won't have you say that sort of thing about Tolstoy, though of course Dostoevsky's more explicit when it comes to exhibiting the Marxist contention that any action's justified—'

'Do stop about Marxism, Books. Marxism has nothing to do with what I'm talking about. I'm talking about Naturalism. I'm in favour of Naturalism. I write that way myself. All I want to make clear is that it's just a way of writing a novel like any other, just as contrived, just as selective. Do you call Hemingway's impotent good guy naturalistic? Think what Dostoevsky would have made of him. After all, Dostoevsky did deal with an impotent good guy in love with a bitch, when he wrote *The Idiot*.'

Bagshaw was silenced for the moment. Trapnel was undoubtedly in an exceptionally excited state, unable to stop pouring out his views. He took a gulp of beer. The pause made comment possible.

'We don't know for certain that Myshkin was impotent.'

'Myshkin was as near impotent as doesn't matter, Nick. In any case Hemingway would never allow a hero of his to be made a fool of. To that extent he's not naturalistic. Most forms of naturalistic happening are expressed in grotesque irrational trivialities, not tight-lipped heroisms. Hemingway's is only one special form of Naturalism. The same goes for Scott Fitzgerald's romantic-hearted gangster. Henry James would have done an equally good job on him in non-naturalistic terms. Most of the gangsters of the classic vintage were queer anyway. James might have delicately conveyed that as an additional complication to Gatsby's love.'

Before literary values could be finally hammered out in a manner satisfactory to all parties, the pub closed. We moved from the table, Trapnel still talking. In the street his incoherent, distracted state of mind was much more apparent. He was certainly in a bad way. All the talk about writing, its flow not greatly different from the termination of any evening in his company, was just a question of putting off the evil hour of having to face his own personal problems. No doubt he had gone into these to some extent with Bagshaw earlier. They had then started up the politico-literary imbroglio in progress when I arrived at the pub. Now, even if nothing were said about Pamela, the problem of getting him home was posed. He was, as Bagshaw so positively believed, perfectly able to walk. There was no difficulty about that. His manner was the disturbing element. An air of dreadful nervousness had descended on him. Now that he had ceased to argue about writing, he seemed to have lost all powers of decision in other matters. He stood there shaking, as if he were afraid. This could have been the consequence of lack of proper food, drinking, pills, or the mere fact of being emotionally upset. Burton had noticed such a condition. 'Cousin-german to sorrow is fear, or rather sister, *fidus Achates*, and continual companion.' That was just how Trapnel looked, a man weighed down by sorrow and fear. Suddenly he reeled. Bagshaw stepped towards him.

'Hold up, Trappy. You're tight.'

That was a fatal remark. Not only did open expression of that opinion make Trapnel very indignant, it also had the effect of physically increasing, anyway for the moment, the lack of control that was overcoming him. Trapnel always hated any suggestion that limits existed to his own powers of alcoholic assimilation. Bagshaw must already have known that. The fact that his comment was true made it no more excusable, except for being equally applicable to Bagshaw himself.

'Tight? I'm always being asked by people how it is I'm never drunk, however much I put back. They can't make it out. I can finish a bottle of brandy at a sitting, get up sober as when I started. Drink just doesn't have any effect on me. You don't suppose the few halves of bitter we've had tonight made me drunk, Books, do you? It's you who are a little tipsy, my boy. You've rather a weak head.'

He waved his stick. If the contrast had to be made, this described their capacities in reverse. Bagshaw took it well, having made the initial error by his comment.

'Drunk or sober, we can none of us stand here all night. Shall we head for your place, Trappy?'

This suggestion had a steadying, immediately subduing effect on Trapnel. He seemed to remember suddenly all he had been trying to forget. The outward appearance of drunkenness left him at once. He might have swallowed an instant sedative. The state of utter dejection returned. He spoke to Bagshaw quietly, almost humbly.

'Does Nicholas know what's happened?'

'Roughly.'

'I'd like to be a bit clearer about what's up.'

'There's been some trouble with Pam. It was all over my new book. We never seem to agree about writing, especially my writing. It's almost as if she hates it, doesn't want me to do it, and yet she thinks about my work all the time, knows just where the weak places are. We have a lot of rows about it. We had one this morning. I left the house in a rage. I told her she was mad on Naturalism. That's why the subject was on my mind. Books and I began talking about it. I'm for it too. I told her I was. I've told everyone, and written it. What I can't stand is people giving it their own exclusive meaning. That's what Pam does. She just uses it to pick on the way I write. She brings up all my own arguments against me. Then when I half agree, she takes an absolutely opposite line. It's like Pavlov's dogs. I think sometimes I'll go up the wall.'

'Why discuss your work with her?' said Bagshawe inconsistently. 'Tell her to get on with the washing-up.'

'It's not the first row we've had by a long chalk. Christ, I don't want her to leave me. I know it's pretty awful living the way we do, but I can't face the thought of her leaving. You know I'm not sure there isn't going to be a film in *Profiles in String*. It was the last thing I thought about when I started, but now I believe there might be. It would go over big, if it went over at all.'

At one moment it looked as if Trapnel were going to break down, at the next, that he was about to indulge in

one of his fantasies about making money, which overwhelmed him from time to time. These sudden changes of
gear were going to require careful handling, if he were to be
conveyed back to the flat. It was much more likely that he
would want to go to a drinking club of some sort. He
usually knew the address of one that would admit him.
Bagshaw, grasping the fact that Trapnel needed soothing,
now took charge quite effectively. He must have had long
experience in persuading fellow-drunks to do what he,
rather than they themselves, wanted. He was ruthless about
getting his own way when he thought that necessary,
showing total disregard for other people's wishes or convenience. That was now all to the good.

'We know what you feel, Trappy. Come on. We'll go
back and see how things are. She's probably longing to see
you.'

'You don't know her.'

'I admit that, but I've seen her. They're all the same.'

'There's not a drop to drink.'

'Never mind. Nick and I will just see you home.'

'Will you really? I couldn't face it otherwise.'

Trapnel was like a child who suddenly decides to be fret-
ful no longer. Now he was even full of gratitude. We
reached Edgware Road with him still in this mood. There
was a small stretch of the main highway to negotiate before
turning off by the Canal. The evening was warm, stuffy,
full of strange smells. For once Trapnel seemed suitably
dressed in his tropical suit. We turned down the south
side of the Canal, walking on the pavement away from the
houses. Railings shut off a grass bank that sloped down to
the tow-path. Trapnel had now moved into a pastoral
dream.

'I love this waterway. I'd like to have a private barge,
and float down it waving to the tarts.'

'Do you get a lot down here?' asked Bagshaw, interested.

'You see the odd one. They live round about, but tend to work other streets. What a mess the place is in.'

Most of London was pretty grubby at this period, the Canal no exception. On the surface of the water concentric circles of oil, undulating in the colours of the spectrum, were illuminated by moonlight. Through these luminous prisms floated anonymous off-scourings of every kind, tin cans, petrol drums, soggy cardboard boxes. Watery litter increased as the bridge was approached. Bagshaw pointed to a peculiarly obnoxious deposit bobbing up and down by the bank.

'Looks as if someone's dumped their unit's paper salvage. I used to have to deal with that at one stage of the war. Obsolete forms waiting to be pulped and made into other forms. An eternal reincarnation. Fitted the scene in India.'

Trapnel stopped, and leant against the railings.

'Let's pause for a moment. Contemplate life. It's a shade untidy here, but romantic too. Do you know what all that mess of paper looks like? A manuscript. Probably someone's first novel. Authors always talk of burning their first novel. I believe this one's drowned his.'

'Or hers.'

'Some beautiful girl who wrote about her seduction, and couldn't get it published.'

'When lovely woman stoops to authorship?'

'I think I'll go and have a look. Might give me some ideas.'

'Trappy, don't be silly.'

Trapnel, laughing rather dementedly, began to climb the railings. Bagshaw attempted to stop this. Before he could be persuaded otherwise, Trapnel had lifted himself up, and was halfway across. The railings presented no very serious obstacle even to a man in a somewhat deranged state, who carried a stick in one hand. He dropped to the other side

221

without difficulty. The bank sloped fairly steeply to the lower level of the tow-path and the water. Trapnel reached the footway. He paused for a moment, looking up and down the length of the Canal. Then he went to the water's edge, and began to poke with the swordstick at the sheets of paper floating about all over the surface.

'Come back, Trappy. You're not the dustman.'

Trapnel took no notice of Bagshaw. He continued to strain forward with the stick, until it looked ominously as if he would fall in. The pieces of paper, scattered broadcast, were all just out of reach.

'We shall have to get over,' said Bagshaw. 'He'll be in at any moment.'

Then Trapnel caught one of the sheets with the end of the stick. He guided it to the bank. For a second it escaped, but was recaptured. He bent down to pick it up, shook off the water and straightened out the page. The soaked paper seemed to fascinate him. He looked at it for a long time. Bagshaw, relieved that the railings would not now have to be climbed, for a minute or two did not intervene. At last he became tired of waiting.

'Is it a work of genius? Do decide one way or the other. We can't bear more delay to know whether it ought to be published or not.'

Trapnel gave a kind of shudder. He swayed. Either drink had once more overcome him with the suddenness with which it had struck outside the pub, or he was acting out a scene of feigned horror at what he read. Whichever it were, he really did look again as if about to, fall into the Canal. Abruptly he stopped playing the part, or recovered his nerve. I suppose these antics, like the literary ramblings in the pub, also designed to delay discovery that Pamela had abandoned him; alternatively, to put off some frightful confrontation with her.

'Do come back, Trappy.'

Then an extraordinary thing happened. Trapnel was still standing by the edge of the water holding the dripping sheet of foolscap. Now he crushed it in his hand, and threw the ball of paper back into the Canal. He lifted the sword-stick behind his head, and, putting all his force into the throw, cast it as far as this would carry, high into the air. The stick turned and descended, death's-head first. A mystic arm should certainly have risen from the dark waters of the mere to receive it. That did not happen. Trapnel's Excalibur struck the flood a long way from the bank, disappeared for a moment, surfaced, and began to float downstream.

'Now he really has become unmoored,' said Bagshaw.

Trapnel came slowly up the bank.

'You'll never get your stick back, Trappy. What ever made you do it? We'll hurry on to the bridge right away. It might have got caught up on something. There's not much hope.'

Trapnel climbed back on to the pavement.

'You were quite wrong, Books.'

'What about?'

'It was a work of genius.'

'What was?'

'The manuscript in the water—it was *Profiles in String*.'

I now agreed with Bagshaw in supposing Trapnel to have gone completely off his head. He stood looking at us. His smile was one of the consciously dramatic ones.

'She brought the MS along, and chucked it into the Canal. She knew I should be almost bound to pass this way, and it would be well on the cards I should notice it. We quite often used to stroll down here at night and talk about the muck floating down, french letters and such like. She must have climbed over the railings to get to the water. I'd like to have watched her doing that. I'd thought of a lot of things she might be up to—doctoring my pills, arranging for me to find her being had by the milkman, giving the bailiffs our address. I never thought of this. I never thought she'd destroy my book.'

He stood there, still smiling slightly, almost as if he were embarrassed by what had happened.

'You really mean that's your manuscript over there in the water?'

Trapnel nodded.

'The whole of it?'

'It wasn't quite finished. The end was what we had the row about.'

'You must have a copy?'

"Of course I haven't a copy. Why should I? I told you, it wasn't finished yet.'

Even Bagshaw was appalled. He began to speak, then stopped, something I had never seen happen before. There was certainly nothing to say. Trapnel just stood there.

'Come and look for the stick, Trappy.'

Trapnel was not at all disposed to move. Now the act had taken place, he wanted to reflect on it. Perhaps he feared still worse damage when the flat was reached, though that was hard to conceive.

'In a way I'm not surprised. Even though this particular dish never struck me as likely to appear on the menu, it all fits in with the cuisine. Christ, two years' work, and I'll never feel the same as when I was writing it. She may be correct in what she thinks about it, but I'll never be able to write it again—either her way or my own.'

Bagshaw, in spite of his feelings about the manuscript, could not forget the stick. The girl did not interest him at all.

'You'll never find a swordstick like that again. It was a great mistake to throw it away.'

Trapnel was not listening. He stood there musing. Then all at once he revealed something that had always been a mystery. Being Trapnel, an egotist of the first rank, he supposed this disclosure as of interest only in his own case, but a far wider field of vision was at the same time opened up by what was unveiled. In a sense it was of most interest where Trapnel was concerned, because he seems to have reacted in a somewhat different fashion to the rest of Pamela's lovers, but, applicable to all of them, what was divulged offered clarification of her relations with men. Drink, pills, the strain of living with her, the destruction of *Profiles in String*, combination of all those, brought about a confession hardly conceivable from Trapnel in other circumstances. He now spoke in a low, confidential tone.

'You may have wondered why a girl like that ever came to live with me?'

'Not so much as why she ever married that husband of hers,' said Bagshaw. 'I can understand all the rest.'

'I doubt if you can. Not every man can stand what's entailed.'

'I don't contradict that.'

'You don't know what I mean.'

'What do you mean?'

Trapnel did not answer for a moment. It was as if he were thinking how to phrase whatever he intended to say. Then he spoke with great intensity.

'It's when you have her. She wants it all the time, yet doesn't want it. She goes rigid like a corpse. Every grind's a nightmare. It's all the time, and always the same.'

Trapnel said this with absolute simplicity. Irony, melodrama, narcissism, fantasy, all his accustomed tendency to play a rôle had been this time completely eliminated. The curtain was at least partially drawn aside. A little light had been let in. Stevens had not told all the truth.

'I could take it, because—well, I suppose because I loved her. Why not admit it? I'm not sure I don't still.'

Bagshaw could not stand that. Excessive displays of amative sensibility always disturbed him.

225

'Even Sacher-Masoch drew the line somewhere, Trappy
—true we don't know where. What did her husband think
about this, I'd like to know.'

'She told me he only tried a couple of times. Gave it up
as a bad job.'

'So that's how things are?'

'For certain reasons it suited him to be married to her.'

'And her to him?'

'She stopped that, if ever true, when she came to live with
me.'

Even after what had taken place, Trapnel spoke defensively.

'It gave him a kind of prestige,' he said.

'Not much prestige the way she was carrying on.'

'You don't understand.'

'I don't.'

'It's not what she does, it's what she is.'

'You mean he's positively flattered?'

'That's what she seemed to think. She may be right.
That's a form of masochism too. It's not my sort. Not that
I can explain my sort, if that's what it is. It doesn't feel unnatural to me. As I said, I love her—at least used to. I don't
think I do now. She'll always go on like this. She's a child,
who doesn't know any better.'

'Oh, balls,' said Bagshaw. 'I've heard men say that sort
of thing about women before. It's rubbish, the scrapings of
the barrel. You must rise above that, Trappy. Let's get back
to your place anyway.'

I had never seen Bagshaw so agitated. This time Trapnel
came quietly. When we reached the bridge, he insisted that
he did not want to look for the stick.

'It's a sacrifice. One of those things you dedicate to the
Gods. I remember reading about a sacred pool in an Indian
temple, where good writing floated on the water, bad
writing sank. Perhaps the Canal has the same property,
and Pam was right to put my book there.'

Those words meant that he was getting back his normal form. Panache was coming into play. I sympathized with Bagshaw's sentiments as to the deliberate throwing away of a good swordstick, but Trapnel's manner of dealing with the situation had not been without its lofty side. Nothing unexpected was found in the flat. Pamela had packed her clothes, and left with the suitcases. The Modigliani and her own photographs were gone too. No doubt she had strolled down to the Canal, disposed of *Profiles in String*, then returned with a taxi to remove her effects. Trapnel glanced for a second at the spaces left by the pictures.

'She can't have been gone more than a few hours. She must have done it after dark. If only I'd come back earlier in the day she'd still have been here.'

He took off the tropical jacket, slipped it on to a wire coat-hanger pendant from a hook in the door, loosened his tie. After that he stretched. That seemed to give him an idea. He began to look about the room, opening drawers, examining the shelf at the top of the inside of the wardrobe, even searching under the bed. Doubtless he was looking for 'pills' of one sort or another. Pamela might well have taken them away with her. He talked while he hunted round.

'I warned you hospitality would be rather sparse if you came back. Not a drop of Algerian left. I'm sorry for that. It was a great help when you're seeing things through. I'll just have to have a think now as to the best way of tackling life.'

'Will you be all right, Trappy?'

'Absolutely.'

'Nothing we can do?'

'Not a thing—ah, here we are.'

Trapnel had found the box. He swallowed a couple of examples of whatever sustaining globules were kept inside it. Possibly they were no more than sleeping pills. There was now no point in our staying a moment longer.

Both Bagshaw and I tried to say something more of a sympathetic sort. Trapnel shook his head.

'Probably all for the best. Who can tell? Still, losing that manuscript takes some laughing off. I'll have to think a lot about that.'

Bagshaw still hung about.

'Are you absolutely cleaned out, Trappy?'

'Me? Cleaned out? Good heavens, no. Thanks a lot all the same, but a cheque arrived this morning, quite a decent one, from a film paper I'd done a piece for.'

Whether or not that were true, it was a good exit line; Trapnel at his best. Bagshaw and I said goodnight. We passed again along the banks of the Canal, its waters still overspread with the pages of *Profiles in String*. The smell of the flat had again reminded me of Maclintick's.

'Will he really be all right?'

'I don't know about being all right exactly,' said Bagshaw. 'It's hard to be all right when you've not only lost your girl, but she's simultaneously destroyed your life work. I don't know what I'd feel like in the same position. I've sometimes thought of writing another novel—a political one. Somehow there never seems time. I expect Trappy'll pull through. Most of us do.'

'I mean he won't do himself in?'

'Trappy?'

'Yes.'

'God, no. I'd be very surprised.'

'People do.'

'I know they do. There was a chap in Spain when I was there. An anarcho-syndicalist. He'd talk about Proudhon by the hour together. He shot himself in a hotel room. I don't think Trappy will ever take that step. He's too interested in his own myth. Not the type anyway. He'd have done it before now, if he were going to.'

'He says something about suicide in the *Camel*.'

'The *Camel*'s not an exact description of Trappy's own life. He is always complaining people take it as that. You must have heard him. There are incidents, but the novel's not a blow-by-blow account of his early career.'

'I've heard X say that readers can never believe a novelist invents anything. He was at least in Egypt?'

'Do you mean to say he's never told you what he was doing there?'

'I'd always imagined his father was in the Consular, or something of the sort—possibly secret service connexions. X is always very keen on spying, says there's a resemblance between what a spy does and what a novelist does, the point being you don't suddenly steal an indispensable secret that gives complete mastery of the situation, but accumulate a lot of relatively humdrum facts, which when collated provide the picture.'

Bagshaw was not greatly interested in how novelists went to work, but was greatly astonished at this ignorance of Trapnel's life when young.

'A spy? Trapnel *père* wasn't a spy. He was a jockey. Rode for the most part in Egypt. That's why he knew the country. Did rather well in his profession, and saved up a bit. Married a girl from one of those English families who've lived for three or four generations in the Levant.'

'But all this is good stuff. Why doesn't X write about it?'

'He did talk of an article for the mag. Then he thought he'd keep it for a book. Trappy has mixed feelings. Of course he got through whatever money there was, as soon as he laid hands on it. He's not exactly ashamed. Rather proud in a way. All the same, it doesn't quite fit in with his own picture of himself. Hints about the secret service seem more exciting. The other was just ordinary home life, therefore rather dull.'

By this time Bagshaw was all but sober. Our paths lay in

different directions. We parted. I made my way home. A great deal seemed to have happened in a comparatively short time. It was still before midnight. A clock struck twelve while I put the key in the door. As if from a neighbouring minaret, a cat muezzin began to call other cats to prayer. The aberrations of love were incalculable. Burton, I remembered, supposed the passion to extend even into the botanic world:

'In vegetal creatures what sovereignty Love hath by many pregnant proofs and familiar example may be proved, especially of palm trees, which are both he and she, and express not a sympathy but a love-passion, as by many observations have been confirmed. *Constantine* gives an instance out of *Florentius* his Georgicks, of a Palm-tree that loved most fervently, and would not be comforted until such time her love applied himself unto her; you might see the two trees bend, and of their own accords stretch out their bows to embrace and kiss each other; they will give manifest signs of mutual love. *Ammianus Marcellinus* reports that they marry one another, and fall in love if they grow in sight; and when the wind brings up the smell to them, they are marvellously affected. *Philostratus* observes as much, and Galen, they will be sick for love, ready to die and pine away . . .'

Now, considering these matters that autumn afternoon under the colonnade, vegetal love seemed scarcely less plausible than the human kind. The damp cobblestones in front gave the illusion of quivering where the sunlight struck their irregular convexities. Rain still fell. The Library presented itself as a preferable refuge from the wet. I was uncertain whether rules permitted casual entry. It was worth trying. At worst, if told to go away, one could remain in the porch until time to move on. It would be no worse than where I was. Abandoning the colonnade, I crossed the road to a grey domed Edwardian building. Beyond its threshold, a parabola of passage-way led into a high circular room, rising to the roof and surrounded by a gallery. The place, often a welcome oasis in the past, seemed smaller than remembered. A few boys were pottering about among the bays of books, with an absent-minded air, or furiously writing at a table, as if life itself depended on getting whatever it was finished in time. A librarian presided at his desk.

Hoping to remain unobserved, I loitered by the door. That was not to be. The librarian looked up and stared. He took off his spectacles, rubbed his eyes, chose another pair from several spectacle-cases in front of him, put them on his nose and stared again. After a moment of this, he beckoned me. Recognizing that I was not to be allowed to kill five or ten minutes in peace, I prepared for expulsion. No doubt there was a regulation against visitors at this hour. The thing to do would be to delay eviction as long as possible, so that a minimum of time had to be spent in the porch. The librarian's beckonings became more urgent. He was a man older than normal for the job, more formally dressed. In fact, this was clearly an assistant master substituting for a regular librarian. Professional librarians were probably unprocurable owing to shortage of labour. I went across the room to see what he wanted. Tactics could be decided by his own comportment. This happy-go-lucky approach was cut short. Sitting at the desk was my former housemaster Le Bas. He spoke crossly.

'Do I know you?'

Boyhood returned in a flash, the instinct to oppose Le Bas —as Bagshaw would say—dialectically. The question was unanswerable. It is reasonable for someone to ask if you know him, because such knowledge is in the hands of the questioned party. How can it be asserted with assurance whether or not the questioner knows one? Powers of telepathy would be required. It could certainly be urged that five years spent under the same roof, so to speak under Le Bas's guidance, gave him a decided opportunity for knowing one; almost an unfair advantage, both in the superficial, also the more searching sense of the phrase. That was the primitive, atavistic reaction. More mature consideration brought to mind Le Bas's notorious forgetfulness even in those days. There was no reason to suppose his memory had improved.

'I was in your house—'

Obviously it would be absurd to call him 'sir', yet that still obtruded as the only suitable form of address. What on earth else could he be called? Just 'Le Bas'? Certainly he belonged to a generation which continued throughout a lifetime to use that excellently masculine invocation of surname, before an irresponsible bandying of first names smothered all subtleties of relationship. In any case, to call Le Bas by a christian name was unthinkable. What would it be, in effect, if so daring an apostrophe were contemplated? The initials had been L. L. Le B.—Lawrence Langton Le Bas, that was it. No one had ever been known to call him Lawrence, still less Langton. Among the other masters, some—his old enemy Cobberton, for example—used once in a way to hail him as 'Le B.' There was, after all, really no necessity to call him anything. Le Bas himself grew impatient at this procrastination.

'What's your name?'

I told him. That made things easier at once. Direct enquiry of that sort on the part of a former preceptor was much to be preferred to Sillery's reckless guessing. Confessed ignorance on the point—as on most points—showed a saner attitude towards life. Le Bas had learnt that, if nothing else. He was probably older than Sillery, a few years the wrong side of eighty. Like Sillery, though in a different manner, he too looked well; leathery, saurian; dry as a bone. Taking off the second pair of spectacles, he again rubbed in the old accustomed fashion the deep, painfully inflamed sockets of the eyes. Then he resumed the earlier pair, or perhaps yet a third reserve.

'What's your generation, Jenkins?'

This was like coming up for sentence at the Last Judgment. I tried to remember, to speak more exactly, tried to decide how best to put the answer clearly to Le Bas.

'Fettiplace-Jones was captain of the house when I arrived . . . my own lot . . . Stringham . . . Templer . . .'

Le Bas glared, as if in frank disbelief. Whether that was because the names conveyed nothing, or my own seemed not to belong amongst them, was only to be surmised. It looked as if he were about to accuse me of being an impostor, to be turned away from the Library forthwith. I lost my head, began to recite names at random as they came into my mind.

'Simson . . . Fitzwith . . . Ghika . . . Brandreth . . . Maiden . . . Bischoffsheim . . . Whitney . . . Parkinson . . . Summers-Miller . . . Pyefinch . . . the Calthorpes . . . Widmerpool . . .'

At the last name Le Bas suddenly came to life.

'Widmerpool?'

'Widmerpool was a year or so senior to me.'

Le Bas seemed to forget that all we were trying to do was approximately to place my own age-group in his mind. He took one of several pens lying on the desk, examined it, chose another one, examined that, then wrote 'Widmerpool' on the blotting paper in front of him, drawing a circle round the name. This was an unexpected reaction. It seemed to have nothing whatever to do with myself. Le Bas now sunk into a state of near oblivion. Could it be a form of exorcism against pupils of his whom he had never much liked? Then he offered an explanation.

'Widmerpool's down here today. I met him in the street. We had a talk. He told me about a cause he's interested in. That's why I made a note. I shall have to try and remember what he said. He's an MP now. What happened to the others?'

It was like answering enquiries after a match—'Fettiplace-Jones was out first ball, sir' . . . 'Parkinson kicked a goal, sir' . . . 'Whitney got his colours, sir'. I tried to recollect some piece of information to be deemed of interest to Le Bas about the sort of boys of whom he could approve, but the only facts that came to mind were neither about these, nor cheerful.

'Stringham died in a Japanese prisoner-of-war camp.'

'Yes, yes—so I heard.'

That awareness was unexpected.

'Templer was killed on a secret operation.'

'In the Balkans. Somebody told me. Very sad.'

Once more the cognition was unforeseen. Its acknowledgment was followed by Le Bas taking up the pen again. Underneath Widmerpool's name he wrote 'Balkans', drew another circle round the word, which he attached to the first circle by a line. It looked more than ever like some form of incantation.

'Now I remember what it was Widmerpool consulted me about. Some society he has organized to encourage good relations with one of the Balkan countries. Now which one? Simson was drowned. Torpedoed in a troopship.'

He mentioned Simson as another relevant fact, not at all as if he did not wish to be outdone in consciousness of widespread human dissolution in time of war.

'What are you doing yourself, Jenkins?'

'I'm writing a book on Burton—the *Anatomy of Melancholy* man.'

Le Bas took two or three seconds to absorb that statement, the aspects, good and bad, implied by such an activity. He had probably heard of Burton. He might easily know more about him than did Sillery. Dons were not necessarily better informed than schoolmasters. When at last he spoke, it was clear Le Bas did know about Burton. He was not wholly approving.

'Rather a morbid subject.'

He had used just that epithet when he found me, as a schoolboy, reading St John Clarke's *Fields of Amaranth*. He may have thought reading or writing books equally morbid, whatever the content. To be fair to Le Bas as a critic, *Fields of Amaranth*—if you were prepared to use the term critically at all—might reasonably be so described. I now agreed, even if on different grounds. The admission had to be made. Time had been on Le Bas's side.

We were interrupted at this moment by a very small boy, who had come to stand close by where we were talking. It would be truer to say we were inhibited by his presence, because no direct interruption took place. Dispelling about him an aura of immense, if not wholly convincing goodness, his intention was evidently to accost Le Bas in due course, at the same time ostentatiously to avoid any implication that he could be so lacking in good manners as to break into a conversation or attempt to overhear it. Le Bas, possibly not unwilling to seek dispensation from further talk about the past, distant or immediate, with all its uncomfortably realistic—Trapnel might prefer, naturalistic—undercurrents, turned in the boy's direction.

'What do you want?'

'I can wait, sir.'

This assurance that his own hopes were wholly unimportant, that Youth was prepared to waste valuable time indefinitely while Age span out its senile conference, did not in the least impress Le Bas, too conversant with the ways of boys not to be for ever on his guard.

'Can't you find some book?'

'Sir—the *Dictionary of Phrase and Fable*.'

'Brewer's?'

235

'I think so, sir.'

'You've looked on the proper shelf?'

'Of course, sir.'

'What's your name?'

'Akworth, sir.

Le Bas rose.

'It will be the worse for you, Akworth, if Brewer turns out to be on the proper shelf.'

I explained to Le Bas why I had come; that it was time to move on to my appointment.

'Good, good. Excellent. I'm glad we had a—well, a chat. Most fortunate you reminded me of that society of Widmerpool's. I don't know why he should think I am specially interested in the Balkans—though now I come to think of it, Templer's . . . makes a kind of link. You know, Jenkins, among my former pupils, I should never have guessed Widmerpool would have entered the House of Commons. Fettiplace-Jones, yes—he was another matter.'

Le Bas paused. He had immediately regretted this implied criticism of Widmerpool's abilities.

'Of course, they need all sorts and conditions of men to govern the country. Especially these days. Sad about those fellows who were killed. I sometimes think of the number of pupils of mine who lost their lives. Two wars. It adds up. Come along, Akworth.'

The boy smiled, conveying at once apology for disruption of our talk, and his own certainty that its termination must have come as a relief to me. As he hurried off towards one of the shelves, beside which he had piled up a heap of books, he gave the impression that quite a complicated intellectual programme for ragging Le Bas had been planned. Le Bas himself sighed.

'Goodbye, Jenkins. I hope the school will have acquired a regular librarian by your next visit.'

It was still wet outside, but, by the time my appointment

was at an end, the rain had stopped. A damp earthy smell filled the air. The weather was appreciably colder. In spite of that a man in a mackintosh was sitting on the low wall that ran the length of the further side of the street in front of the archway and chapel. It was Widmerpool. He looked in great dejection. I had not seen him since the night at Trapnel's flat, when he had, so to speak, expressed his confidence in Pamela's return. Now that had come about. He had prophesied truly. Isobel, about a month before, soon after the destruction of *Profiles in String*, had pointed out a paragraph in a newspaper listing guests at some public function. The names 'Mr Kenneth Widmerpool MP and Mrs Widmerpool' were included. It was just as predicted. In the Governmental reshuffle at the beginning of October Widmerpool had received minor office. In spite of these two matters, both showing himself undoubtedly in the ascendant, he sat lonely and cheerless. I should have been tempted to try and slip by unnoticed, but he saw me, and shouted something. I crossed the road.

'Congratulations on your new parliamentary job.'

'Thanks, thanks. What are you doing down here?'

I told him, adding that I had been talking with Le Bas.

'I ran into him too. I took the opportunity of giving him some account of my Balkan visit. Whatever one may think of Le Bas's capabilities as a teacher, he is supposedly in charge of the young, and should therefore be put in possession of the correct facts.'

'How did your trip go?'

'We hear a lot about what is called an "Iron Curtain". Where is this "Iron Curtain", I ask myself? I found no sign. That was what I told Le Bas. You might think him a person to hold reactionary views, but I found that was not at all the case, now that the idea of world revolution has been dropped. By the way, how are you employed since *Fission* has closed down?'

I mentioned various concerns that involved me. Widmerpool showed no embarrassment in mentioning the magazine. He even asked if it were true that Bagshaw had secured a job in television. However, when I enquired why, on such a damp and increasingly cold evening, he should be sitting on the wall, apparently just watching the world go by, he shifted uneasily, stiffening at the question.

'Pam and I came down for the day.'

He laughed.

'She's got a young friend here whom she met somewhere during his holidays, and he invited her to tea. She's having tea in his room now. I'm waiting for her.'

'A boy, you mean?'

'Yes—I suppose you'd call him a boy still.'

'I meant still at the school?'

'He was leaving, but stayed on for some reason—to captain some team, I think. Son or nephew of one of the Calthorpes. Do you remember them? Pam thought it would be an amusing jaunt. She insisted I mustn't spoil the party by coming too. Rather a good joke.'

All the same, he did not look as if he found it specially funny. Blue-grey mist was thickening round us. I had a train to catch. The Widmerpools had come by car. They had no fixed plan about getting back to London. Pamela hated being tied down by too positive arrangements. She was going to pick her husband up hereabouts when the tea-party was over. I thought of what Trapnel had said of her couplings.

'I must be off.'

'I don't believe I ever sent you details about that society I was telling Le Bas about. My secretary will forward them. I received Quiggin & Craggs's Autumn List recently—their last. There were some interesting titles. Clapham has asked me to continue my association with publishing by joining his board.'

I too had received the list; later heard Quiggin's comments on it. Sillery's *Garnered at Sunset*, unexciting as the selection might be, had been noticed respectfully. Shernmaker, for example, was unexpectedly approving. Sales were not too bad, even if the advance was never recouped. Sillery might be said to have successfully imposed his will in this last fling. So did Ada Leintwardine. *I Stopped at a Chemist* upset several of the more old-fashioned reviewers who had survived the war, but they admitted a novel-writing career lay ahead of her. Even Evadne Clapham was impressed. In fact, *Golden Grime* was the last of Evadne Clapham's books in her former style. Her subsequent manner followed Ada's. *Engine Melody*—truncated title of *The Pistons of Our Locomotives Sing the Songs of Our Workers*—believed to be not too well translated, was by no means ignored, Nathaniel Sheldon's mention including the phrase 'muted beauty'. Vernon Gainsborough's *Bronstein: Marxist or Mystagogue?*, with seven other books on similar subjects, was favourably noticed in a *Times Literary Supplement* 'front'.

'It's a real *apologia pro vita sua*,' said Bagshaw. 'Conversion from Trotskyism expressed in such unqualified terms must have warmed Gypsy's heart after her reverses.'

The last reference was to *Sad Majors*. Odo Stevens had dealt effectively with efforts, such as they were, to suppress his book. He had enjoyed exceptional opportunities for knowing about such things. That may have put him at an advantage. As usual, he also had good luck. So far from being inconvenient, the whole matter worked out in his best interests. Having already grasped that he might have done better financially by going to some publisher other than Quiggin & Craggs, he at once recognized that the loss of the two typescripts would give a potent reason for requiring release from his contract. He did not mention the third typescript, which had been all the time in the hands of Rosie Manasch. Rosie had apparently suggested that her former Fleet Street contacts might be useful in exploiting serial possibilities. She was right. *Sad Majors* was serialized on excellent terms. It was published in book form in the spring.

L. O. Salvidge, rather an achievement in the light of current publishing delays, got out a further volume of essays to follow up *Paper Wine*. The new one, *Secretions*, was much reviewed beside Shernmaker's *Miscellaneous Equities*. It was a notable score for Salvidge to have produced two books in less than a year. After the unsuccessful prosecution, Kydd's *Sweetskin* at first failed to recover from the withdrawal at the time of the injunction, but, given a new wrapper design, Kydd himself alleged that it picked up relatively well. That season also appeared David Pennistone's *Descartes, Gassendi, and the Atomic Theory of Epicurus*, the work of which he used to speak so despairingly when we were in the army together. I busied myself with Burton, even so only just managing to see *Borage and Hellebore: a Study* in print by the following December.

The scattered pages of *Profiles in String*, with the death's-head swordstick, floated eternally downstream into the night. It was the beginning of Trapnel's drift too, irretrievable as they. He went underground for a long time after that night. When at last he emerged, it was to haunt an increasingly gruesome and desolate world. There were odds and ends of film work, stray pieces of journalism, an occasional short story. In the last, possibly some traces reappeared of what had gone into *Profiles in String*, though in a much diminished form. Something of it may even have emerged on the screen. Another novel never got written. Trapnel himself always insisted that a novel is what its writer is. The definition only opens up a lot more questions. Perhaps he had taken a knock from which he never recovered; perhaps he had used up already what was in him, in the way writers do. In these sunless marshlands of existence, a dwindling reserve of pep-pills, a certain innate inventiveness, capacity for survival, above all the mystique of panache—in short, the Trapnel method—just about made it possible to hang on. That was the best you could say.

I once asked Dicky Umfraville—whose own experiences on the Turf made his knowledge of racing personalities extensive—whether he had ever heard of a jockey called Trapnel, whose professional career had been made largely in Egypt.

'Heard of him, old boy? When I was in Cairo in the 'twenties, I won a packet on a French horse he rode called Amour Piquant.'

Temporary Kings

for
Roland

1

THE SMELL OF VENICE SUFFUSED the night, lacustrine essences richly distilled. Late summer was hot here. A very old man took the floor. Hoarse, tottering, a few residual teeth, arbitrarily assembled and darkly stained, underpinning the buoyancy of his grin, he rendered the song in slower time than ordinary, clawing the air with his hands, stamping the floor with his feet, while he mimed the action of the cable, straining, creaking, climbing, as it hauled upward towards the volcanic crater the capsule encasing himself and his girl, a journey calculated to stir her ungrateful heart.

> Iamme, iamme, via montiam su là.
> Iamme, iamme, via montiam su là.
> Funiculì funiculà, via montiam su là.

A first initiatory visit to Italy, travelling as a boy with my parents, had included a week at this same hotel. It overlooked the Grand Canal. Then small, rather poky even, its waterfront now extended on either side of the terrace, where, by tradition, the musicians' gondola tied up. Near-tourist outfits replaced evening dress antique as the troupe itself, in other respects the pattern remained unaltered, notably this veteran and the 'business' of his song. Could he be the same man? A mere forty years—indeed three or four short of that—might well have passed without much perceptible transmutation in a façade already radically weathered by Time when first observed. The gestures were identical. With an operatic out-thrust of the body, he intimated the kingdoms of the earth ranged beneath funicular passengers for their delectation.

> Si vede Francia, Procida, la Spagna,
> E io veggo te, io veggo te.

The century all but within his grasp, the singer might actually recollect the occasion for which the song had been composed; on that great day, as the words postulated, himself ascended Vesuvius accompanied by his inamorata, snug together in the newly installed spaceship, auspicious with potentialities for seduction. Had a dominating personality, the suggestive rotations of the machinery, Procida's isle laid out far below, like a girl spreadeagled on her back, all combined to do the trick? The answer was surely affirmative. Even if marriage remained in question—conceivably the librettist's deference to convention—at least warmer contacts must have been attained.

The stylized movements of the hands were reminiscent of Dicky Umfraville at one of his impersonations. He too should have harnessed his gift, in early life, to an ever renewing art from which there was no retiring age. To exhibit themselves, perform before a crowd, is the keenest pleasure many people know, yet self-presentation without a basis in art is liable to crumble into dust and ashes. Professional commitment to his own representations might have kept at bay the melancholy—all but chronic Frederica and his stepchildren complained—now that Umfraville had retired from work as agent at Thrubworth. Sometimes, after a day's racing, for example, he might return to the old accustomed form. Even then a few misplaced bets would bring the conviction that luck was gone for good, his life over.

'Christ, what a shambles. Feeling my back too. Trumpeter, what are you sounding now?—*Defaulters*, old boy, if your name's Jerry Hat-Trick. You know growing old's like being increasingly penalized for a crime you haven't committed.'

'Which ones haven't you committed?' said Frederica. 'You've never grown up, darling. You can't grow old till you've done that.'

Sufferance, as well as affection, was implied, though Frederica had never tired of Umfraville, in spite of being often cross with him.

'I feel like the man in the ghost story, scrambling over the breakwaters with the Horrible Thing behind him getting closer and closer. There hasn't been a good laugh since that horse-box backed over Buster Foxe at Lingfield.'

As a rule Umfraville disliked mention of death, but the legend of Buster Foxe's immolation under the wheels of a kind of Houyhnhnm juggernaut, travelling in reverse gear, was the exception. It had resolutely passed into Umfraville myth. Captain Foxe's end (he had been promoted during the war) was less dramatic, though certainly brought about by some fatal accident near the course, terminating for ever risk of seeing an old enemy at future race-meetings. It would be worth asking Umfraville if he had his own version of *Funiculì-Funiculà*, an accomplishment by no means out of the question.

The present vocalist to some extent controverted Frederica's argument, supporting more St John Clarke's observation that 'growing old consists abundantly of growing young'. The aged singer looked as if thoughts of death, melancholy in any form, were unknown to him. He could be conceived as suffering from rage, desire, misery, anguish, despair; not melancholy. That was clear; additionally so after the round of applause following his number. The clapping was reasonably hearty considering the heat, almost

3

as oppressive as throughout the day just passed. Dr Emily Brightman and I joined in. Acknowledgment of his talent delighted the performer. He bowed again and again, repeatedly baring blackened sporadic stumps, while he mopped away streams of sweat that coursed down channels of dry loose skin ridging either side of his mouth. Longevity had brought not the smallest sense of repletion where public recognition was in question. That was on the whole sympathetic. One found oneself taking more interest than formerly in the habits and lineaments of old age.

In spite of the singer's own nonchalance, the susceptive tunes of the musicians, the gorgeous dropscene, the second carafe of wine, infected the mind not disagreeably with thoughts of the evanescence of things. At the beginning of the century, Marinetti and the Futurists had wanted to make a fresh start—whatever that might mean—advocating, among other projects, filling up the Venetian canals with the rubble of the Venetian palaces. Now, the Futurists, with their sentimentality about the future, primitive machinery, vintage motor-cars, seemed as antiquely picturesque as the Doge in the *Bucentaur*, wedding his bride the Sea, almost as distant in time; though true that a desire to destroy, a hatred and fear of the past, remained a constant in human behaviour.

'Do you think the soubrette is his mistress, or his great-granddaughter?' asked Dr Brightman. 'They seem on very close terms. Perhaps both.'

From our first meeting, at the opening session of the Conference (when friendly contacts had been achieved by mutual familiarity with *Borage and Hellebore*, my book about Burton, and her own more famous work on The Triads), Dr Brightman had made clear a determination to repudiate the faintest suspicion of spinsterish prudery that might, very mistakenly, be supposed to attach to her circumstances. Discreetly fashionable clothes emphasized this total

4

severance from anything to be thought of as academic stuffiness, a manner of dress quietly but insistently smart. One of her pupils at the university (our niece Caroline Lovell's best friend) alleged a reputation of severity as a tutor, effortless ability to reduce to tears, if necessary, the most bumptious female student. Dr Brightman, it was true, was undoubtedly a little formidable at first impact. We touched on the Dark Ages. She spoke of her present engagement on Boethius, in a form likely to prove controversial. The male don of her name, known to me when myself an undergraduate, appeared to be only a distant relation.

'You mean Harold Brightman, who played some part in organizing a dinner to celebrate the ninetieth birthday of that old rascal Sillery? He's a cousin of some sort. There are scores of them engaged in the learned professions. We all stem from the Revd Salathiel Brightman, named in *The Dunciad* in connexion with some long forgotten squabble about a piece of Augustan pedantry. He composed *Attick and Roman Reckonings of Capacity for Things Liquid and Things Dry reduced to the Common English Mensuration for Wine and Corn*. I believe the great Lemprière acknowledges indebtedness in preparation of his own tables of proportion at the end of the *Bibliotheca Classica*. Salathiel is said to have revolutionized the view held in his own day of the cochlearion and oxybaphon, though for myself I haven't the smallest notion of how many of either went to an amphora. Speaking of things liquid and things dry, shall we have a drink? Tell me, Mr Jenkins, did Mark Members persuade you to come to this Conference?'

'You, too?'

'Not without resistance on my own part. I had planned a lot of work this long vac. Mark positively nagged me into it. He can be very tyrannical.'

'I resisted too, but was in difficulties about a book. It seemed a way out.'

5

To say that was to make the best of things, let oneself down gently. Writing may not be enjoyable, its discontinuance can be worse, though Members himself must by then have been safely beyond any such gnawings of guilt. By now he was a hardened frequenter of international gatherings for 'intellectuals' of every sort. He had been at the game for years. The activity suited him. It brought out hitherto dormant capabilities for organization and oratory, neither given a fair chance in the course of an author's routine dealings with publishers and editors; nor for that matter—Members having tried reversing the rôles—trafficking with authors as editor or publisher. The then ever-widening field of cultural congresses pleased and stimulated his temperament. At one of them he had even found a wife, an American lady, author and journalist, a few years older than himself, excellently preserved, not without name and useful connexions in her own country. She was also, as Members himself boasted, 'inured to writers and their inconsequent ways'. That was probably true, as Members was her fourth husband. The marriage still remained in a reasonably flourishing condition, in spite of hints (from the critic, Bernard Shernmaker, chiefly) that Members had dropped out of the Venetian rendezvous because another, smaller conference was to include a female novelist in whom he was interested. A reason for supposing that particular imputation unjust was that several other literary figures had thought the rival conference more tempting. These differed in this from Members only insomuch as he had played some part in organization of the Venetian gathering at the London end. That was why, to avoid becoming vulnerable in his own apostasy, he had to find, at short notice, one or two substitutes like Dr Brightman and myself. He brushed aside pretexts that I never took part in such activities.

'All the more reason to go, Nicholas, see what such meetings of true minds have to offer. I should not be at all

6

surprised if you did not succumb to the drug. It's quite a potent one, as I've found to my cost. Besides, even at our age, there's a certain sense of adventure at such jamborees. You meet interesting people—if writers and suchlike can be called interesting, something you and I must often have doubted in the course of our *via dolorosa* towards literary crucifixion. At worst it makes a change, provides a virtually free holiday, or something not far removed. Come along, Nicholas, bestir yourself. Say yes. Don't be apathetic.

> Leave we the unlettered plain its herd and crop;
>   Seek we sepulture
> On a tall mountain, citied to the top,
>   Crowded with culture!

It's not sepulture, and a tall mountain, this time, but the Piazza San Marco—my patron saint, please remember—and a lot of parties, not only crowded with culture, but excellent food and drink thrown in. There's the Biennale, and the Film Festival the following week, if you feel like staying for it. Kennst du das Land, wo die Zitronen blühn? Take a chance on it. You'll live like a king once you get there.'

'One of those temporary kings in *The Golden Bough*, everything at their disposal for a year or a month or a day —then execution? Death in Venice?'

'Only ritual execution in more enlightened times—the image of a declining virility. A Mann's man for a' that. Being the temporary king is what matters. The retribution of congress kings only takes the form, severe enough in its way, I admit, of having to return to everyday life. Even that, my dear Nicholas, you'll do with renewed energy. Like the new king, in fact.

> Here upon earth, we're kings, and none but we
> Can be such kings, nor of such subjects be.

7

That's what the Venice Conference will amount to. I shall put your name down.'

'Who else is going?'

'Quentin Shuckerly, Ada Leintwardine. They're certain. Not Alaric Kydd, which is just as well. The new Shuckerly, *Athlete's Footman*, is the best queer novel since *Sea Urchins*. You ought to have a look at it, if you've got time. You won't regret the decision to go to Venice. I'm *désolé* at not being able to attend myself. Unfortunately one can't be in two places at once, and I have a duty to make myself available elsewhere. There will be a lot of international figures there, some of them quite distinguished. Ferrand-Sénéschal, Kotecke, Santos, Pritak. With any luck you'll find a very talented crowd. I'd hoped to hear Ferrand-Sénéschal on the subject of Pasternak and the Nobel Prize. His objections —he will certainly demur at the possibility—will be worth listening to.'

In suggesting that the international fame of several foreign writers liable to attend the Conference was not to be entirely disregarded in assessing its attractions, Members was speaking reasonably enough. To meet some of these, merely to set eyes on them, would be to connect together a few additional pieces in the complex jigsaw making up the world's literary scene; a game never completed, though sometimes garishly illuminated, when two or three unexpected fragments were all at once coherently aligned in place. To addicts of this pastime, the physical appearance of a given writer can add to his work an incisive postscript, physical traits being only inadequately assessable from photographs. Ferrand-Sénéschal, one of the minor celebrities invoked by Members, was a case in point. His thick lips, closely set eyes, ruminatively brutal expression, were familiar enough from newspaper pictures or publishers' catalogues, the man himself never quite defined by them. I had no great desire to meet Ferrand-Sénéschal—on balance

8

would almost prefer to be absolved from the effort of having to talk with him—but I was none the less curious to see what he looked like in person, know how he carried himself among his fellow nomads of the intellect, Bedouin of the cultural waste, for ever folding and unfolding their tents in its oases.

There was another reason, when Members picked Ferrand-Sénéschal's name out of the hat as a potential prize for attending the Conference, why a different, a stronger reaction was summoned up than by such names as Santos, Pritak, Kotecke. During the war, staff-officers, whose work required rough-and-ready familiarity with conditions of morale relating to certain bodies of troops or operational areas—the whole world being, in one sense, at that moment an operational area—were from time to time given opportunity to glance through excerpts, collected together from a wide range of correspondence, inspected by the Censorship Department. This symposium, of no very high security grading, was put together for practical purposes, of course, though not with complete disregard for light relief. The anonymous anthologist would sometimes show appreciation of a letter's comic or ironic bearing. Ferrand-Sénéschal was a case in point. Scrutinizing the file, my eye twice caught his name, familiar to anyone whose dealings with contemporary literature took them even a short way beyond the Channel. Ferrand-Sénéschal's letters were dispatched from the United States, where, lecturing at the outbreak of war, he had remained throughout hostilities. Always a Man of the Left (much in evidence as such at the time of the Spanish Civil War, when his name had sometimes appeared in company with St John Clarke's), he had shown rather exceptional agility in sitting on the fence that divided conflicting attitudes of the Vichy Administration from French elements, in France and elsewhere, engaged in active opposition to Germany.

9

Cited merely to illustrate the current view of a relatively well-known French author domiciled abroad through the exigencies of war, Ferrand-Sénéschal's couple of contributions to the Censor's digest deftly indicated the deviousness of their writer's allegiance. No doubt, in one sense, the phrases were intended precisely to achieve that, naturally implying nothing to be construed as even covertly antagonistic to the Allied cause. Whatever else he might be, Ferrand-Sénéschal was no fool. Indeed, it was his own appreciation of the fact that his letters might be of interest to the Censor —any censor—which provoked a smile at the skill shown in excerpting so neatly the carefully chosen sentences. In addition, personal letters, even when deliberately composed with an eye to examination, official or unofficial, by someone other than their final recipient, give a unique sense of the writer's personality, often lacking in books by the same hand. They are possibly the most revealing of all, like physical touchings-up of personal appearance to make some exceptional effect. In the case of Ferrand-Sénéschal, as with his portraits in the press, the personality conveyed, not to be underrated as a force, was equally not a specially attractive one.

Avoidance, during this expatriate period, of all outward participation, even *parti pris*, in relation to the issues about which people were fighting so fiercely, turned out no handicap to Ferrand-Sénéschal's subsequent career. Not only did he physically survive those years, something he might easily have failed to do had he remained in Europe, but he returned to France unembarrassed by any of the inevitable typifications attached to active combatants of one sort or another. Some of these had, of course, acquired distinction, military or otherwise, which Ferrand-Sénéschal could not claim, but, in this process, few had escaped comparatively damaging sectarian labels. In fact, Ferrand-Sénéschal, who had worked hard during his exile in literary and academic spheres in both American continents, found himself in an improved position, with a wider public, in a greatly changed world. He now abandoned a policy of non-intervention, publicly announcing his adherence to the more extreme end of his former political standpoint, one from which he never subsequently deviated. From this vantage point he played a fairly prominent rôle in the immediately post-war period of re-adjustment in France; then, when a few years later cultural congresses settled down into their swing, became—as emphasized by Members—a conspicuous figure in their lively polemics.

Remembrance of these censored letters had revived when I was 'doing the books' on *Fission*. A work by Ferrand-Sénéschal turned up for review. Quiggin & Craggs had undertaken a translation of one of his philosophico-economic studies. Although the magazine was, in theory, a separate venture from the publishing house producing it, the firm —Quiggin especially—was apt to take amiss too frequent disregard of their own imprint in the critical pages of *Fission*. I should in any case have consulted Bagshaw, as editor, as to whether or not a Quiggin & Craggs book might be safely ignored. Bagshaw's preoccupations with all forms of Marxism, orthodox or the reverse, being what they were, he was likely to hold views on this one. He did. He was at once animated by Ferrand-Sénéschal's name.

'An interesting sub-species of fellow-traveller. I'd like to have a look myself. Ferrand-Sénéschal's been exceedingly useful to the Party at one time or another, in spite of his heresies. There's always a little bit of Communist propaganda in whatever he writes, however trivial. He also has odd sexual tastes. Political adversaries like to dwell on that. In America, they allege some sort of scandal was hushed up.'

Bagshaw turned the pages of Ferrand-Sénéschal's book. He had accepted it as something for the expert, sitting down to make a closer examination.

'You won't find anything about his sexual tastes there. I've glanced through it.'

'I'll take it home, and consider the question of a reviewer. I might have a good idea.'

By the following week Bagshaw had a good idea. It was a very good one.

'We'll give Ferrand-Sénéschal to Kenneth Widmerpool for his routine piece in the mag. It's not unlike his own sort of stuff.'

That was Bagshaw at his best. His editor's instinct, eccentric, unguarded, often obscure of intent, was rarely to be set aside as thoughtless or absurd. He reported Widmerpool as being at first unwilling to wrestle with the Ferrand-Sénéschal translation (having scarcely heard of its author), but, on reading some of the book, changing his mind. The article appeared in the next issue of *Fission*. Widmerpool himself was delighted with it.

'One of my most successful efforts, I think I can safely aver. Ferrand-Sénéschal is a man to watch. He and I have something in common, both of us intellectuals in the world of action. In drawing analogy between our shared processes of thought, I refer to a common denominator of resolution to break ruthlessly with old social methods and outlooks. In short, we are both realists. I should like to meet this Frenchman. I shall arrange to do so.'

The consequences of the Ferrand-Sénéschal article were, in their way, far reaching. Ferrand-Sénéschal, who visited London fairly often in the course of business—cultural business—was without difficulty brought into touch with Widmerpool on one of these trips. Some sort of a fellow-feeling seems to have sprung up immediately between the two of them, possibly a certain facial resemblance contributing to that, people who look like one another sometimes finding additional affinities. In the army, for example, tall cadaverous generals would choose tall cadaverous soldier-servants or drivers; short choleric generals prefer short choleric officers on their staff. Whatever it was, Widmerpool and Ferrand-Sénéschal took to each other on sight. As a member of some caucus within the Labour Party, Widmerpool invited Ferrand-Sénéschal to meet his associates at a House of Commons luncheon. This must have gone well, because in due course Ferrand-Sénéschal returned the compliment by entertaining Widmerpool, when passing through Paris on his way back from Eastern Europe, touring there under the banner of a society to encourage friendship with one of the People's Republics.

This night-out in Paris with Ferrand-Sénéschal had also been an unqualified success. That was almost an understatement of the gratification it had given Widmerpool, according to himself. Either by chance or design, his comments on the subject had come straight back to the *Fission* office. That was the period when Widmerpool, deserted by his wife, was keeping away from the magazine. Not unreasonably, he may have hoped, by deliberately building up a legend of high-jinks with Ferrand-Sénéschal, to avoid seeming an abandoned husband, unable to amuse himself, while Pamela lived somewhere in secret with X. Trapnel. That could have been the motive for spreading broadcast the tidings of going on the Parisian spree; otherwise, it might be thought, an incident wiser to keep private. Certainly highly coloured rumours about their carousal were in circulation months after its celebration. Apart from other considerations, such behaviour, anyway such brazenness, was in complete contrast with the tone in which Widmerpool himself used to deplore the *louche* reputation of Sir Magnus Donners.

This censure could, of course, have been a double-bluff. When we had met at a large party given for the Election Night of 1955—the last time I had seen him—Widmerpool deliberately dragged in a reference to the weeks spent together trying to learn French at La Grenadière, adding that it was 'lucky for our morals Madame Leroy's house had

13

not been in Paris', words that seemed to bear out, on his part, desire to confirm a reputation for being a dog. That was early in the evening, before Pamela's incivility had greatly offended our hostess, or Widmerpool himself heard (towards morning, after Isobel and I had gone home) that he had lost his seat in the House. In *Fission* days, Bagshaw had been sceptical about the Paris story, without dismissing it entirely.

'I suppose some jolly-up may have taken place. The brothels are closed nowadays officially, but that wouldn't make any difference to someone in the know. I'm not sure what Ferrand-Sénéschal is himself supposed to like—being chained to a crucifix, while a green light's played on him —little girls—two-way mirrors—I've been told, but I can't remember. He may have given Kenneth a few ideas. I shall develop sadistic tendencies myself, if that new secretary doesn't improve. She's muddled those proofs of the ads again. I say, Nicholas, we've still too much space to spare. Just cast your eye over these, and see if you've any suggestions. You'll bring a fresh mind to the advertisement problem. It's a blow too we're not going to get any more Trapnel pieces. Editing this mag is driving me off my rocker.'

In the light of what I knew of Widmerpool, the tale of visiting a brothel with Ferrand-Sénéschal was to be accepted with caution, although true that he had more than once in the past adopted a rather gloating tone when speaking of tarts, an attitude dating back to our earliest London days. Moreland used to say, 'Maclintick doesn't like women, he likes tarts—indeed he once actually fell in love with a tart, who led him an awful dance.' That taste could be true of Widmerpool too; perhaps a habit become so engrained as to develop into a preference, handicapping less circumscribed sexual intimacies. Such routines might go some way to explain the fiasco with Mrs Haycock, even the relationship—whatever that might be—with Pamela. That Ferrand-Sénéschal, as Bagshaw suggested, had been the medium for introduction, in middle-age, to hitherto unknown satisfactions, new, unusual forms of self-release, was not out of the question. By all accounts, far more unlikely things happened in the sphere of late sexual development. Bagshaw was, of course, prejudiced. By that time he had decided that Widmerpool was not only bent on ejecting him from the editorship of *Fission*, but was also a fellow-traveller.

'He probably learnt a lot from Ferrand-Sénéschal politically, the latter being a much older hand at the game.'

'But what has Widmerpool to gain from being a crypto?'

Bagshaw laughed loudly. He thought that a very silly question. Political standpoints of the extreme Left being where his heart lay, where, so to speak, he had lost his virginity, the enquiry was like asking Umfraville why he should be interested in one horse moving faster than another, a football fan the significance of kicking an inflated bladder between two posts. At first Bagshaw was unable to find words simple enough to enlighten so uninstructed a mind. Then a lively parallel occurred to him.

'Apart from anything else, it's one of those secret pleasures, like drawing a moustache on the face of a pretty girl on a poster, spitting over the stairs—you know, from a great height on to the people below. You see several heads, possibly a bald one. They don't know where the saliva comes from. It gives an enormous sense of power. Like the days when I used to throw marbles under the hooves of mounted policemen's horses. Think of the same sort of fun when you're an MP, or respected civil servant, giving the whole show away on the quiet, when everybody thinks you're a pillar of society.'

'Isn't that a rather frivolous view? What about deep

convictions, all the complicated ideologies you're always talking about?'

'Not really frivolous. Such spitting itself is an active form of revolt—undermining society as we know it, spreading alarm and despondency among the bourgeoisie. Besides, spitting apart, you stand quite a good chance of coming to power yourself one day. Giving them all hell. The bourgeoisie, and everyone else. Being a member of a Communist *apparat* would suit our friend very well politically.'

'But Widmerpool's the greatest bourgeois who ever lived.'

'Of course he is. That's what makes it such fun for him. Besides, he isn't a bourgeois in his own eyes. He's a man in a life-and-death grapple with the decadent society round him. Either he wins, or it does.'

'That doesn't sound very rational.'

'Marxism isn't rational, Nicholas. Get that into your head. The more intelligent sort of Marxist tells you so. He stresses the point, as one of its highest merits, that, like religion, Marxism requires faith in the last resort. Besides, my old friend Max Stirner covers Kenneth—"Because I am by nature a man I have equal rights to the enjoyment of all goods, says Babeuf. Must he not also say: because I am 'by nature' a first-born prince I have a right to a throne?" That's just what Kenneth Widmerpool does say—not out aloud, but it's what he thinks.'

Bagshaw had begun on his favourite political philosopher. I was not in the mood at that moment. To return instead to sorting the *Fission* books was not to deny there might be some truth in the exposition: that Widmerpool, conventional enough at one level of his life—conventional latterly in his own condemnation of conventionality—might at the same time nurture within himself quite another state of mind to that shown on the surface; not only desire to re-shape the world according to some doctrinaire pattern, but also to be revenged on a world that had found himself insufficiently splendid in doing so. Had not General Conyers, years ago, diagnosed a 'typical intuitive extrovert'; cold-blooded, keen on a thing for the moment, never satisfied, always wanting to get on to something else? In one sense, of course, the world, from a material assessment, had treated Widmerpool pretty well, even at the time when Bagshaw was talking. On the other hand, people rarely take the view that they have been rewarded according to their deserts, those most rewarded often the very ones keenest to be revenged. Possibly Ferrand-Sénéschal was just such another.

Whatever Ferrand-Sénéschal's inner feelings, the meeting with him in Venice was not to be. Not even a glimpse on the platform. His death took place in London only a few days before the Conference opened. He suffered a stroke in his Kensington hotel. The decease of a French author of international standing would in any case have rated a modest headline in the papers. The season of the year a thin one for news, more attention was given to Ferrand-Sénéschal than might have been expected. It was revealed, for example, that he had seen a doctor only a day or two before, who had warned him against excessive strain. Accordingly no inquest took place. Death had come—as Evadne Clapham remarked, 'like the book'—in the afternoon. Later that evening, so the papers said, Ferrand-Sénéschal had been invited to 'look in on' Lady Donners after dinner—'not a party, just a few friends', she had explained to the reporters—where he would have found himself, so it appeared, among an assortment of politicians and writers, including Mr and Mrs Mark Members. Social engagements of this kind, together with a stream of acquaintances and journalists passing in and out of his suite at the hotel, had evidently proved too much for a state of health already impaired.

The London obituaries put Léon-Joseph Ferrand-Sénéschal

in his sixtieth year. They mentioned only two or three of his better known books, selected from an enormous miscellany of novels, plays, philosophic and economic studies, political tracts, and (according to Bernard Shernmaker) an early volume, later suppressed by the author, of verse in the manner of Verlaine. This involuntary withdrawal would make little difference to the Conference. Well known intellectuals were always an uncertain quantity when it came to turning up, even if they did not suddenly succumb. Pritak, Santos, Kotecke, might equally well find something better to do, though not necessarily meet an unlooked-for end. I made up my mind to ask Dr Brightman, when opportunity arose, whether she had ever encountered Ferrand-Sénéschal; if so, what she thought of him.

The youngest and best-looking of the troupe, the one Dr Brightman had called the Soubrette, took a plate round for the collection. The rest burst *en masse* into *Santa Lucia*. The programme came to an end. Preparations began for moving on to another hotel. Before they got under way, the old singer, in participation with the Soubrette, surreptitiously examined the takings, both gesticulating a good deal, whether with satisfaction or irony at the extent of the offering was uncertain.

'To sing Neapolitan songs in Venice is rather like a Scotch ballad in Bath,' said Dr Brightman. 'Naples is unique. Even her popular music doesn't export as far north as this. A taste for Naples is one of the divisions between people. You love the place, or loathe it. The character of the traveller seems to have no bearing on the instinctive choice. Personally I am devoted to the Parthenopean shore, although once victim of a most unseemly episode at Pompeii when younger. It was outside the lupanar, from which in those days ladies were excluded. I should have been affronted far less within that haunt of archaic vice, where I later found little to shock the most demure, except the spartan hardness of the double-decker marble bunks. I chased the fellow away with my parasol, an action no doubt deplored in these more enlightened days, as risking irreparable damage to the responses of one of those all too frequent cases of organ inferiority.'

She briskly shook the crop of short white curls cut close to her head. They looked like a battery of coiled wire (like the Dark Lady's) galvanizing an immensely powerful dynamo. The bearing of the anecdote brought Ferrand-Sénéschal's name to mind again. I asked if she had ever met him.

'Yes, I once was introduced to Ferrand-Sénéschal in the not very inviting flesh. He told me he despised "good writing". I praised his French logic in that respect. As you doubtless know, his early books are ridiculously stilted, his later ones grossly slipshod. I was at once hustled away by his court of toadies. Certain persons require a court. Others prefer a harem. That is not quite the same thing.'

'Some like both.'

'Naturally the one can merge with the other—why, hullo, Russell.'

The young American who had come up to our table seemed to be the only one of his countrymen at the Conference. He was called Russell Gwinnett. We had sat next to each other at luncheon the day before. He had explained that he taught English at a well-known American university for women, where Dr Brightman herself had spent a year as exchange professor, so that they had known one another before meeting again at the Conference.

'How are you making out, Russell? Have you met Mr Nicholas Jenkins? This is Mr Russell Gwinnett, an old friend from my transatlantic days. You have? Come and join us, Russell.'

The serious business of the Conference, intellectuals from all over the world addressing each other on their favourite topics, took place at morning and afternoon sessions on the island of San Giorgio Maggiore. To reanimate enthusiasms imperilled by prolonged exposure to the assiduities of congress life, extension of the syllabus to include an official luncheon or dinner was listed for almost every day of our stay. These banquets were usually linked with some national treasure, or place of historic interest, occasions to some extent justifying the promise of Members that we should 'live like kings'. They gave at the same time opportunity to 'get to know' other members of the Conference. Through the medium of one of these jaunts, which took place at a villa on the Brenta, famous for its frescoes by Veronese, Gwinnett and I had met.

He was in his early thirties, slight in figure, with a small black moustache that showed a narrow strip of skin along the upper lip above and below its length. That he was American scarcely appeared on the surface at first, then something about the thin bone formations of arms and legs, the sallowness and texture of the skin, suggested the nationality. The movements of the body, supple, not without athletic promise, also implied an American, rather than European, nervous tension; an extreme one. He wore spectacles lightly tinted with blue. His air, in general unconformist, did not strongly indicate any recognizable alignment.

I had not sat next to him long the previous day before unorthodoxy was confirmed. Having invoked the name of Dr Brightman, Gwinnett (like her) created the usually advantageous foundation of good understanding between writers—one by no means always available—by showing well-disposed knowledge of my own works. That was an excellent start. He turned out to hold another ace up his sleeve, but did not play that card at once. In showing control, he began as he went on. After the gratifying, if subjective, offering made in the direction of my own writing, he became less easy. In fact he was almost impossible to engage, drying up entirely, altogether lacking in that reserve of light, reasonably well-informed social equipment, on the whole more characteristic of American than British academic life. This lapse into a torpid, almost surly reluctance to cooperate conversationally suggested an American version of the least flexible type of British don, that quiet egotism, self-applauding narrowness of vision, sometimes less than acceptable, even when buttressed with verified references and forward-looking views. If Gwinnett showed signs almost of burlesquing a stock academic figure, he was himself not necessarily lacking in interest on that account, if only as a campus specimen hitherto unsampled; especially as he seemed oddly young to have developed such traits. Even at the outset I was prepared for this diagnosis to be wide of the mark. There was also something not at all self-satisfied about him, an impression of anxiety, a never ceasing awareness of impending disaster.

At table he had messed about the food on his plate, a common enough form of expressing maladjustment, though disconcerting, since the dishes happened to be notably good. He refused wine. It might be that he was a reprieved alcoholic. He had some of that sad, worn, preoccupied air that suggests unquiet memories of more uproarious days. Above all there was a sense of loneliness. I talked for a time with the Belgian writer on my other side. Then the Belgian became engaged with his neighbour beyond, leaving Gwinnett and myself back on each other's hands. Before I could think of anything new to say, he put an unexpected question. This was towards the end of the meal, the first sign of loosening up.

'How does the Veronese at Dogdene compare with the ones on the wall here?'

That was a surprise.

'You mean the one Lord Sleaford's just sold? I've never been to Dogdene, so I haven't ever seen it in anything but reproduction. I only know the house itself from the Constable in the National Gallery.'

The Sleaford Veronese had recently realized at auction what was then regarded as a very large sum. The picture had always been a great preoccupation of Chips Lovell, who used often to grumble about his Sleaford relations never recognizing their luck in ownership of a work by so great a master. Lovell, who agreed with Smethyck (now head of a gallery), and with General Conyers, that the picture ought to be cleaned, was also in the habit of complaining that the public did not have sufficient opportunity to inspect its beauties. In those days admission to Dogdene was about three days a week throughout the summer. After the war, in common with many other mansions of its kind, the house was thrown open, at a charge, all the year round. Even so, the Veronese had to be sold to pay for the basic upkeep of the place. In spite of the publicity given at the time of the sale, I was impressed that Gwinnett had heard of it.

'I've been told it's not Veronese at his best—*Iphigenia*, isn't it?'

That had been Lovell's view in moods of denigration or humility. Gwinnett seemed more interested in the subject of the picture than whether or not Veronese had been on form.

'That's an intriguing story it depicts. The girl offering herself for sacrifice. The calm dignity with which she faces death. Tiepolo painted an Iphigenia too, more than once, though I've only seen the one at the Villa Valmarana. There's at least one other that looks even finer in reproduction. It's the inferential side of the myth that fascinates me.'

Gwinnett sounded oddly excited. His manner had altogether altered. The thought of Iphigenia must have strangely moved him. Then he abruptly changed the subject. For some reason speaking of the Veronese had released something within himself, made it possible to introduce another, quite different motif, one, as it turned out, that had been on his mind ever since we met. This matter, once given expression, a little explained earlier lack of ease. At least it suggested that Gwinnett, when broaching topics that meant a lot to him, was not so much vain or unaccommodating, as nervous, paralysed, unsure of himself. That was the next impression, equally untrustworthy as a judgment.

'You knew the English writer X. Trapnel, Mr Jenkins?'

'Certainly.'

'Pretty well, I believe?'

'Yes, I was quite an authority on Trapnel at one moment.'

Gwinnett sighed.

'I'd give anything to have known Trapnel.'

'There were ups and downs in being a friend.'

'You thought him a good writer?'

'A very good writer.'

'That's OK. Me too. That's why I'd have loved to meet him. I could have done that when I was a student. I was over in London. I get mad at myself when I think of that. He was still alive. I hadn't read his books then. I wouldn't have known where to go and see him anyway.'

'All you had to do was to have a drink at one of his pubs.'

'I couldn't just speak to him. He wouldn't have liked that.'

'If somebody had told you one or two of his haunts— The Hero of Acre or The Mortimer—you could hardly have avoided hearing Trapnel holding forth on books and writers. Then you might have stood him a drink. The job would have been done.'

'Trapnel's the subject of my dissertation—his life and works.'

'So Trapnel's going to have a biographer?'

'Myself.'

'Fine.'

'You think it right?'

'Quite right.'

Gwinnett nodded his head.

'I ought to say I'd already planned to get in touch with you, Mr Jenkins—among others who'd known Trapnel—when I reached England after this Conference. I never calculated to find you here.'

After the statement of Gwinnett's Trapnel project, relations might have been expected to become easier. That did not happen; at least easing was by no means immediate. For a minute or two he seemed even to regret the headlong nature of the confession. Then he recovered some of the earlier more amenable manner.

'You did not go on seeing Trapnel right up to his death, I guess?'

'Not for about four or five years before that. It must be the best part of ten years now since I talked to him—though he once sent me a note asking the date when some book had been published, the actual month, I mean. He went completely underground latterly.'

'What book was that—the one he wanted to know about?'

'A collection of essays by L. O. Salvidge called *Paper Wine*. There had been some question of Trapnel reviewing it, but the notice never got written.'

'Where was Trapnel living when he wrote you?'

'He only gave an accommodation address. A newspaper shop in the Islington part of the world.

'I want to see Mr Salvidge too when I get to London.'

'As you know, he contributed an Introduction to a posthumous work of Trapnel's called *Dogs Have No Uncles*.'

'It's good. Not as great as *Camel Ride to the Tomb*, but good. What a sense of doom that other title gives.'

In contrast with the passing of a prolific writer like Ferrand-Sénéschal, Trapnel's end, in spite of aptness of circumstances, took place unnoticed by the press. That was not surprising. He had produced no 'serious' work during his latter days. Throughout his life he had been accustomed to 'go underground' intermittently, when things took an unfavourable turn; the underground state becoming permanent after the Pamela Widmerpool affair, her destruction of his manuscript, return to her husband. That was when Trapnel disappeared for good. I knew no one who continued to hobnob with him. He must have made business contacts from time to time. His name would occasionally appear in print, or on the air, in connexion with hack work of one kind or another. This was usually radio or television collaboration with a partner, a professional, safely established, to whom Trapnel had passed on a saleable idea he himself lacked energy or will to hammer out to the end. In these exchanges he must have inclined to avoid former friendly affiliations, reminders of 'happier days'. It had to be admitted Trapnel had known 'happier days', even if of a rather special order.

Bagshaw was a case in point of Trapnel deliberately rejecting overtures from an old acquaintance. As he had himself planned after the liquidation of *Fission*, when such fiefs were comparatively easy to seize, Bagshaw had carved out for himself an obscure, but apparently fairly prosperous, little realm in the unruly world of television. Now he was known as 'Lindsay Bagshaw', the first name latent until this coming into his own. I never saw much of him after the magazine ceased publication, though we would run across each other occasionally. Once we met in the lift at Broadcasting House, and he began to speak of Trapnel. Even by then Bagshaw had become rather a changed man. Success, even moderate success, had left a mark.

'I'd have liked Trappy to appear in one of my programmes. Quite impossible to run him to earth. I caught sight of him one day from the top of a 137 bus. It wasn't so much the beard and the long black greatcoat, as that melancholy distinguished air Trappy always had. I couldn't jump off in full flight. It was one of those misty evenings in Langham Place. The lights were shining from all the rows of windows in this building. Trappy was standing by that church with the pointed spire. He was looking up at those thousand windows of the BBC, all ablaze with light. Something about him made me feel very sad. I couldn't help thinking of the Scholar Gypsy, and Christ-Church hall, and all that, even though I wasn't at the university myself, and it wasn't snowing. I thought it would have been a splendid shot in a film. I wondered if he'd agree to do a documentary about his own failure in life—comparative, I mean. About a month later, I ran into one of his understrappers in a pub. He was going to see Trappy later that evening. I sent a note, but it wasn't any good. No answer.'

There was also the occasional Trapnel story or article to appear, nothing to be ashamed of, at the same time nothing comparable with the old Trapnel standard. This submerged period of Trapnel's life could not have been enviable. He abandoned The Hero of Acre, all the other pubs where he had been accustomed to harangue an assemblage of chosen followers. The roving intelligentsia of the saloon bar—cultural nomads of a race never likely to penetrate the international steppe—professional topers, itinerant bores, near-criminals, knew him no more. They were thrown back on their own resources, had to keep themselves instructed and amused in other ways. Where Trapnel himself went, whom he saw, how he remained alive, were all hard to imagine. Probably there remained women to find him still passable enough even in decline; more or less devoted mistresses to maintain survival of a sort. As Trapnel himself might have insisted—one could hear his dry harsh voice speaking the words—a washed-up condition is not necessarily an un-attractive one to a woman. That had also been one of Barnby's themes: 'Ladies like a man to rescue. A job that

26

offers a challenge. They can annex the property at a cheap rate, and ruthlessly develop it.'

Trapnel may have been annexed by a woman, not much development feasible, minimum financial security about the best to be hoped. That in itself was after all something. Gwinnett agreed the plausible assumption, after the collapse of Trapnel's hopes, was personal administration taken over by a relatively prudent wage-earning mistress; even a good-hearted landlady, whose commonsense regulated money matters, such as they were, warding off actual destitution. That is, Gwinnett had nothing else to offer. His accord was not enthusiastic. Comparative reluctance to accept that a woman might have kept Trapnel going, made me wonder whether Gwinnett were not homosexual. He might be a homosexual as well as a redeemed drunk; the former state, possibly repressed, seeking outlet in the latter. Then he brought back the subject of women himself.

'I'd like to ask you about this girl—the castrating one.'

'Pamela Widmerpool?'

'I've been spun so many yarns about her.'

The stories he had been told were, on the whole, garbled in a manner to make the true circumstances of Trapnel's life all but unrecognizable. It was in any case a field where accuracy was hard to come by. At the same time, if Gwinnett's information had percolated through misinformed sources, he himself showed unexpected flashes of insight. Enormous simplifications were possibly necessary to carry a deeper truth than lay on the surface of a mass of unsorted detail. That was, after all, what happened when history was written; many, if not most, of the true facts discarded. Besides, what could be called unreservedly true when closely examined, especially about Trapnel? The stories told to Gwinnett became notably blurred in their inferences about Pamela Widmerpool. Trapnel's relationship with her emerged as little more than a love affair that had gone wrong, something that might have happened to anybody. Naturally, in one sense, it *was* a love affair that had gone wrong, but subtlety was required to express the unusual nature of that love affair, its start, progress, termination. All these had been conveyed with such lack of finesse that no kind of justice was done to the exceptional nature of those concerned: Pamela: Widmerpool: Trapnel himself. For Gwinnett, too, there existed the seldom remittent difficulty of translating the personalities and doings of English material into American terms.

The impression these reports had left with him was of a man's luck—Trapnel's luck—having suddenly, meaninglessly, taken a turn for the worse. From being, in his way, a notable writer, a promising career ahead of him, Trapnel had been suddenly, inexorably, struck down by misfortune, although leading much the same sort of life as he had always led, with girls not so wholly different from Pamela, before he had linked himself to her. Sometimes Gwinnett hedged a little, but that main interpretation was the one he was prepared, even if unwillingly, to accept.

'Trapnel's crack-up is easy for an American to understand. If you don't mind my saying so, to find a writer of even your age on his feet, and working, is not all that common with us.'

'Some of the violent consuming nervous American energy was characteristic of Trapnel too.'

'He'd no American blood?'

'Not that I know of.'

'I'd like to think he had.'

'His father was a jockey in Egypt. If Trapnel had written about that we'd have a completer picture.'

'Completion was one of the things Trapnel aimed at, you said—the idea of the Complete Man. Did he achieve some of that? I think so.'

'Vigny says the poet is not a sport of nature, his destiny is the human predicament.'

'And the concept was challenged by this girl—as it were invalidated.'

Gwinnett thought about that for a moment, almost as if he were hoping to rebut his own conjecture. Then he laughed, and changed his tone.

'It was the god Hercules deserting Antony.'

'As a matter of fact the god Hercules returned in Trapnel's case. There was music in the air again, though only briefly.'

Gwinnett had heard more misleading accounts. The best in existence was probably Malcolm Crowding's. It was at least first-hand. No doubt Crowding's story had been a little ornamented with the passage of time, no worse than that. The basic facts were that Trapnel had found himself in possession of a hundred pounds. No one argued about that, a fact in itself sufficiently extraordinary. What was additionally astonishing, almost a miracle, was the sum being in notes. A cheque might have brought quite different consequences. Where opinion chiefly differed was in the provenance of the money. It was usually designated, rather pedestrianly, as payment for forgotten 'rights', which had finally borne fruit in some medium functioning in long delayed action, possibly from a foreign country. Alternatively, more picturesquely, the hundred pounds was said to be a legacy left to Trapnel's father, the celebrated jockey, as one of the items in the eccentric will of a grateful backer of the winning horse, ridden by Trapnel *père*, at a long forgotten Egyptian race-meeting. By slow but workmanlike processes of the law, the bequest had in due course been deflected to Trapnel himself as heir and successor, the sum delivered to him. If the latter origin were true, the whimsical testator must either have had a long memory, or omitted to overhaul his will for a great many years. In either case, almost equally surprising, Trapnel was traced, the money handed over in cash. The only colourable explanation was that Trapnel, improbable as that might seem, having found his way personally to the intermediary—lawyer, accountant, publisher, agent—by his old skill induced whoever was in charge to accept a receipt for notes. If so, that final mustering of Trapnel's long dormant forces proved dramatically, in a sense appropriately, fatal.

Were the hypothesis of the female guardian a correct one (situation reminiscent of Miss Weedon curing Stringham of drink), she would in the normal course of things certainly intercept any money Trapnel might earn, or, more credibly, derive from 'public assistance'. Even in his less calamitous days, there had been interludes in the past of signing on at 'the Labour'—the Labour Exchange—though what trade or vocation Trapnel claimed at such emergencies was never revealed. When, so transcendentally, the hundred pounds in cash materialized into his hands in the manner of a highly proficient conjuror, Trapnel (like Stringham) must have evaded his keeper, reverted to type in the traditional manner, decided, now the money had come his way in this utterly unforeseen manner, to squander it gloriously in The Hero of Acre.

Malcolm Crowding's account of Trapnel's apotheosis in The Hero was likely to be the most reliable. He had been there in person. Besides, his own works proclaimed him a writer of little or no imagination. He could never have invented such a story. By that time he had ceased to publish verse, and was lecturing on English literature at a newly-founded provincial university, in fact spending the night in London in connexion with the editing of a textbook. He approached the subject of Trapnel, like his own academic work, in a spirit of the severest literary puritanism. On impulse, a wish to call up old times, he had dropped in that night to The Hero.

'I expect he hoped to pick up a boy-friend,' said Evadne Clapham. 'The Hero was full of queers when I was taken there last. It was much against my will in any case. They were all standing round wide-eyed watching that old wretch Heather Hopkins giving an imitation of John Foster Dulles in his galoshes.'

Whatever Malcolm Crowding's original intention, Trapnel's arrival in The Hero offered something worth while; in fact supplied a story to become, ever after, Crowding's most notable set-piece.

'It was Lazarus coming back from the Dead. Better than that, because Lazarus didn't buy everyone a drink—at least there's no mention of that in Holy Writ.'

Somebody present—probably Evadne Clapham again, bent on disorganizing the side-effects of Crowding's story —suggested that free drinks were to be inferred on the earlier resurrectionary occasion from Tennyson:

'When Lazarus left his charnel-cave . . .
The streets were filled with joyful sound.'

Crowding refused to allow his narrative to be obstructed by inconclusive pedantry of that sort. He merely increased the vibrant note of his rather shrill voice. Evadne Clapham, or whoever else it was interrupting, ceased to argue. Crowding, feeling the Tennysonian phrase appropriate enough for Trapnel's sojourn in outer darkness, developed new metaphor in the direction of Shelley.

'The charnel cave was put behind him. It was Trapnel Unbound.'

There were present in The Hero old stagers who had endured in that spot since Trapnel's own great days, when, tall, bearded, loquacious, didactic, draped in his dyed greatcoat, toying with the death's head swordstick, he had laid down the law on literature, commanded the price of a drink (though never as now), dominated the length of the saloon bar. His arrival was a thunderbolt. Even the most complacent of The Hero's soaks were jolted by it from their evening's drinking. Crowding never tired of telling the story.

'X started in at once—Wodehouse and Wittgenstein, Malraux and the Marx Brothers—it was just like the old days, though never before had The Hero known a night like that for free drinks.'

Unlike the mourners of Lazarus—to accept Crowding's apprehension of the incident, rather than Evadne Clapham's —the mourners of Trapnel, as, on the strength of his resurrection, they were soon to become, were stood round after round. The Hero, one of those old-fashioned pubs in grained pitchpine with engraved looking-glass (what Mr Deacon used to call a 'gin palace'), was anatomized into half-a-dozen or more separate compartments, subtly differentiating, in the traditional British manner, social subdivisions of its clientèle, according to temperament or means: saloon bar: public bar: private bar: ladies' bar: wine bar: off-licence: possibly others too. Customers occupied in these peripheries were all included in the Trapnel largesse, no less than those in the saloon bar, where he had manifested himself. Swept in, too, were several birds of passage, transients buying half-a-bottle in the off-licence. The fountains ran with wine, more precisely with bitter and scotch. News of this boundless munificence got round immediately, not only emptying The French-polishers' Arms opposite— according to Crowding, lately a serious rival to The Hero in draining off a sediment of discontented intellectuals—but also considerably reducing numbers in The Marquess of Sleaford round the corner, where intellectuals were virtually unknown. Not only were these two latter pubs practically cleared of customers, but what Crowding called a 'thirsty concourse' poured into The Hero from The Wheelbarrow (at the time of Bagshaw's first marriage, his last port of call on the way home, owing to staying open until eleven), auxiliary drinkers from other taverns being all hospitably received by Trapnel, if they could only get near enough to him. Crowding, telling the story, would here shake his head.

'X looked dreadfully ill. As near the image of Death as the knob of that stick he used to carry round, before he threw it into the Grand Union Canal. His face was even whiter.'

Trapnel had been at the height of his old form, talking at the top of his voice, laughing, shouting, contradicting, laying down the law about books and writers, films and film stars, giving prolonged imitations of Boris Karloff; in general reconstructing in its most intrinsic aspects his own persona of years gone by. Not only Crowding, but many others, agreed The Hero had never known such a night. That could not go on for ever. An end had to come. Finally, inexorably, closing time was announced. This moment always represented the peak of Crowding's narrative.

'X walked through the doors of The Hero like a king. There was real dignity in his stride. It was a royal progress. Courtiers followed in his wake. You can imagine—free drinks—there was quite a crowd by that time, some of them singing, as it might be, chants in a patron's praise. X stopped outside, and they all stood round. He waited for a moment by the kerb. Everyone kept back somehow, as if they didn't dare be too familiar. X gazed up the street, then down it, in that proud way of his. He must have been looking for a taxi. He hadn't said yet where he wanted to go. I noticed for the first time that his beard was turning grey. Suddenly he gave a start, remembering something. He wrung his hands, rushed back, tried to get into the pub again through the outer doors, which they were barring up. They wouldn't let him back. He gave a loud cry.

' "I've forgotten my stick. I've lost my stick. My death's head stick."

33

'Of course they wouldn't let him in again after closing time. Somebody told him he hadn't brought a stick with him. Whoever it was couldn't have known about the sword-stick. X didn't take that in for a second or two. When he did, he began to laugh. He laughed and laughed, like one of his own impersonations of a horror film—and it was pretty horrible too. He went on laughing for some minutes, walking slowly back to the edge of the pavement. People close said his look was quite frightening.

' "No," he said. "Of course I haven't got a stick any longer, have I? I sacrificed it. Nor a bloody novel. I haven't got that either."

'Then he heeled over into the gutter. Everybody thought he was drunk.'

At this point in the narrative Crowding would pause, his face apt to twitch so violently that the more sensitive of his listeners had to turn away. He would then slow up the tempo of the narrative for its termination.

'Drunk? They were sadly in error. I watched Trapnel the whole time we were in the saloon bar together. He consumed exactly one bloody double Three Star in the course of the whole bloody time he was in The Hero.'

After adding this comment as a kind of tailpiece to his chronicle, Crowding always stopped, and glared round like a man expecting contradiction of the most vigorous kind. Contradiction never came. Even Evadne Clapham was silent. Whether that was owed to the force of Crowding's recital, or because most of the audience usually knew Trapnel had never been a great drinker, was uncertain. The surmise that alcohol in itself played no great part in his final collapse was no doubt correct, though he may have allowed himself that night an unwise admixture of drink and 'pills'; simply too many pills. Either could have resulted from finding himself unexpectedly in funds. An inner fatigue, utter moral exhaustion, had to be taken into consideration too. He was removed from the street in due course, to a hospital, dying an hour or two later. By the time the ambulance arrived, the near-criminal potential of the traditional Trapnel entourage had extracted from his pockets all remnants, if such there were, of the hundred pounds. He died quite penniless. At that particular juncture, he appeared to be living alone. That probably explained getting his hands on the money. Crowding never mentioned this last fact, but he would change his tone, from pub crony to academic critic, as he drew to an end.

'I respected the man more than his work. He became a legend in his own lifetime. He often said so himself, and with truth. Sometimes my students ask me to tell them about him—and did you once see Trapnel plain? I reply "I did", and often stopped and spoke with him. At the same time I am put in a quandary. These young people find the intellectual climate of *Camel Ride to the Tomb* unsatisfying. I cannot in all fairness blame them. Where, they say, is the social conscience? I have to reply, they look in vain.'

At the time of his death, Trapnel's *œuvre*, so far as I knew, consisted of *The Camel*; the selection of short stories published as *Bin Ends*; a fair amount of additional stories, never yet collected, some dating back to his early days as a writer before the war (when he had kept himself alive by all sorts of odd employments); a miscellany of occasional pieces, criticism (some of it quite good), articles, parodies, stuff written for papers like *Fission,* and never brought together; finally the *conte* (unpublished in Trapnel's lifetime on account of some legal battle over 'rights') *Dogs Have No Uncles.* A work in Trapnel's liveliest manner, almost long enough to be called a novel, its posthumous appearance with Salvidge's Introduction had done something to prevent Trapnel's reputation from slumping too severely after his death. All this did not constitute a large aggregate of work, but, together with what was available in other material, should make a respectable critical biography. In any case, Trapnel's was still an unexplored period. Gwinnett added another item.

'Did you know he kept a *Commonplace Book* during his last years?'

'Where is it?'

'I have it myself.'

Gwinnett seemed for a moment uncertain as to what he was prepared to say on the subject. Then, after this hesitation, described how the librarian of his university, knowing about Gwinnett's interest in Trapnel, had drawn attention to an English bookseller's catalogue, which listed, among other manscripts offered for sale, certain papers of Trapnel's come on the market. The price was not high, the College authorities uninterested. Gwinnett acquired these odds and ends himself. None of them turned out of startling interest, even the *Commonplace Book*, though there was enough there to make its purchase worth while to a potential biographer. That was Gwinnett's own account.

'I'll show you the book. Some of the notes—they're all abbreviated, almost a code—are surely about the castrating girl. You say she's married to—is the name Widmerpool?'

'Yes, she's still married to him.'

That was strange enough. In the course of a dozen years or more of the Widmerpools' married life many stories had gone round, the least of them lurid enough to imply the union could scarcely persist a week longer, yet it had persisted. They remained together; anyway to the extent of living under the same roof. That phrase did not, in fact, define the situation realistically. Each was usually under the different roof of one or other of Widmerpool's two places of residence. There was the flat in Westminster (one of a large block near the River), and his mother's former cottage in the Stourwater neighbourhood, which (Widmerpool mentioned when we met) had been 'enlarged and improved'.

Stourwater Castle was now a girls' school; rather a fashionable one. The Quiggin twins, Amanda and Belinda, were being educated there.

The existence of these two separate Widmerpool establishments was sometimes offered as explanation of a capacity to remain undivorced, which certainly required elucidation. Pamela would disappear now and then with other men, behaviour apparently accepted by Widmerpool himself, so that it became, as it were, accepted by everyone else, a matter of comparatively little interest. People recently returned from abroad would report that Pamela Widmerpool had been seen in Spain with an ambitious journalist; among the islands of the Ægean with a fashionable don; that one of the generals at a NATO headquarters had fallen out with another senior officer, when she was staying with him; that her visit to an embassy in Asia had resulted in a reshuffle of diplomatic personnel; that the TUC had been put in a flutter one year at their conference by her presence with a delegate at a local hotel. A Pamela Widmerpool anecdote might stop the gap in a languishing dinner-table conversation, but, unless highly spiced, was by now unlikely to hold the attention of the company for long.

'My wife loves travel,' said Widmerpool. 'She likes seeing how other people live.'

No convincing answer had been offered to the question why she did not leave him for one of her many, if soon disillusioned lovers; nor why Widmerpool himself never chose his moment to divorce her. For some reason the *status quo* seemed to suit both. Trapnel, alleging the Widmerpool marriage to exclude sexual relationship (scarcely even tried out), had also spoken in a few tortured sentences of the frustration, agony, alienation, inspired in himself—though he loved her—by Pamela's blend of frigidity with insatiable desire. People who went in for more precise ascriptions in such matters, especially far-fetched or eccentric ones, explained this matrimonial paradox by the theory that Widmerpool actually took pleasure in his wife's infidelities, derived masochistic satisfaction, at the very least felt flattered, by the agitation she inspired. Pamela too, so these amateurs of psychology concluded, on her own side luxuriated no less in enjoyment of a recurrent thrill at being unfaithful. Another husband, less tolerant, could prove less satisfactory. Such hypotheses, if not widely accepted, remained comparatively unchallenged by more convincing speculation. At least they attempted to make sense of an otherwise inexplicable situation. They even offered a dim outline of a genuine, if macabre, bond of union; one very different from Trapnel's enslavement. Even Dicky Umfraville's comment had a certain force.

'Anyway they've remained married. Took me five attempts, even if I placed the right bet in the end.'

Loss of his seat in the Commons did not prevent Widmerpool from remaining a fairly prominent figure in public affairs, though there was some surprise when (a few weeks before the Conference opened in Venice) he was created a Life Peer. This advancement, proceeding through the medium of a Conservative Government, must undoubtedly have been conferred after consultation with Labour sources of authority, then in Opposition. Roddy Cutts, who held a minor post in the Tory administration, agreed that Widmerpool's elevation to the Lords had aroused adverse comment on both sides of the House. At the same time, Cutts was sure the recommendation must have been cleared with the Leader of the Opposition, in spite of his reputed dislike for Widmerpool himself. Cutts was inclined to dismiss talk, such as Bagshaw's, of Widmerpool's fellow-travelling.

'After all, if you're on the Left, you have to take a Leftward line in public. That doesn't necessarily mean you're a Communist. Widmerpool may have had leanings in that direction once—certainly his own side thought so—but after all he's not the only one. Personally I'm inclined to think all that's over and done with. There was a story about his being mixed up with Maclean and Burgess. I can't remember which. It was even said he lent a hand in tipping them off. Somebody did, but I'm sure it wasn't Widmerpool. Besides, I don't believe the man's a bugger for a moment. Labour peers had to be created. It wasn't at all easy to settle on suitable names. Not everyone wants to be kicked upstairs to the Lords. Widmerpool lost his seat. He'd made himself very useful on the financial side at one time or another, no matter what the talk about fellow-travelling. Yes, I mean contribution to Party funds. Why not? The money's got to come from somewhere. Probably undisclosed inner workings of the Labour Party machine played a rôle too. Patronage? Might be. These things happen. No different to ourselves in that respect. A political party has to be operated. The PM would never have gone over Hugh's head. When Widmerpool arrived in the House I found him abrasive about marginal issues. Latterly we've got on pretty well. We may be opponents, that's no reason why one should doubt his sincerity. What is true—probably played a part in the peerage—is the active manner Widmerpool's promoted East/West trade, naturally a sphere where some community of political thought, anyway outward acceptance of the other fellow's point of view, is likely to oil the wheels. Whatever he did in that direction had, of course, the blessing of the Board of Trade. He must have made a packet too. Do you ever drink that wine from round the Black Sea? We don't at all despise it at home. Tastes a bit sultry at times, but has the merit of being cheap. Kenneth Widmerpool's got to do something to bring the pennies in with a wife like that. I daresay he wanted the peerage to induce her to stay.'

This last supposition was unconvincing. It was possible

to accept Bagshaw's theory, up to a point, that Widmerpool dreamed of revenging himself on the world; in addition, that his marriage was one of the areas where that mood might seem to some extent justified. The notion that a Life Peerage would impress Pamela was improbable; typical of the unimaginative side of Roddy's nature. That was one's first thought. Then, reconsidering the evidence, the view emerged as one Widmerpool himself might easily hold. Pamela was unlikely to be interested, one way or the other, in whatever prestige might be supposed to attach to that transmutation. She had never shown the smallest inclination to reach out towards more considerable aggrandizements for herself. They were reported, according to good authority, to have been on offer from lovers at different times. Her disregard for anything of the kind, provided its active expression remained within not too outrageous bounds, was one of his wife's few characteristics potentially advantageous to Widmerpool's public life. He could convincingly point to her behaviour as embodiment of contempt for 'The Establishment', an abstraction increasingly belaboured by him in speeches and articles. In fact, considering the Life Peerage in the light of Pamela's past conduct, so far from its creation—as Cutts put forward—assuring an irreducibly solid foundation for a marriage often rocked by upheaval, the reverse appeared more likely, similar landmarks in her husband's career having been emphasized in the past by proportionately augmented scandals. A Life Peerage, as an extreme example of Moreland's conviction that matrimonial discord vibrates on an axis of envy, rather than jealousy, could even portend final severance.

To explain all that, even a small part of it, to Gwinnett, in hope of enlarging his view of the Widmerpools in relation to Trapnel, was not easy; certainly not within the time allotted for sitting under the Veroneses. Nothing about the Trapnel story was simple. Although Gwinnett was quick to grasp things, nothing about his own personality was simple either. He was an altogether unfamiliar type. He himself seemed almost painfully aware of our mutual difficulties of intercommunication. That made things no easier. There was an innate awkwardness about him. Now, for instance, he stood by the table, unable to make up his mind whether or not to accept Dr Brightman's invitation to sit with us.

'What will you drink?'

Without answering, he caught a passing waiter and ordered a citronade. On such a night nothing was more natural than to prefer a cooling soft drink to something stronger, yet again one speculated for some reason about the possibility of an alcoholic past. Something about him suggested rigid control, concealment, an odd way of life. He had the air of punishing himself, possibly for his own supposed social inadequacies. When he sat down, all Dr Brightman's briskness was required to dispel the threat he brought of damped conversation. He had been carrying a newspaper under his arm, which he laid on the table. It was French, the name folded out of sight.

'We were talking of courts and harems, Russell,' said Dr Brightman. 'Those who need them. I'm sure you must have experienced friends like that.'

Gwinnett smiled, but did not comment. The relationship between himself and Dr Brightman appeared good, the best yet, so far as observable. There was none of the coyness that might be suggested by the idea of a distinguished female professor becoming friends with a young academic colleague of the opposite sex. You felt they liked each other, had perhaps learnt from each other, would not for a second hesitate to be tough with each other, if required by circumstance. There was no suggestion of sentimental feelings, a kind of mother/son relationship, just because Dr Brightman had been far from home, Gwinnett something of an oddity in his own surroundings.

'Talking of harems', she said, 'the owner of the Palazzo we're invited to visit tomorrow bears the famous name of Bragadin, and claims to be descended from Casanova's patron, though not, of course, in the legitimate line.'

Gwinnett showed no great interest in that. I asked which of the several Bragadin palaces this was. I had not studied the extra-mural programme carefully, preferring these excursions to come as a series of bracing surprises.

'One never open to the public. Our Conference is greatly favoured. There's a Tiepolo ceiling there on which I've longed to gaze for years. In fact the hint that Conference members might gain access was the chief weapon of Mark Members in overcoming any hesitation in agreeing to attend.'

'It's the Jacky Bragadin one reads about in gossip columns?'

Dr Brightman nodded.

'The Palazzo wasn't inherited. All sorts of people have lived there at one time or another. Jacky Bragadin—though I've no right to speak of him in this familiar manner—bought it just after the war.'

Gwinnett, who had been looking about him without paying much apparent attention to what Dr Brightman was saying, joined in at that.

'Jacky Bragadin's mother's was one of the big American fortunes of the last century. She was a Macwatters of Philadelphia. That's where the funds for the Bragadin Foundation come from.'

'Which have been of good use to most of us in our time,' said Dr Brightman. 'My knowledge of the benefactor, like that of Mr Jenkins, derives chiefly from gossip columns. His well publicized personality remains, all the same, for me an elusive one, beyond an evident taste for entertaining persons as rich as himself. Remarkable that he should have found time enough from that hobby to have given birth to a Foundation.'

'He's not married, I think?'

'Do you imply the Bragadin Foundation is illegitimate too? A case of parthenogenesis, I expect. In any case, I am more concerned with his Tiepolo.'

Tiepolo ranking with Poussin as one of my most admired Masters, I asked the subject of the ceiling, the very existence of which was unknown to me. The bare fact that members of the Conference could visit the Palazzo had been announced, knowledge of its contents no doubt taken for granted in an assembly of intellectuals.

'One of the painter's classical scenes—*Candaules and Gyges*. The subject, thought to have some contemporary reference, caused trouble at the time the ceiling was painted. That's why the tradition of playing the picture down, keeping it almost a secret, has persisted to the present day. The owner is in any case said to be more than a little neurasthenic in approach to his possessions, and much else too.'

Gwinnett knew about the ceiling.

'I've been told it's not unlike the Villa Valmarana *Iphigenia* in composition,' he said. 'The owner won't allow it to be photographed.'

He turned to me.

'Speaking about the *Iphigenia* again made me think of what we were talking about at that luncheon.'

He picked up from the table the paper he had brought with him, opened it, folding back a page. It was *Détective, Içi Paris*, or another of those French periodicals that explore at greater length cases, usually already reported, which through expansion promise more pungent details of crime or scandal. Gwinnett singled out two sheets, the central spread. He was about to hand them over, but Dr Brightman,

43

catching the name under a photograph, intercepted the paper.

'Good gracious,' she said. 'That ugly little man? I should never have thought it.'

I looked over her shoulder. The headline ran along the top of both pages.

L'APRES-MIDI D'UN MONSTRE?

Two large cut-out photographs stretched across the type-face, the story, whatever it was, fitting round their edges. In spite of Dr Brightman's lack of principle in appropriating the letterpress to herself, and although I was not close enough to read the sub-titles, the likenesses of the two persons portrayed were immediately recognizable. Both photographs had manifestly been taken some years before, ten at least. In fact that of Ferrand-Sénéschal made him look a man in early middle-age. He had been caught on some public occasion, mouth wide open, hands raised above his head in a passionate gesture, almost as if he, too, were singing *Funiculì-Funiculà*, miming the ascending cable. No doubt he had been snapped addressing a large audience on some political or cultural theme.

The other photograph, also far from recent, though less time-expired than Ferrand-Sénéschal's, was more interesting. It was of Pamela Widmerpool. Her hair-do suggested the end of the war, or not long after. The picture could have dated from the year of her marriage to Widmerpool, possibly even taken at the moment of emergence from the ceremony. In spite of heavy touching-up on the part of the blockmaker, the expression was resentful enough for that. This touching-up had added a decidedly French air to her appearance. That could have been acquired not only from the cupid's bow mouth, brutally superimposed on her own, but, more universally, from the manner in which photographic portraiture in the press automatically assumes the national characteristics of whatever country has processed the blocks,

44

fabricated their 'screen'; an extension of the law that makes the photographer impose his personal view of them on individuals photographed. Dr Brightman scrutinized carefully both pictures.

'Lady Widmerpool? A very bedworthy gentlewoman, I understand. But Ferrand-Sénéschal? I am frankly surprised. I should never have guessed . . . assoiffé de plaisir . . . dévoré de désir . . . terrible obsession . . . How unchanged remains the French view of English life—phlegmatic, sadistic aristocrats, moving coldly and silently from one atrocity to another through the fogs of le Hyde Park and les Jardins de Kensington.'

I tried to peer over Dr Brightman's shoulder at what was written. Clutching the paper obstinately, she refused to surrender an inch of its surface.

'The implication is that Lady Widmerpool visited Ferrand-Sénéschal in his luxurious hotel suite—accommodation Sardanapalus would have found over-indulgent—only a few hours before the Reaper. Even that is chiefly my own assumption. Nothing definite is even hinted.'

Gwinnett laughed abruptly, rather uncomfortably. His laugh was high and nervous. He addressed me again.

'Isn't that the lady we talked about—Trapnel's girl?'

'Certainly.'

'The implication is she was in bed with this Frenchman after he was dead.'

'Is that how you read it?'

Dr Brightman disregarded our exchange, too engrossed to hear, or because Trapnel's name meant nothing to her. From time to time she read out a phrase that took her fancy.

'Fougueuse sensualité . . . étranges caprices . . . amitiés équivoques . . . We never seem to get anything solid. Odieux chantages . . . but of whom? Situation genanté . . . Then why not tell us about it? Le scandale éclate. . . It

45

never seems to have done so. I am still not at all sure what happened, scarcely wiser than after reading the headline.'

She handed the paper over at last. Reservations about its interest were more than justified. As usual in such journalism, promise was far short of performance. There was a hint that some scandal about Ferrand-Sénéschal had been hushed up in France fairly recently, no details given, only pious horror expressed. That social engagements since arrival in London sufficiently explained taking an afternoon's rest, even between sheets, in the light of medical advice, was altogether ignored. References to Pamela—called 'Lady Pamela Widmerpool'—were even less specific. Indeed, they were written without serious attempt to fit her into the Ferrand-Sénéschal story, such as it was. Nothing whatever was alleged against her, except that she—apparently other persons too—had visited the hotel suite at one time or another. By implication, Ferrand-Sénéschal's habits so notorious, that visit in itself was damaging enough. Her own pranks were touched on only vaguely, not very accurately, though more directly than the law of libel would have allowed an English paper. Widmerpool was treated simply as a great nobleman of the Old School.

'One of my maiden aunts—a social category no longer extant—used to live permanently in that hotel,' said Dr Brightman. 'I'm sure she had no idea things like that were going on there. The place did not at all suggest gaiety. She would have been surprised. Rather thrilled too, I think.'

The respectable, unpretentious style of Ferrand-Sénéschal's hotel disavowed the *grand luxe* attributed to his two-room suite. It was only a few streets away from the former Jeavons residence in South Kensington, converted by Ted Jeavons after the war into several small flats, one of which he inhabited himself. The fact that Ferrand-Sénéschal was on his way to the Conference later on found no place in the *Détective* story, probably regarded as a banal detail likely to prejudice inferences that he had come to London with the sole purpose of participating in an orgy. Dr Brightman reached out for the paper again. She examined the picture of Pamela.

'I can add my own small contribution to the bulletin,' she said. 'The lady in question is in Venice at this moment.'

Gwinnett, who had been sitting silent, chewing at his thumbnail, shifted forward.

'She is, Emily? You've seen her?'

This time he sounded quite excited. Dr Brightman made a gesture to indicate she had enjoyed no such luck.

'I was so informed by a French colleague, who is also attending the Conference. We normally correspond about Gallo-Roman personal names, with special reference to Brittany. On this occasion I fear we descended to gossip. My friend must be unaware of the reference here to Lady Widmerpool, or I'm sure he would have mentioned it. He had witnessed what he described as an extraordinary incident at the French Embassy in London, where Lady Widmerpool, quite deliberately, broke the back of a small gilt chair during supper. That made such an impression, he immediately recognized her profile seen at Quadri's.'

'I'd give something to meet that lady.'

Gwinnett did not sound hopeful. Dr Brightman and I assured him there should be no difficulty in arranging that.

'You've just got to sit in the Piazza long enough. You see everyone in the world, if you do that.'

'But I don't know Lady Widmerpool.'

'I'll introduce you.'

That was said in the heat of the moment. Afterwards, immediately afterwards, it was to be seen as a rash offer. I hoped she would not walk into the hotel at that moment. The very idea of her being in Venice made Gwinnett restless, a state alternating in him with a kind of torpor. He

47

rose from the table, then paused for a moment, again unsure what he wanted to do. He came to a decision.

'I'll take a stroll in the Piazza right now. Do you mind if I retain this journal?'

That could not be refused, since it belonged to him, though I had not yet studied the piece thoroughly. He folded it again, stood in thought for a moment, said goodnight. We said goodnight to him in return. It was not impossible that he might see Pamela Widmerpool in St Mark's Square. Perhaps he hoped to pick up someone there in any case. A girl? A man? One felt rather ashamed of these speculations, as earlier of wondering whether he was an ex-alcoholic. He had shown no sign whatever of seeking in Venice any sort of dissipation. The notion that he was bent on some such goal, no doubt quite unfounded, attached to his withdrawn mysterious air, a little uncommon in an American, anyway in Gwinnett's form. As soon as he was gone, Dr Brightman, without any prompting, began to speak of him.

'Let me tell you about Russell Gwinnett.'

'Please do.'

'He is a small fragment detached from the comparatively extensive and cavernous grottoes of gothic America. He is part of an Old America—the oldest—yet has become in some respects the New America. I hardly know how to put it.'

'Halfway between Henry Adams and Charles Addams?'

'Not bad. In fact alpha plus, insomuch as Henry Adams says that true eccentricity is in a tone, and only the conventional approach loves to assume unconventionality. Russell is unconventional by nature, not by choice. Even then, only in certain respects. He is good at such sports as racquets, skating, skiing. If there is a superfluity of Edgar Allan Poe brought up to date, there is also a touch of Edwin Arlington Robinson.'

'You outrun my literary bounds.'

48

'But you can at least understand that Russell is at once intensely American, yet allergic to American life. That, in itself, can be paralleled, though not quite in Russell's terms. To quote Adams again, he is not one of those Americans who can only assert or deny. I did not use the comparison of the two poets recklessly. Russell, too, hoped to be a poet. He was sufficiently self-critical to see that was not to be. He also draws quite well. Almost always portraits of himself. We saw a lot of each other when I was over there. He is a nice young man, cagey in certain moods.'

'You know he is writing a book about X. Trapnel. That's why he wants to meet Pamela Widmerpool.'

'Trapnel is only a name to me. One of my pupils used to rave about his books. If Russell does that, he will do it well. He is industrious, in spite of his singularities, perhaps because of them. Had he been an English undergraduate, his rooms would have been equipped with black candles, skulls, the odour of incense. He likes Death. That atmosphere is not the American tradition. The taste has told against him, notwithstanding the significance of his name. There was also some kind of a tragedy in his early college days. He was friendly with a girl who committed suicide—at least she seems to have committed suicide. Perhaps it was an accident. He was not in the smallest degree to blame.'

'Why is his name significant?'

'He is descended—collaterally, I understand—from what is known as a "Signer", one Button Gwinnett, who set his name to the Declaration of Independence. Both halves of the name are of interest to persons like oneself, "Gwinnett", of course, "Gwynedd", meaning North Wales—the Buttons, a South Wales family, probably *advenae*. A small piece of topographical history neatly established by nomenclature.'

'I don't know how these things are looked on in America.'

'Like so much else, the attitude is ambivalent. In general,

49

anyway in the right circles, to be descended from a Signer can be highly regarded, even if many such have passed into obscurity. Some Americans will, of course, deny any interest whatever in such trivial matters.'

'Kind hearts are more than Cabots?'

'And simple faith than Mormon blood. This is something of a paradox in that the transgression—crime perhaps —of America has been to reject Classicism for Romanticism. The national distaste for moderation—to which Henry Adams referred—inevitably leads to such a choice. Russell himself is far from immune, though you might not guess that from outward bearing. Profound Romanticism is bound in due course to dilate towards its gothic extremities. In his particular case, family history may have helped.'

'It is often pointed out that one form of Romanticism is to be self-consciously Classical, but what you say accords with Gwinnett's choice of Trapnel as a subject. Let's hope he treats Trapnel's own Romanticism in a Classical manner.'

'Naturally the terms are hopelessly imprecise. That does not make them valueless. Baudelaire and Swinburne have Classical statements to make—more than many people are aware who regard them as pure Romantics—but their gothic side is equally undeniable. Underneath Russell Gwinnett's staid exterior I suspect traces of an American Byron or Berlioz. I spoke of Poe, the preoccupation with Death. When there was trouble about this girl, it was because he had broken into the place where her body was. Some found it deeply touching... others... well...'

'Were there a lot of girls?'

'Apparently none after that. No one seems to know why. Again, some look on that with admiration, others deem it unsatisfactory.'

'As to Byron—what you said about Button Gwinnett— was this Gwinnett brought up in a similar tradition of high descent, I mean in American terms?'

'His grandfather was a fairly successful lawyer, the father some sort of a bad lot, alcoholic, spendthrift, deserted Russell's mother at an early age. He is still alive, I believe. There were money difficulties about going to college, and so on. But we will talk more of Russell Gwinnett, and American gothicism, another time. Now I must go to bed. Fatigue comes on one suddenly here, delayed action after listening to all those speeches in demotic French about the Obligations of the Intellectual. I shall bid you goodnight. Tomorrow we meet under the Tiepolo ceiling.'

Not long after that I turned in too. The night had become a trifle cooler. Through the window of my bedroom the musicians' refrain was to be heard in the distance. Perhaps the songs were no longer theirs, cadences wafted now synthetically from the radio. For a while I tried to read in bed, *The Castle of Fratta*, a translation brought with me as appropriate. Nievo's view of Bonaparte's invasion of Italy was an antidote to Stendhal's. The novel might make a good film in the epic manner. I rather regretted not staying on for the Film Festival, more since I had never attended a Film Festival than because of anything very exciting on offer. A German picture about a prostitute who blackmailed her clients aroused a faint sense of curiosity. Then there was a British one, much recommended, adaptation of a Thomas Hardy story, in which Polly Duport was playing the lead.

I had seen Polly Duport act quite often, never again met her, since the day when we had travelled back to the War Office, with her mother and stepfather, Colonel Flores, in his official car, after the Victory Day Service at St Paul's. Then she had seemed charming, well brought up, a beauty too, with that unfledged look of a young, shy, slender animal. Now she was quite a famous actress. Her gifts had turned out for the Theatre, rather than everyday life, public rather than private. Anyone immersed in the English

Theatre would undoubtedly put her among the three or four of her age and sex at the top of the profession. It was, so it seemed to me, not a very 'interesting' talent, though immensely 'finished'. She had been married for a time to a well-known actor. They had separated. Far from given to love affairs, she lived almost as a nun, it was said, devoted to the stage and its life. This was unlike her mother, whose voice and gestures Polly Duport sometimes recalled on the stage, without any of the mystery Jean had once seemed to exhale. Possibly something of her father's business ability, in one sense, taste for work, accounted for his daughter's serious approach to her profession, lack of interest in private life. The Hardy part was a new line for her. She was said to excel in it anything she had done before. That estimate might be consequence of an energetic publicity campaign.

Musings about the past shifted to the time when I had stayed in this hotel as a boy, to that eternal question of what constitutes experience. A close examination of what happened at any given period in itself provokes an unnatural element, like looking at a large oil painting under a magnifying glass, the over-all effect lost. Nievo, for example, was an over-all effect writer, even when he dealt with childhood. I tried to reconstruct the earlier visit. We had come to Venice because my father liked spending his 'leave' in France or Italy. However much they might be wanting in other respects, he approved of the Latin approach to sex and food. That did not mean he was always at ease on the Continent, but then, in any fundamental sense, he was rarely at ease in his own country. His temperament, a craft of light tonnage, borne effortlessly into heavy seas no matter how calm the weather on setting sail, was preordained to violent ups and downs in foreign waters. Language, currency, timetables, passports, cabmen, waiters, guides, touts, all the paraphernalia and hubbub incidental to travel, were scarcely required for the barometer to register gale force. He was, at the same time, always prepared to undertake any expedition, intricate or arduous, in the interests of sightseeing—or ingenious economy, like sitting up on a station platform for a special train in the small hours —though not necessarily displaying a tolerant spirit while such excursions were in progress. His aesthetic tastes were varied, sometimes comparatively daring, sometimes stolidly conventional, but, once he had taken a fancy to a work of art, monument, building, landscape, that another critic might set a lower value on it than himself was altogether beyond his comprehension. He never stood in front of the Mona Lisa without remarking that, in the eyes of trivial people, the chief interest of Leonardo's masterpiece was to have once been stolen from the Louvre; thereby—as with much else in life—managing to have his cake and eat it, taste the sweets of banality, while ostensibly decrying their flavour.

My mother, too, liked these Continental trips. She enjoyed sightseeing, to which she brought a good deal of general knowledge, wholly untouched by intellectual theory; except possibly as provided by a much earlier, almost pre-Victorian tradition of upbringing. Garlic apart, she too was well disposed to the menus of France and Italy, insomuch as she ever allowed herself any self-indulgence; except perhaps indulgence of an emotional kind, even that rather special in expression. More important, for this last reason, was the manner in which foreign travel, at least in theory, offered relaxation to my father from a pretty chronic state of tension about his career, health, money, housing, hobbies, everything that was his; an innate fretfulness of spirit that seemed automatically to generate good reason to fret.

To emerge from a bank in Rome, notecase filled a moment before with the relatively large sum drawn to settle a week's hotel bill for three persons, and buy tickets for the return journey to England, then have your pocket picked while standing on the outside platform of a crowded tram, is a misadventure to fall to anyone's lot. On the other hand, for a French porter's carrying-strap to split assunder as he mounted the gangway of a Channel steamer with two suitcases across his shoulder, precipitating both into Dieppe harbour, was likely to befall only a traveller in a peculiar degree subject to such tribulations. It was additionally characteristic that the submerged suitcases (home forty-eight hours later in the immutably briny condition of a sea-god's baggage) contained not only a comparatively new dinner jacket (then a feature of Continental hotels), but also the two volumes of Pennells' *Life of Whistler*. Whistler was a painter my father admired. He had bought the books in Paris because his old friend Daniel Tokenhouse reported the French edition to have the same illustrations as the English, the price appreciably cheaper. To recall that was a reminder that I must make an effort to see Tokenhouse before I left Venice.

My father had few friends. The cause of that was not, I think, his own ever smouldering irascibility. People put up surprisingly well with irascibility, some even finding in it a spice to life otherwise humdrum. There is little evidence that the irascible, as a class, are friendless, and my father's bursts of temper may, for certain acquaintances, have added to the excitement of knowing him. It was more a kind of diffidence, uncertainty of himself (to some extent inducing the irascibility) that also militated against intimacy. Whatever the reason, by the time he reached later life, he had quarrelled with the few old friends who remained, or given them up as a matter of principle. Daniel Tokenhouse hung on longer than most, possibly because he too was decidedly irascible. In the end a row, brisk and rigorous, parted them for good.

Tokenhouse, going back to earliest days, had been a Sandhurst contemporary, though friendship, from the first tempered by squabbles, took root in the years after the South African War. The relationship had some basis in a common leaning towards the arts, a field in which Tokenhouse was the more instructed. It was strengthened by a shared taste for arguing. Those were the similarities. They differed in that Tokenhouse—like Uncle Giles—complained from the beginning that the army did not suit him, while my father, addicted to grumbling like most professional soldiers, never seriously saw himself in another rôle. Tokenhouse had specific ambitions. My father put them in a nutshell.

'For reasons best known to himself, Dan always hankered after publishing picture books.'

At the outset of the 'first' war, Tokenhouse, serving with the Expeditionary Force, contracted typhoid. He remained in poor health, through no fault of his own, doing duty in a series of colourless military employments, which took him no further than the rank of major. Whether or not he would have remained in the army had not some relation died, I do not know. As it was, he was left just enough money to be independent of his pay. He resigned his commission, taking immediate steps to gratify the aspiration towards 'picture books'. Tokenhouse did that with characteristic thoroughness, learning the business from the beginning, then investing his capital in a partnership of the kind he had in mind, a firm trafficking not only in 'the fine arts', but also topography and textbooks. One consequence of this was that I myself spent several years of early life in the same business, Tokenhouse my boss. We got on pretty well together. He had an unusual flair for that sort of publishing, making occasional errors of judgment—St John Clarke's Introduction to *The Art of Horace Isbister* one of the minor miscalculations—but on the whole a mixture

55

of hard work, shrewdness, backing his own often eccentric judgment, produced successful results.

When it came to being hasty in temper, idiosyncratic in conduct, my father and Tokenhouse could, so to speak, give each other a game, but, acceptable as a brother-officer less successful than himself, Tokenhouse became gradually less admissible as a very reasonably prosperous civilian; more especially after my father himself was forced to leave the army on account of ill health. Minor skirmishes between them began to take on a note of increasing asperity.

'Dan would have been axed anyway,' said my father. 'Just as well there was a trade to which he could turn his hand, and money enough to buy his way into it. Dan would never have wriggled himself through the bottleneck for officers of his type and seniority. You know, as a young man, old Dan seriously thought of going into the Church. It was touch and go. Then some bishop made a public statement of which he disapproved, and he decided for the army, which his family had always wanted.'

Whether or not that was true, there could be no doubt Tokenhouse's nature included an inveterate puritanism, which army life had by no means decreased. Having abandoned the idea of taking Holy Orders, he developed an absolutely fanatical hatred for religion in any form, even the association of his own forename with a biblical character, thereby suggesting involuntary commitment, becoming a vexation to him. This puritanism also showed itself in dislike for any hint of sensuality in the arts, almost to the extent of handicapping a capacity for making money out of them. Even my parents, who knew him well, admitted that Tokenhouse's sex life had remained undisclosed throughout the years. Not the smallest interest in women had ever been uncovered; nor, for that matter, in his own sex either. He seemed quite unaware of the physical attributes of those he came across, though perhaps an unusually good-looking

56

lady would just perceptibly heighten his accustomed brusqueness. That was my own impression after working for several years in the same office, a condition that can reveal a colleague, especially a superior, with an often devastating clarity.

This apparent non-existence of sexual partiality could have been due to the fact that Tokenhouse was aware of none. General Conyers (had they met, which never happened) might have hazarded a favourite solution, 'a case of exaggerated narcissism'. The peculiarities of Tokenhouse's subsequent conduct may have had their roots there; reaction perhaps from too rigid control, physical and emotional. The only personal relaxation he ever allowed himself, so far as was known, consisted in fairly regular practice of sparetime painting. Otherwise he was always engaged in business, direct or indirect in form.

Painting was a hobby of long standing. The pictures, if a school had to be named, showed faintly discernible traces of influence filtered down from the Camden Town Group. Rising to no great heights as masterpieces of landscape, they did convey an absolutely genuine sense of inner moral discomfort. A Tokenhouse canvas possessed none of the self-conscious professionalism of Mr Deacon's scenes from Greek and Roman daily life, flashy in their way, even when handled without notable competence. Tokenhouse, on the contrary, took pride in being an amateur. He always made a point of that status. It was therefore a surprise to his friends—matter of disapproval to my father—when he announced that he was going to retire from publishing, and take up painting as a full-time occupation. That was about six months before 'Munich'. By that time I had left the firm for several years.

For some little while before taking that decision, Tokenhouse had been behaving in rather an odd manner, having rows with publisher colleagues, laying down the law at dinner parties, in general showing signs of severe nervous tension. This condition must have come to a head when he exchanged publishing for painting; being simultaneously accompanied by a comparatively violent mental crisis about political convictions. No one had previously supposed Tokenhouse to possess strong political feelings of any sort, his desultory grumblings somewhat resembling those of Uncle Giles, even less coherently defined, if possible. To invoke Mr Deacon again, Tokenhouse had never shown the least sign of leanings towards pacifist-utopian-socialism. In making these two particular comparisons, it should equally be remembered that neither Uncle Giles nor Mr Deacon had ever showed any of Tokenhouse's sexual constraint.

Whatever the reason for this metamorphosis, the final row between Tokenhouse and my father took place on the subject of 'Munich'. It was an explosion of considerable force, bursting from a substratum of argument about world strategy, detonated by political disagreement of the bitterest kind. They never spoke again. It was the final close of friendship, so that by the time of the Russo-German Pact in 1939—when Tokenhouse suffered complete breakdown and retired to a psychiatric clinic—there could be no question of going to visit him. There he stayed for the early part of the war, emerging only after the German invasion of the USSR. When I ran across him buying socks in London, not long after I came out of the army, Tokenhouse said he was making preparations to live in Venice.

'Always liked the place. Couldn't go there for years because of Mussolini. Now they've strung him up, it may be tolerable again. Better than this country, and Attlee's near-fascist Government. Come and see me, if you're ever there. Ha, yes.'

Although he had long since shaved off the scrubby tooth-brush moustache of his army days, the ghost of its bristles still haunted his upper lip, years of soldiering for ever perpetuating in Tokenhouse the bearing of a retired officer of infantry. He must have carried out this migration expeditiously and in good order. Not long after our meeting, letters with a Venetian address began to appear in the papers, especially the weeklies, excoriating American foreign policy, advocating the 'Nuclear Campaign', protesting about the conduct of British troops in occupation of Germany, a great many kindred subjects too, signed 'D. McN. Tokenhouse, Maj. (retd)'. Once he sent me a roneo-ed letter of protest about several persons imprisoned in South America for blowing up a power station. Since then we had lost touch with each other.

Before coming to Venice, I had felt that I should see Tokenhouse for old times' sake, at least speak with him on the telephone. We had not met for twenty years or more, so that any such renewal of contact would require tactful handling. In short, I had thought it best to send a note announcing date of my arrival. The telephone, even if Tokenhouse had installed one, might seem too much like holding a pistol to his head. He had always been a man to treat with caution. A note gave time to think things over, make an excuse, also by letter, if he did not wish the matter to be carried further. The Conference he was likely to view with irony, if not open laughter. He had always affected to find the goings-on of self-styled 'intellectuals' ridiculous, although not wholly detached from appertaining to that category himself. I reckoned that Tokenhouse must be in his middle to late seventies. One thought of the ancient singer. If he were really the same man, he was much older than that, still going strong enough. His voice or another's echoed on the summer night.

> Iamme, iamme, via montiam su là.
> Iamme, iamme, via montiam su là.
> Funiculì funiculà, via montiam su là.

2

THE BRAGADIN PALACE WAS APPROACHED on foot. Gwinnett and I walked together. Shared acquaintance with some of the circumstances of Trapnel's life had not made Gwinnett's behaviour less reserved. If anything, he was more farouche than before. Possibly he felt that to speak of the *Commonplace Book* had been indiscreet. Although he had emphasized that Trapnel's 'remains' contained little of interest, many researchers in Gwinnett's place might have kept the fact of its existence to themselves. In that respect he could not be called 'cagey', as Dr Brightman had characterized him at times. This lack of response was something less crude than 'caginess', almost suggesting terms like 'alienation' or 'withdrawal.' No doubt he was merely one of those persons, not so very uncommon, with whom every subsequent meeting after the first entails a fresh start from the beginning. The anxious air always remained. I should have liked to probe his views on the Ferrand-Sénéschal article, no more than skimmed, but something about Gwinnett's manner made this not the moment.

'Did you run across anyone you knew when you reconnoitred the Piazza last night?'

'How do you mean?'

'See anyone from the Conference?'

Gwinnett wriggled his neck.

'No.'

He drawled out the negative, making it sound as if he thought the question in itself uncalled for, a trifle intrusive. I asked if he knew what the Palazzo would be like. Gwinnett was more responsive to that. He began to speak of Venetian architecture, of which he evidently knew something, going on to recommend the book written about Venice by William Dean Howells when American consul here. Then he abandoned porticos and pediments, and fell into a long silence, suggesting a mood to be left alone. We made our way through narrow calles towards an area beyond the Accademia. I wondered how best we could disembarrass ourselves of each other's company without too blatantly seeming to do so. Suddenly Gwinnett came out of his dream with a sort of jerk, one of his characteristic nervous movements, which were not necessarily resentful. He spoke now as if referring to a matter he had been pondering for some little time, using that habitually low tone often hard to catch.

'It seems Louis Glober is house-guest at the Palazzo.'

'The publisher?'

'Glober was that one time. He's been a heap of other things too.'

'When I met him years ago he was in publishing. That's why I think of him as a publisher. I was in a firm that produced art books myself. He came to see us.'

'Glober's been more associated with pictures.'

'Paintings, you mean, or films?'

'Movies. I guess he owns some sort of a modern picture collection too.'

'He was keen on paintings thirty years ago. He wanted my firm to do a series on the Cubists. That was when we met. It was quite a funny occasion. I wonder whether he remembers. Do you know him?'

Gwinnett shook his head.

'I just saw a paragraph about him in the Continental *Herald-Tribune*. It said the well-known playboy-tycoon Louis Glober was here for the Film Festival, and was staying with Mr Jacky Bragadin.'

'I thought Glober an amusing figure. Since then I've never done more than read about him in the paper in his playboy-tycoon capacity. I suppose he's a typical Jacky Bragadin guest. Did the *Herald-Tribune* name any others?'

'Just Glober. It seems he's come on here from the German Grand Prix.'

'Racing?'

'Automobile racing. World Championship.'

'He's in that game too?'

'Sure.'

To the eye of a fellow American I saw Glober must present a very different outline to that of my own remembrance. If not exactly the daily meat of the columnist, Louis Glober was a reasonably tasty snack, always available on the back shelf of the larder, where public personalities of a minor sort are stored in case of need. He was neither dished up too often to cause surfeit, nor left too long on ice to become stale. Contradictory features hampered his definition. The *Herald-Tribune* had termed him playboy-tycoon, this type-casting to cover publisher, film-producer, sportsman, 'socialite', a lot of other more or less news-valued labels, most with some basis in fact. The last photograph I had seen of Glober had been driving a vintage car. Gwinnett thought activities like sailing or motor racing had latterly taken the form of promotion, rather than too laboriously personal a rôle. That did not prevent Glober from still figuring as a noted rider, shot, golfer, yachtsman, or whatever else was required by the context. A taste for amusing himself had not inhibited making money, though again Glober was said to lose fortunes as easily as win them.

'The point I remember about Glober was that he seemed rather intelligent.'

'Ah-ha.'

The answer was non-committal, possibly disapproving, either because Gwinnett thought such a judgment, even if favourable, impertinent to pass on another human being, or because he was himself reluctant to allow the laurels of intelligence to decorate a brow of Glober's type. As not seldom when Americans utter that sound, hard to trans-literate, I was uncertain. We talked of some of the reputed exploits; the blazing Hollywood restaurant from which Glober had carried shoulder-high down a ladder a famous film star—Dietrich, Hepburn, Harlow—neither of us was certain of the heroine; the methusalem of champagne that burst celebrating the return from Europe of Texas Guinan; the fight (almost won) in some night-club with an ex-middle-weight champion of Australia. A reporter never seemed far away to chronicle these vignettes of Glober as a picturesque or glamorous figure, his own clear-cut sense of the dramatic occasion endearing him to press and public wherever he went. Even in England, where he was not much known, editors instinctively printed the intermittent Glober item, compressed into a couple of lines on the back page. I mentioned that.

'Would they report him today?'

'Perhaps not.'

'Glober must be about washed up.'

'What is he? In his sixties? Just about.'

Gwinnett gave the impression of not greatly caring for the idea of Glober, at the same time granting some respect to a romantic so unusually successful at giving public expression to his romanticism; showing ability too, even if a fluctuating one, in making a success of financial ventures. My own memory of Glober was far from unsympathetic, even if he now sounded rather different—though not all that different—from the young American first set eyes on. The mere fact that he was staying with Jacky Bragadin for the Film Festival, that he had been car-racing in Germany, argued survival powers of a sort; resilience not always found in characters of his type.

'Who's he married to now?'

Glober's wives had always been beauties. Once, very briefly, he had been husband of a world-famous film star. These unions lasted only a few years before being dissolved; soon renewed in similar fashion to the accompaniment of further widespread exudations of publicity in the appropriate quarters.

'No one, so far as I know. His last wife died quite a long while ago. They'd been wed only a very short time. It was leukemia, I think. Glober was photographed kneeling at her grave. There was a blanket of lilies, and, on a card written large enough to read in a newspaper picture, a message: *Farewell, Fleurdelys, farewell, fair one.*'

'Fleurdelys was her name?'

'It looked almost as if Glober was lying in the grave.'

Gwinnett spoke with an odd sense of excitement. He stared at me hard. I did not know quite whether he were criticizing Glober, or applauding him, expressing irony or admiration. The thought of what Dr Brightman had said about the dead girl came back.

'He was in a different mood when I met him.'

That had been towards the end of the nineteen-twenties. Glober had arrived in London as representative of a recently founded New York publishing house. Even before he landed, his name went round among the London publishers as a young American colleague with a head full of bright new ideas; by no means an unqualified recommendation to that particular community. Glober came to call on my own firm. He saw Daniel Tokenhouse. One of the bright ideas was the Cubist series. The suggestion was to produce generously illustrated, cheaply produced studies of these painters, blocks to be made in Holland or Germany by some newly devised process. Apart from the fact that the Cubists were still very generally regarded as wild men, if not worse, certainly unwise to encourage, transactions that included overseas production always entailed risks not every publisher was prepared to take. That was where Tokenhouse came in. Tokenhouse did not mind an element of risk. His predisposition for certain forms of rebellion against a humdrum approach to life was one of his unexpected sides. He also derived pleasure from the thought of how much the series would annoy other publishers, not to mention booksellers. Then at quite an early stage, something went wrong in connexion with the issue of the series. I did not remember exactly what upset the project, but it never went forward. There had been rather a row, money and tempers lost. I was in too subordinate a position at the time to be concerned, or greatly interested, except so far as being well disposed to 'modern art'. There were other things to think about, better ones, it then seemed, the business aspects forgotten among elements more memorable.

Tokenhouse was still occupied when Glober arrived for his appointment. Negotiations on the matter of St John Clarke's Introduction to *The Art of Horace Isbister* had just begun. St John Clarke was still haggling about payment. He was too well known a novelist to be dismissed out of hand, so Glober could not be received. The manager, with whom I shared a not over-luxurious office, was wrangling with a binder in the firm's waiting-room, a cubicle from its austerity in any case unsuitable for reception of another publisher, especially an American one. Tokenhouse rang through on the house-telephone with instructions to hold Glober in play for the further few minutes required to dislodge St John Clarke. The room where the manager and I passed our days, its walls grimly lined with file copies, was almost as comfortless as the waiting-room, but Glober was shown in. From the moment he entered, there was no need to provide distraction from the frugality of the surroundings. Glober himself took charge. In a matter of seconds we seemed already on the friendliest of terms. That was Glober's speciality. I made some apology for this delay after an appointment had been made.

'Don't worry. It's great to draw breath. There's a lot of running round in London. I didn't get to bed till late last night.'

He sat down in the collapsed armchair, and looked about him.

'You've got a real Dickensian place here.'

'*Bleak House?*'

Glober laughed his quiet attractive laugh.

'*The Old Curiosity Shop*,' he said. 'In the illustration.'

I supposed him thirty, possibly a year or two more, to my own twenty-two or twenty-three, but his self-confidence, maturity of manner, separated us by several decades. Unusually tall, incontrovertibly good-looking, Glober's features —in the later words of Xenia Lilienthal—were those of a 'young Byzantine emperor'. One saw what she meant. It showed she had taken in that aspect of him, in spite of her bad cold. His quietly forceful manner suggested a right to command, inexhaustible funds of stored up energy, overwhelming sophistication, limitless financial resource. At that age I did not notice a hard core of melancholy lurking beneath these assets. Perhaps in those days that side of his nature was better concealed. The instinct he so essentially possessed was getting on the right terms with everybody, no matter how transiently encountered. This intuitive impulse caused him to move from illustrating Dickens to pictures in general, the fact that he himself wanted to buy an Augustus John drawing before he left England. The gallery handling John's work had shown him nothing he fancied. Had I any ideas? I suggested direct approach to the painter himself, all the time feeling there was some quite easy answer, which Glober's flow of questions had put from my head.

'John's out of the country. If I could meet some private person that had a drawing he was willing to trade.'

Then I remembered such an opportunity had been announced the previous week. The Lilienthals were trying to sell a John drawing for Mopsy Pontner. Moreland had mentioned the fact. Moreland had been searching for a secondhand copy of *The Atheist's Tragedy* in the Lilienthals' bookshop, and Xenia Lilienthal had told him that Mopsy Pontner—more correctly, Mopsy Pontner's husband—had an Augustus John drawing to sell. The Lilienthals were accustomed to take books off Mr Deacon's hands, when included in miscellaneous 'lots' acquired by him at auction to add to his stock of antiques. Mr Deacon was not above marketing the odd volume of *curiosa*—eroticism preferably confined to the male sex—but did not care to be bothered with the sale of more humdrum literary works. The Lilienthal's shop was just around the corner. They were familiar with his quirks, like the Pontners, frequenters of The Mortimer, though not regularly.

Moreland (these were days before marriage to Matilda) always commended Mopsy Pontner's looks, but was a friend of Pontner, who was musically inclined in a manner Moreland could approve, a qualification by no means common. Moreland tended to keep off his friends' wives. Pontner, who knew several languages pretty well, earned a living by translating. He also bought paintings and drawings, when he could afford them, partly because he had a taste for pictures too, partly as a speculation. I ought to have thought of that when Glober raised the subject. This must have been a moment when money was required to tide over a financial crisis, take a holiday, or, as likely as either, invest in another work of art, which Pontner considered a better bet for a rise on the market. Pontner was older than his wife. The fact that Moreland found Mopsy attractive, liked talking about her, probably accounted for his passing on the information. At that time I had never met her, though knew she was reputed quite a beauty in her way. Suddenly remembering about this drawing, I told Glober it had been on offer a week or more before.

'Do you think it's still unsold?'

'Shall I make enquiries?'

'Go ahead. This is great. Mr Jenkins, we just had to meet.'

Glober was full of enthusiasm. He must have recognized one of his own characteristic situations taking shape before his eyes. His next reaction was that everyone must come to dinner with him to discuss the deal. By now he was certain the drawing remained unsold. Its existence revealed, it was now his by law of nature. Before the matter could be gone into further, Tokenhouse appeared in the doorway, having disembarrassed himself of St John Clarke, who could be heard coughing painfully, in a disgruntled manner, as he made his way down the stairs. Tokenhouse uttered his characteristically rather brusque apologies for the delay. Before they disappeared together Glober took my hand.

'Call me up at the hotel between four and five this evening, Mr Jenkins. Even suppose the drawing is sold, I'd like to have you dine with me.'

Tokenhouse heard that a shade suspiciously. He was jealous of outside contacts, not least American ones. Glober stayed for about an hour. I did not see him when he left. In the course of the day I made several telephone calls, finding the Augustus John drawing still available, Pontners and Lilienthals delighted to find a buyer. I informed Glober.

'And they'll all have dinner with me?'

'Of course.'

68

Everyone was pleased with the idea. The party took place in Glober's sitting-room on one of the upper floors of the hotel, an old-fashioned establishment (pulled down a couple of years later) in the Curzon Street neighbourhood. It was a favourite haunt at that period of the more enlightened sort of American publisher. The place was just Glober's mark. When I arrived, he was inspecting the table laid for dinner.

'Good to see you. I've asked quite a crowd.'

Mopsy Pontner, bringing the drawing with her, arrived alone. At the last moment her husband had been prevented from coming by another engagement, arisen at short notice, having professional bearing on one of his translations. Pontner rightly judged his wife fully competent to negotiate the business of the drawing on her own. There were a dozen or more guests by the time we sat down. The Lilienthals arrived late, and rather drunk, having had a long session at The Mortimer with a customer who could not make up his mind whether or not to buy a Conrad first-edition in their catalogue. Xenia Lilienthal, small, with ginger corkscrew curls and a beseeching expression, was suffering from a heavy cold in her nose. Lilienthal, his mind on business, kept fingering the hairs of his sparse black beard. Glober had roped in another American publisher and wife, met the previous day in London, both hitherto unknown to him. They were on their way to the south of France. He wanted them to deliver by hand a present to a friend they had in common, who was staying at Antibes. A young man with a lisp and honey-coloured hair, come to the hotel earlier in the evening to sell Glober a Georgian silver tankard, had been asked to stay for dinner. This young man told the Lilienthals he had once met them with Mr Deacon, to which they assented without much warmth. There was a lesbian called 'Bill' (apparently lacking a surname), seen much at parties, who admitted soon after arrival that she was uncertain as to how firm her invitation had been to this one. Old Mrs Maliphant was present, who had been on the stage in the 'seventies. She was alleged to have slept with Irving; some said Tree; possibly both. Glober had encountered her at the house of one of the several publishers to whom she had promised her Memoirs. Moreland, to some extent responsible for the whole assembly, arrived in poorish form, absent in manner, probably weighed down with a current love affair gone wrong. Other guests, now forgotten, may also have been entertained. If so, their presence did not affect what happened.

The years invest the muster-roll of Glober's dinner-party with a certain specious picturesqueness, if anything increased by being a shade grotesque. At the time, at least on the surface of things, the evening turned out heavy going. That was Glober's fault only so far as he had been over-reckless in mixing people, always risky, sometimes fatal. In this particular venture, he had, as an American, underrated the intractable strain in English social life, even at this undemanding London level, an easy thing to do for anyone not conversant with its heterogeneous elements, their likes and dislikes. Food and drink were both reasonably good. Conversation never got properly under way. Something was lacking.

Glober bought the Augustus John drawing on sight. He made no demur about the price, a fairly steep one in the light of the then market. It was a three-quarter length of a model called Conchita, a gipsy type Barnby, too, sometimes employed. Glober's own demeanour, as when he had visited the office, was enormously genial, but even he did not appear to find the going easy with Mopsy Pontner, whom he had placed next to himself at table. He sat between her and the American publisher's wife, a statuesque lady from Baltimore. Mopsy, with dark straggling hair and very red lips, perfectly civil, was uncommunicative in manner. She made Glober do all the talking. He probably did not mind that, but had earned the right to a little more notice than he seemed to be getting. He had also to work hard with the Baltimore lady, though not because she did not talk. The trouble was her anxiety about reservations on the Blue Train the following day. She continually returned to this preoccupation. When Xenia was not snuffling, she and Lilienthal exchanged secondhand-book chat across the table. The young silver salesman and 'Bill', recognizing no harmony in common, did not communicate with each other at all. Mrs Maliphant rambled on in a monologue about old Chelsea days, saying 'Wilde' when she meant 'Whistler', and 'Sargent' for 'Shannon'. Moreland left early. I left early too; early that is in the light of the sort of party intended, and the fact that my flat in Shepherd Market was only a few yards away. Glober said an effusive goodbye.

'Call me up when you're next in New York, Mr Jenkins. I'd like to have you meet James Branch Cabell.'

That was the last I saw of Glober. His firm fell into liquidation the following year. Several go-ahead American publishing houses went bust about that time. The fact was regarded as an amelioration of whatever row had taken place about the Cubists, indicating our own firm was well out of the commitment.

Glober's character was further particularized when, also about a year later, I came to know Mopsy Pontner better. It appeared that the evening at the hotel, anyway the latter part of it, had been less prosaic than might have been supposed at the time. Mopsy herself gave me an account of its consummation; no vague term in the context. She had, so she related, stayed on after the rest of the party had gone home. Glober, it seemed, had been more attractive to her, far more attractive, than outwardly revealed by her demeanour at dinner. In admitting that, she went so far as to declare that she had greatly approved of him at sight, as soon as she entered the room where we were to dine. Glober must have felt the same. The natural ease of his manner concealed such feelings, like Mopsy's exterior reserve. Later that night mutual approval took physical expression.

'Glober did me on the table.'

'Among the coffee cups?'

'We broke a couple of liqueur glasses.'

'You obviously found him attractive.'

'I believe I'd have run away with him that night, if he'd asked me. I was all right a day or two later, quite recovered. The affair stopped dead there. In any case he was sailing the next day. Some men are like that. Isn't it funny? One rather odd thing about Glober, he insisted on taking a cutting from my bush—said he always did that after having anyone for the first time. He produced a pair of nail-scissors from a small red leather case. He told me he carried them round with him in case the need arose.'

'We all of us have our whims.'

Mopsy laughed. So far as Glober was concerned, I do not put her conquest unduly high, though no doubt she was quite a beauty in her way. To exaggerate Glober's achievement would be mistaken, lacking in a sense of proportion, even though Mopsy was capable of refusal, having turned Barnby down. Barnby made a good story about his failure to please on that occasion, which was one way of dealing with the matter. Such sudden adventures as this one of Glober's can be misleading, unless considered in their context, time and place (as Moreland always insisted) both playing so vital a part. Nevertheless, this vignette, taken at an early stage of his career, suggests Glober's vivacity, liberality, wide interests, capacity for attack; Mopsy's footnote adding a small touch of the unusual, the exotic. These were no doubt the qualities that had carried him advantageously through the years of the Depression; New York to

Hollywood, and back again; lots of other places too; until here he was at Jacky Bragadin's Venetian palace. I enquired about Glober's background. Gwinnett gave a rather satirical laugh.

'Why do the British always ask that?'

'One of our foibles.'

'That's not what Americans do.'

'But we're not Americans. You must humour our straying from the norm in that respect.'

Gwinnett laughed again.

'Glober's people were first generation Jewish emigrants. They were Russian. They took a German name to assimilate quicker, so I've heard said. Glober was from the Bronx.'

'What we'd call the East End?'

'His father made a sizeable pile in building. Glober himself didn't begin on the breadline.'

'You mean there was plenty of money before he started his publishing and film career?'

'He made plenty more. Lost plenty too. Money is no problem to Glober.'

Gwinnett spoke with conviction. The comment that Glober was a man to whom money-making was no problem recalled Peter Templer having once made the same remark about Bob Duport. Duport, of course, had always been on a smaller scale financially than Glober, also without any claims to newspaper fame. I felt that side of Glober, the newspaper fame, was not without a certain fascination for Gwinnett, even if he hesitated to approve of Glober as an individual. An idea suddenly struck me.

'Does he write?'

'Does Glober write?'

'Yes?'

'Sure—did he refuse to sign his name to a contract you showed him in London on the grounds he couldn't write? I'll bet it wasn't true, and he can.'

Gwinnett was unbending a little.

'I meant books. It's always a temptation for a publisher to have a go at writing a book. After all, they think, if authors can do that, anybody can.'

'Glober's withstood the temptation so far.'

'What I was leading up to is Glober having something of Trapnel about him—a Trapnel who brought off being a Complete Man. Of course if Glober can't write, the comparison ceases to be valid, unless you accept as alternative Glober's experience as entrepreneur in the arts. That might to some extent represent Trapnel's literary sensibility.'

Gwinnett seemed unprepared for a comparison of that kind.

'I just can't imagine Trapnel without his writing,' he said.

'Certainly in his own eyes that would be a contradiction in terms. But all the beautiful girls, all the publishing and movie triumphs of one sort or another, all the publicity—yet the implied failure too. Experience of the other side of fortune. Losses, as well as gains, in money. Sadness in love, implicit in the changes of wives. In business, changes of interests. Nothing fails like success. Surely all that's part of being complete in Trapnel's eyes? Why shouldn't Glober be Trapnel's Complete Man at sixty?'

Gwinnett thought for a moment, but did not answer. The concept, even if it possessed a shred of interest, did not please him. He smiled a little grimly. There was no point in pressing the analogy. In any case, we had now reached the campo, along one side of which stood the palace to be visited; a Renaissance structure of moderate size, its exterior, as Gwinnett had explained on the way, severely restored in the eighteenth century. In the Venetian manner, the more splendid approach was by water, but it had been found more convenient to admit members of the Conference through the pillared entrance opening on to the square.

74

We passed between massively sententious caryatids towards a staircase carpeted in crimson. Dr Brightman drew level.

'This Palazzo is not even mentioned in most guide-books,' she said.

'I've ascertained the whereabouts of the Tiepolo, and will lead you to it. Follow me, after we've made our bow.'

At the top of the stairs, supported by a retinue of the Conference's Executive Committee, and civic officials, Jacky Bragadin was receiving the guests. The municipality had helped to promote the Conference, in conjunction with the Biennale Exhibition, which fell that year, as well as the Film Festival. A small nervous man, in his fifties, Jacky Bragadin's mixed blood had not wholly divested him of that Venetian physiognomy, noticeable as much in the contemporary city as in the canvases of its painters; somewhat as if most Venetians wore Commedia dell'Arte masks fashioned in the Orient, only a guess made at what Europeans look like. Into such features Jacky Bragadin had fused those of his American ancestry. He did not appear greatly at ease, fidgeting a good deal, a scarcely discernible American accent overlaying effects of English schooldays. The more consequential members of the Conference, after shaking hands, paused to have a word, or chat with the entourage, standing about on a landing ornamented with baroque busts of Roman emperors. The rest moved forward into a frescoed gallery beyond.

'Come along,' said Dr Brightman. 'The ceiling is in an ante-room further on, not at all an obvious place. These Luca Giordanos will keep most of them quiet for the time being. We shall have a minute or two to inspect the Tiepolo in peace.'

Gwinnett, preferring to go over the Palazzo at his own speed, strolled away to examine the Roman emperors on their plinths. He may also have had an interest in Luca Giordano. I followed Dr Brightman through the doors leading into the gallery of frescoes. We passed on through further rooms, Dr Brightman expressing hurried comments.

'These tapestries must be Florentine—look, *The Drunkenness of Lot*. The daughter on the left greatly resembles a pupil of mine, but we must not tarry, or the mob will be upon us again.'

She also disallowed for inspection a rococo ball-room, white walls, festooned with gold foliage and rams' heads, making a background for Longhi caricatures, savants and punchinellos with huge spectacles and bulbous noses.

'How much they resemble our fellow members of the Conference. The ante-room should be at the far end here.'

We entered a small almost square apartment, high ceilinged, with tall windows set in embrasures.

'Here we are.'

She pointed upward. Miraculous volumes of colour billowed, gleamed, vibrated, above us. Dr Brightman clasped her hands.

'Look—*Candaules and Gyges*.'

At our immediate entry the room had seemed empty. A second later, the presence of two other persons was revealed. The unconventional position both had chosen to assume, for a brief moment concealed, as it were camouflaged, their supine bodies, one male, the other female. In order the better to gaze straight ahead at the Tiepolo in a maximum of comfort, they were lying face upwards, feet towards each other, on two of the stone console seats, set on either side of the recess of a high pedimented window. The brightness of the sun flowing in had helped to make this couple invisible. At first sight, the pair seemed to have fainted away; alternatively, met not long before with sudden death in the vicinity, its abruptness requiring they should be laid out in that place as a kind of emergency mortuary, just to get the bodies out of the way pending final removal. Dr Brightman, noticing these recumbent figures too, gave a quick disapproving glance, but, without comment on their posture, began to speak aloud her exposition on the ceiling.

'As Russell Gwinnett said, one is a little reminded of Iphigenia in the Villa Valmarana, or the Mars and Venus there. The usual consummate skill in handling aerial perspectives. The wife of Candaules—Gautier calls her Nyssia, but I suspect the name invented by him—is obviously the the same model as Pharaoh's daughter in *Moses saved from the water* at Edinburgh, also the lady in all the Antony and Cleopatra sequences, such as those at the Labia Palace, which I was once lucky enough to see.'

To make no mistake, I took another swift look at the couple lying on the ledges under the window. There was no mistake. They were sufficiently far away to convey quietly to Dr Brightman that we were in the presence of her 'very bedworthy gentlewoman', heroine, by implication, of 'L'après-midi d'un monstre'. The horizontal figure on the left was certainly Pamela Widmerpool; the man on the right, lying like an effigy of exceptional length on a tomb, was not known to me. Dr Brightman as usual kept her head. Adjusting her spectacles, so as to make a more thorough survey of Pamela when the moment came, she continued to gaze for a few seconds upwards, her tone, at the same time, showing the keen interest she felt in this disclosure.

'Lady Widmerpool? Indeed? I'll curb my aesthetic enthusiasms in a moment in order to scan her surreptitiously.'

She concentrated for at least a minute on the Tiepolo, before making an inspection in her own time and manner. Leaving her to do that, I crossed the floor to where Pamela had brought her body into almost upright position in order to cast a disdainful glance on whoever had entered the room. As I advanced she gave one of her furious

77

looks, then, without smiling, accepted that we knew each other.

'Hullo, Pamela.'

'Hullo.'

Much of the beauty of her younger days remained in her late thirties. She had allowed her hair to go grey, perhaps deliberately engineered the process, silver tinted, with faint highlights of strawberry pink that glistened when caught by sunlight. She looked harder, more angular in appearance, undiminished in capacity for putting less aggressive beauties in the shade. Apart from the instant warning of general hostility to all comers that her personality automatically projected, an unspoken declaration that no man or woman could remain unthreatened by her presence, she did not appear displeased at this encounter, merely indifferent. Even indifference was qualified by a certain sense of suppressed nervous excitement, suggesting tensions almost compliant to interruption of whatever she was doing. Usually her particular form of self-projection excluded conceding an inch in making contacts easier, outward expression, no doubt, of an inner sexual condition. She was like a royal personage, prepared to converse, but not bestowing the smallest scrap of assistance to the interlocutor, from whom all effort, every contribution of discursive vitality, must come. Now, on the other hand, she unbent a little.

'Jacky didn't mention you were staying. I suppose you arrived in that ghastly middle-of-the-night plane. Who's the old girl? One of Jacky's dykes?'

That was about the furthest I had ever heard Pamela go in the way of taking conversational initiative, for that matter, in showing interest in other people's doings. I explained that neither Dr Brightman nor myself was the latest addition to the Bragadin house-party; for fun, subjoining a word about Dr Brightman's academic celebrity. Pamela did not answer. She had the gift of making silence as vindictive as speech. Dr Brightman continued to examine the ceiling, while at the same time she moved discreetly in our direction. When she was near enough I introduced them. Dr Brightman's manner was courteously firm, Pamela in no way uncivil, though she did not attempt to name the man with her. He, also risen from the flat of his back, had now manifestly put himself into an attitude preparatory for meeting strangers. Evidently he was familiar with Pamela's distaste for social convention of any kind, in any case well able to look after himself. After giving her a statutory moment or two to make his identity known, he announced himself without her help. The intonation, deep and pleasant was American.

'Louis Glober.'

He held out a large white hand, much manicured. The voice came back over the years, the tone just the same, quiet in pitch, masterful, friendly, full of hope. Otherwise hardly a trace remained of the smooth dominating young man who had interviewed Tokenhouse about the Cubist series, given the dinner-party for the John drawing, 'done' Mopsy Pontner on the dinner-table in the private suite of that defunct Mayfair hotel. He was still tall, of course, no less full of assurance, though that assurance took rather a different form. It was in one sense less flowing—less like, say, Sunny Farebrother's determination to charm—in another, tougher, more outwardly ruthless. What Glober had lost, physically speaking (a good deal, including, naturally enough, all essentially youthful adjuncts), was to a certain extent counterbalanced by transmutation into a different type of distinguished appearance. The young Byzantine emperor had become an old one; Herod the Tetrarch was perhaps nearer the mark than Byzantine emperor; anyway a ruler with a touch of exoticism in his behaviour and tastes. What was left of Glober's hair, scarcely more than a suggestion he once had owned some,

79

was still black—possibly from treatment artificial as Pamela's—his handsome, sallow pouchy face become richly senatorial. Never particularly 'American' in aspect (not, at least, American as pictured by Europeans), now he might have come from Spain, Italy, any of the Slav countries. A certain glassiness about the eyes recalled Sir Magnus Donners, though Glober was, in general, quite another type of tycoon. Before I could reintroduce myself to him, Dr Brightman went into attack with Pamela.

'Tell me, do tell me, Lady Widmerpool, where did you get those quite delectable sandals?'

Pamela accepted the tribute. They went into the question together. I explained to Glober how we had met before.

'Do you remember—the Augustus John drawing?'

He thought for a moment, then began to laugh loudly. Putting a hand on my shoulder, he continued to laugh.

'This warms me like news from home. Is it really thirty years? I just don't believe you. The charming Mrs Pontner. It was a privilege to meet her. How is she?'

'No more with us, I'm afraid.'

'Passed on?'

'Yes.'

Glober shook his head in regret.

'Was that recently?'

'During the war. I hadn't seen her for ages, even by then. She'd married Lilienthal, the bookseller with the beard, who came to your party too. When Pontner died, Mopsy went to help in the bookshop. Then Xenia went off with an Indian doctor, and Mopsy married Lilienthal.'

'Mrs Lilienthal was the little redhead with the bad cold?'

Glober certainly possessed astonishing powers of recall. I could hardly bring his guests to mind myself, the facts just offered having come from Moreland a comparatively short time before. Otherwise, I should never have remembered (nor indeed known about) most of what I had just related. Whenever we met, which was not often, Moreland loved to talk of that period of his life, days before marriage, ill health, living with Mrs Maclintick, had all, if not overwhelmed him, made existence very different. On that particular meeting, he had dredged up the story of Mopsy Pontner's sad end; for sad it had been. Glober shook his head, and sighed.

'Mrs Pontner, too. I recall her so well.

The forehead and the little ears
Have gone where Saturn keeps the years.'

'You didn't produce that extempore?'
'Edwin Arlington Robinson.'

I was glad to hear a representative quotation from a poet named by Dr Brightman as contributing a small element to Gwinnett's makeup, and wondered how often, when obituary sentiments were owed in connexion with just that sort of personal reminiscence, Glober had found the tag apposite. Frequently, his promptness suggested. The possibility in no manner abated its felicity. We talked for a minute or two about other aspects of that long past London visit of his. I told him Tokenhouse now lived in Venice, but Glober did not rise to that, reasonably enough. The strange thing was how much he remembered. This conversation did not please Pamela. Abandoning an apparently amicable chat about footgear with Dr Brightman, she now pointed to the ceiling.

'You haven't explained yet what's happening up there.'

When she addressed Glober, the tone suggested proprietary rights. One of the paradoxes about Pamela was a sexuality, in one sense almost laughably ostentatious, the first thing you noticed about her; in another, something equally connected with sex that seemed reluctant, extorted, a possession she herself utterly refused to share with anyone.

'What's happening? That's what I want to know.'

She stood, legs thrust apart, staring upward. White trousers, thin as gauze, stretched skintight across elegantly compact small haunches, challengingly exhibited, yet neatly formed; hard, pointed breasts, no less contentious and smally compassed, under a shirt patterned in crimson and peacock blue, stuck out like delicately shaped bosses of a shield. These colours might have been expressly designed— by dissonance as much as harmony—for juxtaposition against those pouring down in brilliant rays of light from the Tiepolo; subtle yet penetrating pinks and greys, light blue turning almost to lavender, rich saffrons and cinnamons melting into bronze and gold. Pamela's own tints hinted that she herself, only a moment before, had floated down out of those cloudy vertical perspectives, perhaps compelled to do so by the artist himself, displeased that her crimson and peacock shades struck too extravagant a note, one that disturbed rather than enriched a composition, which, for all its splendour, remained somehow tenebrous too. If so, reminder of her own expulsion from the scene, as she contemplated it again, increasingly enraged her.

'Can't anybody say anything?'

Glober, half turning in her direction, and smiling tolerantly, parodied the speech of a tourist.

'Oh, boy, it sure is a marvellous picture, that Tee-ay-po-lo.'

All of us, even Dr Brightman, fixed attention once more on the ceiling, as if with the sole object of producing an answer to Pamela's urgent enquiry. There was plenty on view up there. Pamela's desire to have more exact information, even if ungraciously expressed, was reasonable enough once you considered the picture. Dr Brightman took up her former exposition, now delivered to a larger audience.

'The Council of Ten made trouble at the time. Objection was not, so many believe, to danger of corrupting morals in the private residence of a grandee, so much as to the fact that the subject itself was known to bear reference to the habits

82

of one of the most Serene Republic's chief magistrates, another patrician, with whom the Bragadin who owned this palace had quarrelled. The artist has illustrated the highspot of the story's action.'

The scene above was enigmatic. A group of three main figures occupied respectively foreground, middle distance, background, all linked together by some intensely dramatic situation. These persons stood in a pillared room, spacious, though apparently no more than a bedchamber, which had unexpectedly managed to float out of whatever building it was normally part—some palace, one imagined—to remain suspended, a kind of celestial 'Mulberry' set for action in the upper reaches of the sky. The skill of the painter brought complete conviction to the phenomena round about. Only a sufficiently long ladder—expedient perhaps employed for banishing Pamela from on high—seemed required to reach the apartment's so trenchantly pictured dimension; to join the trio playing out whatever game had to be gambled between them by dire cast of the Fates. That verdict was manifestly just a question of time. Meanwhile, an attendant team of intermediate beings—cupids, tritons, sphinxes, chimaeras, the passing harpy, loitering gorgon—negligently assisted stratospheric support of the whole giddy structure and its occupants, a floating recess perceptibly cubist in conception, the view from its levels far outdoing anything to be glimpsed from the funicular; moreover, if so nebulous a setting could be assigned mundane location, a distant pinnacle, or campanile, three-quarters hidden by cloud, seemed Venetian rather than Neapolitan in feeling.

'Who's the naked man with the stand?' asked Pamela.

An unclothed hero, from his appurtenances a king, reclined on the divan or couch that was the focus of the picture. One single tenuous fold of gold-edged damask counterpane, elsewhere slipped away from his haughtily muscular body, undeniably emphasized (rather than concealed) the physical anticipation to which Pamela referred, of pleasure to be enjoyed in a few seconds time; for a lady, also naked, tall and fair haired, was moving across the room to join him where he lay. To guess what was in the mind of the King—if king he were—seemed at first sight easy enough, but closer examination revealed an unforeseen subtlety of expression. Proud, self-satisfied, thoughtful, more than a little amused, he seemed to be experiencing mixed emotions; feelings that went a long way beyond mere expectant sensuality. No doubt the King was ardent, not to say randy, in the mood for a romp; he was experiencing another relish too.

The lady—perhaps the Queen, perhaps a mistress—less intent on making love, anxious to augment pending pleasure by delicious delay, suddenly remembering her own neglect of some desirable adjunct, or necessary precaution, incident on what was about to take place, had paused. Her taut posture, arrested there in the middle of the bedchamber, immediately proposed to the mind these, and other possibilities; that she was utterly frigid, not at all looking forward to what lay ahead; that—like Pamela herself—she was frigid but wanted a lot of it all the same; that her excitement was no less than the King's, but her own attention had been suddenly deflected from the matter in hand by a disturbing sound or movement, heard, perceived, sensed, in the shadows of the room. She had scented danger. This last minute retardation in coming to bed had, at the same time, something of all women about it; the King's anticipatory complacence, something of all men.

The last possibility—that the lady had noticed an untoward happening in the background of the bedchamber—was the explanation. Her eyes were cast on the ground, while she seemed to contemplate looking back over her shoulder to scrutinize further whatever dismayed her. Had she glanced behind, she might, or might not, have been in time to mark down in the darkness the undoubted source of her uneasiness. A cloaked and helmeted personage was slipping swiftly, unostentatiously, away from the room towards a curtained doorway behind the pillars, presumably an emergency exit into the firmament beyond. At that end of the sky, an ominous storm was plainly blowing up, dark clouds already shot with coruscations of lightning and tongues of flame (as if an air-raid were in progress), their glare revealing, in the shadows of the bedchamber, an alcove, where this tall onlooker had undoubtedly lurked a moment beforehand. Whether or not the lady was categorically aware of an intruding presence threatening the privacy of sexual embrace, whether her suspicions had been only partially aroused, was undetermined. There was no doubt whatever some sort of apprehension had passed through her mind. That was all of which to be certain. The features of the cloaked man, now in retreat, were for the most part hidden by the jutting vizor of the plumed helmet he wore, so that his own emotions were invisible. The calmly classical treatment of the scene, breathtaking in opulence of shapes and colours, imposed at the same time a sense of awful tension, imminent tragedy not long to be delayed.

'I wonder whether the model was the painter's wife,' said Dr Brightman. 'She occurs so often in his pictures. I must look into that. If so, she was Guardi's sister. Gyges looks rather like the soldier in *The Agony in the Garden*, who so much resembles General Rommel.'

'I don't remember the story. Didn't Gyges possess a magic ring?'

'That was my strong conviction too,' said Glober.

Dr Brightman offered no apology for settling down to the comportment of a professional lecturer, one she fulfilled with distinction.

'Candaules was king of Lydia—capital, Sardis, of the

New Testament—Gyges his chief officer and personal friend. Candaules was always boasting to Gyges of the beauty of his wife. Finding him, as the King thought, insufficiently impressed, Candaules suggested that Gyges should conceal himself in their bedroom in such a manner that he had opportunity to see the Queen naked. Gyges made some demur at that, public nakedness being a state the Lydians considered particularly scandalous.'

'The Lydians sound just full of small-town prejudices,' said Glober.

'On the contrary,' said Dr Brightman.' The Greeks did not know what being rich meant until they came in contact with the Lydians, now thought to be ancestors of the Etruscans.'

I remembered the text, from the Book of Revelation, inscribed in gothic lettering on the walls of the chapel that had been the Company's barrack-room, when I first joined. Now it seemed particularly apt.

'Thou hast a few names even in Sardis which have not defiled their garments, and they shall walk with me in white, for they are worthy.'

'Exactly,' said Dr Brightman. 'Gyges tried to be one of the worthy at first, but Candaules insisted, so he gave in, and was hidden in the royal bedchamber. Unfortunately for her husband, the Queen noticed the reluctant voyeur stealing away—we see her doing so above—and was understandably incensed. She sent for Gyges the following day, and presented him with two alternatives: either he could kill Candaules, and marry her *en secondes noces*, or—no doubt a simple undertaking in their respective circumstances at the Lydian court—she would arrange for Gyges himself to be done away with. In the latter event, familiarity with her unclothed beauty would die with him; in the former, become a perfectly proper aspect of a respectably married man's—or rather married king's—matrimonial relationship. Gyges chose the former course of action. His friend and sovereign, Candaules, was liquidated by him, he married the Queen, and ruled Lydia with credit for forty years.'

There was pause after Dr Brightman's terse recapitulation of the story. Everyone seemed to be thinking it over. Glober was the first to speak.

'Then the owner of the magic ring was another guy—another Gyges rather? Not the same Gyges that saw the lady nude?'

Dr Brightman gave the smile reserved for promising pupils.

'Versions vary in all such legends. According to Plato, Gyges descended into the earth, where he found a brazen horse, within which lay the body of a huge man wearing a brazen ring on his finger. Gyges took the ring, which had the property of rendering its wearer invisible. This attribute may well have facilitated the regicide. The Hollow Horse, you remember, is a widespread symbol of Death and Rebirth. You probably came across that in the works of Thomas Vaughan, the alchemist, Mr Jenkins, in the course of your Burton researches. The historical Gyges may well have excavated the remains of some Bronze Age chieftain, buried within a horse's skin or effigy. Think of the capture of Troy. I don't doubt they will find horses ritually buried round Sardis one of these days, where a pyramid tomb may still be seen, traditionally of Gyges—whose voyeurism brought him such good fortune.'

This was getting a long way from Tiepolo, but, seasoned in presentation of learning, Dr Brightman had dominated her audience. Even Pamela, who might have been expected to interrupt or walk away, had listened with attention. So far from becoming restless or rebellious, she too showed signs of being impressed, in her own way stimulated, by the many striking features of the Candaules/Gyges story.

87

Her cheeks had become less pale. Glober responded to the legend too, though in quite a different manner. He seemed almost cowed by its implications.

'That's a great tale,' he said. 'David and Uriah the other way round.'

'An excellent definition,' said Dr Brightman. 'You mean Candaules, by so to speak encouraging a Peeping Tom, put himself, without foreseeing that, in the forefront of the battle. One thinks of Vashti and Ahasuerus too, where much less was required. Nowadays such a treat would be in no way comparable. You need to go no further than the Lido to contemplate naked bodies—all but naked at least— but in Lydia, Judah too for that matter, the bikini would not have been tolerated.'

'There's a difference between a bikini, and nothing at all, Dr Brightman,' said Glober. 'You've got to grant that much.'

Pamela was full of contempt for such a comment. Now she showed herself getting back to her more normal form.

'What are you talking about? What the King wanted was to be watched screwing.'

If she supposed that observation likely to discompose Dr Brightman, Pamela made a big mistake, though she was herself by then likely to be beyond such primitive essays in shocking. She had always spoken out exactly as she felt on any given occasion; at least exactly as it suited her to give public expression to whatever she wished to pass as her own feelings. In this particular case, she seemed genuinely interested in the true aim of Candaules, the theory put forward, a matter of psychological accuracy, rather than lubricious humour. Dr Brightman did not hesitate to take up the challenge.

'Others, as well as yourself, have supposed mere nakedness an insufficient motif, Lady Widmerpool. Gautier, in his conte written round the legend, characteristically adum-

88

brates a melancholy artist-king, intoxicated by the beauty of his artist-model queen, whom he displays secretly to his friend Gyges, drawn as a French lieutenant of cavalry. Gide, on the other hand, takes quite a different view, somewhat reorganizing the story. Gide's Gyges is a poor fisherman, who delivers to the King's table a fish, in which the ring of invisibility is found. Candaules, a liberal, forward-looking, benevolent monarch—no less melancholy than Gautier's prince, though not, like him, a mere Ivory Tower aesthete—decides as a matter of social conscience to bestow on his impoverished subject, the fisherman, some of the privilege a king enjoys. Among such treats is the sight of the Queen naked. To this end, Candaules lends Gyges the ring. Gyges, once invisible, is master of the situation. He spends a night with the wife of Candaules, who thinks her husband in unusually high spirits. Naturally, Gyges slays his benefactor in the end, taking over Queen and Kingdom.'

'That taught His Majesty to brag about his luck,' said Glober. 'He went that much too far.'

Dr Brightman allowed such a point of view.

'Gide's political undertones insinuate that Candaules represents a too tolerant ruling class, over anxious to share personal advantages, some of which are perhaps better left unshared, anyway that sharing, in the case of Candaules, led to disaster. You must remember the play was written nearly half a century ago. I need hardly add that both Gautier and Gide treat the theme in essentially French terms, as if the particular events described could have taken place only in France.'

Pamela remained unsatisfied.

'That wasn't what I meant. I didn't say having an affair. I said watching—looking on, or being looked at.'

She spoke the words emphatically, in a clearer tone than that she was accustomed to use. Her attention had undoubtedly been captured. Dr Brightman, not in the least denying that to 'watch' was quite another matter, nodded again to show she fully grasped the disparity.

'You mean one facet of the legend links up with kingship in another guise? I agree. Sacrifice is almost implied. Public manifestation of himself as source of fertility might be required too, to forestall a successor from snatching that attribute of regality. You have made a good point, Lady Widmerpool. To speak less seriously, one cannot help recalling a local example here in Venice—or rather the island seclusion of Murano—of the practice to which you refer. I mean Casanova's divertissement with the two nuns under the eye of Cardinal de Bernis.'

Pamela, perhaps from ignorance of the Memoirs, appeared out-manoeuvred for the moment, at least attempted no comeback. The subject could already have begun to pall on her, though for once she was looking thoughtful rather than impatient. Moreland, too, was fond of talking about Casanova's threesome with the nuns.

'I've never myself been more than one of a pair,' Moreland said. 'How inexperienced one is, even though the best things in life are free. For the more venturesome, the song is not *How happy could I be with either*, but *How happy could I be with two girls*.'

By now the rest of the Conference had begun to infiltrate the Longhi room, the vanguard of oncoming intellectuals substantiating Dr Brightman's comparison with the sages, abbés, punchinellos, pictured on the white-and-gold walls. Gwinnett was among this advance party, which also included two other British representatives, Ada Leintwardine and Quentin Shuckerly. Both of these accommodated at an hotel on the Lido, I had done no more than exchange a few words with them. They were taking the Conference with great seriousness, from time to time addressing sessions, an obligation for which Gwinnett and myself had substituted contribution to the organ devoted to its 'dialogues'. Ada, not least because she retained some of the girlish good-looks of her twenties, had been warmly received in her observations regarding the necessity of assimilating European culture to that of Asia and Africa, delivered in primitive but daring French. Shuckerly, too, won applause by the artlessness and modesty with which he emphasized the many previous occasions on which he had made his now quite famous speech about culture being the scene-shifter to ring up the Iron Curtain.

Shuckerly was a great crony of Ada's. Tall, urbane, smiling, businesslike, with a complexion so richly tanned by the sun that his enemies (friends, too) hinted at artifice, he had by now begun almost to rival Mark Members himself as a notable figure at international congresses. In earlier days, both as intimate friend and committed poet, he had been closely associated with Malcolm Crowding. Bernard Shernmaker, always irked by even comparative success in others, had designated Shuckerly 'the air-hostess of English Letters' at some literary party. 'Better than the ad-man of french ones,' had been Shuckerly's retort, a slanting gloss on Shernmaker's recently published piece about Ferrand-Sénéschal. Ada and Shuckerly sat on the same committees, signed the same protests, seemed to share much the same temperament, except that Ada, so far as was known, required no analogous counterpoise to Shuckerly's alleged taste (Shernmaker again the authority) for being intermittently beaten-up.

Shernmaker had been malicious about Ada, too, in days of her first appearance as a novelist, though latterly, having in general somewhat lost his critical nerve, allowing her from time to time temperate praise. Some explained this unfriendly tone by rejected advances, at the period when Ada was new to London, and certainly Shernmaker remained always insistent that, in spite of marriage, Ada's emotional interests lay chiefly with her own sex. There may have been some truth in this assertion. If so, that had not prevented her from giving birth to twins soon after marriage to Quiggin, their identical, almost laughable, resemblance to their father scotching another of Shernmaker's disobliging innuendos. Quiggin did not by now at all mind his wife being a better known figure than himself. The sales of her books may even have played some part in his own evolvement, after Clapham's death, as chairman of the firm. In the delicate rôle—compared by Evadne Clapham to a troika—of publisher, husband, critic, Quiggin had judged his wife's first book, *I Stopped at a Chemist* (a tolerable film as *Sally Goes Shopping*), too short commercially. In consequence of this advice, Ada had written two long novels about domestic life, which threatened literary doldrums. She had extracted herself with *Bedsores* and *The Bitch Pack Meets on Wednesday*, since these never looked back as a successful writer. Ada's personality—what Members called her 'petits soins'—played a considerable part, too, in the Quiggins' notorious literary dinner parties.

As they advanced into the Tiepolo room, Shuckerly made for Dr Brightman, Ada for Pamela. She seemed very surprised to find her old friend in the Bragadin palace. As Ada passed him, Glober shot out an appraising glance, reminiscent of those Peter Templer used to give ladies he did not know, Glober's all-inclusive survey suggesting recognition of Ada's valuable qualities, additional to her good looks. Always a shade on the plump side (even when she had worked for Sillery), she was no thinner, but carried herself well, retaining that air of bright, blonde, efficient, self-possessed secretary, who knows the whereabouts of everything required in a properly run office, much too sensible to allow more than just the right minimum of flirtatious behaviour to pervade business hours. No doubt Ada had learnt a lot from contact with Sillery. At the ninetieth birthday celebrations mentioned by Dr Brightman, the names of both the Quiggins had appeared as present, Quiggin himself reported as having delivered one of the many speeches.

Ada hurried up to Pamela, and embraced her warmly. It looked as if they had not met for some time. Pamela's reception of this greeting was less obviously approving of reunion, though her accustomed coldness of manner was not to be constructed as pointer in one direction more than another. Ten years ago they had been on good terms. Since then they might well have quarrelled, moved apart, made friends again, never ceased to be friends. It was impossible to judge from outward signs. Pamela allowed herself to be kissed. She made no attempt to return the ardent flow of words from Ada that followed. No such display of sentiment was to be expected, even if Ada could claim, in the past, to have been Pamela's sole female friend and confidante. No doubt mere acceptance of Ada's continued devotion confirmed no rift had taken place.

'Pam, what are you doing here? You're the last person I'd expected to see. You can't be a member of the Conference?'

Pamela made a face of disgust at the thought.

'What are you doing then?'

'I'm staying here.'

'In the Palazzo—with Mr Bragadin?'

'Of course.'

'Both of you?'

Ada allowed too much unconcealed curiosity to echo in that question for Pamela's taste. Her face hardened. She began to frown. As it turned out, that seemed more from contempt for Ada's crude inquisitiveness, than from displeasure at what she wanted to know. Whatever Pamela's feelings about her husband, she was not prepared to plunge into the heart-to-heart talk about him which Ada's question posed. Ada's tone sounded as if she too had heard Pamela's name connected with the Ferrand-Sénéschal affair. It was more than a conventional enquiry to a wife about her husband. The conventional assumption would in any case have been that Pamela was not accompanied by Widmerpool. Ada was no doubt dying to learn how he was taking this new scandal involving his wife's name; Pamela, perfectly grasping what her friend was after, not at all inclined, there and then, to make a present of the latest news. Instead, she gave Ada a look, hard, understanding, half-threatening, which declared for the present a policy of adjournment in relation to more exciting items.

'He's arriving today.'

'In Venice?'

'Yes.'

This manner of stating Widmerpool's movements re-called the habit of referring always to 'him', rather than using a name. Ada's question was at least answered.

'That awful night-flight? I was a wreck when I arrived at four in the morning.'

Pamela laughed derisively.

'He wasn't man enough to take the night-flight this time. He's on a plane as far as Milan, from there by train.'

Ada was persistent.

'Is he feeling worried then?'

'Why should he be?'

'I don't know. I just wondered. He always has such a lot on his plate, as he himself always says. I must congratulate him on becoming a lord—and you too, darling.'

'Oh, that?'

'Aren't you pleased?'

Pamela did not bother to answer.

'I'm longing for a talk.'

Pamela did not answer that either. She began to frown again. It did not look as if she herself were longing for a talk at all. Her bearing suggested quite the contrary. In spite of such discouragement, Ada rattled on. She was,

94

after all, used to Pamela and her ways. An affection of simplicity was simply part of Ada's tactic. She judged, probably rightly, that even if Pamela's prevailing aspect did not at present show a good disposition towards old acquaintance, that could in due course be overcome.

'How long are you both staying in Venice?'

'I don't know.'

'I've a story I must tell you.'

Ada lowered her voice. Gwinnett, finished with the Longhis, had proceeded on to examination of the Tiepolo. He was moving steadily in our direction. At any moment now opportunity would be offered for putting him in touch with Pamela. Obligation to effect an introduction, so that he could relate her to his work on Trapnel, was not to be ignored. On the other hand, was this the right moment? From Gwinnett's point of view the risk was considerable. Head-on presentation might—almost certainly would—result in one of Pamela's sudden capricious antagonisms, possibly aversion so keen that all further enquiry in her direction woud be at an end. Nevertheless, in whatever manner Gwinnett were to approach her, that eventuality had to be faced. There was no way of guarding against their temperaments proving mutually antipathetic. This was as good a chance as likely to occur. In the case of flat refusal to cooperate, he would have to do the best he could. To bring them together in this neutral spot, even if Gwinnett did not, here and now, speak of Trapnel—an awkward subject to broach in the first few seconds after introduction —circumstances would at least allow him to absorb something of Pamela's personality, useful material for his book he might never secure again, if opportunity were missed. Before I could make up my mind how best to act, Glober, left on his own by Ada's monopoly of Pamela, Shuckerly's of Dr Brightman, began to speak of the ceiling again.

'The way the painter's contrived to illuminate those

locations of dark pigmentation is just great. Dwell on that multi-coloured luminosity of cloud effect. To think I spent twenty-four hours in Jacky's Palazzo before stepping over to gaze.'

Continuous companionship, with the conversation that brought, was necessary to Glober all the time. His manner made one feel even momentary isolation of himself required ending instantly, if he were not to risk grave nervous strain. His words postponed need for decision about bringing together Gwinnett and Pamela. Gwinnett himself came up at that moment, and started off an enquiry of his own.

'Do you know the legend depicted up there? It's not familiar to me.'

Glober, recognizing another American, but taking charge probably more from instinct to speak authoritatively, than because a fellow-countryman had asked the question, stepped in with an answer.

'We've just been told the story by Dr Brightman. It's a great one.'

He proceded to recapitulate, briefly and proficiently. Gwinnett listened with attention. I did not know whether he recognized Glober, nor, if so, whether he wanted to meet him. His own vague manner almost suggested un-awareness that Glober and I had been talking together; that nothing was further from his mind than that Glober should reply to his question. At the same time, one never quite knew with Gwinnett; what he was thinking, how he would behave. That his action in approaching us at that moment was deliberate, premeditated, could not be entirely ruled out.

'Thanks a lot. That's an interesting story.'

Gwinnett evidently meant what he said. Although I was aware of hazards incident on introducing to each other nationals of the same country (Americans not least), without carefully reconnoitring the ground, no alternative was offered. I spoke their names, coupled with that of the college where Gwinnett taught English. He smiled faintly when this was done, but with an impassivity that gave nothing away, least of all any hint that he was already conversant with Glober's reputation. If interested in making this encounter, Gwinnett did not show it, holding his cards to his chest in a manner, to the popular European view, 'un-American'. Anyway, it was in contrast with Glober's exuberance, intact from younger days, tempered with that unnoisy manner which so well suited him. There was nothing in the least forced about Glober's friendliness, none of that sense of inadequacy sometimes noticeable after a gushing approach has lacked basic vitality to sustain its first impact. Glober possessed that inner strength. When he caught Gwinnett's two hands, the gesture managed to be warm, amusing, not at all reckless or overdone.

'One of the rarest signatures too,' he said.

Although he spoke in that quiet way, he might just as well have shouted, from the punch he put into this piece of banter, for, even if complimentary, banter was what it turned out to be. At the time, the bearing was obscure to me, unconnected with Dr Brightman's reference to the surname's link with a 'Signer' family; though I noted inwardly the odd coincidence of Gwinnett himself speaking ironically of Glober being 'able to sign his name'. The conjunction of phrase, a mere chance, made Gwinnett's reply seem the more enigmatic. Later, I wondered whether, in fact, he ever signed his own name without thinking of his ancestor. That was not impossible. At the moment he appeared a little put out, laughing in a deprecatory manner, as he tried to withdraw his fingers from Glober's grip.

'I take care my own signature's a rare one too,' he said. 'Anyway on cheques.'

There was a touch of reproof in this rather knockabout

rejoinder. Gwinnett was probably flattered too. How much flattered was hard to assess, the incident not immediately explicable, its implications only subsequently revealed. Gwinnett was in any case, so it seemed to me, too good an American to persist, after all that, in his earlier, more distant air; to make absolutely unambiguous a preference for different, less overpowering, modes of address between strangers. There was no question of 'putting Glober in his place', an inclination that might easily have emerged in England from a personality of Gwinnett's type. At the same time, to the extent of showing the smallest spark of exuberance himself, he did not at all retreat from his own chosen position, just keeping a dead level of civility, to which exception could not possibly be taken.

In due course, Dr Brightman explained that, among endorsements of the Declaration of Independence, Button Gwinnett's signature happened to be much prized among collectors purposing to possess an example of each. In Gwinnett's light dismissal, as an individual, of Glober's commendatory teasing, in quite another form, something was reminiscent of Pamela's neutralization of Ada's affectionate embrace. Neutralization was the process Gwinnett's manner often called to mind. Pamela's exterior, to the uninformed observer, could have been interpreted as hostile. No hostility was present in Gwinnett's reply, just unspoken announcement of another way of life. If that were hostility, it was to be detected by only the most delicate instrument. Glober himself showed not the smallest awareness of even that antithesis. Constitutionally habituated, simply as a man, to being liked by people, he could have become insensitive to antipathy, unless explicit, alternatively, so intensely conscious of any attitude towards himself short of total surrender, that he was conditioned utterly to conceal any such awareness.

The dissimilarities of these two Americans seemed to put

them into almost every direct opposition in relation to one another: Gwinnett, much the younger, a disturbed background, chancy fortunes, a small but appreciable stake in American history: Glober, of mature age, easy manner, worldly success, recent—not necessarily easy—family origins. One thought of the gladiator with the sword and shield; the one with the net and trident. No doubt gladiators too had in common the typical characteristics of their trade, and something bound Gwinnett and Glober together, perhaps merely their 'Americanness'. One struggled for a phrase to define this characteristic in common, if indeed it existed. An appropriate term warbled across the room from the lips of Quentin Shuckerly.

'So I told Bernard he was just like the lame boy in the Pied Piper, getting left behind as a critic, whenever a fashionable tune was played. I clinched my argument by using a word he didn't know—allotropic—a variation of properties that doesn't change the substance. My dear, the poor man was completely crushed.'

That seemed the term for Glober and Gwinnett, at least how they looked to one across the abyss of uncertainty that precluded definition, with any subtlety, of American types and ways. Meanwhile, the question of whether or not to introduce Gwinnett to Pamela, without saying some preliminary word first, was becoming more urgent than ever. Thinking about allotropy was no help. Then all at once, in a flash, the problem was solved, the Gordian Knot cut, possibly in interplay of that allotropic element. Personal responsibility was all at once removed. Glober, taking Gwinnett by the arm, broke in between Pamela and Ada.

'I want you to meet Professor Gwinnett, Pam. This is Lady Widmerpool, who's stopping in the Palazzo.'

Why Glober did that I could not guess at the time, have never since quite decided. The step may have been due to a compulsive, all-embracing need to arrange, in a manner satisfactory to himself, everyone within orbit—creating an instant court, as Dr Brightman might have said—the spirit in Glober that brought together the Mopsy Pontner dinner party. He may, on the other hand, having favourably marked down Ada, grasped that the simplest way to talk with her for a minute or two would be to occupy Pamela with Gwinnett. Alternatively, the consigning of Gwinnett to Pamela might have appealed to him as a delicate revenge for Gwinnett's latent superciliousness, at least refusal to fall in more amicably with Glober's own more effusive mood. To introduce Gwinnett to Pamela was as likely as not to cause a clash. That clash might be what Glober wished, not necessarily in a mood of retaliation, but with the object of bringing the two of them together for the spectacle, the sheer fun, mildly sadistic, of watching what was likely to be a 'scene'—any scene—in which Pamela was involved. What he certainly did not know was that Gwinnett's highest ambition at that moment was just what had taken place through Glober's own instrumentality.

If Glober sought drama, he was disappointed. At least he was disappointed if he wanted fireworks in the form of violent opposition or bad temper. In another sense—for anyone who knew the stakes for which Gwinnett was playing—the reception he received was intensely dramatic, more so than any brush-off could have been, however defiant. The mere fact that Gwinnett himself, not Pamela, took the offensive was in itself impressive.

'I'd hoped very much to meet you while I was in Venice, Lady Widmerpool. I didn't know I'd have this luck.'

He spoke very simply. Pamela gave him one of her blank stares. She did not speak. At that stage of their meeting it looked as if Gwinnett were going to get, if nothing worse, a characteristic rejection. She allowed him to take her hand, withdrawing it quickly.

'I'm writing a book on X. Trapnel,' Gwinnett said.

He paused. This frontal attack, taking over an active rôle, thrusting Pamela even momentarily into the passive, suggested something of Gwinnett's potential. He said the words quietly, quite a different quietness from Glober's, though suggesting something of the same muted strength. They were spoken almost casually, a statement just given for information, no more, before going on to speak of other things. There was no question of blurting out in an uncontrolled manner the nature of his 'project', what he wanted for it from her. To use such a tone was to tackle the approach in an effective, possibly the only effective, manner. It exhibited a fine appreciation of the fact that to gain Pamela's cooperation with regard to the biography was a matter of now or never. He must sink or swim. Gwinnett undoubtedly saw that. I admired him for attempting no compromise. There was again a parallel between Gwinnett's tone with Pamela, and the way he had replied to Glober, the one conveying only the merest atom of overt friendliness, just as the other conveyed possibly the reverse, difference between the two almost imperceptible. While this had been taking place, Glober had transferred his attention to Ada. They were chattering away together as if friends for years.

'I think you knew him,' said Gwinnett. 'Trapnel, I mean.'

Pamela, who had as usual registered no immediate outward reaction to his first statement, still remained silent. Gwinnett was silent too. In that, he showed his strength. After making the initial announcement of his position, he made no effort to develop the situation. They stood looking at each other. There was a long pause during which one felt anything might happen: Pamela walk away: burst out laughing: overwhelm Gwinnett with abuse: strike him in the face. After what seemed several minutes, but could only have been a second or two, Pamela spoke. Her voice was low.

'Poor X,' she said.

She sounded deeply moved, not far from tears. Gwinnett inclined his head a little. That movement was no more than a quiver, quick, awkward, at the same time reverential in its way, wholly without affectation. He too seemed to feel strong emotion. Something had been achieved between them.

'Yes—Trapnel wasn't always a lucky guy it seems.'

Now, it had become Trapnel's turn to join the dynasty of Pamela's dead lovers. Emotional warmth in her was directed only towards the dead, men who had played some part in her life, but were no more there to do so. That was how it looked. The first time we had ever talked together, she had described herself as 'close' to her uncle, Charles Stringham, almost suggesting a sexual relationship. Stringham's circumstances made nothing more unlikely, in any physical form, although, in the last resort, close relationship of a sexual kind does not perhaps necessarily require such expression, something even undesired, except in infinitely sublimated shape. When, for example, Pamela had been racketing round during the war, with all sorts of lovers, from all sorts of nations, she had refused to give herself to Peter Templer (in his own words 'mad about her'); after he was killed calling him the 'nicest man I ever knew'.

Trapnel, whose rapid declension as a writer had been substantially accelerated by Pamela's own efforts, notably destruction of his manuscript, was now to be rehabilitated, memorialized, placed in historical perspective, among those loves with whom, but for unhappy chance, all might have been well. It was Death she liked. Mrs Erdleigh had hinted as much on the night of the flying-bombs. Would Gwinnett be able to offer her Death? At least, in managing to catch and hold the frail line cast to him, he had not made a bad beginning. There was hope for his book. Glober, after instigating the Gwinnett/Pamela conversation, must now have decided to put an end to it, having said all he wanted to say to Ada. Seeing out of the corner of his eye that Gwinnett's communion with Pamela produced no immediately lively incident, he may have judged it better to cut it short. Pamela herself anticipated anything he might be about to say.

'Why didn't you explain at first Professor Gwinnett was the man you need for the Trapnel film?'

Glober was not quite prepared for that question. It opened up a new subject. Pamela turned to Gwinnett again.

'Louis wants to make a last film. I've told him it's to be based on the Trapnel novel that got destroyed. X himself said there was a film there. I've been telling Louis the best parts of the book, which I remember absolutely. He's not very quick about taking facts in, but he's got round to this as a proposition.'

Glober smiled, but made no effort to elaborate the subject put forward.

'Naturally I never read the last novel,' said Gwinnett. 'Did it have close bearing on Trapnel's own life.'

'Of course.'

Circumstances came to Glober's aid at that moment, in the manner they do with persons of adventurous temperament put in momentary difficulty. He brought an abrupt end to the matter being discussed by jerking his head towards the far side of the room.

'Here's Baby—with your husband.'

Two persons, without much ceremony, were forcing a channel between the dense accumulation of intellectuals, pottering about or gazing upward. One of these new arrivals was Widmerpool, the other a smartly dressed woman of about the same age-group. Widmerpool was undoubtedly seeking his wife. Even at a distance, symptoms of that condition were easily recognizable. They were a little different, a little more agitated, than any of his other outward displays of personal disturbance. As he pushed his way through the crowd, he had the look of a man who had not slept for several nights. No doubt the journey, even by train, had been tiring, but hardly trying enough to cause such an expression of worried annoyance, irritation merging into fear.

Thinner than in his younger days, Widmerpool was less bald than Glober, even if such hair as remained was sparse and grizzled. Rather absurdly, I was a little taken aback by this elderly appearance, physical changes in persons known for a long time always causing a certain inner uneasiness— Umfraville's sense of being let down by the rapidity with which friends and acquaintances decay, once the process has begun. Widmerpool's air of discomfort was by no means decreased by the heavy texture, in spite of the hot weather, of the dark suit he wore. Built for him when more bulky, it hung about his body in loose folds, like clothes on a scarecrow. He seemed to have come straight from the City; having regard to recent elevation in rank, more probably the House of Lords.

The woman with him was Baby Wentworth—or whatever she was now called. When last heard of, she had been married to an Italian. I remembered her beauty, sly look, short curly hair, thirty years before, when, supposedly mistress of Sir Magnus Donners, she had also been pursued, at different levels, by both Prince Theodoric and Barnby. Now in her fifties, Baby had not at all lost her smart appearance—she too wore trousers—but, if she looked less than her age, her features also registered considerable ups and downs of fortune. She made towards Glober, abandoned again by Pamela who had resumed talk with Gwinnett. Widmerpool went straight for his wife, inserting himself without apology between her and Gwinnett, in order to reduce delay in speaking to a minimum.

'Pam—I want a word in private at once.'

Gwinnett took a step back to allow Widmerpool easier passage. No doubt he guessed the relationship. Pamela, on the other hand, showed not the least recognition of the fact that her husband had just arrived. She took no notice of him whatsoever. Instead of offering any facility for speech, she quickly moved sideways and forward, again decreasing distance between Gwinnett and herself, blocking Widmerpool's way, so that she could continue a conversation, which, so far as could be judged, was going relatively well.

'Pam . . .'

Pamela threw him a glance. Her manner suggested that a man—a very unprepossessing man at that—was trying to pick her up in a public place; some uncouth sightseer, not even a member of the Conference, having gained access to the Palazzo because the door was open, was now going round accosting ladies encountered there. Widmerpool persisted.

'You must come with me. It's urgent.'

She answered now without turning her head.

'Do go away. I heard you the first time. Can't you take a hint? I'm being shown round the house by Louis Glober. You knew he was going to be staying with Jacky. At the moment I'm talking about a rather important matter to Professor Gwinnett.'

Widmerpool's reaction to this treatment was complex. On the one hand, he was obviously not at all surprised by blank refusal to cooperate; on the other, he could not be said to have received that refusal with anything like indifference. He paused for a moment, apparently analysing means of forcing his wife to obey; then he must have decided against any such attempt. His expression suggested the existence of one or two tricks up his sleeve, to be played

105

when they were alone together. He was about to move away, return from wherever he had come, but, catching sight of me, stopped and nodded. Recognition evidently suggested more to him than the fact that we had not met since the night of the Election party. He went straight to the point, his manner confirming existence of some problem on his mind desperate to solve.

'Nicholas, how are you? Staying with Jacky Bragadin? No—then you are almost certainly a member of this Conference going round? That is what I expected. Just the man I want to talk to.'

'Congratulations on the peerage.'

'Ah, yes. Thank you very much. Not very contemporary, such a designation sounds today, but it has its advantages. I didn't want to leave the Commons, no one less. 1955 may have been a moral victory—several of my constituents described my campaign as a greater *personal* triumph than the previous poll, when I was returned—but past efforts were forgotten in a fight that was not always a clean one. As I still have a lot of work in me, the Upper Chamber, so long as it hangs on, seemed as good a place to do that work as any other. As it happens, my normal activities are rather impeded at the moment by a number of irksome matters, indeed one domestic tragedy, since my mother passed away only a few days ago at her cottage in Kirkcudbrightshire, which she always spoke of as an ideal home for her declining years. She had reached a ripe age, so that the end was not unexpected. Unfortunately, it was quite impossible for me to make a journey as far as Scotland at this particular moment. I could not attempt it. At the same time, it was painful to leave a matter like my mother's burial in the hands of a secretary, competent as my own secretary happens to be. Something a little over and above routine competence is required at such a moment. None the less, that was what had to be done. I couldn't be in Kirkcudbright-

106

shire and Venice at the same time, and, little as I like the place, I had to come to Venice.'

He stopped, overwhelmed by his troubles. I did not know why I was being told all this. Widmerpool's jaws worked up and down. He gave the impression of hesitation in asking some question. I enquired if he were in Venice on business, since he did not care for the city in other respects.

'Yes—no—not really. A slight rest. Pamela wanted a short rest. To be quiet, out of things, just for a little. You may be able to help me, as a matter of fact, in something I want to know. Your Conference has been going on for a day or two?'

'Yes.'

'You meet and mix with the other members—the foreign ones, I mean?'

'Some of them.'

'I was hoping to kill two birds with one stone. Pamela was given an open invitation to stay in this imposing residence. The owner—Bragadin—is one of the smart international set, I understand, what the papers call café society, I'm told. All that sort of thing is a mystery to me. Distasteful too, in the highest degree. At the same time, it was convenient for Pamela to take a rest, even if in a style I myself cannot approve. But to get back to the Conference, am I right in supposing all these people round about are its members? I am. There chances to be one of them I am particularly anxious to meet, if here. It is a most lucky opportunity the two things coincided.'

'The Conference, and your visit?'

'Yes, yes. That is what I mean. Have you run across Dr Belkin? He is familiar to me only by name, through certain cultural societies to which I belong. By an unhappy mischance, we have never set eyes on each other, though we have corresponded—on cultural matters, of course. He was, incidentally, a mutual friend of poor Ferrand-Sénéschal.

107

How sad that too. I am, of course, not sure that Dr Belkin will have been able to put in an appearance. He could have become too much occupied in the cultural affairs of his own country, in which he plays a central part. They may not have been able to spare him at the last moment. He is a busy man. Belkin? Dr Belkin? Have you heard anything of him, or seen him?'

I was about to answer that the name was unknown to me, when Pamela, overhearing Widmerpool's strained, eager tone, got her word in first. She turned from where she stood with Gwinnett, looked straight at her husband, and laughed outright. It was not a friendly laugh.

'You won't find your friend Belkin here.'

She spoke under her breath, almost in a hiss, still laughing. Widmerpool's face altered. He swallowed uneasily. When he replied he was quite calm.

'What do you mean?'

'What I say.'

'You only know about Belkin because you've heard me refer to him.'

'That's sufficient.'

'What information have you got regarding him then?'

'Just what you've told me. And a few small items I've picked up elsewhere.'

'But I haven't told you anything—I—that was what I wanted to talk to you about.'

'You don't have to.'

'Why should you think he won't be here? You don't know him personally any more than I do. Nothing I've said gave you any reason to draw that conclusion. Only quite a recent development makes me want to meet him rather urgently.'

'It wasn't what *you* said. It was what Léon-Joseph said.'

Considering the circumstances, Widmerpool took that comment stoically, though he was showing signs of strain.

He seemed to want most to get to the bottom of Pamela's insinuation.

'He told you this before he . . .'

Widmerpool put the question composedly, as if what had happened to Ferrand-Sénéschal did not matter much, only out of respect he did not name it.

'No,' said Pamela, also speaking quietly. 'He told me after he'd died, of course—Léon-Joseph appeared to me as a ghost last night, and gave the information. He was gliding down the Grand Canal, walking on the water like Jesus, except that he was carrying his head under his arm like Mary Queen of Scots. I recognized the head by those blubber lips and rimless spectacles. The blubber lips spoke the words: "A cause de ses sentiments stalinistes, Belkin est foutu." '

Widmerpool appeared more disconcerted by the implications of Pamela's words than resentful of their ironic intonation. She said no more for the moment, returning to Gwinnett, who had politely moved a little to one side, when she broke off to take part in this last interchange. He must by then know for certain she was engaged with her husband. Opportunity was now more available than earlier to estimate Pamela's potentialities. This readiness of Gwinnett's to withdraw into the background showed comprehension. Widmerpool again thought things over for a moment. Then he made a step in his wife's direction. Once more Gwinnett moved away. Widmerpool was fairly angry now. Anger and fright seemed to make up his combined emotions.

'If this is true—Léon-Joseph really told you something of the kind before he died—why on earth didn't you pass it on?'

'Why should I?'

'*Why should you?*'

'Yes?'

Widmerpool, almost shaking now, was just able to control himself.

'You know its importance—if true ... which I doubt ...
the whole point of making this contact ... the consequences
... you know perfectly well what I mean ...'

It looked as if the consequences, whatever they were likely
to be, remained too awesome to put into words. Pamela
turned her head away, and upward. Resting lightly the tips
of her fingers on her hips, she leant slowly back on her
heels, revealing to advantage the slimness of her still
immensely graceful neck. She tipped her head slightly to
one side, apparently lost once more in fascination by the
legend of Candaules and Gyges. Widmerpool could stand
this treatment no longer. He burst out.

'What are you looking at? Answer my question. This is
a serious matter, I tell you.'

Pamela did not reply at once. When she did so, she spoke
in the absent strain of someone who has just made an
absorbing discovery.

'There's a picture up there of a man exhibiting his naked
wife to a friend. Have you inspected it yet?'

Widmerpool did not reply this time. His face was yellow.
The look he gave her suggested that, of all things living,
she was the most abhorrent to him. Pamela continued her
soft, almost cooing commentary, a voice in complete contrast with her earlier sullenness.

'I know you can't tell one picture from another, haven't
the slightest idea what those square, flat, brightly coloured
surfaces are, which people put in frames, and hang on their
walls, or why they hang them there. You probably think
they conceal safes with money in them, or compromising
documents, possibly dirty books and postcards. The favourite
things you think it better to keep hidden away. All the
same, the subject of this particular picture might catch your
attention—for instance remind you of those photographs
shut up in the secret drawer of that desk you sometimes
forget to lock. I didn't know about them till the other day.

I didn't even know you'd taken them. Wasn't that innocent of me? How Léon-Joseph laughed, when I told him. You were careless to forget about turning the key.'

Widmerpool had gone a pasty yellowish colour when his wife quoted Ferrand-Sénéschal's alleged conjecture about Dr Belkin's reasons for absenting himself from the Conference. Now the blood came back into his face, turning it brick red. He was furious. Even so, he must have grasped that whatever had to be said must wait for privacy. He made a powerful effort at self-control, which could not be concealed. Then he spoke quite soberly.

'You don't know how things stand, why it was necessary for me to come here. When you do, you will see you are being rather silly. There have been unfortunate developments certainly, absurd ones. Even if Belkin does not turn up, there will be a way out, but, if he is here, that will be easier. We'll have a talk later about the best way of handling matters. This may concern you as much as me, so please do not be frivolous about it.'

Pamela was uninterested.

'I haven't the least idea what matters need handling. Oh, yes—the picture on the ceiling? You mean that? You want more explanation? Well, the wife there, whose husband arranged for his chum to have a peep at her in that charming manner, handled things by getting the chum who'd enjoyed the eyeful to do the husband in.'

She looked about for Gwinnett again. He was on the other side of the room, in front of a highly coloured piece of Venetian eighteenth-century sculpture, torso of a Turk. Gwinnett was examining the elaborate folds of the marble turban. Pamela went to join him. There could be no doubt she was interested in Gwinnett. What had taken place between the Widmerpools had attracted no attention from surrounding members of the Conference, nor Bragadin guests. Gwinnett himself could hardly have failed to notice its earlier pungency, but may not have caught the drift. Pamela might well be on her way to give him an account of that. Perhaps his Trapnel studies had prepared him for something of the sort; perhaps he supposed this the manner English married couples normally behaved. Considering the things said, both Widmerpools could have appeared outwardly unruffled, the colour of Widmerpool's face reasonably attributable to the heat of the day, and texture of his clothes. He still seemed uncertain whether or not his wife had spoken with authority on the subject of Belkin. He looked at her questioningly for a second. When he turned to me again, his thoughts were far away.

'I wonder what's the best course to take about Belkin. The first thing to do is to make sure whether or not he's here. How can I find that out?'

'Ask one of the Executive Committee. Dr Brightman, over there, would know whom to tackle. She's talking to our host.'

Jacky Bragadin, not paying much attention to whatever Dr Brightman was saying to him, was casting anxious glances round the room. A few members of the Conference had begun to drift into the farther gallery, by far the larger majority continuing to contemplate the Tiepolo. Jacky Bragadin seemed to fear the story of Candaules and Gyges had hypnotized them, caused an aesthetic catalepsy to descend. Their state threatened to turn his home into a sort of Sleeping Beauty's Palace, rows of inert vertical figures of intellectuals, for ever straining sightless eyes upward towards the ceiling, impossible to eject from where they stood. He waved his hands.

'This way,' he cried. 'This way.'

He may have been merely regretful that his guests should exhaust so much appreciation on this single aspect, even if a highly prized one, of his treasures, anxious that should not be done to detriment of other splendid items. Most likely of all, he wanted to get us out of the place, hoped our sightseeing would be undertaken with all possible dispatch, leaving him and his guests in peace; or whatever passed for peace in such a house-party. One wondered how he could ever have been foolhardy enough to have presented Pamela with an open invitation to stay any time she liked. The cause, in his case, would not have been love. Possibly he had never done so. She had forced herself on him. It was waste of time to speculate how the Widmerpools had managed to install themselves in the Palazzo. Jacky Bragadin, like most rich people, was well able to attend to his own interests. He must have had his reasons.

'This way,' he repeated. 'This way.'

He tried to encourage the more obdurate loiterers with smiles and beckonings. They would not be persuaded. He gave it up for a moment. Dr Brightman pinned him down again. Glober reappeared beside Widmerpool and myself.

'Mr Jenkins, I want you and Signora Clarini to meet. Signora Clarini is stopping in the Palazzo too. Her husband's name you'll know, the celebrated Italian director.'

I explained Baby and I had already met, though contacts had been slight, ages before. In those days, soon after her own association with Sir Magnus Donners, the Italian husband had then been spoken of as satisfactory to herself, even if of dubious occupation. Now he was no longer dubious, he must also have become less satisfactory, because Baby seemed displeased at his name being dragged in. Glober, on hearing she and I had met, struck an amused pose, as always personal to himself, if to some extent drawn from that deep fund of American schematized humour, of which, in a more sparing and austere technique, Colonel Cobb had been something of a master. Glober was not at all displeased to find earlier knowledge of Baby would un-equivocally demonstrate the sort of woman prepared to run after him; an undertaking on which she certainly seemed engaged.

'Baby, I believe you've met every man in the Eastern Hemisphere, and quite a few in the Western too.'

Possibly a small touch of malice was voiced. Baby may have thought that. She looked sulky. I remembered Barnby's passion for her, his comment how Sir Magnus never minded his girls having other commitments. That was hardly a subject to bridge our once slender acquaintance. Her manner, not outstandingly friendly, minimally accepted former meetings had taken place.

'Aren't you fed up with this heat?' she said. 'Everybody's dripping. Look at Louis. Isn't he a disgusting sight?'

Glober murmured consciously good-natured protests. 'Am I, Baby? But not everyone. Look at Lord Widmerpool, he's fresh as a daisy. I believe he's right to take that Milan route. I'll do the same myself next time.'

Drawing attention in this manner to Widmerpool's appearance was indication that Glober made no pretence of liking him. Baby did not even smile. Her demeanour wafted through the Tiepolo room a breath of the Nineteen-Twenties. Like one who hands on the torch of a past era of folk culture, she had somehow preserved intact, from ballroom and plage, golf course and hunting field, a social technique fashionable then, even considered alluring. This rather unblissful breeze blowing across the years recalled a little Widmerpool's former fiancée, Mrs Haycock (Baby's distant cousin), though Baby herself had always been far the better-looking. She stopped a long way short of displaying the stigmata a lifetime of late parties and casual love affairs had bestowed on Mrs Haycock. Nevertheless, she had developed some of the same masculine hardening of the features, voice rising to a bark, elements veering in the direction of sex-change, threatened by too constant adjustment of husbands and lovers; comparable with the feminine characteristics acquired from too pertinacious womanizing.

'Are you hopping over to the Lido for a dip this evening, Louis? A bathe will do you good. Freshen you up. Then I'm going to visit Mrs Erdleigh, the famous clairvoyante, who's in Venice. Why don't you come there too? She'll tell your fortune.'

Glober shook his head glumly at the thought of looking into the future. He showed no great keenness to bathe either.

'I'll have to think about the Lido. Get my priorities straight.'

Widmerpool was becoming impatient again.

'Your Dr Brightman is talking for a very long time,' he said. 'Who is she?'

'A very distinguished scholar.'

'Oh.'

Jacky Bragadin was as eager to get away from Dr Brightman as Widmerpool to be put in contact with her. In Jacky Bragadin's efforts to escape, the two of them arrived beside us. Dr Brightman swept everyone in.

'I've been talking to our host about his Foundation. I thought something might be done for Russell Gwinnett. Where's he gone?'

'It must be on paper,' said Jacky Bragadin. 'Always on paper. The name sent to the Board. They look into such matters.'

He sounded desperate. Dr Brightman, pausing to explain that I wrote novels, ignored his misery. The information made Jacky Bragadin horribly uneasy, but at least resulted in a let-out from further discussion of his Foundation. I told Dr Brightman that Widmerpool wanted to meet one of the Executive Committee. At that she began to question Widmerpool too. Without great originality of subject matter, I spoke to Jacky Bragadin of the beauty of the ceiling.

'Nice colour,' he said, his heart not in the words.

'We were discussing the story—'

Jacky Bragadin's despair began rapidly to increase again at that. He laid his hand on my sleeve beseechingly.

'You must see the other rooms . . . They all must . . .'

He peered, without much hope, at Baby, still trying to persuade Glober to bathe. Widmerpool and Dr Brightman went off together, presumably to try and find a member of the Executive Committee. Most of the other members of the Conference, including Ada and Shuckerly, had begun to filter into the next room, a small backwash of Tiepolo enthusiasts from time to time borne back on an incoming current to take another look. Among these last was Gwinnett. Pamela was no longer to be seen. Gwinnett seemed by then rather dazed.

'How was it? You seemed to be making good going?'

'Lady Widmerpool's agreed to talk about Trapnel.'

'She has?'

'That's as I understand it.'

'Fine.'

'If she sticks to that. She's said some amazing things already.'

'You brought off quite a quick bit of work.'

'Do you think so?'

He appeared uncertain.

'At least we're going to meet again,' he said.

'What could be better than that?'

'Where do you think she's arranged to meet?'

'I can't guess.'

'Try.'

'Harry's Bar?'

Gwinnett shook his head.

'St Mark's.'

'In the Piazza?'

'In the Basilica.'

'Any particular place in the church?'

'She just said she'd be there at a certain time.'

'On, on . . .' pleaded Jacky Bragadin. 'On, on . . .'

3

Daniel Tokenhouse rang up the following morning to acknowledge my notification of arrival in Venice. I was still in bed when he telephoned, though breakfast had been ordered. In keeping with an instinctive determination to hold the moral advantage, he made a point of ascertaining that I was not yet up. On the line, he sounded in tolerably good form, brisk, peremptory, as always. I had not expected him to be in the least senile, but the sharpness of his manner may have been amplified by some apprehension, shared by myself, that changes must have taken place in both of us during the last twenty years, which could prove mutually disenchanting.

'How are you, Dan?'

'In rude health. Working hard, as ever. Been up painting since half-past six this morning. Hate staying in bed. You'll find developments in my style. I shall be interested to hear what you think of them.'

Complete absorption in himself, and his own doings, always characterized Tokenhouse, a temperament that had served him pretty well in getting through what must have been, on the whole, rather a solitary life, especially of late years. He had in no way relaxed this solipsistic standpoint.

'When can your works be seen?'

'I've been thinking about that. Sunday morning would

suit me best. You will not be in conference then, I trust, with your fellow intellectuals? I hope they are proving themselves worthy of their proud designation. Come about twelve o'clock midday—half-past eleven, if you prefer. That will give us more time. Do not fear. I shall not be attending matins.'

He gave his high, unamused laugh.

'How do I reach you, Dan?'

'I live, I am thankful to say, in a spot quite off the beaten track of that horrible fellow, the tourist. Among the people of Venice. The real people. I could not remain here an hour otherwise. My flat is in the quarter of the Arsenal, if you know where that is, a calle off the Via Garibaldi. You take an accelerato, then a short walk along the Riva Ca Di Dio and Riva Biagio. Let me explain the exact whereabouts, for it is not at all easy to find.'

He gave minute instructions, forcibly bringing back the years when I had worked under him, something establishing a relationship which can never wholly fade.

'Afterwards, I thought, we might walk as far as the Biennale together. I have not seen the latest Exhibition yet. I should like you to lunch with me at the restaurant in the Giardini.'

'I'll be with you, Dan, between half-past eleven and twelve on Sunday.'

'You may not care for the sort of work I am doing now. I warn you of that. Are you sure you know how to get here? Let me repeat my instructions.'

He went over the directions with that pedantic attention to detail natural to him, dilated by army training.

'Have you got it? Remember, an accelerato. When you disembark, turn to the right, walk straight on, then bear left, left again, then right—not left, remember—then right again. It's over a greengrocer's. Walk straight up.'

When Sunday morning came, the place turned out quite

easy to find. It was a characteristic Tokenhouse abode, which, freedom from sound of traffic apart, might have been situated in an alley-way of some down-at-heel district of London, or anywhere else, all architectural and local emphasis as negative as possible; exceptional only insomuch as to discover—elect to inhabit—so featureless a location in Venice was in itself a shade impressive. I climbed the stairs and knocked. The door opened immediately, as if Tokenhouse had been already gripping the handle, impatiently awaiting someone to arrive.

'Hullo, Dan.'

'Come in, come in. Through here. This is the room where I paint.'

The windows faced on to a blank wall. Except for a pile of canvases, none of great size, stacked in one corner, the room showed no sign of being an artist's studio. It was scrupulously neat, suggesting for some perverse reason— possibly actual by-product of its owner's intense anti-clericalism—sense of arrival in the study of an urban vicarage or rectory, including an indefinably churchly smell.

'Did it take you long to get here? No? Not after my detailed instructions, I expect. They were necessary. How are you? What is your hotel like? I know it by name. I can't bear that fashionable end of the Canal. It gets worse every year. I continue to live in Venice only because I am used to the place by now. At my age it would be a great business to move. Besides, there are advantages. One can make oneself useful.'

He rapped his knuckles together several times, and nodded. In spite of the parsonic overtones of the sitting-room-studio, Tokenhouse himself did not look at all like a clergyman; nor even the very reasonably successful publisher of art books he had been in his time. Acquired erudition, heterodox opinions, expatriate domicile, none had done anything to alter deep dyed marks of the military

119

profession, an appearance, one imagined, Tokenhouse would not have chosen. At the same time, if aware of looking like a retired soldier, even heartily disliking that, he would have considered dishonest any effort at diminishment brought about by artificial means, such as wearing relatively unconformist clothes. His clothes, in one sense, certainly were unconformist, but not at all with that object in view. Spare, wiry, very upright, he could be thought dried up, wizened, ascetic; considering his years, not particularly old. His body seemed made up of gristle, rather than flesh; grey hair, trimmed severely, almost *en brosse*, remaining thick. He peered alertly, rather peevishly, through gold-rimmed spectacles set well forward on a long thin reddish nose. An all-enveloping chilliness of manner hung about him, sense of being utterly cut off from the rest of the world, a personality, even physique, no sun could warm. Unlike Widmerpool, sweltering in his House of Lords suit, the ancient jacket Tokenhouse wore, good thick serviceable tweed, designed to keep out damp wind on the moors, his even older flannel trousers punctiliously pressed, seemed between them garments scarcely substantial enough to prevent him looking blue with cold, in spite of blazing Venetian sunlight outside.

'How are your family? You have children of your own almost grown up now, I believe? Is that not so?'

He spoke as if procreation of children were an extraordinary fate to overtake anyone, consequence of imprudence, if not worse. We talked for a time of things that had happened since our last meeting.

'Your father and I parted on bad terms. There was no other way. He could never see reason. An entirely unphilosophic mind. Childish view of politics. Now he is dead. Most of the people I used to know are dead. I don't find that makes much difference to me. I have learnt to be self-supporting. It is the only way. No good thinking about the past. The future is what matters. But you said you would like to see some of my work. Then we'll go to the Exhibition. The Gardens are within walking distance. The pictures aren't much good this year, I'm told, but let's look at my work first, if that is what you would like.'

Moving jerkily across the room, he returned once more with some of the unframed canvases, chosen from the pile that lay in the corner. He spread out several of these, propping them up against chairs.

'You've certainly changed your style, Dan.'

'True, O King.'

That had always been a favourite expression of Tokenhouse's, especially when not best pleased. I tried to think of something to say. The Camden Town Group had been wholly superseded, utterly swept away, so far as the art of Daniel Tokenhouse was concerned. What had taken its place was less easy to define; a sort of neo-primitivism. The light was bad for forming a judgment. So revolutionary was the transformation that a happy phrase to cover just what had happened did not come easily to mind. The new Tokenhouse style, in one of its expressions, suggested frescoes, frescoes on a very small scale; not at all in the manner of, say, Barnby's murals once decorating the entrance to the Donners-Brebner Building. After some minutes, Tokenhouse himself making no comment, I felt compelled to pronounce a judgment, however insipid.

'The garage scene has considerable force. Its colour emotive too, limiting yourself in that way to an almost regular monochrome, picked out with passages of flat heavy black.'

'You mean this study?'

'Both of those. Aren't they the same group from another angle?'

'Yes, this is another shot. Three in all. The subject is *Four priests rigging a miracle*. The rather larger version here, and its fellow, are less successful, I think. At the same time both have merit of a sort.'

'You always make several studies of the same subject nowadays?'

'I find that produces the best results. I work slowly. That comes from lack of early training. My difficulty is usually to get the values correctly.'

'The browns, greys and blacks seem to create an effective recession.'

'Ah, you have misunderstood me. Having, so to speak, forged ahead politically myself, it is easy to forget other people remain content with old notions of painting, formalistic ones. I meant, of course, that it is not always plain sailing so far as political values are concerned. I am no longer interested in such purely technical achievements as correct recession, so called, or making a kind of pattern.'

'Still, incorrect recession can surely play havoc—unless, of course, deliberate distortion is in question. Was your change of technique gradual?'

Tokenhouse gave a restive intake of breath to show how wildly he had been misunderstood.

'One forgets, one forgets. Let me explain. I had begun to feel very impatient with Formalism, the sort of painting that derived from Impressionists and Post-Impressionists, not to mention their successors, such as the Surrealists—as I prefer to call them, Pseudo-Realists. I thought about it all a lot. I long pondered the phrase read somewhere: "A picture is an act of Socialism." I don't expect you're familiar with that approach. You may not agree anyway. Your dissent is immaterial to me. I made up my mind to embark on a fresh start. I began by taking a bus over the bridge to Mestre, and attempting some *plein air* studies. I set about one of those large installations there—hydro-electric, or whatever they are—a suitably functional conception. Absurd as that may seem, I created the impression of being engaged on some sort of industrial espionage. Nothing serious happened, but it was all rather tedious and discouraging. Much more important than the interfering attitude of the authorities was my own fear that Impressionist errors were creeping back, just as fallaciously as if I was one of the old ladies sitting on a camp-stool in front of the Salute. In short, I comprehended I was still hopelessly aesthetic.'

'I'd never call you an aesthete, Dan.'

Tokenhouse laughed shortly.

'Certainly not in the nineteenth-century use of the word. All the same, you have to watch yourself. We all have to. That was specially true of my next phase, when I thought I would try Political Symbolism. The effect was very mixed. I've painted-over quite a lot of them, wiped them out completely. This is one of the rather better efforts I preserved. It was completed quite soon after my breach with retrospection—accepting the past, I mean, simply as a point of departure. The important thing was I had learnt by then that Naturalism was not enough.'

'Like patriotism?'

Tokenhouse paid no attention, either because he never cared for flippancy, or, more likely, had passed beyond paying attention to most remarks made by other people. He had begun to speak quickly, excitedly, almost gabbling this account of his own development as a painter, reciting his painting creed like a lesson learnt by heart.

'I suddenly saw in a flash, a revelation, that I could not retain any remnant of self-respect, if I gave way to Formalism again in the slightest degree. I *must* satisfy my own conviction that a new ideological content had to be infused into painting, one free of all taint of neutrality. That was just as important for an amateur like myself, as for a professional painter of long standing and successful attainment.'

Like an onlooker dexterously exposing an attempt to deceive in manipulation of the Three-Card Trick, Tokenhouse seized the three studies of miracle-rigging priests, two in his right hand, one in his left, with incredible speed setting in their place a single example of his interim period. It was larger in size than earlier exhibits, brighter in colour. Most of his pictures, Formalist or Reformed, were apt to end up a superfluity of brownish-carmine tones. This latest canvas, vermilion and light cobalt, showed the origins of the fresco technique in representation of what were evidently factory workers, stripped to the waist, pushing over a precipice a disordered group of kings and bishops, easily recognizable by their crowns and mitres. Perhaps deliberately, treatment of posture and movement was a trifle wooden, but the painter had clearly taken a certain pleasure in depicting irresolute terror in the features of monarchs and ecclesiastics toppling into the abyss. The subject suggested, not for the first time in the character of Tokenhouse, a touch of muted sadism, revealed occasionally in conversation, otherwise kept, so far as one knew, in check.

'I found Politico-Symbolism, for a person of my limited imaginative faculties, a *cul de sac*. My aim latterly has been to depict social injustice in as straightforward a manner as possible, compatible with avoiding that too passive Realism of which I have spoken. My own constricted skill' has prevented me from attempting some of the more ambitious subjects I have in mind, though I like to think there are signs of improvement. Ah-ha, you do too? I am glad. It is simply a question of documentation in the last resort. You meditate along the correct political lines, the picture almost paints itself. Look at this—and this.'

We inspected a representative collection of Tokenhouse's more recent work.

'I don't want to bore you with my efforts. Shall we set out for the Biennale? If you want to see more, we could look in again after lunch, but I expect you've had enough by now.'

He found an ashplant walking-stick, placed on his head a battered grey hat with a greenish-black ribbon, turned down the brim all round, opened the door of the flat. We set off for the Giardini, Tokenhouse at his habitual short rapid stride, a military quickstep, suggesting chronic fear of unpunctuality. He hurried along, hobnailed shoes grinding the cobbles.

'I'm feeling rather pleased about a letter received this morning. I've been revising my will, terms that may surprise some people, among others making the lawyers agree to insert a clause for no religious ceremony at the funeral. They didn't like it. Don't like that sort of thing, even these days. I had my way. No nonsense of that sort. Well, tell me about your Conference. What do you all discuss? Plenty of nonsense talked there, I'll be bound.'

'The Philosophy of Engagement—Obligations of the Writer—the Arts in relation to World Government—all that sort of thing.'

'Ah-ha, yes. There can be serious sides to such questions, but they are rarely tackled. Now those attending your Conference, do any emigré writers from the USSR, or Balkan countries, turn up there? One would be interested to hear what such people are saying and thinking, especially the Russians. For example how they react to the "thaw", as people call it. I've been looking through a novel called *Dr Zhivago*. I expect you've heard of it. It's been given a good deal of publicity. I suppose that sort of book, purporting as it does to present the point of view of certain members of a generation very much on their way out, might give a certain amount of satisfaction to expatriate Russians? Those who've chosen to dissociate themselves from the great developments taking place in their country. It would gratify them, a book like that, by stilling their self-reproach. Have you come across instances of that? One would be interested to hear.'

'I haven't met any emigré Russians at the Conference. I couldn't swear none are there.'

'Which again reminds me. There's a certain Dr Belkin who might have turned up. He visits Venice from time to time. Usually lets me know at the last moment.'

'Not an emigré?'

'No, no. Far from it. A man of the soundest views in his own country. He informed me some little while ago he might be looking in on this congress, or one about this time. He enjoys coming to Venice, because he's devoted to painting. He's even kind enough to be interested in my own humble brush. Of course my sort of painting is practised comparatively little in Western Europe. Nice of him to include a novice like myself in his survey. He's been to visit me several times. Naturally we see eye to eye politically.'

'Somebody else was asking about him.'

'Belkin has many friends. I do what I can to keep him up to date about books and things. Hold them for him some-times, if he's afraid they'll go astray in the post. That avoids delay in the long run. He admits his own impatience with some of the bureaucracy unavoidable in getting an entirely new system of government working, a revolutionary one. We all have to face that. There's quite a lot of stuff he prefers to collect personally when he turns up here.'

'Somebody said they thought he wouldn't be able to come to the Conference.'

'Very possibly not. It's of no great importance. I can hold his stuff for him. I always like to see Belkin. Such a cheerful fellow. Full of ideas. Where does this Conference of yours meet?'

'Over there on San Giorgio.'

A mist of heat hung over the dome and white campanile, beyond the glittering greenish stretch of water, across the surface of which needles of light perpetually flashed. It was so calm the halcyon's fabled nest seemed just to have floated by, subduing the faintest tremor of wind and wave. We reached the Gardens, and entered the cool of the lime trees. Tokenhouse made for the enclosure permanently consecrated to the cluster of strange little pavilions, which, every two years, house pictures and sculpture by which each country of the world chooses to be known to an international public.

'We'll look at everything. Just to get an idea how low the art of painting has fallen in these latter days of capitalism. You were speaking of the obligations of the artist. I hope someone has pointed out that art has been in the hands of snobs and speculators too long. Indeed, I can guarantee that the only sanctuary from subjectless bric-à-brac here will be in the national pavilions of what you no doubt term the Iron Curtain countries. We will visit the USSR first.'

The white pinnacled kiosk-like architecture of a small building, no doubt dating from pre-Revolutionary times, seemed by its outwardly church-like style to renew the ecclesiological atmosphere that pursued Tokenhouse throughout life. Within, total embargo on aesthetic abstraction proved his forecast correct. We loitered for a while over Black Sea mutineers and tractor-driving peasants. Never able wholly to control a taste for antagonism, even against his own recently voiced opinions, Tokenhouse shook his head more than once over these images of a way of life he approved, here found wanting in executive ability.

'Don't think I'm lapsing into aestheticism in complaining that some of these scenes from the Heroic Epoch seem a little lacking in inspiration. Not all of this expresses with conviction the Unity of the Masses. I shall return for a further assessment. Now we will marvel at the subjective inanities you probably much prefer.'

Tokenhouse showed no ill will in exploring the other

national selections on view, my own presence giving excuse to examine what, alone, might have caused him to suffer guilt at inspecting at all.

'Absurd,' he kept muttering. 'Preposterous.'

In the French pavilion we came upon Ada Leintwardine and Louis Glober. They were standing before a massive work, seven or eight foot high, chiefly constructed from tin or zinc, horsehair, patent leather and cardboard. Ada was holding forth on its points, good and bad, Glober listening with a tolerant smile. Glober saw us first.

'Hi.'

As neither of them seemed attached to a party, it was to be supposed they had become sufficiently friendly at the Bragadin palace to arrange a visit to the Biennale together. There was the possibility, a remote one, that both had decided to spend Sunday morning at the Exhibition, run across each other by chance. Ada wore a skirt and carried a guidebook, outer marks of serious sightseeing, but the idea of Glober setting out on his own for such a trip was scarcely credible. Ada's immediate assumption of the exaggeratedly welcoming manner of one caught in compromising circumstances was not very convincing either. The Biennale was hardly the place for a secret assignation.

'Why, hullo,' she said. 'Everyone seems to have decided to come here today. What fun. We're having such an argument about the things on show, especially this one. Mr Glober sees African overtones, influenced by Ernst. To me the work's much more redolent of Samurai armour designed by Schwitters.'

To recognize a potential pivot of Conference gossip, a touch of piquancy, in detection of the pair of them together, was reasonable enough on Ada's part. Glober's greeting too, his serenely hearty manner always retaining a certain degree of irony, was seasoned this time with a small injection of deliberately roguish culpability. Nevertheless, their combined acceptance of giving cause for interesting speculation could not be taken at absolute face value. Pretence to an exciting vulnerability was more likely to be demanded by sexual prestige, an implied proposition that something was 'on', no more than mutual tribute to each other's status as 'attractive people'. That was to take a cool commonsense-inspired view. At the same time, the significance of so rapid a move towards association together was not to be altogether ignored, even if Glober, as playboy-tycoon, was no longer in his first youth; Ada, near-bestseller, mother of twins, alleged to prefer her own sex.

Ada's pronouncements on the subject of the artefact in front of us, extensive and well informed, continued for some minutes, so there was no immediate opportunity to introduce Tokenhouse. He was contemplating the metal-and-leather framework with unconcealed dislike, dissatisfied, too, at prospect of meeting strangers, particularly an American, representing by his nationality all sorts of political and social attitudes to be disapproved. A pause in Ada's talk giving opportunity to tell him she was a well-known novelist, also active force in a publisher's office, so to speak, on the other side of the counter, he showed no awareness of her writing, but grudgingly muttered something about having heard of her husband. When, on the other hand, Glober's name was announced, Tokenhouse displayed an altogether unexpected remembrance of him. He seemed positively glad to meet Glober again after thirty years.

'You're the man who put up the idea of the Cubist series. Of course you are. I'm not in the least interested in Cubists now, with their ridiculous aesthetic ideas, but I thought them a good proposition at the time, and I haven't changed my mind about that. It was a good proposition then. I was quite right.'

This looked, at first, an altogether remarkable example of

Glober's mastery of those attributes which impose their owner's personality for life; even after so trivial a business contact as that which had brought Tokenhouse and himself together. Then there turned out to exist a more tangible cause than Glober's charm, in itself, to stimulate Tokenhouse's memory. He began to chatter away in his rapid, assertive, disconnected manner, which, once under way, was impossible to check, however ill-adapted, or unintelligible, to his listeners.

'We made the blocks for the Cubist illustrations. They were never used. Your firm went out of business, but it wasn't due to that. Several American publishers went bust about that time. Some of the most active, as regards what were then new ideas. The whole thing was called off for quite other reasons. It was a great pity. I always held we could have made a success of things. I had a row with my board about it. They accused me of behaving in a high-handed manner. Very well, I said, if you think that, I'll pay for the blocks myself. I'll buy them at cost price. I'll stand the damage. They'll be my property. They could make no objection to that. So long as publishing remains in private hands, it might just as well be for my profit, as for that of any other speculator. I'd use them in my own good time. That was what happened. They've been in store ever since. I own them to this day. I stick to it that they would have made a good series in the light of what was being thought at the time.'

Tokenhouse was quite breathless by the end of his speech, excitement similar to that displayed by him when expatiating on what painting should be. Glober took in the situation at once. He grasped that he was dealing with an eccentric, one in a high class of his category, and roared with laughter. Glober may not have remembered much about Tokenhouse personally (he had shown no sign when I spoke of him earlier), but he appreciated that he was in the presence of an oddity, from whom amusement might, for the moment, be derived. Perhaps the notion of Tokenhouse buying the Cubists blocks appealed to Glober as, on however infinitesimal a scale, a touch of his own method, an element of playboy-tycoonery. That was in spite of Tokenhouse being, on the surface, about as far from a playboy as you could get, while his former status of tycoon, if ever to be so called, was an inconceivably modest one. Perhaps that was a misjudgment, however diluted, the characteristics being present in Tokenhouse too. The important fact was that, reunited with Glober, he was pleased to see him.

'Maybe we were men before our time, Mr Tokenhouse. Too ready to experiment with new ideas too early. I'm sorry it all ended that way. Not long after we met in London, I abandoned publishing for motion pictures. When I came back to publishing for a while, things had greatly changed. That was why I returned to the Coast.'

'Yes, yes.'

Tokenhouse spoke inattentively, still thinking about the blocks, certainly unapprised of 'the Coast', or why Glober should return there. This talk of publishing must have struck Ada as a useful opening. She had accepted without the least umbrage lack of acquaintance with herself as a novelist. The blocks offered as good, if not better, opportunity for impressing Glober with her own abilities.

'I should like to hear more about the Cubist blocks, Mr Tokenhouse. My husband's firm would certainly be glad to consider the question of taking them over from you, should you be interested in an advantageous price. In these days of steeply mounted production charges, they might find a place in our list.'

Tokenhouse, never much at ease with women, especially good-looking ones, approached this proposition with caution, but without open hostility. The incomparable training of having worked as Sillery's secretary behind her, Ada had made rather a speciality of handling the older generation of Quiggin & Craggs authors, becoming so accomplished in that respect that she might now be indulging in mere display of that dexterity for its own sake. Whether or not she wanted the blocks, Tokenhouse accepted the principle of a tender. He began to discuss a lot of not specially interesting technical particulars. Retirement from publishing, changed taste in art, revised ideological opinions, had none of them blunted a keen business sense. Ada showed no less briskness about the potential deal. Glober looked at his watch.

'Have you and Mr Tokenhouse any plans for luncheon? Mrs Quiggin and I—should I say Miss Leintwardine?—were going to the restaurant here. Why don't you both join us?'

Ada looked for a moment as if she might have preferred to keep Glober to herself, a natural enough instinct, then changed her mind, welcoming the suggestion.

'Do let's all lunch together—and call me Ada.'

Tokenhouse also hesitated for a moment at thus entangling himself with forms of social life against which he had openly declared war, but he had by no means finished what he had to say about the blocks. Having in any case planned to eat at the restaurant, refusal was difficult. Even if his reluctance, and Ada's, had been more determined, Glober's pressure to enlarge the party might have surmounted that too. To deny him would have required a lot of energy. If he had an ulterior motive, long or short term, nothing of the sort was apparent. As before in the Palazzo, he seemed to hope for no more than to collect round him as many persons as available. That was simply because collecting people round him (creating one of those rudimentary courts adumbrated by Dr Brightman) brought a sense of confidence in himself. Finally, everyone had by that time seen as much of the Exhibition as desired, whether to praise or blame. Art was abandoned. It was agreed the party should lunch together. We strolled across to the restaurant, finding a table to allow a good view of the water. Glober enquired about drinks.

'A nerone,' said Ada. 'With an urgent request for plenty of gin.'

Tokenhouse declared that he never took more than a single glass of wine in the middle of the day. Glober would not hear of that. So gently importunate was he about everyone having an aperitif that in the end Tokenhouse, obstinate in his habits as a rule, surprisingly gave way, agreeing to begin with a 'punt è mes'. That was more of a triumph than Glober knew. He went on to make suggestions about what we should eat, judicious so far as that went, even if originating in a wish to impose the will. They were not acceptable to Ada. When Quiggin had married her, he had still taken pride in being an austere man—like most persons of that pretension, imposing frugality on his acquaintances, while making a lot of fuss himself, if food happened not to be absolutely to his own taste. Ada put an end to all that. Under her sway, Quiggin would now discuss bad wine, salad dressings, regional dishes, with the best. Such gastronomic ascendancy behind her, Ada was not likely to accept dictation from Glober.

Tokenhouse did not join in this chatter about food. He ordered spaghetti for himself, and sat back in silence. He would probably have liked to continue talking about blocks, but Ada must have decided nothing more could be settled about the matter until put before Quiggin. The fact was, Tokenhouse had lost the habit of this sort of party. In his publishing days he had gone out a good deal, possessing the reputation of an aggressive talker when the evening was well advanced, and he had taken a fair amount to drink. Even dead sober, he was usually prepared to shout down the rest of the party, if there were disagreements. Now he gave the impression of once more beginning to disapprove, earlier distrust of such company rearoused in him. He was rather cross when Glober nodded for a repetition of the drinks, but swallowed the second glass of vermouth, also took several deep gulps of wine when it arrived. Ada switched her attention to him, now offering a clue to her own easy acceptance of breaking up a tête-à-tête with Glober.

'You never published any of St John Clarke's novels, Mr Tokenhouse, did you?'

Tokenhouse, who had been particularly irritated when St John Clarke failed to produce the promised Introduction to *The Art of Horace Isbister*, made some non-commital answer about his firm not dealing in fiction, which Ada must have known already. She pressed the subject, not, so it appeared, because Tokenhouse was likely to throw light on St John Clarke, as from some wish of her own to emphasize the almost forgotten novelist's unrecognized merits. Then her aim became clearer.

'Louis—I shall call you Louis, Mr Glober—has come to Europe to look for a story to film. Of course, I hoped he would want one of my own novels—in default of one of yours, Nick—but we've been talking together, and he was saying the moment must have arrived for something nostalgic, something Edwardian. Then I had the brilliant idea that St John Clarke was the answer.'

This was rather a different story from Pamela's statement that Glober was going to film something by Trapnel. What subject Glober should choose struck me at the time as a perfectly endurable topic, during luncheon in these fairly idyllic surroundings, not one to take for a moment seriously. The same applied to Pamela's earlier words on the matter, in that case easing the way for Gwinnett. Commercial deals like selling stories to film companies are more likely to emerge from tedious negotiation undertaken by agents in prosaic offices. Such was one's melancholy conclusion. Glober, if not a producer in the top class, had been quite a figure in Hollywood; he was therefore tough. No doubt his mood accorded with this sort of chit-chat. To conclude any true buyer's interest had been aroused would be to misconstrue the ways of film tycoons. All the same, to be too matter-of-fact about such possibilities could be wide of the mark, as to be too susceptive to pleasing possibilities. With businessmen, you can never tell; least of all when movies are in question. On Ada's part, this looked like declaration of war on Pamela. She sounded very sure of herself.

'Perhaps you don't know, Nick, that we control the St John Clarke rights now. Clapham got the lot before he died. Just for the sake of tidiness—but I forgot, you probably do know, because St John Clarke left the royalties to your Warminster brother-in-law, and of course they came back to Quiggin & Craggs in the Warminster Trust. JG secured our own interest before Craggs died.'

What Ada stated made sense. I had not known about the St John Clarke rights; at least never thought out that aspect. She was undoubtedly going to do her best to sell a St John Clarke novel to Glober.

'A strange man I used to know in the army was devoted to *Match Me Such Marvel*. He'd worked in a provincial theatre or cinema, so he might be the right pointer for popular success.'

Bithel's view, twenty years later, could represent the winning number. Ada was enthusiastic.

'*Match Me Such Marvel* is the one I suggested. There's a homosexual undercurrent. Of course, you Americans are so jumpy about homosexuality. It would be a great pity to leave that sequence out.'

'Who says we're going to leave it out?' said Glober lazily. 'We Americans are getting round to hearing about all sorts of things of that kind these days. You don't do us justice. When were you last in the States, Ada?'

They were a well matched couple when it came to that

sort of teasing, as cover for business negotiation. Token-house, likely to disapprove of such levity, was ruminating on some matter of his own. Suddenly he joined in.

'St John Clarke was a vain fellow. I never cared for such novels of his as I read. He behaved in a most unsatisfactory manner dealing with my firm. It was only quite by chance I came across a pamphlet he had written in the latter part of his life dealing with an interest of my own, that is to say Socialist Realism in painting. That pamphlet was not without merit.'

Ada showed herself more than equal to this comment too. Her policy was, I think, to ventilate in a general way the claims of St John Clarke; get his name thoroughly into Glober's head, without bothering too much whether the impression was good or bad. When St John Clarke had sunk in as a personality, she would plug the book she wanted to be filmed. She showed warm appreciation of this new aspect of the novelist.

'Exactly, Mr Tokenhouse. St John Clarke is no back-number. His style may seem a little old-fashioned today, but there is nothing old-fashioned about his thought. He is full of compassion—compassion of his own sort, sometimes a little crudely expressed to the modern ear. I am most interested in what you say about his art criticism. I had missed that. Of course I know about Socialist Realism. I expect you used to read a magazine called *Fission*, which ran for a couple of years just after the war, and remember the instructive analysis Len Pugsley wrote there, called *Integral Foundations of a Fresh Approach to Art for the Masses*.'

Tokenhouse got out his pencil. Making Ada repeat the title of Pugsley's article, he wrote it on a paper table napkin. I recalled Bagshaw's editorial irritation at having to publish the piece.

'If we've got to print everything written by whoever's

rogering Gypsy, we'll have to get a new paper allocation. Even our Commy subscribers don't want to read that stuff.'

Bagshaw's comment, partially disproved by Tokenhouse's interest, was borne out to the extent that Gypsy (retaining her name and style) had gone to live with Pugsley, when she became a widow. Tokenhouse now found himself assailed by Ada with an absolute barrage of expertise on his own subject. She began to reel off the names of what were evidently Socialist Realist painters.

'Svatogh? Gaponenko? Toidze? I can only remember a few of the ones Len mentioned. Of course you'll be familiar with all their pictures, and lots more. There is so much in art of which one remains so dreadfully ignorant. I must look into all that side of painting again, when I have a moment to spare.'

Tokenhouse, who had certainly begun luncheon in a mood of refusal to truckle to undue demands on making himself agreeable, could not fail to be impressed. I was impressed myself. In her days as employee at Quiggin & Craggs, the Left Wing bias of the firm had naturally demanded a smattering of Marxist vocabulary, but to retain enough political small talk of that period to meet Tokenhouse on his own Socialist Realist ground was no small achievement; not less because Quiggin himself, anyway commercially, had so far abrogated his own principles as to have lately scored a publishing bull's eye with the Memoirs of a Tory 'elder statesman'. Glober laughed quietly to himself.

'You two take me back to the Film Writers' Guild. Give me two minutes notice to beat it, before you throw the bomb.'

Seen closer, over a longer period, he was observable as a little tired, a little melancholy, amusing himself with mild jaunts such as this one, which made small demand on valuable reserves. He was husbanding his forces. To suppose that, in no way implied a state of total exhaustion. You felt there was quite a lot left for future effort, even if requirement for everything to be played out in public, in a manner at once striking and elegant, increased need for exceptional energy. What did not happen in public had no reality for Glober at all. In spite of the quiet manner, there was no great suggestion of interior life. What was going on inside remained there only until it could be materially expressed as soon as possible. The tress of hair had to record the sexual conquest.

To unAmerican eyes, probing the mysteries of American comportment and observance, this seemed the antithesis of Gwinnett. Much going on in Gwinnett was never likely to find outward expression. That was how it looked. No doubt a European unfamiliarity heightened, rather than diminished, the contrast; even caricatured its salient features. That did not remove all substance, the core seeming to be the ease with which Glober manipulated the American way; Gwinnett's awkwardness in its employment. That was to put things crudely, possibly even wrongly, just consequence of meeting both in Europe. Glober, only recently sprung from the Continent, had about him something of the old fashioned Jamesian American, seeking new worlds to conquer. Gwinnett was not at all like that. With Gwinnett, everything was within himself. He had, so it seemed, come to Europe simply because he was passionately interested in Trapnel, obsessed by him, personally identified with him; again, one felt, inwardly, rather than outwardly.

Dr Brightman had called Gwinnett a 'gothic' American. What, in contrast, would she call Glober? She had invoked Classicism and Romanticism. Here again it was hard to apportion epithets. In one sense, Glober, the practical man, was also the 'romantic'—as often happens—Gwinnett, working on his own interior lines, the 'classical'. Gwinnett wanted to see things without their illusory trimmings; Glober forced things into his own picturesque mould. In doing that, Glober retained some humour. Could the same be said of Gwinnett? Would Gwinnett, for example, be capable of taking pleasure in Tokenhouse as a medium for amusement? Was the analogy to be found in quite other terms of reference: Don Juan for Glober, Gwinnett in Faust?

The wine, passing round rather rapidly, may have played some part in these reflections. Tokenhouse was by now a little tight. Age, or abstinence, must have weakened his head. Perhaps solitude, sheer lack of opportunity to air his views, caused a few glasses to release the urgent need to hold forth again at a crowded table. He now proceeded to reproduce, in greatly extended form, the lecture he had given me earlier on the necessity for rejecting Formalism. In doing this, Tokenhouse passed all reasonable bounds of dialectical prosiness. Glober, showing American tolerance for persons outlining a favourite theme with searching thoroughness, did not interrupt him, but, when coffee came, Tokenhouse had gone too far in presuming on national forbearance in indicating to a compulsive talker that he has become a bore. By that time Tokenhouse had admitted he painted himself. Glober leant across the table.

'Now see here, Mr Tokenhouse. We're going to drink a glass of strega, then we're all coming back to your studio to admire your work.'

That took Tokenhouse so much by surprise that he scarcely demurred at the strega, protesting only briefly, as a matter of form. It was hard for an amateur painter—he kept on making a point of this status—to be other than flattered. It was agreed the party should make their way to the flat after leaving the restaurant. When the bill arrived, Glober insisted on paying. He swept aside energetic, if rambling, efforts on the part of Tokenhouse to prevent this on grounds that I was his guest. They argued for a time, Tokenhouse producing a ten-thousand-lire note, Glober thrusting it aside. We set off at last, Tokenhouse still talking hard. He was not drunk in any derogatory sense, had merely taken a little more than accustomed, which had transformed a prickly detachment into discursiveness not to be checked. He hurried along, the old grey hat jammed down on his head, swinging his stick, Glober taking long strides to keep up. Ada and I followed a short way behind.

'How on earth did you know the names of those painters, Ada? Are they Russian?'

Ada smiled, justifiably pleased with herself.

'Len Pugsley's at our Lido hotel. He'd brought the article with him, as basis of a speech he's going to make at the Conference. Getting something published in *Fission* was his first real step in life.'

'His last one too. Why hasn't he appeared?'

'Len's got a stomach upset. He's in bed. He wanted to rehearse his speech. He read it all to me. I say, I hear from Glober the Widmerpools have had a terrible row.'

'Isn't that a permanent state?'

'This one's worse than usual.'

Ada could offer no more at that moment, because Glober, fearing dispersal of his court, or that its courtiers were plotting against him, turned back to make sure we were included in whatever he was discussing with Tokenhouse. A few minutes later we entered the narrow calle in which the flat was situated. Tokenhouse led the way up the stairs. He opened the door, pointing ahead.

'Seat yourselves. I'm afraid there is nothing luxurious about my way of life. You must excuse that, take me as you find me, a humble amateur painter.'

He stumped off in the direction of the canvases in the corner.

Glober looked round the room.

'Mr Tokenhouse, you ought to advertise your studio as Annex to the Biennale Exposition.'

'I should, I should. I shall have to wait another two years now.'

Tokenhouse laughed excitedly, shuffling about arranging pictures at every angle. Glober's interest must have encouraged him to widen the scope of what he was prepared to display. In addition to those shown in the morning were others stacked in two cupboards.

'Do I detect the influence of Diego Rivera, Mr Tokenhouse?'

'Ah-ha, you may, you may.'

'Or is it José Clemente Orozco, who did those frescoes at Dartmouth? There is something of that artist too.'

Tokenhouse was in ecstasies, if such a word could be used of him at all.

'I would not deny influence of the former. I am less familiar with the work of the latter. I flatter myself in these experiments in style, now wholly abandoned, I have caught a small touch of Rivera's gift for speaking in a popular language. This, for instance—now who the devil can that be?'

A heavy knock had been given on the outside door. Tokenhouse set down the two pictures he was holding. He did not go to the door at once. Instead, he took a small diary from his pocket, and studied it. The knock came again. Tokenhouse, put out by this interruption, went into the passageway. The sound came of the door being opened, followed by muffled conversation. The caller's enquiry had not been audible. Tokenhouse's answer was testy, almost shrill.

'Yes, yes. Of course he mentioned your name to me. More than once in the past. I had no idea you were attending the Conference. You're not? Ah-ha, I see. Well, come in then. It's not very convenient, but now you're here, you'd better stay. I have some people looking at my pictures. Yes, my pictures, I said—but you can wait till they're gone. Then we can have a talk.'

He returned to the studio-room accompanied by Widmerpool.

'This is—did you say *Lord*—yes, Lord Widmerpool. Ah-ha, you know everybody. That makes things easier.'

Tokenhouse spoke the word 'Lord' with great contempt. Neither he, nor Widmerpool himself, looked in the least as if they believed the fact of 'knowing everyone' made things easier. Tokenhouse had spoken the words bitterly, ironically. In his own eyes nothing much worse could happen, now that his Private View had been interrupted, the chance of a lifetime mucked up; Widmerpool, armed with an introduction, arriving at this particular moment. Tokenhouse seemed to know instinctively that Widmerpool felt no interest whatever in pictures, good or bad.

'Take a seat.'

Widmerpool looked round. There was no very obvious place to do so. He was undoubtedly surprised at finding Glober, Ada, myself, here; not more so than I, that he should suppose it advantageous to visit Tokenhouse. The connexion could hardly be publishing. By the time Widmerpool, in an advisory capacity, had been on the Quiggin & Craggs board, Tokenhouse's days as a publisher were over. Possibly some link went back to Widmerpool's time in a solicitor's office; his former firm perhaps that recording the ban on religious rites at the Tokenhouse obsequies. Widmerpool had plainly not been warned that painting was Tokenhouse's hobby. He stared rather wildly at the pictures propped up all over the room, then nodded to each of us in turn.

'Yes—we all know each other. How are you, Ada? We haven't met since *Fission*. I expect you're at the Conference, or come for the Film Festival?'

The last suggestion seemed to have struck him on the spur of the moment, probably on account of Glober's film connexions. Ada pretended to be piqued.

'Didn't you notice me at the Bragadin palace, Kenneth? I saw you. Pam and I talked away. I should have thought she'd have mentioned that to you.'

Widmerpool, discerning a probe for information, rather than expression of wounded feelings, gave nothing away. He smiled.

'Pam often forgets to tell me things. We think it best not to live in each other's pockets. It makes married life easier. You would agree, wouldn't you, Louis?'

'I sure would.'

Glober laughed in his usual quiet friendly way, which did not at all conceal dislike. He also took the opportunity of stating his own situation.

'Mrs Quiggin and I were discussing the Biennale the time her Conference was looking over Jacky's place. We thought we'd take a look at the Biennale pictures together too. Who should we meet but Mr Jenkins and Mr Tokenhouse. Now we're admiring Mr Tokenhouse's pictures instead of those at the Biennale.'

That was brief, exact description of just what had happened. If Glober had designs on Pamela—it was hard to think otherwise—he might welcome opportunity of emphasizing to Widmerpool that he had 'picked up' Ada, accordingly was not to be taken as too serious a competitor for Pamela. Such was just a notion that occurred. If it displayed Glober's intention, Widmerpool showed no sign of appreciating the point.

'I see.'

He spoke flatly, staring round again at the rows of small canvases that cluttered the studio. Obviously they conveyed nothing to him. He appeared more than ever worried, but made an effort.

143

'Have you collected these over the years, Mr Tokenhouse?'

Tokenhouse looked furious.

'I painted them.'

He snapped out the answer.

'Yourself. I see. How clever.'

Widmerpool said that without the smallest irony.

'Merely a hobby. Not at all clever. The last thing they are—or I should wish them to be—is clever.'

Tokenhouse did not conceal his annoyance. Widmerpool had ruined the afternoon. Here were all his pictures spread out, a relatively sympathetic audience, to whom he could preach his own theories of art, a unique occasion, in short, wrecked by the arrival of a self-important stranger—a 'lord' at that—with an introduction, presumably about some business matter. Again, it was hard to see what business interests Widmerpool and Tokenhouse could share, yet the connexion was clearly not a friendly one, some common acquaintance's suggestion that the two of them would get on well together. Although nettled, Tokenhouse did not seem exactly taken aback. Widmerpool, after whatever had been said at the door, must represent some burden liable to be shouldered sooner or later. The botheration was for such responsibility to have descended at this moment. Tokenhouse, accepting the party was over, like a child putting away its toys, began gloomily replacing the canvases in the nearer cupboard. Then one of Glober's gestures went some way towards saving the situation.

'Just a moment, Mr Tokenhouse. Don't be in such a hurry with those pictures of yours. Would you consider a sale? If you would—and don't tell me to hell with it—I'd like to know your price for the shipwreck scene.'

He pointed to one of the illustrations of social injustice, such it must be, seemingly enacted on the crowded deck of a boat, where several persons were in trouble. Tokenhouse paused in his tidying up. He visibly responded to the enquiry.

'Sell a picture?'

'That's what I hoped.'

Tokenhouse considered.

'I've only been asked that once before, apart from an occasion years ago—in my Formalist days—when requested to present a picture of mine to be raffled for a charity. It was one of those typical feckless efforts to bolster up the capitalist system—some parson at the bottom of it, of course—attempting to launch that sort of ameliorating endeavour, which I now recognize as worse, more deliberately harmful, than brutal indifference, and should now naturally refuse to have anything to do with.'

Tokenhouse turned to Widmerpool. He spoke rather spitefully.

'The only other occasion when I sold one of my pictures was to our mutual friend. The friend who sent you here. He very kindly bought one of my efforts.'

Widmerpool seemed further embarrassed. He started slightly. Then he made a movement of the hand to express appreciation.'

'Oh, yes. Did he, indeed? I didn't know he liked painting.'

'Of course he does. He bought one of the army incidents. I called it *Any Complaints?* A typical mess-room injustice about rations. To buy it was a charming return for a small service I had been able to perform for him. I had, of course, expected no such return, having acted entirely from principle.'

'I'm sorry I didn't know you were an artist,' said Widmerpool.

There was silence. Tokenhouse blew his nose. Glober returned to the question of buying a picture himself.

'Then I take it you will sell one, Mr Tokenhouse?'

145

'I see no reason why not, no reason at all.'

'The emigrant ship?'

'They are a poor family found travelling without a ticket on the vaporetto.'

'Better still. A souvenir of Venice. That's fine.'

Glober, certainly aware of Widmerpool's impatience to speak with Tokenhouse alone, was determined not to be hurried. Tokenhouse, equally recognizing Widmerpool's claim on him, whatever that was, also showed no scruple about keeping him waiting. He seemed almost to enjoy doing so. Glober enquired about terms. Widmerpool was getting increasingly restive. He fidgeted about. Glober began to argue that the sum Tokenhouse had named as price for his picture was altogether inadequate. A discussion now developed similar to that about paying the restaurant bill. At last Widmerpool could bear it no longer. He interrupted them.

'I expect you know our mutual friend was unable to come?'

He addressed himself to Tokenhouse, who took no notice of this comment.

'Our friend is not here,' Widmerpool repeated.

Although clear we should have to go soon, the strain of waiting for that moment was telling on him. Tokenhouse merely nodded, as much as to say he accepted that as regrettable, though of no great importance.

'He mentioned when I last saw him he might not be able to undertake the trip this time... Now, about wrappings. It will have to be newspaper. You must not mind it being a not very pro-American journal.'

Tokenhouse laughed quite heartily at his own joke. The all but unprecedented sale of a picture had for the moment quite altered him. He could not be bothered with Widmerpool's problems, however grave, until the negotiation was completed.

'It's all—well—a bit unfortunate,' said Widmerpool.

146

'Ah-ha, it is? I'm sorry ... Now, string? Here we are. We'll have to unknot this. I think it good to have to make use of your hands from time to time. A bourgeois up-bringing has given me no aptitude in that direction. I always tie granny knots. There we are. Not a very neat parcel, I fear, but people don't fuss about that sort of thing in this quarter of Venice. There we are. There we are.'

He handed Glober the picture, enclosed now in several sheets of *Unità*. Glober took it. Tokenhouse stood back.

'Luckily my pictures are a manageable size. Patrons of Veronese or Tiepolo would need more than the painter's morning paper to bring their purchases home wrapped up.'

The name of Tiepolo seemed to cause a moment's faint embarrassment, not only to Widmerpool, but also, for some reason, to Ada and Glober. In any case, if we did not leave, Widmerpool was soon going to request our withdrawal in so many words. I could recognize the signs. Glober, too, seeing a showdown imminent, and deciding against a head-on clash at that moment, brought matters to a close, shaking hands with Tokenhouse. Tokenhouse saw us to the top of the stairs.

'I may get in touch with you again. Nick, before you leave Venice. There might be a small package I should like you to post for me in England. The mails are very uncertain here. Ah-ha, yes. Goodbye to you then, goodbye. I'm glad we had opportunity to meet again, Mr Glober. Yes, yes. I do my poor best. Ah-ha, ah-ha. I hope I may at least have acted as a signpost away from Formalism. Yes, do let me know about the blocks, Mrs Quiggin. I quite see your position. Goodbye, goodbye.'

We left him to Widmerpool, whatever dialogues lay ahead of them. After reaching the street, nothing was said for a minute or two. Then Glober spoke.

'That was a most interesting experience—and a superb addition to my collection of twentieth-century primitives.'

'I adored Mr Tokenhouse,' said Ada. 'Those blocks could be quite a snip, if he's prepared to consider a reasonable price. I remember JG talking of him now. I'm not sure JG didn't know the psychiatrist—a Party member—who treated Tokenhouse for his breakdown, anyway treated some ex-publisher for a breakdown. He used to treat a friend of Howard Craggs, an old girl called Milly Andriadis, who died in Paris last year.'

'I once went to a party given by Mrs Andriadis,' said Glober. 'That shows how old I am.'

Neither he nor Ada spoke of Widmerpool. There seemed something almost deliberate about their avoidance of his name. Then Glober stopped suddenly.

'Oh, hell.'

'What's happened?'

'I'd forgotten that contact man I was due to see at the Gritti.'

He looked at his watch.

'I'm going to be late. What's to be done in a town without taxis, and not a gondola in sight?'

Ada pointed.

'If you run, you'll catch the circolare. It's coming up. You could just about make it.'

Glober, with a shout that we must meet again soon, seemed delighted to show his mettle as a short-distance sprinter. Taking Tokenhouse's picture from under his arm, he bounded off. We saw him catch the boat, just as the rope was thrown across the rails. He turned and waved in our direction. We waved back.

'What energy.'

'All quite unnecessary too. He's surrounded by secretaries and hangers-on of one kind or another, who are only there to give an impression big business is being transacted. I'm going to make for the Lido. Have a rest, before going out this evening with Emily Brightman.'

We walked on towards the stazione.

'Who's this American called Gwinnett that Pam's taken a fancy to?'

'Has she taken a fancy to him? He's writing a book about our old friend X. Trapnel. If you don't deflect Glober's film interests to St John Clarke, Gwinnett might help in making a Trapnel film. Did she tell you she liked him?'

Ada laughed at such an idea.

'I was hearing about Gwinnett from Glober. Can you keep a secret? Glober wants to marry Pam, not just have an affair with her. Don't breathe a word to anyone. You won't, will you? He revealed that to me when he found I was her old friend. Only in the strictest confidence.'

'What does her husband think about that? He must have had plenty of opportunities to divorce her, if he wanted. Anyway, why should she herself decide to marry Glober?'

'I doubt if Kenneth knows yet. He just thinks Glober's one of her usuals. So far as Pam is concerned, the bait Glober holds out is the lead in this great film he's going to make.'

'Pamela? But she's never acted in her life, has she?'

Ada thought that a naive reaction.

'What does that matter? Besides, Pam's no fool. If she wants a thing, she'll force herself to do it. What Glober's worried about is this young American turning up, who's a Trapnel fan. He doesn't want Gwinnett sticking round, if he does a Trapnel film. That's why he's begun to look about for another book to make his picture from. There's a character just like Pam in *Match Me Such Marvel*. Of course, St John Clarke didn't know anything about women, but a competent script-writer could alter all that.'

'Why should she want to act at all?'

'Because Pam longs for fame.'

'You mean publicity?'

'Anything you like to call it. Nobody's ever heard of her. She doesn't care for that. For one thing, she isn't keen on nobody having heard of her, and quite a lot of people having heard of me.'

'Where did Glober meet her?'

'At her father's place in Montana. Cosmo Flitton married an American, and they run a dude ranch together. Wouldn't you adore to meet some dudes? Anyway, Pam went up there to stay, when she was in the States with Kenneth, and Louis Glober fell.'

'So Cosmo Flitton's still going?'

'Not only still going, but a highly regarded figure out there, with his one arm and reputation of an old hero. Everybody's mad about him. About Pam too, Glober says. He also described a scene that took place last night at Jacky Bragadin's, which went rather far even for Pam. It all arose from the Tiepolo ceiling. That was why Kenneth Widmerpool winced when Tiepolo was mentioned by Mr Tokenhouse, just before we left. Do you know the subject of the picture? I was brought up on significant form, colour values, all that sort of thing, so I hadn't particularly noticed what was being illustrated. Unlike Mr Tokenhouse, and Len Pugsley, my family always rather looked down on people who thought a picture told a story. I know about Socialist Realism, but this is an Old Master. I just saw a classical subject, and left it at that. Apparently it's a man showing his naked wife to a friend.'

Ada spoke with clinical objectivity.

'Perfectly right.'

'For some reason Pam was determined to talk about that picture all through dinner. There were a lot of people there, Glober said. She was between a monsignore and a maharaja. You know how silent she is as a rule. That night she chattered incessantly. Went on and on. Nothing would stop her. She seemed to be doing this partly to get under the skin of a lady Glober knows, called Signora Clarini, the English wife of the Italian film director, but living apart. Apparently Signora Clarini was a girl-friend of Sir Magnus Donners years ago, and now wants to marry Glober. He conveyed that in his quiet way. Pam may decide not to marry him herself, she was going to make sure Signora Clarini didn't either. She kept on talking about Donners, implying he was a voyeur.'

'Pamela's hardly in a position to take a high moral line, if only after some of the things being said about her at the more sensational end of the French press.'

Ada had not heard about the Ferrand–Sénéschal revelations. She brushed them aside. Borrit, a War Office colleague, who had served in Africa, once spoke of the Masai tribe holding, as a tenet of faith, that all cows in the world belong to them. Ada, in similar manner, arrogated to herself all the world's gossip, sources other than her own a presumption.

'Pam didn't take a high moral line. Quite the reverse. She spoke as if she and Signora Clarini were sister whores. That, according to Glober, was what made Signora Clarini so cross.'

'This was all in front of Widmerpool?'

'That's what Glober found so fascinating. Kenneth didn't attempt to shut her up. Of course he knows by now that's impossible, but Glober thought he was not only afraid of her—almost physically afraid—but got a kind of kick from what she was saying.'

'How did their host enjoy this small talk at his table?'

'Jacky Bragadin wasn't feeling well that evening, thought he was going to have one of his attacks, so wasn't bothering much. The monsignore was one of those worldly priests, who take anything in their stride, but the maharaja didn't know where to look. Louis Glober, to relieve the tension, persuaded the maharaja to teach him cricket. Jacky Bragadin found a Renaissance mace that belonged to some famous condottiere, and they used that for a bat. The maharaja bowled a peach, Glober hit it so hard he caught Kenneth on the jaw. That made further trouble.'

'Somebody once did that with a banana at school. His face must have a radar-like attraction for fruit. Glober still wants to marry Pamela in spite of all this?'

'I think so. He's quite tough. He says all his contemporaries have drunk themselves crazy, undergone major surgery, discharged both barrels with their big toe, dropped down dead on the set, and he's not going to fall for any of that. All the same, he's disturbed about Gwinnett. Pam asked Louis if Gwinnett was queer. That's what worried him. Her interest. Is he?'

'Homosexual?'

'Of course.'

'I don't think so. I don't think he's very normal either.'

'Will Gwinnett's book about Trapnel be good? Ought we to publish it? We'll talk about that later. Here's my vaporetto. See you at the *Men of Letters/Men of Science* session. I must polish up my speech. Don't breathe a word about anything I've said, will you?'

She boarded a vessel bound for the Lido. I waited for the next boat heading towards the Grand Canal. To present Sir Magnus Donners as Candaules at the Bragadin dinner party showed imagination on Pamela's part. Bob Duport had offered much the same solution as to what Sir Magnus 'liked'.

'Donners never minded people getting off with his girls. I've heard he's a voyeur.'

Barnby, without arriving at that logical conclusion, had expressed the same mild surprise at Sir Magnus's lack of jealousy. The subject, reduced to the crude medium of the peep-hole, recalled the visit to Stourwater, when, without warning, its owner had suddenly appeared through a concealed door, decorated with the spines of dummy books, just as if he had been waiting at an observation post. The principle could clearly be extended from a mere social occasion to one with intimate overtones. The power element in both uses was obvious enough.

'Peter may have developed special tastes too,' Duport said. 'Very intensive womanizing sometimes leads to that, and no one can say Peter hasn't been intensive.'

In days when Peter Templer had been pursuing Pamela, he might easily have talked to her about Sir Magnus, even taken her to see him, but not at Stourwater, the castle by then converted to wartime uses. The fact that his former home was now a girls' school, rather a fashionable one, could hardly be unpleasing to the shade of Sir Magnus, if it walked there. The practices attributed to him, justly or not, had to be admitted as inescapably grotesque, humour never more patently the enemy of sex. Perhaps Gyges, too, had felt that; as king, living his next forty years in an atmosphere of meticulous sexual normality. I should have liked to discuss the whole matter with Moreland, but, although he was no longer married to Matilda, the habits of Sir Magnus and his mistresses remained a delicate one to broach. He was like that. Moreland was not well. In fact, things looked pretty bad. He would work for a time with energy, then fall into a lethargic condition. There had been financial strains too. One of his recordings becoming in a small way a popular hit, made that side easier lately. We rarely met. He and Audrey Maclintick—whom he had never married—lived, together with a black cat, Hardicanute, an obscure, secluded life.

At the hotel desk they handed out a letter from Isobel. I took it upstairs to read. Across the top of the page, an afterthought from personal things, that amorphous yet intense substance of which family life is made up, she had scribbled a casual postscript.

'Have you seen about Ferrand–Sénéschal? Probably not as you never read the papers abroad. Fascinating rumours about Pamela Widmerpool.'

I lay on the bed and dozed. It would have been wiser to have drunk less at lunch. I felt Glober was to blame. Quite a long time later the telephone buzzed, waking me.

'Hullo?'

'Is that Mr Jenkins?'

It was a man's voice, an American's.

'Speaking.'

'It's Russell Gwinnett.'

'Why, hullo?'

There was a pause at the other end of the line. I was not sure we had not been cut off. Then Gwinnett cleared his throat.

'Can we have a talk?'

'Of course. When?'

He seemed undecided. While he was thinking, I looked to see the time. It was well after six.

'Now, if you like. We could have a drink somewhere.'

'I can't manage right now.'

There was another long pause. He seemed to regret having called. At least he sounded as if he required help in making up his mind whether or not to ring off. It seemed as if he would do that, unless I could suggest an alternative. I had no plans for the evening. Dinner with Gwinnett would solve that problem. In an odd way, prospect of his company gave a sense of adventure.

'How about dining together?'

Gwinnett considered the proposal for some seconds. The idea seemed not greatly to appeal, but in the end he concurred.

'OK.'

He made it sound a concession.

'Where shall that be?'

'Not in the hotel, I guess.'

'I agree.'

Talk took place about restaurants. Gwinnett showed himself unexpectedly knowledgeable. In this, as in other matters, he was a dark horse. We fixed on one at last, arranging to meet at the table. He showed no immediate sign of getting off the line, but did not speak, nor appear, at that juncture, to have more to say.

'Eight o'clock then?'

'OK.'

'I'll be there.'

'OK.'

I hung up. He was not an easy man. All the same, I liked him. Later, at the restaurant, he turned up punctually. The fact that I liked him was just as well, otherwise dinner, anyway at the start, would have been tedious. I had supposed, rather complacently, that Gwinnett wanted to talk about his assignation with Pamela; report on it, ask an opinion, perhaps discuss future tactics. As the meal progressed, he showed no sign of approaching that subject. The appointment might well have foundered. Nothing was more probable. The more one thought about it, the less likely seemed any possibility of Pamela having turned up. Gwinnett had almost certainly waited, perhaps for an hour or two, in the porch of the Basilica, then trudged back to the hotel. That was the picture. In any case, now we were together, he had to be allowed to approach the matter on his own terms. To force an issue would be fatal. Without going into details about Tokenhouse, I mentioned meeting Glober at the Biennale, lunching in his company. Gwinnett showed no interest. He talked of Conference matters. He was preparing a report for his College. The College, so it appeared, had arranged his attendance with that in view, the Venetian visit combined with London, for Trapnel research. He asked if I had known Dr Brightman for long.

'I met her for the first time here. I'd read some of her books.'

Gwinnett spoke highly of Dr Brightman, the good impression she had made on the Faculty, when exchange professor, her influence on his own way of looking at things. He said all that quite simply, in the manner Americans achieve, without self-consciousness or affectation, serious comment that, in English terms, would require—at least almost certainly receive—less direct unvarnished treatment. He let fall that his family had moved to New England after the Civil War. The impression was of an unusual, rather lonely young man, who had sustained a kind of intellectual nourishment from an older woman, with whom no sort of cross-currents of gender, not the slightest, were in question. I still wondered what was his trouble, the wound that had somehow maimed him. Dr Brightman must have been understanding about whatever that might be. Dinner was nearly at an end, when, quite suddenly, he turned to the subject of Pamela. This employment of two personalities in himself was possibly deliberate; voluntary or involuntary, characteristic of him.

'She showed up at San Marco.'

'She did?'

'Yes.'

Gwinnett's follow-up took so long to arrive that there were moments when it looked as if these words were all the information he proposed to give about the meeting.

'Is she likely to produce any usable Trapnel material?'

His silence extorted that. Gwinnett did not answer the question. Instead, he suggested we should leave the restaurant, drink more coffee elsewhere.

'All right.'

'Where shall we go?'

'Florian's?'

'OK.'

As soon as we were outside he began about Pamela. What he had to say may have seemed easier to express in comparative darkness of the street, rather than across the table at an over brightly lighted restaurant. Now he sounded thoroughly excited, not at all inert.

'I'm going to meet her in London.'

'That sounds all right.'

'I don't know so much.'

'Did she suggest that?'

'Yes—when she saw me in San Marco.'

'The interview there went off well?'

'She turned up on time.'

'That in itself must have been a surprise.'

Gwinnett laughed uneasily. He was evidently making a great effort, no doubt for the sake of his book, to be clear, uncomplicated, unlike how he usually felt, how at least he behaved.

'You know how dark it is in the Basilica? I was standing by the doors. I didn't recognize her for a moment, although I was thinking I must be careful not to miss her. She had dressed up all in black, a skirt, dark glasses, a kind of mantilla. She looked—I just don't know how to put it. I was almost scared. She didn't say a word. She took me by the hand, down one of those side aisles. It was the darkest part of the church. She stopped behind a pillar, a place she seemed to know already.'

Gwinnett was momentarily prevented from continuing his story by thickening of the crowd, as we approached the Piazza along a narrow street, necessitating our own advance in single file. Two nuns passed. Gwinnett turned back, indicating them.

'Do you know the first thing Lady Widmerpool said?

She asked if the place we were in didn't make me want to turn to the religious life?'

'How did you answer that one?'

'I said it might be a good experience for some people. It wasn't one I felt drawn to myself. I asked if she herself was thinking of taking the veil.'

'Good for you.'

'I said her clothes looked more religious than in the Palazzo.'

'How did she take that?'

'She laughed. She said she often felt that way. I wasn't all that surprised. It fits in.'

The comment showed Gwinnett no beginner in female psychology. He and Pamela might be well matched. This was the first outward indication of a mystic side to her. Gwinnett for the moment had shaken off his own constraint.

'I began to speak of Trapnel. She listened, but didn't give much away. The next thing did startle me.'

He gave an embarrassed laugh.

'She grabbed hold of me,' he said.

'You mean—'

'Just that.'

'By the balls?'

'Yeah.'

'Literally?'

'Quite literally. Then she hinted the story about Ferrand-Sénéschal was true.'

Coming out from under the pillars, we entered the Piazza. The square was packed with people. They trailed rhythmically backwards and forwards like the huge chorus of an opera. One of the caffè orchestras was playing selections from *The Merry Widow*, Widmerpool's favourite waltz, he had said, just before Barbara Goring poured sugar over his head. The termination of the Pamela story had to be left in Gwinnett's discretion. It was not to be crudely probed.

'That was when she told me to call her up when I got to London. I just said I'd do that.'

'By that time she'd let go—or was she still holding on?'

He laughed. He seemed past embarrassment now.

'I'd disengaged her—told her to lay off.'

'How did she take that?'

'OK. She laughed the way she does. Then she took off.'

'To contemplate the religious life elsewhere?'

Gwinnett did not offer an opinion on that point.

'You heard no more from her about Trapnel?'

'Not a word.'

Most of the tables at Florian's seemed occupied. People from the Conference were scattered about among multitudes of tourists. Gwinnett and I moved this way or that through the crowded caffè, trying to find somewhere to sit. Then two chairs were vacated near the band. Making for them, we were about to settle down, when someone from the next table called out. They were a party of four, revealed to be Rosie Manasch—Rosie Stevens now for some years—her husband, Odo Stevens, and an American couple.

'Switch the chairs round and join us,' said Stevens. 'We've just finished a Greek cruise, staying in Venice a day or two to get our breath.'

Rosie introduced the Americans, middle-aged to elderly, immensely presentable. I played Gwinnett in return. It was more characteristic of Stevens than his wife that Gwinnett and I should not be allowed to sit by ourselves. Like Glober, he had a taste for forming courts. He was a little piqued, or pretended to be, at hearing about the Conference.

'Why do I never get asked to these international affairs? Not a grand enough writer, I suppose. Who's turned up? Mark Members? Quentin Shuckerly? The usual crowd?'

Now in his early forties, Odo Stevens, less unchanged

159

than Rosie, had salvaged a fair amount of the bounce associated with his earlier days; Rosie, for her part, entirely retaining an intrinsic air of plump little queen of the harem. Having decided, possibly on sight, to marry Stevens, she seemed perfectly satisfied now the step was taken. So far as that went, so did Stevens. They had two or three children. There had been ups and downs during the years preceding marriage, but these had been survived, the chief discord when Matilda Donners had shown signs of wanting to capture Stevens for herself. Owing either to Matilda's tactical inferiority, or loss of interest in the prize, nothing had come of that, Rosie carrying Stevens off in the end. His temporary seizure by Matilda may have been planned more as a foray into her rival's territory—war considered as a mere extension of foreign policy—a sortie into the enemy's country, not intended as permanent advance beyond foremost defended localities, already recognized as such. At the time, Rosie took the aggression calmly, in that spirit preparing for withdrawal just as far as necessary, never losing her head. Matilda's punitive raid was, so to speak, driven off in due course, after admittedly inflicting a certain measure of casualty; both sides afterwards possessing some claim to have achieved their objective. During this little campaign, explosive while it lasted, Stevens was rumoured to have gone with Matilda to Ischia.

The battle over Stevens could claim a certain continuity from the past, Matilda and Rosie not only rivals at giving parties, but Rosie's first husband, Jock Udall, having belonged to a newspaper-owning family, traditionally opposed to Sir Magnus Donners and all his works. Some thought the pivot of the Ischia incident Stevens himself, bringing pressure on Rosie to force marriage. If so, the manoeuvre was successful. When his body was finally recovered from the battlefield, marriage took place, although only after a decent interval, to purge his contempt. The story that

Stevens had given Rosie a black eye during these troubled times was never corroborated. After marriage, a greater docility was, on the contrary, evident in Stevens. He hovered about on the outskirts of the literary world, writing an occasional article, reviewing an occasional book. It was generally supposed he might have liked some regular occupation, but Rosie would not allow that, imposing idleness on her husband as a kind of eternal punishment for the brief scamper with Matilda. Stevens had never repeated the success of *Sad Majors*, a work distinguished, in its way, among examples of what its author called 'that dicey artform, the war reminiscence'. The often promised book of verse—'verse, not poetry', Stevens always insisted—had never appeared. I had heard it suggested that Stevens worked part-time for the Secret Service. War record, general abilities, way of life, none of them controverted that possibility, though equally the suggestion may have been quite groundless. When Rosie, and the two Americans, began to talk to Gwinnett, Stevens swivelled his chair round in my direction.

'Do you know who's in this town, Nick?'

'Who?'

'My old girl friend Pam Flitton. I saw her wandering across the Piazzetta soon after we arrived. She didn't see me.'

He spoke in a dramatically low voice. There was no doubt a touch of facetiousness in pretending his wartime affair with Pamela was a desperate secret from his wife, even if true he was more than a little in awe of Rosie.

'She's staying with someone called Jacky Bragadin. Both the Widmerpools are.'

'Somebody called Jacky Bragadin? Don't be so snobbish, old cock. I know Jack Bragadin. Rosie's known him for years. He was a friend of her father's. He once came to a party of ours in London. Don't try and play down your smart friends, as if I was too dim to have heard of them.

We were actually thinking of ringing Jacky up tomorrow, asking if we could come and see him.'

'Keep calm, Odo. He's not a friend of mine. I never met him before the Conference went over his Palazzo. That was how I knew the Widmerpools were staying with Jacky Bragadin.'

Rosie caught the name. She left the Americans to chat together with Gwinnett, who had assumed, with his compatriots, a blunt, matter-of-fact, all-purposes air.

'Did you mention Jacky Bragadin? How is he? His heart wasn't too good when I last saw him, also that trouble with his chest. We thought of getting into touch. Do you know who's staying there?'

'I was telling Odo—the Widmerpools, among others.'

'Good heavens, the Frog Footman, and that *ghastly* wife of his. What can Jacky be thinking of? Thank goodness you warned me. Who are the other unfortunates?'

'An American film tycoon called Louis Glober. Baby Clarini, who used to be Baby Wentworth. Those are the only ones I know about, in addition to the Widmerpools.'

Rosie made a face at the name of Baby Wentworth.

'Jacky certainly can take it on the chin, Baby and Pamela Widmerpool under the same roof. What about Louis Glober? I seem to know the name. Is he up to the weight of the others? I hope so.'

One of the Americans enquired about Glober.

'What's he up to now? Louis Glober hasn't made a picture in years. The last I heard of him was automobile racing, in fact saw him at the Indianapolis Speedway.'

They talked of Glober and his past exploits. Gwinnett remained silent. I had not caught the name of the Americans, indeed never found that out. The husband began to enlarge on the Glober legend.

'Did you ever hear of Glober's Montana caper?'

That looked a possibility as the story of Glober's meeting with Pamela, but turned out to have bearings of interest chiefly on Glober's many-sidedness. It explained, too, a Montana connexion.

'One time Glober was in Hollywood, he went north with a cowboy actor—I'll think of the name—who was starring in a picture of Glober's. The Indians were bestowing some sort of a tribal honour on this actor, who'd invited Glober to accompany him, and watch the ceremony. Montana, it seems, went to Glober's head. That's how he is. He talked of starting life again up there, buying a defunct cattle business, refinancing Indian leases, that sort of stuff. He was crazy about it all.'

'Wouldn't mind that kind of life myself,' said Stevens. 'In the open all day.'

'Oh, darling?' said Rosie. 'Do you think so?'

'Glober stayed up there quite a while, talking of becoming a cattleman. All sorts of yarns came back to the Coast about his doings. There was supposed to have been a gun fight. A rancher found Glober in compromising circumstances with his wife. He pulled a gun, took a shot at Glober, and missed. Glober must have been prepared for trouble, because he had his own gun by him, blazed back, and missed too. They ran out of shells, or the lady herself intervened, so they settled to cut the cards for her. Glober lost, and returned to Hollywood.'

'His luck was in,' said Stevens.

The story suggested the *monde* in which Cosmo Flitton had come to rest. I caught Gwinnett's eye.

'That's all pure Trapnel—the sort of thing X would have loved, but never managed to bring off.'

Gwinnett nodded, without giving any indication whether or not he agreed.

'When the tale got back to Beverly Hills, Dorothy Parker said Glober planned to take the lead in his next

163

picture himself. It was to be called *The Western of the Playboy World*.'

The American lady broke in.

'Louis Glober's got a fine side too. All that money he gave for the mental health research project, that institution for schizophrenics. It was all done on the quiet. Not a soul knew it was Glober, until—'

Stevens kicked me under the table. I lost track of the precise history of Glober's generous act, but caught enough to gather it had been brought about in deliberate secrecy, the teller of the story having happened quite by chance on the magnanimous part Glober had played. I could not at once understand whatever Stevens was signalling. His eyes stared fixedly in front of him. Glancing round in the direction towards which they were set, I was now able to observe Pamela Widmerpool moving between the closely packed tables and chairs. As usual she gave the impression almost of floating through the air. She was apparently looking for someone thought likely to be sitting at Florian's. At least that was the impression given. Possibly she was merely taking an evening walk, choosing to wander through the crowded caffè to give spice to a stroll, cause a little inconvenience, draw attention to herself. The people at the tables stared at her. As she wove her way amongst them, she paused from time to time to stare haughtily back. Stevens was rather rattled.

'She's bloody well making in our direction,' he muttered.

Pamela had hit him in the face the last time I had seen them together, but no doubt he feared her unhappy moral impact on his wife, rather than physical violence. The others had not noticed Pamela's onset. Rosie, always a great talker, had a conspicuous rival in the American lady. Gwinnett seemed resigned to the position in which he found himself. Pamela had marked down our table. She was steering for it, without the least hurry. The course unquestionably was intentional. She was still wearing her white trousers, carrying from her shoulder a bag hung from a gold chain. Stevens was surprisingly disturbed.

'Has this got to happen?'

Pamela halted behind the chair of the male American. He was unaware of her presence there.

'Have you seen Louis?'

'Glober?'

'No, Louis the Fourteenth.'

'I haven't seen either since lunch.'

'Did you lunch with Louis?'

'Yes, Glober—not the Roi Soleil.'

'I thought he was giving lunch to that old cow Ada. Do you know she put round a story that I left a picador in Spain because I found a basket-ball player twice his size?'

'Ada was there too.'

'Where?'

'The restaurant in the Giardini.'

'Did he take Ada back to screw her—if he can still manage that, or can't she face a man any longer?'

'So far as I know Glober left for the Gritti Palace to meet a business acquaintance, and Ada returned to the Lido to work on a speech she's going to make at the Conference.'

'Louis's been seen at Cipriani's since he was at the Gritti.'

'Then I can't help.'

'I want some dope from him.'

Although the word might be reasonably used for any entity too much trouble to particularize, Pamela spoke as if she meant a drug, rather than, say, schedule of airflights to London, programme of tomorrow's sightseeing, name of a recommended restaurant. She sounded as if she felt a capricious desire for a narcotic Glober could supply, no breathless despairing longing, just what she wished at the moment. The possibility was not to be wholly dismissed as

165

an aspect of Glober's courtship. The men of the party had risen, standing awkwardly beside their chairs, while this conversation proceded, waiting for her to move on.

'How are you, Pam?' asked Stevens.

He still sounded nervous. She glanced at him, but gave no sign of having seen him before. Stevens himself may have hoped matters would rest there, that Pamela, failing to obtain the information she sought, would continue on her way without further acknowledgment. She remained, not speaking, looking coldly round, regarding Gwinnett with as chilly an eye as the rest. There was no suggestion they had met, far less touched on the religious life, shared some sort of physically sexual brush. Gwinnett himself was hardly more forthcoming. Absolutely poker-faced, his expression was that of a man determined not to fall below the standard of politeness required by convention towards an unknown woman pausing by the table at which he had been sitting, at the same time not unwilling that she should move on as quickly as possible to enable him to resume his seat. Pamela had no intention of moving on.

'I'm not going to drag the canals for Glober. I'll get the stuff from him tomorrow.'

She stepped forward to occupy the chair temporarily vacated by the American husband, thereby putting an end to any hope that she was not going to stay. The American managed to find another chair, then good-naturedly asked what she wanted to drink.

'A cappuccino.'

Stevens was forced into mumbling some sort of general introduction. Rosie, of course, knew perfectly well who Pamela was, but either the two of them, by some chance, had never met, or it suited the mood of both to pretend that. Gwinnett, without emphasis, allowed recognition of previous acquaintanceship of some sort by making a backward jerk of the head. Rosie, undoubtedly angry at

Pamela imposing herself in this manner, was at the same time, unlike Stevens, quite unruffled in outward appearance.

'We heard you and your husband were staying with Jacky,' she said. 'How is he? Free from that catarrh of his, I hope?'

She expertly eyed Pamela's turn-out, letting the assessment pause for a second on what appeared to be a wine-stain, at closer range revealed, on the white trousers, which Pamela, in spite of other signs of grubbiness, had not bothered to change. Rosie also contemplated for a moment the crocodile-skin bag. Its heavy chain of gold looked rather an expensive item. This was all very cool on both sides, the sense of tension—though neither glanced at the other—between Pamela and Gwinnett, rather than Pamela and Rosie. When the cappuccino arrived, Pamela did not touch it. She sat there quietly, taking no notice of anyone. Then she seemed to decide to answer Rosie's question.

'Jacky's no worse than usual. Only worried about having a couple like us staying with him.'

'You and your husband?'

'Yes.'

Rosie laughed lightly.

'Why should he be worried by that?'

'One accused of murder, the other of spying.'

'Oh, really. Which of you did which?'

Still smiling, Rosie spoke quite evenly. Pamela allowed herself a faint smile too.

'The French papers are hinting I murdered Ferrand-Sénéschal.'

'The French writer?'

Rosie's tone suggested that to have murdered Ferrand-Sénéschal was an act, however thoughtless, anyone might easily have committed.

167

'They haven't said in so many words I did it yet.'

'Oh, good—and the spying?'

Pamela laughed.

'Only those in the know, like Jacky, are fussing about that at present.'

'I see.'

'Jacky thinks he'll get in wrong with one lot, or the other, through us. Jacky's got quite a lot of Communist chums, movie people, publishers, other rich people like himself. Some of them are Stalinists, and quarrelling with the new crowd. Jacky doesn't want a stink. It looks as if a stink's just what he's going to get. He didn't bargain for that when he said we could come and stay, though he wasn't too keen in the first place. I had to turn the heat on. He thought I'd keep an American called Louis Glober quiet, and we might both be useful in other ways. Now he wants to get rid of us. That may not be so easy.'

She laughed again. The joke had to be admitted as rather a good one, even if grimmish for Jacky Bragadin. Rosie smiled tolerantly. She did not pursue further inflexions of the story by asking more questions. She picked up the bag resting on the table, its long chain still looped round Pamela's shoulder.

'How pretty.'

'Do you think so? I hate the thing. This man Glober gave it me. He keeps saying he'll change it. He'll only get something worse, and I can't be bothered to spend hours in a shop with him.'

'Is Mr Glober over for the Film Festival?' asked one of the Americans.

'That's what he's put out. He probably wants to pick up some hints from the German film about the blackmailing whore.'

'I rather wish we were staying for the Film Festival,' said Rosie. 'I'd like to see Polly Duport in the Hardy picture.'

We know her. She's so nice, as well as being such a good actress.'

There was a lull in conversation. Stevens remarked that his new interest was in vintage cars. The Americans said they would have to be thinking of returning to their hotel soon. Rosie confirmed the view that it had been a tiring day. Stevens looked as if he might have liked to linger at Florian's, but any such intractability would clearly be inadvisable, if matrimonial routines were to operate harmoniously. He did not openly dissent. Within the limits of making no pretence she found the presence of Pamela welcome, Rosie had been perfectly polite. Stevens could count himself lucky the situation had not hardened into open discord. Retirement from the scene had something to offer. Pamela appeared indifferent to whether they stayed or went. Goodbyes were said. She nodded an almost imperceptible farewell and dismissal. The Stevens party withdrew. They were enclosed almost immediately by the shadows of the Piazza. We sat for a minute or two in silence. The orchestra sawed away at *Tales of Hoffmann*.

'What a shit Odo is,' said Pamela.

'Rosie is nice.'

It seemed best to make that statement right away, declare one's views on the subject, rather than wait for attack. That would be preferable to a follow-up defending Rosie, as a friend. Rather surprisingly, Pamela agreed.

'Yes, she's all right. I suppose she gets a kick out of keeping that little ponce.'

'You must admit his war record was good.'

'What's that to me?'

To stay longer at the table would be not only to prejudice Gwinnett's opportunity for further pursuit of Trapnel investigations, but also, if Pamela had taken a fancy to him, risk being told in uncompromising terms to leave them *à deux*.

'I'm off too.'

Pamela herself rose at that.

'I've had enough of this place,' she said.

That remark had all the appearance of being Gwinnett's cue, a chance not to be missed to take her elsewhere, get out of her whatever he wanted. Florian's could reasonably be regarded as a distracting spot for serious discussion. Gwinnett himself stood up, but without putting forward any alternative proposal. There was a pause. As a matter of form, I offered to see Pamela back to the Bragadin palace. If Gwinnett did not want to settle immediately on another port of call, he could easily suggest the duty of taking her home should fall to him. He said nothing. Pamela herself categorically refused escort.

'Where's your hotel?'

I named it.

'Both of you?'

'Yes.'

She turned to Gwinnett.

'Are you going back too?'

'That was my intention.'

Pamela fully accepted the implication that he did not propose to take her on at that moment. She showed no resentment.

'I'll walk as far as your hotel, then decide what I want to do. I like wandering about Venice at night.'

Gwinnett was certainly showing himself capable of handling Pamela in his own manner. He seemed, at worst, to have accomplished a transformation of rôles, in which she stalked him, rather than he her. That might produce equally hazardous consequences, not least because Pamela herself showed positive taste for the readjustment. The hunter's pursuit was no doubt familiar to her from past experience, only exceptional, in this case, to the extent that Gwinnett was already in her power from need to acquire Trapnel material.

'OK,' he said.

The three of us set off together. Nothing much was said until we were quite close to the hotel. Then, on a little humped bridge crossing a narrow waterway, Pamela stopped. She went to the parapet of the bridge, leant over it, looking down towards the canal. Gwinnett and I stopped too. She stared at the water for some time without saying anything. Then she spoke in her low unaccentuated manner.

'I've thought of nothing but X since I've been in Venice. I see that manuscript of his floating away on every canal. You know Louis Glober wants to do it as a film, with just that ending. It might have happened here. This place just below.'

Gwinnett seemed almost to have been waiting for her to make that speech.

'Why did you do it?'

He asked that quite bluntly.

'You think it was just to be bitchy.'

'I never said so.'

'But you think it.'

He did not answer. Pamela left the parapet of the bridge. She moved slowly towards him.

'I threw the book away because it wasn't worthy of X.'

'Then why do you want Glober to make a picture of something not worthy?'

'Because the best parts can be preserved in a film.'

I supposed by that she meant her own part, in whatever Trapnel had written, could be recorded that way; at least her version of it. Then Gwinnett played a trump. Considering contacts already made, he had shown characteristic self-control in withholding the information until now.

'Trapnel preserved the outline himself in his *Common-place Book*.'

'What's that?'

'Something you don't know about.'

171

'Where is it?'

'I've got it.'

'He says there what he said in *Profiles in String*?'

'Some of it.'

'I'll destroy that too—if it isn't worthy of him.'

Gwinnett did not answer.

'You don't believe me?'

'I entirely believe you, Lady Widmerpool, but you don't have the *Commonplace Book*.'

In another mood she would certainly have shown contemptuous amusement for Gwinnett's prim formality of manner. Now she was working herself up into one of her rages.

'You won't take my word—that I threw the manuscript into the Canal because it wasn't good enough?'

'I take your word unreservedly, Lady Widmerpool.'

Gwinnett himself might have been quite angry by then. It was impossible to tell. As usual he spoke, like Pamela herself, in a low unemphatic tone.

'X himself knew it was a necessary sacrifice. He said so after. He liked to talk about that sort of thing. It was one side of him.'

What she stated about Trapnel was not at all untrue, if strange she had appreciated that aspect of him. She was an ideal instance of Barnby's pronouncement that for a woman being in love with a man does not necessarily imply behaving well to him. Some comment of Trapnel's about the destruction of the manuscript must have come to her ears later.

'That was why he threw away his swordstick too.'

This settled the fact of someone having given her an account of the incident. Not myself, unlikely to have been Bagshaw, the story had just travelled round.

'You knew that?'

She was insistent.

'I'd been told,' Gwinnett admitted.

He was stonewalling obstinately.

'You don't know what sacrifice is.'

Gwinnett gave an odd smile at that.

'What makes you think so?'

If Pamela were an uncomfortable person, so was he. The way he asked that question was dreadfully tortured. If she noticed that fact—as time went on one suspected she did not miss much—she gave no sign.

'I'll show you.'

She slipped from off her shoulder the bag Glober had given her, wound the chain quickly about it, forming a rough knot. Then, holding the shortened links of gold, whirled round the bundle in the air, like a sort of prayer-wheel, and tossed it over the side of the bridge. There was the gentlest of splashes. The crocodile-skin (returned to its natural element) bobbed about for a second or two on the surface of the water, the moonlight glinting on metal clasps, a moment later, weighed down by the weight of its chain, sinking into the dark currents of the little canal. Gwinnett still did not speak. Pamela returned from the parapet from which she had watched the bag disappear.

'That shows you what X did with something he valued.'

She had evidently intended to play out for Gwinnett's benefit a figurative representation of the offering up of both manuscript and swordstick. Gwinnett did not propose to allow that. He showed himself prepared for a tussle.

'You said just a short while back you didn't think all that of the purse.'

He stood there openly unimpressed. For the moment it looked as if Pamela were going to hit him in the face, register one of those backhand swings she had dealt Stevens in the past. She may have contemplated doing so, thought better of it. Instead, she took hold of his right arm with her left hand, and hammered on his chest with her fist. She must have hit him quite hard. He retreated a step or two from the force of the onset, laughing a little, still not speaking. Pamela ceasing to pound Gwinnett at last, stood back. She gave him a long searching look. Then she turned, and walked quickly away in the direction from which we had come. Gwinnett did nothing for a minute or two. Either a lot of breath had been knocked out of him, and he was recovering, or he remained lost in contemplation of the whole strange incident; probably both. Then at last he shook his head.

'I'd best go see what she's after.'

He too set off into the night. He did that at a more moderate speed than Pamela's. I left them to make whatever mutual coordination between them, physical or intellectual, seemed best in the light of whatever each required from the other. Even in the interests of getting a biography written about Trapnel, it was not for a third party to intervene further. Gwinnett had certainly entered the true Trapnel world in a manner no aspiring biographer could discount. It was like a supernatural story, a myth. If he wanted to avoid becoming the victim of sorcery, being himself turned into a toad, or something of that kind—in moral terms his dissertation follow *Profile in String* into the waters of the Styx—he would have to find the magic talisman, and do that pretty quickly. It might already be too late.

Dr Brightman was in the hall of the hotel. She too had just come in. The evening with Ada had been a great success.

'What a nice girl she is. I hear you both met at the Biennale. Russell Gwinnett suggested we should go there together. I must speak to him about it.'

'Russell Gwinnett's just been beaten up by Lady Widmerpool.'

Dr Brightman showed keen interest in the story of what had been happening. At the end she gave her verdict.

'Lady Widmerpool may be what Russell is looking for.'

'At least she could hardly be called a mother-substitute.'

'Mothers vary.'

'You called him gothic?'

'To avoid the word decadent, so dear to the American heart, especially when European failings are in question. It is rarely used with precision here either. Of course there were the *Décadents*, so designated by themselves, but think of the habits of Alexander the Great, or Julius Ceasar, neither of whom can be regarded as exactly decadent personalities.'

'Are you implying sexual ambivalence in Gwinnett?'

'I think not. His life might have been easier had that been so. Of course he remains essentially American in believing all questions have answers, that there is an ideal life against which everyday life can be measured—but measured only in everyday terms, so that the ideal life would be another sort of everyday life. It is somewhere at that point Russell's difficulties lie.'

We said goodnight. I slept badly. Tokenhouse rang up early again the following morning. He brushed aside reference to the visit to his studio. He was, in his own terms, back to normal, comparative gaieties of the Glober luncheon obliterated entirely.

'I think you said you were going to be in Venice another day or two?'

I told him when the Conference broke up.

'In that case we shall not be able to meet again—and I shall not require the package, of which I spoke, posted in England. I find I am falling seriously behind in my work. Got to buckle down, not waste any more time with visitors, if the job is to be properly done. Of course I was glad to see you after so many years, hear your news. Painting is like

175

everything else, it must be taken seriously. No good other-wise. That does not mean I was not pleased we fell in with each other. Let me know if you come to Venice again on a similar peregrination with your intellectual friends.'

'Did you clear up Widmerpool's problem?'

'Widmerpool?'

'The man who came in while we were looking at your pictures.'

'Widmerpool? Ah, yes, Lord Widmerpool. For the moment I could not place the name. Yes, yes. I did my best for him. Only a small matter. I don't know why he seemed so concerned about it. He simply wanted to ascertain the whereabouts of a friend we have in common. By the way, keep it to yourself, will you, that you met Lord Widmerpool at my studio. He asked me to say that. I have no idea why. He rather gave me to understand that he had offered some excuse, other than that he was coming to see me, to avoid some social engagement—I can sympathize with that—and did not want so flimsy a motive to be revealed. Well, I mustn't waste the whole morning coffee-housing on this vile instrument. Has your Conference settled anything by its coming together? No? I thought not. Goodbye to you, goodbye.'

He rang off. When I saw Gwinnett later in the morning, before one of the sessions, I asked if he had caught up with Pamela. He replied so vaguely that it remained uncertain whether he had managed to find her; or found her, and been sent about his business. He said he was not packing up with the Conference, having decided to stay on for the Film Festival. Then he spoke as an afterthought.

'There's something I'd be glad for you to do for me when you get back to England—tell Trapnel's friend, Mr Bagshaw, whom you mentioned, I'll be calling him up. Just so he doesn't think I'm some crazy American dissertation-writer, and give me the brush-off.'

'He won't do that. Where are you staying in London?'

Gwinnett named an hotel in Bloomsbury, a former haunt of Trapnel's.

'That will be fairly spartan.'

'I'll get the atmosphere there. Later I might try some of the more rundown locations too.'

'You're going to do it in style.'

'Sure.'

I saw Gwinnett only once again, the day the Conference closed. He appeared carrying a small parcel, which looked like a paper-wrapped book. This he handed to me.

'It's Trapnel's *Commonplace Book*. You'll like to see it, though there isn't all that there.'

'Won't you need it? When will I be able to return it to you, and where?'

'You keep it for the next few weeks. I'd rather it wasn't in my own hands for the time being. I'll get in touch when I want it back.'

That was all he would say, except also implying a preference not to be called up, otherwise contacted, at the hotel. Apart from the loan of the *Commonplace Book*, a generous one, our parting was as stiff as our meeting had been. Thinking over the unsolicited lending of the *Commonplace Book*, I could only surmise he felt the Trapnel notes, after what she had said, safer right away from Pamela. Did he not trust himself, or was it that he thought her capable of anything? Dr Brightman, not remaining for the Film Festival, was also delaying immediate return to England.

'It seemed a pity to be in this part of Italy, and not idle away a few days with the Ostrogoths and Lombards. The Venetian air overcomes one with dilettantism. That nice little Ada Leintwardine says she will join me for a night or two, when the Film Festival is over, at whatever place I have reached by then. Such an adventure to have met Lady Widmerpool. My colleagues will be green with envy.'

At that period, when one travelled to and from Venice direct by air (the route avoided by Widmerpool), a bus picked up, or set down, airport passengers in the Piazzale Roma. By night this happened at an uncomfortable hour. You waited in a caffè, the bus arriving about one o'clock in the morning. Ennui and dejection were to be associated with the small hours spent in that place. Even in daytime the Piazzale Roma, flanked by two garages of megalomaniac dimension, overspread with parked charabancs and trucks, crowded throughout the twenty-four hours with touts and loiterers, is a gloomy, dusty, untidy, rather sinister spot. These backblocks, raw underside of the incredible inviolate aqueous city, were no doubt regarded by Tokenhouse as the 'real Venice'—though one lot of human beings and their habitations cannot be less or more 'real' than another—purlieus that, in Cassanova's day, would have teemed with swindlers, thieves, whores, pimps, police spies, flavours probably not wholly absent today.

Waiting for the airport bus, I watched gangs of young men circling the huge square again and again. They seemed to wander about there all night. As one of these clusters of itinerant corner-boys prowled past the caffè, a straggler from the group turned aside for a moment to utter the hissing accolade owed to any female passer-by not absolutely monstrous of feature.

'Bella! Bellissima!'

A confrère ahead of him looked round too, and the wolf-whistler, forgetting his own impassioned salutation of a moment before, entered into argument with his friend, quite evidently about another subject. They all trudged on, chattering together. Through the shadows, recurrently dispersed by flashing headlights of cars passing and repassing, a slim trousered figure receded through murky byways, slinking between shifting loafers and parked vehicles. It certainly looked like Pamela Widmerpool. She was alone, roving slowly, abstractedly, through the Venetian midnight.

4

BAGSHAW WAS AT ONCE ATTENTIVE to the idea of an American biographer of X. Trapnel seeking an interview with himself. In fact he pressed for a meeting to hear a fuller account of Gwinnett's needs. Television had made him more prolix than ever on the line. One was also increasingly aware that he was no longer Books-do-furnish-a-room Bagshaw of ancient days, but Lindsay Bagshaw, the Television 'personality', no towering magnate of that order, but, if only a minor scion, fully conscious of inspired status. He suggested a visit to his own house, something never before put forward. In the past, a pub would always have been proposed. Bagshaw himself was a little sheepish about the change. Complacent, he was also a trifle cowed. He attempted explanation.

'I like to get back as early as possible after work. May prefers that. There's always a lot to do at home.'

The idea of Bagshaw deferring, in this manner, to domesticity, owning, even renting, a house was an altogether unfamiliar one. In early life, married or single, his quarters had been kept secret. They were in a sense his only secret, everyone always knowing about his love affairs, political standpoint, prospects of changing his job, ups and downs of health. Where he lived was another matter. That was not revealed. One pictured him domiciled less vagrantly

than Trapnel, all the same never in connexion with anything so portentous as a house. There was no reason why
Bagshaw should not possess a house, nor in general be
taken less seriously than other people. No doubt, for his
own purposes, he had done a good deal to encourage a view
of himself as a grotesque figure, moving through a world
of farce. Come to rest in relatively prosperous circumstances,
he had now modified the rôle for which he had formerly
typecast himself. Dynamic styles of life required one
'image'; static, another. How deep these changes went
could not be judged. Bagshaw remained devious.

'We're a bit north of Primrose Hill. I got the lease on
quite favourable terms during the property slump some
years after the war, when I left *Fission*. I shall look
forward to hearing all about Professor Gwinnett, when I
see you.'

Bagshaw's house, larger than surmised, was of fairly
dilapidated exterior. Waiting on the doorstep, I wondered
whether the upper storeys were let off. Children's voices
were to be heard above, one of them making rather a fuss.
Children had never played a part in the Bagshaw field of
operation. They seemed out of place there. I rang a couple
of times, then knocked. The door was opened by a girl of
about sixteen or seventeen. Rather vacant in expression,
reasonably good-looking, she was not on sight identifiable
as member of the family or hired retainer. The point could
not be settled, because she turned away without speaking,
and set off up some stairs. At first I supposed her a foreign
'au pair', speaking no English, possibly seeking an interpreter, but, as she disappeared, she could be heard complaining.

'All right, I'm coming. Don't make such a bloody row.'

The protest was a little hysterical as uttered. There was
an impression, possibly due to a naturally tuberous figure,
that she might be pregnant. That could easily have been a

mistaken conclusion. I waited. Several doors could be explored, if no one appeared. I was about to experiment with one of these, when an elderly man, wearing a woollen dressing-gown, came slowly down the stairs up which the girl had departed. It was evident that he did not expect to find me in the hall. His arrival there would pose action of some sort, but, suddenly aware of my presence, he muttered some sort of apology, retreating up the stairs again. Even if Bagshaw's way of life had in certain respects altered, become more solid, a fundamental pattern of unconventionality remained. The problem of what to do next was solved by the appearance, from a door leading apparently to the basement, of Bagshaw himself.

'Ah, Nicholas. When did you arrive? How did you get in? Avril opened the door, I suppose. Where is she now? Gone off to quieten the kids, I expect. You haven't been here long, have you?'

'No, but a white-haired gentleman came down the stairs just now, apparently seeking help.'

Bagshaw dismissed that.

'Only my father. May didn't appear, did she? The gas-cooker's blown. Come in here, shall we?'

He had changed a good deal since last seen. At that period we did not have a television set, so I had never watched a Bagshaw programme. He looked not only much older, also much more untidy, which once would have seemed hard to achieve. The room we entered was even untidier than Bagshaw himself. The mess there was epic. It seemed half-study, half-nursery, in one corner a bookcase full of works on political theory, in another a large dolls' house, lacking its façade. The tables and floor were covered with type-scripts, income-tax forms, newspapers, weeklies, mini-cars, children's bricks. Bagshaw made a space on the sofa, at the far end from that where the stuffing was bursting out.

'Now—a drink?'

'Who is Avril?'

'One of my stepdaughters.'

'I didn't know—'

'Three of them. Avril's not a bad girl. Not very bright. A bit sub, to tell the truth. She's in rather a jam at the moment. Can't be helped.'

Bagshaw made a despairing, consciously theatrical gesture, no doubt developed from his professional life.

'Are the other stepchildren upstairs?'

He looked surprised. Certainly the ages seemed wrong, if anything were to be inferred from the noises being made.

'No, no. The ones upstairs are my own. The stepchildren are more or less grown-up. Getting into tangles with boy-friends all the time. You see I'm quite a family man now.'

Bagshaw said that in a whimsical, rather faraway voice, probably another echo of his programme. His whole de-meanour had become more histrionic, at least histrionic in a different manner from formerly. He sat down without pouring himself out a drink, something not entirely without precedent, though unlikely to be linked now with curative abstinences of the past.

'Aren't you having anything?'

'I hardly drink anything these days. Find I feel better. Get through more work. Here's May. How's your migraine, dear? Have a drink, it may make you feel better. No? Too busy?'

Mrs Bagshaw, in her forties, with traces of the same blonde good-looks as her daughter, had the air of being dreadfully harassed. She was also rather lame. Evidently used to people coming to see her husband about matters connected with his work, perfectly polite, she obviously hoped to get out of the room as soon as possible, after giving some sort of a progress report about the cooking-stove crisis. This problem solved, or postponed, she excused herself and retired again. Bagshaw, who had listened gravely, replied

183

with apparent good sense to his wife's statements and questions, clearly accepted this new incarnation of himself. In any case, it was no longer new to him. When Mrs Bagshaw had gone, he settled down again to his professionally avuncular manner.

'Where will this American friend of yours stay in London, Nicholas?'

'In one of those bleak hotels X used to frequent. He hopes to get the atmosphere first-hand. He really is very keen on doing the book well.'

'Which one?'

Bagshaw groaned at the name, and shook his head. To judge from the exterior of the place, that reaction was justified.

'I spent a night there myself once years ago—rather a sordid story I won't bore you with—in fact recommended the place to Trappy in the first instance. The bathroom accommodation doesn't exactly measure up to the highest mod. con. standards. You know how strongly Americans feel about these things.'

'Gwinnett wants the Trapnel ethos, not the best place in London to take a bath.'

'I see.'

That fact impressed Bagshaw. He thought about it for a moment.

'Look here, this idea occurred to me as soon as you mentioned your American. Why doesn't Professor Gwinnett —I mean only when he's completed his stint of Trapnel ports of call, not before—come and PG with us? The spare room's free at the moment. Our Japanese statistician went back to Osaka. I think we made him comfortable during his stay. At least he never complained. That may have been Zen, of course, overcoming of illusory dualisms. I got quite interested in Zen while he was with us.'

The idea of lodging with Bagshaw, a guest paying or

non-paying, would once have seemed almost as extra-ordinary as the fact of his possessing a house. Even in the reformed state of his ménage there were disrecommend-ations. If anyone were to be 'lodger', Bagshaw himself had always appeared prototype of the kind, one of Nature's lodgers; coaxing the landlady, when behind with the rent, seducing her daughter, storing (in his revolutionary days) subversive pamphlets under the bed. He was imaginable in all such stylized circumstances; even meeting his death as a lodger—the Passing of the Third Floor Back, with Bagshaw as the body. Although that picture had to be revised, the thought of paying to live with Bagshaw was still to be accepted with some demur. That was what I felt as Bagshaw himself digressed on the subject.

'The Icelander, an economist, was rather a turgid fellow, the Eng. Lit. New Zealander, a charming boy. We're looking for a replacement just like your friend—and what could be better from his point of view, if he's writing a book about poor old Trappy? I'll tell you what, Nicholas, I'll send a line to Professor Gwinnett to await arrival, so that he can arrange to see me whenever it suits his purpose. We'll have a talk. If all goes well, I'll suggest he comes and beds down here. I'll put it this way, that he doesn't dream of doing any such thing until he's made an exhaustive study, in depth, of Trapnel haunts, thoroughly absorbed the Trapnel *Weltanschauung*. That should not take long. The essentials are not difficult to grasp.'

Gwinnett was, after all, well able to look after himself. He needed no surveillance, would resent anything of the sort. Besides, from Gwinnett's point of view, there was something to be said for hearing about Trapnel, while living side by side with Bagshaw. If he decided that to stay with the Bagshaws was convenient to his purpose, he would do so; if not, either refuse, or after brief trial withdraw. That was the situation. In any case, Gwinnett was not concerned with living a life of ease, but—something very different—living the life of Trapnel. To lodge with the Bagshaws would in no way run counter to that ambition, in spite of Trapnel himself never having undergone the experience. He must have done similar things. At that moment a girl, recognizable as sister of Avril, probably a year or so older, came into the room. She took no notice of us, but knelt down, and began hunting about in the bookcase. She, too, was fairly good-looking.

'What do you want, Felicity?'

'A book.'

'This is Mr Jenkins.'

'Hullo,' she said, without turning round.

'Where's Stella?' asked Bagshaw.

'God knows.'

She found her book, and went away, slamming the door after her. Bagshaw grimaced at the noise.

'That one's rather a worry too. Young people are nowadays. It's either Regan or Goneril. Look here, have you seen this? Only one paper reported the item.'

He searched about among the assortment of journals lying on the floor, indicating a short paragraph on the foreign news page, when he found the special one he wanted. Its subject was a recent state trial in one of the countries of Eastern Europe, action somewhat unexpected in an atmosphere, in general, of relaxed international tension. Representatives of an outgoing Government had been expelled from the Party, and a former police minister, with one or two others, imprisoned by the new administration taking over. No great prominence was being given by the London press to these proceedings, which appeared to be of a fairly stereotyped order in the People's Republic concerned. That morning a modest headline in my own paper had drawn attention to allegations that some of the accused had been in the pay of the British Secret Service. The three or four persons named as having set out to corrupt members of the fallen Government (together with certain officials and 'intellectuals') were all British Communists of some public standing, or at least prominent fellow-travellers, making little or no concealment of their political affiliations; in short, as little likely to be connected with the British Secret Service, as the accused of being in touch with that organization. An additional name, unintelligibly translated, had been put within inverted commas in Bagshaw's newspaper paragraph.

'Who is . . .?'

The row of consonants, unlinked by vowels, was not to be spoken aloud. Bagshaw was quite excited. He was no longer an oppressed family man, nor even a television 'personality'.

'Is it one of their own people?'

'You don't recognize the name?'

'Not at all.'

'Try speaking it.'

On the tongue the syllables were no more significant.

'An old friend.'

'Of yours?'

'Both of us.'

'A hanger-on of Gypsy's?'

That was just a shot at possibles.

'Once, I believe. A *Fission* connexion.'

'A foreigner?'

'Not at all.'

'You're not suggesting the name's "Widmerpool"?'

'What else could it be?'

'Denounced as—what amounts to being denounced as a Stalinist?'

'In fact, a Revisionist, I think.'

'But—'

'I always said he was at the game.'

'Does a certain Dr Belkin mean anything to you?'

Among the scores of such names proverbial to Bagshaw, Dr Belkin's did not figure. That did not alter the conviction Bagshaw had already reached about Widmerpool.

'There have been some odd stories going round about both the Widmerpools since Ferrand-Sénéschal died.'

Bagshaw was not greatly interested in whatever part Pamela had played. It was the political angle he liked.

'That woman may have invented the whole tale about herself and Ferrand-Sénéschal. A sexual fantasy. It wouldn't surprise me at all. The denunciations at the trial are another matter. It's become a routine process. Nagy in Hungary, earlier in the year. Slansky in Czechoslovakia. I'd like to know just what happened about Widmerpool. He probably didn't move quite quick enough. Might be a double bluff. You can't tell. He himself could have felt he needed a little of that sort of attention to build up his reputation as an anti-Communist of the extreme Left. Make people think he's a safe man, because he's attacked from the Communist end. Pretend he's an enemy, when he's really a close friend.'

Bagshaw rambled on. Time came to leave. I was rather glad to go. The Bagshaw house was on the whole lowering to the spirit. Its other members did not appear again, but, when Bagshaw opened the front door, discordant sounds were still audible from the higher floors, together with the noise of loud hammering in the basement. Bagshaw came down the steps.

'Well, goodbye. I expect you're hard at work. I've been thinking a lot about Widmerpool. He's a very interesting political specimen.'

The Venetian trip, contrary to the promises of Mark Members, had not renewed energies for writing. All the same, established priorities, personal continuities, the confused scheme of things making up everyday life, all revived, routines proceeding much as before. The Conference settled down in the mind as a kind of dream, one of those dreams laden with the stuff of real life, stopping just the right side of nightmare, yet leaving disturbing undercurrents to haunt the daytime, clogging sources of imagination—whatever those may be—causing their enigmatic flow to ooze more sluggishly than ever, periodically cease entirely.

Gwinnett showed no sign of arrival in England. In the light of his general behaviour, changing moods, estrangement from social life, distaste for doing things in a humdrum fashion, that was not at all surprising. If still engaged in the unenviable labour of sampling first-hand former Trapnel anchorages, he might well judge that enterprise liable to prejudice from outside contacts. Some writers require complete segregation for getting down to a book. Gwinnett could be one of them. He was, in any case, under no obligation to keep me, or anyone else, informed of his movements. He might quite easily have decided that, so far as I was concerned, any crop of Trapnel memories had been sufficiently harvested by him in Venice. When it comes to recapitulation of what is known of a dead friend, for the benefit of a third party (whether or not writing a biography), remnants transmissible in a form at once lucid, unimpeded by subjective considerations, are astonishingly meagre.

I felt a little concerned by being left with the *Commonplace Book* on my hands, and would have liked opportunity to return it to Gwinnett. Scrappy, much abbreviated, lacking the usual neatness of Trapnel's holographs, its contents were not without interest to a professional writer, who had also known Trapnel. The notes gave an idea, quite a good idea, of what the novel destroyed by Pamela might have been like, had it ever been finished. Certain jottings, not always complimentary, had obvious reference to herself. Clearly obsessive, they were not always possible to interpret. If Pamela had her way, a film based on *Profiles in String*

—more likely on Trapnel's own life—made by Glober, the *Commonplace Book* could be of assistance.

If Gwinnett wanted to 'understand' Trapnel, two aspects emerged, one general, the other peculiar to Trapnel himself. There was the larger question, why writers, with apparent reserves of energy and ideas, after making a good start, collapse, or fizzle out in inferior work. In Trapnel's case, that might have been inevitable. On the other hand, its consideration as an isolated instance unavoidably led to Pamela. Gwinnett's approach, not uncommon among biographers, seemed to be to see himself, at greater or lesser range, as projection of his subject. He aimed, anyway to some extent, at reconstructing in himself Trapnel's life, getting into Trapnel's skin, 'becoming' Trapnel. Accordingly, if, in the profoundest sense, he were to attempt to discover why Trapnel broke down, failed to surmount troubles, after all, not greatly worse than many other writers had borne—and mastered—the inference could not be dodged that Gwinnett himself must have some sort of a love affair with Pamela. So far as he had revealed his plans, Gwinnett appeared to aim at getting into Trapnel's skin, but not to that extent. In fact everything about Gwinnett suggested that he did not at all intend to have a love affair with Pamela. If he accepted the possibility, he was playing his cards with subtlety, holding them close to his chest. It was, of course, possible something of the sort had already taken place. Instinctively, one felt that had not happened.

This conjecture was endorsed—anyway in one sense— in an odd manner. To express how things fell out is to lean heavily on hearsay. That is unavoidable. Trapnel himself, speaking as a critic, used to insist that every novel must be told from a given point of view. An extension of that fact is that every story one hears has to be adjusted, in the mind of the listener, to prejudices of the teller; in practice, most listeners increasing, reducing, discarding, much of what they have been told. In this case, the events have to be seen through the eyes of Bagshaw's father. What Bagshaw himself later related was not necessarily untrue. Bagshaw was in a position to get the first and best account. He must also have been the main channel to release details, even if other members of the household added to the story's volume. Nevertheless, Bagshaw's father, in his son's phrase 'the man on the spot', was the only human being who really knew the facts, he himself only some of them.

The first indication that Gwinnett had accepted Bagshaw's offer, gone to live in the house, was a story purporting to explain why he had left. This was towards Christmas. It looks as if the alleged happenings were broadcast to the world almost immediately after taking place, but only a long time later did I hear them from Bagshaw's own lips. Dating is possible, because, on that occasion, Bagshaw made a great point of the Christmas decorations being up, imparting a jovial grotesqueness to the scene. Knowledge of the Christmas decorations did certainly add something. Through thick and thin, Bagshaw always retained vestiges of a view of life suggesting a thwarted artist, no doubt the side that finally brought him where he was.

'My father enacted the whole extraordinary incident under a sprig of mistletoe. In the middle of it all, some of the holly came down, with that extraordinary scratchy noise holly makes.'

Although I had not expected Bagshaw's father to be descending the stairs in his dressing-gown, when I called at the house, I had, in the distant past, more than once heard Bagshaw speak of him. They were on good terms. Even in those days, that had seemed a matter of interest in the light of the manner Bagshaw himself used to go on. Bagshaw senior had been in the insurance business, not a notable success in his profession, being neither energetic nor ambitious, but with the valuable quality that he was prepared to put up in a good-natured spirit with his son's irregularities of conduct. On this account there was a certain justice in Bagshaw apparently more or less supporting his father in retirement.

Mr Bagshaw had risen in the night to relieve himself. He was making his way to a bathroom in, or on the way down to, the basement. This fact at once raises questions as to the recesses of the Bagshaws' house, its interior architectural complications. An upper lavatory may not have existed, been out of order, possibly occupied, in view of what took place later. On the other hand, some preference or quirk may have brought him downstairs. He could have been making a similar journey, when I had seen him. Perhaps sleeping pills, digestive mixtures, medicaments of some sort, were deposited at this lower level. The essential thing was that Mr Bagshaw had to pass through the hall.

It seems to have been a mild night for the time of year. That did not prevent Mr Bagshaw from being surprised, even for a moment startled, when, turning on one of the lights, he saw a naked woman standing in the passage or hall. Here again the narrative lacks absolute positiveness. In a sense, the truth of its essential features is almost strengthened by the comparative unimportance adjudged to exact locality. Bagshaw's insistence on the mistletoe suggests the hall; other circumstances, a half-landing, or alcove, on the first-floor; not uncommon in a house of that date, possibly also offering a suitable nook or niche for mistletoe.

Bagshaw's father, short-sighted, had not brought his spectacles with him. His immediate assumption was that the dimly outlined female shape was one of his son's stepchildren, who, having taken a bath at a relatively unorthodox hour, had considered dressing not worth while for making the short transit required to her bedroom. Bagshaw, telling the story, admitted the girls behaved in a sufficiently unmethodical, not to say disordered manner, to make that possibility by no means out of the question. What seemed to have caused his father most surprise was not so much lack of clothing, but extinction of all movement. The naked lady was lost in thought, standing as if in silent vigil.

Mr Bagshaw made a conventional remark to the effect that she 'must not catch cold'. Then, probably owing to receiving no reply, grasped that he was not speaking to one of the family. He may also, in spite of his poor sight, have observed the lady's hair was grey, even if scarcely seeing well enough to appreciate threads of strawberry-pink caught by artificial light. Whatever he did or did not take in, one must concur in Bagshaw's praise of his father for showing good sense, in no manner panicking at this unforeseen eventuality. At one time or another, he had undoubtedly experienced testing incidents in the course of existence with Bagshaw as a son, but by then he was a man of a certain age, and, however happy-go-lucky the atmosphere of the household, this was exceptional. Speculation as to what Mr Bagshaw thought is really beside the point. What happened was that (as when I myself saw him) he muttered an apology, and moved on; his comportment model of what every elderly gentleman might hope to display in similar circumstances.

Whether or not he associated in his mind the midnight nymph with Gwinnett is another matter. Gwinnett by then had lived in the house some little time, probably a couple of months. Equally unknown is how Pamela, in the first instance, effected entry into the Bagshaw house. Even Bagshaw himself never claimed to be positive about that. His theory was she had somehow ascertained the whereabouts of Gwinnett's bedroom, then more or less broken in. That seems over-dramatic, if not infeasible. A more probable explanation, that one of the stepdaughters, the rather dotty, possibly pregnant one likeliest, had admitted her earlier in the evening, then denied doing so during subsequent investigations; Pamela finding Gwinnett in his room, or waiting there for his return. If the former, the two of them, Pamela and Gwinnett, had spent quite a long time, several hours, in the bedroom together, before Bagshaw's father encountered her, wherever he did, in an unclothed state.

She was no longer in the hall, or on the half-landing, when Mr Bagshaw reappeared on his return journey. He seems to have taken this as philosophically as he had earlier sight of her, simply retiring to bed again. If he hoped after that for a good night's rest, that hope was nullified by a further complication, a more ominous one. This development had taken place while he was himself down in the basement incommunicado. Bagshaw's other stepdaughter, Felicity, now played a part. Woken by the interchange, slight as that had been, between Pamela and Bagshaw's father, or (another possibility) herself cause of Mr Bagshaw's descent to the basement by excluding him from an upstairs retreat, perhaps noticing the light on, came down to see what was afoot. She was faced with the same spectacle, a slim grey-haired lady wearing no clothes. Bagshaw, when he spoke of the matter, added a gloss to the circumstances.

'The truth seems to be—I'd noticed it myself—Felicity had taken a fancy to Gwinnett. That was why she drew the obvious conclusions, and kicked up the hell of a row. So far as I know, Gwinnett hadn't made any sort of a pass at her. Perhaps that was what made her so keen on him. Before you could quote Proudhon's phrase about equilibrium of competition, her sister Stella heard the talking, and came down too. The whole lot were quarrelling like wild cats.'

Just what happened at this stage is not at all clear; nor at what moment were spoken the words to put in some sort of perspective subsequent events. Gwinnett, of course, himself appeared. He dealt as well as he could with Bagshaw's stepdaughters, while Pamela dressed and slipped away. Probably she retired on Gwinnett's arrival, leaving him to cope. She was not present by the time Bagshaw, made aware by the noise that something exceptional was taking place, joined the party. Mrs Bagshaw, like her father-in-law, assuming some comparatively minor domestic contingency in progress, still suffering from migraine, did not leave her bed. Avril, incurious or occupied with her own problems, also remained in her room. Bagshaw said that, insofar as it were possible to behave with dignity throughout the whole affair, Gwinnett contrived to do so.

'He didn't say much. Just offered some apologies. Of course, it was obviously Pamela Widmerpool's fault, not his. He didn't attempt to excuse himself on that account.'

The night's disturbances appear to have died down in a fairly banal family quarrel, nothing to do with Pamela or Gwinnett. In fact, the following day, Bagshaw—so far as I know, May Bagshaw too—was prepared for all to be forgiven and forgotten. On this point Bagshaw's father and stepdaughters do not seem to have been consulted. Gwinnett himself was firm that he must leave. He moved to an hotel (another of Trapnel's haunts) the same afternoon. Bagshaw said he was uncertain what he felt after Gwinnett had gone.

'I was sorry to lose him. At the same time I saw, from his own point of view, it would be difficult to stay on. The whole thing might happen again, if that woman knew he was still living with us. Of course, I thought they were having an affair, that she had come to the house to sleep with him. If so, I couldn't see why either of them needed to make all that to-do. Couldn't he have done whatever her other lovers do? That was how it looked at the moment.'

By the time Bagshaw told the story himself, a good deal had happened to give opportunity for improving its framework, accentuating highspots of the narrative. One could not be quite sure he had not seen things differently during the embroilment. For example, he spoke of words, possibly apocryphal, murmured by Pamela, as she withdrew (however that had happened) from the house. Bagshaw put this scarcely coherent sentence forward as key to what took place later, explanation, too, of the night's doings, or lack of them; for that matter, general relationship with Gwinnett.

Bagshaw could not swear to the exact phrase. It had something to do with 'dead woman' or 'death wish'. He also asserted that Gwinnett, while staying in the house, had spoken more than once of Pamela's conjunction with Ferrand-Sénéschal, bearing out Dr Brightman's theory that Gwinnett himself was more than a little taken up with mortality. Bagshaw gave other instances. At the time, naturally, emphasis immediately afterwards was laid on the question why Pamela had been wandering about without any clothes. Reflecting on similar instances in my own experience, there was the time (actually not witnessed) when the parlourmaid, Billson, had walked naked into the drawing-room at Stonehurst; more tangibly, when the front door of her flat had been opened to myself by Jean Duport in the same condition. Unlike Candaules's queen, these two had deliberately chosen to appear in that state, not, as the Queen—anyway vis-à-vis Gyges—involuntarily nude. Perhaps the Tiepolo picture had done something to disturb the balance of Pamela's mind, in the light of her reported behaviour at the Bragadin dinner party. The situation—just what had really caused the doings at the Bagshaws'—remained, at the end of that year, still obscure. Most people who took any interest in the matter simply assumed Pamela and Gwinnett had been 'having an affair', some row taken place, notable only for Pamela's incalculable manner of handling things.

About January or February, Gwinnett himself sent a line saying he would like to meet. He wished the *Commonplace*

Book returned to him, unless I particularly needed to keep it longer. We arranged to lunch together on a day I was coming to London. Gwinnett had not remained unaffected by the months spent in England. Whether the change was due to odd experiences undergone, or simply because he felt a sense of release in making a start on his book, was impossible to say. The transformation itself was not easy to define. Not exactly loosened up, he gave at the same time an impression of being on better terms with himself. Here in London he looked more 'American' than in Venice. He still wore his light blue lenses, only just observably tinted against the sun. It was not the effect of these. The spectacles, thin filament of moustache, secretive manner, implied quite other origins. One thought, for some reason, of the Near East, though he was not in the least oriental. Perhaps his air was Mexican. The Americanism had something to do with the intense whiteness of his shirt, cut low in the neck, the light shade of the heavily welted rubber-soled shoes, almost yellow in colour. The shoes were the first thing you noticed about him. Ignorant still of just what had happened at the Bagshaws', I had no way of rationalizing to myself the slight, but apparent alteration. The *Commonplace Book* was handed over. Gwinnett mentioned that he had stayed with the Bagshaws, then decided he would work more easily in another of Trapnel's hotels.

'How much of the book have you done?'

'I might have roughed out the first quarter.'

He spoke of some of his discoveries. From various sources, he had unearthed material about Trapnel's early life in Egypt. Perhaps concentrating on Egypt had given Gwinnett the Near East look. He could list, among other things, racehorses Trapnel's father had ridden, and their owners. There were striking facts about the schools Trapnel had attended, which were many and various. Gwinnett had worked hard.

'Have you traced any of the girls?'

'I have.'

Tessa, who had immediately preceded Pamela as object of Trapnel's love, was doing extremely well. She was secretary, evidently a high-powered one, to the chairman of a noted firm of merchant bankers. Tessa had been helpful to Gwinnett in a straightforward way, giving him a clear, unvarnished account of Trapnel's daily life, its interior economy, seen from the point of view of an intelligent, capable mistress, who wanted her lover to become a success as a writer. Although retaining affectionate memories of Trapnel, she decided in due course, she said, that he lacked the necessary stamina. That was an interesting first-hand view. Gwinnett had appreciated its good points.

'Then there was Pat.'

Pat, now married to a don, Professor of Social Science, had been less willing to have her past dredged up. She had replied with a tactful letter saying she preferred not to see Gwinnett.

Sally was dead. That was all he had been able to find out about her.

'I'd have liked to know more—how and why she died.'

Jacqueline had married a journalist, and was living abroad, where her husband was foreign correspondent to a daily paper. Linda could not be traced.

'Did you know Pauline?'

'I never met her. I've heard Trapnel speak of her. He thought her depraved. Those were his words. They remained on good terms after parting.

'I ran Pauline to earth.'

'What's she doing?'

'She's become a call-girl.'

'Trapnel said that was where Pauline would end.'

'Well, not much short of that, I'd say.'

Gwinnett seemed uncertain whether or not to qualify the

description. He thought for a moment, then decided against amendment.

'I went to see her. She told me some facts.'

'Such as?'

'What some of her clients like.'

'Anything out of the usual run?'

'Not much, I guess.'

'I'd have thought Trapnel pretty normal.'

'She said he was.'

Gwinnett changed the subject. I thought he had abandoned it. I was wrong. He was choosing another conversational angle, one of his habits, at times effected in a manner a little disconcerting.

'Did Lindsay Bagshaw say there'd been some trouble at his place?'

'I haven't seen him, but I heard something of the sort. I knew you'd left.'

'You heard Lady Widmerpool kicked up a racket there?'

'Her name was mentioned.'

'As raising hell?'

'Well, yes.'

'If you run across Lady Widmerpool, do you mind not telling her my address?'

'OK.'

'You heard about Lord Widmerpool being denounced on the radio as a British agent? Lindsay Bagshaw talked his head off about it. I'm not that interested in politics, though I couldn't but be interested in such a thing happening. Just because of all the Trapnel tie-up with her. What do you think?'

'He might be in deep water. Hard to say, at this stage.'

Gwinnett hesitated, seeming, as he sometimes did, uncertain of the exact ground he wanted to occupy.

'Lady Widmerpool—Pamela—I wouldn't be in her husband's shoes, if she's left to decide his fate.'

'She's got it in for him?'

'That's how it looks.'

'You're avoiding her for the time being?'

That was a reasonable question in the circumstances. Gwinnett did not answer it. At the same time he accepted its inferences.

'Just to duck back to Pauline for a spell—she had dealings with Lord Widmerpool.'

'Professional ones, you mean?'

'Sure.'

'He picked her up somewhere? Answered an ad?'

'When his wife was living with Trapnel, Widmerpool had her shadowed. As a former girl friend of Trapnel's, whom he saw once in a while, Pauline's name was given to Widmerpool.'

'And he went to see her?'

'They met somehow.'

'Continued to meet?'

'It seems arrangements were made satisfactory to both sides. Pauline later figured at several parties attended by Widmerpool—and the Frenchman, too, who died all that sudden, when Pamela was around.'

'Pauline told you that?'

Gwinnett nodded. He had a way with him when he sought information. At least information was what he acquired.

'Was Pamela herself included in these Pauline jaunts?'

'I don't know for certain. I don't believe so.'

Thought of Pamela seemed to depress Gwinnett. He fell into one of his glooms. Their relationship was an enigma. Perhaps he was in love with her, in spite of everything. We parted on good terms, the best. Gwinnett spoke as if we were likely to talk together again as a matter of course, do that quite soon. At the same time he parried any suggestion of coming to see us; even arranging another meeting in London. This determination that initiative should remain in his hands was a reminder of Trapnel methods. Possibly it was one of the ways in which Gwinnett was growing to resemble Trapnel.

During the next month or so, Gwinnett's problems receded in my mind as a matter of immediate interest, Widmerpool's too. Fresh information about the second of these came from two rather unexpected sources. These followed each other in quick succession, although quite unconnected.

For several years after the war, I had attended reunion dinners of one of the branches of the army in which I had served, usually deciding to do so at the last moment, even then never quite knowing what brought me there. Friends made in a military connexion were, on the whole, to be seen more conveniently, infinitely more agreeably, in settings of a less deliberate character, where former brother officers, now restored to civilian life in multitudinous shapes, had often passed into spheres with which it was hard to make conversational contact. Intermittent transaction in the past of forgotten military business provided only a frail link. All the same, when something momentous like a war has taken place, all existence turned upside down, personal life discarded, every relationship reorganized, there is a temptation, after all is over, to return to what remains of the machine, examine such paraphernalia as came one's way, pick about among the bent and rusting composite parts, assess merits and defects. Reunion dinners, to the point of morbidity, gave the chance of indulging in such reminiscent scrutinies. Not far from a vice, like most vices they began sooner or later to pall. Even the first revealed the gap, instantaneously come into being on demobilization, between what was; what, only a moment before, had been. On each subsequent occasion that hiatus widened perceptibly, moving in the direction of an all but impassable abyss.

There were, of course, windfalls. One evening, at such an assemblage, my former Divisional Commander, General Liddament (by then promoted to the Army Council) turned up as guest of honour, making a lively speech about the country's military commitments 'round the map', ending with a recommendation that everyone present should read Trollope. That was an exceptional piece of luck. In the same way, an old colleague would sometimes appear; Hewetson, who had looked after the Belgians, now senior partner in a firm of solicitors: Slade, Pennistone's second-string with the Poles, headmaster of a school in the Midlands: Dempster, retired from selling timber, settled in Norway, still telling his aunt's anecdotes about Ibsen. Finn, Commanding Officer of the Section, was dead. At the end of the war he had gone back briefly to his cosmetic business in Paris, soon after left, to end his days in contemplation of his past life and his VC, near Perpignan. Pennistone (married to a French girl, said to have taken an energetic part in the Resistance) had stepped into Finn's place in the firm. His letters reported good sales. He rarely came to England, spare time from the office taken up with writing a book on the philosophical ideas of Cyrano de Bergerac.

Usually there was less on offer, fewer, still fewer, even known by sight. That was especially true when the thinned ranks of branches, originally designed to be reunited on this particular occasion, were augmented by other elements. These, if remotely related in duties, had once been regarded with a certain professional suspicion, but their attendance too dwindled through death and inanition, requiring, as we did, bolstered numbers to make the party worth while. In short, feeling increasingly isolated, I lost the habit of attending these dinners. Then, a son likely to become liable for military service, it seemed wise to re-establish bearings in a current army world, find out what was happening, pick up anything to be known. I put down my name again, without much hope of seeing anyone with whom closer bonds were likely to be evoked than shared memory of whether or not some weapon, piece of equipment, had 'come off the security list' for release to the Allies, or by swopping stories about the shortcomings, as an officer and a man, of the unpopular brigadier.

That year the dinner was held on the premises of a club or association of vaguely patriotic intent, unfamiliar to myself both in membership and situation. The dining-room was decorated in a manner sober to the point of becoming sepulchral, drinks obtainable from a bar at one end. No one standing about there was an acquaintance. At the table assigned to my former Section, faces were equally unknown. Mutual introductions took place. My righthand neighbour, Lintot, fair, bald, running to fat, had looked after some of the Neutrals—a 'dismal crowd', he said—before Finn commanded, later posted to Censorship in the Middle East. He worked in a travel agency. We talked of the best places to take an autumn holiday abroad.

Macgivering, on the other side, also belonged to a War Office epoch earlier than my own. His duties had been in the Section handling in-coming telegrams, where he remembered the stunted middle-aged lieutenant, for ever polishing his Sam Browne belt. We had both forgotten his name. Macgivering himself, tall, spare, haggard, with a slight stutter, had been invalided out of the army, consequent on injury from enemy action, while in bed at his flat one early night of the blitz. We split a bottle of indifferent Médoc, and discussed car insurance, as he had some sort of public relations connexion with the motor business.

Only towards the end of dinner did I notice Sunny Farebrother sitting at the end of a table on the far side of the room. During the war he had operated in several areas of army life, including at least one of those branches now joined to the increasingly disparate elements of this dinner. He had found himself a place at right angles to the 'high table', where more important members or guests sat. He was talking hard. His neighbour looked like a relatively senior officer, whom Farebrother appeared to be indoctrinating with some ideas of his own. Farebrother looked in the best of form. He must be close on seventy, I thought. At the end of these dinners movement away from table places was customary, so that people could circulate. I decided to have a word with Farebrother at this interspersion. He was still in earnest conversation with the supposed general, when the time came. He could be pushing a share in which he was interested. I had not seen him at or near the bar on arrival. Probably he had deliberately turned up at the last moment to avoid threatened liability for buying a drink.

While I waited for a suitable moment to move across to Farebrother's table, a man with woolly grey hair and wire spectacles (the latter not yet a fashionable adjunct) came to speak with Lintot. Macgivering had already left, to make contact elsewhere in the room. I changed into his former seat, to allow the wire-spectacled man to talk in more comfort sitting next to Lintot. They appeared to know each other through civilian rather than army connexions. Lintot was astonished at the wire-spectacled man's presence at this dinner. His wonderment greatly pleased the other.

'Didn't expect to find your accountant here, did you, Mr Lintot? We can both of us forget the Inland Revenue for once, can't we? To tell the truth, I'm attending this dinner under rather false pretences. The fact is a friend of mine told me he was coming to London for this reunion. We wanted to talk together about certain matters, one thing and another, so as I'd gained a technical right to be deemed Intelligence personnel, I applied to the organizers of this 'I' dinner. They said I could come. I always enjoy these get-togethers. My old mob have one. There's a POW one too. Why not roll up, I said to myself.'

'Never knew you were in the army. Of course we've always had a lot of other things to talk about, so that wasn't surprising.'

Lintot appeared rather at a loss what to say next. He drew me into the conversation, mentioning we had been in the same Section, though not in the War Office at the same period.

'This is—well, I've got to be formal, and call you Mr Cheesman, because I only know your initials—this is Mr Cheesman, whose accountancy firm acts for mine. For me personally too. We do our best against the taxman between us, don't we? I didn't expect to find him here. Never thought of Mr Cheesman as a military man somehow, though I never think of myself as one either, if it comes to that.'

'Yes, but you see my point. If I'm eligible, no reason why I shouldn't come to the dinner, is there?'

Cheesman was insistent. He was not in the least put out by Lintot's emphasis on the unmilitary impression he gave. What he was keen on, pedantically keen, consisted in establishing his, so to speak, legal right to be at the party. He spoke in a precise, measured tone, as if attendance at the dinner were a matter of logic, as much as free choice.

'Of course, of course. Glad to see you here. You're about the only man in the room I've met before.'

Lintot was quite uninterested in Cheesman's bona fides as 'I' personnel. Cheesman accepted that his point had been understood, even if unenthusiastically. Now, I remembered that manner, at once mild and aggressive. It brought back early days in the army—Bithel, Stringham, Widmerpool.

'Didn't you command the Mobile Laundry?'

I appended the number of General Liddament's Division to that question.

'You were there just for a short time, the Laundry only attached. Then it was posted to the Far East.'

Cheesman drew himself up slightly.

'Certainly I commanded that sub-unit. May I ask your name?'

I told him. It conveyed nothing. That was immaterial. Cheesman's own identity was the important factor.

'Surely you fetched up in Singapore?'

Cheesman nodded.

'In fact, you were a Jap POW?'

'Yes.'

Cheesman gave that answer perfectly composedly, but for a brief second, something much shorter than that, something scarcely measurable in time, there shot, like forked lightning, across his serious unornamental features that awful look, common to those who speak of that experience. I had seen it before. Cheesman's face reverted—the word suggests too extended a duration of instantaneous, petrifying exposure of hidden feeling—to an habitual sedateness. I remembered his arrival at Div. HQ; showing him the Mobile Laundry quarters; making this new officer known to Sergeant-Major Ablett. Bithel had just been slung out. I had left Cheesman talking to the Sergeant-Major (who had the sub-unit well in hand), while I myself went off for a word with Stringham. One of Cheesman's peculiarities had been to wear a waistcoat under his service-dress tunic. He had been surprised at that garment provoking amused comment in mess.

'A waistcoat's always been part of any suit I wore. Why change just because I'm in the army? I've got to keep warm in the army, like anywhere else, haven't I?'

He did not give an inch, either, in adapting himself to military manners and speech, behaving to superiors as he

206

would in a civilian firm, where he was paid to give the best advice he could in connexion with his own employment. He dressed nothing up in the forms and terms traditional to the military subordinate. Colonel Hogbourne-Johnson had been particularly irked by that side of Cheesman. He used to call him 'our Mr Cheesman', a phrase in which Cheesman himself would have found nothing derogatory. Thirty-nine when he joined the army at the beginning of the war, he wanted to 'command men'. He must be nearly sixty now. Except when that frightful look shot across his face, the features were scarcely more altered than Sunny Farebrother's.

'How the hell did you survive your Jap POW camp?' asked Lintot cheerfully.

Cheesman brushed the question aside.

'A bit of luck. The Nips were moving some of their prisoners in '44. Don't know where they were taking us. When we were at sea, the Nip transport was sunk by an American warship. No arrangements made for POWs, of course, when ship's company took to the boats, but the Americans rescued most of us—and a lot of the Nips too.'

'Don't expect you were feeling too good by that time?'

'Naturally I wasn't fit for normal duties for a month or two. When I was on my feet again, I got a change of job. They were short of Intelligence wallahs where I was. I'd picked up a few words of Japanese. It was thought better to make use of me in 'I', rather than go back to Mobile Laundry duty, though I'd have liked to return to the job for which I'd been trained. That's why I'm allowed here, without being strictly speaking applicable. Funny meeting you, Mr Jenkins. I don't remember your face at all at that Div HQ. The officer I recall is the DAAG, Major Widmerpool. He made quite an impression on me. Very efficient, I should say. A really good officer. You can always tell the type. I expect he's done well in civilian life too.'

'Do you remember a man in your sub-unit called Stringham?'

Cheesman looked surprised at the question.

'Of course I do. How did you know Stringham?'

'We were friends in civilian life.'

'You were?'

Cheesman found that statement hard to credit. He thought about it for a second or two. Stringham and I —that was the impression—seemed miles apart. He wrestled with the question inwardly. When at last he answered, it was as if prepared to accept my word, even then the claim scarcely believable.

'I see. I do recall now Stringham wasn't just the ordinary bloke you find in the ranks. I was taken aback at first when you said you'd known him. Of course, you get all sorts in a war. He was a superior type, an educated man. You could see that. All the same I never thought about it much. He never made any difficulties. I'd forgotten altogether. Just remember him in the jobs he used to do. I could never place him myself. What was his work in civilian life?'

That was a hard question to answer. What did Stringham do? Cheesman must be told something. What about the time when (with Bill Truscott as dominant colleague) he had been a sort of personal secretary to Sir Magnus Donners? I fell back on that. To be a secretary implied at least a measure of professional identity. That would serve the purposes of the moment.

'Stringham was private secretary to a business tycoon.'

'Oh, was he?'

Cheesman seemed at first more surprised than ever. He did not pursue the matter. His own job could well have brought him face to face with eccentric business tycoons. Either that struck him, or he decided to leave the question vague in solution.

'He was very fond of making jokes, but I always found him an excellent worker in my sub-unit.'

Cheesman said that without the least disapproval. He spoke as one merely registering an unusual characteristic. So far as jokes were concerned, his own features proclaimed a state of intact virginity as to any experience or sense of them, immaculately so. Cheesman had never made a joke, never seen a joke, could live—and die—without jokes, even if he knew they existed. It did him credit to have so far rationalized Stringham's behaviour as to be capable of thus defining it. Stringham might have been worse typified.

'Stringham made jokes in the camp,' he added.

'He wasn't taken from Singapore too?'

'No.'

Again the ghastly forked lightning flashed, a flicker of Death's vision, reflected for a dreadful instant behind the wire spectacles' plates of glass. The flesh of Cheesman's face, softly wrinkled, made one think of those old servants of the past, who had worked unquestioningly for a lifetime in a single household. In Cheesman's case this unchanging interior had been, no doubt, his own austere, limited—one might reasonably say—heroic personality. There was the same self-assurance as Dan Tokenhouse, the same impression of having dispensed with sex. There was something else too.

'Stringham died in the camp. He behaved very well there.'

Cheesman thought for a moment after saying that.

'Very well. Yes. A good man. He wasn't too strong, you know. Fancy your having met him. They're odd these things. Sergeant-Major Ablett, you may remember him. He was rescued. He's quite prosperous now.'

The matter was better pressed no further. More information could easily become too much, too much anyway for one's peace of mind. Cheesman gave no sign that might be so. He also made no attempt to enlarge. Lintot, under-

standably, had not been much interested in these reminiscences. If Cheesman were his personal accountant, as well
as his firm's, he may have felt he had a better right than
myself to Cheesman's attention, even if he had brought us
together again.

'Don't mind my talking shop for a moment, Mr
Cheesman. It will save a letter. Now about Tax Reserve
Certificates ...'

By then Farebrother's senior officer had managed to get
away, with or without buying the shares remained unknown. Farebrother himself was making preparations to
leave the party, giving a final look round the room to
make sure he had missed no one worthy of a few minutes'
conversation. I went across to him. His friendliness was
positively enormous. The powerful extrusion of Farebrother
charm remained altogether undiminished by age. He was
specially pleased about something, possibly success in whatever he had recommended his neighbour.

'There's an empty stretch of table over there, Nicholas.
Let's sit at it. I don't feel like any more to drink, do you?
Got to cut down on the pleasures of life nowadays. Something I want to ask you. What do you think of the latest
development in the Widmerpool case?'

'I didn't know there was a case.'

'You haven't read the evening paper? The Question in
the House? I think he's for it now.'

Farebrother was amazed anyone should have missed such
a pleasure as that night's evening paper. His handsome
greyhound profile, additionally distinguished with increased
age, lighted up while he supplied a commentary. He made
clear that, in his opinion, this news was going to offer no
minor revenge. The Parliamentary Question had been on
the subject of Widmerpool's commercial activities in Eastern
Europe. To outward appearance worded in terms not at all
sensational, they were, to an initiate in that form of attack,

ominous in the extreme. The country concerned was the one where Widmerpool had been named in connexion with the State trial. Farebrother said he understood there had also been a denunciation on the air in one of their official broadcasts.

'The implications arc of the most damaging order.'

'What's he really been up to?'

Farebrother, usually in the habit of cloaking his own imputations or reprisals in mild, vaguely expressed language, now made no bones about the disaster threatening his old enemy. He seemed to know more than was easily to be drawn from the mere wording of the Question, however much that were open to sophisticated interpretation. His war service (like that of Odo Stevens) had given Farebrother contacts from which such enlightenment might be derived. Someone in a position to 'know' could have dropped a hint. That was certainly the impression Farebrother himself, truly or not, hoped to give.

'Some underling on their side was accepting bribes, and has now defected, so I've heard said. That had been done with Widmerpool's connivance. He had been giving encouragement, too, by passing across little bits of information himself from time to time. How valuable that information was remains to be seen. In any case, I'm just putting two and two together. Most of it guesswork.'

'Will it come to arrest, a trial?'

'That depends what the employee reveals—if that story is true.'

'In any case that would be *in camera*?'

'You can't say. Some evidence probably.'

'The Question is just a ranging shot?'

'Not far from the target. Give him a jolt. I can tell you something else too.'

Farebrother looked about to make sure no one was sitting near us, who might overhear what he was going to say.

Most of the diners were now congregated round the bar. Many had left, or were leaving. He put his arm over the back of my chair.

'I've just retired from one of the smaller merchant banks. We deal with European and overseas commercial activities and investments. Fascinating work.'

I toyed with the fantasy that Trapnel's former girl, Tessa, was going to abut on to what Farebrother had to say, then remembered Gwinnett had described her as working for the chairman of a large, rather than small, merchant bank.

'I don't mind telling you some of the Eastern European deals of our friend might be of interest from the taxation angle, if figures had to be produced in a court of law. Nothing to do with treasonable dealings, just bank statements. I make no accusations. Just of interest, I suggest.'

Farebrother smiled his charming smile. He settled back into his own chair. Then he looked at his watch.

'Good gracious me, I must be getting home. Geraldine and I are not at all late birds.'

'She is well, I hope.'

Farebrother snapped his fingers in the air to give some idea of his wife's overflowing health and spirits. He was in his gayest mood. The Parliamentary Question had made his day. It provided something far better, in a different class, from the occasion when Widmerpool's career had been threatened by nothing worse than the disapproval of General Liddament.

'We've found a nice little flat, not too expensive, well appointed as you could wish. Geraldine has a wonderful instinct for the right sort of economies, so we don't have to be thinking about the pennies all the time now. In fact we find we can run a country cottage too. Roses are my interest these days. I don't mind telling you, Nicholas, I'm rather proud of my roses. You and your wife must look us up, if you're ever passing. We can't always manage luncheon. Tea certainly. Well, it's been a most enjoyable evening. I heard Ivo Deanery was to be present as a guest —can't remember if you know him, he's a major-general now—and we settled some useful matters. Don't forget that invitation—preferably when the roses are in bloom.'

He repeated the address of the cottage, waved one of his genial goodbyes, was gone. The following day, the Parliamentary Question was brought up again at another party, in very different circumstances. This occasion owed something to the diplomatic détente, of which Bagshaw had spoken. The so-called 'thaw' had been reflected, in a minor manner, by the tour through some of the European capitals of a well-known Russian author, bestseller in his own country. To give a few of our own literary world opportunity to meet a confrère, not in general encountered in the West, a luncheon, to which I found myself invited, was given at the Soviet Embassy.

At this gathering, a foreseen profusion of literary figures had been perceptibly infused with a sprinkling of MPs, other notabilities, official and semi-official, either with a view to imparting additional robustness of texture to the party, or, more probably, simply to work off individuals, whose names were listed for entertainment, sooner or later, on the ambassadorial roster. Including our hosts of the Embassy staff, a large number of whom were present, about forty or fifty persons were drinking vodka, sampling zakuski, sitting in small groups scattered about a long, austerely decorated drawing-room. There was a faint atmosphere of constraint, as if someone or something essential to the party had not yet been manifested, but that would happen in a moment, when, from then on, all would be well, much easier, more relaxed.

The invitation had not included wives of writers asked as guests, but both the Quiggins were there, Quiggin's status as a publisher no doubt judged of sufficient eminence to be considered out of context, permitting accompaniment of his novelist consort. Alaric Kydd—to use a favourite phrase of Uncle Giles's—was behaving as if he owned the place. Other writers included L. O. Salvidge, Bernard Shernmaker, Quentin Shuckerly, a lot more, men greatly predominating in numbers over women. Mark Members was absent, known to be ill; Len Pugsley, not important enough, or considered too closely 'committed' to be asked to a purely social party. Evadne Clapham had also been overlooked, more probably barred from acceptance by a too relentless social programme of her own. Dr Brightman, sprucely dressed in a fur cap and high fur collar, revealing a rather chilly manner to Ada Leintwardine, passed her with a smile, moving on to where L. O. Salvidge and I were chatting to one of the secretaries of embassy.

'I hope you don't think my clothes too *voulu*?'

The secretary nodded, and laughed. He was a tall fair young man, of surface indistinguishable from any other member of London's diplomatic corps, of similar age and seniority. We discussed signs of spring in the London parks. The young secretary moved away for a moment to receive incoming guests. Salvidge caught my eye. His silent lips formed the words 'KGB'. The secretary returned before any sort of secretly uttered return comment was possible. Dr Brightman shared none of Salvidge's trepidation about our surroundings.

'Have you seen anything of Russell Gwinnett? I've quite lost touch with him. He was staying at one moment with some people called Bagshaw. He wrote to me from their house. Rather a depressed letter. I hear he left after some sort of trouble. The most extraordinary story I was told.'

Salvidge must have thought this subject dangerously controversial, perhaps because Gwinnett was American. He showed disquiet. At the same time he did not want to appear excluded from the circles of which Dr Brightman spoke.

'Gwinnett came to see me. We had a talk. A nice young man. Not very exciting. I was not sure he was up to tackling so picturesque a figure as Trapnel.'

Salvidge turned to the secretary to explain what he was talking about.

'This is a young writer called Gwinnett—G-W-I-N-N-E-T-T—who is writing a book about a novelist, now dead, called Trapnel—T-R-A-P-N-E-L—a good writer. One of our best.'

'Yes?'

Salvidge must have thought this the moment to change the subject, probably what he had been leading up to.

'Dr Brightman here, you know, is writing a book about Boethius—B-O-E-no diphthong—'

The secretary nodded politely, but cut Salvidge off.

'See, we must go into luncheon.'

We were firmly shepherded into the dining-room. So far as Salvidge was concerned, not a moment too soon. Here again was a faint sense of austerity, an impression of off-white walls sparsely decorated with pictures, landscapes light in tone—the steppe—birch trees—sunset on snow—nothing in the least reminiscent of Tokenhouse and his school. My place at table was between another secretary, possibly counsellor, somewhat older than the first, equally trimmed to outward diplomatic convention; on the other side, a personage not encountered for years, Bill Truscott.

Tipped, as a young man, for at least a place in the Cabinet, even if by some mischance he failed to become Prime Minister, Truscott, after a promising start at Donners-Brebner, had come to rest in some governmental corporation, possibly the Coal Board. The Russian engaged with his other neighbour when I sat down, Truscott and I went through the process of recalling where we had last met. He still carried some of his old, rather distinguished style, a touch, too, of the old underlying toughness that had made people think he would forge ahead. Fresh from observing Farebrother as a professional charmer, one could not help feeling Truscott, at least ten years younger, had worn worse. His manner dated. If he had become the 'great man' predicted, no doubt it would have been perfectly serviceable. As he was, the demeanour was a trifle laboured, ponderous.

I thought of my undergraduate days, when Truscott had been not merely an imposing, but positively frightening figure, setting up, by his flow of talk, standards of sophistication never to be contemplated as attainable. This brilliance of exterior, again, had been of quite a different sort from Glober's. Even in those days, Truscott had been far less lively. There could be no great difference in age, even if the advantage was slightly on Truscott's side. Unlike Glober, he had remained a bachelor. I spoke of Sillery's ninetieth birthday party. It appeared Truscott had not been invited. He showed a little bitterness about that. It was true he had been one of the staunchest vassals of Sillery's court. He should not have been forgotten. He asked if I often found myself in this embassy.

'My first visit—and you?'

'I'm asked from time to time. I'm afraid I'm not at all conversant with the current work of the guest of honour. I never read novels nowadays . . .'

Possibly thinking that admission, for more than one reason, suggested a too headlong falling-off from what had once been an all embracing intellectual coverage, Truscott corrected himself. He gave one of his winning smiles.

'That is, you understand, I don't find much time, with so many things going on—as we all have—of course I fully intend . . . and naturally . . .'

I told him what I had heard about Stringham, once his fellow secretary. Truscott showed interest.

'Very sad. Poor Charles. He was a pleasant companion. One of the nicer people round Donners.'

Thought of his days working for Sir Magnus must have brought Widmerpool to mind; more specifically, as agent of his own sacking from Donners-Brebner. He lowered his voice.

'Hardly a subject for discussion here, but one cannot help being a little intrigued by the embarrassments, at the moment, of another protégé of Sir Magnus of that period.'

'What's going to happen to him?'

By that time, having read the morning paper, I saw what Farebrother meant by speaking of Widmerpool's position as insecure. Truscott certainly thought the same. He coughed, in a semi-official manner.

'I should expect various enquiries of a—well, not exactly public nature—not immediately public, I mean—likely to be set on foot.'

'You think it pretty serious?'

'That would certainly be . . .'

'Might come to a trial?'

'One cannot tell. I—'

Massive middle-aged waitresses had been bustling about the room, snapping out a sharp commentary to each other in their own language, as they clattered with the plates. Now, one of them interposed a large dish of fish between Truscott and myself, severing our connexion. At the same moment, my Russian neighbour began a conversation. Soon, by natural processes, we were discussing Russian writers. After Lermontov and Pushkin, Gogol and Gontcharov, Tchekov and Tolstoy, Dostoevsky's name cropped up. Pennistone—who would never allow intellectual standards to be lowered, just because he was in the army, a war on—had complained that, when he spoke of

Dostoevsky's Grand Inquisitor to General Lebedev, the Soviet military attaché (unconvincing as a regular soldier) had recommended Nekrasov's truer picture of Russian life. In short, Dostoevski, impossible to ignore, equally impossible to assimilate into Communist life, a monolithic embarrassment to his countrymen, was a tendentious subject for the present luncheon party, however unequivocally political the tradition of the Russian novel. Remembering Trapnel once speculated on the meaning of the surname 'Karamazov', I put the question.

'Am I right in thinking "kara" has some implication of blackness? The former Serbian royal house, Karageorgevitch, was not that founded by Black George? But "mazov"? How would that be translated into English?'

My Russian neighbour laughed. He seemed very willing that a Dostoevskian commentary should move into etymological channels, away from potentially political ones. The idea of giving The Brothers an English surname pleased him.

'I shall consult a colleague.'

He spoke quickly in his own language across the table. There was a short discussion. He returned to me.

'He says "kara" means "black" in Turkish. There is a Russian adjective "chernomazy"—do you say "swarthy"? Then "maz", it is "grease", the verb, to smear or to oil. Would that be "varnish" in English?'

Dr Brightman, sitting next to the informant on the other side of the table, was not to be left out of a discussion of this nature. She showed interest at once.

'*The Brothers Blackvarnish?* No, that would hardly do, I think. We must find something better than that.'

She shook her head, giving the matter her full attention.

'How would *The Blacklacquer Brothers* be?'

We discussed the question. While we did so, I reflected how this was all based on Trapnel's meditation on the meaning of the name, his argument with Bagshaw in that dreary pub came back, Trapnel's contention that there was no such thing as Naturalism in novel writing, one of his favourite themes.

'Reading novels needs almost as much talent as writing them,' he used to say.

The occasion had been just before Bagshaw and I had taken him home, on the way found that Pamela had thrown his manuscript into the Regent Canal. Trapnel had said something else that evening too. Now the words came back, in the way spoken words do, with quite a new meaning.

'Call Hemingway's impotent good guy naturalistic? Think of what Dostoevsky would have made of him? After all, Dostoevsky did deal with an impotent good guy in love with a bitch.'

Was that the answer? Was he a good guy? Was he in love? Was the condition only released by Death? The train of thought was interrupted by Dr Brightman offering a new suggestion.

'Simply making use of the connexion with linseed oil— *The Linseed Brothers*?'

'That omits the element of blackness, of darkness, which obviously broods over the story, and must be conveyed by the name.'

When it was time to thank for the party, leave, Truscott, who was by then talking with the Ambassador, gave a smile that indicated he had hopes of the very worst for Widmerpool. Coming down the steps of the Embassy, I found myself with the Quiggins. We walked along Kensington Palace Gardens together, moving south towards the High Street. I asked Ada if any progress had been made in deciding what was to be Glober's last great film.

'Do you mean to say you don't know? Louis is coming over next month. Everything is arranged.'

'What's it to be?'

'*Match Me Such Marvel*, of course. I'm sure it's going to make a box-office record. I can't wait.'

'So Trapnel's off?'

Ada showed more pity than astonishment.

'Trapnel?'

'Glober was going to do a Trapnel film when we were in Venice. Probably a kind of life of Trapnel, with Pamela Widmerpool in the lead. You'd only just begun to make St John Clarke propaganda with him.'

'He saw at once the St John Clarke novel was a much better idea.'

'Is Pamela equally happy?'

Quiggin cut in.

'I'm bored to death with this film of Glober's. I don't believe we're really going to make any money out of it, even if he does it. You never know with these people. Set against Ada's time writing her own novels, or working in the firm, I've always doubted whether it's worth while.'

'Oh, shut up,' said Ada.

She turned to me again.

'Do you really not know about Louis deciding on another girl for his leading lady, as well as ditching the Trapnel idea? That was all settled months ago.'

'Glober found Pamela too much in the end?'

'He fell for someone else.'

Quiggin continued to show irritation about the film.

'Do let's discuss another subject. The food at lunch wasn't too bad. I'm never sure Caucasian wine suits me. I thought he seemed rather a sulky little man, when I had a word with him through the interpreter.

'Who's Glober fallen for now?'

'Why, Polly Duport, of course. You must live absolutely out of the world not to know that. He saw her in the Hardy film at the Venice Festival. She turned up there herself. It was an instantaneous click.'

'Didn't that cause trouble?'

'With Pam?'

'Yes.'

'I don't think Pam really cared by then, even if she cared much before. She was already mad about that other American, what was he called—Russell Gwinnett. She still is. Haven't you heard about what happened at the Bagshaws'?'

'I know about that, more or less, but not about Polly Duport.'

'You remember how horrid Pam was to me in Venice, considering what friends we'd been. She's been ringing me up almost daily lately, trying to find out what's become of Gwinnett. How should I know? I barely met him. The most I did was to ask for us to be allowed to consider his book on X. Trapnel, when it's finished.'

This upset Quiggin again.

'A book on X. Trapnel is never going to sell. Why get us involved in it at all. It would only mean more money down the drain.'

'So any question of Pamela marrying Glober is at an end?'

'Why should she marry Glober?'

'You said he wanted to marry her—not just have an affair with her.'

'I did?'

'Yes.'

'I'm sure I didn't. Anyway, if I did, I shouldn't have done so. Forget about it. Of course, it's all off. How could it be anything else? Louis's terribly sweet and kind, but you never know what he's going to do next.'

'That's just what I've already stated,' said Quiggin.

'All film people go on like that. Never mind. I do think he really is keen on *Match Me Such Marvel*. Of course it's not going to be called that. We haven't decided on the best title yet. Polly is a marvellous girl too. Not only glamorous, but a real professional.'

'What I can't believe is Pamela making no row.'

'Even Pam realized she'd never get the part once Louis began taking Polly out to dinner.'

'Did Pamela meet Polly Duport?'

'I didn't think so. The Widmerpools went back to England halfway through the Film Festival. It was Pam's thing about Gwinnett, as much as anything else, that caused Louis to give her up. It serves Pam right. I believe she really did think she was going to become famous.'

'Why did Glober object so much? Gwinnett was positively running away from the situation, so far as anything Glober might object to. He still is. Even in the early stages, he only wanted Trapnel information.'

'Louis didn't think so. Anyway there was Pam. Perhaps it was because he was another American.'

'Is Glober going to marry Polly Duport now?'

'Isn't she married already, to an actor, though they're living apart? She was on her own when she came to Venice. Perhaps he will.'

'What does Widmerpool think about it all? His feelings don't seem to have been considered much, whether Pam leaves him or stays. Your idea was that he would be quite glad to get her taken off his hands. Now, if he goes to prison for spying, she'll be able to visit him in the Scrubs or Dartmoor, wherever he's sent—give him additional hell.'

Quiggin was outraged.

'You think that a matter to joke about?'

'Isn't that what it looks like?'

'That Parliamentary Question was disgraceful. Our own particular form of McCarthyism. All very gentlemanly, of course, none the less smearingly vindictive.'

'You think he'll emerge without a stain on his character?'

Quiggin was prepared to be less severe on that point.

'Haven't we all sins to forgive? Sins of over-enthusiasm, I mean. Look, Ada, there's our bus.'

5

EACH RECRIMINATIVE DECADE POSES NEW riddles, how best to
live, how best to write. One's fifties, in principle less acceptable than one's forties, at least confirm most worst suspicions about life, thereby disposing of an appreciable tract
of vain expectation, standardized fantasy, obstructive to
writing, as to living. The quinquagenarian may not be
master of himself, he is, notwithstanding, master of a
passable miscellany of experience on which to draw when
forming opinions, distorted or the reverse, at least up to a
point his own. After passing the half-century, one unavoidable conclusion is that many things seeming incredible on
starting out, are, in fact, by no means to be located in an
area beyond belief. The 'Widmerpool case' fell into that
category. It remained enigmatic so far as the public were
concerned. People who liked to regard themselves as 'in
the know' were not much better off, one rumour contradicting another, what exactly Widmerpool had done to put
himself in such an awkward spot remaining undefined. One
extraneous item came my own way, which, as purely
negative evidence, could have been added to material sifted
by whatever official body was undertaking an enquiry. It
was expressed in the form of a picture postcard of the
Doge's Palace.

'Have to date heard nothing from your friend about blocks. Weather here good. D. McN. T.'

That, at least, indicated none of the disaster, threatening Widmerpool on account of Dr Belkin's absence from the Conference, had resulted in Tokenhouse suffering comparable repercussions. I had intended to ask the Quiggins about the blocks for the Cubist series, when walking with them after luncheon at the Soviet Embassy. More personally engrossing matters had intervened. The blocks remained forgotten. I sent Tokenhouse a postcard of Nelson's Column, saying (in army parlance) the matter would be looked into, a report forwarded.

In early summer, Isobel and I went by chance to a musical party organized by Rosie and Odo Stevens. It was a charity affair, our inclusion nothing to do with the meeting in Venice. In fact, the people who brought us knew the Stevenses hardly at all. I make this point to emphasize that guests present at this particular entertainment were not handpicked. No doubt everyone who received an invitation, in the first instance, was an acquaintance of some sort. Beyond such intermediaries stretched a relatively anonymous conflux of persons, whose passport to the house lay only in willingness to buy a ticket. Had things been otherwise, the evening might have turned out differently; possibly not certain other events that followed.

The Stevens house in Regent's Park, not large by the standards of Rosie's parents, though done up inside with a touch of the old Manasch resplendence, had room for a marquee to be built out on to a flat roof at the back to create an improvised auditorium, accommodating a respectable number of persons. Rosie had inherited two or three very acceptable pictures, and pieces of furniture, which Hugo Tolland, speaking from an antique dealer's point of view, regarded with respect. He had sold her two French commodes from his own shop, so they had not been acquired cheaply. Offering this sort of show for a charitable purpose was, on Rosie's part, a pious memento of the days when Sir Herbert and Lady Manasch, great patrons of the arts, had mounted similar projects. Stevens himself, claiming musical enthusiasms, as well as a strong taste for parties, may on this occasion have been at least as responsible as his wife. The 'good cause' was connected with one or more of the emergent African countries; the piece to be performed, Mozart's *Die Entführung aus dem Serail*—the '*Seraglio*'. The price of a ticket included supper after the opera had been performed.

Like the Soviet luncheon party—some of the same guests—there was a distinctly political flavour about the people collected, before the performance, in the Stevens drawing-room, MPs from both sides of the house, some African diplomatic representatives. This time the musical world, Rosie always maintaining links there, took the place of writers. Many of those present were not known to me. I recognized a Tory Cabinet Minister, and a female member of the Labour Shadow Cabinet, from pictures in the press. The music critic, Gossage, and Norman Chandler, who directed now, rather than dancing or acting, had come together. Gossage, a trifle more dried up and toothy than formerly, had exchanged his former pince-nez for rimless spectacles. His little moustache had gone white. Chandler, slightly filled out from the skeletal thinness of his younger days, retained a marionette-like appearance, a marionette now of a certain age. Living in one of the Ted Jeavons flats, Chandler had developed into rather a crony of Jeavons. They used to watch television together.

'Don't think there's much fear I'll be suspected,' Jeavons said. 'All the same, you never know what people will say behind your back.'

On arrival, Isobel had paused to talk with Rosie, who had been a former friend of Molly Jeavons. Moving through the crowd, I came on Audrey Maclintick. She announced the unforeseen fact that Moreland had advised on the *Seraglio*'s production. Quite apart from his poor health, that was unexpected. Moreland had always set his face against charity performances, although there had been occasions in the past when he had been more or less forced to take part in them. Audrey Maclintick agreed their presence was unlooked for. She added that it was not at all the sort of party she was used to. She had said just the same thing when Mrs Foxe had given a party for Moreland's Symphony, more than twenty years before. She herself was not much altered from then, even to the extent of still wearing a version, modified into a more contemporary style, of the dress which, at Mrs Foxe's, had caused Stringham to address her as 'Little Bo-Peep.'

'Hugh's name isn't on the programme?'

'He didn't want it there. The word "Africa" did it. Moreland's cracked about Africa. Always has been, always will be, I suppose. Goes off on the quiet to the British Museum to gaze on the African idols there. Mrs Stevens only had to say the money was going to Africa for Moreland to knock off all his other work, and set about the Mozart. Doesn't matter what worry it causes me. Of course, Moreland knew Mrs Stevens in what he loves to call The Old Days, so The Old Days might have been sufficient anyway, without being clinched by Africa. Whatever I said wasn't going to make any difference.'

Moreland, it was true, had always responded strongly to things African, rather as fountainhead of fetish and voodoo, than aspects of the African continent likely to be benefited by funds raised that night. The fascination exercised on his imagination by such incantatory cults was not unlike Bagshaw's unquenched curiosity about the ritual and dogma of Marxism, neither believers, both enthralled. Once Moreland's attention had been imaginatively aroused, he would find no difficulty in ignoring the fact that witch-doctors, zombies, cults of the dead, might not greatly profit from his help. Moreland himself came up at that moment. Audrey Maclintick did not give him time to speak.

'I expect you've seen who's here tonight—Lady Donners. That was bound to happen. Just her sort of party. I don't expect she wants to see me, any more than I do her. Well, I'll leave you two together to have a talk about The Old Days, which I've no doubt you'll start off on at once. Don't let Moreland have another drink before the curtain goes up. It isn't good for him. He ought to be in bed in any case, not mooning about at a place like this.'

She made off. So far as Moreland having another drink, she was probably right. He did not look at all well. Once, he would have been put out by such an injunction from wife, mistress, anyone else, made a great fuss about being treated as if not able to look after himself. Now, he was not at all concerned, taking the admonition as a matter of course, almost a demonstration of affection, which no doubt in a sense it was. Audrey Maclintick was said to look after him well, in what were not always easy circumstances. Moreland, too, showed signs of accepting her view that his own presence in the Stevens house required excuse.

'Never again. Not after what I've been through with the *Seraglio* committee ladies. Valmont's valet remarked the big difference between persuading a woman to sleep with you, which she really wants to do—though personally I've often found to the contrary—and inducing her to agree to something that offers no comparable satisfaction. My God, he was right.

> Put me
> To yoking foxes, milking of he-goats,
> Gathering all the leaves fall'n this autumn.

228

Drawing farts from dead bodies,
Mustering of ants and numbering of atoms,
There is no hell to a lady of fashion.

I don't mean Rosie. She's all right. It was the rest of them.
They expected me to do just the very things I've mentioned
—every one of them.'

'You've been saying for years you live beyond the pleasure principle. Why boggle at ladies of fashion? Do they
still exist?'

'Believe me they do. Matty's one now. I've just been
having a word with her. Almost the first since we were
husband and wife, beyond saying hullo, when we saw each
other at the Ballet or the Opera. She seems to have supported the death of the Great Industrialist remarkably
well.'

Matilda Donners was standing on the far side of the
room. I had the impression Moreland had never managed
to fall entirely out of love with her.

'I got her to introduce me to Polly Duport, whom she's
talking to now. I've always been rather a fan. What I mean
about Matty's social manner is that, having brought Polly
Duport and myself together, she then had to suggest that I
do the musical settings for some film Polly Duport's going
to play the lead in. It's made from a St John Clarke novel, if
you can imagine anything more grotesque. I remember my
aunt thinking me too young to read *Fields of Amaranth*, but
it isn't that one, and that isn't my objection. The producer,
an American called Glober, was also pressed on me by
Matty. He's that tall, bald, melodramatic character, talking to her now, looking as if he's going to play Long John
Silver in a Christmas production of *Treasure Island*.'

'You've met Glober before.'

I recalled to Moreland the Mopsy Pontner dinner party.
The effect was almost startling. The blood came rushing

into his face as if he were about to have apoplexy. He began to laugh uncontrollably, quite in the old manner. Then, with an effort, he stopped. He was almost breathless, coughing hard. At the end of this near paroxysm he looked less ill, more exhausted. The information had greatly cheered him.

'No, really, that's too much. Am I to be suffocated by nostalgia? Will that be my end? I should not be at all surprised. I can see the headline:

MUSICIAN DIES OF NOSTALGIA

They'd put someone like Gossage on to the obit. "Mr Hugh Moreland—probably just Hugh Moreland these days —(writes our Music Critic), at a fashionable gathering last night—I'm sure Gossage still talks about fashionable gatherings—succumbed to an acute attack of nostalgia, a malady to which he had been a martyr for years. His best known works, etc, etc. . ." Are you aware, quite apart from Matty turning up here tonight, there hangs on the stairs of this very house Barnby's drawing—in his naturalistic manner, I'm glad to say—of Norma, that little waitress at Casanova's Chinese Restaurant? All this, and Mopsy Pontner too. I can't bear it. I shall mount the stage, and announce that, instead of Mozart tonight, I am myself going to entertain the company with a potpourri of nostalgic melodies.'

Moreland paused. He stepped back, clasping his hands, intoned gently:

> 'Dearest, our day is over,
> Ended the dream divine.
> You must go back to your life,
> I must go back to mine.

Nothing short of some such outward expression of my own nostalgic feelings would be at all adequate. You shouldn't have told me about Mopsy Pontner. It wasn't the act of a friend.'

Although still laughing, Moreland, as before sometimes in such moods, had stirred himself emotionally by his own irony, his eyes filling with tears. Stevens came up to us.

'Look, Hugh, the curtain isn't going to rise absolutely on time. A Second Violin was a minute or two late. The regular player went down with flu at the last moment, and a substitute had to be found at short notice. We've been assured he's all right. He's upstairs peeing at the moment, but he'll be along when he's finished, and start fiddling away. Don't get worked up about the delay.'

'You speak as if I was a temperamental impresario about to throw a scene. It's no affair of mine when the curtain goes up. I'd much rather have another drink, which the delay gives me the right to do, whatever Audrey says.'

It was remarkable he should admit to being defiant about what she said. Moreland went off. There was no means of putting a veto on drink into operation. He moved as if his joints were rather stiff these days. Stevens laughed.

'Isn't Hugh splendid? Rosie thought he wasn't well, but he seems perfectly all right to me. I say, who do you think have turned up tonight? The Widmerpools. I suppose he's celebrating.'

'What's he got to celebrate about? I thought he was going to be sent to the Tower, hanged, drawn and quartered.'

'Not now. It's been found "not in the public interest" to proceed with the case. I was hearing about it earlier in the day. A journalist I know told me some quite interesting things. Widmerpool was damned lucky. You can take it from me he was in a tight corner. I suppose he thought this a good opportunity to show himself in public. You can't exactly say with an untarnished reputation, but at least not serving twenty-five years for espionage.'

'Did he apply to you for a ticket, as a once close friend of his wife's?'

'The Widmerpools, old cock, were brought by a friend of Rosie's, Sir Leonard Short, a civil servant with musical leanings, who used to frequent her parents' house. As luck will have it, Tompsitt's here too, our ambassador in the place where Widmerpool was having his trouble. They'll be able to dish it up together. All very respectable.'

'Is the large grim lady Tompsitt's wife?'

'She's rather rich. Schweizer Deutsch. Been married before. Ah, things are moving quicker now. I see Rosie is making signs. Do you and Isobel know where your seats are? I want to talk to Isobel. I haven't seen her for ages.'

He obviously had no idea how much Isobel disliked him. We all passed into the marquee. The Widmerpools, with Short (knighted at the last Birthday Honours), were several rows in front. Short, although his prim buttoned-up exterior allowed few inner doubts to be observed, looked less happy than the occasion seemed to demand, if what Stevens reported about Widmerpool were true. Pressure had perhaps been put on him to arrange this public appearance signalizing exculpation. Less dramatically than that, Widmerpool could simply have wished to hear the opera performed because he hoped to be identified with this particular charity. Love of music was unlikely to have brought him, whatever other reason. He, too, was looking more aggrieved than triumphant. Short's apparent uneasiness—Widmerpool's too, for that matter—may have been due to discovering that Pamela was far from popular with her hostess. If it came to that, Short was not at all well disposed to Pamela himself. She sat beside him, a look of utter contempt on her face, at the same time, rare with her, smiling faintly. She had got herself up in her smartest manner. Only those who knew her reputation might have reflected that, in another, more perverse mood, she might easily have turned up to watch the *Seraglio* wearing an old pair of jeans.

Rosie, Stevens, the Tory Cabinet Minister, his wife, Matilda Donners (who seemed to have brought the last two), were all sitting rather to the side of the front row. Their group, which included Polly Duport and Glober, had probably dined together. Behind the Widmerpools sat the Tompsitts, whom I had noticed on arrival. I had not set eyes on Tompsitt since hearing him, at the close of some inter-service committee, deplore, with Widmerpool, the Poles' lack of circumspection in making representations about Katyn to the International Red Cross. The air of disorder, marking out Tompsitt in his early days as a young diplomatist free from the conventionality ascribed to his kind, had settled down to a middle-aged unkemptness, implying chronic irritability, as much as a free spirit. The exceptionally peevish expression on his face at that moment could be attributed to Widmerpool himself, who, leaning back in a manner threatening to repeat his wife's chair-breaking incident at the French Embassy, showed no sign of ceasing to talk, in deference to the opening notes of the Overture. Finally, Tompsitt's wife raised her programme menacingly. Widmerpool, bowing to force, turned away from them. The curtain rose revealing the Pasha's palace.

During the first interval, on the way out of the marquee, we came on Glober. He was holding Polly Duport lightly by the arm.

'Why, hullo, Nick. Fancy meeting you here. What a hell of a good time we all had in Venice. I'm not going to forget your Major Tokenhouse in years. I had that picture of his packaged, and sent back to the States, where it's to become one of the treasures of the Glober collection of twentieth-century primitives. Why didn't you stop over for the Film Festival, and meet Polly here?'

In saying all this Glober managed also to convey an odd sense of added remoteness, not only in speaking of our Venetian meeting, also somehow in relation to himself. He was not in the least unfriendly, absolutely the reverse, still enormously cordial, at the same time in a manner that set him at a distance, put a cordon round him, entrenched his position. It was a little like the rays people seem to emit when they have promised a job, promotion, invitation, satisfaction of one sort or another, then withdrawn the offer. He continued to speak for a minute or two about the Tokenhouse picture, imprisoning all around him within the net of his own social technique, moving on to the Film Festival, then the St John Clarke novel. He was not quite prepared for Isobel's knowledge (in certain areas rivalling Trapnel's) of obscure or forgotten fiction.

'How well you handle the scene where Phyllida and Prosper get lost in the mist on the glacier at Schwarenbach?'

While Glober dealt with that question, I reminded Polly Duport of our drive back from the St Paul's service, with her mother and stepfather. Undeniably a beauty, less remarkably so off the stage, she had now, I thought, come to resemble Duport more than Jean. She had her father's cool, wary scepticism, as well as Jean's figure and grey eyes. In her thirties, already well known, she had in the film at Venice somehow achieved this additional prestige, a flowering which had instinctively caught Glober's fancy, aroused his untiring interest in the immediate.

'I remember an English officer joining us. So that was you? I suppose you were keeping an eye on my stepfather, making sure he behaved properly in church?'

The comment recalled her mother.

'How is Colonel Flores?'

'Very well indeed. He's a general now, but more or less retired from the army, and in politics.'

'And your mother?'

'She's all right. Fine, in fact. Carlos's new job suits her. You see he's Head of the Government.'

'I didn't know that.'

'For a year now.'

'Dictator?'

'We don't call it that.'

'Your mother must enjoy being Dictatress—Dictatrix, more correctly.'

Polly Duport laughed. She was charming, in spite of resemblance to her father, much 'nicer', one felt, than her mother, but without, so far as I was myself concerned, any of her mother's former bowling-over endowments. Glober must have felt the reverse. Her professionalism of the Theatre, a seriousness her mother could never have achieved, in the Theatre, or any other of the arts, possibly exerting some of that effect on him.

'I think Mama would certainly rather do the job herself.'

'And your father?'

'Do you know him too? You are well up in our family. Papa's in the crude still.'

'The crude?'

This seemed an enormously suitable calling, whatever it was, for Duport to follow, but one could not in the least imagine financial or administrative shape taken by such employment.

'Crude oil. That's how it's known in the trade. His business is mixed up with importing into Canada for processing. He doesn't do too badly. That's his life. Has been for quite a long time now. He's rather crotchety these days. Trouble with his inside. He never really recovered from that upset in the war. Still, Papa has his moments.'

The way she said that recalled Jean again. Glober, who had been explaining to Isobel how he was going to shoot

Match Me Such Marvel in Spain, returned to holding Polly Duport's arm.

'More Mozart now. We'll see you at the next intermission.'

The Widmerpools, Tompsitts, and Short, were standing not far away, the men discussing something in an undertone. Mrs Tompsitt, no beauty, looked less than pleased. As Stevens remarked, she had the air of being rich. She and Pamela were not talking together. Pamela's eye was on us. She was still smiling a little to herself. Glober glanced in her direction, raising his hand slightly in greeting. From the gesture, they appeared not to have met earlier that evening. Pamela made no sign in return, not altering her faint smile. If Glober felt himself in a delicate position, he gave no outward evidence of that. As he strolled away, hand on Polly Duport's elbow, he was perfectly at ease.

'That was the American who planned to run away with Lady Widmerpool, but is to do so no longer?'

'That's the one.'

'She's looking rather frightening tonight.'

Isobel's comment, although it could not possibly have been heard by Pamela at that range, appeared in some manner to react on her. As we approached the marquee again, she broke off from the Tompsitt group, and came towards us. We said good evening.

'I've just this afternoon found where Gwinnett's staying.'

Pamela spoke that like a comment on something we had already discussed together.

'You have?'

'He's been in hiding.'

She laughed. The laugh sounded a little mad.

'You'll never guess who gave me the address.'

'I'm sure I can't.'

'A tart.'

'Indeed?'

'Does it surprise you, him knowing a tart?'

'I'll have to think about the answer to that.'

'Perhaps you know her too?'

'I've no reason to suppose so.'

'She's called Pauline.'

'As it happens, I never met her.'

'A girl of X's.'

'Of course.'

'So it's all above board, so far as Gwinnett's concerned.'

'I agree.'

The music began. She laughed again, and turned away. We found our seats. The Second Act took place, the drunken scenes, the setting to rest of fears that the girls might join the Pasha's harem. When we came out for the second interval, Moreland reappeared. Gossage and Chandler came up.

'I'm always fond of the English maid, Blonde,' Moreland said. 'Unlike the Pasha's gardener, I find that vixenish touch sympathetic.'

'I'm mad about Osmin,' said Chandler.

Gossage giggled nervously, a giggle unaltered by increased age. He brought conversation back to more serious criticism.

'The man's more of a baritone than a bass. Some cardinal appoggiaturas went west in the last Act, I'm afraid. No harm in subordinating virtuosity to dramatic expression once in a way. Not least in a work of this kind. We can't deny a lyrical tenderness, can we? I expect you agree with that, Mrs . . .'

Hesitating to call her 'Mrs Maclintick', after all these years of living with Moreland, at the same time, never having graduated to addressing her as 'Audrey', Gossage's voice trailed gently away. Audrey Maclintick took no notice of him. She spoke quietly, but there was a rasp in her tone.

'Have you seen the Second Violin, Moreland?'

Moreland guessed from her manner of speaking trouble was on the way. He was plainly without a clue what form that might take, why she had asked the question.

'Has he arrived tight, or something? I've conducted unshaved myself before now. One mustn't be too critical. This one's a substitute for the regular man, who's ill. The orchestra wasn't too bad. Allowing for Gossage's just strictures on the subject of appoggiaturas.'

'You haven't noticed one of the Violins, Moreland?'

'No, should I? Has he got two heads, or a forked tail emerging from the seat of his trousers?'

Moreland said that in a conciliatory manner, one he used often to employ with Matilda. Audrey Maclintick brought out the answer through her teeth.

'It's Carolo.'

Moreland was not at all prepared for that. It was not a contingency anyone was likely to foretell; at the same time, the musical world being what it was, one not in the least unheard of in the circumstances. At first Moreland looked dreadfully upset. Then, seeing the matter in clearer proportion, his face cleared. There were signs that he was going to laugh. He successfully managed not to do so, his mouth trembling so much in the effort that it looked for a second as if he might burst into an almost hysterical peal, similar to that brought on by news of Glober's identity. Audrey Maclintick, for her part, showed no sign of seeing anything funny in the presence of her former lover—the man for whom she had left Maclintick—turning up in the *Seraglio* orchestra. Her demeanour almost suggested suspicion that Moreland himself had deliberately engineered transposition of violinists, just to disturb her own feelings. Seeing she was thoroughly agitated about what seemed to himself merely comic—another nostalgic enrichment of the Stevens party—he pulled himself together, plainly with an effort, and spoke soothingly.

'Is this really true? Are you sure it's Carolo? Musical types often resemble each other facially, especially violinists. I've noticed when conducting.'

Audrey Maclintick would have none of that.

'I lived with the man for three years, didn't I? Why should I say he was Second Violin, if he wasn't? I got to know him by sight, even if he didn't spend much time in the house.

Her fluster about the matter was unforeseen. On the whole, one would have been much more prepared for complete indifference. Objecting to the presence of Matilda was another matter. The intensity of feeling that bound Audrey Maclintick to Moreland was all at once momentarily revealed. Moreland made a face in my direction. He must have been wondering whether Matilda—actually married to Carolo for a short period in her early life—had also noticed the presence of her former husband. All this talk caused Gossage to suffer one of his most severe conjunctions of embarrassment. Like a man playing an invisible piano, he made wriggling movements in the air with fingers of both hands, while he mused aloud in a kind of aside.

'I did hear Carolo was not so very prosperous some years ago. No reason why he shouldn't have substituted tonight, prosperous or not. Did it to oblige, I expect.'

Chandler disagreed.

'Who ever heard of Carolo being obliging, since the days when he was fiddling away at Vieuxtemps, in a black velvet suit and lace collar? He's not dressed like that tonight, is he? Now that we're none of us so young, I'm wearing quieter clothes myself.'

That gave Moreland a chance to deflect the conversation.

'Nonsense, Norman, you're known as London's most eminent Teddy Boy.'

The measure was successful so far as putting an end to further discussion about Carolo, until time to return to the marquee. On the way there, Gossage was still muttering to himself.

'They've got polish. Vivacity.'

That was safely to relegate Carolo to a collective group. The orchestra could not be seen from where we sat. So far as I know, direct contact was never made during the further course of the evening between Carolo and his former ladies, but, at the termination of the opera, expression was given to a kind of apotheosis of the situation. This juncture, brief but striking, to be appreciated only by those conversant with Carolo's earlier fame, was too dramatic, too trite, to be altogether good art. Nevertheless, it had its certain splendour, however banal. This happened when, praise of the Pasha's renunciation of revenge chanted to a close, the curtain fell to much applause; then rose again for the reappearance of the cast. The audience was enthusiastic. The curtain rose, fell again, several times. The cast bowed their way off. It was the turn of the orchestral players. They trooped on to the stage.

'Which is Carolo?' whispered Isobel.

I was not sure I should have recognized him among the Violins without prompting. That was not because Carolo's appearance had become in any manner less picturesque than when younger. On the contrary, the romantic raven locks, now snow white, had been allowed to grow comparatively long, in the manner of Liszt, to whom Carolo bore some slight resemblance. His whole being continued to proclaim the sufferings of the artist, just as in days gone by, in the basement dining-room of the Maclinticks. He bowed repeatedly (without the warmth of the old singer in Venice) to the charity-performance guests, with his colleagues, the general acknowledgment of the orchestra.

Then the orchestral players turned, in unison, towards the side of the auditorium, where Rosie and Stevens sat, together with Matilda, the Cabinet Minister and his wife. To these, as begetters of the show, Carolo and his fellows now made a personal tribute, Matilda, of necessity, included in this profound obeisance. The faint smile she gave, while she clapped, was not, I think, illusory. It marked her recognition that rôles had changed since Carolo, young and promising musician, had picked up, married, a little girl from the provinces, just managing to keep afloat as an actress. Matilda's attitude, more philosophic than Audrey Maclintick's, had not been of the temperament to remain married to Moreland. A few minutes later, illustration was provided of unlikely ties that can, on the other hand, keep a couple together, without marriage, probably without sexual relationship. This took place on the way to the supper-room. Odo Stevens came up with two people for whom he wanted to find a place.

'Do you remember, when you and I lived in that block of flats during the war—just before I went off with my Partisans? Of course you do. Here's Myra Erdleigh, who was there too, and this is Mr Stripling. Jimmy Stripling is teaching me a lot about my new passion I was talking about in Venice, vintage cars. Let's find a table.'

Age—goodness knows how old she was—had exalted Mrs Erdleigh's unsubstantiality. She looked very old indeed, yet old in an intangible, rather than corporeal sense. Lighter than air, disembodied from a material world, the swirl of capes, hoods, stoles, scarves, veils, as usual encompassed her from head to foot, all seeming of so light a texture that, far from bringing an impression of accretion, their blurring of hard outlines produced a positively spectral effect, a Whistlerian nocturne in portraiture, sage greens, sombre blues, almost frivolous greys, sprinkled with gold.

Jimmy Stripling, certainly a lot younger than Mrs Erdleigh, had become old in a different, more conventional genre. Tall, shambling, what remained of his hair grey, rather greasy, his bulky figure, which took up more room than ever, was shapeless and bent. Even so, he seemed in certain respects less broken down, morally speaking, than in his middle period. To be old suited him better, gave excuse to a bemused demeanour, pulled it together. Stevens was delighted with both of them.

'Myra and I met again in Venice. That was after you'd left. We talked a lot about those wartime flats, and the people who lived there. All those Belgians. Myra told my fortune then. She predicted a *belle guerre* for me. I didn't have too bad a one, so she prophesied right.'

Mrs Erdleigh took my hand. As in the past, her touch brought a sense of intercommunication, one conveyed by vibrations that imposed themselves almost more by not-being, than by being. They emphasized the inexistence of the flesh, rather than, by direct contact, extending its pressures and undercurrents.

'We have not met since that night of dangers.'

She smiled her otherworldly smile, misted hazel eyes roaming over past and future, apportioning to each their substance and shadow, elements to herself one and indivisible. I asked if she had been staying at the Bragadin palace. She shook her head in a faraway manner.

'I went only a few times to see Baby Clarini. She is a very old friend. Under Scorpio, like that other lady at the Palazzo, who is here tonight. Baby has had a sad life. She has never delved down to those eternal foundations, of which Thomas Vaughan speaks—Eugenius Philalethes, as we know him—that transform the hard stubborn flints of the world into chrysolites and jasper.'

She did not seem at all surprised when I told her Dr Brightman had also, speaking of *Borage and Hellebore*, invoked the name of Thomas Vaughan in Venice.

'His spirit was moving there. The Lion of St Mark could symbolize that green lion he calls the body, the magical entity that must clip the wings of the eagle. Do you remember planchette on that dark afternoon in the country? It was Baby's planchette that had beeen borrowed.'

I had forgotten that fact. The occasion, in any case, was not one desirable for resurrection at that moment. Better reminiscence should stop there. Mrs Erdleigh, who had perhaps been teasing, allowed that view to prevail. I followed up her astrological connotation of Baby Clarini by drawing attention to Isobel's horoscope.

'My wife is under Pisces. She rebels against that.'

Isobel made some complaint about the trials to which Piscians are subject. Mrs Erdleigh turned on to her a soothsayer's gaze, friendly but all-seeing.

'Remember always The Fishes are ruled by Jupiter—give no credence to Neptune. There is the safeguard. When first I put out the cards for your husband, I told him you two would meet, and all would be well.'

If my acknowledgment fell short of absolute agreement that Mrs Erdleigh had seen so far ahead, it also fell much farther short of truthful denial that she had said anything of the sort. Sorceresses, more than most, are safer allowed their professional *amour propre*. Stripling leant across the table. He had sat down opposite, next to Stevens. He was probably under permanent orders to remain directly within Mrs Erdleigh's eye.

'Are you one of these musical people? I expect so. I don't know a thing about Mozart opera, or anyone else's, but Myra wanted to come. Myra and I have been friends for years. I have to do what she wants. She's such a wonderful

243

person. What she knows is uncanny, far more than that.
No, it is, Myra, I mean it.'

Mrs Erdleigh had made no attempt to deny omniscience,
but Stripling may have felt the whole speech necessary to
establish his own standing. I attempted some remark about
having met him at the Templers' years before.

'Of course, of course. Poor old Peter.'

Stripling did not seem very capable of taking in chronological bearings about people any longer, only motor-cars,
as it turned out a moment later, when I told him about
seeing Sunny Farebrother some months before. Farebrother,
too, then a butt of Stripling's derision, had been at the
Templer house when we first met.

'Sunny Farebrother? Do you know I was thinking of
Sunny the other day. He used to own an old Ford car years
ago—thirty or forty, old even then—so much so, people
like me ragged him about it. No hope he's kept it, I suppose? He's always been a very economical man, but I don't
expect there's any hope of that. I'd give a lot to possess that
car. Cars are the only things I know about. Are you
interested in cars?'

'I possess one, so I have to be to that extent.'

Stripling shook his head. That was not enough.

'I've loved cars all my life. Love's the only word.
Passionate love. Some feel like that about them. Probably
why my marriage wasn't a success. I loved cars over
well. I'm too old to race them now, but I study them,
and collect them. Not a rally, not a *concours d'élégance*,
I miss. You know Odo's got very keen on vintage cars
too.'

When people speak of a subject close to them, they can
look transformed. Almost as mystically absorbed in car lore
as Mrs Erdleigh in a transcendental vision, Stripling suddenly changed from his dreamy state to one of intense
excitement. He had just thought of something he could not

244

wait to communicate to Stevens, something of paramount importance to both of them.

'I say, Odo, do you know there's an American at this party who's keen on vintage cars? A fellow called Glober. Told me quite by chance a minute before the opera started. It's just come back to me. I'd mentioned I owned two Armstrong Siddeleys, '26 and '27, which both still go like smoke. Powerful as dreadnoughts, the pair of them. He was as keen as mustard at once. They're 14 h.p., o.h.v., four-cylinder, sparely raked windscreens, both absolute treasures the way they pound along. What do you think Glober told me? He owns a 4½ litre supercharged '31 Bentley, which he's got here tonight. Only bought her last week. Of course, he wanted to see the Armstrong Siddeleys, when he's got a chance to let up on the film he's making —he's a film producer—and he's going to show me the Bentley when we leave. He's pondering a Bugatti 35.'

Stevens took charge of Stripling at this stage.

'Of course I know Louis Glober's in the vintage market, Jimmy. What are you thinking about? But, look here, tell me again what you were saying the other day about the 1902, 5 h.p., Renault Voiturette. It's the big stuff I'm getting interested in now. There was also a 1903 Panhard et Levassor, 10 h.p., tonneau, I wanted to discuss.'

They settled down to the subject.

'Though many desire these treasures, none enter but he who knows the key and how to use it.'

For a moment, Mrs Erdleigh sounded as if he she, too, had embarked on the subject of vintage cars, but occult practices were still her theme.

'I remember Dr Trelawney saying much the same not long before he—'

I stopped just in time, at the last minute remembering no one, least of all a mage like Dr Trelawney, should be disparaged by the statement that Death had overtaken him.

Providential suspension on my lips of that misnomer was barely accepted by Mrs Erdleigh. She had already begun to shake her head at such a near lapse, congenital lack of insight, all but openly displayed.

'You mean not long before he achieved the Eighth Sphere to which Trismegistus refers?'

'Exactly.'

'Where, as again Vaughan writes, the liberated soul ascends, looking at the sunset towards the west wind, and hearing secret harmonies. He calls this world, where we are now, an outdoor theatre, in whose wings the Dead wait their cue for return to the stage—an image from the *opéra bouffe* we have just witnessed. In a short space now, I too shall leave for the wings. Perhaps before the drama is played out, of which the opening Act was in the Bragadin palace. The rumble of wheels sounds. Once set in motion, the chariot of the soul does not long linger.'

'What was begun at Jacky Bragadin's?'

'Much to disorder the hierarchy of being. Elsewhere too. Pluto disports himself in the Eighth House.'

I should have liked to continue, try to persuade Mrs Erdleigh to show herself a little more explicit, but her attention was distracted by a young Labour MP, politely sceptical, also anxious to enquire into his own astrological nativity. Mrs Erdleigh's engagement in this, other similar interrogations, took up the rest of supper. After we had moved away from the table, further opportunity came to talk to Stevens, who had for the moment renounced vintage cars, about Widmerpool, what had taken place to extricate him from his embarrassments. Stevens himself was greatly preoccupied with this question.

'It's been suggested he wrote an indiscreet letter. Realised he'd gone too far, then tried to withdraw. That might have been in office hours, or when he was being cultured in Eastern Europe. You can't tell. It's not denied now he's a close sympathizer. Even so, he didn't want to get in trouble with his own security authorities. A spot of blackmail seems to have been the result. I know the form. One of my own mob found himself in a tangle that way. Thought it all in the interests of "international goodwill" to hand over one or two quite important little items. They asked for more, he stalled—got cold feet—they gave him away to us.'

'Somebody said there was a defection on their side.'

Stevens gave a sharp look.

'Perhaps there was. Whatever happened, he's got away with it.'

Stevens moved at ease through the world of secret traffickings of this kind. He was about to continue an exposition of what happened to such suspects, when—when not—convenient to prosecute, but was interrupted by Rosie. She came up in a state of some disquiet. Her little black eyes were popping out of her head with agitation.

'Odo, come at once. Something rather worrying has happened.'

Stevens went off with her. Rosie's anxiety might have any cause, the house on fire, an undesired invitation she wanted help in refusing, one of the children been sick, the degree of seriousness could not be estimated. Stevens's comments had interest. What dreams of power, practical or phantasmic had long tantalized Widmerpool's heart, what plans meditated to put them into effect? Stevens had spoken ironically of betrayals in the interest of 'international goodwill'; Bagshaw, speculating on less highflown motives, satisfaction of a taste for wholesale destruction, vicarious individual revenge against society. Neither Bagshaw nor Stevens spoke without experience. Perhaps, in Widmerpool's case, he managed to coalesce in himself both aspects. Chandler and Gossage passed. They said goodnight.

'A nice turn of power in the middle notes, didn't you think?' said Gossage. 'A fine sensibility of phrase?'

'Hugh didn't look too well,' said Chandler. 'I hope he's all right. I hadn't seen him for an age.'

They passed on. It was time to leave. I began to look about for Isobel. Before I found her, Stevens returned to the room. I took this opportunity of saying goodbye, as he seemed on his way somewhere. He confirmed, as it were, the words spoken a minute before by Chandler.

'Hugh Moreland's not very well. He's gone to lie down in the study. I'm on my way to get the car. I can run them home.'

Stevens, many of his characteristics uncommendable, was good at taking charge when certain kinds of awkward situation arose.

'Is Hugh bad?'

'Doesn't look too good. He had a blackout, and fell. He's all right now, all right in the sense that he doesn't want to leave, because he says there are a lot of things about the *Seraglio* he still wants to discuss. We've persuaded him to take it easy for the moment. He'll be better when he gets to bed.'

'Can one see him?'

'Yes, do go up. Might keep him quiet. Don't bring a crowd with you. The room's the little study on the second floor, to the left.'

I found Isobel, and we both went upstairs. Moreland was lying on a small sofa, Rosie and Audrey Maclintick standing over him. The sofa was not big enough to contain his body comfortably at full length. He was drinking a glass of water, something I had never before seen him do, except after a heavy evening the night before. As Chandler had said, he did not look at all well. He was refusing to compromise with his own situation further than agreement to be driven home, when Stevens returned. Audrey Maclintick was trying to persuade him to rest quietly, until the car was announced as at the front door. When he saw us, he began to laugh in his old way.

'I told you nostalgia would get me. It did. Absolutely spun me over like a ninepin. It was Carolo put the finishing touch. I can't take it as I used. They say you lose your head for nostalgia, as you get older. That's also the time when waves of it come sweeping down without warning. You have to ration yourself, or a sudden dose knocks you out, as it did me.'

'You stop talking so much, and take it easy,' said Audrey Maclintick. 'I'm going to get that precious doctor of yours round as soon as you're in bed, no matter what the time is, and how much he's had to drink, if he hasn't passed out cold. Even he told you to be careful, the last time he looked you over. You're going to stay in bed for a week or two now, if I have anything to do with it.'

Moreland did not listen. In spite of Rosie's added protest that he would be wiser to remain quiet, he continued to insist he would be perfectly recovered the following day. He also kept on returning to what had been happening that evening.

'There were a lot of people near me talking about vintage cars. There's nostalgia, if you like.

For some we loved, the loveliest and the best,
That from his vintage rolling Time hath pressed.

That's a striking image. I remember, years ago, a man who kept on quoting Omar at that party of Mrs Foxe's, after my Symphony. I've only just grasped that the verse refers to a car. Life's vintage car, in which we're all travelling. Better than Trapnel's Camel, more Hegelian too. Then you're suddenly told to get out and walk—pressed to, as the poet truly says.'

There was nothing to be done until Stevens returned.

Staying with Moreland was only to encourage running on like this, tiring himself, so Isobel and I spoke a word or two, then said goodnight. It was not quite clear what sort of a fall he had suffered. He seemed to have lost his senses for a minute or so, afterwards felt no worse than a little dazed.

'I was pretty normal when I got up from the floor. If one could ever truthfully say that about oneself.'

A large proportion of the guests had already left when we arrived downstairs again.

'Poor Hugh,' said Isobel. 'He didn't look at all well to me.'

'Nor me.'

Outside, the night was dark. There was no moon. A breeze, fresh, almost country-scented, blew in from the Park's tall clusters of trees. We were aiming to cut through from the terrace, where the Stevens house stood, making for a street beyond, which ran parallel, where a taxi could be picked up. A few doors away from the Stevens entrance, two or three persons, standing against the railings, were having some sort of argument. Having attended the party, they seemed now to be squabbling. Numbers and sex were not at first distinguishable in the gloom, but turned out as a woman, two men, in fact the Widmerpools and Short. Widmerpool was giving Short a dressing-down. He was very angry. Short was defending himself mildly, but with bureaucratic obstinacy. He could be heard maintaining that administrative breakdowns were from time to time unavoidable.

'I've already told you, Kenneth, that I quite plainly instructed the car to be outside waiting. The driver must have mistaken the address. If so, he will be along in a minute or two.'

As we went by, Widmerpool recognized us.

'Have you by any chance got a car? Our hired vehicle

hasn't turned up. Leonard has made some sort of muddle. I suppose you couldn't give us a lift?'

'We're on our way to pick up a taxi.'

'Oh.'

'Why not do the same? They come down fairly frequently in the street behind here.'

'Pam doesn't want to walk that far. Oh, hell and blast. Why must this have happened?'

Widmerpool was not merely cross, put out by the car not being on time, but wrought up to an extent almost resembling drunkenness. Drink, which he hardly touched as a rule, was unlikely to have played any part in this highly strung state, unless, quite exceptionally, he had felt the *Seraglio* an occasion to swallow a few glasses, more to impress others with his own improved situation, than because he enjoyed their effect. Apart from threat of prosecution, he could have been suffering more than usual domestic strain, Pamela's design to leave him—if all alleged about Glober were true—now suddenly put into reverse gear. Even if Widmerpool did not know the reason, her change of plans, involvement with Gwinnett, might well have caused more than usually uncomfortable repercussions at home. The fact that she would not walk the few yards necessary to find a taxi showed her mood. Widmerpool stamped his feet. Short addressed us in a more temperate manner.

'If you should see anything looking like a hired car waiting round the corner, please ask the chauffeur if he's booked in the name of Sir Leonard Short, will you? He may have mistaken the address. If so, just send him along here.'

We said we would do that.

'Goodnight.'

'Goodnight.'

The only answer was Short's.

'I told you Lady Widmerpool was looking frightening,' said Isobel.

'Will they wait there all night?'

'I think she's planning something. That was how she looked to me.'

By that time we had reached the main road. A taxi cruised by. So far as we were both concerned, that closed the *Seraglio* evening.

As with stories of Trapnel's last hours, others in connexion with Gwinnett's decampment from the Bagshaws', what followed, outside the Stevens house in Regent's Park, appeared afterwards in various versions. One hears about life, all the time, from different people, with very different narrative gifts. Accordingly, not only are many episodes, in which you may even have played a part yourself, hard enough to assess; a lot more must be judged from haphazard accounts given by others. Even if reported in good faith, some choose one aspect on which to concentrate, some another. This truth, obvious enough, was particularly applicable to the events following the *Seraglio* party. Even so, essential facts were scarcely in question. My own informants were Moreland and Stevens.

There was no irreplaceable divergence between these two accounts, although, when it came to telling a story in which veracity had to be measured against picturesque detail, neither could be called pedantically veracious; Moreland, in this respect the more reliable, being, if the more imaginative, the one who also best appreciated the graphic power of fact. Moreland talked about the scene right up to the end. He never tired of it. There can be no doubt it cheered his last months, added, as he himself said, to the richness of his own experience. His powerful gift of creative imagery led him, over and over again, to reconstruct the incidents, whenever anyone came to visit him.

Stevens, in principle to be thought of as a type used to

violent scenes, was in a sense more taken by surprise, worse shocked, than Moreland. Marriage may have enervated Stevens, accustomed him by then to sedate, well-behaved routines. The rational, utilitarian, unruffled point of view, tempered with toughness, that directed most of his life —had so directed it in the past—could mislead, as well as stimulate. Like many persons who had enjoyed a comparatively adventurous career, knocked about the world a good deal, he retained a strain of naivety, naivety penetrating just the areas of the mind which, in Moreland's case, were quite free from any such inhibition. Indeed, Moreland used to complain himself that 'naivety in short supply' could be a disadvantage in practising the arts, where it is often necessary to see one thing only, that particular thing with supreme clarity. In fact, when it came to giving a convincing description of what took place that night, the details Stevens produced, except for a few useful appendices, were little more than confirmation of Moreland's epic account. Stevens himself excused the scrappiness of his own narration.

'It was so bloody dark, and I was worrying all the time about getting Hugh home, before he had another fit, or whatever it was.'

The Stevens garage was in a mews behind the house. When Stevens drove the car back towards his own front door, he noticed figures talking together a few yards up the terrace. He did not identify them, merely supposing they were guests having a final musical dispute before parting on their separate ways. Moreland, Audrey Maclintick, several others, were by then chatting with Rosie in the hall, Moreland having become so restless lying on the sofa that it seemed best to come downstairs to wait for the car. There they found Mrs Erdleigh, Stripling, Glober, Polly Duport, all about to leave. Moreland at once recognized the potentialities of Mrs Erdleigh, whom he had not met earlier that evening. Within a matter of minutes—as he himself admitted—they were discussing together the magical writings of Cornelius Agrippa. Moreland and Mrs Erdleigh had already reached the Book of Abramolin the Mage, spells for surrounding an enemy with a vision of trellis-work, others for causing the Pope to fall in love with you, when Stevens came up the steps. Meanwhile Glober and Stripling had returned to vintage cars.

'Now we'll take a look at the Bentley, Mr Stripling. My automobile's parked at the end of the block.'

Stripling must already have obtained permission from Mrs Erdleigh to inspect the Bentley, before restoring her to whatever witch's lair she inhabited, but there is some uncertainty as to how exactly the outgoing party came on the Widmerpools and Short, still hanging about in the terrace, waiting for their car. It seems possible that Moreland refused to enter the Stevens car before he had finished his occult conversation with Mrs Erdleigh. Alternatively, his interest by now aroused in vintage cars, he too could have wanted to inspect Glober's vehicle. Moreland seems to have been strolling with Mrs Erdleigh; Stevens and Audrey Maclintick behind; Stripling, Glober, Polly Duport, a short way ahead. The talk of cars may have been carried to the ears of Short, who (having made contact with Glober at supper on the subject of the French political situation vis-à-vis Algeria) now repeated a request for a 'lift'. Polly Duport was alleged to have thrown back a comment to the effect that the '31 Bentley was the 'size of a bus', thereby raising Short's hopes. Another possibility is that Pamela had intended that something of this sort should happen. She had been waiting for a chance not arisen at the party. She could hardly have foreseen the lateness of the hired car, but might have grasped that Glober, still in the Stevens house, was bound sooner or later to pass that way. Short, having no reason to connect Glober with the Widmerpools, stepped forward, and made a little speech.

'If your car is really so commodious, Mr Glober, I wonder whether you could include in it a party of three—for our own hired vehicle does not seem to have turned up. It would be too kind were you able to manage that good office. We all live in the Westminster direction, if you happened to be going that way. It ill becomes a native of this country to seek transport from a transatlantic visitor, guest to our shores, but, not for the first time in recent years, we must needs throw ourselves upon the goodwill of American resources.'

Uncertainty prevails whether or not, at this stage, Glober immediately grasped that the other applicants for help were the Widmerpools. On the whole, it seems likely he did not. In the dark, there was no reason why he should recognize them. At the same time, Glober, out of sheer love of living dangerously, may have accepted this as a challenge. Moreland was ignorant of Glober's former affiliations with Pamela, of whom he knew little or nothing at that time. Stevens, too, had not kept up with Pamela's ever varying situation, by then of no particular interest to him, provided his own married life was not embarrassed by it. In Venice, he had no doubt thought of the Widmerpools as guests of Jacky Bragadin, rather than connecting either of them with Glober; Pamela's own references to Glober giving no reason to convey the comparative seriousness of her relationship with him.

'I'd just love to give you all a ride in my new automobile. Come with us.'

Only after Glober had made that statement, so it appears, did Widmerpool join the group. Pamela still remained a little apart.

'This is very kind,' said Widmerpool. 'We have not seen each other since Venice.'

255

That indicated he and Glober had exchanged no word at the party. Glober bowed.

'You're welcome.'

Glober then introduced Mrs Erdleigh, Jimmy Stripling, Moreland, and Audrey Maclintick. If Widmerpool was to make a convenience of his car, Glober was determined to have some amusement too. Audrey Maclintick, of course, wanted to get Moreland into the Stevens car—and home— but for once does not seem to have succeeded in making her voice heard. Moreland, telling the story, emphasized the formality of Glober's introductions. That was the moment when Pamela joined the group. She came towards them hesitantly, as if she wanted to be introduced too. Her arrival impressed Moreland, not on account of any foreseeable dis- harmony that might include Glober, but because of the look given her by Mrs Erdleigh, more precisely rays of mystic disapproval trajected with force noticeable even in the dark. That perception was characteristic of Moreland. Mrs Erdleigh had made a deep impression on him.

'The Sorceress seemed to know Lady Widmerpool al- ready. At least she gave her extraordinary smile—one I would rather not have played on myself.'

Pamela had smiled in return. She took no other notice of Mrs Erdleigh, nor the rest of them. The person to whom she addressed herself was Polly Duport. Pamela did not come close, but it was plain to whom she was speaking.

'I hear you're going to be the star in Louis's new film.'

Pamela said that very gently, barely audibly. Her tone almost suggested she was shy of mentioning the matter at all, though beyond words delighted at hearing such a rumour. All she wanted was to have the good news con- firmed. Both Moreland and Stevens agreed there was not the smallest hint of unfriendliness in Pamela's voice. At the same time, Stevens, knowing Pamela to the extent of having lived with her for at least a few weeks, had no doubt something ominous was brewing. Moreland, it seemed, had not bothered to categorize Pamela at all; so far as he was concerned, another 'lady of fashion', full of every sort of nonsense about music, to be avoided at all costs. He admitted to having been struck by her looks, when he came to examine her.

Polly Duport, whether she knew much or little about Pamela, can have had few illusions as to friendliness. She could hardly have failed to hear of Glober's comparatively recent intention to cast Pamela for the lead she herself— anyway for the moment—was intended by him to play. Beyond that knowledge, of a purely business sort, the extent of her awareness of Pamela's character, even nature of relationship with Glober, could well be over-estimated. The segregated life of the Theatre, separated by its nature from so much going on round about, might easily have prevented her from hearing more than essential; so to speak, her own cue in taking Pamela's place. Polly Duport herself may not have been, over and above that, at all interested. She would know that Pamela, not a professional actress, had been in the running as 'star' of Glober's film, had probably experienced some sort of love affair with him. That was not necessarily significant. There was no reason for her to guess Glober had planned to marry Pamela.

Polly Duport, replying to Pamela's question, seems to have let fall a scrap of stylized stage banter adapted to such an enquiry, one of those conventional sets of phrase, existing in every professional world, in this case designed for use in counteracting another player, complimentary, spiteful, a mixture of both; clichés probably often in demand throughout the give-and-take of life in the Theatre. Moreland could not remember the actual comeback employed. He suggested several known to himself from his own backstage undertakings. Whatever form Polly Duport's answer presented was amicably accepted by Pamela, but she did not abandon the subject.

'I'm sure you'll like working with Louis.'

'Who could doubt that?' said Polly Duport.

She spoke lightly, of course. Pamela was behaving as if so pleased about the whole arrangement, that she was even a little anxious that it might not all go as well as deserved.

'You mean because all women love Louis?'

'All the world, surely?'

That was a neat reply. Pamela recognized it as such. She smiled, rather sadly, even though the idea seemed to please her. There was an instant's pause. Moreland said this was the point when the atmosphere became very highly charged. One of the elements causing him to notice that was Stripling suddenly ceasing to reel off names and dates of vintage cars, which, until this tenseness made itself felt, he had, up to the last possible moment, continued to recite to Glober. Pamela spoke again, this time reflectively.

'Quite a lot of people have loved Louis.'

'They couldn't help it,' said Polly Duport.

Pamela laughed softly.

'I expect you know,' she said. 'Louis's stuffed a charming little cushion with hair snipped from the pussies of ladies he's had?'

Stevens said afterwards that he 'recognized that enquiry as signal for trouble starting'. Both he and Moreland, in whatever other respects their stories differed, stood shoulder to shoulder as regards those precise words of Pamela's. Where they disagreed was as to the manner in which Polly Duport took them. Stevens thought her outraged. Moreland's view was of her merely raising an eyebrow, so to speak, at the crudeness of phrasing. She was not in the least disconcerted by the eccentricity of the practice. Moreland was absolutely firm on that.

'Miss Duport showed not the slightest sign of wilting.'

He agreed with Stevens that she made no comment. No one else made any comment either. They just stood, 'as if hypnotized', Moreland said. Pamela laughed quietly to herself, giving the impression that thought of Glober's whim amused her. She turned towards him.

'You have, haven't you, Louis?'

'Have what, honey?'

Glober was absolutely relaxed. Stevens, again fancying other people as scandalized as himself, supposed him taken aback a moment before. If so, Glober was now completely recovered.

'Stuffed a cushion?'

'Sure.'

'As well as the ladies themselves?'

'Correct.'

Glober remained unrattled. Pamela laughed this time shrilly. She was working herself up to a climax, possibly a sexual one. Stevens said her behaviour reminded him of a scene made at a black-market night-club during the war, when she had started a sudden row, calling out to the people at the next table that he was impotent. Stevens never minded telling that sort of story about himself. It was one of his good points. In any case, even if at one time or another he had failed to satisfy Pamela, the charge was hard to substantiate, in her case not a specially damaging one. As Barnby used to say in that connexion, 'There's a boomerang aspect.' Glober remained equally undisturbed. His conversational tone matched Pamela's.

'I thought Miss Duport would just like to know what's expected. Perhaps you've been at work with the nail-scissors already, Louis? Anyway, it's a cheaper hobby than his.'

She pointed at Widmerpool. At this stage of the proceedings, Mrs Erdleigh seems to have taken charge. One imagines that, in her own incorporeal manner, she floated from the exterior of the group to its moral centre, wherever that might be. She appears to have laid a hand on Pamela's arm, a movement to suggest restraint. This was the interlude Moreland most enjoyed describing, what he called 'the Sorceress in the ascendant, Lady Widmerpool afflicted'. He said that Pamela, at contact of Mrs Erdleigh's fingers, shot out a look of intense malevolence, hesitating for a second in whatever she was about to say.

'My dear, beware. You are near the abyss. You stand at its utmost edge. Do not forget the warning I gave when you showed me your palm on that dread night.'

Stevens took the line later that neither second-sight nor magical powers were required to foretell the way things were moving. He may have been right. At the same time, however obscurely phrased, Mrs Erdleigh's presentiments were near the mark.

'The vessels of Saturn must not be shed to their dregs.'

Stevens, incapable himself of reproducing cabalistic dialectic, was no less impressed than Moreland, in whose repetition such specialized language lost none of its singularity. The unwonted nature of Mrs Erdleigh's invocations did not so much in themselves bewilder Stevens as in their practical effect on Pamela.

'The extraordinary thing was Pam more or less understood the stuff. That was how it looked. At least she stopped in her tracks for a second or two. I've never seen anything like it.'

Stevens was certainly taken aback, but the spell, as it turned out, was short lasting. Briefly quelled, Pamela recovered herself.

'Then you know?'

'Time yet remains to evade the ghastly cataract.'

'But you know?'

'Knowledge is the treasure of our unsealed fountains.'

Pamela gave what Stevens, in his flamboyant manner,

called a 'terrible laugh'. Moreland admitted he, too, had found that laugh uncomfortable.

'Then I'll unseal them—and him.'

Mrs Erdleigh made some sort of motion with her hand, one of her mystic passes, conceivably no more than an emotional gesture, at which Pamela drew herself away, Moreland said, 'like a serpent'. Mrs Erdleigh issued her final warning.

'Court at your peril those spirits that dabble lasciviously with primeval matter, horrid substances, sperm of the world, producing monsters and fantastic things, as it is written, so that the toad, this leprous earth, eats up the eagle.'

Then Pamela began to scream with laughter again, shriller even than before.

'You know, you know, you know. You're a wonderful old girl. You don't have to be told Léon-Joseph croaked in bed with me. You know already. You know it's true, what nobody else quite believes.'

To what extent that plain statement was at once comprehended by those standing round remains uncertain. Probably the words did not wholly sink in until later. At moment of utterance they could have sounded all part of this extraordinary interchange, at once metaphorical and coarsely earthy. Some doubt existed, in due course, as to the exact phrases Pamela used. Whatever they were, positiveness of assertion was in no way diminished. She turned to Widmerpool again.

'You tell them about it. After all, you were there.'

She pointed at him, now speaking to the others.

'He thought I didn't spot he was watching through the curtain.'

Up to this stage of things, it appears, no one except Mrs Erdleigh had attempted to tackle Pamela. Mrs Erdleigh, so far as it went, having done that with success; spoken her warning, withdrew into the shadows. Widmerpool had

261

remained all the time silent. Even now he did not at once answer this imputation on himself. He heard it to the end without speaking. Glober, uncharacteristically at a loss for the inspired wisecrack to ease the situation, was equally mute. After that, from the moment Pamela voiced these revelations, there is difficulty in pinpointing order of events, reliable continuity almost impossible to establish. Accounts given by Moreland and Stevens were at odds with each other. What appears to have taken place is that Pamela, dissatisfied at her words being received with comparative calm, at best so stunning that her bearers lacked reaction, chose another line of attack. It is no less possible she was building up, in any case, to that. Stevens, more at home this time with plain statements, rather than Mrs Erdleigh's oracular sayings, gave a convincing imitation of Pamela's hissing denunciation.

'You might think that enough. Watching your wife being screwed. Naturally it wasn't the first time. It was just the first time with a blubber-lipped Frenchman, who couldn't do it, then popped off. Of course he had arranged it all with Léon-Joseph beforehand—except the popping off —and in some ways it made things easier to have two of us to explain to the hotel people that Monsieur Ferrand-Sénéschal had just passed away, while we were visiting him. Then there's a tart called Pauline he has games with. He used to photograph her. I found the photographs. He didn't guess I'd meet Pauline too.'

Even then Widmerpool seems to have made no active protest. What really upset him was Pamela's next item.

'He's been telling everybody that he hasn't the slightest idea why they thought he was spying. I can explain that too, all his little under-the-counter Communist games. How he's got out of his trouble, in spite of their holding an interesting little note in his own handwriting. He's given the show away as often, and as far, as he dares. Unfortunately, he gave it away to his old pals, the Stalinists. The lot who are in now want to discredit some of those old pals. That's where Léon-Joseph comes in again. Poor old Ferrand-Sénéschal was playing just the same sort of game—as well as an occasional orgy, when he felt up to it. So what he did was to hand over all the information he possessed about Ferrand-Sénéschal, some of that quite spicy. That's why he was let off this time with a caution.'

Stevens, his mind, as I have said, adjusted to secret traffickings, his nature to physical violence, reported Pamela's words as cut short at Widmerpool seizing her by the throat. Moreland disagreed that anything so forcible had happened, at least immediately. Moreland thought Widmerpool had simply caught her arm, possibly struck her on the arm, attempting to silence his wife. The scene partook, in far more savage temper, of that enacted at the Huntercombes' ball, when, after Barbara Goring had cut his dance, Widmerpool grasped her wrist. The upshot then had been Barbara pouring sugar over his head. Widmerpool's onslaught this time might be additionally menacing, stakes of the game, so to speak, immensely higher; the physical protest was the same, final exasperation of nerves kept by a woman too long on edge. Another analogy with this earlier grapple was Pamela, no more daunted at the assault than Barbara by her clutched wrist, dragged herself away, screaming with laughter. The scene was not without its horrifying, morally upsetting, side. Moreland emphasized that; Stevens, too, in his own terms.

'In fact, I thought I was going to be sick,' Moreland said. 'Nausea might have been caused by my recent *crise*. If I had vomited, that would scarcely have added at all to other gruesome aspects.'

In emerging from this hand-to-hand affray with Pamela, possibly beaten off by her own counter-attack, Widmerpool seems to have stepped back without warning, retreating heavily on to Glober, who may himself have moved forward with an idea of separating husband and wife. Stevens thought Stripling had made some ponderous, ineffectual attempt to intervene. That is to some extent controverted by subsequent evidence. The view of Stevens was that Stripling had tried to catch Widmerpool round the waist, with the idea of restraining him, an act misattributed by Widmerpool to Glober. Both Moreland and Stevens agreed that, in the early stages of the Widmerpools' clinch, Glober took no special initiative. Perhaps, for once, he felt a certain diffidence, owing to the intricacies of his own position. Possibly, too, he was not unwilling to watch them fight it out on their own. There is some corroboration of Stripling playing a comparatively active part at this stage, but things moving so quickly, it was hard to know what he did, how long remained present.

What does seem fairly certain is that Widmerpool, stepping backwards, immediately supposed himself to have been in some manner curbed or coerced. Simultaneously, Mrs Erdleigh, foreseeing trouble when Stripling laid a hand on Widmerpool, may at once have spirited Stripling away by some more or less occult means. That would to some extent explain why Widmerpool, finding Glober, rather than Stripling, made an angry, presumably derogatory comment. It is possible, of course, Glober had indeed taken hold of him. They faced one another. That was when Glober hit Widmerpool.

'It's never a KO on these occasions,' said Stevens. 'I've seen it happen before, though not with men of quite that age. Widmerpool just staggered a bit, and put his hand up to his face. No question of dropping like a sack of potatoes, being out for the count, floored by a straight left, or right hook. That only happens professionally, or in the movies. The chief damage was his spectacles. They were knocked off his nose, and broke, so the midnight match had to be called off.'

No one watching denied the light had been too bad for the fracas to be critically assessed blow by blow. For this latter stage of the story, Stevens was probably the better equipped reporter. Moreland, his own nervous tensions by this time strongly reacting, not to mention the recent collapse he had suffered, was by now partly repelled by what was happening, partly lost in a fantastic world of his own, in which he seemed to be dreaming, rather than observing. He admitted that. Stevens, more down to earth in affecting to regret unachieved refinements of the boxing-ring, seems also to have been a little shocked, a condition vacillatingly induced, in this case, by the age of the antagonists. It is impossible to say how matters would have developed had not interruption taken place from outside. A large car drove jerkily down the terrace, the chauffeur slowing up from time to time, while he looked out of its window to ascertain the number of each house as he passed. He drew up just beside the spot where everyone was standing.

'None of you gentlemen Sir Leonard Short by any chance?'

Short stepped forward. Until then he had been inactive. He may have withdrawn completely, while the imbroglio was at its worst. Now he entered the limelight.

'Yes. I am Sir Leonard Short. I should like some explanation. I cannot in the least understand why this car should be so late.'

'I am a trifle after time, sir. Sorry about that. Went to the wrong address. There's a Terrace, and a Place, and a Gate. Very confusing.'

'This unpunctuality is not at all satisfactory. I shall take the matter up.'

Short opened the door of the car with a consciously angry jerk. He brusquely indicated to Widmerpool that he was to get in, do that quickly. Short was in command. Stevens said one saw what he could be like in the Ministry. Widmerpool, who had already picked up the remains of his spectacles from the pavement, obeyed. Short followed, slamming the door. The car drove slowly down the terrace. Moreland said it was a good, an effective exit.

'When I looked round, the three of us—Audrey, Odo, myself—were alone. It was like a fairy story. The Sorceress was gone, taking off, no doubt, on her broomstick, the tall elderly vintage-car-bore riding pillion. Lady Widmerpool was gone too. That was the most mysterious. I have the impression she made some parting shot to the effect that none of us would see her again. The American tycoon and Polly Duport were almost out of sight, heading for the far end of the terrace. I don't exactly know how any of them faded away. I was feeling I might pass out again by then. Much relieved when Odo drove us home.'

6

GWINNETT WROTE ME A LONGISH letter about a year later. By then he was living in the south of Spain. He referred only indirectly to the embarrassments ('to use no harsher term') suffered during the latter period of his London visit. He said he wrote chiefly to confirm details I had given him in Venice concerning Trapnel's habits, dress, turns of phrase. The notes he had then made seemed to conflict, in certain minor respects, with other sources of research. Apart from checking this Trapnel information, he just touched on the comparatively smooth manner in which dealings with the police, other persons more or less officially concerned, had passed off, including journalists. The briefness, relatively unsensational nature of the inevitable publicity, had impressed him too.

Pamela's name did not occur in the letter. At the same time, Gwinnett's emphasis on Trapnel, in what he wrote, may have been a formality, something to supply basis for communication, felt to be needed, of necessity delicate to express. The Trapnel enquiries were plainly not urgent. In their connexion, Gwinnett spoke of returning to his critical biography only after sufficient time had elapsed to ensure the dissertation's approach remained objective, ran no risk of being too much coloured by events that concerned himself, rather than his subject. Characteristically, he added that he still believed in 'aiming at objectivity, however much that method may be currently under fire'. As well as reducing immediate attention to the Trapnel book—though not his own fundamental interest in Trapnel himself— Gwinnett had abandoned academic life as a formal profession for the time being. He might return to the campus one of these days, he said, at the moment he only wanted to ruminate on that possibility. His new job, also teaching, was of quite a different order. He had become instructor of water-skiing at one of the Mediterranean seaside resorts of the Spanish coast. He said he liked the work pretty well.

Gwinnett also touched on Glober's death. The accident (on the Moyenne Corniche) had been one of those reflecting no marked blame on anyone, except that the car had been travelling at an unusually high speed. A friend of Glober's, a well-known French racing-driver, had been at the wheel. The story received very thorough press coverage. It was the sort of end Glober himself would have approved. Although the last time I saw him—of which I will speak later—he was with Polly Duport, *Match Me Such Marvel* was soon after abandoned as a project. No one seemed to know how far things had gone between them in personal relationship. The general view was that her profession, rather than love affairs, came first in her life. She may have been well out of the Glober assignment, because, about a month before Glober died, she acquired a good part (not the lead, one in some ways preferable to that) in a big 'international' film made by Clarini, Baby Wentworth's estranged husband.

I had the impression that Gwinnett and Glober had never much cared for one another. Beyond appreciating the obvious fact of their differing circumstances, I had no well defined comprehension of how they would have mutually reacted in their own country. In his letter, Gwinnett—like Gwinnett in the flesh—remained enigmatic, but he did comment on the way Death (he gave the capital letter) had been in evidence all round. There was nothing in the least obsessive in the manner he treated the subject. He did not, of course, disclose whether he had 'known' Pamela's condition before she came to the hotel. How could he disclose that?

The fact is, Gwinnett must have known. Otherwise there would have been no point in Pamela making the sacrifice of herself. Her act could only be looked upon as a sacrifice— of herself, to herself. So far as sacrifice went, Gwinnett could accept Pamela's, as much as Iphigenia's. The sole matter for doubt, in the light of inhibitions existing, not on one side only, was whether, at such a cost, all had been achieved. One hoped so. I wrote a letter back to Gwinnett. I told him how I had seen Glober, without having opportunity to speak with him, in the autumn of the previous year. I did not mention I had seen Widmerpool too on that occasion. It seemed better not. I always liked Gwinnett. I liked Glober too.

During the months that remained to Moreland, after the *Seraglio* party, we often used to talk about the story of Candaules and Gyges. He had never heard of the Jacky Bragadin Tiepolo. The hospital was on the south bank of the River.

'One might really have considered the legend as a theme for opera,' Moreland said. 'I mean, if other things had been equal.'

He lay in bed with an enormous pile of books beside him, books all over the bed too. He would quote from these from time to time. He was very taken with the idea of the comparison Pamela herself had made.

'Candaules can obviously be better paralleled than Gyges. Most men have a bit of Candaules in them. Your friend Widmerpool seems to have quite a lot, if he really liked exhibiting his wife. She was the Queen all right, if she's to be believed as being put on show. Also, in knowing that, herself intending to kill the King. Not necessarily physical killing, but revenge. Who was Gyges?'

'Hardly Ferrand-Sénéschal. In any case, through no fault of his own, he failed in that rôle. Others seemed to have enjoyed his Gyges-like privileges without dethroning the King. Candaules-Widmerpool continues to reign.'

'No, it doesn't really work,' said Moreland. 'All the same, it's a splendid fable of Love and Friendship—what you're liable to get from both—but the bearings are more general than particular, in spite of certain striking resemblances in this case. You really think she took the overdose, told him, then . . .'

'What else could have happened?'

'Literally dying for love.'

'Death happened to be the price. The sole price.'

'All other people's sexual relations are hard to imagine. The more staid the people, the more inconceivable their sexual relations. For some, the orgy is the most natural. On that night after the *Seraglio*, I was very struck by the goings-on with which Lady Widmerpool taxed her husband. I've next to no voyeurist tastes myself. I lack the love of power that makes the true voyeur. When I was in Marseilles, years ago, working on *Vieux Port*, there was a brothel, where, allegedly unknown to the occupants, you could look through to a room used by other clients. I never felt the smallest urge to buy a ticket. It was Donners's thing, you know.'

Moreland reflected a moment on what he had said. While still married to Matilda, he had, rather naturally, always avoided reference to that side of Sir Magnus's life. This was the first time, to my own knowledge, he had ever brought up the subject.

'Did I ever tell you how the Great Industrialist once confided to me that, when a young man—already doing pretty well financially—the doctors told him he had only a year to live? Of course that now seems the hell of a long time, in the light of one's own medical adviser's admonitions —not that I'm greatly concerned about keeping the old hulk afloat for another voyage or two, in the increasingly stormy seas of contemporary life, especially by drastic cutting down of the rum ration, and confining oneself to ship's biscuit, the régime recommended. That's by the way. The point is, I now find myself in a stronger position than in those days for vividly imagining what it felt like to be the man in the van Gogh pictures, so to speak Donners-on-the-brink-of-Eternity. Do you know what action Donners took? I'll tell you in his own words.'

Moreland adopted the flat lugubrious voice, conventionally used by those who knew Sir Magnus, to imitate—never very effectively, because inimitable—his manner of talking.

'I rented a little cottage in The Weald, gem of a place that brought a lump to the throat by its charm. There I settled down to read the best—only the best—of all literatures, English, French, German, Italian, Scandinavian.'

Moreland paused.

'I don't know why Spanish was left out. Perhaps it was included, and I've forgotten. Between these injections of the best literature, Donners listened to recordings of the best —only the best—music.'

'Interrupted by meals composed of the best food and the best wine?'

'Donners, as you must remember to your cost, like most power maniacs, was not at all interested in food and drink. Although far more in his line, I presume the best sexual sensations were also omitted. That would be not so much because their physical expression might hasten ringing down the curtain, as on account of the apodictic intention. Is "apodictic" the right word? I once used it with effect in an article attacking Honegger. The *villeggiatura* was very specifically designed to rise above coarser manifestations of the senses.'

'In the end did all this culture bring about a cure?'

'It wasn't the culture. The medicos made a mistake. They'd got the slides mixed, or the doctrine changed as to whatever Donners was suffering from being fatal. Something of the sort. Anyway they guessed wrong. Everything with Donners was right as rain. After spending a month or two at his dream cottage, he went back to making money, governing the country, achieving all-time records in utterance of conversational clichés, diverting himself in his own odd ways, all the many activities for which we used to know and love him. That went on until he was gathered in at whatever ripe old age he reached—not far short of eighty, so far as I remember.'

'Also, if one may say so, without showing much outward sign of having concentrated on the best literature of half-a-dozen nations.'

'Not the smallest. I was thinking that the other day while reading a translation of *I Promessi Sposi*. It sounds as if I were modelling myself on Donners, but I've got a lot of detective stories too. There was a special reason why *I Promessi Sposi* made me think of Donners, wonder whether it figured on his list, when he put on that final spurt to become cultured before *rigor mortis* set in. Like so many romantic novels, the story turns to some extent on the Villain upsetting the Hero by abducting the Heroine, unwilling victim threatened by the former's lust. That particular theme always misses the main point in the tribulations of Heroes in real life, where the trouble is that the Heroine, once abducted, is likely to be only too anxious to suffer a fate worse than death.'

'You mean Sir Magnus and his girls?'

For the moment I had not thought of Matilda.

'I meant when he abducted Matty, and married her. Not

exactly a precise parallel with Manzoni, I admit, but you'll see what I mean.'

I did not know what to answer. This was the first time Moreland had ever spoken in such terms of Matilda leaving him for Sir Magnus Donners. He sighed, then laughed.

'I suppose she liked being married to him. She remained in that state without apparent stress. She knew him, of course, from their first round together. In his odd way, he must have been attached to her too. All the same, I believe her when she said—consistently said—that she herself always refused to play his games, the way some—presumably most—of his girls did. I mean his taste, like your friend Lord Widmerpool's, for watching other people make love.'

'He was a friend of Donners too, but I don't think Widmerpool got the habit there. What you say was certainly one of the things alleged. So it was true?'

'Let's approach the matter in the narrative technique of *The Arabian Nights*—the world where Donners really belonged—with a story. In fact, two stories. You must be familiar with both, favourite tales of my youth. To tell the truth, I've heard neither of them since the war. I've no doubt they survive in renovated shape.'

Moreland sighed again.

'The first yarn is of a man making his way home late one night in London. He finds two ladies whose car has broken down. It is in the small hours, not a soul abroad. The earliest version ever told me represented the two ladies— one young and beautiful, the other older, but very distinguished—as having failed to crank their car with the starting-handle. Thought of this vintage jewel would make the mouths water of those vintage-hounds at the *Seraglio*, and shows the antiquity of the legend. No doubt the help required was later adapted to more up-to-date mechanics. In yet earlier days, the horses of their phaeton were probably restive, or the carriage immobilized for some other contemporary reason. Anyway, the man gets the engine humming. The ladies are grateful, so much so, they ask him back to their home for a drink. He accepts. After placing the glass to his lips, he remembers no more. He is found the following day, unconscious, in the gutter of some alley in a deserted neighbourhood. He has been castrated.'

'A favourite anecdote of my father's.'

'Of all that generation. The other story concerns a man —I like to think the same man, before he was so cruelly incapacitated—who is accosted by a beautiful girl, again late at night, no one about. He thinks her a tart, though her manner does not suggest that. She says she wants not money, but love. At first he declines, but is at last persuaded by assurances that something about him attracted her. They adjourn to her flat, conveniently near. The girl leads the way up some stairs into a room, unexpectedly large, hung with dark curtains up to the ceiling. Set in the middle of the floor is a divan or bed. On it, in one form or another, perhaps several, they execute together the sexual act. When all is ended, the man, still incredulous, makes attempt to offer payment. The girl again refuses, saying the pleasure was its own reward. The man is so bewildered that, when he leaves, he forgets something—umbrella, hat, overcoat. Whatever it is, he remembers at the foot of the stairs. He remounts them. The door of the curtained room is shut— locked. Within, he can hear the babble of voices. A crowd of people must have emerged from behind the curtains. His sexual activities—possibly deviations—have been object of gratification for a concealed clientèle.'

'I've heard that one too.'

'We all have. It's gone the round for years. Just within the bounds of possibility, do you think?'

'Why was the situation complicated by refusal of payment?'

'To make sure he agreed. The appeal to male vanity may have added to the audience's fun. If he swallowed the declaration that she thought him so attractive, the display would not be over too quickly. Do you suppose Sir Magnus was behind the curtain?'

'He may have watched the castration too.'

'Some of his ladies would have been well qualified as surgeons,' said Moreland.

He lay back in the bed. I suppose he meant Matilda. Then he took a book from the stack of works of every sort piled up on the table beside him.

'I always enjoy this title—*Cambises, King of Percia: a Lamentable Tragedy mixed full of Pleasant Mirth.*'

'What's it like?'

'Not particularly exciting, but does summarize life.'

One day in November, having a lot of things to do in London, before returning to the country that afternoon, I went to see Moreland earlier than usual. It was bleak, rainy weather. When I crossed the River, by Westminster Bridge, two vintage cars were approaching the Houses of Parliament. Another passed before I reached the hospital. Some sort of rally was in progress, for others appeared. I watched them go over the bridge, then went on. Moreland had no one with him. Audrey Maclintick would turn up later in the morning, possibly someone else drop in. Usually these friends were musical acquaintances, unknown to myself. I reported that droves of vintage cars were traversing the Thames in convoy. Moreland reached out for one of the books again.

'I've been researching the subject, since quoting to you the Khayyám reference. Keats was an addict too. I found this yesterday.

Like to a moving vintage down they came,
Crowned with green leaves, and faces all on flame . . .
Within his car, aloft, young Bacchus stood . . .

What could be more specific than that? Interesting that you stood upright to drive those early models. One presumes the vintage, where the Grapes of Wrath were stored, was a tradesman's van of Edwardian date or earlier.'

He threw the book down, and chose another. He was full of nervous energy. The impression one derived of his state was not a good one.

'I've been haunted by the story of Lady Widmerpool. Have you ever read *The Dutch Courtezan*? Listen to her song—forgive me quoting so much verse. Things one reads become obsessional, while one lies here.

> The darke is my delight,
> So 'tis the nightingale's.
> My musicke's in the night,
> So is the nightingale's.
> My body is but little,
> So is the nightingale's.
> I love to sleep next prickle
> So doth the nightingale.

It makes her sound nice, but she wasn't really a very nice girl.'

'The Dutch Courtezan, or Pamela Widmerpool?'

'I meant the former. Lady Widmerpool had her failings too, if that evening was anything to go by. Still, it's impressive what she did. How some men get girls hotted up. No, what I was going to say about the Dutch Courtezan was—if there'd been time to spare—I might have toyed with doing a setting for her song, whatever she was like. One could have brought it into the opera about Candaules and Gyges perhaps. That would have made Gossage sit up.'

He sighed, more exhaustedly than regretfully, I thought. That morning was the last time I saw Moreland. It was also the last time I had, with anyone, the sort of talk we used to have together. Things drawing to a close, even quite suddenly, was hardly a surprise. The look Moreland had was the one people take on when a stage has been reached quite different from just being ill.

'I'll have to think about that song,' he said.

Drizzle was coming down fairly hard outside. I walked back over the bridge. Vintage cars still penetrated the traffic moving south. They advanced in small groups, separated from each other by a few minutes. More exaggerated in style, some of the period costumes assumed by drivers and passengers recalled the deerstalker cap, check ulster, General Conyers had worn, when, on the eve of the 'first' war, he had mastered the hill leading to Stonehurst, in his fabled motor-car. I wondered if the Conyers car had survived, to become a collector's piece of incalculable value to people like Jimmy Stripling. Here and there, from open hoodless vehicles, protruded an umbrella, sometimes of burlesque size or colour. I paused to watch them by the statue of Boadicea—Budicca, one would name her, if speaking with Dr Brightman—in the chariot. The chariot horses recalled what a squalid part the philosopher, Seneca, with his shady horse-dealing, had played in that affair. Below was inscribed the pay-off for the Romans.

> Regions Ceasar never knew
> Thy posterity shall sway.

Whatever else might be thought of that observation, the Queen was obviously driving the ultimate in British vintage makes. A liability suddenly presented itself, bringing such musings sharply to a close, demanding rapid decisions. Widmerpool, approaching from right angles, was walking along the Embankment in the direction of Parliament. It might have been possible to avoid him by crossing quickly in front, because, as usual when alone, his mind seemed bent on a problem. At that moment something happened to cause the attention of both of us to be concentrated all at once in the same direction. This was the loud, prolonged hooting of one of the vintage cars, which, having crossed Parliament Square, was approaching Westminster Bridge.

Widmerpool stopped dead. He stared for a second with irritated contempt. Then his face took on a look of enraged surprise. The very sight of the vintage cars appeared to stir in him feelings of the deepest disgust, uncontrollable resentment. That would not be altogether out of character. His deep absorption in whatever he was regarding gave opportunity to avoid him. Instead, I myself tried to trace the screeching noises to their source. They were issuing from the horn, whimsically shaped like a dragon's head, of a vintage car driven by a man wearing neo-Edwardian outfit, beside whom sat a young woman in normal dress for an outing. The reason for Widmerpool's outraged expression became clear, even then not immediately. I am not sure I should have recognized Glober, in his near-fancy-dress, had not Polly Duport been there too. My first thought, complacently self-regarding, had been to suppose they had seen me, hooted, if not in a mere friendly gesture, at least to signalize Glober's own glorious vintage progress. A similar explanation of why the horn had sounded offered itself to Widmerpool. He, too, thought they had hooted at him. He took for granted that Glober was hooting in derision.

The doubtful taste of such an act—given all the circumstances—had time to strike me, slightly appal me, before I became aware that the imputation was altogether unjust. Glober had noticed neither Widmerpool, nor myself. The crescendo of resonances on the dragon-horn had been prompted by Odo Stevens, with Jimmy Stripling, at that moment passing Glober's Boadicean machine, in one of similar date, though without a hood. Stevens, clad even more exotically than Glober, was driving; Stripling, wear-

278

ing a simple cap and mackintosh, holding a large green umbrella over their heads. Widmerpool turned away from contemplation of the scene. He was red with anger. There could be no doubt he supposed himself the object of ridicule. All this had taken a moment or two to absorb. Escape was now out of the question. We were only a few yards apart. He could not fail to see me. I spoke first, as the best form of defence.

'I'm glad I'm not driving a long distance on a day like this in a car liable to break down.'

That was not a particularly interesting nor profound observation. Nothing better came to mind to bridge the moments before mutation of the traffic lights allowed evasion by crossing the road. Widmerpool accepted this opening by giving an equally flat reply.

'I'm on my way to the House of Lords.'

The statement carried conviction. The block of flats in which he lived was only a few minutes walk from where we stood. Riverside approach to Parliament would be preferable to the Whitehall route. He showed outward mark of the stresses endured. His body was thinner, the flesh of his face hanging in sallow pouches. So deeply, so all envelopingly, was he dressed in black, that he looked almost ecclesiastical.

'After what I've been through, I think it my duty to show I can rise above personal attack—and, I might add, personal misfortune.'

I made some acknowledgment, one not conspicuously glowing, of these sentiments. Short of turning on one's heel, which would have been overdramatic, it was still impossible to get away. Widmerpool, for his part, appeared quite pleased at this opportunity for uttering a short address on his own situation, possibly some sort of informal rehearsal of material later to be used in a speech.

'I do not propose for one moment to abandon the cause

of genuine internationalism. It has been said that a presumption of innocence is a peculiarity of bourgeois liberal law. My own experience of bourgeois liberal law is the reverse. From the first, in my own case, there was a presumption of culpability. Fortunately, I was in a position to rebut my accusers. In the Upper House, wherever else I am called upon to serve the purposes of political truth, I shall continue to assail the limitations of contemporary empiricism, and expose the bankruptcy of cold-war propagandists.'

He sounded more than a little unhinged. Widmerpool had not finished. Without altering his tone, he changed the subject.

'The squalor—the squalor of that hotel.'

Traffic, beginning to slow up at the amber, came at last to a halt at red. Grinding noises provided exemption from need to produce an audible reply. Widmerpool showed no sign of expecting anything of the sort.

'The sheer ingratitude,' he said.

'I must be getting on. There's a lot to do. I want to get home before dark.'

He was never greatly interested in other people's doings. I added some platitude about the evenings drawing in. Widmerpool did not question the notation of the days. He turned to wait for the other lights to change, enabling him to proceed towards his destination. I crossed Whitehall swiftly. Another burst of vintage cars was advancing towards the bridge.

Hearing Secret Harmonies

for
Robert Conquest

1

DUCK, FLYING IN FROM THE south, ignored four or five ponderous explosions over at the quarry. The limestone cliff, dominant oblong foreground structure, lateral storeyed platforms, all coral-pink in evening sunlight, projected towards the higher ground on misty mornings a fading mirage of Babylonian terraces suspended in haze above the mere; the palace, with its hanging gardens, distantly outlined behind a group of rather woodenly posed young Medes (possibly young Persians) in Mr Deacon's *Boyhood of Cyrus*, the picture's recession equally nebulous in the shadows of the Walpole-Wilsons' hall. Within this hollow bed of the stream the whole range of the quarry was out of sight, except for where the just visible peak of an escarpment of spoil shelved up to the horizon's mountainous coagulations of floating cottonwool, a density of white cloud perforated here and there by slowly opening and closing loopholes of the palest blue light. It was a warm windy afternoon. Midday thunder had not brought back rain. Echoes of the blasting, counterfeiting a return of the storm, stirred faintly smouldering wartime embers; in conjunction with the duck, recalling an argument between General Bobrowski and General Philidor about shooting wildfowl. The angular formation taken by the birds (mimed by Pole and Frenchman with ferocious gestures) was now neatly exhibited, as the flight spiralled down deliberately, almost vertically, settling among reeds and waterlilies at the far end of the pool. Two columns of smoke rose above a line of blueblack trees thickly concentrated together beyond the dusty water, scrawling slate-coloured diagonals across the ceiling of powdered grit, inert and translucent, that swam above the screened workings. Metallic odours, like those of a laboratory, drifted down from a westerly direction, overlaying a nearer-by scent of fox.

'Here's one,' said Isobel. 'At least he's considering the matter.'

After the dredging of crevices lower down the brook, expectation was almost at an end. The single crayfish emerging from under the stones was at once followed by two more. Luck had come at last. The three crayfish, swart miniature lobsters of macabrely knowing demeanour, hung about doubtfully in a basin of mud below the surface. The decision was taken by the crayfish second to enter. He led the way with fussy self-importance, the other two bustling along behind. The three of them clawed a hold on to opposite sides of the outer edge of the iron rim supporting the trap's circle of wire-netting submerged at the water's edge, all at the same moment hurrying across the expanse of mesh towards a morsel of flyblown meat fastened at the centre.

'Do you want to hold the string, Fiona?' asked Isobel. 'Wait a second. A fourth has appeared.'

'Give it to me.'

The dark young man spoke with authority. Presented under the name of Scorpio Murtlock, he was by definition established as bossing the other three. As Fiona made no attempt, either as woman or niece, to assert prior right, Isobel handed him the lengths of twine from which the trap dangled. His status, known on arrival, required observation to take in fully. The age was hard to estimate. He could be younger than Barnabas Henderson, the other young man, thought to be in his later twenties. Fiona herself was twenty-one, so far as I could remember. The girl introduced as Rusty (no surname attached) looked a battered nineteen. I felt relieved that crayfish, as such, had not proved illusory, a mere crazy fancy, recognizable from the start as typical of those figments of a superannuated imagination older people used to put forward when one was oneself young. Four crayfish had undeniably presented themselves, whether caught or not hardly mattered. In any case the occasion had been elevated, by what had been said earlier, to a level above that of a simple sporting event. This higher meaning had to be taken into consideration too.

'The trap must be hauled up gently, or they walk off again,' said Isobel. 'The frustration of the Old Man and the Sea is nothing to it.'

Murtlock, still holding the strings, gathered round him the three-quarter-length bluish robe he wore, a kind of smock or kaftan, not too well adapted to country pursuits. He went down on one knee by the bank. Sweeping out of his eyes handfuls of uncared-for black hair, he leant forward at a steep angle to inspect the crustaceans below, somehow conveying the posture of a priest engaged in the devotions of a recondite creed. He was small in stature, but impressive. The shining amulet, embossed with a hieroglyph, that hung round his throat from a necklace of beads, splashed into the water. He allowed it to remain for a second below the surface, while he gazed fixedly into the depths. Then, having waited for the fourth crayfish to become radically committed to the decomposing snack, he carefully lifted the circle of wire, outward and upward as instructed, from where it rested among pebbles and weed under the projecting lip of the bank.

'The bucket, Barnabas—the gloves, one of you.'

The order was sternly given, like all Murtlock's biddings.

3

Barnabas Henderson fumbled with the bucket. Fiona held out the gardening gloves. Rusty, grinning to herself uneasily, writhed her body about in undulating motions and hummed. Murtlock snatched a glove. Fitting on the fingers adroitly, without setting down the trap, by now dripping over his vestment-like smock, he picked a crayfish off the wire, dropping the four of them one by one into a pail already prepared quarter-full with water. His gestures were deft, ritualistic. He was totally in charge.

This gift of authority, ability to handle people, was the characteristic attributed by hearsay. At first the outward trappings, suggesting no more than a contemporary romantic vagabondage, had put that reputation in doubt. Now one saw the truth of some at least of what had been reported of him; that the vagabond style could include ability to control companions—notably Fiona—as well as crayfish and horses; the last skill demonstrated when they had arrived earlier that day in a small horse-drawn caravan. Murtlock's rather run-of-the-mill outlandishness certainly comprised something perceptibly priestly about it. That was over and above the genuflexion at the water's edge. There was an essentially un-sacerdotal side, one that suggested behaviour dubious, if not actively criminal. That aspect, too, was allied to a kind of fanaticism. Such distinguishing features, more or less, were to be expected after stories about him. A novice in a monastery of robber monks might offer not too exaggerated a definition. His eyes, pale, cold, unblinking, could not be denied a certain degree of magnetism.

Barnabas Henderson was another matter. He was similarly dressed in a blue robe, somewhat more ultramarine in shade, a coin-like object hanging from his neck too, hair in ringlets to the shoulder, with the addition of a Chinese magician's moustache. His spectacles, large and square, were in yellow plastic. The combination of moustache and spectacles created an effect not unlike those one-piece cardboard

4

contraptions to be bought in toyshops, moustache and spectacles held together by a false nose. That was unfair. Henderson was not a badlooking young man, if lacking Murtlock's venturesome bearing, as well as his tactile competence. Henderson's garments, no less eclectically chosen, were newer, a trifle cleaner, less convincingly part of himself. The genre was carried off pretty well by Murtlock, justly heralded as handsome. Henderson's milder features remained a trifle apologetic, his personality, in contrast, not by nature suited to the apparent intent. He was alleged to have abandoned a promising career as an art-dealer to follow this less circumscribed way of life. Perhaps that was a wrong identification, the new life desirable because additionally circumscribed, rather than less so. There could be little doubt that Henderson owned the caravan, painted yellow, its woodwork dilapidated, but drawn by a sound pair of greys. Probably Henderson was paying for the whole jaunt.

The girls, too, were dressed predominantly in blue. Rusty, whose air was that of a young prostitute, had a thick crop of dark red hair and deep liquid eyes. These were her good points. She was tall, sallow-skinned, hands large and coarse, her collar-bones projecting. Having maintained total silence since arrival, except for intermittent humming, she could be assessed only by looks, which certainly suggested extensive sexual experience.

Fiona, daughter of Isobel's sister Susan and Roddy Cutts, was a pretty girl ('Fiona has a touch of glamour,' her first-cousin, Jeremy Warminster, had said), small, fair-skinned, baby-faced, with her father's sandy hair. Otherwise she more resembled her mother, without the high spirits (an asset throughout her husband's now closed political career) brought out in Susan by any gathering that showed signs of developing into a party. Susan Cutts's occasional bouts of melancholy seemed latterly to have descended on her

5

daughter in the form of an innate lugubriousness, which had taken the place of Fiona's earlier tomboy streak.

The upper halves of both girls were sheathed in T-shirts, inscribed with the single word HARMONY. Rusty wore jeans, Fiona a long skirt that swept the ground. Dragging its flounces across the damp grass, she looked like a mediaeval lady from the rubric of an illuminated Book of Hours, a remote princess engaged in some now obsolete pastime. The appearance seemed to demand the addition of a wimple and pointed cap. This antique air of Fiona's could have played a part in typecasting Murtlock as a reprobate boy-monk. Equally viewed as whimsical figures in a Tennysonian-type Middle Age, the rôles of Rusty and Henderson were indeterminate; Rusty perhaps a recreant knight's runaway mistress disguised as a page; Henderson, an unsuccessful troubadour, who had mislaid his lute. This fanciful imagery was not entirely disavowed by the single word motto each girl bore on her breast, a lettered humour that could well have featured in the rubric of a mediaeval manuscript, inscribed on banner or shield of a small figure in the margin. The feet of all four were bare, and—another mediaeval touch—long unwashed.

Fiona (whose birth commemorated her parents' reconciliation after Roddy Cutts's misadventure with the cipherine during war service in Persia) had given a fair amount of trouble since her earliest years. This was in contrast with her two elder brothers: Jonathan, married, several children, rising rapidly in a celebrated firm of fine arts auctioneers; Sebastian, still unmarried, much addicted to girlfriends, though no less ambitious than his brother, 'in computers'. Both the Cutts sons were tireless conversationalists in their father's manner, uncheckable, informative, sagacious, on the subject of their respective jobs. Fiona, who had run away from several schools (been required to leave at least one), had strengthened her status as a difficult subject by

6

catching typhoid abroad when aged fourteen or fifteen, greatly alarming everyone by her state. Abandonment of boisterous forms of rebellion, in favour of melancholic opposition, dated from the unhappy incident with the electrician, handsome and good-natured, but married and not particularly young. Since then nothing had gone at all well. Fiona's educational dislodgements had not impaired education sufficiently to prevent her from getting a living on the outskirts of 'glossy' journalism.

No one seemed to know where exactly Fiona had run across Scorpio Murtlock, nor the precise nature of this most recent association. It was assumed—anyway by her parents —to include cohabitation. Her uncle, Isobel's brother, Hugo Tolland, cast doubts on that. Hugo's opinions on that sort of subject were often less than reliable, a taste for exaggeration marring the accuracy that is always more interesting than fantasy. In this case, Hugo coming down on the side of scepticism—on grounds that, if Murtlock liked sex at all, he preferred his own—the view had to be taken into consideration. How Murtlock lived seemed as unknowable as his sexual proclivities. The Cutts parents, Roddy and Susan, always very 'good' about their daughter's vagaries, continued to be so, accepting the Murtlock régime with accustomed resignation.

The member of the family best equipped to speak with anything like authority of Fiona, and her friends, was Isobel's unmarried sister, Blanche Tolland, who had, in fact, rung up to ask if we were prepared to harbour a small caravan in our field for one night, its destination unspecified. The easygoing unambitious nature that had caused Blanche, in early days, to be regarded—not wholly without reason—as rather dotty, had latterly given her a certain status in dealing with a generation considerably younger than her own; Blanche's unemphatic personality providing a diplomatic contact, an agency through which dealings

7

could be negotiated by either side without prejudice or loss of face. This good nature, allied to a deep-seated taste for taking trouble in often uncomfortable circumstances, led to employment in an animal sanctuary, a job that had occupied Blanche for a long time by now.

'Blanchie meets the animals on their own terms,' said her sister, Norah, also unmarried. 'The young people too. She really runs a sanctuary for both.'

'Do you mean the young people think of Blanchie as an animal, or as another young person?' asked her brother.

'Which do you suppose, Hugo?' said Norah sharply. 'It's true they might easily mistake you for an ape.'

Hugo, rather a sad figure after the death of his partner, Sam, could still arouse the mood in Norah that had caused her to observe he would 'never find a place for himself in the contemporary world'. Working harder than ever in the antique shop, now he was on his own, Hugo's career could be regarded, in general, as no less contemporary than anyone else's. Sam (said to have begun life as a seaman) had remained surnameless (like Rusty) to the end, so far as most of the family were concerned. It was during this exchange in Norah's Battersea flat that I first heard the name of Scorpio Murtlock.

'Blanchie says Fiona's turned over a new leaf under the influence of this new young man, Scorp Murtlock. Sober, honest, and an early riser, not to mention meditations. No hint of a drug. It's a kind of cult. Religious almost. Harmony's the great thing. They have a special greeting they give one another. I can't remember the exact words. Quite impressive. They don't wash much, but then none of the Cutts family ever did much washing.'

'How did he come to be christened Scorp?' I asked.

'Short for Scorpio, his Zodiac sign.'

'What's he like?'

'Blanche says attractive, but spooky.'

At this point Hugo showed unexpected knowledge.

'I didn't know Fiona's latest was Scorpio Murtlock. I've never met him, but I used to hear about him several years ago, when he was working in the antique business. Two fellow antique dealers told me they had engaged a very charming young assistant.'

Norah was not prepared for Hugo to take over entirely in the Murtlock field.

'Blanchie says he has a creepy side too.'

'You can be creepy and attractive. There are different forms of creepiness, just as there are different forms of attractiveness.'

'The antique dealers are presumably queers?'

'Even so, that's hardly the point. Murtlock made himself immensely useful in the business—which ranges from garden furniture to vintage cars—so useful that the owners suddenly found they were being relegated to a back place themselves. Murtlock was slowly but surely elbowing them out.'

'Did their passion remain unsatisfied?'

'I'm not sure.'

'Unlike you, Hugo, not to be sure about that sort of thing.'

'One of them implied he'd brought off something. That was not the rather nervy one. The nervy one complained he had begun to feel like a man bewitched. Those were his own words. The unnervy one agreed after a while that there was something uncomfortable about Murtlock. They were wondering how best to solve their problem, when Murtlock himself gave notice. He'd found someone more profitable to work over. His new patron—a man of some age, even older than oneself, if that can be imagined—was apparently more interested in what Blanchie calls Murtlock's spooky side than in his sex appeal. They met during some business deal.'

9

'Murtlock doesn't sound a particularly desirable friend for Fiona.'

'Blanche says he makes her behave herself.'

'Even so.'

'Susan and Roddy are thankful for small mercies.'

'Taking exercise, meditation, no alcohol, sound quite large ones.'

'They sound to me like the good old Simple Life,' said Hugo. 'Still it's a relief one won't catch one's foot in a hypodermic when next at Blanchie's cottage.'

'You always talk about your nephews and nieces in the way Aunt Molly used to talk about you,' said Norah.

Hugo was not at all discomposed by the comparison.

'And you, Norah dear—and you. Think how Aunt Molly used to go on about you and Eleanor Walpole-Wilson. As a matter of fact, I quite agree I've turned into Aunt Molly. I'd noticed it myself. Old age might have transformed one into something much worse. Everybody liked her. I flatter myself I'm much what she'd have been had she remained unmarried.'

'I shall begin to howl, Hugo, if you talk like that about poor Eleanor.'

The Norah Tolland/Eleanor Walpole-Wilson ménage had not been revived after the war, their ways dividing, though they remained friends. Norah, never so fulfilled as during her years as driver in one of the women's services, had taken a job with a small car-hire firm, where she continued to wear a peaked cap and khaki uniform. Later she became one of the directors of the business, which considerably enlarged itself in scope, Norah always remaining available to drive, especially if a long continental trip were promised. Eleanor Walpole-Wilson, for her part, securing a seat on the Urban District Council, became immersed in local politics. Of late years she had embarked on a close relationship with a Swedish woman-doctor. Staying with this friend in Stockholm, Eleanor had been taken ill and died, bequeathing to Norah, with a small legacy, a pair of short-tempered pugs. Sensing mention of their former mistress, this couple now began to rush about the flat, snuffling and barking.

'Oh, shut up, pugs,' said Norah.

The commendation accorded to Scorpio Murtlock—that he could keep Fiona in order—limited in compass, was not to be lightly regarded, if valid. It was reiterated by Blanche, when she rang up about the caravan party. Never very capable of painting word pictures, she was unable to add much additional information about Murtlock, nor did she know anything, beyond her name, of the girl Rusty. Barnabas Henderson, on the other hand, possessed certain conventional aspects, notably a father killed in the war, who had left enough money for his son to buy a partnership in a small picture-dealing business; a commercial venture abandoned to follow Murtlock into the wilderness.

Blanche's assurance of comparatively austere behaviour— what Hugo called the good old Simple Life—had been to some extent borne out, on the arrival of Fiona and her friends, by refusal of all offers of food and drink. Provided with a bivouac under some trees, on the side of the field away from the house, they at once set about various minor tasks relative to settling in caravan and horses, behaviour that seemed to confirm the ascription of a severe standard of living. When, early in the afternoon, Isobel and I went to see how they were getting on, they had come to the end of these dispositions. Earlier negotiations about siting the caravan had been carried out with Fiona, Murtlock standing in silence with folded arms. Now he showed more sign of emerging as the strong personality he had been billed.

'Is there anything you'd all like to do?'

Fiona had been addressed. Murtlock took it upon himself to answer.

'Too late in the year to leap the fires.'

He spoke thoughtfully, without any touch of jocularity. This was evidently the line Blanche had denominated as spooky. Since we had agreed to put up the caravan, there was no reason, if kept within bounds, why Beltane should not be celebrated, or whatever it was he had in mind.

'We could make a bonfire.'

'Too near the solstice.'

'Something else then?'

'A sacrifice.'

'What sort?'

'One in Harmony.'

'Like Fiona's shirt?'

'Yes.'

He did not laugh. He did not even smile. This affirmative somehow inhibited further comment in a frivolous tone, imposing acquiescence in not treating things lightly, even Fiona's shirt. At the same time I was uncertain whether he was not simply teasing. On the face of it teasing seemed much more likely than all this assumed gravity. Nevertheless uncertainty remained, ambivalence of manner leaving one guessing. No doubt that was intended, after all a fairly well recognized method of establishing one sort of supremacy. The expressed aim—that things should be in Harmony—could not in itself be regarded as objectionable. It supported the contention that Fiona's latest set of friends held to stringent moral values of one sort or another. How best to achieve an act of Harmony was another matter.

'Harmony is not easy to define.'

'Harmony is Power—Power is Harmony.'

'That's how you see it?'

'That's how it is.'

He smiled. When Murtlock smiled the charm was revealed. He was a boy again, making a joke, not a fanatical young mystic. At the same time he was a boy with whom it was better to remain on one's guard.

'How are we going to bring off an act of Harmony on a Saturday afternoon?'

'Through the Elements.'

'What elements?'

'Fire, Air, Earth, Water.'

The question had been a foolish one. He smiled again. We discussed various possibilities, none of them very sparkling. The other three were silent throughout all this. Murtlock seemed to have transformed them into mere shadows of himself.

'Is there water near here? I think so. There is the feel of water.'

'A largish pond within walking distance.'

'We could make a water sacrifice.'

'Drown somebody?'

He did not answer.

'We could go crayfishing,' said Isobel.

Since demands made by improvisation at a moment's notice of the necessary tackle for this sport were relatively onerous, the proposal marked out Isobel, too, as not entirely uninfluenced by Murtlock's spell.

'The crayfish are in the pond?'

'In the pools of the brook that runs out of it.'

He considered.

'It can't be exactly described as a blood sport,' I added.

I don't know why inserting that lame qualification seemed required, except that prejudice against blood sports could easily accord with an outlook to be inferred from people dressed in their particular style. If asked to rationalize the comment, that would have been my pretext. Aggressive activities against crayfish might be, by definition, excluded from an afternoon's programme devoted to Harmony. Who could tell? Harmony was also Power, he said. Power would be exercised over crayfish, if caught, but possibly the wrong sort of Power. He pretended to be puzzled.

'You mean that without blood there is no vehicle for the spirit?'

'I mean that you might not like killing.'

'I do not kill, if not killed.'

He seemed glad to have an opportunity to make that statement, gnomic to say the least. It sounded like a favourite apophthegm of a luminary of the cult to which they all belonged, the familiar ring of Shortcuts to the Infinite, Wisdom of the East, Analects of the Sages. For some reason the pronouncement seemed also one recently brought to notice. Had I read it not long before in print? The Murtlock standpoint, his domination over Fiona and the others, was becoming a little clearer in a certain sense, if remaining obscure in many others.

'I don't think we'll be killed. Deaths crayfishing are comparatively rare.'

'You spoke not of death, but of killing.'

'The latter is surely apt to lead to the former?'

'There is killing—death is an illusion.'

This was no help so far as deciding how the afternoon was to be spent.

'The point is whether or not you would consider the killing of crayfish to be in Harmony?'

Once more his smile made me feel that it was I, rather than he, who was being silly.

'Not all killing is opposed to Harmony.'

'Let's kill crayfish then.'

The odd thing was that he managed never to be exactly discourteous, nor even embarrassing, when he talked in this way. It was always close to a joke, though a joke not quite brought to birth. At least you did not laugh. You accepted on its own merits what he said, unintelligible or the reverse. I wondered—had not some forty years stretched between us—

14

whether, as a contemporary, I should have been friends with Scorpio Murtlock. Indications were at best doubtful. That negative surmise was uninfluenced by his manner of talking, mystic and imperative, still less the style of dress. Both might have been acceptable at that age in a contemporary. In any case fashions of one generation, moral or physical, are scarcely at all assessable in terms of another. They cannot be properly equated. So far as they could be equated, the obstacles set up against getting on with Murtlock were in themselves negligible.

The objection to him, if objection there were, was the sense that he brought of something ominous. He would have been ominous—perhaps more ominous—in a City suit, the ominous side of him positively mitigated by a blue robe. His accents, liturgical, enigmatic, were also consciously rough, uncultivated. The roughness was imitated by Fiona and Henderson, when they remembered to do so. Rusty never uttered. No doubt Murtlock's chief attraction was owed to this ominousness, something more sexually persuasive than good looks, spectacular trappings, even sententious observations. Certainly Fiona was showing an altogether uncharacteristic docility in allowing, without any sign of dispute or passive disapproval, someone else to make all the going. It might be assumed that she and Rusty were 'in love' with Murtlock. Probably Henderson shared that passion. Murtlock himself showed no sign of being emotionally drawn to any of them. In the light of what had been reported, it would have been surprising had he done so.

'What do we need?'

He spoke this time in a tone of practical enquiry.

'A circle of wire mesh kept together by a piece of iron. Something like the rim of an old saucepan or fryingpan does well.'

'The circle, figure of perfection—iron, abhorred by demons.'

15

'Those aspects may help too.'

'They will.'

'Then a piece of preferably rotting meat.'

'Nothing far different from a sacrifice for a summoning.'

'In this case summoning crayfish.'

'Crayfish our sacrifice, rather.'

The requirements took a little time to get into order. A morsel of doubtful freshness was found among bones set aside for stock. The four of them joined in these preparations usefully, shaping the wire-netting, measuring out cords, fixing the tainted bait. When the trap was assembled Murtlock swung it gently through the air. Even in undertaking this trial of weight, which showed grasp of the sport, there was something of the swaying of a priest's censer.

'And now?'

'The crayfish beds, such as they are, lie about a quarter of a mile away.'

The brook flowed through fields of poorish pasture, tangled with undergrowth as they sloped down more steeply to the line of the stream. Once the trap was slung among its stones Murtlock seemed satisfied. If the others were bored, they did not dare show it during the long period when there was no sign of a catch. Conversation altogether flagged. Murtlock himself possessed to a marked degree that characteristic—perhaps owing something to hypnotic powers—which attaches to certain individuals; an ability to impose on others present the duty of gratifying his own whims. It seemed to matter that Murtlock should get what he wanted—in this case crayfish—while, if the others were bored, that was their affair. No particular obligation was laid on oneself to prevent it. When at last the circle of iron showed signs of possessing the supposedly magical properties he had attributed, four crayfish caught, this modest final success, obviously pleasing to Murtlock, was for some reason exceptionally pleasing to oneself too. By then afternoon was turning to evening. Again he took the initiative.

'We'll go back now. There are things to do at the caravan. Barnabas must water the horses.'

'Sure you won't dine?'

'Yes.'

'I can easily run up something,' said Isobel.

'The day is one of limited fast.'

Fiona had not explained that when the dinner invitation had been issued some hours earlier.

'Nothing else you want?'

'No.'

'A bottle of wine?'

Then I remembered that they abstained from alcohol.

'No—have you a candle?'

'We can lend you an electric torch.'

'Only for a simple fire ritual.'

'Come back to the house. We'll look for candles.'

'Barnabas can fetch it, if needed. It may not be.'

'Don't start a forest fire, will you?'

He smiled at that.

'Only the suffusion of a few laurel leaves.'

'As you see, laurel is available.'

'Pine-cones?'

'There are one or two conifers up the road to the right.'

'We'll go back then. Take the bucket, Barnabas. The gloves are on the ground, Fiona. Rusty, carry the trap—no, Rusty will carry it.'

None of them was allowed to forget for a moment that he or she was under orders. When the crayfishing paraphernalia had been brought together we climbed the banks that enclosed this length of the stream. After crossing the fields the path led through trees, the ground underfoot thick with wild garlic. At one point, above this Soho restaurant smell,

17

the fox's scent briefly reasserted itself. Here Murtlock stopped. Gazing towards a gap between the branches of two tall oaks, he put up a hand to shade his eyes. The others imitated his attitude. In his company they seemed to have little or no volition of their own. Murtlock's control was absolute. The oak boughs formed a frame for one of the blue patches of sky set among clouds, now here and there flecked with pink. Against this irregular quadrilateral of light, over the meadows lying in the direction of Gauntlett's farm a hawk hovered; then, likely to have marked down a prey, swooped off towards the pond. Murtlock lowered his arm. The others copied him.

'The bird of Horus.'

'Certainly.'

'Do you often see hawks round here?'

He asked the question impatiently, almost angrily.

'This particular one is always hanging about. He was near the house yesterday, and the day before. He's a well-known local personality. Perhaps a retired kestrel from a 'Thirties poem.'

The allusion might be obscure to one of his age. So much the better. Obscurity could be met with obscurity. A second later, either on the hawk's account, or from some other disturbing factor in their vicinity—the quarry end of the pond—the duck flew out again. Rising at an angle acute as their former descent, the flight took on at once the disciplined wedge-shaped configuration used in all duck transit, leader at apex, main body following behind in semblance of a fan. Mounting higher, still higher, soaring over copper and green beechwoods, the birds achieved considerable altitude before a newly communicated command wheeled them off again in a fresh direction. Adjusting again to pattern, they receded into creamy cavernous billows of distant cloud, beyond which the evening sun drooped. Into this opaque glow of fire they disappeared. To the initiated, I reflected—to ancient soothsayers—the sight would have been vaticinatory.

'What message do the birds foretell?'

Even allowing for that sort of thing being in his line, Murtlock's question, put just at the moment when the thought was in my own mind, brought a slight sense of shock. He uttered the words softly, as if now gratified at being able to accept my train of thought as coherent, in contrast with earlier demur on the subject of death and killing. Even with intimates that sort of implied knowledge of what is going on in one's head, recognition of unspoken thoughts passing through the mind—in its way common enough—can be a little disconcerting, much more so to be thought-read by this strange young man. The ducks' coalescence into the muffled crimsons of sunset had been dramatic enough to invoke reflection on mysterious things, and such a subject as ornithomancy was evidently of the realm to which he aspired. The process was perhaps comparable with the intercommunication practised by the birds themselves, their unanimous change of direction, well ordered regrouping, rapid new advance, disciplined as troops drilling on the square; more appositely, aircraft obeying a radioed command.

This well disciplined aspect of duck behaviour must have been partly what entranced the generals, when with such fervour both of them had demonstrated the triangular formation. The evening came back vividly. Duties of the day over—I had been conducting officer with a group of Allied military attachés—we had been sitting in the bar of the little Normandy auberge where we were billeted. Bobrowski had almost upset his beer in demonstrating the precise shape of the flight. Philidor was calmer. Some years after the war—he was in exile, of course, from his own country—Bobrowski had been knocked down by a taxi, and killed. Oddly enough Philidor, too, had died in a car accident—so a Frenchman at their Embassy said—having by then attained quite high rank. Perhaps such deaths were appropriate to men of action, better than a slow decline. Aware that a more than usually acute consciousness of human mortality had descended, I wondered for a moment whether Murtlock was responsible for that sensation. It was not impossible.

'I was thinking of the Roman augurs too.'

'They also scrutinized the entrails of animals for prophecy.'

He added that with a certain relish.

'Sometimes—as the Bard remarks—the sad augurs mocked their own presage.'

One had to fight back. Murtlock made no comment. I hoped the quotation had floored him. The rest of the walk back to where the caravan was parked took place in silence and without incident. At the caravan our ways would divide, if the four of them were not to enter the house. Separation was delayed by the appearance of Mr Gauntlett advancing towards us.

'Good afternoon, Mr Gauntlett.'

Mr Gauntlett, wearing a cowslip in his buttonhole, greeted us. He showed no sign whatever of thinking our guests at all unusually dressed, nodding to them in a friendly manner, without the least curiosity as to why the males should be wearing blue robes.

'Happen you've seen my old bitch, Daisy, this way, Mr Jenkins? Been gone these forty-eight hours, and I don't know where she's to.'

'We haven't, Mr Gauntlett.'

A farmer, now retired as close on eighty, Mr Gauntlett lived in an ancient tumbledown farmhouse not far away, where—widower, childless, sole survivor of a large family —he 'did for himself', a life that seemed to suit him, unless rheumatics caused trouble. His house, associated by local legend with a seventeenth-century murder, was said to be haunted. Mr Gauntlett himself, though he possessed a keen sense of the past, and liked to discuss such subjects as whether the Romans brought the chestnut to Britain, always asserted that the ghosts had never inconvenienced him. This taste for history could account for a habit of allowing himself archaisms of speech, regional turns of phrase, otherwise going out of circulation. In not at all disregarding the importance of style in facing life—even consciously histrionic style—Mr Gauntlett a little resembled General Conyers. They both shared the same air of distinction, firmness, good looks that resisted age, but above all this sense of style. Mr. Gauntlett had once told me that during service (in the first war) with the Yeomanry, he had found himself riding through the Khyber Pass, a background of vast mountains, bare rocks, fierce tribesmen, that seemed for some reason not at all out of accord with his own mild manner.

'Maybe Daisy's littered in the woods round here, as she did three years gone. Then she came home again, and made a great fuss, for to bring me to a dingle down by the water, where she'd had her pups. The dogs round about knew of it. They'd been barking all night for nigh on a week to drive foxes and the like away, but I haven't heard 'em barking o' nights this time.'

'We'll keep an eye out for Daisy, Mr Gauntlett. Tell her to go home if we find her, report to you if we run across a nest of her pups. We've all been crayfishing.'

I said that defensively, speaking as if everyone under thirty always wore blue robes for that sport. I felt a little diminished by being caught with such a crew by Mr Gauntlett.

'Ah?'

'We landed four.'

Mr Gauntlett laughed.

'Many a year since I went out after crayfish. Used to as a boy. Good eating they make. Well, I must go on to be looking for the old girl.'

He was already moving off when Murtlock addressed him.

'Seek the spinney by the ruined mill.'

He spoke in an odd toneless voice. Mr Gauntlett, rare with him, showed surprise. He looked more closely at Murtlock, evidently struck not so much by eccentricity of dress as knowledge of the neighbourhood.

'Ah?'

'Go now.'

Murtlock gave one of his smiles. Immediately after speaking those two short sentences a subtle change in him had taken place. It was as if he had fallen into—then emerged from—an almost instantaneous trance. Mr Gauntlett was greatly pleased with this advice.

'I'll be off to the spinney, instead of the way I was going. That's just where Daisy might be. And my thanks to you, if I find her.'

'If you find her, make an offering.'

'Ah?'

'It would be well to burn laurel and alder in a chafing dish.'

Mr Gauntlett laughed heartily. The suggestion seemed not to surprise him so much as might be expected.

'I'll put something extra in the plate at church on Sunday. That's quite right. It's what I ought to do.'

'Appease the shades of your dwelling.'

Mr Gauntlett laughed again. I do not know whether he took that as an allusion to his haunted house, or even if such were indeed Murtlock's meaning. Whatever intended, he certainly conveyed the impression that he was familiar with the neighbourhood. Perhaps he had already made enquiries about haunted houses round about, the spinney by the old mill entering into some piece of information given. Murtlock would have been capable of that. Mr Gauntlett turned again to continue his search for Daisy. Then, suddenly thinking of another matter, he paused a moment.

'Is there more news of the quarry and The Fingers, Mr Jenkins?'

'They're still hoping to develop in that direction,' said Isobel.

'Ah?'

'We mustn't take our eye off them.'

'No, for sure, that's true.'

Mr Gauntlett repeated his farewells, and set off again, this time in the direction of the old mill.

'How on earth did you know about Daisy being at the spinney?'

'The words came.'

Murtlock spoke this time almost modestly. He seemed to attach no great importance to the advice given, in fact almost to have forgotten the fact that he had given it. He was clearly thinking now of quite other matters. This was where we should leave them. Henderson had set down the bucket containing the crayfish. Rusty was sitting on the grass beside the trap. When Fiona handed over the gardening gloves she allowed a faint gesture in the direction of humdrum usage to escape her.

'Thanks for letting us put up the caravan.'

She looked at Murtlock quickly to make sure this was not too cringing a surrender, too despicable a retreat down the road of conventionality. He nodded with indifference. There was apparently no harm in conceding that amount in the circumstances. Henderson, blinking through the yellow specs, simpered faintly under his Fu Manchu moustache. Rusty, rising from the ground, scratched under her armpit thoughtfully.

'Why not take the crayfish as hors d'oeuvres for supper—or would they be too substantial for your limited fast?'

Fiona glanced at Murtlock. Again he nodded.

'All right.'

'They have to be gutted.'

Murtlock seemed pleased at the thought of that.

'Fiona can do the gutting. That will be good for you, Fiona.'

She agreed humbly.

'You'll be able to prophesy from the entrails,' I said.

No one laughed.

'Bring the bucket back before you leave in the morning,' said Isobel. 'I expect we shall see you in any case before you go, Fiona?'

The matter was once more referred to Murtlock for a ruling. He shook his head. The answer was negative. We should not see them the following day.

'No.'

Murtlock gruffly expanded Fiona's reply.

'We take the road at first light.'

'Early as that?'

'Our journey is long.'

'Where are you making for?'

Instead of mentioning a town or village he gave the name of a prehistoric monument, a Stone Age site, not specially famous, though likely to be known to people interested in those things. Aware vaguely that such spots were the object of pilgrimage on the part of cults of the kind to which Fiona and her friends appeared to belong, I was not greatly surprised by the answer. I supposed the caravan did about twenty miles a day, but was not at all sure of that. If so, the group of megaliths would take several days to reach.

'We were there some years ago, coming home from that

24

part of the world. Are you planning to park near the Stones?'

It was a characteristic 'long barrow', set on the edge of a valley, two uprights supporting a capstone, entrance to a chambered tomb. The place had been thoroughly excavated.

'As near as sanctity allows.'

Murtlock answered curtly.

'Sanctity was being disturbed a good deal by tourists when we were there.'

A look of anger passed over his face, either at the comment, or thought of the tourists. He was quite formidable when he looked angry.

'If you're interested in archaeological sites, we've a minor one just over the hill from here. You probably know about it. The Devil's Fingers—The Fingers, as Mr Gauntlett calls it.'

If he knew something of Mr Gauntlett's house being haunted, he might well have heard of The Devil's Fingers. The name seemed new to him. He became at once more attentive.

'It's worth a visit, if you like that sort of thing. Only a short detour from the road you'll probably be taking in any case.'

'A prehistoric grave?'

'No doubt once, though that's been disputed.'

'What remains?'

'Two worn pillars about five foot high, and the same distance apart.'

'No portal?'

'Only the supports survive, if that's what they are.'

'The Threshold.'

'If a tomb, the burial chamber has long disappeared through ploughing. The general consensus of archaeological opinion accepts the place as a neolithic grave. There have been dissentient theories—boundary stones in the Dark Ages, and so on. They don't amount to much. Local patriotism naturally makes one want the place to be as ancient as possible. The lintel probably went for building purposes in one of the farms round about. The uprights may have been too hard to extract. In any case there's usually a superstition that you can't draw such stones from the earth. Even if you do, they walk back again.'

'Why the name?'

'One Midsummer night, long ago, a girl and her lover were lying naked on the grass. The sight of the girl's body tempted the Devil. He put out his hand towards her. Owing to the night also being the Vigil of St John, the couple invoked the Saint, and just managed to escape. When the Devil tried to withdraw his hand, two of his fingers got caught in the outcrop of rock you find in these quarrying areas. There they remain in a petrified condition.'

Murtlock was silent. He seemed suddenly excited.

'Any other legends about the place?'

'The couple are sometimes seen dancing there. They were saved from the Devil, but purge their sin by eternal association with its scene.'

'They dance naked?'

'I presume.'

'On Midsummer Night?'

'I don't know whether only on the anniversary, or all the year round. In rather another spirit, rickety children used to be passed between the Stones to effect a cure.'

That was one of Mr Gauntlett's stories.

'Is the stag-mask dance known to have been performed there?'

'I've never heard that. In fact I've never heard of the stag-mask dance.'

Murtlock was certainly well up in these things.

'Do the Stones bleed if a dagger is thrust in them at the Solstices?'

'I've never heard that either. There's the usual tale that at certain times—when the cock crows at midnight, I think —the Stones go down to the brook below to drink.'

Murtlock made no comment.

'Covetous people have sometimes taken that opportunity for seeking treasure in the empty sockets, and been crushed on the unexpected return of the Stones. The Stones' drinking habits are threatened. They will have to remain thirsty, unless the efforts of various people are successful. One of the quarries is trying to extend in that direction. They want to fill up the stream. Local opposition is being rallied. Where else will the Stones be able to quench their thirst? That was what the old farmer who talked to us was referring to.'

This time Murtlock showed no interest. The threat to The Devil's Fingers might have been judged something to shock anyone who had spoken of the sanctity of another prehistoric site, but he seemed altogether unmoved. At least he enquired no further as to the conservation problem as presented to him. He did, however, ask how the place could be reached, showing close attention when Isobel explained. He discarded all his elaborately mystical façade while listening to instructions of that sort.

'Is it a secluded spot?'

'About half-a-dozen fields from the road.'

'On high ground?'

'I'd guess about five or six hundred feet.'

'Surrounded by grass?'

'Plough, when we were last there, but the farmer may have gone back to grass.'

'Trees?'

'The Stones stand in an elder thicket on the top of a ridge. It's one of those characteristic settings. The land the other side slopes down to the stream.'

Murtlock thought for a moment or two. His face was

pallid now. He seemed quite agitated at what he had been told. This physical reaction on his part suggested in him something more than the mere calculating ambition implied by Hugo's story. Forces perhaps stronger than himself dominating him, made it possible for him also to dominate by the strength of his own feelings. He turned abruptly on the others, standing passively by while his interrogation was taking place.

'Tomorrow we'll go first to The Devil's Fingers. We'll reach there by dawn.'

They concurred.

'You'll find it of interest.'

He made an odd gesture, indicative of impatience, amazement, contempt, at the inadequacy of such a comment in the context. Then his more mundane half-amused air returned.

'Barnabas will leave the bucket by the kitchen door when we set out in the morning.'

'That would be kind.'

'Don't forget, Barnabas.'

Henderson's lip trembled slightly. He muttered that it would be done.

'Then we'll bid you goodbye,' said Isobel.

Fiona, assuming the expression of one taking medicine, allowed herself to be kissed. Henderson rather uneasily offered a hand, keeping an eye on Murtlock in case he was doing wrong. Rusty gave a grin, and a sort of wave. Murtlock himself raised his right hand. The gesture was not far short of benediction. There was a feeling in the air that, to be wholly correct, Isobel and I should have intoned some already acquired formula to convey that gratitude as to the caravan's visit was something owed only by ourselves. There was a short pause while this antiphon remained unvoiced. Then, since nothing further seemed forthcoming on either side, each party turned away from the other. The four

28

visitors moved towards the caravan, there to perform whatever rites or duties, propitiatory or culinary, might lie before them. We returned to the house.

'I agree with whoever it was thought the dark young man creepy,' said Isobel.

'Just a bit.'

Departure the following morning must have taken place as early as announced. No one heard them go. A candle had apparently proved superfluous, because Henderson never arrived to demand one. His own responsibilities, material and moral, must have turned out too onerous for him to have remembered about the bucket. It was found, not by the kitchen door, but on its side in the grass among the tracks of the caravan. The crayfish were gone. Traces of a glutinous substance, later rather a business to clean out, adhered to the bucket's sides, which gave off an incense-like smell. Isobel thought there was a suggestion of camphor. A few charred laurel leaves also remained in an empty tomato juice tin. Whatever the scents left behind, they were agreed to possess no narcotic connotations. This visit, well defined in the mind at the time, did not make any very lasting impression, Fiona and her companions manifesting themselves as no more than transient representatives of a form of life bound, sooner or later, to move into closer view. Their orientation might be worth attention, according to mood; meanwhile other things took precedence.

2

Two compensations for growing old are worth putting on record as the condition asserts itself. The first is a vantage point gained for acquiring embellishments to narratives that have been unfolding for years beside one's own, trimmings that can even appear to supply the conclusion of a given story, though finality is never certain, a dimension always possible to add. The other mild advantage endorses a keener perception for the authenticities of mythology, not only of the traditional sort, but—when such are any good— the latterday mythologies of poetry and the novel. One such fragment, offering a gloss on the crayfishing afternoon, cropped up during the summer months of the same year, when I was reading one night after dinner.

The book, Harington's translation of *Orlando Furioso*— bedside romance of every tolerably well-educated girl of Byron's day—now requires, if not excuse, at least some sort of explanation. Twenty years before, writing a book about Robert Burton and his *Anatomy of Melancholy*, I had need to glance at Ariosto's epic, Burton being something of an Ariosto fan. Harington's version (lively, but inaccurate) was then hard to come by; another (less racy, more exact), just as suitable for the purpose. Although by no means all equally readable, certain passages of the poem left a strong impression. Accordingly, when a new edition of Harington's *Orlando Furioso* appeared, I got hold of it. I was turning the pages that evening with the sense—essential to mature enjoyment of any classic—of being entirely free from responsibility to pause for a second over anything that threatened the least sign of tedium.

In spite of the title, Orlando's madness plays a comparatively small part in the narrative's many convolutions. This does not mean Ariosto himself lacked interest in that facet of his story. On the contrary, he is profoundly concerned with the cause—and cure—of Orlando's mental breakdown. What happened? Orlando (Charlemagne's Roland), a hero, paladin, great man, had gone off his head because his girl, Angelica, beautiful, intelligent, compassionate, everything a nice girl should be—so to speak female counterpart of Orlando himself—had abandoned him for a nonentity. She had eloped with a good-looking utterly boring young man. Ariosto allows the reader to remain in absolutely no doubt as to the young man's total insignificance. The situation is clearly one that fascinates him. He emphasizes the vacuity of mind shown by Angelica's lover in a passage describing the young man's carving of their intertwined names on the trunks of trees, a whimsicality that first reveals to Orlando himself his own banal predicament.

Orlando's ego (his personal myth, as General Conyers would have said) was murderously wounded. He found himself altogether incapable of making the interior adjustment required to continue his normal routine of living the Heroic Life. His temperament allowing no half measures, he chose, therefore, the complete negation of that life. Discarding his clothes, he lived henceforth in deserts and waste places, roaming hills and woods, gaining such sustenance as he might, while waging war against a society he had renounced. In short, Orlando dropped out.

Ariosto describes how one of Orlando's friends, an

English duke named Astolpho, came to the rescue. Riding a hippogryph (an intermediate beast Harington calls his 'Griffith Horse', like the name of an obscure poet), Astolpho undertook a journey to the Moon. There, in one of its valleys, he was shown all things lost on Earth: lost kingdoms: lost riches: lost reputations: lost vows: lost hours: lost love. Only lost foolishness was missing from this vast stratospheric Lost Property Office, where by far the largest accretion was lost sense. Although he had already discovered in this store some of his lost days and lost deeds, Astolpho was surprised to come across a few of his own lost wits, simply because he had never in the least missed them. He had a duty to perform here, which was to bring back from his spacetrip the wits (mislaid on an immeasurably larger scale than his own) of his old friend and comrade-in-arms, Orlando. It was Astolpho's achievement—if so to be regarded—to restore to Orlando his former lifestyle, make feasible for him the resumption of the Heroic Life.

Journeys to the Moon were in the news at that moment (about a year before the astronauts actually landed there) because Pennistone had just published his book on Cyrano de Bergerac, whose *Histoire comique des états et empires de la lune* he used to discuss, when we were in the War Office together. Pennistone was more interested in his subject as philosopher and heresiarch than space-traveller, but, all the same, Cyrano had to be admitted as an example of a remark once made by X. Trapnel: 'A novelist writes what he is. That is equally true of authors who deal with mediaeval romance or journeys to the Moon.' I don't think Trapnel had ever read Ariosto, feel pretty sure he had never attempted Cyrano—though he could surprise by unexpected authors dipped into—but, oddly enough, *Orlando Furioso* does treat of both Trapnel's off-the-cuff fictional categories, mediaeval romance and an inter-planetary journey.

Among other adventures on the Moon, during this expedition, Astolpho sees Time at work. Ariosto's Time—as you might say, Time the Man—was, anthropomorphically speaking, not necessarily everybody's Time. Although equally hoary and naked, he was not Poussin's Time, for example, in the picture where the Seasons dance, while Time plucks his lyre to provide the music. Poussin's Time (a painter's Time) is shown in a sufficiently unhurried frame of mind to be sitting down while he strums his instrument. The smile might be thought a trifle sinister, nevertheless the mood is genial, composed.

Ariosto's Time (a writer's Time) is far less relaxed, indeed appallingly restless. The English duke watched Ariosto's Time at work. The naked ancient, in an eternally breathless scramble with himself, collected from the Fates small metal tablets (one pictured them like the trinkets hanging from the necks of Murtlock and Henderson), then moved off at the double to dump these identity discs in the waters of Oblivion. A few of them (like Murtlock's medallion at the pond) were only momentarily submerged, being fished out, and borne away to the Temple of Fame, by a pair of well disposed swans. The rest sank to the bottom, where they were likely to remain.

On the strength of this not too obscure allegory, I decided to go to bed. Just before I closed the book, my eye was caught by a stanza in an earlier sequence.

And as we see straunge cranes are woont to do,
First stalke a while er they their wings can find,
Then soare from ground not past a yard or two,
Till in their wings they gather'd have the wind,
At last they mount the very clouds unto,
Triangle wise according to their kind:
So by degrees this Mage begins to flye,
The bird of *Jove* can hardly mount so hye;

And when he sees his time and thinks it best,
He falleth downe like lead in fearfull guise,
Even as the fawlcon doth the foule arrest,
The ducke and mallard from the brooke that rise.

The warm windy afternoon, cottonwool clouds, ankle-
deep wild garlic, rankness of fox, laboratory exhalations
from the quarry, parade ground evolutions of the duck,
hawk's precipitate flight towards the pool, all were suddenly
recreated. Duck, of course, rather than cranes, had risen
'triangle wise', but the hawk, as in Ariosto's lines (or
rather Harington's), had hung pensively in the air, then
swooped to strike. I tried to rationalize to myself this
coincidental passage. There was nothing at all unusual in
mallard getting up from the water at that time of day, nor a
kestrel hovering over the neighbouring meadows. For that
matter, reference to falconry in a Renaissance poem was far
from remarkable. Something in addition to all that held
the attention. It was the word Mage. Mage carried matters
a stage further.

Mage summoned up the image of Dr Trelawney, a mage
if ever there was one. I thought of the days when, as a
child, I used to watch the Doctor and his young disciples,
some of them no more than children themselves, trotting
past the Stonehurst gate on their way to rhythmical callis-
thenics—whatever the exercises were—on the adjacent
expanse of heather. In those days (brink of the first war)
Dr Trelawney was still building up a career. He had not yet
fully transformed himself into the man of mystery, the
thaumaturge, he was in due course to become. The true
surname was always in doubt (Grubb or Tibbs, put forward
by Moreland), anyway something with less body to it than
Trelawney. In his avatar of the Stonehurst period he had
been less concerned with the predominantly occult engagement of later years; then seeking The Way (to use his own

phrase) through appropriate meditations, exercises, diet, apparel.

Once a week Dr Trelawney and his neophytes would jog down the pine-bordered lane from which our Indian-type bungalow was set a short distance back. The situation was remote, a wide deserted common next door. Dr Trelawney himself would be leading, dark locks flowing to the shoulder, biblical beard, grecian tunic, thonged sandals. The Doctor's robe (like the undefiled of Sardis) was white, somewhat longer and less diaphanous than the single garment—identical for both sexes and all weathers—worn by the disciples, tunics tinted in the pastel shades fashionable at that epoch. People who encountered Dr Trelawney by chance in the village post-office received an invariable greeting:

'The Essence of the All is the Godhead of the True.'

The appropriate response can have been rarely returned.

'The Vision of Visions heals the Blindness of Sight.'

One of the firmest tenets—so Moreland always said—in the later teachings of Dr Trelawney was that coincidence was no more than 'magic in action'. There had just been an example of that. *Orlando Furioso* had not only produced that evening a magical reconstruction of considerable force, it had also brought to mind the reason why such activities as Dr Trelawney's were already much in the air. A recent newspaper colour supplement article, dealing with contemporary cults, had mentioned that—with much of what Hugo Tolland called the good old Simple Life—a revival of Trelawneyism had come about among young people. That was probably where Murtlock had acquired the phrases about killing, and no death in Nature. It was Dr Trelawney's view—also that of his old friend and fellow occultist, Mrs Erdleigh—that death was no more than transition, blending, synthesis, mutation. To be fair to them both, they seemed to some extent to have made their

35

point. However much the uninstructed might regard them both as 'dead', there were still those for whom they were very much alive. Mrs Erdleigh (quoting the alchemist, Thomas Vaughan) had spoken of how the 'liberated soul ascends, looking at the sunset towards the west wind, and hearing secret harmonies'. Perhaps Vaughan's words, filtered through a kind of Neo-Trelawneyism, explained the girls' T-shirts.

In any case it was impossible to disregard the fact that, while a dismantling process steadily curtails members of the cast, items of the scenery, airs played by the orchestra, in the performance that has included one's own walk-on part for more than a few decades, simultaneous derequisition-ings are also to be observed. Mummers return, who might have been supposed to have made their final exit, even if—like Dr Trelawney and Mrs Erdleigh—somewhat in the rôle of Hamlet's father. The touching up of time-expired sets, reshaping of derelict props, updating of old refrains, are none of them uncommon. An event some days later again brought forcibly to mind these lunar rescues from the Valley of Lost Things. This was a television programme devoted to the subject of the all-but-forgotten novelist, St John Clarke.

Above all others, St John Clarke might be judged, criti-cally speaking, as gone for good. Not a bit of it. Here was a consummate instance of a lost reputation—in this case a literary one—salvaged from the Moon, St John Clarke's Astolpho being Ada Leintwardine. Keen on transvestism, Ariosto would have found nothing incongruous in a woman playing the part of the English duke. Maidens clad in armour abound throughout the poem. Ada Leintwardine, as a successful novelist married to the well-known publisher, J. G. Quiggin, could be accepted as a perfectly concordant Ariosto character. In any case she had latterly been taking an increasingly executive part in forming the policy of the firm of which her husband was chairman. Quiggin used to complain that St John Clarke's novels (all come finally to rest under his firm's imprint) sold 'just the wrong amount', too steady a trickle to be ruthlessly disregarded, not enough comfortably to cover production costs. Nor was there compensatory prestige—rather the reverse—in having a name in the list unknown to a younger generation. In fact Quiggin himself did not deny that he was prepared to allow such backnumbers to fall out of print. Ada, on the other hand, would not allow that. Her reasons were not wholly commercial; not commercial, that is, on the short-term basis of her husband's approach.

Ada's goal was to have a St John Clarke novel turned into a film. This had become almost an obsession with her. Ten years before she had failed—she alleged by a hair's breadth—to persuade Louis Glober to make a picture of *Match Me Such Marvel*, and, after Glober's death, vigorous canvassing of other film producers, American or British, had been no less fruitless. Meanwhile, St John Clarke's literary shares continued to slump. Ada, though she made fairly frequent appearances on television, had not herself produced a novel for some years. Remaining preoccupied with the St John Clarke project, she at last achieved the small advance in her plans that a television programme should be made about the novelist's life and work. This she regarded as a start, something to prepare the ground for later adaptation of one of the books.

Even their old friend, Mark Members, agreed that the Quiggins' marriage, whatever its ups and downs, had been on the whole a success. Members, who had no children himself, used to laugh at the disparity between Quiggin's former views on rebellion, and present attitude towards his twin daughters, Amanda and Belinda, now of university age and troublemakers. Quiggin's grumbling on that subject usually took place when Ada was not about. One of the twins had recently been concerned (only as a witness) in a drug prosecution; the other, about the same time, charged (later acquitted) with kicking a policeman. Quiggin was less reconciled to that sort of thing than, say, Roddy Cutts in relation to Fiona's caprices. In business matters the Quiggins got on well together too, showed a united front. It was the exception that there should be disagreement about St John Clarke.

Quiggin was doubtful as to the wisdom of propagating the novelist's name at this late stage. He feared that a small temporary increase in demand for the books would merely add to his own embarrassments as their publisher. His objection did not hold out very long. In due course Ada had her way. She seems to have brought about her husband's conversion to the idea by pointing out that he himself, as former secretary of St John Clarke, would play a comparatively prominent part in any documentary produced. Quiggin finally gave in at one of their literary dinner parties, choosing the moment after his wife had produced an aphorism.

'The television of the body brings the sales everlasting.'

Quiggin bowed his head.

'Amen, then. I resign St John Clarke to the makers of all things televisible.'

As a fellow ex-secretary of St John Clarke, Members would also have to be included in any programme about the novelist. That was no great matter. Members and Quiggin had been on goodish terms now for years, even admitting the kinship (second-cousins apparently), always alleged by Sillery, nowadays disputing with each other only who had enjoyed the more modest home. Both had come to look rather distinguished, Quiggin's dome-like forehead, sparse hair, huge ears, gave him a touch of grotesquerie, not out of place in a prominent publisher. Members, his white hair worn long, face pale and lined, had returned to the

38

Romantic Movement overtones of undergraduate days. His air was that of an eighteenth-century sage too highminded to wear a wig—Blake, Benjamin Franklin, one of the Encyclopaedists—suitable image for a figure of his eminence in the cultural world. When in London, his American wife, Lenore, fell in with this historical mood, doing so with easy assurance. They remained married, though Lenore spent increasingly long spells in her own country, an arrangement that seemed to suit both of them.

A graver problem than Members, in relation to the St John Clarke programme, was Vernon Gainsborough—now generally styled Dr Gainsborough, as holding an academic post in political theory—who (under his original name of Wernher Guggenbühl) had as a young man, finally displaced both Members and Quiggin in St John Clarke's employment. Quiggin (in those days writing letters to the papers in defence of the Stalinist purges) used to complain that Guggenbühl (as he then was) had perverted St John Clarke to Trotskyism. Some sort of a rapprochement had taken place after the war, when the firm of Quiggin & Craggs had published the recantation of Gainsborough (as he had become) in his study *Bronstein: Marxist or Mystagogue?* Gainsborough could not, therefore, be omitted from the programme. The only other performer who had known St John Clarke in the flesh was L. O. Salvidge, the critic. In his early days, when in low water, Salvidge had done some devilling, when St John Clarke was without a secretary, collecting French Revolution material for *Dust Thou Art*. The cast was made up with several self-constituted friends of the deceased novelist, professional extras, who appeared in all such literary resuscitations on the TV screen.

Isobel and I watched this rescue job from the Valley of Lost Things, to which another small item was added by the opening shot, St John Clarke's portrait (butterfly collar, floppy bow tie), painted by his old friend, Horace Isbister, RA. A few minutes later, Isbister's name appeared again, this time in an altogether unexpected connexion, only indirectly related to painting.

For some years now fashion had inclined to emphasize, rather than overlook, the sexual habits of the dead. To unearth anything about a man so discreet as St John Clarke had proved impossible, but Salvidge ventured to put forward the possibility that the novelist's 'fabulous parsimony' had its origins in repressed homosexuality. Members then let off a mild bombshell. He suggested that the friendship with Isbister had been a homosexual one. The contention of Members was that the central figure in an early genre picture of Isbister's—*Clergyman eating an apple*—was not at all unlike St John Clarke himself as a young man, Members advancing the theory that Isbister could have possessed a fetishist taste for male lovers dressed in ecclesiastical costume.

Quiggin questioned this possibility on grounds that Isbister had finally married his often painted model, Morwenna. Members replied that Morwenna was a lesbian. Gainsborough—who had never heard of Morwenna, and found some difficulty with the name—attempted to shift the discussion to St John Clarke's politics. He was unsuccessful. Something of an argument ensued, Gainsborough's German accent thickening, as he became more irritable. St John Clarke, rather a prudish man in conversation, would have been startled to hear much surmised, before so large an audience, on the subject of his sexual tastes. It was not a very exciting forty minutes, of which Ada was to be judged the star. Isbister's portrait of his friend—perhaps more than friend—flashed on the screen again as finale.

'Shall we stay for the News?'

'All right.'

There was some routine stuff: the Prime Minister in a

safety helmet at a smelting plant; royalty launching a ship; strike pickets; tornado damage. Then, from out of the announcer's patter, a name brought attention—'... Lord Widmerpool, where he was recently appointed the university's chancellor ...'

The last time I had seen Widmerpool, nearly ten years before, was soon after the troubles in which he had been involved: his wife's grim end; official enquiries into his own clandestine dealings with an East European power. We had met in Parliament Square. He said he was making for the House of Lords. He looked in poor shape, his manner wandering, distracted. We had talked for a minute or two, then parted. Whatever business he had been about that morning, must have been the last transacted by him for a longish period. The following week he disappeared for the best part of a year. He was probably on his way to wind up for the time being his House of Lords affairs.

Pamela Widmerpool's death, in itself, had caused less stir than might be supposed. Apart from the bare fact that she had taken an overdose in an hotel bedroom, nothing specially scandalous had come to light. Admittedly the hotel—as Widmerpool had complained in Parliament Square —had been a sordid one. Russell Gwinnett, the man with whom Pamela was believed to be in love, was staying there, but Gwinnett had an explicable reason for doing so, the place being a haunt of the novelist, X. Trapnel, whose biography he was writing. Pamela had occupied a room of her own. In any case her behaviour had long burst the sound barrier of normal gossip. It was thought even possible that, having heard of the hotel through Gwinnett, she had booked a room there as a suitably anonymous setting to close her final act. Sympathetic comment gave Pamela credit for that.

From the point of view of 'news', Gwinnett's scholarly affiliations, adding a touch of drabness, detracted from such public interest as the story possessed. The suicide of a life peer's wife obviously called for some coverage. That was likely to be diminished by the addition of professorial research work on a novelist unknown to the general public. The coroner went out of his way to express regret that a young American academic's visit to London should have been clouded by such a mishap. Gwinnett had apparently made an excellent impression at the inquest. In short, the whole business was consigned to the ragbag of memories too vague to remain at all clear in the mind. That was equally true of Widmerpool's dubious international dealings, regarding which, by now, no one could remember whether he was the villain or the hero.

'People say he was framed by the CIA,' said Lenore Members. 'The CIA may have fixed his wife's death too.'

By the time that theory had been put forward—and largely accepted—Widmerpool himself had recovered sufficiently to have crossed the Atlantic, reappearing in the United States after his year's withdrawal from the world. Whether by luck, or astute manipulations, no one seemed to know, he had been offered an appointment of some kind at the Institute of Advanced Study of an Ivy League university; ideal post for making a dignified retreat for a further period from everyday life in London. His years of engagement on the Eastern Seaboard were succeeded by a Westward pilgrimage. He was next heard of established at a noted Californian centre for political research. That was where Lenore Members had come across him. Widmerpool had impressed her as a man who had 'been through' a great deal. That was now his own line about himself, she said, one that could not reasonably be denied. Lenore Members was a woman with considerable descriptive powers. She conveyed a picture of undoubted change. Among other things, Widmerpool had spoken with contempt of parliamentary institutions. In public addresses he had been very generally expressing his scorn for such a vehicle of government. In his opinion the remedy lay in the hands of the young.

'Lord Widmerpool said he was working on a book that puts forward his views. It's to be called *Pogrom of Youth*.'

'How does he go down in the States?'

'He has strong adherents—strong opponents too. There's a pressure group to put his name forward for the Nobel Prize. Others say he's crazy.'

'You mean actually mad?'

'Mentally disturbed.'

'How long is he going to stay in the US?'

'He said he might be taking out naturalization papers.'

Whatever the reason, Widmerpool's vision of American citizenship must have been abandoned. He had returned to England. How, in general, he had been occupying himself, I did not know. During the past two or three years since arriving back there had been fairly regular appearances on television. These were usually in connexion with the sort of subjects Lenore Members had indicated as his latest interest, his new axis for power focus. He had played no part in the Labour administration of 1964. He may not even have been back in England by then. I had not watched any of his TV appearances, nor heard about this appointment to a university chancellorship. The post would not be at all inconsistent with the latest line he seemed to be designing for himself. I had no idea what were its duties and powers, probably a job that was much what the holder made of it.

The university to which Widmerpool had been nominated was a newish one. Malcolm Crowding (main authority on the last hours of X. Trapnel) taught English there. Crowding was not to be observed in the procession of capped and gowned figures on the screen; nor, for that matter, was Widmerpool. They had just reached the foot of a flight of steps. In the background were buildings in a contemporary style of scholastic architecture. The persons composing the crocodile of dons and recipients of honorary degrees were preceded by a man in uniform bearing a mace. The cortège was making its way across an open space, shut in by what were probably lecture-halls. A fairly large crowd, students of both sexes, parents, friends, onlookers of one sort or another, stood on either side of the route, watching the ceremony. It was probably a more grandiose affair than usual owing to the installation of the new chancellor. I did not pick out Widmerpool immediately, my attention being caught for a moment by a black notability in national dress of his country, walking between two academically gowned ladies, all three recipients of doctoral degrees. Then Widmerpool came into sight. As he did so there was scarcely time to take in more of him than that he was wearing a mortarboard and gold brocaded robe, its train held up by a page.

Widmerpool, advancing towards the camera, had turned to say a word to this small boy, apparently complaining that the hinder part of his official dress was being borne in a manner inconvenient to its wearer, when the scene suddenly took on a new and startling aspect. What followed was acted out so quickly that only afterwards was it possible to disentangle specific incident from overall confusion. On different sides of the path, at two points, the watching crowd seemed to part. From each of these gaps figures of indeterminate sex briefly emerged, then withdrew themselves again. Some sort of a scuffle arose. An object, perhaps two objects, shot up in the air. In the background a flimsy poster, inscribed with illegible words outlined in shaky capital letters, fluttered for a second in the air, hoisted on the end of a long pole, then appeared to collapse. All these things, flitting by too quickly to be taken into proper account, were accompanied by the sound of singing or chanting. By the time I had grasped the fact that some sort

44

of a demonstration was afoot, Widmerpool was no longer in sight.

Before the scene changed—which it did in a flash—I had just time to recollect Moreland's words, uttered at Stourwater nearly thirty years before. It was the night we had all dressed up as the Seven Deadly Sins, and been photographed by Sir Magnus Donners, with whom we were dining—'One is never a student at all in England, except possibly a medical student or an art student. Undergraduates have nothing in common with what is understood abroad by a student—young men for ever rioting, undertaking political assassination, overturning governments.'

Moreland had offered that opinion about the time of 'Munich'. Sir Magnus Donners had not shown much interest. Perhaps the innate shrewdness of his own instincts in such matters already told him that, within a few decades, Moreland's conviction about students would fall badly out of date, an epoch not far distant when the sort of student Moreland adumbrated would be accepted as a matter of course. This Stourwater memory had scarcely time to formulate, dissolve, before the announcer's voice drew attention to a close-up of Widmerpool, now standing alone.

'Lord Widmerpool, newly installed chancellor, wishes to give his own comments on what happened.'

At first sight, so ghastly seemed Widmerpool's condition that it was a wonder he was alive, much less able to stand upright and address an audience. He had evidently been the victim of an atrocious assault. His wounds were appalling. Dark stains, apparently blood, covered the crown of his bald head (now capless), streaking down the side of his face, dripping from shoulder and sleeve of the gold embroidered robe. When he raised his hands, they too were smeared with the dark sticky marks of gore. Nevertheless, mangled as the fingers must have been to display this

45

condition, he removed his bespattered spectacles. It was amazing that he had the strength to do so.

'Not the smallest resentment. Even glad this has taken place. Let me congratulate those two girls on being such excellent shots with the paint pot...'

All was explained. There were no wounds. The dark clots, at first seeming to flow from dreadful gashes, were no more than paint. Widmerpool was covered with paint. Paint spread all over him, shining in the sun, dripping off face and clothes, since it was not yet dry. He ignored altogether the inconceivable mess he was in. Now the origin of his condition was revealed he looked like a clown, a clown upon whom divine afflatus had suddenly descended. He was in a state of uncontrolled excitement, gesticulating wildly in a manner quite uncharacteristic of himself. It was like revivalist frenzy. Face gaunt, eyes sunk into the back of his head, he had lost all his former fleshiness. What Lenore Members had tried to convey was now apparent. He said a few words more. They were barely intelligible owing to excitement. It was noticeable that his delivery had absorbed perceptibly American intonations and technique, superimposed on the old hearty unction that had formerly marked his style. Before more could be assimilated, the scene, like the previous one, was wiped away, the announcer's professional tones taking over again, as the News moved on to other topics.

'That was livelier than the St John Clarke programme.'

'It certainly was.'

Setting aside the occasion—a very different one—when Glober had hit him after the Stevenses' musical party, the last time Widmerpool had suffered physical assault at all comparable with the paint-throwing was, so far as I knew, forty years before, the night of the Huntercombes' dance, when Barbara Goring had poured sugar over his head. More was to be noted in this parallel than that, on the one hand, both assaults were at the hands of young women; on the other, paint created a far more injurious deluge than castor sugar. The measure of the latest incident seemed to be the extent to which the years had taught Widmerpool to cope with aggressions of that kind. In many other respects, of course, the circumstances were far from identical. Widmerpool had been in love with Barbara Goring; for the girls who had thrown the paint—he had spoken of them as girls —there was no reason to suppose that he felt more than general approval of a politico-social intention on their part. Possibly love would follow, rather than precede, persecution at their hands. Yet even if it were argued that all the two attacks possessed in common was personal protest against Widmerpool himself, the fact remained that, while he had endured the earlier onslaught with unconcealed wretchedness, he had now learnt to convert such occasions—possibly always sexually gratifying—to good purpose where other ends were concerned.

What would have been the result, I wondered, had he been equipped with that ability forty years before? Would he have won the heart of Barbara Goring, proposed to her, been accepted, married, produced children by her? On the whole such a train of events seemed unlikely, apart from objections the Goring parents might have raised in days before Widmerpool had launched himself on a career. Probably nothing would have altered the fates of either Widmerpool or Barbara (whose seventeen-year-old granddaughter had recently achieved some notoriety by marrying a celebrated Pop star), and the paint-throwing incident, like the cascade of sugar, was merely part of the pattern of Widmerpool's life. It was not considered of sufficient importance to be reported in any newspaper. On running across L. O. Salvidge in London, I heard more of its details.

'I enjoyed your appearance in the St John Clarke programme.'

47

Salvidge, who had a glass eye—always impossible to tell which—laughed about the occasion. He seemed well satisfied with the figure he had cut.

'I was glad to have an opportunity to say what I thought about the old fraud. Did you watch the News that night, see the Quiggin twins throw red paint over the chancellor of their university?'

'It was the Quiggin twins?'

'The famous Amanda and Belinda. What a couple. I was talking about it to JG yesterday. At least I tried to, but he would not discuss it. He changed the subject to the Magnus Donners Prize. He's got a grievance that no book published by his firm has ever won the award. Who are you giving it to this year?'

'Nothing suitable has turned up at present. Something may appear in the autumn. Has JG's firm got anything special? We'll see it, no doubt, if they have. It's my last year on the Magnus Donners panel. Do you want to take my place there?'

'Not me.'

Both Salvidge's eyes looked equally glassy at the suggestion. That was no surprise. Almost as veteran a figure on literary prize committees as Mark Members, Salvidge always had a dozen such commissions on hand. They took up more time than might be supposed. I was glad of my own approaching release from the board of the Magnus Donners judges. This was my fourth and final year.

The origins of the Magnus Donners Memorial Prize went back a long way, in fact to the days when Sillery used to speculate about a project of Sir Magnus Donners to endow certain university scholarships for overseas students, young men drawn from places where the Company's interests were paramount. They were to be called Donners-Brebner Fellowships. Such a possibility naturally opened up a legitimate field for academic intrigue, Sillery in the forefront, if the fellowships were to take practical shape. Sillery (in rivalry, he lamented, with at least three other dons) made no secret of his aim to control the patronage. He had entangled in this matter Prince Theodoric (lately deceased in Canada, where his business ventures, after exile, had been reasonably successful), in those days always anxious to draw his country into closer contacts with Great Britain.

The Donners-Brebner Fellowships were referred to in Sillery's obituary notices (highly laudatory in tone, as recording a sole survivor of his own genus, who had missed his century only by a year or two), where it appeared that the project had been to some extent implemented before the outbreak of war in 1939. Post-war changes in the international situation prevented much question of the fellowships' revival in anything like their original form. Sir Magnus himself, anxious to re-establish a benefaction of a similar kind, seems to have been uncertain how best it should be reconstituted, leaving behind several contradictory memoranda on the subject. In practice, this fund seems to have been administered in a rather haphazard fashion after his death, a kind of all-purposes charitable trust in Donners-Brebner gift. That, any rate, was the version of the story propagated by his widow, Matilda Donners, when she first asked me to sit as one of the judges at the initiation of the Prize. That was four years before. Now—as I had told Salvidge—my term on the Prize committee was drawing to an end.

In Matilda's early days of widowhood it looked as if the memory of Sir Magnus was to be allowed to fade. She continued to circulate for some years in the world of politics and big business to which he had introduced her, to give occasional parties in rivalry with Rosie Stevens, more musically, less politically inclined, than herself. Latterly Matilda had not only narrowed down her circle of friends, but begun to talk of Sir Magnus again. She also moved to smaller

49

premises. Sir Magnus had left her comfortably off, if in command of far smaller resources than formerly, bequeathing most of his considerable fortune to relations, and certain public benefactions. No doubt such matters had been gone into at the time of their marriage, Matilda being a practical person, one of the qualities Sir Magnus had certainly admired in her. Moreland, too, had greatly depended on that practical side of Matilda as a wife. In short, disappointment at having received less than expected at the demise of Sir Magnus was unlikely to have played any part in earlier policy that seemed to consign him to oblivion.

Then there was a change. Matilda began, so to speak, to play the part of Ariosto's swans, bringing the name of Donners—she had always referred to him by his surname—into the conversation. A drawing of him, by Wyndham Lewis, was resurrected in her sitting-room. She was reported to play the music he liked—*Parsifal*, for instance, Norman Chandler said—and to laugh about the way he would speak of having shed tears over the sufferings of the Chinese slavegirl in *Turandot*, no less when watching Ida Rubinstein in *The Martyrdom of St Sebastian*. Chandler remarked that, at one time, Matilda would never have referred to 'that side' of Sir Magnus. No doubt this new mood drew Matilda's attention to the more or less quiescent fund lying at Donners-Brebner. On investigation it appeared to be entirely suitable, anyway a proportion of it, for consecration to a memorial that would bear the name of its originator. One of the papers left on the file seemed even to envisage something of the sort. Matilda went to the directors of Donners-Brebner, with whom she had always kept up. They made no difficulties, taking the view that an award of that nature was not at all to be disregarded in terms of publicity.

Why Matilda waited not much less than fifteen years to commemorate Sir Magnus was never clear. Perhaps it was simply a single aspect of the general reconstruction of her life, desire for new things to occupy her as she grew older. Regarded as a *jolie laide* when young, Matilda would now have passed as a former 'beauty'. That was not undeserved. Relentless discipline had preserved her appearance, especially her figure. Once fair hair had been dyed a darker colour, a tone that suited the green eyes—a feature shared with Sir Magnus, though his eyes lacked her sleepy power—which had once captivated Moreland. A touch of 'stageyness' in Matilda's clothes was not out of keeping with her personality.

Another change had been a new inclination towards female friends. Matilda had always been on good terms with Isobel, other wives of men Moreland had known, but in those days, anyway ostensibly, she seemed to possess no female circle of her own. Now she had begun to show a taste for ladies high-powered as herself. They did not exactly take the place of men in her life, but the sexes were more evenly balanced. With men she had always been discreet. There had been no stories circulated about her when married to Sir Magnus. In widowhood there had been the brief affair with Odo Stevens, before his marriage to Rosie Manasch; that affair thought more to tease Rosie than because she specially liked Stevens. Hardly any other adventure had even been lightly attributed.

Some people believed Gibson Delavacquerie had been for a short time Matilda's lover. That was not my own opinion, although a closer relationship than that of friends was not entirely to be ruled out as a possibility. Matilda was, of course, appreciably the elder of the two. If there were anything in such gossip, its truth would have suggested a continued preference for the sort of man with whom her earlier life had been spent, rather than those who had surrounded her in middle years. She had certainly known Delavacquerie quite well before the Magnus Donners Prize was instituted.

His job—Delavacquerie was employed on the public relations side of Donners-Brebner—offered a good listening-post for Matilda to keep in touch with the affairs of the Company. Undoubtedly she liked him. That could very well have been all there was to the association.

This Delavacquerie connexion may well have played a part in the eventual decision to raise a memorial in literary form. Books were by no means the first interest of Sir Magnus. Notwithstanding Moreland's story that, as a young man, believing himself on the brink of an early grave, 'Donners had spoken of steeping himself in all that was best in half-a-dozen literatures', his patronage had always been directed in the main towards painting and music. According to Matilda various alternative forms of remembrance were put forward, a literary prize thought best, as easiest to administer. Delavacquerie may not only have influenced that conclusion, but, once the principle was established, carried weight as to the type of book to be encouraged.

In the end it was settled that the Prize (quite a handsome sum) should be presented annually for a biographical study dealing with (not necessarily written by) a British subject, male or female, born not earlier than the date of Sir Magnus's own birth. I think discretion was allowed to the judges, if the birth was reasonably close, the aim being to begin with the generation to which Sir Magnus himself belonged. Just how this choice was arrived at I do not know. It is worth bearing in mind that an official 'life' of Sir Magnus himself had not yet appeared. Possibly Matilda—or the Company—hoped that a suitable biographer might come to light through this constitution of the Prize. Any such writer would have to be equal to dealing with formidable perplexities, if the biography was to be attempted during the lifetime of its subject's widow; especially in the light of new freedoms of expression, nowadays to be expected, in the manner of the St John Clarke TV programme.

The possibility that a Donners biographer might be sought was borne out by the additional condition that preference would be given to works dealing with a man of affairs, even though representatives of the arts and sciences were also specifically mentioned in the terms of reference.

Delavacquerie, known to me only casually when Matilda opened up the question of the Magnus Donners committee, was then in his middle forties. He was peculiarly fitted to the rôle in which he found himself—that is to say a sort of unofficial secretary to the board of judges—having been one of the few, possibly the sole candidate, to have benefited by a Donners-Brebner fellowship, when these first came into being. This had brought him to an English university (he had somehow slipped through Sillery's fingers) just before the outbreak of war. During the war he had served, in the Middle East and India, with the Royal Signals; after leaving the army, working for a time in a shipping firm. No doubt earlier connexion with the Company, through the fellowship, played a part in ultimately securing him a job at Donners-Brebner. Although a British subject, Delavacquerie was of French descent, a family settled in the Caribbean for several generations. He would speak of that in his characteristically dry manner.

'They've been there a century and a half. An established family. You understand there are no good families. The island does not run to good families. The Gibsons were an established family too.'

Small, very dark, still bearing marks of French origins, Delavacquerie talked in a quick, harsh, oddly attractive voice. Between bouts of almost crippling inertia—according to himself—he was immensely energetic in all he did. We had met before, on and off, but became friends through the Magnus Donners Prize committee. By that time Delavacquerie had achieved some fame as a poet; fame, that is, over and above what he himself always called his 'colonial' affiliations. Matilda asserted, no doubt truly, that the Company was rather proud of employing in one of its departments a poet of Delavacquerie's distinction. She reported that a Donners-Brebner director had assured her that Delavacquerie displayed the same grasp of business matters that he certainly brought to literary criticism, on the comparatively rare occasions when he wrote articles or reviews, there being no easy means of measuring business ability against poetry. This same Donners-Brebner tycoon had added that Delavacquerie could have risen to a post of considerably greater responsibility in the Company had he wished. A relatively subordinate position, more congenial in the nature of its duties, tied him less to an office, allowing more time for his 'own work'. Moreland—not long before he died—had spoken appreciatively of Delavacquerie's poetry, in connexion with one of Moreland's favourite themes, the artist as businessman.

'I never pay my insurance policy,' Moreland said, 'without envisaging the documents going through the hands of Aubrey Beardsley and Kafka, before being laid on the desk of Wallace Stevens.'

Before we knew each other at all well, Delavacquerie mentioning army service in India, I asked whether he had ever come across Bagshaw or Trapnel, both of whom had served in the subcontinent in RAF public relations, Bagshaw as squadron-leader, Trapnel as orderly-room clerk. It was a long shot, no contacts had taken place, but Bagshaw, Delavacquerie said, had published one of his earlier poems in *Fission*, and Trapnel had been encountered in a London pub. Although I had read other Delavacquerie poems soon after that period, I had no recollection of that which had appeared when I had been 'doing the books' for the magazine. I had then liked his poetry in principle, without gaining more than a rough idea where he stood among the young emergent writers of the post-war era. Most of his early verse had been written in the army, most of it rhymed and scanned. Trapnel, prepared to lay down the law on poets and poetry, as much as any other branch of literature, a great commentator on his own contemporaries, had never mentioned Delavacquerie's name. At that period, before Delavacquerie's reputation began to take shape—kept busy earning a living—he was not often to be seen about. Trapnel, living in a kaleidoscope world of pub and party frequenters, must have forgotten their own meeting. Perhaps he had not taken in Delavacquerie's name.

'When I was working in the shipping firm I didn't know London at all well. I wanted to explore all its possibilities—and of course meet writers.'

Delavacquerie made a slight grimace when he said that.

'Somebody told me The Hero of Acre was a pub where you found artists and poets. I went along there one night. Trapnel was at the bar, with his beard, and swordstick mounted with the ivory skull. I thought him rather a Ninetyish figure, and was surprised when his work turned out to be good. He was about the only one in the pub to qualify as a writer at all. Even he had only published a few stories then. Still, to my colonial eyes, it was something that he looked the part, even the part as played fifty years before. I didn't talk to him that night, but on another occasion we discussed Apollinaire over a bitter, a drink I have never learned to like. Trapnel's dead, isn't he?'

'Died in the early nineteen-fifties.'

This conversation between Delavacquerie and myself had taken place several years before Matilda's invitation to join the Magnus Donners Prize committee, which at first I refused, on general grounds of reducing such commitments to a minimum. Matilda, explaining she wanted to start off with a panel known to her personally, was more pressing than expected. She added that she was determined to get as much fun out of the Prize as possible, one aspect of that being a committee made up of friends.

'One never knows how long one's going to last,' she said.

I still declined. Matilda added an inducement. It was a powerful one.

'I've found the photographs Donners took, when we all impersonated the Seven Deadly Sins at Stourwater in 1938. I'll show them to you, if you join the committee. Otherwise not.'

In supposing these documents from a bygone age would prove irresistible as the Sins themselves, Matilda was right. I accepted the bribe. With some people it might have been possible to refuse, then persuade them to produce the photographs in any case. Matilda was not one of those. The board met twice annually at a luncheon provided by the Company. The judges, as constituted in the first instance, were Dame Emily Brightman, Mark Members, and myself. Delavacquerie sat with us, representing the Company, supplying a link with Matilda, acting as secretary. He arranged for publishers to submit books (or proofs of forthcoming books), kept in touch with the press, undertook all the odd jobs required. These were the sort of duties in which he took comparative pleasure, carried out with notable efficiency. He did not himself vote on final decisions about works that came up for judgment, though he joined in discussions, his opinions always useful. He particularly enjoyed arguing with Emily Brightman (created DBE a couple of years before for her work on The Triads, and polemical study of Boethius), who would allow Delavacquerie more range of teasing than was her usual custom, though sometimes he might receive a sharp rebuke, if he went too far.

Members, on the other hand (once publicly admonished by Dame Emily for a slip about the Merovingians), was rather afraid of her. His inclusion was almost statutory in assembling a body of persons brought together to judge a literary award of any type, quite apart from his own long acquaintance with Matilda Donners. It was from this semi-official side of his life, rather than the verse and other writings, that he had come to know Matilda, whose interests had always been in the Theatre, rather than books. Members had been included in her parties when Sir Magnus was alive. Emily Brightman, in contrast, was a more recent acquisition, belonging to that sorority of distinguished ladies Matilda now seemed to seek out. It was clear, at the first of these Magnus Donners luncheons, that Emily Brightman (whom I had seen only once or twice since the Cultural Conference in Venice, where Pamela Widmerpool first met Gwinnett) had lost none of her energy. The unobtrusive smartness of her clothes also remained unaltered.

'I have a confession to make. It should be avowed in the Dostoevskian fashion on the knees. You will forgive me if I dispense with that. To kneel would cause too much stir in a restaurant of this type. During our Venetian experience, you will remember visiting Jacky Bragadin's palazzo—our host didn't long survive our visit, did he?—the incomparable Tiepolo ceiling? Candaules showing Gyges his naked wife? How it turned out that Lord Widmerpool—such an unattractive man—had done much the same thing, if not worse? You remember, of course. That poor little Lady Widmerpool. I took quite a fancy to her, in spite of her naughtinesses.'

Emily Brightman paused; at the thought of those perhaps.

'It turns out that I was scandalously misinformed, accordingly misleading, in supposing Gautier to have invented the name Nysia for Candaules's queen. The one he exhibited in so uncalled for a manner. Nysia was indeed the name of the nude lady in Tiepolo's picture. I came on the fact, quite by chance, last year, when I was reading in bed one night. She is categorically styled Nysia in the *New*

History of Ptolemy Chennus—first century, as you know, so respectably far back—and I was up half the night establishing the references. In fact I wandered about almost as lightly clad as Nysia herself. I hope there was no Gyges in the College at that hour. It was sweltering weather, I had not been able to sleep, and allowed myself a gin and tonic, with some ice in it, while I was doing so. I found that Niklaus of Damascus calls her Nysia, too, in his *Preparatory Exercises*. He also ridicules the notion of an oriental potentate of the Candaules type becoming enamoured of his own wife. I thought that showed the narrowness of Greek psychology in dealing with a subtle people like the Lydians. Another matter upon which Nicholas of Damascus —wasn't he Herod the Great's secretary?—throws doubt is the likelihood of the ladies of Sardis undressing before they went to bed. He may have a point there.'

'Perhaps the sheer originality of his queen undressing was what so enthralled Candaules,' said Members. 'I can never sufficiently regret having missed that Conference. Ada Leintwardine and Quentin Shuckerly talk of it to this day. What was the name of the American who got so involved with Kenneth Widmerpool's wife there?'

'Russell Gwinnett. An old friend of mine. He was put in an unfortunate position.'

Emily Brightman said that rather sharply. Members took the hint. I asked if she had seen anything of Gwinnett lately.

'Not a word from him personally. Another American friend, former colleague of both of us, said Russell was back in academic life again. The name of his college escapes me.

'Has he returned to the book he was writing about X. Trapnel?'

'There was no mention of what he was writing, if anything. I had myself always thought Trapnel, as a subject, a little lightweight. I hear, by the way, that Matilda Donners has some amusing photographs of the Seven Deadly Sins, in which you yourself figure. I must persuade her to produce them for me.'

Matilda had made good her promise by showing the photographs to Isobel and myself a few weeks before. The Eaton Square flat, where she lived (on the upper floors of a house next door to the former Walpole-Wilson residence, now an African embassy), was neither large, nor outstandingly luxurious, except for some of the drawings and small oil paintings. Matilda had sold the larger canvases bequeathed to herself. Apart from the high quality of what remained, the flat bore out that law which causes people to retain throughout life the same general characteristics in any place they inhabit. Matilda's Eaton Square flat at once called to mind the garret off the Gray's Inn Road, where she had lived when married to Moreland. The similarities of decoration may even have been deliberate. Moreland had certainly remained a little in love with Matilda until the end of his days. Something of the sort may have been reciprocally true of herself. Unlike Matilda's long silence about Sir Magnus, she had never been unwilling to speak of Moreland, often talking of their doings together, which seemed, some of them, happy in retrospect.

'Norman Chandler's coming to see the photographs. I thought he would enjoy the Sins. They belong to his period. Norman was always such a support to Hugh, when there was anything to do with the Theatre. The Theatre was never really Hugh's thing. He wasn't at all at ease there, even when he used to come round and see me after the performance. I particularly didn't want Norman to miss Hugh's splendid interpretation of Gluttony.'

'What's Norman directing now?'

'Polly Duport's new play. I haven't seen it yet. It sounds rather boring. Do you know her? She was here the other night. Polly's having a very worrying time. Her mother's married to a South American—more or less head of the government, I believe—and there are a lot of upheavals there. Here's Norman. Norman, my pet, how are you? We were just saying how famous you'd become. That new fringe makes you look younger than ever—like Claudette Colbert. And what a suit. Where did you get it?'

Chandler, whose air, even in later life, was of one dancing in a perpetual ballet, was not at all displeased by these comments on his personal appearance. He looked down critically at what he was wearing.

'This little number? It's from the Boutique of the Impenitent Bachelor—Vests & Transvests, we regular customers call the firm. The colour's named Pale Galilean. To tell the truth I can hardly sit down in these trousers.'

'Our brother-in-law, Dicky Umfraville, always refers to his tailor as Armpits & Crotch.'

'Their cutter must have moved over to the Boutique. How are you both? Oh, Isobel, I can't tell you how much I miss your uncle, Ted Jeavons. Watching the telly will never be the same without his comments. Still, with that piece of shrapnel, or whatever it was from the first war, inside him, he never thought he'd last as long as he did. Ted was always saying how surprised he was to be alive.'

Inhabiting flats, both of them, in what had formerly been the Jeavons house in South Kensington, Chandler and Jeavons had developed an odd friendship, one chiefly expressed in watching television together. Jeavons, who had always possessed romantic feelings about theatrical life, used to listen in silence, an expression of deep concentration on his face, while Chandler rattled on about actors, directors, producers, stage designers, most of whose names could have meant little or nothing to Jeavons. Umfraville—who always found Jeavons a bore—used to pretend there was a homosexual connexion between them, weaving elaborate fantasies in which they indulged in hair-raising orgies at the South Kensington house. Umfraville himself did not change much as the years advanced, spells of melancholy alternating with bursts of high spirits, the last latterly expressed by a rather good new impersonation of himself as an old-fashioned drug-fiend.

When Matilda spread out the photographs on a table the manner in which the actual photography 'dated' was immediately noticeable; their peculiarity partly due to the individual technique of Sir Magnus as photographer, efficient at everything he did, but altogether unversed in any approach to the camera prompted by art. This was especially true of his figure subjects. Painfully clear in outline (setting aside the superimposed exoticism of the actions portrayed), they might have been taken from the pages of a mail-order catalogue, the same suggestion of waxworks, in this case, rather sinister waxworks. Details of costume scrupulously distinct, the character of the models was scarcely at all transmitted. This method did not at all diminish the interest of the pictures themselves. Sir Magnus had remarked at the time that he had taken up photography with a view to depicting his own collections—china, furniture, armour—in the manner he himself wished them photographically recorded, something in which no professional photographer had ever satisfied him. One speculated whether—the Seven Deadly Sins pointing the way—he had later developed this hobby in a manner to include his own tastes as a voyeur. A certain harshness of technique would not necessarily have vitiated that sphere of interest. That Sir Magnus had actually introduced Widmerpool to the practices of which Pamela had so publicly accused her husband at Venice, was less likely, though there, too, photography, of a dubious intention, was alleged. Matilda set out the photographs, as if playing a game of Patience.

'So few of one's friends qualify for all the Sins. Quite a lot of people can offer six, then break down at the seventh.

They're full of Lust, Envy, Gluttony, Pride, Anger, Sloth—
then fall down on Avarice. One knows plenty of good per-
formers at Avarice, but they so often lack Gluttony or Sloth.
Of course it helps if you're allowed to include drink, in
place of food, for Gluttony.'

She picked up the picture of herself as Envy.

'It was unjust of Donners to make me take on Envy. I'm
not at all an envious person.'

That was probably true, notwithstanding her green eyes.
Matilda had never shown any strong signs of being envious.
Then one thought of her rivalry with Rosie Stevens. Even
that was scarcely Envy in the consuming sense that certain
persons display the trait. It was competitive jealousy, something rather different, even if partaking of certain envious
strains too. Matilda liked her friends to be successful, rather
than the reverse. That in itself was a rare characteristic.

'I suppose Donners thought I was envious of that silly
girl he was then having one of his fancies for. What is she
called now? Her maiden name was Lady Anne Stepney.
She's married to a Negro much younger than herself, rather
a successful psychedelic painter. Donners knew at the time
that Anne was conducting a romance with your friend
Peter Templer. Do you remember? You and Isobel were
staying at our cottage. This man, Peter Templer, picked us
up in his car, and drove us over to Stourwater for dinner
that night? There's Anne herself, as Anger, which wasn't
bad. She had a filthy temper. Here she is again, with Isobel
as Pride. That's not fair on Isobel either, anyway not the
wrong sort of Pride. And Sloth's absurd for you, Nick.
Look at all those books you've written.'

'Sloth means Accidie too. Feeling fed up with life. There
are moments when I can put forward claims.'

'Hugh, too, I can assure you. Better ones than yours, I
feel certain. But Hugh was so good as Gluttony, one
wouldn't wish him doing anything else. Look at him.'

Even the lifeless renderings of Sir Magnus's photography had failed to lessen the magnificence of Moreland's Gluttony. He had climbed right on top of the dining-room table, where he was lying supported on one elbow, gripping the neck of a bottle of Kümmel. He had already upset a full glass of the liqueur—to the visible disquiet of Sir Magnus—the highlights of the sticky pool on the table's surface caught by the lens. Moreland, surrounded by fruit that had rolled from an overturned silver bowl, was laughing inordinately. The spilt liqueur glass recalled the story told by Mopsy Pontner (whom Moreland had himself a little fancied), her romp on another dining-room table with the American film producer, Louis Glober. That was a suitable inward reminiscence to lead on to the photographs of Templer as Lust; three in number, since he had insisted on representing the Sin's three ages, Youth, Middle Years, Senility.

'It was Senile Lust that so upset that unfortunate wife of his. She rushed out of the room. What was her name? Donners made her play Avarice. The poor little thing wasn't in the least avaricious. Probably very generous, if given a chance. Somebody had to do Avarice, as we were only seven all told. She might have seen that without kicking up such a to-do. Of course she was pretty well nuts by then. Peter Templer as a husband had sent her up the wall. Donners insisted she should go through with Avarice. That was Donners at his worst. He could be very sadistic, unless you stood up to him, then he might easily become masochistic. Betty—that's what she was called. She ought to have seen it was only a game, and numbers were short. I believe she had to be put away altogether for a time, but came out after her husband was killed, and had lots of proposals. You know how men adore mad women.'

'Women like mad men, too, Matty, you must admit that. Besides, she wasn't really mad. Did she accept any of the proposals?'

'She married a man in the Foreign Office, and became an ambassadress. They were very happy, I believe. He's retired now. Most of these pictures are pretty mediocre. Hugh's the only star.'

Chandler turned the pictures over.

'I think they're wonderful, Matty. What fun it all was in those days.'

Matilda made a face.

'Oh, it wasn't. Do you truly think that, Norman? I always felt it was dreadfully grim. I don't believe that was only because the war was going to happen. Do you remember that awful man Kenneth Widmerpool coming in wearing uniform? He ought to have played the eighth Sin—Humbug.'

I was a little surprised by the violence of Matilda's comment. So far as I knew Widmerpool had taken no particular part in her life, though she might have heard about him from Sir Magnus. She was, in any case, a woman who said —and did—unexpected things, a strangeness of character reflected by her marriages to Carolo, Moreland and Sir Magnus, even if the marriage to the violinist had been a very brief one.

'I think I rather like humbugs,' said Chandler. 'People like old Gossage, the music critic, he's always been quite a friend of mine.'

Matilda laughed.

'I mean something much above poor old Gossage's bumblings. I'm speaking of making claims to a degree of virtue, purity, anything you like to call it—morals, politics, the arts, any field you prefer—which the person concerned neither possesses, nor is seriously attempting to attain. They just flatter themselves they are like that. How solemn I'm getting. That sounds just like the speeches I used to make in my early days from behind the footlights. Tell Norman about the Magnus Donners Memorial Prize, Nick.'

She began to put the photographs away. I described the Prize to Chandler.

'My dear, you ought to link the Prize with the photographs. Do the Seven Deadly Sins in rotation. The book wins, which best enhances the Sin-of-the-Year.'

'Oh, Norman, I wish we could.'

That emendation would have added spice to the Magnus Donners Prize, which got off to an unspirited start, with a somewhat pedestrian biography of Sir Horrocks Rusby. A contemporary of Sir Magnus, this once celebrated advocate's life-story was the only book of that year falling within the terms required. The frontispiece, a florid portrait of Rusby in wig and gown, was from the brush of Isbister, foreshadowing the painter's later resurgence. The following year there were sufficient eligible candidates to make me regret ever having let myself in for so much additional reading of an unexciting kind. It was won with a lively study of a wartime commander, written by a military historian of repute. The third year's choice, reflecting a new mood of free expression, was of greater interest than its forerunners; a politician, public personality rather than statesman, chronicled by a journalist friend, who provided, in generous profusion, details of his subject's adventures (he had been homosexual), which would have remained unrecorded only a few years before. Emily Brightman made one of her pronouncements, when this book had been finally adopted for the Prize.

'In its vulgar way, a painstaking piece of work, although one must always remember—something often forgotten today—that because things are generally known, they are not necessarily the better for being written down, or publicly announced. Some are, some aren't. As in everything else, good sense, taste, art, all have their place. Saying you prefer to disregard art, taste, good sense, does not mean that those elements do not exist—it merely means you lack them yourself.'

On the fourth and final year of the panel, the existing committee was confronted with much the same situation as that of the first presentation of the award, except that then there had been at least one eligible book, if no very inspiring one. This year, as I had told Salvidge, nothing at all seemed available. For one reason or another every biography to appear, or billed to appear within the publishing period required, fell outside the Magnus Donners category. When I arrived at the table for the second annual meeting, Emily Brightman and Mark Members were discussing procedure for announcing that, this year, the Prize would not be presented. A minute or two later Delavacquerie came into the restaurant. He held under his arm what looked like the proof copy of a book. When he sat down Emily Brightman tried to take it from him. Delavacquerie resisted. He would not even let her see the title, though admitting he had found a possible entrant for the Prize.

'The publishers got in touch with me yesterday.'

'Who's it about?'

'I'd like to speak of a few things first, before we get on to the actual merits of the book. There are complications. Other copies of this proof are in the post to the private addresses of all members of the Magnus Donners committee. If you decide in favour, the publishers can get the book out within the appointed time. Let's order luncheon before we go into the various problems.'

Delavacquerie kept the proof copy hidden on his knee. He always gave the impression of knowing exactly what he wanted to say, how he was going to behave. Emily Brightman, aware that to show impatience would undermine the strength of her position, displayed self-control. Delavacquerie possessed several of her own characteristics, firmness, directness, grasp of whatever subject had to be considered.

66

If they opposed each other, she was prepared to accept him on equal terms as an adversary, by no means true of everyone. When food and drink had been ordered, Delavacquerie began to make his statement. Even at the outset this was a sufficiently startling one.

'You remember, a long time ago, the name came up at one of these meetings of the novelist, X. Trapnel, author of *Camel Ride to the Tomb, Dogs Have No Uncles*, and other works? He died in the nineteen-fifties. You knew him quite well, I think, Nick?'

Members broke in.

'I knew Trapnel well too. We all knew him. Did he leave a posthumous biography of somebody, which has just been discovered?'

'I never knew Trapnel,' said Emily Brightman. 'Not personally, that is. I'm always promising myself to read his books, but this must be—'

'Please,' said Delavacquerie.

Smiling, he held Emily Brightman in check.

'I'm sorry, Gibson, but I'm sure I know more about this subject than you do.'

Delavacquerie, still smiling, shook his head. He continued. In relation to Trapnel he was determined to clarify his own position before anything else was said.

'I met Trapnel himself only once, and that not for long, more than twenty years ago, but I believe him to be a good writer. We have a life of Trapnel here. His career was not altogether uneventful. This book is by an American professor, a doctoral dissertation, none the worse for that. I have read the book. I think you will like it.'

Emily Brightman was not to be held in any longer. She raised a fork threateningly, as if about to stab Delavacquerie, if he did not come quickly to the point. Members, too, was showing signs of wanting to ventilate his own Trapnel experiences, before things went much further. I myself felt the same impelling urge.

'Gibson, this book must be written by Russell Gwinnett.'

Delavacquerie, who, reasonably enough, had forgotten that Emily Brightman once announced herself an old friend of Gwinnett's, looked a little surprised that she should know the name of the biographer.

'Have the publishers sent your proof copy already, Emily?'

'Not yet, but I knew Russell Gwinnett was writing a life of Trapnel. So did Nicholas. We could have told you at once, Gibson, had we been allowed to speak. Russell is an old friend of mine. Nicholas, too, met him when we were in Venice. We talked of it at the first meeting of this committee. You could not have been attending, Gibson. You see you sometimes underrate our capabilities.'

Delavacquerie laughed. Before he could defend himself, Members pegged out his own claim.

'I don't know Gwinnett, but I knew Trapnel. You count as knowing a man reasonably well after he's borrowed five pounds off you. Is that incident mentioned? I hope so.'

If Delavacquerie considered Gwinnett's book good, the judgment was likely to be sound. I was less surprised to hear that Gwinnett's biography of Trapnel was well done, than that it had ever been completed at all. If the work was accomplished, Gwinnett was likely to have brought to it the powers he certainly possessed. Personally, I had doubted that the study would ever see light. Emily Brightman must have thought the same. She was greatly excited by the news. When they had both been teaching at the same women's college in America, in a sense Gwinnett had been a protégé of hers. She had always supported a belief in his abilities as a writer. How much she was prepared to face another, more enigmatic, even more sinister, side of his character, was less easy to assess.

68

'I told you Russell was an industrious young man, Nicholas. A capable one too. I suppose he can't be spoken of as young any longer. He must be well into his forties. At last it looks as if we've found someone for the Prize. There is no writer to whom I would rather award it than Russell. It's just what he needs to give him self-assurance, and what the Prize itself needs, to lift it out of the rut of the commonplace. Show me the proof at once, Gibson.'

Delavacquerie continued to withhold the proof copy.

'Not yet, Emily.'

'Gibson, you are intolerable. Don't be absurd. Hand it over immediately.'

'I'm prepared to be magnanimous about the fiver,' said Members. 'I could ill afford forfeiture of five pounds at the time, but we were all penniless writers together, and bygones shall be bygones. The point is whether the book is good.'

'The merits of Gwinnett's book are not so much the issue,' said Delavacquerie. 'The difficulty is quite another matter.'

'I know what you're going to put forward,' said Emily Brightman. 'Libel. Am I right? I can see a book of that sort might be libellous, but that is surely the publisher's affair. We shall have given the Prize before the row starts.'

'That is not exactly the problem. At least the publishers are not worried in a general way on that ground. They think the possibility of anything of the sort very remote. The libel, if any, would be in connexion with Trapnel's love affair with Pamela Widmerpool. As you know, she destroyed the manuscript of his last novel. That business was largely responsible for Trapnel's final débâcle.'

'An interesting legal point,' said Members. 'Is it libellous to write that someone's deceased wife was unfaithful to him? I always understood, in days when I myself worked in a publisher's office, that you can't libel the dead. That was one of the firmest foundations of the publishing profession. On the other hand, I suppose the surviving partner might consider himself libelled, as being put on record as a trompé'd husband. At the time I was speaking of, my ancient publishing days, there also existed the element Emily brought up, rather severely, at one of our meetings—good taste—but fortunately we don't have to bother about that now—even if it does platonically exist, as Emily assures us. Don't say it's good taste that makes you waver, Gibson. I believe you're frightened of Emily's disapproval.'

Members and Delavacquerie, outwardly well disposed towards each other, anyway conversationally, were not much in sympathy at base. Delavacquerie, formal as always, may all the same have revealed on some occasion his own sense of mutual disharmony. If so, Members was now getting his own back. Delavacquerie, recognizing that, smiled.

'You may be right, Mark. At the same time you will agree, I think, when I state the problem, that it is a rather special one. Meanwhile, let me release these proofs.'

He handed the bundle to Emily Brightman, who almost snatched it from his hands. She turned at once to the title-page. I read the layout over her arm.

DEATH'S-HEAD SWORDSMAN
The Life and Works of
X. TRAPNEL
by
RUSSELL GWINNETT

In due course the proofs came my way. Gwinnett's academic appointment, named at the beginning of the book, was held at an American college to be judged of fairly obscure status, though lately in the news, owing to exceptionally severe student troubles on its campus. On the page where a dedication might have stood, an epigraph was set.

My study's ornament, thou shell of death,
Once the bright face of my betrothèd lady.
                    The Revenger's Tragedy.

For those who knew anything of Gwinnett, or of
Trapnel for that matter, the quotation was, to say the
least, ambiguous. The longer the lines were considered,
the more profuse in private meaning they seemed to
become. Moreland, too, had been keen on the plays of
Cyril Tourneur. He used often to quote a favourite image
from one of them: '... and how quaintly he died, like a
politician, in hugger-mugger, made no man acquainted
with it ...'

Tourneur, as Gwinnett himself, was obsessed with Death.
The skull, carried by the actor, his 'study's ornament', was
no doubt, in one sense, intended to strike the opening note
of Gwinnett's book, his own 'study'. The couplet drew
attention also to the melodramatic title (referring presumably to the death's-head, mentioned by Delavacquerie, on
the top of Trapnel's sword-stick); but had it deeper meaning as well? If so, who was intended? The lines could be
regarded as, say, dedication to the memory of Gwinnett's
earlier girlfriend (at whose death he had been involved in
some sort of scandal); alternatively, as allusion to Pamela
Widmerpool herself. If the latter, were the words conceived as spoken by Trapnel, by Gwinnett, by both—or,
indeed, by all Pamela's lovers? Even if ironical, they were
appropriate enough. At least they defined the tone of the
book. Then another thought came. Not only was the quotation about a skull, the title of Tourneur's play had also to
be considered. It was called *The Revenger's Tragedy.* Did
revenge play some part in writing the book? If so, Gwinnett's revenge on whom? Trapnel? Pamela? Widmerpool?
There were too many questions to sort out at that moment.
Delavacquerie allowed everyone to examine the proofs as

long as they wished, before he brought out the information he was holding in reserve.

'With regard to libel,' said Emily Brightman. 'I see that neither Lord Widmerpool, nor his late wife, is named in what is evidently a very full index. I am, by the way, hearing all sorts of strange stories about Lord Widmerpool's behaviour as a university chancellor. He seems to have the oddest ideas how the duties of that office should be carried out.'

I, too, had noticed the omission of the names of the Widmerpools, husband and wife, from the book's index. That did not mean that their identities were necessarily unrecognizable in the text. Members protested at all this talk about libel.

'I can't see that we need be punctilious about the susceptibilities of Lord Widmerpool, whatever Emily feels as to maintaining standards of good taste. Especially as she herself now draws attention to his much advertised broadmindedness, in various recent statements made by him, on the subject of students at his own university.'

This gave Delavacquerie the opportunity he was waiting for to produce an effective climax to what he had been saying.

'What you put forward, Mark, is quite true. Only last week I was watching a programme of Lord Widmerpool's dealing with protest, counterculture, alternative societies, all the things that he is now interested in. That does not entirely meet our problem, which is a rather more delicate one. The fact is that Lord Widmerpool acts as one of the trustees of the fund from which the Magnus Donners Memorial Prize derives.'

This piece of information naturally made a considerable impression. None of the committee came out with an immediate response. My own first thought was how on earth Widmerpool could have come to occupy such a position in relation to this literary prize, or any other. He might be planning to write a book, but, after all, he had been talking of doing that from his earliest days. More than this was needed as explanation. Who could have been insane enough to have made him trustee of the Magnus Donners Prize? Then, when Delavacquerie continued, the reason became plain.

'Lord Widmerpool, in his early business life, was for quite a long time associated with Donners-Brebner. He did many miscellaneous jobs for Sir Magnus himself. At one time he might almost have been called Sir Magnus's right-hand man, so I've been told, though I've never known Lord Widmerpool personally, only seen him at meetings.'

'The term jackal has been used,' said Members.

Delavacquerie ignored the comment. He was always determined that the formalities should be observed.

'Putting in work on organizing this fund for the Donners-Brebner Fellowships was one of the tasks allotted. In that capacity, as benefiting from them myself, I might even be considered in his debt. For some reason when the Prize was, so to speak, detached from the general sum, Lord Widmerpool's name remained as a trustee.'

Even Members agreed that a ticklish problem was posed. Any hypothetical question of libel sank into the background, compared with the propriety of awarding a substantial monetary prize, administered—at least in theory—by Widmerpool himself, to an author, who had been one of his wife's lovers, and written the biography of another man, of whom she had also been the mistress. Besides, Gwinnett had not merely been Pamela's lover, he was considered by some to be at least the indirect cause of her death; even if she herself had chosen that to be so. After quite a long pause, Emily Brightman spoke.

'I feel dreadfully sure that I am going to vote for Russell

73

getting the Prize, but I do agree that we are faced with a very delicate situation.'

Delavacquerie, who had no doubt given a good deal of thought to the perplexity which he knew would confront the panel, appeared quite prepared for its attitude to be one of irresolution.

'The first thing to do is for the committee to read the book, decide whether or not you want the Prize to be given to Professor Gwinnett. If you do, I am prepared to take the next step myself. I will approach Lord Widmerpool in person, and ask him where he stands on the matter. It will no doubt be necessary for him to read *Death's-head Swordsman* too, before he can make up his mind.'

Members showed uneasiness about that. I felt a little doubtful myself. It seemed going out of the way to meet trouble.

'But Kenneth Widmerpool may forbid publication. What shall we do then? Why should we be bullied by him? Surely it would be better to leave Widmerpool alone. What can he do?'

Delavacquerie was firm.

'The question to some extent involves the Company. The directors may not care tuppence what Widmerpool feels in the matter, but they would not wish attention to be drawn to the fact that he is still connected with the Company to that extent, and at the same time objects to publication. I should like to get Lord Widmerpool's attitude clearly stated, if I have to consult them. His name could be quietly removed. All sorts of things might be done. They can be gone into, when we know his own views. To remove his name right away, for instance, might induce trouble, rather than curtail it.'

That sounded reasonable. Members withdrew his objection. What had worried him, he said, was thought that the award could turn on Widmerpool's whim. In other respects, the idea that the committee's choice might cause a stir greatly pleased Members, who always enjoyed conflict.

'This is a courageous offer, Gibson,' said Emily Brightman.

Delavacquerie laughed.

'In not knowing Lord Widmerpool personally, I have the advantage of ignorance. That is sometimes a useful weapon. I am perhaps not so foolhardy as you all seem to think. There are aspects of the Trapnel story with which, in his latest frame of mind, Lord Widmerpool might even welcome association. I mean Trapnel the despised and rejected—insomuch as Trapnel was despised and rejected.'

I felt confidence in Delavacquerie's judgment, and could grasp some of what he meant. Nevertheless his train of thought was not wholly clear.

'But even the new Widmerpool will hardly stomach such an association with Gwinnett, will he?'

'We'll see. I may be wrong. It's worth a try.'

Delavacquerie was giving nothing away at this stage. During what remained of the meeting no matter of consequence was discussed. *Death's-head Swordsman* had first to be read. That was the next step. Luncheon came to an end. Emily Brightman said she was on her way to the British Museum. Members was going to his hairdresser, before attending another literary prize committee later that afternoon. After saying goodbye to the others, Delavacquerie and I set off for Fleet Street.

'How do you propose to tackle Widmerpool?'

Delavacquerie's manner changed a little from its carefully screened air employed at the table.

'Tell me, Nicholas, did not Pamela Widmerpool take an overdose that she might be available to the necrophilic professor?'

'That was how things looked at the time. She may have decided to do herself in anyway.'

75

'But it might be said that Gwinnett—by, perhaps only indirectly, being the cause of her end—avenged Trapnel for destruction of his novel, and consequent downfall?'

'You could look at it that way.'

'In a sense Gwinnett represents Widmerpool's revenge on Pamela too?'

'That also occurred to me. *The Revenger's Tragedy*. All the same, the point is surely not going to be easy to put, as man-to-man, when you confront Widmerpool?'

'Nevertheless, I shall bear it in mind.'

'I never thought Gwinnett would get the book finished. He gave up academic life when all the trouble happened. I last heard of him teaching water-skiing.'

'A promising profession for a man keen on Death?'

'I don't think Gwinnett does away with his girls. He is not a murderer. He just loves where Death is. The subject enraptures him. Emily Brightman says there was an earlier incident of his breaking into a mortuary, where a dead love of his lay.'

Delavacquerie thought for a moment.

'I can understand the obsession, like most others. People love where Beauty is, where Money is, where Power is— why not where Death is? An American poet said Death is the Mother of Beauty. No, I was being perhaps unduly secretive at lunch. I'll tell you. I have a special line on Lord Widmerpool. My son is at the university of which he is the chancellor.'

I knew Delavacquerie's wife had died ten or fifteen years before. I had never met her. They had come across each other in England, the marriage, so far as I knew, a happy one. Delavacquerie sometimes spoke of his wife. The son he had never before mentioned.

'In the ordinary way, of course, Etienne would scarcely know who was the chancellor of the university. Lord Widmerpool, as we were saying at lunch, has for some little time been laying stress on his own closeness to the younger generation, and its upheavals. You may have seen his letters —always signed nowadays "Ken Widmerpool", rather than just "Widmerpool", as a peer of the realm—a matey approach habitually brought into play so far as students of the university are concerned. He has made his house a centre for what might be called the more difficult cases.'

'Was your son involved in the Quiggin twins' paint-throwing?'

Delavacquerie laughed at the suggestion.

'On the contrary, Etienne is a hard-working boy, who wants to get a good economics degree, but naturally he does the things his own contemporaries do up to a point—knows all about them, I mean, even if he isn't the paint-throwing type. He has talked a lot about Lord Widmerpool. Quite a personality cult has been established there. Lord Widmerpool has made himself a powerful figure in the student world—which, I need hardly remind you, is by no means entirely made up of students.'

'You think your knowledge of Widmerpool's latest stance is such as to persuade him to create no difficulties about Gwinnett's book?'

'It is my own self-esteem that prompts me to attempt this. That is what I am like. I want to come back to the Magnus Donners Prize committee, and inform them that Lord Widmerpool is perfectly agreeable to *Death's-head Swordsman* receiving the award—that is, if you and the rest of the panel wish the book to be chosen.'

This statement of his own feelings in the matter was very typical of Delavacquerie; to admit ambitions of a kind not necessarily to be expected from a poet, anyway the poet of popular imagination. By the time we had this conversation the habit had grown up of our lunching together in London at fairly regular intervals (quite apart from the Magnus Donners meetings), so that I was already familiar with a

77

side of him that was competitive in a manner he rather liked to emphasize. Then he came out with something for which I was not at all prepared.

'Isn't a girl called Fiona Cutts some sort of a relation of yours?'

'A niece.'

'She used to be a friend of Etienne's.'

'Lately?'

'A year or two ago. For a short time she and Etienne saw quite a lot of each other—I mean enough for me to have met her too. A nice girl. I think in the end she found Etienne too humdrum, though they got on well for a while.'

'Did they meet with the odd crowd Fiona is now going round with?'

'No, not at all. At some musical get-together, I think. The thing broke up when this other business started.'

Fiona's friendship with Etienne Delavacquerie had never percolated down through the family grapevine. There was no particular reason why it should. Even Fiona's parents were unlikely to keep track of all their daughter's current boyfriends. It was a pity Susan and Roddy Cutts had never known about this apparently reliable young man. They would have felt relieved, anyway for a short period of time. Delavacquerie, also regretting the termination of the relationship, was probably in ignorance of the extent to which Fiona could show herself a handful. I asked if he knew about Scorpio Murtlock.

'I knew she was now mixed up with some mystic cult. I didn't know Murtlock had anything to do with her. I thought he was a queer.'

'Hard to say.'

'All I know about Murtlock is that Quentin Shuckerly picked him up somewhere ages ago. Shuckerly, expecting an easy lay, put Murtlock up in his flat. Shuckerly can be quite tough in such matters—that former intellectual black

boyfriend of his used to call him the Narcissus of the
Nigger—but his toughness, or his narcissism, didn't stand
up to Murtlock's. Shuckerly had to leave the country to get
Murtlock out of his flat. A new book of Shuckerly poems
was held up in publication in consequence. I wouldn't have
thought Murtlock a wise young man to get mixed up with.
Etienne never told me that.'

Delavacquerie looked quite disturbed. Here our ways
had to part.

'I should like to bug your conversation with Widmerpool,
anyway your opening gambit.'

Delavacquerie made a dramatic gesture.

'I shall take the bull by the horns—adopt the directness
of the CIA man and the Cuban defector.'

'What was that?'

'He asked him a question.'

'Which was?'

'You know how it is in Havana in the Early Warning?'

Delavacquerie waved goodbye. I went on towards the
paper, to get a book for review. In the anxiety he had
shown about his son's abandoned love affair—and Fiona's
own involvement with Murtlock—Delavacquerie had displayed more feeling than he usually revealed. It suggested
that Etienne Delavacquerie had been fairly hard hit when
Fiona went off. I was interested that Delavacquerie himself
had met her, and would have liked to hear more of his
views on that subject. There had been no opportunity. In
any case the friendships of later life, in contrast with those
negotiated before thirty, are apt to be burdened with
reservations, constraints, inhibitions. Probably thirty was
placing the watershed too late for the age when both parties
begin more or less to know (at least think they know) what
the other is talking about; as opposed to those earlier friendships—not unlike love affairs, with all sexual element

79

removed—which can exist with scarcely an interest in common, mutual misunderstanding of character and motive all but absolute.

In earlier days, given our comparative intellectual intimacy, there would have been no embarrassment in enquiring about Delavacquerie's own sexual arrangements. The question would have been an aspect of being friends. In fact, Delavacquerie himself would almost certainly have issued some sort of statement of his own on the matter, a handout likely to have been given early priority, when we were first getting to know one another. That was why the rumoured brush with Matilda remained altogether blurred in outline. There was no doubt that Delavacquerie liked women, got on well with them. His poetry showed that. If he possessed any steady company—hard to believe he did not—the lady herself never seemed to appear with him in public.

Thinking of the information now accumulating about Scorpio Murtlock, an incident that had taken place a few years before came to mind. It might or might not be Murtlock this time, the principle was the same. The occasion also marked the last time I had set eyes on an old acquaintance, Sunny Farebrother. I was in London only for the day. Entering a comparatively empty compartment on a tube train, I saw Farebrother sitting at the far end. Wearing a black overcoat and bowler hat, both ancient as his wartime uniforms, he was as usual holding himself very upright. He did not look like a man verging on eighty. White moustache neatly trimmed, he could have passed for middle sixties. In one sense a figure conspicuously of the past in turnout, there was also something about him that was extremely up-to-date, not to say brisk. He was smiling to himself. I took the vacant seat next to him.

'Hullo, Sunny.'

Farebrother's face at once lost its smile. Instead, it

assumed an expression of rueful compassion. It was the face he had put on when Widmerpool, then a major on the staff, seemed likely to be sacked from Divisional Headquarters. Farebrother, an old enemy, had dropped in to announce that fact.

'Nicholas, how splendid to meet again after all these years. You find me on my way back from a sad occasion. I am returning from Kensal Green Cemetery. The last tribute to an old friend. One of these fellows I'd known for a mighty long time. Life will never be quite the same again without him. We didn't always hit it off together—but, my goodness, Nicholas, he was someone known to you too. I've just been to Jimmy Stripling's funeral. Poor old Jimmy. You must remember him. You and I stayed at the Templers', a hundred years ago, when Jimmy was there. He was the old man's son-in-law in those days. Tall chap, hair parted in the middle, keen on motor-racing. I always remember how Jimmy, and some of the rest of the house-party, tried to play a trick on me, after we'd come back from a ball, and I had gone up to bed. Poor old Jimmy hoped to put a po in my hatbox. I was too sharp for him.'

Farebrother shook his head in sadness at the folly of human nature, folly so abjectly displayed by Jimmy Stripling in hoping to outwit Farebrother in a matter of that sort. I saw now that a black tie added to the sombre note struck by the rest of his clothes.

'Jimmy and I used to do a lot of business together in our early City days. He always pretended we didn't get on well. Then, poor old boy, he gave up the City—he was in Lloyd's, hadn't done too badly there, and elsewhere—gave up his motor-racing, got a divorce from Peter Templer's sister, and began mixing himself up with all sorts of strange goings-on that couldn't have been at all good for the nerves. Old Jimmy was a highly strung beggar in his way. Took up with a strange lady, who told fortunes. Occultism, all that.

Not a good thing. Bad thing, in fact. The last time I saw him, only a few years ago, he was driving along Piccadilly in a car that could have been fifty years old, if it was a day. Jimmy must have lost all his money. His cars were once his pride and joy. Always had the latest model before anyone else. Now he was grinding along in this old crock. I could have wept at seeing Jimmy reduced to an old tin can like that.'

Farebrother, a habit of his when he told almost any story, suddenly lowered his voice, at the same time looking round to see if we were likely to be overheard, though no one else was sitting at our end of the compartment.

'It was even worse than that, I fear. There weren't many at the funeral but those who were looked a rum lot, to say the least. I got into conversation with one of the few mourners who was respectably dressed. Turned out he was a member of Lloyd's, like Jimmy, though he hadn't seen him for a long time. Do you know what had happened? When that fortune-telling lady of Jimmy's was gathered in, he took up with a *boy*. Would you have believed it? Jimmy may have behaved like a crackpot at times, but no one ever guessed he had *those* tastes. This bloke I talked to told me he'd heard that a lot of undesirables used to live off Jimmy towards the end. I don't think he'd have invented the tale on account of the funny types at the funeral. Jimmy's boy was there. In fact he was more or less running the show. He wore a sort of coloured robe, hair not much short of his shoulders. Good-looking lad in his way, if you'd cleaned him up a bit. Funnily enough, I didn't at all take against him, little as I'm drawn to that type as a rule. Even something I rather liked, if you can believe that. He had an air of efficiency. That always gets me. It was a cremation, and this young fellow showed himself perfectly capable of taking charge. All these strange types in their robes sang a sort of dirge for Jimmy at the close of the proceedings.'

'Perhaps it was the efficiency Jimmy Stripling liked?'

'I hope you're right, Nicholas. I hadn't thought of that. Jimmy just needed somebody to look after him in his old age. I expect that was it. We all need that. I see I've been uncharitable. I'm glad I went to the funeral, all the same. I make a point of going to funerals and memorial services, sad as they are, because you always meet a lot of people at them you haven't seen for years, and that often comes in useful later. Jimmy's was the exception. I never expect to set eyes on mourners like his again, Kensal Green, or anywhere else.'

The train was approaching my station.

'How are you yourself, Sunny?'

'Top-hole form, top-hole. Saw my vet last week. Said he'd never inspected a fitter man of my age. As you probably know, Nicholas, I'm a widower now.'

'I didn't. I'm sorry to hear—'

'Three years ago. A wonderful woman, Geraldine. Marvellous manager. Knew just where to save. Never had any money of her own, left a sum small but by no means to be disregarded. A wonderful woman. Happy years together. Fragrant memories. Yes, I'm in the same little place in the country. I get along somehow. Everyone round about is very kind and helpful. You and your wife must come and see my roses. I can always manage a cup of tea. Bless you, Nicholas, bless you . . .'

As I walked along the platform towards the Exit staircase the train moved on past me. I saw Farebrother once more through the window as the pace increased. He was still sitting bolt upright, and had begun to smile again. On the visit to which he had himself referred, the time when Stripling's practical joke had fallen so flat, Peter Templer had pronounced a judgment on Farebrother. It remained a valid one.

'He's a downy old bird.'

83

3

IRRITATED BY WHAT HE JUDGED the 'impacted clichés' of some review, Trapnel had once spoken his own opinions on the art of biography.

'People think because a novel's invented, it isn't true. Exactly the reverse is the case. Because a novel's invented, it is true. Biography and memoirs can never be wholly true, since they can't include every conceivable circumstance of what happened. The novel can do that. The novelist himself lays it down. His decision is binding. The biographer, even at his highest and best, can be only tentative, empirical. The autobiographer, for his part, is imprisoned in his own egotism. He must always be suspect. In contrast with the other two, the novelist is a god, creating his man, making him breathe and walk. The man, created in his own image, provides information about the god. In a sense you know more about Balzac and Dickens from their novels, than Rousseau and Casanova from their Confessions.'

'But novelists can be as egotistical as any other sort of writer. Their sheer narcissism often makes them altogether unreadable. A novelist may inescapably create all his characters in his own image, but the reader can believe in them, without necessarily accepting their creator's judgment on them. You might see a sinister strain in Bob Cratchit, conventionality in Stavrogin, delicacy in Molly Bloom. Besides, the very concept of a character in a novel—in real life too—is under attack.'

'What you say, Nick, strengthens my contention that only a novel can imply certain truths impossible to state by exact definition. Biography and autobiography are forced to attempt exact definition. In doing so truth goes astray. The novelist is more serious—if that is the word.'

'Surely biographers and memoir-writers often do no more than imply things they chronicle, or put them forward as uncertain. A novelist is subjective, and selective, all the time. The others have certain facts forced on them, whether they like it or not. Besides, some of the very worst novelists are the most consciously serious ones.'

'Of course a novelist is *serious* only if he is a good novelist. You mention Molly Bloom. She offers an example of what I am saying. Obviously her sexual musings—and her husband's—derive from the author, to the extent that he invented them. Such descriptions would have been a thousand times less convincing, if attributed to Stephen Dedalus—let alone to Joyce himself. Their strength lies in existence within the imaginary personalities of the Blooms. That such traits are much diminished, when given to a hero, is even to some extent exemplified in *Ulysses*. It may be acceptable to read of Bloom tossing off. A blow by blow account of the author doing so is hardly conceivable as interesting. Perhaps, at the base of it all, is the popular confusion of self-pity with compassion. What is effective is art, not what is "true"—using the term in inverted commas.'

'Like Pilate.'

'Unfortunately Pilate wasn't a novelist.'

'Or even a memoir-writer.'

'Didn't Petronius serve as a magistrate in some distant

85

part of the Roman Empire? Think if the case had come up before him. Perhaps Petronius was a different period.'

The *Satyricon* was the only classical work ever freely quoted by Trapnel. He would often refer to it. I recalled his views on biography, reading Gwinnett's—found on return home—and wondered how far Trapnel would have regarded this example as proving his point. That a biography of Trapnel should have been written at all was surprising enough, an eventuality beyond all guessing for those to whom he had been no more than another necessitous phantom at the bar, to stand or be stood a half pint of bitter. Now, by a process every bit as magical as any mutations on the astral plane claimed by Dr Trelawney, there would be casual readers to find entertainment in the chronicle of Trapnel's days, professional critics adding to their reputation by analysis of his style, academics rummaging for nuggets among the Trapnel remains. It seemed unlikely that much was left over. Gwinnett had done a thorough job.

I had been friends with Trapnel only a few years, but in those years witnessed some of his most characteristic attitudes and performances. Here was a good instance of later trimmings that throw light on an already known story. Gwinnett had not only recorded the routine material well, he had dealt judiciously with much else of general interest at that immediately post-war period; one not specially easy to handle, especially for an American by no means steeped in English life. Prudently, Gwinnett had not always accepted Trapnel (given to self-fantasy) at his own estimation. The final disastrous spill (worse than any on the race-course by his jockey father)—that is to say Trapnel's infatuation with Pamela Widmerpool—had been treated with an altogether unexpected subtlety. Gwinnett had once implied that his own involvement with Pamela might impair objectivity, but only those who knew of that already were likely to recognize the extent to which author identified himself with subject. I wrote to Delavacquerie recommending that *Death's-head Swordsman* should receive the year's Magnus Donners Memorial Prize. He replied that, Emily Brightman and Mark Members being in agreement, he himself would, as arranged, approach Widmerpool. If Widmerpool objected to our choice, we should have to think again. In due course, Delavacquerie reported back on this matter. His letters, like his speech, always possessed a touch of formality.

'There are to be no difficulties for the judges from that quarter. Lord Widmerpool's assurances justify me in my own eyes. You would laugh at the professional pleasure I take in being able to write this, the quiet satisfaction I find in my own skill at negotiation. To tell the truth no negotiation had to take place. Lord Widmerpool informed me straightaway that he did not care a fart—that was his unexpected phrase—what was said about him in Professor Gwinnett's book, either by name or anonymously. He gave no reason for this, but was evidently speaking without reservation of any kind. At first he said he did not even wish to see a copy of *Death's-head Swordsman*, as he held all conventional writings of our day in hearty contempt, but, thinking it best to do so, I persuaded him to accept a proof. It seemed to me that would put the committee of judges in a stronger position. Lord Widmerpool said that, if he had time, he would look at the book. Nothing he found there would make any difference to what he had already told me. That allays all fears as to the propriety of the award. Have you seen Lord Widmerpool lately? He is greatly altered from what I remember of him, though I only knew him by sight. Perhaps the American continent has had that effect. As you know, I regard the Western Hemisphere as a potent force on all who are brought in contact with its influences, whether or not they were born or live there—and of course I do not merely mean the US. Possibly I was right in my assessment of how Lord Widmerpool would react towards Professor Gwinnett's book. At present I cannot be sure whether my triumph—if it may so be called—was owed to that assessment. Lord Widmerpool made one small condition. It will amuse you. I will tell you about it when we next lunch together—next week, if you are in London. I have kept Matilda in touch with all these developments.'

The news of Widmerpool's indifference to whatever Gwinnett might have written, unanticipated in its comprehensive disdain of the whole Trapnel—and Gwinnett—story, certainly made the position of the Prize committee easier. It looked as if the publishers had already cleared the matter with Widmerpool. They seemed to have no fear of legal proceedings, and Delavacquerie's letter gave the impression that his interview might not have provided Widmerpool's first awareness of the book. Even so, without this sanction, there could have been embarrassments owed to the Donners-Brebner connexion. I wrote to Gwinnett (with whom I had not corresponded since his Spanish interlude), addressing the letter to the English Department of the American college named at the beginning of his book.

The recipient of the Magnus Donners Prize was given dinner at the expense of the Company. A selection of writers, publishers, literary editors, columnists, anyone else deemed helpful to publicity in the circumstances, was invited. Speeches were made. It was not an evening-dress affair. Convened in a suite of rooms on the upper floor of a restaurant much used for such occasions, the party was usually held in the early months of the year following that for which the book had been chosen. As a function, the Magnus Donners Memorial Prize dinner was just what might be expected, a business gathering, rather than a social one. Delavacquerie, who had its arranging, saw that food and drink were never less than tolerable. When he and I next met for one of our luncheons together I asked what had been Widmerpool's condition for showing so easygoing an attitude.

'That he should himself be invited to the dinner.'

'Did he make the request ironically?'

'Not in the least.'

As a public figure of a sort, although one fallen into comparative obscurity, issue of an invitation to Widmerpool would in no way run counter to the general pattern of guests; even if his presence, owing to the particular circumstances, might strike a bizarre note. It was likely that a large proportion of those present would be too young to have heard—anyway too young to take much interest in—the scandals of ten years before.

'No doubt Widmerpool can be sent a card. You were right in thinking the stipulation would amuse me.'

'You haven't heard it all yet.'

'What else?'

'He wants to bring two guests.'

'Donners-Brebner can presumably extend their hospitality that far.'

'Of course.'

'Who are to be Widmerpool's guests?'

'Whom do you think?'

The answer was not so easy as first appeared. Whom would Widmerpool ask? I made several guesses at personalities of rather his own kind, figures to be judged useful in one practical sphere or another. In putting forward these names, I became aware how little I now knew of Widmerpool's latest orientations and ambitions. Delavacquerie shook his head, smiling at the wrongness of such speculation.

'I told you Lord Widmerpool had greatly changed. Let me give you a clue. Two ladies.'

I put forward a life peeress and an actress, neither in their first youth.

89

'Not so elderly.'
'I give it up.'
'The Quiggin twins.'
'The girls who threw paint over him?'
'The same.'
'But—is he having an affair with both of them?'

Delavacquerie laughed. He was pleased with the effect of the information he had given.

'Not, I feel fairly sure, in any physical sense, although I gather he has no objection to girls who frequent his place— boys too, Etienne assures me—being good to look at. If the weather is warm, undressing is encouraged. I doubt if he contemplates sleeping with either sex. You know Widmerpool is not far from making himself into a Holy Man these days, certainly a much venerated one in his own circle.'

'What will Gwinnett think of this, if he comes to the dinner himself? I imagine it is quite possible he will. Have you heard from him about getting the Prize? I wrote a line of congratulation, but have had no reply.'

That Gwinnett had not replied was no surprise. It did not at all diverge from the accustomed Gwinnett manner of going on. If anything, lack of an answer suggested that Gwinnett's harassing London experiences had left him unchanged.

'Professor Gwinnett wrote to me, as secretary of the Prize committee, to say he would take pleasure in travelling over here to receive the Prize in person.'

'That will add to the drama of the dinner.'

'He said he was on the point of visiting this country in any case. He would speed up his plans.'

'Was Gwinnett pleased his book was chosen?'

'Pleased—far from overwhelmed. He wrote a few conventional phrases, saying he was gratified, adding that he would turn up for the dinner, if I would let him know time and place. No more. He was not at all effusive. In fact, from my own experience of Americans, his appreciation was restrained to the point of being brusque.'

'That's his line.'

The publishers issued *Death's-head Swordsman* just in time to be eligible for the Prize, though not at an advantageous moment to receive much attention from reviewers. That was inevitable in the circumstances. Such notices as appeared were favourable, but still few in number by the time of the Magnus Donners dinner, which took place, as usual, in the New Year.

'I'm asking the committee to come early,' said Delavacquerie. 'It's going to be rather an exceptional affair this year. Last-minute problems may arise.'

When I arrived he was moving about the dining-room, checking that seating was correct. Emily Brightman and Mark Members had not yet turned up.

'Professor Gwinnett is on Matilda's right, of course, and I've put Isobel on his other side. Emily Brightman thought it might look too much as if she had been set to keep an eye on him, if she were next door. Emily is sitting next to you, Nick, and a Donners-Brebner director's wife on the other side. Let me see, Mrs—'

The winner of the Prize was always beside Matilda Donners, at a long table, which included judges, representatives of the Company, and wives of these. At the end of dinner Delavacquerie's duty was to say a few words about the Prize itself. One of the judges' panel then introduced the recipient, and spoke of his book. Members, a compulsive public speaker, had been easily persuaded to undertake this duty. Brevity would not be attained, but it was more than possible that, having known Trapnel personally, he would in any case have risen to his feet. To tell the story of the borrowed five pounds would be tempting. Members had once before 'said a few words', after the scheduled speeches were at an end, followed by Alaric Kydd, who also felt that a speech was owed from him. Kydd had been expatriate for some years now, so there was no risk of that tonight. Delavacquerie took a last look round the tables.

'I've placed Lord Widmerpool and the Miss Quiggins out of the way of the winner of the Prize and the judges. In the far corner of the room by the other door. I think that is wise, don't you? A quiet table. Elderly reviewers and their wives or boyfriends. No young journalists. That's just being on the safe side.'

'I doubt if the present generation of young journalists remember about Gwinnett's connexion with Widmerpool. They may recall that the Quiggin twins threw paint over him. Even that's back last summer, and ancient history. What sort of form is Gwinnett himself in?'

'I haven't seen him.'

'Didn't he call you up on arrival?'

'I've heard nothing from him since his reply to my second letter. I suggested we should make contact before this dinner. He answered that he had all the information he needed. He would just turn up at the appointed time.'

'Where's he staying?'

'I don't even know that. I offered to fix him up with an hotel. He said he'd make his own arrangements.'

'He's being very Gwinnett-like. I hope he will turn up tonight. On second thoughts, it might be better if he did not appear. We can easily go through the motions of awarding the Prize *in absentia*. The presence of the author is not required for voicing correct sentiments about his book. Various potential embarrassments might be avoided without Gwinnett himself.'

'Gwinnett will be here all right. He writes the letter of a man of purpose.'

I agreed with that view. Gwinnett was, without doubt, a

man of purpose. Before we could discuss the matter further Emily Brightman came in, followed a moment later by Members. She was dressed with care for her rôle of judge, a long garment, whitish, tufted, a medal hanging from her neck that suggested a stylish parody of Murtlock's medallion. Delavacquerie fingered this ornament questioningly.

'Coptic, Gibson. I should have thought a person of your erudition would have recognized its provenance immediately. Is Lenore coming tonight, Mark?'

'Lenore was very sad at not being able to attend. She had to dash over to Boston again.'

'Congratulations on your own award.'

Members bowed. He was in a good humour. Emily Brightman referred to the poetry prize he had just received —nothing so liberal in amount as the Magnus Donners, but acceptable—for his *Collected Poems*, a volume which brought together all his verse from *Iron Aspidistra* (1923) to *H-Bomb Eclogue* (1966), the latter, one of the few poems Members had produced of late years.

'Thank you, Emily.'

'You have heard that the Quiggin twins are to be here tonight?'

'Rather hard on JG and Ada, who are also coming. They've done their best for those girls. The only reward is that they throw paint over Kenneth Widmerpool, and then turn up with him at their parents' parties.'

The disapproval with which Members spoke did not conceal a touch of excitement. If the Quiggin twins were to be present there was no knowing what might not happen. The room began to fill. L. O. Salvidge, an old supporter of Trapnel's (he had taken some trouble to give *Death's-head Swordsman* a send-off review), brought a new wife, his fourth. Wearing very long shiny black boots, much blue round the eyes, she was a good deal younger than her predecessors. They were followed by Bernard Shernmaker, who, in contrast with Salvidge, had always remained un-married. Shernmaker, by not reviewing Gwinnett's book had still avoided committing himself about Trapnel. He was in not at all a good temper, in fact seemed in the depths of rage and despair. If looks were anything to go by, he was never going to write a notice of *Death's-head Swordsman*. Members, as an old acquaintance, did not allow Shern-maker's joyless façade to modify his own consciously jocu-lar greeting.

'Hullo, Bernard. Have you heard the Quiggin twins are coming tonight? What do you think about that?'

Shernmaker's face contorted horribly. Nightmares of boredom and melancholy oozed from him, infecting all the social atmosphere round about. Somebody put a drink in his hand. Tension relaxed a little. A moment later the Quiggin parents appeared. Ada, as customary with her, was making the best of things. If she knew about her daughters attending the party with Widmerpool, she was determined to carry the situation off at this stage as natural enough. The probability was that she did not yet know the twins were to be present. Fifty in sight, Ada had kept her looks remark-ably well. She began to profess immense enthusiasm at the prospect of meeting Gwinnett again.

'Is he here yet? I scarcely took him in at all, when we were all in Venice that time. I long to have another look. Fancy Pamela, of all people, going to such lengths for a man.'

'Gwinnett hasn't arrived yet.'

'Now that he's won the Magnus Donners, JG is furious we never signed him up for the Trapnel biography. I sug-gested that at the time. JG wasn't in the least interested. He said books about recently dead writers were dead ducks. He's specially angry because L. O. Salvidge gave it such a good notice. I told him that was only because there's nothing about at this time of year. JG's not only cross on

94

account of none of our books ever winning the Magnus Donners, but he's got a bad throat too. It makes him full of *Angst*, worries, regrets of all sorts. He mustn't stay late.'

Quiggin was certainly looking sorry for himself. Giving off an exhalation of cold-cures, he was wrinkling his high forehead irritably. Contrary to Ada's words, he showed little or no interest in who might, or might not, have won the Prize, brushing off Evadne Clapham, when she tried to get his opinion about the selection this time. Evadne Clapham herself had recently made something of a comeback with *Cain's Jawbone* (her thirty-fifth novel), a story that returned to the style which had first made her name.

'The title of Mr Gwinnett's book is curiously like that of my own last novel, JG. Do you think he could have had time to be influenced by reading it? I'm so anxious to meet him. There's something I *must* tell him in confidence about Trappy.'

Quiggin, offering no opinion on book-titles, restated his own position.

'I oughtn't to have come tonight. I'm feeling rotten.'

'Do you think Kenneth Widmerpool knows Mr Gwinnett is in London?' Ada remarked.

That gave Members his chance.

'Hadn't you heard Widmerpool's coming tonight, Ada? He's bringing Amanda and Belinda.'

Members could not conceal all surprise at his luck in being able to announce that to the twins' parents. Ada controlled herself, but looked extremely put out. The information was altogether too much for her husband. Quiggin and Members might be on good terms these days, even so, there were limits to what Quiggin was prepared to take from his old friend. He received this disclosure as if it were a simple display of spite on the part of Members, whose genial tone did not entirely discount that proposition. Quiggin, pasty-faced from his indisposition, went red. He gave way to a violent fit of coughing. When this seizure was at an end, he burst out, in the middle of the sentence his voice rising to a near screech.

'Amanda and Belinda are coming to this dinner?'

Members was not prepared for his words to have had so violent an effect. He now spoke soothingly.

'Kenneth Widmerpool simply asked if he could bring them. There seemed no objection.'

'But why the buggery is Widmerpool coming himself?'

'He was just invited.'

Members said that disingenuously, as if inviting Widmerpool was the most natural thing in the world. In one sense it might be, but not within existing circumstances. Quiggin was too cross to think that out.

'Why the bloody hell didn't you tell us before, Mark? I didn't realize all the thing with Widmerpool and the twins was still going on. Anyway why should they want to turn up at a party like this?'

Ada intervened. Even if the announcement were just as irritating for herself, she was better able to conceal annoyance.

'Oh, do shut up about the girls, JG. They're all right. We know about their seeing a lot of Widmerpool. No harm in that. They joke about it themselves. After all he's chancellor of their bloody university. If anybody's got a right to be friends with them, he has. They might easily have been sent down, even these days, if it hadn't been for him. Why shouldn't they come and hear who's won the Prize. Do have some sense. Why, hullo, Evadne. Congratulations on *Cain's Jawbone*. I haven't read it yet, but it's on my list. Hullo, Quentin. What news on the cultural front? I enjoyed your piece on Musil, Bernard. So did JG. Have you read the Gwinnett book?'

Isobel arrived. She and I were talking with Salvidge, and

his new wife, when Delavacquerie came up. He brought with him a smallish bald thick-set man, wearing a dark suit of international cut, and somewhat unEnglish tie.

'Here's Professor Gwinnett, Nick.'

Delavacquerie, rather justly, said that a little reprovingly, as if I might have been expected, if not to mark down Gwinnett's entry into the room, at least to show quicker reaction, when brought face to face with him in person. Whatever Delavacquerie's right to take that line, I should have been quite unaware who the man in the dark suit might be, without this specific statement of identity. It was lucky I had not been close to the door when Gwinnett entered the room. So far as I was concerned, he was un-recognizable. Since Venice, a drastic transformation had taken place. Gwinnett held out his hand. He did not speak or smile.

'Hullo, Russell.'

'Good to see you, Nicholas.'

'You got my letter?'

'Thanks for your letter, and congratulations. I didn't reply. I was pretty sure I'd be seeing you, after what Mr Delavacquerie told me.'

'It was only meant as a line to say how much I'd enjoyed the book, Russell. Delighted it won the Prize. Also glad to see you over here again. You haven't met Isobel. You're sitting next to each other at dinner.'

Giving her a long searching look, Gwinnett took Isobel's hand. He remained unsmiling. When I had last seen him, his appearance seemed young for his age, then middle thirties. Now, in middle forties, he might have been con-sidered older than that. He had also added to his personality some not at once definable characteristics, a greater com-pactness than before. Perhaps that impression was due only to a changed exterior. All physical slightness was gone. Gwinnett was positively heavy now in build. He had shaved off the thin line of moustache, and was totally bald. Such hair as might have remained above his ears had been rigorously clipped away. Below were allowed two short strips of whisker. The shaven skull—which made one think at once of his book's title—conferred a tougher look than formerly. He had always something of the professional gymnast. The additional fleshiness might have been that of a retired lightweight boxer or karate instructor. Pale blue lenses, once worn in his spectacles, had been exchanged for large rimless circles of glass girdered with steel.

'I've heard a lot about you, Mr Gwinnett.'

Gwinnett slightly inclined his head. He wholly accepted Isobel must have heard a lot about him, that others in the room might have heard a lot about him too. Such was what his manner suggested. It was surprising how little to be regarded as authentic was available even now. The Pamela Widmerpool episode apart, he was scarcely less enigmatic than when I had first sat next to him at one of the luncheons of the Venice conference, and we had talked of the Sleaford Veronese. Delavacquerie returned, bringing with him Emily Brightman and Members, the last of whom had not previously met Gwinnett. Old friend as she was, Emily Brightman had observed Gwinnett's arrival no more than myself. She, too, may have found him unrecognizable. If so, she covered that by the warmth of greeting when she took his hand. I think, in her way, she was much attached to him. If she felt doubts about some of the complexities of Gwinnett's nature, she put into practice her belief that certain matters, even if known to be true, are not necessarily the better for being said aloud.

'How are you, Russell? Why have you never written and told me about yourself for all these years? Wasn't it nice that we were able to give you the Prize? You have produced a work to deserve it. How long are you remaining in this country?'

'Just a week, Emily. I'll be back again next year. I've got research to do over here.'

'Another great work?'

'I guess so.'

'What's the subject. Or is that a secret?'

'No secret at all—*The Gothic Symbolism of Mortality in the Texture of Jacobean Stagecraft.*'

Gwinnett, always capable of bringing off a surprise, did so this time. Neither Emily Brightman nor I were quite prepared for the title of his new book.

'Some people—I think you among them, Emily—judged X. Trapnel a little lightweight as a theme. I do not think so myself, but that has been suggested. I decided to look around for a new focus. I see the Jacobean project as in some ways an extension, rather than change, of subject matter. Trapnel had much in common with those playwrights.'

This offered yet another reason for the epigraph introducing *Death's-head Swordsman*. Gwinnett had been speaking with the enthusiasm that would suddenly, though rarely, come into his voice. Members, who had no reason to be greatly interested in Gwinnett's academic enterprises, strayed off to examine the new Mrs Salvidge. There was a pause. Even Emily Brightman seemed to have no immediate comment to make on the Jacobean dramatists. Gwinnett had the characteristic of imposing silences. He did so now. I broke it with a piece of seventeenth-century pedantry that seemed at least an alternative to this speechlessness.

'Beaumont, the dramatist, was a kind of first-cousin of my own old friend, Robert Burton of the *Anatomy of Melancholy.*'

'Sure.'

Gwinnett spoke as if every schoolboy knew that. Emily Brightman, abandoning seventeenth-century scholarship, asked where he was staying in London. Gwinnett named an hotel.

'Wait, I'll write that down.'

She took an address-book from her bag. Either the name conveyed nothing, or Emily Brightman was showing more then ever her refusal to find human behaviour, notably Gwinnett's, at all out of the ordinary, anyway when his was removed from the purely academic sphere. I was not sure I should myself have been equally capable of concealing the least flicker of recognition at the name. Gwinnett had chosen to visit again the down-at-heel hostelry in the St Pancras neighbourhood, where he had spent the night— her last—with Pamela Widmerpool. He drawled the address in his usual slow unemphasized scarcely audible tone. Emily Brightman's impassivity in face of this taste for returning to old haunts, however gruesome their associations, could have been due as much to forgetfulness as to pride in accepting Gwinnett's peculiarities. Nevertheless, she changed the subject again.

'Now tell me of your other doings, Russell. I don't know much about your college, beyond reading in the papers that it had been suffering from campus disturbances. Sum up the root of the trouble. What is the teaching like there?'

Gwinnett began speaking of his academic life. Emily Brightman, listening with professional interest, made an occasional comment. Delavacquerie, who was now standing by in silence, drew me aside. He had perhaps been waiting for a suitable opportunity to do that.

'As soon as Professor Gwinnett arrived I informed him that Lord Widmerpool was attending the dinner.'

'How did he take that?'

'He just acknowledged the information.'

'There's no necessity for them to meet.'

'Unless one of them feels the challenge.'

'Widmerpool probably wants to do no more than re-examine Gwinnett. He barely met him when we were in Venice. Widmerpool is not at all observant where individuals are concerned. Also, he had plenty of other things to think about at the time. It would be reasonable to have developed a curiosity about Gwinnett, after what happened, even if this is not a particularly sensitive way of taking another look at him.'

'Didn't they see each other at the inquest?'

'How are such enquiries arranged? Perhaps they did. All I know is that Gwinnett was exonerated from all blame. I find it more extraordinary that Widmerpool should choose to bring the Quiggin twins, rather than that he should wish to gaze at Gwinnett.'

'Aren't the girls just a way of showing off?'

Delavacquerie put on an interrogative expression that was entirely French. He was probably right. Commonplace vanity was the explanation. Widmerpool felt satisfaction, as a man of his age, in appearing with a pair of girls, who, if no great beauties, were lively and notorious. They could be a spur to his own exhibitionism, if not his masochism.

'I see Evadne Clapham making towards us. She tells me she has something vital to convey to Professor Gwinnett about Trapnel. Can Trapnel have slept with her? One never knows. It might be best to get the introduction over before dinner.'

Delavacquerie went off. By now Matilda had arrived. As queen of the assembly, she had got herself up even more theatrically than usual, a sort of ruff, purple and transparent, making her look as if she were going to play Lady Macbeth; an appearance striking the right note in the light of Gwinnett's new literary preoccupations. When Delavacquerie presented him to her this seemed to go well. Matilda must often have visited New York and Washington with Sir Magnus, and Gwinnett showed none of the moodiness of which he could be capable, refusal to indulge in any conversational trivialities. By the time dinner was announced the two of them gave the appearance of chatting together quite amicably. There was no sign yet of Widmerpool, nor the Quiggin twins. They would presumably all arrive together. As Delavacquerie had said, I found myself between Emily Brightman, and the wife of a Donners-Brebner director; the latter, a rather worried middle-aged lady, had put on all her best clothes, and most of her jewellery, as protection, when venturing into what she evidently regarded as a world threatening perils of every kind. We did not make much contact until the soup plates were being cleared away.

'I'm afraid I haven't read any of your books. I believe you write books, don't you? I hope you won't mind that.'

I was in process of picking out one of the several routine replies designed to bridge this not at all uncommon conversational opening—a phrase that at once generously accepts the speaker's candour in confessing the omission, while emphasizing the infinite unimportance of any such solicitude on that particular point—when need to make any reply at all was averted by a matter of much greater interest to both of us. This was entry into the room of Widmerpool and the Quiggin twins. My neighbour's attention was caught simultaneously with my own, though no doubt for different reasons. Widmerpool led the party of three, Amanda and Belinda following a short distance behind. As they came up the room most of the talk at the tables died down, while people stopped eating to stare.

'Do tell me about that man and the two girls. I'm sure I ought to know who they are. Isn't it a famous author, and his two daughters? He's probably a close friend of yours, and you will laugh at my ignorance.'

In the circumstances the supposition of the director's lady was not altogether unreasonable. If you thought of authors as a grubby lot, a tenable standpoint, Widmerpool certainly filled the bill; while the age of his companions in relation to his own might well have been that even of grandfather and granddaughters. Since I had known him as a schoolboy, Widmerpool had been not much less than famous for looking ineptly dressed, a trait that remained with him throughout life, including his army uniforms. At the same time—whether too big, too small, oddly cut, strangely patterned—his garments had hitherto always represented, even at his most revolutionary period, the essence of stolid conventionality as their aim. They had never been chosen, in the first instance, with the object of calling attention to himself. Now all was altered. There had been a complete change of policy. He wore the same old dark grey suit—one felt sure it was the same one—but underneath was a scarlet high-necked sweater.

'As a matter of fact he's not an author, though I believe he's writing a book. He's called Lord Widmerpool.'

'Not *the* Lord Widmerpool?'

'There's only one, so far as I know.'

'But I've seen him on television. He didn't look like that.'

'Perhaps he was well made-up. In any case he's said to have changed a good deal lately. I haven't seen him for a long time myself. He's certainly changed since I last saw him.'

Her bewilderment was understandable.

'Are the girls his daughters?'

'No—he's never had any children.'

'Who are they then? They look rather sweet. Are they twins? I love their wearing dirty old jeans at this party.'

'They're the twin daughters of J. G. Quiggin, the publisher, and his novelist wife, Ada Leintwardine. Their parents are sitting over there at the table opposite. J. G. Quiggin's the bald man, helping himself to vegetables, his wife the lady with her hair piled up rather high.'

'I believe I've read something by Ada Leintwardine—*The Bitch*—*The Bitches*—something like that. I know bitches came into the title.'

'*The Bitch Pack meets on Wednesday.*'

'That's it. I don't remember much about it. Are the girls with Lord Widmerpool, or are they just joining their parents?'

'They're with him.'

'Are they his girlfriends?'

The party was evidently coming up to expectations.

'He's chancellor of their university. They threw paint over him last summer. I don't know how close the relationship is apart from that.'

'Those two little things threw paint over him?'

'Yes.'

'Didn't he mind?'

'Apparently not.'

'And now they're all friends?'

'That's what it looks like.'

'What do you think about the Permissive Society?'

Widmerpool had entered the dining-room with the air of Stonewall Jackson riding into Frederick, that is to say glaring round, as if on the alert for flags representing the Wrong Side. Amanda and Belinda, apart from looking as ready for a square meal as the rebel horde itself seemed otherwise less sure of their ground, sullen, even rather hangdog. Their getup, admired by my neighbour, was identical. As companions for Widmerpool they belonged, broadly speaking, to the tradition of Gypsy Jones, so far as physical appearance was concerned. (A couple of lines had announced, not long before, the death of 'Lady Craggs, widow of Sir Howard Craggs, suddenly in Czechoslovakia'; and I had made up my mind to ask Bagshaw, when next seen, if he knew anything of Gypsy's end.) This Gypsy Jones resemblance gave a certain authenticity to the twins' Widmerpool connexion. Their bearing that evening, on the other hand, had none of her aggressive self-confidence. It more approximated to that of Baby Wentworth

104

(also deceased the previous year, at Montego Bay, having just married a relatively rich Greek), when, as his discontented mistress, Baby entered a room in the company of Sir Magnus Donners. In the case of the Quiggin twins, as Delavacquerie had observed, sexual relations with Widmerpool highly improbable, the girls may have been embarrassed by merely appearing in front of this sort of public as his guests. If so, why did they accompany him? Perhaps there was a small gratifying element of exhibitionism for them too; in that a meeting of true minds. Emily Brightman allowed a murmur to escape her.

'I hope those young ladies are going to behave.'

Delavacquerie, already on the look out and seeing action required, had risen at once from his seat, when the Widmerpool party came in. Now he led them to the table indicated earlier, where three chairs remained unoccupied. The Donners-Brebner lady lost interest after they disappeared.

'What do you think about Vietnam?'

Widmerpool and the twins once settled at their table, dinner passed off without further notable incident. Isobel reported later that Gwinnett had given no outward sign of noticing Widmerpool's arrival. Possibly he had not even penetrated the disguise of the red sweater. That would have been reasonable enough. Alternatively, Gwinnett's indifference could have been feigned, a line he chose to take, or, quite simply, expression of what he genuinely felt. Neither with Isobel, nor Matilda, did he display any of his occasional bouts of refusing to talk. He had, Isobel said, continued to abstain from alcohol.

'What do you think of Enoch?' asked the Donners-Brebner lady.

The time came for speeches. Delavacquerie said his usual short introductory word. He was followed by Members, who settled down to what sounded like the gist of an undelivered lecture on The Novel; English, French, Russian;

notably American, in compliment to Gwinnett, and recognition of the American Novel's influence on Trapnel's style. Members went on, also at some length, to consider Trapnel as an archetypal figure of our time. The final reference to his own gone-for-ever five pounds was received with much relieved laughter.

'Was the last speaker a famous writer too?'

'A famous poet.'

Members seemed owed this description, within the context of the question. Gwinnett followed. He did not speak for long. In fact, without almost impugning the compliment of the award, he could hardly have been more brief. He said that he had admired Trapnel's work since first reading a short story found in an American magazine, taken immediate steps to discover what else he had written, in due course formed the ambition to write about Trapnel himself. His great regret, Gwinnett said, was never to have met Trapnel in the flesh.

'I called my book *Death's-head Swordsman*, because X. Trapnel's sword-stick symbolized the way he faced the world. The book's epigraph—spoken as you will recall, by an actor holding a skull in his hands—emphasizes that Death, as well as Life, can have its beauty.

> 'Whether our death be good
> Or bad, it is not death, but life that tries.
> He lived well: therefore, questionless, well dies.'

Gwinnett stopped. He sat down. The audience, myself included, supposing he was going to elaborate the meaning of the quotation, draw some analogy, waited to clap. Whatever significance he attached to the lines, they remained unexpounded. After the moment of uncertainty some applause was given. Emily Brightman whispered approval.

'Good, didn't you think? I impressed on Russell not to be prosy.'

Conversation became general. In a minute or two people would begin to move from their seats—a few were doing so already—and the party break up. I turned over in my mind the question of seeing, or not seeing, Gwinnett, while he remained in England. Now that his work on Trapnel was at an end we had no special tie, although in an odd way I had always felt well disposed towards him, even if his presence imposed a certain strain. The matter was likely to lie in Gwinnett's hands rather than mine, and in any case, he was only to stay a week. It could be put off until research brought him over here again.

'In the end we decided against the Bahamas,' said the director's lady.

At the far end of the dining-room a guest at one of the tables had begun to talk in an unusually loud voice, probably some author, publisher or reviewer, who had taken too much to drink. There had been enough on supply, scarcely an amount to justify anything spectacular in the way of intoxication. Whoever was responsible for making so much row had probably arrived tipsy, or, during the time available, consumed an exceptional number of pre-dinner drinks. Members, for instance—who put away more than he used—was rather red in the face, no more than that. Conceivably, the noise was simply one of those penetrative conversational voices with devastating carrying power. Then a thumping on the table with a fork or spoon indicated a call for silence. Somebody else wanted to make a speech. There was going to be another unplanned oration, probably on the lines of Alaric Kydd's tribute to the memory of the homosexual politician, whose biography had received the Prize that year.

'Look—Lord Widmerpool is going to speak. He was awfully good when I heard him on telly. He talked of all sorts of things I didn't know about in the most interesting way. He's not at all conventional, you know. In fact he said he hated all conventions. The American was rather dull, wasn't he?'

The moment inevitably recalled that when, at a reunion dinner of Le Bas's Old Boys, Widmerpool had risen to give his views on the current financial situation. I had seen little or nothing of his later career as a public man, so this occasion could have been far from unique. Even if he made a practice nowadays of impromptu speaking, the present gathering was an extraordinary one to choose to draw attention to himself.

'Magnus Donners Prize winner, judges and guests, there is more than one reason why I am addressing you tonight without invitation.'

The parallel with the Old Boy dinner underlined the changes taken place in Widmerpool's oratory. In former days a basic self-assurance had been tempered with hesitancy of manner, partly due to thickness of utterance, partly to consciousness of being on uneasy terms with his contemporaries. All suggestion of unsureness, of irresolution, was gone. When a sentence was brought out too quickly, one word, rasping over the next in a torrent of excited assertion, the meaning might become blurred, but, on the whole, the diction had become more effective with practice, and a changed accentuation.

'I address you in the first place as the once old friend and business colleague of the late Magnus Donners himself, the man we commemorate tonight by the award of the Prize named after him, and by the dinner we have just eaten. In spite of this, no more than a few words have been spoken of Donners, as public man or private individual. In certain respects that is justified. Donners represented in his public life all that I most abhor. Let me at once go on record as expressing this sentiment towards him. All that I hold most pernicious characterized Donners, and his doings, in many different ways, and in many parts of the world. Nevertheless

Donners put me in charge, many years ago, of the sources from which the monies derive that make up the amount of the Prize, and pay for our dinner tonight. That, as I say, was many years ago. I do not wish to speak more of my own work than that. It was hard work, work scrupulously done. I make these introductory remarks only to convince you that I have strong claims to be given a hearing.'

Widmerpool paused. He gazed round. The room was quite silent, except for the Quiggin twins, who, paying no attention whatever to Widmerpool's words, were muttering and giggling together. No one could blame them for that. It looked as if we were in for a longish harangue. Quiggin, from a table over the way, kept an eye on his daughters. On the other hand, Ada seemed riveted by Widmerpool himself. Half smiling, she sat staring at him, possibly musing how extraordinary that Pamela Flitton, her old friend, should once have been his wife. Matilda was watching Widmerpool too. Her face had assumed a look of conventional stage surprise, one appropriate to an actress, no longer young, playing a quizzical rôle in comedy or farce. This expression remained unchanged throughout Widmerpool's strictures on Sir Magnus. The dark profile of Delavacquerie, grave, firm, rather sad in repose, gave nothing away. Nor did Gwinnett, either by look or movement, show any reaction. Gwinnett might have been listening to the most banal of congratulatory addresses, delivered by the official representative of some academic body. Widmerpool passed his hand inside the neck of his sweater. He was working himself up.

'We are often told we must establish with certainty the values of the society in which we live. That is a right and proper ambition, one to be laid down without reticence as to yea or nay. Let me say at once what I stand for myself. I stand for the dictatorship of free men, and the catalysis of social, physical and spiritual revolution. I claim the right to do so in the name of contemporary counterculture, no less than in my status as trustee of the fund of which I have already spoken. But—let me make this very plain—neither of these claims do I regard as paramount. I have yet another that altogether overrides the second, and expresses in an intrinsic and individual formula a point of contact to be looked upon as the veritable hub of the first.'

Widmerpool again stopped speaking. He was sweating hard, though the night was far from warm. He took a long drink of water. No one interrupted—as some of the more impatient had done in the course of Alaric Kydd's extempore harangue—probably kept silent from sheer surprise. Widmerpool also managed to give the impression he was coming on to something that might be worth hearing. In fact the Donners-Brebner director's wife had been to some extent justified in her assessment.

'There are persons here tonight aware that I am myself referred to—even if not by name—in the biography that has received this year's Magnus Donners Memorial award, the work we have come together to celebrate at this dinner. For the benefit of those not already in possession of that information—those who do not know that, under the cloak of a specious anonymity, the story of my own married life is there recorded—I take the opportunity to announce that fact. I was the husband of the woman who destroyed the wretched author Trapnel's manuscript book—or whatever it was of his literary work that she destroyed—one of the steps on the downfall of Trapnel, and of herself.'

To describe as somewhat horrified the silence that continued to exist throughout the dining-room would be no undue exaggeration. These words were far more than the committee had bargained for. Delavacquerie especially must at the moment be feeling that, I thought, though in a sense Widmerpool's line was the one Delavacquerie himself had predicted; even if infinitely more aggressive. There was no way of stopping Widmerpool. He would have to be heard to the end.

'Some of you—not, I hope, the younger section of my audience—may be surprised at my drawing attention to my own case in playing a part—that of the so-called betrayed husband—once looked upon as discreditable and derisory. I go further than merely proclaiming that fact to you all. I take pride in ridiculing what is—or rather was—absurdly called honour, respectability, law, order, obedience, custom, rule, hierarchy, precept, regulation, all that is insidiously imposed by the morally, ideologically, and spiritually naked, and politically bankrupt, on those they have oppressed and do oppress. I am grateful to the author of this book—the title of which for the moment escapes me—for bringing home to so large an audience the irrelevance of such concepts in this day and age, by giving me opportunity to express at a gathering like ours, the wrongness of the way we live, the wrongness of marriage, the wrongness of money, the wrongness of education, the wrongness of government, the wrongness of the manner we treat kids like these.'

Widmerpool extended his hand in the direction of Amanda and Belinda. They were still conferring together. Neither took any notice of this reference to themselves. Perhaps they were unaware of it.

'I have brought these two children tonight by special request on my own part, and for a good reason. They are the couple who threw paint over me in my capacity as university chancellor. It was the right thing to do. It was the only thing to do. I was taking part in a piece of pompous and meaningless ceremonial, which my own good sense, and social opinions, should have taught me to avoid. I am now eternally glad that I did not avoid that. I learnt a lesson. Even now there are marks of red paint on my body, that may remain until my dying day, as memorial to a weak spirit. The entirely commendable act of Amanda and

Belinda brought to the surface many half-formulated ideas already in my mind. Crystallized them. These children are right to have abandoned the idea that they can get somewhere without violence. Festering diseases need sharp surgery. These kids were articulate in their own way, and, in a different manner, the book by Professor—Professor—this book, the one that has won the Prize, has crystallized my views—'

Quiggin was not taking Widmerpool's speech at all well. If he had been looking in poor health at the start of the evening, he now appeared almost at the end of his tether with his cold, and the unlooked for imposition of this flow of revolutionary principles. Ada, too, had begun to show signs of stress. Then Quiggin's expression suddenly changed. From sourness, irritability, air of being out of sorts, the features became distorted with alarm. He had noticed something about Widmerpool, so it seemed, that disturbed him out of all proportion to the words spoken, many of which he must often have heard before, even if exceptional in the present circumstances. I turned towards Widmerpool's table to see what the cause of this anxiety might be. The movement was too late. Whatever preparations Quiggin apprehended had by then passed into the sphere of active operation. There was a loud crackling explosion, like fireworks going off in an enclosed space, followed by a terrific bang. Widmerpool's table was enveloped in a dark cloud that recalled 'laying down smoke' in army exercises. Within half a second all that end of the room was hidden in thick fumes, some of which reached as far as the judges' table. At the same time a perfectly awful smell descended.

'I knew it would be a mistake to allow those girls in. I have some experience.'

Emily Brightman's voice was calm. Academic administration had accustomed her to such things as were taking place.

The smell that swept through the room was of stupefying nastiness. When the smoke cleared away—which for some reason it did quite quickly, the smell, in contrast, dilating in volume and foulness—the Quiggin twins had disappeared. They must have made a quick exit through the door at that end of the dining-room. A few wisps of blue smoke hung round Widmerpool himself, like a penumbra, where he still stood upright at the table. He seemed as unprepared as anyone else present for these discharges. His mouth continued to open and close. Either no words came out, or they could be heard no longer at this distance on account of the general turmoil made by people rising from their seats in an effort to escape the nauseating reek. The last I saw of the Donners-Brebner lady was a backview hurrying down the room, handkerchief raised to face. Emily Brightman, puckering her nostrils, fanned herself with a menu.

'This compares with the Mutilation of the Hermae. Fortunately Russell is used to the antics of students. He is always self-possessed in trying situations. I told you that Lord Widmerpool had become very strange. No one showed much interest in that information at the time.'

Delavacquerie was the first to reach Gwinnett to make some sort of an apology for what had happened. He was followed by others, including the Quiggin parents. Gwinnett himself was behaving as if fire-crackers, artificial smoke, stinkbombs, were all normal adjuncts of any literary prize-giving, in London, or anywhere else. Matilda, too, was taking it all quietly. The scene may even have appealed a little to her own adventurous side.

'Here's the maître d'hotel,' she said. 'We shall probably be asked to hold the party in another restaurant next year.'

The origin of all this tumult—Widmerpool and his speech, more precisely, Widmerpool and his guests—had been for the moment forgotten in the general confusion.

Now Widmerpool himself appeared in the crowd clustering round Gwinnett. He was in a state of almost uncontrollable excitement, eyes gleaming through his spectacles, hands making spasmodic jerky movements.

'That was a Happening, if you like. Amanda and Belinda don't do things by halves. I wouldn't have missed that for a cool million—I mean had money meant anything to me these days.'

He made for Gwinnett, whom Evadne Clapham had at last managed to pin down; Delavacquerie having moved away to speak with Matilda. Widmerpool—something of a feat—elbowed Evadne Clapham aside. He faced Gwinnett. They did not shake hands.

'Professor Gwinnett—at last I recall the name—I hope you did not mind what I said in my speech.'

'No, Lord Widmerpool, I did not mind.'

'Not at all?'

'Not at all.'

'You are probably familiar with its trend.'

'I am.'

'You have heard some of those concepts ventilated in academic circles?'

'I have.'

'Are you staying in this country?'

'Just a week.'

'I should like to see you. Where are you staying?'

Gwinnett expressed no view as to whether or not he himself wished to renew such acquaintance as already experienced with Widmerpool. He simply gave the name of his hotel. Widmerpool, who had taken out a pencil, was about to write the address on the back of a menu picked up from the table. He showed immediate signs of recognizing the place, which he must almost certainly have been required to enter in the course of clearing up his wife's affairs. His mouth twitched. Having gone thus far in making overtures to Gwinnett, expressly stating that he would like to see more of him while he was in England, he firmly went through with noting down the information given. The hotel, macabre as the choice might be, was a minor matter, it might be supposed, compared with the general wish to consort with Gwinnett himself.

'Will you have time to visit me, Professor Gwinnett—I should like you, as an academic, to inspect my little community in the country? There are young people there you might enjoy meeting. I flatter myself I have bridged the age-gap with success—and in a manner that could be of interest in connexion with your own students. It was a problem to which I gave special attention when I was in the USA.'

Gwinnett said nothing. His silence was altogether uncommitted. It carried neither approval and acceptance, nor disapproval and rejection. His own position was absolutely neutral so far as outward gesture was concerned. It recalled a little his treatment in Venice of Glober, the film tycoon. Widmerpool tore off half the menu he held, and wrote on it his own address.

'Here you are. Let me know, if you have a moment to come down. I shall leave here now, as I do not propose to stay any longer than necessary at a bourgeois gathering of a sort deeply repugnant to me. I came only to state in public certain things I deeply feel, and this seemed an ideal occasion for stating. I did not guess my words would be reinforced by militant action. So much the better. Why it took place, I myself do not know. Perhaps because you yourself—the winner of the Prize—are of American nationality, a citizen of the United States. If so, you will understand, Professor, that it was called for by your country's policies, not your own book, and will recognize a gesture of cultural paranoia, from representatives of Youth, in which nothing the least personal is intended.'

Widmerpool grinned unpleasantly for a second, then turned away. He did not say goodbye to Matilda, Delavacquerie, myself, nor anyone else. In fact he now seemed not only unaware that other persons were present, but altogether insensible to the smell, hardly at all abated in frightfulness. The transcendent beauty of the performance put on by the Quiggin twins alone absorbed him; as it were, levitated him into a world of almost absolute moral and political bliss. Deep in thought, he walked slowly down the room, now rapidly emptying.

4

IN DAYS WHEN UNCLE GILES had been (to borrow the expressive idiom of Dr Trelawney) a restless soul wandering the vast surfaces of the Earth, it had seemed extraordinary that a man of his age—by no means what I now considered venerable—should apparently regard his life as full of incident, take his own doings with such desperate seriousness. These arbitrarily accepted conjectures of one's earlier years—to the effect that nothing of the slightest interest happens to people, who, for reasons best known to themselves, have chosen to grow old—were not wholly borne out by observation of one's contemporaries, nor even to some degree by personal experience. Widmerpool was certainly a case in point. The backwash of the Magnus Donners dinner tended, naturally enough, to emphasize the action of the Quiggin twins, rather than Widmerpool's own performance that night, but, after all, Amanda and Belinda would never have had opportunity to break up the party, if Widmerpool had not negotiated the invitation.

Widmerpool himself had explained in the clearest terms, at the time, his reasons for taking the course he had, including the wish to be accompanied by the Quiggin twins, but not everyone was able to comprehend his latest standpoint. There were even found those to echo the conclusion of Lenore Members that he had become 'mentally disturbed.'

Then the answer dawned on me. Widmerpool was Orlando. The parallel with Ariosto's story might not be exact at every point, its analogy even partake of parody, but here was Widmerpool, for years leading what he certainly regarded himself as the Heroic Life, deserted by his Angelica, not for one but a thousand (in Widmerpool's eyes) nonentities. If Pamela lacked some of Angelica's qualities, Angelica, too, had sometimes drunk at enchanted fountains that excited violent passions. It was the consequence of this situation that seemed so apposite; the signs Widmerpool was showing, at least morally speaking, of stripping himself naked like Orlando, taking to the woods, in the same manner dropping out. It remained to be seen whether Widmerpool would find an Astolpho.

Later that spring there was another small reminder of Ariosto, this time in connexion with the Mage beginning to fly; in short, Scorpio Murtlock—perhaps annually incarnate at this season as a vernal demigod—whose name appeared in a newspaper paragraph. It reported some sort of a row that had taken place in the neighbourhood of the megalithic site to which the caravan had been travelling just about a year before. Whether the same party, or other members of the cult, had been in that area all the time was not clear. Only Murtlock was mentioned by name. I did not know whether Fiona still belonged to his community, enquiries about her doings from her parents being a delicate matter. The local inhabitants seemed to have objected to ceremonies, performed in and about the neolithic site, by Murtlock and his followers. The police were reported as undertaking investigations. Murtlock himself was represented as making vigorous protest against alleged persecution of the group for their beliefs. That was the sole reference to the incident at the time, anyway the only one I saw.

In a writer's life, as time shortens, work tends to predominate, among other things resulting in a reduction of attendance at large conjunctions of people. In relation to work itself there are arguments against this change of rhythm. An affair like the Magnus Donners dinner might be exceptional in what it had provided, but even assemblages of a calmer nature staved off that reclusion which seems to offer increasing attractions, keeping one in some sort of circulation, in a position to hear the latest news. Such jaunts prevented a repletion of ideas, mulled over constantly in the mind, wholly taking the place of experience. Thinking —as General Conyers used to insist—damages feeling. No doubt he had got the idea from a book. That did not make it less valid. Something can get lost, especially in the arts, by thinking too much, which sometimes confuses the instinct for what ought to go down on paper.

These professional reflexions, at best subjective, at worst intolerably tedious, are pretext for inclusion of yet another public dinner; though my life was far from consisting in a succession of such functions. When an invitation arrived for the Royal Academy banquet the phrase conjured up a tempting vision of former days: forgotten Victorian RAs, their names once a household word; vast canvases in vaster gilt frames; 'society' portraits of famous beauties and eminent statesmen; enigmatic Problem Pictures: fashionable crowds; a whole aesthetic and social cosmos with a myth of its own. The institution that had welcomed Isbister, excluded Mr Deacon, had now undergone a deathbed conversion to Modernism. Yet was the Academy on its deathbed? The reality of the occasion—as opposed to such reveries—had by no means discarded all vestige of the old tradition. If the pictures hanging on the now whitewashed walls might be called temperately avant-garde in treatment, a reassuring suspicion remained that techniques, long sunk in oblivion, were to be found tucked away in obscure corners. The company, too, was no less traditional, minor royalty likely to be present, not to mention a member of the Cabinet—possibly the Prime Minister himself—making, at this relatively free and easy party, a speech that could touch on some grave matter of policy.

The suggestion thus given of a kind of carnival, devoted to the theme of Past and Present, was heightened by the contrasted attire of the guests. White ties and black tail-coats, orders and decorations, mingled with dinner-jackets, the intermittent everyday suit. The last were rare. Those who despised evening-dress usually adopted an out-and-out knock-about-the-studio garb, accompanied by beard and flowing hair. The odd thing was that the appearance of these rebels against convention—alienated against a background of stiff white shirts, coloured ribands, sparkling stars and crosses—made the rebels themselves seem as much survivors from an early nineteenth-century romantic bohemianism, as swallow-tailed coats and medals recalled the glittering receptions of the same era.

The seating plan showed my own place between an actor and a clergyman, both professions to strike the right archetypal note for an evening of that sort. The actor (who had performed a rather notable Shallow the previous year) was now playing in an Ibsen revival, of which Polly Duport was the star. The clergyman's name—the Revd Canon Paul Fenneau—familiar, was not immediately placeable. A likely guess would be that he was incumbent of a London parish, a parson known for active work in some charitable sphere, possibly even the preservation of ancient buildings. Celebrity in such fields could have brought him to the dinner that night. The last possibility might also explain the faintly scholarly associations, not necessarily theological, that the name set in motion.

A crowd of guests was already collected by the bar in the gallery beyond the circular central hall. Members was there, talking to Smethyck (recently retired from the directorship of his gallery), both of them, Members especially, giving the impression that they intended to make a mildly uproarious evening of it. The flushed cheeks of Members enclosed by fluffy white hair and thick whiskers, contrasted with Smethyck's longer thinner whiskers, and elegantly shaped grey corkscrew curls, increased the prevailing atmosphere of Victorian jollification. Both were wearing white ties, an order round the neck. I had not seen Members since the Magnus Donners dinner, nor should we meet in future in that connexion, the panel of judges having been reconstituted. He was still taking immense pleasure in the scenes there enacted.

'I've been telling Michael about the Quiggin twins. Do you know he had never heard of them? What do you think of that for an Ivory Tower?'

Smethyck smoothed his curls and smiled, gratified at the implications of existing in gloriously rarefied atmosphere.

'True, I live entirely out of the world these days, Mark. How should I know of such things as stinkbombs?'

'I may have done some indiscreet things in my time,' said Members. 'I've never fathered any children. That's notwithstanding a few false alarms. Poor old JG. The great apostle of revolt in the days of our youth. Do you remember Sillers calling him our young Marat? Marat never had to bring up twins. What a couple.

> Dids't thou give all to thy daughters?
> And art thou come to this?

It won't be long before JG's out on Hampstead Heath asking that of passers-by.'

Smethyck pedantically demurred, thereby somewhat impugning his claim to know nothing of contemporary life.

'In Lear's case it was the father seeking an alternative society. The girls supported the Establishment. They're my favourite heroines in literature, as a matter of fact.'

Members accepted correction.

'Lindsay Bagshaw told me the other day that he regarded himself as a satisfied Lear. Since his wife died, he divides his time between his daughters' households, and says their food is not at all bad.'

'Your friend Bagshaw must be temperamentally equipped to accept the compromises that Lear rejected,' said Smethyck. 'I do not know him—'

He had evidently heard as much as he wanted about the Magnus Donners dinner, and moved away to speak with a well-known cartoonist. Members continued to brood on the Quiggin twins and their activities.

'Do you think Widmerpool arranged it all, to get his own back on Gwinnett?'

'Widmerpool was as surprised as anyone when the bang went off.'

'That's what's being generally said. I wondered whether it was true. He's here tonight.'

'Widmerpool?'

'Looking even scruffier than at the Magnus Donners. What does it all mean dressing like that? Do you think he will make another speech off the cuff?'

Members, speaking as one in a position to deplore slovenliness of dress, fingered the cross at his throat. A life peeress, also connected with the world of culture, passed at that moment, and he buttonholed her. A moment later Widmerpool came into sight at the far end of the gallery. He was prowling about by himself, speaking to no one. Members had called him scruffy, but his disarray, such as it was, did not greatly differ from that of the Magnus Donners evening. He was still wearing the old suit and red polo jumper, though closer contact might have revealed the last as unwashed since the earlier occasion. Widmerpool's appearance afforded an example of the curiously absorbent nature of the RA party. At almost any other public dinner the getup would have looked out of place. Here, clothes and all, he was unified with fellow guests. Those who did not know him already might easily have supposed they saw before them a professional painter, old and seedy—Widmerpool looked decidedly more than his later sixties—who had emerged momentarily, from some dilapidated artists' colony, to make an annual appearance at a function to which countless years as an obscure contributor had earned him the prescriptive right of invitation. In this semi-disguise, seen at long range, he could be pictured pottering about with an easel, in front of a row of tumbledown whimsically painted shacks lying along the seashore. Widmerpool moved out of sight. I did not see him again until we went into dinner, when he reappeared sitting a short way up the table on the other side from my own.

The clergyman, Canon Fenneau, was already engaged in conversation with the Regius Professor on his left, when I sat down. The actor and I talked. I had not seen the Ibsen production in which he was playing, but I told him that I had met Polly Duport, and knew Norman Chandler, who had directed a play in which my neighbour had acted not long before. Talk about the Theatre took us through the first course. The actor spoke of Molnar, a dramatist known to me from reading, on the whole, rather than seeing on a stage.

'Molnar must be about due for a revival.'

The actor agreed.

'Somebody was saying that the other day. Who was it? I know. It was after the performance last week. Polly Duport's friend with the French name. He's a writer of some sort, I believe. He thought Molnar an undervalued playwright in this country. What is he called? I've met him once or twice, when he's come to pick her up.'

'I wouldn't know. I don't know her at all well.'

'A French name. De-la-something. Delavacquerie? Could it be that?'

'There's a poet called Gibson Delavacquerie.'

'That's the chap. I remember Polly calling him Gibson. Small and dark. They're two of the nicest people.'

I heard no more about this revelation—it graded as a revelation—because someone on the far side of the table distracted the actor's attention by saying how much he had enjoyed the Ibsen. Almost simultaneously a voice from my other flank, soft, carefully articulated, almost wheedling, spoke gently.

'We met a long time ago. You will not remember me. I'm Paul Fenneau.'

Smooth, plump, grey curls (rather like Smethyck's, in neat waves), pink cheeks, Canon Fenneau stretched out a hand below the level of the table. It seemed rather unnecessary to shake hands at this late juncture, but I took it. The palm surprised by its firm even rough surface, electric vibrations. I had to admit he was right about my not remembering him.

'At a tea-party of Sillery's. I should place it in the year 1924. I may be in error about the date. I am bad at dates. They are so meaningless.'

For some reason Canon Fenneau made me feel a little uneasy. His voice might be soft, it was also coercive. He had small eyes, a large loose mouth, the lips thick, a somewhat receding chin. The eyes were the main feature. They were unusual eyes, not only almost unnaturally small, but vague, moist, dreamy, the eyes of a medium. His cherubic side, increased by a long slightly uptilted nose, was a little too good to be true, with eyes like that. In the manner in which he gave you all his attention there was a taste for mastery.

'In those days I was a frightened freshman from an obscure college. I can't tell you how impressed I was by the august company gathered in Sillery's room—if I rightly remember the afternoon we met. I didn't dare open my mouth. There was Mark Members, for instance, whom I noticed you talking with before dinner. I'd never seen a large-as-life poet in the flesh before. How I envied Mark for the fuss Sillers made of him. I remember Sillers pinched his neck. I'd have given the world in those days to have my neck pinched by Sillers. Then there was the famous Bill Truscott. Truscott, already working London, so tall, so distinguished, a figure entirely beyond my purview in the undergraduate world I frequented.'

Fenneau sighed, and smiled. It was hard to believe he had ever been frightened of anybody. I still had no recollection of meeting him, even while he recalled that particular tea-party of Sillery's; which, for various reasons, had made a strong impression on myself too. Fenneau could easily have been one of several undergraduates present, who were—and remained—unknown to me; though no doubt introduced at the time, Sillery being keen on introductions. Subsequent silence about Fenneau on Sillery's part would indicate not so much Fenneau's own pretensions to obscurity—Sillery rather liked to glory in the obscurity of some of his favourites—as cause given that afternoon, or at a later period, for Sillerian disapproval. Fenneau was probably one of the young men passed briskly through the Sillery machine, and found wanting; tried out once, never reprocessed. So far as being speechless went, Sillery did not necessarily mind that. The occasional speechless guest could be a useful foil. Some of his own pupils in that genre were quite often at the tea-parties. They set off more ebullient personalities. I hoped Fenneau would not produce embarrassing reminiscences of my own undergraduate behaviour at Sillery's, or elsewhere in the University.

'Did you often go to Sillery's?'

'Very few times after the first visit. I was not encouraged to pay too frequent calls. Just the necessary tribute from time to time. Rendering unto Sillers the things which were Sillers'. My claims could not have been less high, even for pennies that bore, so to speak, Sillery's own image and superscription.'

He smiled again, making, with a morsel of bread, a gesture indicative of extreme humility.

'Claims on Sillers?'

'Rather his claims on myself. My late father was an English chaplain on the Riviera. For a number of reasons Sillers found useful a South of France contact of that kind. Besides, my father was a personal friend of the Bishop of Gibraltar, a prelacy to attract the regard of Sillers, owing to the farflung nature of the diocese.'

'I can see that.'

'But my manner of talking about Sillers sounds most ungenerous. I would not speak a word against him. He did me, as a poor student, kindnesses on more than one occasion, although he could never reconcile himself to some of my interests.'

'You mean Sillery did not like you going into the Church?'

Fenneau smiled discreetly.

'Sillery had no objection to the Church—no objection to any Church—as such. He liked to have friends of all sorts, even clergymen. He did not at all mind my living in an undergraduate underworld, the *bas fond* of the University. The underworld, too, had its uses for Sillers—witness J. G. Quiggin, who attended that same historic tea-party.'

'You know Quiggin?'

'I do not often see JG these days. For a time—after meeting at Sillery's—we became quite close friends.'

Canon Fenneau made a sound that was not much short of a giggle, then continued.

'Like Sillers, JG found some of my interests ill advised. Socially unacceptable to Sillers, they were politically decadent to JG. Hopelessly unprogressive. JG wanted everyone he knew to be interested in politics in those days. He was a keen Marxist, you may remember. I have never liked politics.'

'May I ask what are these interests of yours that arouse so much antipathy?'

Fenneau smiled, this time gravely. He did not speak for a moment. His small watery eyes gazed at me. There was a touch of melodrama in the look.

'Alchemy.'

'The Philosopher's Stone? Turning base metal into gold?'

'I prefer to say more in the sense of turning Man from earthly impurity to heavenly perfection. It is a conception that has always gripped me—naturally in a manner not to run counter to my cloth. Some knowledge of such matters can indeed stand a priest in good stead.'

He spoke the last sentence a little archly. The reason for his name's familiarity was now revealed. Fenneau's signature would appear from time to time under reviews of books about Hermetic Philosophy, the Rosicrucians, Witchcraft, works that dealt with what might be called the scholarly end of Magic. His own outward physical characteristics—not in themselves exceptional ones in priests of any creed—were, more than in most ecclesiastics, those to be associated with the practice of occultism; fleshiness of body allied to a misty look in the eye. Dr Trelawney and Mrs Erdleigh, hierophants of other mysteries, were both exemplars of that same physical type, in spite of what was no doubt a minor matter, difference of sex. These preoccupations of Fenneau's would explain the faintly uncomfortable sensations his proximity generated. He seemed to convey, especially when he fixed his stare, that he hoped, without making too much fuss about it, to hypnotize his interlocutor; at the very least to read what was in his mind. That, too, was a trait not unknown among conventional priests of all denominations. Canon Fenneau, clearly not at all conventional, possessed the characteristic in a marked degree.

'Do you still see Mark Members?'

'Not for a long time until this evening. We have never entirely lost touch, although Mark—unlike JG—considered me less than the dust beneath his chariot wheels, when we were undergraduates. Years ago I was able to help him. He carelessly wrote somewhere that Goethe mentions Paracelsus in *Faust*, a slip confusing Paracelsus with Nostradamus. Mark was attacked on that account by a rather unpleasant personage, of whom you will certainly have heard, who called himself Dr Trelawney.'

'I've even met him.'

'I assisted Mark in rebutting these aggressions by pointing out that Trelawney's long and abstruse letter on the subject darkened counsel. I added that, even if Paracelsus supposed every substance to be made up of mercury, sulphur, and salt, mercury was only one of the elements. Trelawney recognized the warning.'

'What was the warning?'

'Mercury is conceived in alchemy as hermaphroditic. Trelawney was at that time engaged in certain practices to which he did not wish attention to be drawn. He sheered off.'

Fenneau's features had taken on a menacing expression. Dr Trelawney had evidently found an adversary worthy of crossing swords; perhaps, more appropriately, crossing divining rods. I retailed some of my own Trelawney contacts, beginning with the Doctor and his disciples running past the Stonehurst gate.

'That too? How very interesting. May I say that you bear out a deeply held conviction of mine as to the repetitive contacts of certain individual souls in the earthly lives of other individual souls.'

Fenneau again fixed his eyes on me. He gave the impression of a scientist who has found a useful specimen, if not a noticeably rare one. His stare was preferably not to be endured for too long. He may have been aware of that himself, because he immediately dropped this disturbing inspection. Perhaps he had settled to his own satisfaction whatever was in his mind. I took the initiative.

'Nietzsche thought individual experiences were recurrent, though he put it rather differently. But what did you mean by saying "that too"?'

'I was astonished to hear that as a child you should have known Trelawney.'

'Only by sight. I did not meet him till years later. It is true that, as a child, he haunted my imagination—at times rather more than I liked. Haunting the imagination was the closest we came to acquaintance at that early period.'

'Haunters of the imagination have already come close to the imagination's owner. From that early intimacy would you give any credence to the claim of Scorpio Murtlock that in him—Scorpio—Trelawney has returned in the flesh? Some proclaim that as well as Scorpio himself.'

The question was asked this time very quietly, put forward in this unemphatic manner, I think, deliberately to startle. In fact there can be little doubt that Canon Fenneau had such a motive in view. I took the enquiry as matter-of-factly as possible, while accepting its unexpectedness as an impressive conversational broadside. It would have been bad manners to admit less.

'You know Murtlock too?'

'Since he was quite a little boy.'

Fenneau spoke reflectively, almost sentimentally.

'What was he like as a child?'

'A beautiful little boy. Quite exceptionally so. And *very* intelligent. He was called Leslie then.'

Fenneau smiled at the contrast between Murtlock's nomenclature, past and present.

'You still see him?'

'From time to time. I have been seeing something of him recently. That was why I was aware he would be known to you. You may have read about certain antagonisms Scorpio was encountering. I believe a good deal never got into the papers. In consequence of this rumpus there was some talk of a television programme about the cult—one of the series *After Strange Gods*, in which Lindsay Bagshaw recently made a comeback, but perhaps you don't watch television—and I was approached as a possible compère. I had to say that I had long been a friend of Scorpio's, but could not publicly associate myself, even as a commentator, with his system, if it can be so called. Mr Bagshaw himself came to see me. It transpired, in the course of conversation, that Scorpio had visited you in the country.'

'That was produced as a reference?'

'Mr Bagshaw seemed to think it a good one.'

I did not often see Bagshaw these days, but made a mental note to take the matter up with him, if we ran across each other.

'Murtlock was one of your flock in his young days?'

That was an effort to set the helm, so far as Fenneau was concerned, in a more professionally clerical direction; not exactly a call to order, so much as a plea for better defined premises for discussion of Murtlock's goings-on. If I were to be brought in by Bagshaw as a sort of reference for Murtlock's respectability—on the strength of allowing the caravan to be put up for one night—I had a right to be told more about Murtlock. That he had been a pretty little boy might be a straightforward explanation for extending patronage to him, but, anyway as a clergyman, it seemed up to Fenneau to provide a less sensuous basis for their early association together. After further biographical background was given, enquiries could proceed as to whether Fenneau himself had set Murtlock on the path to become a mage. Fenneau was in no way unwilling to elaborate the picture.

'Scorpio once sang in my choir. That was when I was in south London. His parents kept a newspaper shop. As ever in these cases, there was an interesting heredity. Both mother and father belonged to a small fanatical religious sect, but I won't go into that now. It was with great difficulty that I secured their son for the choir. I should never have done so, had Leslie himself not insisted on joining. His will was stronger than theirs.'

'Did you yourself introduce him to what might, in general terms, be called alchemy?'

'On the contrary, Scorpio—Leslie as he was then— already possessed remarkable gifts of a kinetic kind. As you certainly know, there has been of late years a great revival of interest in what can only be called, in many cases, the Black Arts, I fear. It was quite by chance that Scorpio's natural leanings fell within a province with which I had long concerned myself. Mystical studies—my Bishop agrees —can be unexpectedly valuable in combating the undesirable in that field.'

Fenneau's mouth went a little tight again at mention of his Bishop, the eyes taking on a harder, less misty surface. It was permissible to feel that the Bishop himself—elements of exorcism perhaps out of easy reach at that moment— could have agreed, not least from trepidation at prospect of being transformed into a toad, or confined for a thousand years within a hollow oak.

'What happened to Murtlock after he left your choir?'

'A success story, even if a strange one. After singing so delightfully—I wish you could have heard his solo:

Now we are come to the sun's hour of rest,
The lights of evening round us shine.

131

—Leslie won a scholarship at a choir-school. He was doing splendidly there. Then a most unfortunate thing happened. It was quite out of the ordinary. He developed a most unhappy influence over the choirmaster. Influence is a weak word in the circumstances.'

'You mean—'

Fenneau smiled primly this time.

'That is certainly what one might expect. There had been trouble of that sort earlier. Leslie was quite a little boy then, hardly old enough to understand. The man was not convicted—I think rightly—as there was a possibility that Leslie had—well—invented the whole thing, but, as people said at the time, no smoke without fire. That unhappy possibility did not arise with the choirmaster. I knew him personally, a man of blameless life. There are, of course, men of blameless life, who yield to sudden temptation— lead us not into Thames Station, as the choirboys are said to have prayed—and there is no question but Leslie was an unusually handsome boy. No one could fail to notice that. Not that he wasn't a boy with remarkable qualities other than physical ones. At the same time I am satisfied that not a hint of improper conduct took place on the part of the choirmaster.'

The thought extended the smile of Fenneau's long mouth into ogreish proportions. He moved quickly from the prim to the blunt.

'Not even pawing. Leslie assured me himself.'

'Murtlock gave the impression of being tough when I met him. I should have thought he would be as tough about sex, as about anything else.'

'You are right. Let me speak plainly. Leslie—Scorpio by now—is tough. That does not mean he is necessarily badly behaved in matters of sex. I have always thought him not primarily interested in sex. What he seeks is moral authority.'

'Mightn't he use sex to gain moral authority?'

Fenneau gave me an odd look.

'That is another matter. Possibly he might. I can only say that all who had anything to do with the choirmaster affair agreed that sex—in any commonplace use of the word —did not come into it. At the same time, having known Leslie from his earliest years, I was not altogether surprised at what happened. I felt sure something of the sort would take place sooner or later. I knew it would grieve me.'

'Had he ever tried to impose his moral authority in your own case?'

I thought Fenneau deserved the question. He showed no disposition to resent or sidestep it. When he spoke he gazed into the distance beyond me.

'Fortunately I knew how to handle the gifts Leslie had been granted.'

'How did the choir-school story end?'

'Most tragically. The choirmaster was going to be a difficult man to replace. Good men are always at a premium, let alone good schoolmasters. Leslie—or should I already call him Scorpio?—was leaving at the end of the following term to take up another scholarship. He had done nothing against the rules. Every effort was made to persuade the choirmaster to exert his own will sufficiently to contend with the few months that remained. It was no good. His will had altogether gone. He was in too demoralized a state to stay on. He wished to be relieved of his appointment without delay.'

'The choirmaster left, Murtlock remained?'

'That was so. The unfortunate man took a job at another school, in quite a different part of the country. He was thought to be doing well there. Alas, just before the opening of the summer term, the poor fellow was found drowned in the swimming-pool.'

Fenneau sighed.

'What's Murtlock's present position, over and above people objecting to what he does at prehistoric monuments? How far does he model himself on Trelawney? When he stayed with us he appeared to have indulged in nothing worse than burning laurel leaves, and scenting a bucket with camphor.'

'Camphor? I am glad to hear of that. Camphor traditionally preserves chastity. With regard to Trelawney, I hope Scorpio has purged away the more unpleasant side. Harmony is the watchword. Harmony, as such, is not to be disapproved. I fear things are not always allowed to rest there. An element of Gnosticism emphasizes the duality of austerity and licence, abasement as a source of power, also elements akin to the worship of Mithras, where the initiate climbed through seven gates, or up seven ascending steps, imagery of the soul's ascent through the spheres of the Planets—as Eugenius Philalethes says—hearing secret harmonies.'

'I remember Trelawney's friend, Mrs Erdleigh, quoting that. Did you know her?'

'Myra Erdleigh was ubiquitous.'

Toasts and speeches began to take place. When these were over, lighting a cigar, Fenneau began to speak of Gnosticism, and the Mithraic mysteries. I was relating how Kipling's Song to Mithras had so much puzzled my former Company Commander, Rowland Gwatkin (whose obituary, recently printed in the Regimental Magazine, said he had taken an active interest in Territorial and ex-Service organizations to the end), when, several seats opposite having been vacated by guests rising to relieve themselves, or stroll round the pictures, Widmerpool moved down to one of these empty chairs. I had forgotten all about him, even the possibility put forward by Members that another unscheduled speech of Widmerpool's might take place. Close up, he looked even more like a down-at-heel

artist than at a distance. The scarlet sweater was torn and
dirty. Nodding to me, he addressed himself to Fenneau.

'Canon Fenneau, I think?'

'Your servant.'

Fenneau said that like a djinn rising vaporously from an
unsealed bottle.

'May I introduce myself? My name is Widmerpool—Ken
Widmerpool. I am called by some Lord Widmerpool. Don't
bother about the Lord. It is irrelevant. We have never met,
Canon. I am no churchgoer nowadays, though once I
served my turn as a churchman.'

Hoping to disengage myself from whatever business
Widmerpool had with Fenneau—impossible to imagine
what that could be—I was about to make off, having myself
planned to do a lightning tour of the pictures, in search
of interesting specimens from the past. Widmerpool delayed
this.

'Nick Jenkins here will vouch for my credentials. We've
known each other more years than I like to think. Canon
Fenneau, I have a request to make.'

Fenneau watched Widmerpool with the eye of a croupier,
fixed on the spinning roulette wheel, ready to deal with any
number that might turn up, in this case none endowed
with power to break the bank, whatever sum put on, at
whatever odds.

'Let me say at once, Lord Widmerpool, that it is supererogatory to tell me about yourself. You are, if I may say so,
too famous for that to be necessary.'

Widmerpool accepted this definition without demur.

'All the same don't keep on Lord-Widmerpooling me,
Canon. Ken will do.'

Fenneau smiled deprecatingly, making no reciprocal request that he should be called Paul. Widmerpool seemed
a little uncertain how to proceed. He drummed on the
tablecloth with his knuckles.

135

'I could not help hearing snatches of your conversation during dinner. You were speaking of someone in whom I am interested. I had, in fact, made enquiries, and learnt already that this personage was known to you, Canon.'

Fenneau raised his almost non-existent eyebrows, and set his hands together as if in prayer. Widmerpool had perhaps hoped to be helped out in what he wanted to say. If so, he was disappointed.

'This young man Scorp Murtlock.'

'Ah, yes?'

'I am interested in him.'

'Scorpio is an interesting young man.'

Widmerpool, seeing he was to get no assistance, became somewhat more hectoring in manner.

'I am not—to speak plainly—attracted by mumbo-jumbo. What concern me, on the contrary, are the social aspects of Murtlock's community, if so to be called. Its importance as a vehicle of dissent. I read about his persecution by the police. That set me to making enquiries. I found—from certain young people with whom I am already in touch—that there was a clear case of injustice that ought to be taken up in law.'

'If you listened to our conversation, Lord Widmerpool, you will by now be aware that I have already confessed myself, at this very table, as something of an amateur of mumbo-jumbo. Believe me, Lord Widmerpool, mumbo-jumbo has its place in this world of ours. Make no mistake about that.'

Fenneau spoke mildly. Widmerpool recognized the underlying firmness. He modified his tone.

'You may be right, Canon. I was not thinking along quite those lines. What I mean is that mumbo-jumbo has never played any part in my own life. I am—even now with my greatly changed views—a man of affairs, somebody who wants to get things done, and, since I want to get things

done, let us move to more concrete matters. Young Murtlock, living much of his time in a caravan, is not an altogether easy person to contact. My informant—who had
himself had some truck with him—said that he, Murtlock,
sometimes visited you. I thought that perhaps a meeting,
or at least the forwarding of a letter, could be arranged
through your good self. What struck me about Scorp
Murtlock—as I understand he is usually called—was his
vigorous sense of rebellion. He is a genuinely rebellious
personality. They are rarer than you might think, even
today. He seems to have been treated scandalously, indeed
ultra vires. His way of life, in certain details, may not be
my own, but I am in sympathy with his determination to
revolt. Would you be with me, Canon?'

Fenneau was not committed so easily.

'If you meet Scorpio, Lord Widmerpool, you will find he
holds no less strong views on laws that he himself regards
as binding, than is his desire to break the bonds that he
feels fetter those laws.'

'That is just what I mean. He seems the prototype of
what has become a positive obsession with me, that is to
say the necessity to uproot bourgeois values, more especially
bourgeois values in connexion with legality. On top of that
I am told that young Scorp has a most attractive personality.'

'Scorpio's personality can be very attractive.'

Fenneau showed a few teeth when he said that.

'As you may know, I hold a certain academic appointment. A number of the young people with whom I am
brought in contact have made my house something of a
centre. I might almost use the word commune. Do you
think that Scorp Murtlock would pay me a visit?'

'That is something on which I cannot pronounce with
certainty, Lord Widmerpool.'

Fenneau placed his fingers together again, this time the

hands a little apart, in a conventionally parsonic position. He repeated his statement.

'No. I cannot be sure of that. For one thing I am myself uncertain of Scorpio's precise whereabouts at the moment.'

'They could no doubt be ascertained.'

'I could make enquiries.'

'I am sure you could run him to earth.'

'Do you really wish me to do so? I should issue a warning. Charming as Scorpio can be in certain moods, he has what can only be called a darker side too. I cannot advise contact with him to anyone not well versed in the mysteries in which he traffics—not always then.'

Fenneau spoke the words with profound gravity. Widmerpool showed no sign whatever of noticing this change of tone. He did not laugh, because he rarely laughed, but he made little or no attempt to hide the fact that he found this warning absurd. For some reason he was absolutely set on getting Murtlock into his clutches.

'I think I can assert, by this time, that I am something of an expert on the ways of young people at least as tricky to handle as Master Murtlock. As I said earlier, I should like to add him and his followers—if only temporarily—to our own community, anyway persuade him to come and see us. There is something about him that I have greatly taken to. It may be his refusal to compromise. The question is only whether or not you yourself will be able to bring us together.'

'Was there any particular aspect, in the difficulties Scorpio was having with the local people, that you found of interest —ones that I could tell him about, if we were to meet in the near future?'

Widmerpool hesitated.

'I understand there was some rather absurd complaint about nudity, which Murtlock sensibly answered by pointing out that, in the past, stripping to the skin was accepted as a sign of humility and poverty.'

'That worship should take place unclothed—in the manner of Adam—was a familiar heresy in the Middle Ages. If Scorpio practised such rites, they are ones which I cannot approve.'

Fenneau spoke severely. Widmerpool must have felt that he had got on to the wrong tack. He quickly abandoned what seemed to have become a delicate subject.

'That was just one of the points, Canon, just one of the points. It may even have been untrue. May I assume then that, if I send a letter through your good self, young Murtlock will get it sooner or later?'

'If you really wish that, Lord Widmerpool, but I advise against.'

'In spite of your advice.'

'Then I will do my best.'

Widmerpool made a gesture of thanks. He withdrew. He rightly saw that further conversation might harm rather than forward his aims. Fenneau asked one of the waiters whether it would be possible to have another cigar. He sat back in his chair.

'That was interesting.'

'You dealt with Widmerpool almost as if you were prepared for his approach.'

'To those familiar with the rhythm of living there are few surprises in this world. Not only is Lord Widmerpool anxious to meet Scorpio, Scorpio has already spoken of his intention to make himself known to Lord Widmerpool.'

'You kept that dark.'

'For a number of reasons I judged it best. I am by no means satisfied that their conjunction is desirable. At the same time, what happened tonight convinces me that no purpose is served by refusal to collaborate in transmission of a message. Other more powerful forces are on the march. *Che sarà sarà.*

'Why should Murtlock wish to meet Widmerpool?'

'Scorpio's plans are not often crystal clear.'

'He can hardly hope to bring Widmerpool into his cult.'

'There may be more material considerations. Scorpio is not unpractical in worldly matters. You have probably noticed that.'

'You mean Widmerpool's place might provide a convenient temporary base?'

'That is possible.'

'Which would make putting up with Widmerpool himself worth while?'

'To gain mastery is also one of Scorpio's aims.'

'Power?'

'The goal of the Alchemists.'

'Perhaps a mutual attraction in those terms?'

'We live in a world in which much remains—and must remain—unrevealed.'

Fenneau looked at his watch.

'I think I shall have to be wending my way homeward. We have had a most pleasant talk. Ah, yes. Something else. I expect that, in your profession, a lot of books pass through your hands for which you have little or no use, review copies and the like. Books of all kinds flow into a writer's daily life. Do please remember some of them for my Christmas bazaar. I will send you a reminder nearer the season. Let me have your address. Write it down here. Goodnight, goodnight.'

5

To BE TOLD SOMETHING THAT comes as a surprise, then find everyone has known about it for ages, is no uncommon experience. The remarks on the subject of Delavacquerie and Polly Duport, dropped by the actor at the Royal Academy dinner, were a case in point. Mere chance must have been the cause of having heard nothing of this close association. It had been going on for some little time, and there appeared to be no secret about their relationship. Mention of it cropped up again, not long after, in some quite other connexion. All the same, although we continued to meet at comparatively regular intervals, Delavacquerie himself never brought up the matter. When he did so, that was about a year later than this first indication that they even knew each other.

During that year, among many other events in one's life, two things happened that could have suggested achievement of the mutually desired meeting between Widmerpool and Murtlock. The month of both indications was roughly dated as December, by the arrival of Canon Fenneau's reminder about books for his bazaar, and the fact that, when Greening and I ran across each other in London, we were doing our Christmas shopping. Neither event positively brought home the Widmerpool/Murtlock alliance at the time. The first of these was the bare announcement in the paper that Widmerpool, having resigned the chancellorship of the university, was to be replaced by some other more or less appropriate figure. After his various public pronouncements there seemed nothing particularly notable in Widmerpool preferring to disembarrass himself of official duties of any sort whatsoever.

Greening's information was rather another matter. It should have given a clue. We met in the gift department of some big shop. Greening, who had been badly wounded in the Italian campaign, had a limp, but was otherwise going strong. He had been ADC to the General at the Divisional Headquarters on which we had both served in the early part of the war; later rejoined his regiment, and, it had been rumoured, died of wounds. He looked older, of course, but his habit of employing a kind of schoolboy slang that seemed to predate his own generation had not changed. He still blushed easily. He said he was a forestry consultant, married, with three children. We talked in a desultory way of the time when we had soldiered together.

'Do you remember the DAAG at that HQ?'

'Widmerpool?'

'That's the chap. Major Widmerpool. Rather a shit.'

'Of course I remember him.'

'He was always getting my goat, but what I thought was really bloody awful about him was the way he behaved to an old drunk called Bithel, who commanded the Mobile Laundry.'

'I remember Bithel too.'

'Bithel had to be shot out, the old boy had to go all right, but Widmerpool boasted in the Mess about his own efficiency in getting rid of Bithel, and how Bithel had broken down, when told he'd got to go. It may have happened, but we didn't all want to hear about it from Widmerpool.'

'If it's any consolation, Widmerpool's become very odd himself now.'

'You know that already? I was coming on to that. He's gone round the bend. Nothing less.'

'You've seen him?'

'I was looking at some timber—woodland off my usual beat—and was told an extraordinary story by the johnny I was dealing with. Widmerpool—it must be the same bugger, from what he said—runs a kind of—well, I don't know what the hell to call it—sort of colony for odds and sods, not far away from the property I was inspecting. Widmerpool's place has been going for a year or two—a kind of rest-home for layabouts—but lately things have considerably hotted up, my client said. A new lot had arrived who wore even stranger togs, and went in for even gaudier monkey-tricks. This chap talked of Widmerpool as having made himself a sort of Holy Man. Not bad going after starting as a DAAG.'

Greening, unable to paraphrase the narrative of the owner of the woodland, could produce no revelation beyond that. Nevertheless the account of Widmerpool had evidently made a strong impression on him. I don't think the possibility of the new arrivals being Murtlock's adherents occurred to me at the time. If that had been at all conveyed, the conclusion would have been that Murtlock had been absorbed into Widmerpool's larger organization. In short, what Greening spoke of seemed little more than what had been initially outlined some time before by Delavacquerie's son. Greening began to collect his parcels.

'Well, I must go on my way rejoicing. Nice to have had a chin-wag. Best for the Festive Season. I'm determined not to eat too much plum pudding this year.'

When, Christmas over, I next saw Delavacquerie, it was well into the New Year. He gave news of Gwinnett being in London again.

'I thought him rather standoffish when he was over here

before. This time he got in touch with me at once. In his own remote way he was very friendly.'

'Has he returned to that gruesome dump in St Pancras?'

'I picked him up there the other day, and we lunched at the buffet at King's Cross Station.'

'How's he getting on with *Gothic Symbols, etc?*'

'I think it will be rather good. The Elizabethan and Jacobean dramatists happen to be a subject of mine too. In fact I was able to assist in a minor way by taking him to a Jacobean play that's rarely staged. It's ascribed to Fletcher. *The Humorous Lieutenant,* not particularly gothic, nor full of mortality, but Gwinnett seemed glad to have an opportunity to see it.'

Without reading the notices very carefully, I had grasped that a play of that name was being given a limited run of a few weeks at a theatre where such productions once in a way found a home. An energetic young director (more influential in that line than Norman Chandler) had been responsible for the revival of this decidedly obscure comedy, interest in it, so Delavacquerie now said, having been to to some extent aroused by himself.

'I once toyed with the idea of calling my own collected war poems *The Humorous Lieutenant,* from this play. Then I thought the title would be misunderstood, even ironically.'

'Why was he humorous?'

'He wasn't, in the modern sense, not a jokey subaltern, but moody and melancholy in the Elizabethan meaning of humorous—one of your Robert Burton types. The Lieutenant had reason to be. He was suffering from a go of the pox. Having a dose made him unusually brave, fighting being less of a strain than sitting about in camp feeling like hell. One sees the point. When he was cured all the Lieutenant's courage left him.'

'How did you persuade them to put the play on?'

'I infiltrated the idea through Polly Duport, who is rather a friend of mine. She thought she'd like to play Celia, though a bit old for the part of a young girl.'

This was Delavacquerie's first mention of Polly Duport. There was some parallel with the way in which Moreland had first produced Matilda, when she had been playing in *The Duchess of Malfi*. I was quite unable to tell whether this casual method of introducing the name was deliberate, or Delavacquerie supposed I had always known about the association. Clinging to privacy was characteristic of both of them. Apparent secrecy might be partly explained by the shut-in nature of Polly Duport's life of the Theatre, scarcely at all cutting across Delavacquerie's two-fold existence, divided between poetry and public relations.

'I believe you've met Polly?'

'I haven't seen her for ages. I used to know her parents —who are divorced of course.'

I did not add that, when we were young, I had been in love with Polly Duport's mother. There seemed no moral obligation to reveal that, in the light of Delavacquerie having kept quiet for so long about her daughter; an example of the limitations, mentioned before, set round about the friendships of later life.

'You knew both Polly's parents? It is almost unprecedented to have met the two of them. I myself have never seen either, though Polly spends a lot of time looking after her father, who has been very ill. She's marvellously good about him. He never sounds very agreeable. Her mother— as you probably know—was married to that South American political figure who was murdered by terrorists the other day.'

'Poor Colonel Flores? Was he murdered?'

'Wasn't he a general? He was machine-gunned from behind an advertisement hoarding, so Polly told me. It wasn't given much space in the English papers. I didn't see it reported myself. He was retired by then. It was bad luck.'

I felt sorry about Colonel Flores, a master of charm, even if other qualities may have played a part in his rise to power. Delavacquerie returned to the subject of Gwinnett and the play.

'He seemed to enjoy it a great deal. I had never seen Gwinnett like that before. He became quite talkative afterwards, when we all had supper together.'

'What's it about?'

'A King falls in love with his son's girlfriend—that's Celia, played by Polly—while the son himself is away at the wars. When the son returns, his father says the girl is dead. The King has really hidden Celia, and is trying to seduce her. As he has no success, he decides to administer a love potion. Unfortunately the love potion is drunk by the Humorous Lieutenant. In consequence the Lieutenant falls in love with the King, instead of Celia doing so.'

'Did the Lieutenant's exaggerated sense of humour cause him to drink the love philtre?'

'It was accidental. He had been knocked out in a fight, and someone, thinking a bowl of wine was lying handy, gave him the love philtre as a pick-me-up. The incident is quite funny, but really has nothing to do with the play— like so many things that happen to oneself. As a neurotic figure, the Lieutenant is perhaps not altogether unlike Gwinnett.'

'Possibly Gwinnett too should drink a love philtre?'

'Gwinnett is going to risk much stronger treatment than that. Do you remember that Lord Widmerpool, after making that speech at the Magnus Donners, asked Gwinnett to come and see him? Widmerpool has returned to the charge, as to a visit, and Gwinnett is going to go.'

'That sounds a little grisly.'

'Precisely why Gwinnett is going to do it. He wishes to

have the experience. Widmerpool's situation has recently become more than ever extraordinary. From being, in a comparatively quiet way, an encourager of dissidents and dropouts, the recent addition to his community of Scorpio Murtlock, the young man we talked about some little time ago, has greatly developed its potential. Murtlock provides a charismatic element, and apparently Widmerpool thinks there are immense power possibilities in the cult. He's got enough money to back it, anyway for the moment.'

'But surely it's Murtlock's cult, not Widmerpool's.'

'We shall see. Gwinnett thinks that a struggle for power is taking place. That is one of the things that interests him. Gwinnett's angle on all this is that the cult, with its rites and hierarchies, is all as near as you can get nowadays to the gothicism of which he is himself writing. He has seen something of the semi-mystic dropout groups of his own country, but feels this one offers a more Jacobean setting, through certain of its special characteristics.'

'Does Gwinnett approve or disapprove? I expect he doesn't show his hand?'

'On the contrary, Gwinnett disapproves. He talked quite a lot about his disapproval. As I understand it, one of the tenets of the cult is that Harmony, Power, Death, are all more or less synonymous—not Desire and Death, like Shakespeare. Gwinnett disapproves of Death being, so to speak, removed from the romantic associations of Love—his own approach, with which his book deals—to be prostituted to the vulgar purposes of Power—pseudo-magical power at that. At the same time he wants to examine the processes as closely as possible.'

'Some might think it insensitive of Gwinnett, in the circumstances, to visit Widmerpool, even in the interests of seventeenth-century scholarship.'

'On that question Widmerpool himself has made his own standpoint unambiguously clear by going out of his way to invite Gwinnett to come and see him. You said that Gwinnett, when writing about Trapnel, saw himself as Trapnel. Now Gwinnett, writing about gothic Jacobean plays, sees himself as a character in one of them. I regret to say that I shall not be in England when Gwinnett pays his visit to Widmerpool, and therefore won't hear how things went—that is, if Gwinnett chooses to tell me.'

'You're taking a holiday?'

'Polly and I may be going to get married. We've known each other for a long time now. In the light of the way we both earn a living, neither of us liked the idea of being under the same roof. We might be changing that now. She's coming to have a look at my Creole relations.'

Delavacquerie raised his eyebrows, as if that were going to be an unpredictable undertaking. I said some of the things you say when a friend of Delavacquerie's age announces impending marriage. He laughed, and shook his head. All the same, he seemed very pleased with the prospect. So far as I knew anything of Polly Duport, she seemed a nice girl.

'We shall see, we shall see. That is why we are visiting the Antilles.'

During the next month or so I did not go to London. Over and above the claims of 'work'—put forward earlier as taking an increasing stranglehold—attention was required for various local matters; the chief of these—and most tedious—the quarry question.

One of the neighbouring quarries (not that recalling the outlines of Mr Deacon's picture) was attempting encroachment, as mentioned earlier, in the area of The Devil's Fingers. The matter at issue had begun with the quarrying firm (using a farmer as 'front', at purchase of the land) acquiring about seventy agricultural acres along the line of the ridge on which the archaeological site stood. The firm was seeking permission from the Planning Authority to extend in the direction of the monument. Among other projects, if this were allowed, was creation of a 'tip', for quarry waste, above the stream near The Devil's Fingers; the waters of the brook to be channelled beneath by means of a culvert. If local opposition to workings being allowed so near the remains of the Stone Age sepulchre could be shown to be sufficiently strong, a Government Enquiry was likely to be held, to settle a matter now come to a head, after dragging on for three if not four years.

The quarry-owners were offering undertakings as to 'landscaping' and 'shelter belts', to demonstrate which an outdoor meeting had been arranged. Men carrying flags would be posted at various spots round about, indicating both the proposed extension of the workings, and related localities of tree-plantation. The assembly point for those concerned, timed at nine o'clock in the morning in order to minimize dislocation of the day's work, was a gap in the hedge running along a side road, not far from the scene of action. A stile led across the fields to the rising ground on which The Devil's Fingers stood, within a copse of elder trees.

'Quite a good turnout of people,' said Isobel. 'I'm glad to see Mrs Salter has shown up. She won't stand any nonsense from anyone.'

The previous night had been hot and muggy, a feeling of electricity in the atmosphere. The day, still loaded with electrical currents, warm, was uncertain in weather, bright and cloudy in patches. Cars were parked against gates, or up narrow grass lanes. All sorts were present, representatives of the quarry, officials from local authorities, members of one or two societies devoted to historical research or nature preservation, a respectable handful of private individuals, who were there only because they took an interest in the neighbourhood. Mrs Salter, noted by Isobel, was in charge of the Nature Trust. A vigorous middle-aged lady in sweater and trousers, whitehaired and weatherbeaten, she carried a specially designed pruning-hook, a badge of office from which she was never parted.

'Who are the three by the stile?'

'Quarry directors. Mr Aldredge and Mr Gollop. I don't know who the midget is.'

The small energetic henchman with Mr Aldredge and Mr Gollop, almost as if he were shouting the odds, began to pour out a flow of technicalities on the subject of landscaping and arboriculture. Mr Aldredge, pinched in feature, with a pious expression, seemed at pains to prove that no mere hatred of the human race as such—so he gave the impression of feeling himself accused—caused him to pursue a policy of wholesale erosion and pollution. He denied those imputations pathetically. Mr Gollop, younger, aggressive, would have none of this need to justify himself or his firm. Instead, he spoke in a harsh rasping voice about the nation's need for nonskid surfacing on its motorways and arterial roads.

'I shall not make for Mr Todman immediately,' said Isobel. 'I shall choose my moment.'

Mr Todman was from the Planning Authority. Upstanding and hearty, he had not entirely relinquished a military bearing that dated from employment during the war on some aspect of constructing The Mulberry. That had been the vital experience of his life. He had never forgotten it. He had the air of a general, and brought a young aide-de-camp with him. Mr Todman was talking to another key figure in the operation, Mr Tudor, Clerk of the Rural District Council. Mr Tudor's appearance and demeanour were in complete contrast with Mr Todman's. Mr Tudor, appropriately enough, possessed a profile that recalled his shared surname with Henry VII, the same thoughtful shrewdness, if necessary, ruthlessness; the latter, should the interests of the RDC be threatened.

'I can't remember the name of the suntanned, rather sad figure, who looks like a Twenties film star making a comeback.'

'Mr Goldney. He's retired from the Political Service in Africa, now secretary of the archaeological society.'

There were quite a lot of others, too, most of whom I did not know by sight. The thicket of The Devil's Fingers was not to be seen from the stile. We set off across the first field. It was plough, rather heavy going. Mr Aldredge, the quarryman putting up a policy of appeasement, addressed himself to Mrs Salter, with whom he had probably had passages of arms before.

'Looks like being a nice Midsummer's Day. We deserve some decent weather at this time of year. We haven't seen much so far.'

Mrs Salter shook her head. She was not to be lulled into an optimistic approach to the weather, least of all by an adversary in the cause of conservation.

'It will turn to rain in the afternoon, if not before. Mark my words. It always does in these parts at this time of year.'

Mr Gollop, the pugnacious quarryman, took the opportunity, a good one, to draw attention to rural imperfections unconnected with his own industry.

'We quarry people get shot at sometimes for the fumes we're said to cause. It strikes me that's nothing to what's being inflicted on us all at this moment by the factory farms.'

The smell through which we were advancing certainly rivalled anything perpetrated by the Quiggin twins. Mrs Salter, brushing away this side issue, went into action.

'It's not so much the fumes you people cause as the dust. The rain doesn't wash it away. The leaves are covered with a white paste all the year round. After they've had a lot of that, the trees die.'

151

Mr Tudor, a man of finesse, must have thought this conversation too acrimonious in tone for good diplomacy. He had steered the Council through troubled waters before, was determined to do so this time.

'We do receive occasional complaints about intensive farming odours, Mr Gollop, just like those we get from time to time regarding your own industry. The Council looks on animal by-products as the worst offenders, even if poultry and pig-keepers cannot be held altogether blameless, and some of the silage too can be unpleasing to the nostrils. The air will be fresher, I hope, when we are over the next field. There's a lovely view, by the way, from the top of the ridge.'

Individual members of the party being concerned with different aspects of what was proposed, the group began to string out in all directions. Isobel, discussing with Mr Goldney the contrasted advantages of stone walls and hedges, a tactical feint, would quickly disengage herself, when opportunity arose, to obtain a good position to command the ear of Mr Todman, the figure likely to be most influential in the outcome of the morning's doings. Somebody, who had not joined the party at its point of departure by the stile, was now coming across the fields from the west. When he drew level this turned out to be Mr Gauntlett. He would usually appear on any occasion of this kind. Today he was wearing an orchid in his buttonhole.

'Good morning, Mr Gauntlett.'

'Morning, Mr Jenkins. Beautiful one too just now, tho' t'won't last.'

'That's what Mrs Salter says.'

'Not where the clouds do lie, nor the manner the rooks be flying.'

Mr Gauntlett's professional rusticity did not entirely cloak his faintly military air, which was in complete contrast with Mr Todman's soldierliness. Mr Todman suggested modern scientific warfare; Mr Gauntlett, military levies of Shakespearean days, or earlier.

'How are you keeping, Mr Gauntlett? Haven't seen you for a long while.'

'Ah, I can't grumble. There was a sad thing last week. Old Daisy died. She was a bad old girl, but she'd been with me a long time. I'll miss her.'

'I remember you were looking for her—it must have been two years ago or more—when those strange young people came to see us in their caravan.'

Still feeling rather self-conscious about being caught by Mr Gauntlett with the caravan party, I said that with implied apology. Mr Gauntlett brushed anything of the sort aside.

'Daisy was just where your young friend said. She'd whelped, and there was one pup left alive. It were a good guess on his part.'

'So he was right?'

'It were a good guess. A very good guess. He must know the ways o' dogs. Well, what are we going to be shown this morning, Mr Jenkins?'

'I wonder. There's quite a fair lot of people have come to see. It means local interest in preventing what the quarry want to do.'

Mr Gauntlett laughed at some amusing thought of his own in this connexion. When he voiced that thought the meaning was not immediately clear.

'Ernie Dunch won't be joining us today.'

'He won't?'

There was nothing very surprising about this piece of information. It looked as if Mr Gauntlett had cut across the fields from Dunch's farm, which was out to the west from where we were walking. Mr Dunch farmed the meadow on which The Devil's Fingers stood. He was not the farmer who had acted as figurehead in purchase by the quarry of the neighbouring fields, his land running only to the summit of the ridge, but his own attitude to quarry development was looked upon as unreliable by those who preferred some restriction to be set on the spread of quarry workings. Dunch was unlikely to bother much about what infringements might be taking place on territory with scenic or historical claims. Idle curiosity could have brought him to the meeting, nothing more. He would be no great loss. For some reason Mr Gauntlett found the fact immensely droll that Mr Dunch would not be present.

'Ernie Dunch didn't feel up to coming,' he repeated.

'I don't expect Mr Dunch cares much, one way or the other, what the quarry does.'

'Nay, I don't think 'tis that. Last Tuesday I heard Ernie saying he'd be out with us all today, to know what was happening nextdoor to him. I said I'd drop in, and we'd go together. I thought I'd see, that way, Ernie did come.'

Mr Gauntlett laughed to himself.

'That's natural enough, since the quarry would extend quite close to his own land. I'm glad he feels himself concerned. What's wrong with Mr Dunch?'

Obviously, from Mr Gauntlett's manner, that question was meant to be asked. He had a story he wanted to tell. I was not particularly interested myself why Dunch had made his decision to stay away.

'Ernie's quite a young fellow.'

'So I've been told. I don't know him personally.'

'Two-and-thirty. Three-and-thirty maybe.'

Mr Gauntlett pondered. We plodded on through the heavy furrows. Mr Gauntlett, having presumably settled in his own mind, within a few days, the date of Ernie Dunch's birth, changed his tone to the rather special one in which he would relate local history and legend.

'I'll warrant you've heard tell stories of The Fingers, Mr Jenkins?'

'You've told me quite a few yourself, Mr Gauntlett—the Stones going down to the brook to drink. That's what we want to make sure they're still able to do. Not be forced to burrow under a lot of quarry waste, before they can quench their thirst. I should think the Stones would revenge themselves on the quarry if anything of the sort is allowed to happen.'

'Aye, I shouldn't wonder. I shouldn't wonder.'

'Smash up the culvert, when the cock crows at midnight.'

'Ah.'

I hoped for a new legend from Mr Gauntlett. He seemed in the mood. They always came out unexpectedly. That was part of Mr Gauntlett's technique as a story-teller. He cleared his throat.

'I've heard tales o' The Fingers since I was a nipper. All the same, it comes like a surprise when young folks believe such things, now they're glued to the television all day long.'

Mr Gauntlett watched television a good deal himself. At least he seemed always familiar with every programme.

'I'm pleased to hear young people do still believe in such stories.'

'Ah, so am I, Mr Jenkins, so am I. That's true. It's a surprise all the same.'

I thought perhaps Mr Gauntlett needed a little encouragement.

'I was asked by a young man—the one who told you where to find Daisy—if the Stones bled when a knife was thrust in them at Hallowe'en, or some such season of the year.

'I've heard tell the elder trees round about The Fingers do bleed, and other strange tales. I can promise you one thing, Mr Jenkins, in Ernie Dunch's grandfather's day, old Seth Dunch, a cow calved in the dusk o' the evening up there one spring. Old Seth Dunch wouldn't venture into The Fingers thicket after dark, nor send a man up there neither—for no one o' the men for that matter would ha' gone—until it were plain daylight the following morning. Grandson's the same as grandfather, so t'appears.'

'If Ernie Dunch is afraid of The Fingers, he ought to take more trouble about seeing they're preserved in decent surroundings.'

Mr Gauntlett laughed again. He did not comment on the conservational aspect. Instead, he returned to young Mr Dunch's health.

'Ernie's not himself today. He's staying indoors. Going to do his accounts, he says.'

'Accounts make a bad day for all of us. You've just been seeing him, Mr Gauntlett, have you?'

I could not make out what Mr Gauntlett was driving at.

'Looked in on the farm, as I said I would, on the way up. I thought Ernie ought to come to the meeting, seeing we were going through his own fields, but he wouldn't stir.'

'Just wanted to tot up his accounts?'

'Said he wasn't going out today.'

'Has he got flu?'

'Ernie's poorly. That's plain. Never seen a young fellow in such a taking.'

Mr Gauntlett found Ernie Dunch's reason for not turning up excessively funny, then, pulling himself together, resumed his more usual style of ironical gravity.

'Seems Ernie went out after dark last night to shoot rabbits from the Land Rover.'

Rabbit-shooting from a Land Rover at night was a recognized sport. The car was driven slowly over the grass, headlights full on, the rabbits, mesmerized by the glare of the lamps, scuttling across the broad shaft of light. The driver would then pull up, take his gun, and pick them off in this field of fire.

'Did he have an accident? Tractors are always turning over, but I'd have thought a Land Rover ought to be all right for any reasonable sort of field.'

'No, not an accident, Mr Jenkins. I'll tell you what Ernie said, just as he said it. He passed through several o' these fields, till he got just about, I'd judge, where we are now, or a bit further. He was coming up to the start o' the meadow where The Fingers lie, so Ernie said, in sight o' the elder copse—and what do you think Ernie saw there, Mr Jenkins?'

'The Devil himself.'

'Not far short o' that, according to Ernie.'

Again Mr Gauntlett found difficulty in keeping back his laughter.

'What happened?'

'Ernie hadn't had no luck with the rabbits so far. There didn't seem none o' them about. Then, as soon as he drove into the big meadow, he noticed a nasty light round The Fingers. It seemed to come in flashes like summer lightning.'

'Nasty?'

'That's what Ernie called it.'

'Probably was summer lightning. We've had quite a bit of that. Or his own headlights reflected on something.'

'He said he was sure it wasn't the car's lamps, or the moonlight. Unearthly, he said. It didn't seem a natural light.'

'When did he see the Devil?'

'Four o' them there were.'

'Four devils? What form did they take?'

'Dancing in and out o' the elder trees, and between the Stones, it looked like, turning shoulder to shoulder t'ords each other, taking hold o'arms, shaking their heads from side to side.'

'How did he know they were devils?'

'They had horns.'

'He probably saw some horned sheep. There are a flock of them round about here.'

'It was horns like deer. High ones.'

157

'How were they dressed?'

'They weren't dressed, 'cording to Ernie.'

'They were naked?'

'Ernie swears they were naked as the day they were born —if they were human, and were born.'

'Men or women?'

'Ernie couldn't properly see.'

'Can't he tell?'

Mr Gauntlett gave up any attempt to restrain the heartiness of his laughter. When that stopped he agreed that Ernie Dunch's sophistication might well fall short of being able to distinguish between the sexes.

'Appearing and disappearing they were, Ernie said, and there might ha' been more than four, though he didn't stop long to look. He figured there might ha' been two male, and two female, at least, but sometimes it seemed more, sometimes less, one of 'em a real awful one, but, such was the state he was in hisself, he was uncertain o' the numbers. Even in his own home, when he was telling the tale—Mrs Dunch and me nigh him—Ernie began to shake. He said he didn't go any nearer to The Fingers, once he saw what he saw, just swivelled the Land Rover round as quick as might be, and made for the farm. He said to me 'twas a wonder he didn't turn the Land Rover the wrong way up on the run back, banging through the tussocks o' grass and furrows o' ploughland. His forewheel did catch in one rut, but he managed to right the wheel again. Mrs Dunch says he was more dead than alive, when he got back. She says she never saw him like that before. Ernie swears he don't know how he did it.'

'He thought they were supernatural beings?'

'I don't know what Ernie thought—that the Devil had come to take him away.'

'They must have been some jokers.'

'You tell Ernie Dunch they were jokers, Mr Jenkins.'

158

'If they'd been the genuine ghosts of The Fingers there'd only have been two of them.'

'Ernie may have seen double. He wasn't at all positive about the numbers. All he was positive about was that he wouldn't go up there again that night for a thousand pounds.'

'This happened last night as ever is?'

'St John's Eve.'

Mr Gauntlett, always an artist in effects, mentioned the date quite quietly.

'So it was.'

'Mrs Dunch reminded Ernie o' that herself.'

'What did Mrs Dunch think?'

'Told Ernie it was the last time she'd let him out after dark with the Land Rover. She said she'd never spent such a night. Every time the young owls hooted, Ernie would give a great jump in the bed.'

'What do you think yourself, Mr Gauntlett?'

Mr Gauntlett shook his head. He was not going to commit himself, however much prepared to laugh at Ernie Dunch about such a matter.

'Ernie looked done up. That's true enough. Not at all hisself.'

'Would you be prepared to visit The Devil's Fingers, Mr Gauntlett, say at midnight on Hallowe'en?'

Mr Gauntlett looked sly.

'Don't know about Hallowe'en, when it might be chilly, but I wouldn't say I'd not been on that same down on a summer night as a lad—nor all that far from The Fingers —and never took no harm from it.'

Mr Gauntlett smiled in reminiscence.

'You must have struck a quiet night, Mr Gauntlett.'

'Well, it were pretty quiet some o' the time. Some o' the time it were very quiet.'

Mr Gauntlett did not enlarge on the memory. It sounded

a pleasant enough one. At that moment Mr Tudor appeared beside us. I don't think Mr Gauntlett had more to say, either about Ernie Dunch's experiences at The Devil's Fingers, or his own in the same neighbourhood. He now transferred his attention to Mr Tudor. Mr Tudor either wanted to ask Mr Gauntlett's advice, as a local sage of some standing, or the two of them had been hatching a plot, before the meeting, which now required to be carried a stage further. They moved off together towards the easterly fork of the ridge. I pushed on alone.

This final field, plough when Isobel and I had visited the place several years before, was now rough pasture. In their individual efforts to obtain an overall picture of what would be the effect on the landscape of the various proposals, the assembled company had become increasingly spread out. Several were studying maps, making notes as they tried to estimate the position of proposed new constructions and plantations represented by the markers with their different coloured flags. Mrs Salter, pruning-hook under one arm, writing in a little book, was furthest in advance. Now, she fell back with the rest to gain perspective. I found myself alone in that part of the field. Over to the east, the direction where Mr Gauntlett and Mr Tudor had disappeared together, lay the workings of the quarry scheduled by its owners for expansion. High chutes, sloping steeply down from small cabins that looked like the turrets of watchtowers, rose out of an untidy jumble of corrugated iron sheds and lofty mounds of crushed limestone. The sun, still shining between dark clouds that had blown up, caught the reflection on the windscreens of rows of parked cars and trucks. To the west, over by Ernie Dunch's farm, still more clouds were drifting up, in confirmation of knowledgeable forecasts that the day would end in rain.

The scene in the fields round about resembled a TEWT —Tactical Exercise Without Troops—such as were held in the army, groups of figures poring over maps, writing in notebooks, gazing out over the countryside. My own guilty feelings, on such occasions, came back to me, those sudden awarenesses at military exercises of the kind that, instead of properly concentrating on tactical features, I was musing on pictorial or historical aspects of the landscape; what the place had seen in the past; how certain painters would deal with its physical features. That was just what was happening now. Instead of trying to comprehend in a practical manner the quarrymen's proposals, I was concentrating on The Devil's Fingers themselves.

The elder thicket was flowering, blossom like hoar frost, a faint sprinkling of brownish red, powdered over the green and white ivy-strangled tree-trunks, gnarled and twisted, as in an Arthur Rackham goblin-haunted illustration. In winter, the Stones would have been visible from this point. Now they were hidden by the ragged untidy elders. The trees might well have been cleared away, leaving The Fingers on the skyline. Possibly the quasi-magical repute attributed to elderberries—the mysterious bleedings of which Mr Gauntlett spoke—had something to do with their preservation.

I was mistaken in supposing Mrs Salter the foremost of our party, that none of the others had pressed so far as the elder thicket. That was what I had decided to do myself, a small luxury, before bending the mind to practical problems. Somebody else from the morning's expedition must have had the same idea; got well ahead at the start, then moved on at high speed across the big field. Now he was slowly returning towards the rest of us. I did not know him by sight. The dark suit probably meant an official. Most of the other representatives of local authorities had moved off to the right and left by now, or withdrawn again some way to the rear. As this figure emerged from the elder trees, advanced down the hill, I felt pretty sure he had not been among those collected earlier at the stile. He must be a stray visitor, a tourist, even professional archaeologist, who had hoped to avoid sightseers by picking a comparatively early hour to visit the monument. Usually there was no one to be seen for miles, except possibly a farmer herding cows or driving a tractor. This man could not have chosen a worse morning for having the place to himself.

He did seem a little taken aback by the crowd of people fanned out across the landscape, the markers on the higher ground, their coloured flags looking like little pockets of resistance in a battle. He paused, contemplated the scene, then continued to walk swiftly, almost painfully, down the slope. There was something dazed, stunned, about his demeanour. The dark suit, bald head, spectacles, looked for some reason fantastically out of place in these surroundings, notwithstanding the fact that others present were bespectacled, bald, dark-suited.

'Russell?'

'Hi, Nicholas.'

Gwinnett was far less astonished than myself. In fact he did not seem surprised at all. He was carrying under his arm what looked like a large black notebook, equipment that had at first assimilated him with other note-takers in the fields round about.

'I was told you live near here, Nicholas.'

'Fairly near.'

'What's going on?'

He managed to establish a situation in which I, rather than he, found it necessary to give an explanation for being on that spot at that moment. I tried to summarize briefly for him the problem of the quarry and The Devil's Fingers. Gwinnett nodded. He made some technically abstruse comment on quarrying. In spite of outward calmness he was not looking at all well. This was very noticeable at close quarters. Gwinnett's appearance was ghastly, as if he had drunk too much, been up all night, or—on further inspection—slept on the ground in his clothes. The dark suit was covered in dust and scraps of grass. His shoes, too, were caked with mud. He brought with him even greater disquiet than usual; a general sense of insecurity increased by the skies above becoming all at once increasingly dark.

'Have you been visiting The Devil's Fingers?'

'Yeah.'

'You're staying near here?'

'Not far.'

'With friends?'

'No.'

He named an inn at a small town a few miles distant. It appeared from what he said that he was alone there.

'I didn't know you were interested in prehistoric stuff—or has this something to do with your Jacobean dramatists?'

Gwinnett, as was often his habit, did not answer at once. He seemed to be examining his own case, either for a clue as to what had indeed happened to him, or, already knowing that, in an effort to decide how much to reveal.

'I've lost my way. Just now I came up the same path, as well as I could remember it. I don't know how to get down to the road from here.'

'You've been to The Devil's Fingers before?'

'We came up on foot last night. I couldn't sleep when I got back. I thought I'd drive out here again. Make more notes on the spot. It's because I'm tired I've forgotten the path down, I guess.'

'You've got a car with you?'

'It's parked in a gully off the road. Beside some old cars that have been dumped there. I took the steep path up the hill. It stops after a while. That's why I can't find the place.'

'You were here last night?'

'Some of the night.'

His manner was odd even for Gwinnett. He talked like a man in a dream. It occurred to me that he was recovering from a drug. The suspicion was as likely to be unfounded as earlier ones, in Venice, that he was a homosexual, or a reclaimed drunk.

'Were you one of the party dancing round The Devil's Fingers last night?'

Gwinnett laughed aloud at that. He did not often laugh. To do so was the measure of the state he was in. His laughter was the reverse of reassuring.

'Why? Were they seen? How do you know about that?'

'They were seen.'

'I wasn't one of the dancers. I was there.'

'What the hell was going on?'

'The stag-mask dance.'

'Who was performing?'

'Scorp Murtlock and his crowd.'

'Are they at your pub too?'

'They're on their own. In a caravan. Those taking part in the rites travelled together. Scorp thought that necessary. I met them near here. We came up to the place together.'

'Who were the rest of the party?'

'Ken Widmerpool, two girls—Fiona and Rusty—a boy called Barnabas.'

'Was Widmerpool in charge?'

'No, Scorp was in charge. That was what the row was about.'

'There was a row?'

Gwinnett puckered up his face, as if he was not sure he had spoken correctly. Then he confirmed there had been a row. A bad row, he said. Its details still seemed unclear in his mind.

'Did Widmerpool dance?'

'When the rite required that.'

'Naked?'

'Some of the time.'

'Why only some of the time?'

'Ken was mostly recording.'

'How do you mean—recording?'

'Sound and pictures. It was a shame things went wrong. I guess that was bound to happen between those two.'

The flashes of light seen by Ernie Dunch were now explained. Gwinnett seemed to find the operation, in which he had himself been anyway to some extent engaged, less out of the ordinary, less regrettable, than the fact that some untoward incident had marred the proceedings.

'Russell, what was all this about? Why were you there? Why was Widmerpool there? I can just understand Murtlock and his crew going on in that sort of way—one's reading about such things every day in the paper—but what on earth were you and Widmerpool playing at?'

Gwinnett's features took on an expression part obstinate, part bewildered. It was a look he had assumed before, when asked to be more explicit about something he had said or done. No doubt his present state added to this impression of being half stunned, a condition genuinely present; if not the result of a drug, then fatigue allied to enormously heightened nervous tension. Again, seeming to consider how best to justify his own standpoint, he did not answer for a moment or two.

'Gibson Delavacquerie said you'd seen something of the Widmerpool set-up, the commune, or whatever he runs. He said Murtlock had joined up with it. Murtlock seems to have taken over.'

Delavacquerie's name appeared for some reason to bring relief to Gwinnett. His manner became a trifle less tense.

'I like Delavacquerie.'

'You probably know he's abroad at the moment.'

'He told me he was going. I talked to him about seeing

Ken Widmerpool again, but I didn't tell Delavacquerie the whole story. When Ken sent me a letter after the Magnus Donners Prize presentation last year I said I just didn't have time, which was true. Anyhow I wasn't that anxious to see him. I thought he'd forget about it this time, though I may have mentioned I was coming over again. I don't know how he found out I was in London. I hadn't told anyone here I was coming over. I only was in touch with Gibson after I arrived. Then someone called me up, and said he was speaking for Ken, who had a young friend—and master—whom he wanted me to meet.'

'Master?'

'It was Scorp himself telephoning, I guess. I hadn't met him then. That was how it started. While he was speaking —and I've wondered whether Scorp didn't somehow put the idea in my head—it came to me in a flash that I'd often thought these weirdos linked up with the early seventeenth-century gothicism I was writing about. Here was an opportunity not to throw away. I was right.'

'It was worth it?'

'Sure.'

This was much the way Gwinnett had talked of his Trapnel researches.

'As soon as I went down there, I knew my hunch was right. Ken was altogether different from the man he had been the year before. He was crazy about Scorp, and Scorp's ideas. It was Scorp's wish that I should be present at the rites they were planning. A summoning. Scorp thought my being there might even make better vibrations, if I didn't take part.'

Gwinnett stopped. He passed his hand over a face of light yellowish colour. He looked uncommonly ill.

'Scorp said these rites can't be performed with any hope of success, if those taking part are in a normal state of mind and body. I haven't had anything to eat or drink myself now for thirty-six hours. I didn't want to miss the chance of a lifetime, to see played out in the flesh all the things I'd been going over and over in my mind for months—like Tourneur's scene in the charnel house.'

'What were they trying to do?'

'The idea was to summon up a dead man called Trelawney.'

'How far did they get?'

Gwinnett gave a slight shudder. He was detached, yet far from calm, perhaps no more than his normal state, now aggravated by near collapse.

'They got no further than the fight between Ken and Scorp.'

Gwinnett's use of these abbreviated first-names gave a certain additional grotesqueness to what was already a sufficiently grotesque narrative.

'Did they have a scrap during the rite?'

'In the middle of it.'

'The horned dance?'

'No—during the sexual invocations that followed.'

'What did those consist of?'

'Scorp said that—among the ones taking part in the rite— they should have been all with all, each with each, within the sacred circle. I was a short way apart. Not in the circle. Scorp thought that best.'

Gwinnett again put up his hand to his head. He looked as if he might faint. Then he seemed to recover himself. Heavy spots of rain were beginning to fall.

'Did everyone in the circle achieve sexual relations with everyone else?'

'If they could.'

'Were they all up to it?'

'Only Scorp.'

'He must be a remarkable young man.'

'It wasn't for pleasure. This was an invocation. Scorp was

the summoner. He said it would have been far more likely to be successful had it been four times four.'

'Not Widmerpool?'

'That was the quarrel.'

'What was?'

'It had something to do with the union of opposites. I don't know enough about the rite to say exactly what happened. Ken was gashed with a knife. That was part of the ritual, but it got out of hand. There was some sort of struggle for power. After a while Scorp and the others managed to revive Ken. By then it was too late to complete the rites. Scorp said the ceremony must be abandoned. It wasn't easy to get Ken back over the fields, and down the hill. As well as doing the recording—it was all wrecked when he fell—he'd been concentrating the will. He'd been giving it all he had. He wasn't left with much will to get back to the caravan.'

'And they just let you take notes?'

'Scorp didn't mind that. He even urged me to.'

Gwinnett spoke as if that permission surprised him as much as it might surprise anyone else. He took the black notebook from under his arm, and began to turn its pages. They were full of small spidery handwriting.

'Listen to this. When I first went to Ken Widmerpool's place, and met Scorp, I was reminded of something I read not long before in one of the plays by Beaumont and Fletcher I'd been studying. I couldn't remember just what the passage said. When I got back I hunted it up, and wrote the lines down.'

Gwinnett's hand shook a little while he held the notebook in front of him, but he managed to read out what was written there.

'Take heed! this is your mother's scorpion,
That carries stings ev'n in his tears, whose soul

Is a rank poison thorough; touch not at him;
If you do, you're gone, if you'd twenty lives.
I knew him for a roguish boy
When he would poison dogs, and keep tame toads;
He lay with his mother, and infected her,
And now she begs i' th' hospital, with a patch
Of velvet where her nose stood, like the queen of spades,
And all her teeth in her purse. The devil and
This fellow are so near, 'tis not yet known
Which is the ev'ler animal.'

'Scorpio Murtlock to the life.'
'He did shed tears during the rite. They poured down his
cheeks. That was just before he gashed Ken.'
'The familiar contemporary slur of our own day gains
force of imagery in additionally giving your mother a dose.'
'The kid in the play was the prototype maybe. Scorp's in
the same league.'
'The girl called Fiona is a niece of ours.'
Gwinnett seemed taken aback at that. The information
must have started him off on a new train of thought.
'I don't know how that nice kid got mixed up with that
kind of stuff. Rusty's another matter. She's just a tramp.'
He brushed some of the mud from his sleeve. He
appeared to feel quite strongly on the subject of Fiona, at
the same time was unwilling to say more about her. That
was like him.
'I have to get back. I just wanted to make a few notes
on the spot. I've done that. They'll be useful. How do I find
where I've parked, Nicholas?'
'We'll go as far as the top of the hill, and have a look
round. You'll probably be able to recognize the country
better from there. Why don't you have a sleep at your pub,
then come over to us for lunch?'
'No, I'll sleep for an hour or two, if I can, then get back

to London. I want to write while it's all in my mind, but I've got to have my books handy too.'

He made a movement with his shoulders, and gave a sort of groan, as if that had been painful. He was not at all well. I was rather relieved that he had refused an invitation to lunch. It would not have been an easy meal to sit through. We walked up the field together in silence. Round about the circle of elder trees the grass had been heavily trodden down. Rain was descending quite hard now. Gwinnett's story had distracted attention from the weather. The men with flags were beginning to pack up, the inspecting party massing together again, on the way back to their cars; a few hardy individuals, Mrs Salter, for instance, continuing to talk with the quarry representatives, or make notes. Gwinnett and I reached the summit of the rise.

'Have a look from here.'

The far side sloped down to the waters from which The Fingers drank, when at midnight the cock crew. The Stones would probably need an extra drink after all that had happened during the past twelve hours. I did not mention the legend of their drinking to Gwinnett. It might seem a small matter, after whatever he himself had witnessed up there. We stood side by side on the edge of the hill. Fields and hedges stretched away in front; a few scattered farms; clumps of trees; telegraph poles; a pylon; far distant bluish uplands. The roofs of the small town, where Gwinnett was staying, were just visible in rainy haze. Main roads, hard to pick out in light diminished by heavy cloud, were marked from time to time by the passage of a lorry. Gwinnett stared for some seconds towards the country spread before us, rather than looking immediately below for his recent place of ascent. He pointed.

'There they are.'

He spoke in his usual low voice, quite dispassionately. A long way off, where two hedges met at a right angle, what might be the shape of a yellow caravan stood in the corner of a field. The sight of it seemed to cheer Gwinnett a little, convince him that he had not dreamt the whole experience. Now he was able to turn his attention to the land below, from which he had first approached The Fingers. While rain continued to fall he established his bearings.

'That was the path.'

He pointed down to a sharp decline in the ground, not far from where we stood. Away below to the left, in a hollow overgrown with yet more elder, thick in thistles and ragwort, two or three abandoned cars were slowly falling to pieces. They must have been driven in there, and dumped, from a nearby grass lane. Gwinnett's vehicle, not visible from where we stood, was somewhere beyond these. He raised his hand in farewell. I did the same.

'See you in London perhaps?'

'I'll be having to work hard through the summer and fall.'

The answer seemed to indicate a wish to be left alone. That was understandable after all the things he had by now tolerated from the presence of other people. He edged unsteadily down the incline towards the brook. Rain was pouring so hard that I did not wait to see him negotiate its breadth, shallow and muddy, but too wide to jump with convenience. Probably he waded through. That would not have added much to the general disarray of his clothing. There was a flicker of forked lightning, a clatter of thunder. The whole atmosphere quivered with fluxes of electricity, discernible running through one's limbs. At the same time the rain itself greatly abated, diminishing to a few drops that continued to fall. The lightning flickered again, this time across the whole sky. I hurried to rejoin the rest of the party, hastening away like an army in full retreat. In the big field I noticed the ruts, where Ernie Dunch had so violently reversed the Land Rover. They were now filled with water. Mr Goldney, of the archaeological society, collar turned up, hands in pockets, appeared. He was half running, but slowed up, supposing I was looking for something.

'No weather to search for flints. I once picked up a piece of Samian ware not far from here. It's an interesting little site. Not up to The Whispering Knights, where I was last month. That's an altogether grander affair. Still, we have to be grateful for what we have in our own neighbourhood.'

'Why is it called The Whispering Knights? I've heard the name, but never been there.'

'During a battle some knights were standing apart, plotting against their king. A witch passed, and turned them into stone for their treachery.'

'Perhaps a witch will be waiting at the stile, and do the same to the quarry directors. Then we'll have a second monument up here.'

Mr Goldney did not reply. He looked rather prim, shocked at so malign a concept, or unwilling to countenance light words on the subject of folklore. Rain had possibly soaked him past the threshold of small-talk. Mr Tudor, in company with Mrs Salter, both very wet, joined us. Mr Tudor showed signs of a tempered optimism so far as to the outcome of the meeting.

'The Advisory Committee will have to get together again, Mr Goldney. Will Thursday at the same hour suit you? There's the correspondence with the Alkali Inspector we ought to go through again in relation to new points raised in consequence of today's meeting.'

'That's all right for me, Mr Tudor, and I'd like to bring up haulage problems.'

Mrs Salter sliced at a bramble with her pruning-hook.

'Even Mr Gollop admits haulage problems. At first he was evasive. I wouldn't have that.'

Isobel, after a final word with Mr Todman, caught us up.

'Who was the man you were talking to on the ridge?'

'I'll tell you about it on the way home.'

'You looked a very strange couple silhouetted against the skyline.'

'We were.'

'A bit sinister.'

'Your instincts are correct.'

The company scattered to their cars. Mr Gauntlett, an elderly woodland sprite untroubled by rain—if anything, finding refreshment in a downpour—disappeared on foot along a green lane. The rest of us drove away. The meeting had been a success in spite of the weather. Its consequence, assisted by the findings of the Advisory Committee, and the individual activities of Mr Tudor, was that a Government Enquiry was ordered by the Ministry. To have brought that about was a step in the right direction, even if the findings of such an Enquiry must always be unpredictable. That was emphasized by Mr Gauntlett, when I met him some weeks later, out with his gun, and the labrador that had replaced Daisy.

'Ah. We shall see what we shall see.'

He made no further reference to nocturnal horned dancers round about The Devil's Fingers. Neither did I, though their image haunted the mind. It was not quite the scene portrayed by Poussin, even if elements of the Seasons' dance were suggested in a perverted form; not least by Widmerpool, perhaps naked, doing the recording. From what Gwinnett had said, a battle of wills seemed to be in progress. If, having decided that material things were vain, Widmerpool had turned to the harnessing of quite other forces, it looked as if he were losing ground in rivalry with a younger man. Perhaps the contest should be thought of— if Widmerpool were Orlando—as one of Orlando's frequent struggles with wizards. Or—since the myth was in every

173

respect upsidedown—was Murtlock even Widmerpool's Astolpho, playing him false?

I did not see Delavacquerie again until the early autumn. I wanted to hear his opinion about Gwinnett's inclusion in the rites at The Devil's Fingers. As someone belonging to a younger generation than my own, coming from a different hemisphere, a poet with practical knowledge of the business world, who possessed personal acquaintance with several of the individuals concerned in an episode that took a fairly high place for horror, as well as extravagance, Delavacquerie's objective comment would be of interest. For one reason or another—I, too, was away for a month or more—we did not meet; nor did I hear anything further of Gwinnett himself, or his associates of that night.

When a meeting with Delavacquerie took place he announced at once that he was feeling depressed. That was not uncommon. It was usually the result of being put out about his own business routine, or simply from lack of time to 'write'. He did not look well, poor states of health always darkening his complexion. I thought it more than possible that the trip with Polly Duport had not been a success; projected marriage decided against, or shelved. On the principle of not playing out aces at the start of the game, I did not immediately attack the subject of The Devil's Fingers. Then Delavacquerie himself launched into an altogether unforeseen aspect of the same sequence of circumstances.

'Look, I'm in rather a mess at the moment. Not a mess so much as a tangle. I'd like to speak about it. Do you mind? That's more to clear my own head than to ask advice. You may be able to advise too. Can you stand my talking a lot about my own affairs?'

'Easily.'

'I'll start from the beginning. That is always best. My own situation. The fact that I like it over here, but England isn't my country. I haven't got a country. I'm rootless. I'm not grumbling about being rootless, especially these days. It even has advantages. At the same time certain problems are raised too.'

'You've spoken of all this on earlier occasions. Did going home bring it back in an acute form?'

Delavacquerie dismissed that notion with a violent gesture.

'I know I've talked of all this before. It's quite true. Perhaps I am over-obsessed by it. I am just repeating the fact as a foundation to what I am going to say, a reminder to myself that I'm never sure how much I understand people over here. Their reactions often seem to me different from my own, and from those of the people I was brought up with. Quite different. I've written poems about all this.'

'I've read them.'

Delavacquerie stopped for a moment. He seemed to be deciding the form in which some complicated statement should be made. He began again.

'I spoke to you once, I remember, of my son, Etienne.'

'You said he'd had some sort of thing for our niece, Fiona, which had been broken off, probably on account of that young man, Murtlock. I'm in a position to tell you more about all that—'

'Hold it for the moment.'

'My additions to the story are of a fantastic and outrageous kind.'

'Never mind. I don't doubt what you say. I just want to put my own case first. That is best. We'll come to what you know later—and I'm sure it will help me to hear it, even if I've heard some of it already. But I was speaking of Etienne. He has been doing well. He got a scholarship, which has taken him to America. By then he had found a new girl. She's a nice girl. It seems fairly serious. They keep up a regular correspondence.'

'How does he like the States?'

'All right.'

Whether or not Etienne liked the US did not seem to be the point. Delavacquerie paused again. He laughed rather uncomfortably.

'When Fiona was about the place, with Etienne, I noticed that I was getting interested in the girl myself. It wasn't more than that. I wasn't in love. Not in the slightest. Just interested. You will have had sufficient experience of such things to know what I am talking about—appreciate the differentiation I draw.'

'Of course.'

'I examined myself carefully in that connexion at the time. I found it possible to issue an absolutely clean bill of health, temperature, pulse, blood pressure, above all heart, all quite normal. I didn't even particularly want to sleep with her, though I might have tried to do so, had the situation been other than it was. The point I want to make is that the situation was not in the least like that of *The Humorous Lieutenant,* the King trying to seduce his son's girlfriend, as soon as the son himself was out of the way.'

'No love potions lying about.'

'You never know when you're not going to drink one by mistake, but in this case I had not done so.'

'May I ask a question?'

'Questions might clarify my own position. I welcome them. All I wish to curtail, for the moment, is competing narrative, until I've finished my own.'

'How was this feeling of interest in Fiona related to your other more permanent commitment?'

'To Polly? But, of course. That is just what I meant. How shall I put it? If, as I said, the case had been other, the possibility of a temporary run around might not have been altogether ruled out. You understand what I mean?'

'Keeping it quiet from Polly?'

'I suppose so.'

'Would Fiona herself have been prepared for a temporary run around—I mean had the situation, as you put it, been quite other?'

'Who can say? You never know till you try. Besides, if things had been different, they would have been totally different. That is something that perhaps only those—like ourselves—engaged in the arrangement of words fully understand. The smallest alteration in a poem, or a novel, can change its whole emphasis, whole meaning. The same is true of any given situation in life too, though few are aware of that. It was because things were as they were, that the *amitié* was formed. Perhaps that *amitié* would never have been established had we met somewhere quite fortuitously.'

'I see what you mean.'

'Then—as I told you—Etienne's thing with Fiona blew over. She went off with Murtlock, whether immediately, I'm not sure, but she went off. Passed entirely out of Etienne's life, and, naturally, out of mine too. I was rather glad. For one thing I preferred what existed already to remain altogether undisturbed. It suited me. It suited my work. I forgot about Fiona. Even the interest—interest, as opposed to love—proved to have been of the most transient order.'

I wholly accepted Delavacquerie's picture. Everything in connexion with it carried conviction—several different varieties of conviction. I could not at all guess where his story was going to lead. Inwardly, I flattered myself that my own narration, when I was allowed to unfold it, would cap anything he could produce.

'I told you, before I went away, that Gwinnett was going to see Widmerpool. That visit took place.'

'I know. You haven't heard my story yet. I've seen Gwinnett since he told you that.'

177

'I myself have not seen Gwinnett, but keep your story just a moment longer. Gwinnett, in fact, seems to have disappeared, perhaps left London. Murtlock, on the other hand, has been in touch with me.'

'Did he appear in person, wearing his robes?'

'He sent a message through Fiona.'

'I see.'

'Fiona arrived on my doorstep one evening. She knew the flat from her Etienne days.'

Delavacquerie lived in the Islington part of the world, not far from where Trapnel had occasionally camped out in one form or another. I had never seen Delavacquerie on his own ground.

'This without warning?'

'No, she called me up first, saying she had something to tell me. I asked her in for a drink. I had forgotten that none of them drink, owing to the rules of the cult, but she came at drinks time of day.'

I thought—as it turned out quite mistakenly—that I saw how things were shaping.

'May I interpolate another question?'

'Permission is given.'

'You remain still living single in your flat?'

Delavacquerie laughed.

'You mean did the combined trip to the Antilles have any concrete result? Well, purely administratively, it was decided that Polly and I would remain in our separate establishments, anyway for a short time longer, on account of various not at all interesting pressures in our professional lives. Does that answer the substance of your enquiry?'

'Yes. That was what I wanted to know. A further query. Had Fiona more or less invented an excuse for coming to see you again?'

Delavacquerie smiled at that idea. It seemed to please him, but he shook his head. On the face of it, the suggestion was reasonable enough. If Delavacquerie had taken what he called an interest in Fiona, when she had frequented the house, she herself was likely to be at least aware of something of the sort in the air, an *amitié*, to use his own term. She could have decided later, if only as a caprice, that she might experiment with his feelings, see how far things would go. Delavacquerie stuck to his uncompromising denial.

'No, she was sent by Murtlock all right. I'm satisfied as to that. Murtlock's motive for wanting to get into communication with me was an odd one. Not a particularly pleasant one.'

'He is not a particularly pleasant young man.'

'Nevertheless people are attracted to him.'

'Certainly.'

'They come under his influence. They may not even like him when they do so. They may not even be in love with him—naturally they could be in love with him without liking him. My first thought was that Fiona was in love with Murtlock. I'm not sure now that's correct. On the other hand, she's certainly under Murtlock's influence.'

It sounded a little as if Delavacquerie was explaining all this to himself, rather than to me, establishing confidence by an opportunity of speaking his hopes aloud. He had, after all, more or less suggested that as his aim, when he broached all this.

'Does Murtlock hope to rope you into his cult? Surely not? That would be too much.'

'It wasn't me he was after. It was Gwinnett.'

'They met, I suppose, when Gwinnett went down to see Widmerpool.'

'That hadn't happened, when Fiona came to see me.'

'Murtlock knew about Gwinnett already.'

'It appears that Gwinnett has won quite a name for himself in occult circles—if that is what they should be called—by having allegedly taken part in an act of great magical significance—in modern times almost making magical history.'

'You mean—'

'By release of sexual energy in literally necromantic circumstances—if we are to accept Gwinnett did that—in short, direct contact with the dead. In performing a negative expression of sex, carried to its logical conclusions, Gwinnett took part in the most inspired rite of Murtlock's cult.'

'I knew that, according to Murtlock doctrine, pleasure was excluded. There is no reason to suppose Gwinnett himself believed that.'

'You are right. Such an attitude seems even to have shocked Gwinnett. At the same time he felt that, as a scholar, he should study this available form of the gothic image of mortality. I do not think Gwinnett exactly expected that the theme would be, so to speak, played back to himself by Murtlock when he paid his visit to Widmerpool. I understand that the reason for Murtlock's interest in him was never put—the metaphor is appropriate—in cold blood. How much Gwinnett himself guessed, I do not know.'

'You learnt all this from Fiona?'

'Yes.'

'Is it time to tell my story yet?'

Delavacquerie laughed. He looked at me rather hard.

'You knew some of this already—I mean in connexion with Fiona?'

'As it happens, yes.'

He hesitated, perhaps more tormented than he would admit to himself.

'Let me say one thing more. What I have been talking about is not quite so simple as the way I've told it. There is another side too. You imply that you know for a fact that Fiona was involved—physically involved—in some of these highly distasteful goings-on. Do you know more, Nicholas, than that she has been for quite a long time a member of the cult, therefore they would inevitably come her way?'

'Yes. I do know more.'

'Involved without love—even in the many heteroclite forms of that unhappy verb.'

'Yes.'

'My first thought—when Fiona came to me with Murtlock's message that he wanted to know Gwinnett's whereabouts—was to have nothing to do with the whole business. That was more on grounds of taste than morals. As Emily Brightman is always pointing out, they are so often hopelessly confused by unintelligent people.'

'Murtlock knew Gwinnett was in England?'

'He'd already found that out somehow.'

'He finds out a lot. I'm surprised, having got so far, he hadn't traced Gwinnett's whereabouts.'

'He may, in any case, have preferred a more tortuous approach. I felt it an imposition on the part of this young visionary—whatever his claims as a magician—to force his abracadabras on an American scholar, engaged over here on research of a serious kind, however idiosyncratic Gwinnett's own sexual tastes may be. Would you agree?'

'Besides, as you've said, so far as we know, Gwinnett pursues these for pleasure, rather than magical advancement.'

'Exactly. Love and Literature should rank before Sorcery and Power. There was, however, an additional aspect. That was why I was not speaking with absolute truth when I denied that Fiona was in some degree playing her own game, when she came to see me. On the other hand, that possibility did not possess quite the flattering slant you implied.'

'She told you in so many words why Murtlock wanted to meet Gwinnett?'

'Certainly. No embarrassments at all about that. More so

regarding the ulterior motive for her visit. That emerged while we were talking. The fact was that Fiona was getting tired—more than that, absolutely desperate—about the life she has been living for a long time now.'

'That's good news.'

'Of course.'

Delavacquerie paused again. He did not sound quite so enthusiastic about Fiona cutting adrift from Murtlockism as might have been expected. The chronological sequence of when these things happened—Fiona come to Delavacquerie, Gwinnett gone to visit Murtlock and Widmerpool, the period between—was not very clear to me. I was also uncertain as to Delavacquerie's present feelings about Fiona. Whatever she had said to him did not appear to have affected her doings at The Devil's Fingers. I fully believed what Delavacquerie had described as his attitude towards Fiona as his son's girlfriend; I believed, more or less, that he later put her from his mind; but this new Fiona incarnation remained undefined. It was quite another matter. Also there was Polly Duport in the background. More must be explained. When he spoke again it was in an altogether detached tone.

'Fiona more or less broke down while we were talking. Even then she was unwilling to say she would give up the whole thing. This was at our first meeting.'

'There were subsequent ones?'

'Several. Murtlock wouldn't accept no for an answer, so far as Gwinnett's whereabouts were concerned.'

'You had refused to reveal them?'

'Yes.'

'That showed firmness.'

'Firmness, in any sphere, is ultimately the only thing anyone respects. Murtlock seems to have foreseen a refusal at first. Either that, or he enjoyed linking Fiona and myself in a kind of game.'

'He would be capable of both.'

'His instincts told him that he could force Gwinnett's address out of me, sooner or later, through Fiona herself. Murtlock, as you know by now, is exceedingly cunning in getting what he wants. He was well aware that Fiona felt that he, Scorpio Murtlock, must in some manner release her, personally, from his domination—give her leave to go, before she herself, of her own volition, could escape the net.'

'All she had to do, in plain fact, was to walk out.'

'That is just what Fiona could not bring herself to do. Murtlock knew that perfectly. He knew she must have some sort of legal dismissal from his service, one afforded by himself.'

'An honourable discharge?'

'Even a dishonourable one, I think—since all abandoning of himself and the cult must be wrong—but it had to come from Murtlock. It was no good arguing with her. That was how she felt. We talked it over exhaustively—and exhaustingly—during various meetings.'

Delavacquerie seemed to have established a more effective relationship with Fiona than any up-to-date achieved by her own family.

'So what happened?'

'In the end I revealed Gwinnett's sleazy hotel. The price of that was that Fiona should be free to leave. Even then Murtlock would not allow her to go immediately. He said she could only go when she had taken part in a ceremony that included the presence of Gwinnett.'

'So it was through you, in a sense, that Gwinnett went to see Widmerpool. He said it was because he wanted to observe gothic doings done in a gothic way.'

'That was true too. It was a bit of luck for Murtlock—unless he bewitched Gwinnett too, put the idea into his head. I prefer to think it luck. No doubt he always has luck.

183

Those people do. Once I had told Murtlock where to find Gwinnett, Gwinnett himself decided there was a good reason to fall in with what Murtlock wanted all along the line.'

'Where's Fiona now? Has she got away from Murtlock yet?'

Delavacquerie looked for a moment a little discomposed.

'As a matter of fact Fiona's living in the flat—not living with me, I mean—but it was somewhere to go. In fact it seemed the only way out. She didn't want to have to live with her parents—obviously she could, for a time anyway, if she felt like doing that—and, if she set up on her own, there was danger that Murtlock might begin to pester her again. A spell of being absolutely free from Murtlock would give a chance to build up some resistance, as against a disease. There's no one in Etienne's room. It was her own suggestion. As you can imagine, she's rather off sex for the moment.'

'I see.'

That was untrue. I did not in the least see; so far as seeing might be held to imply some sort of understanding of what was really taking place. A complicated situation appeared merely to be accumulating additional complicated factors. Delavacquerie himself evidently accepted the in-adequacy of this acknowledgment in relation to problems involved. He seemed to expect no more.

'When I say we talked things over, that isn't exactly true either. Fiona doesn't talk things over. She's incapable of doing that. That's partly her trouble. One of the reasons why it was better for her to be in the flat was that it offered some hope of finding out what she was really thinking.'

He abruptly stopped speaking of Fiona.

'Now tell me your story.'

To describe what had happened at The Devil's Fingers, now that Fiona was living under Delavacquerie's roof, was an altogether different affair from doing so in the manner that the story had first rehearsed itself to my mind. Then, planning its telling, there had been no reason to suppose her more than, at best, a sentimental memory; if—which might be quite mistaken—I had been right in suspecting him a little taken with her, when, in connexion with his son, Delavacquerie had first spoken Fiona's name. Nevertheless, there was no glossing over the incident at The Devil's Fingers. It had, in any case, been narrated by Gwinnett with his accustomed reticences, and, after all, Delavacquerie knew from Fiona herself more or less what had been happening. That was only a specific instance, though, for various reasons, an exceptional one. If he felt additional dismay on hearing of that night's doings, he showed nothing. His chief interest was directed to the fact that Gwinnett had been present in person at the rites. This specific intervention of Gwinnett had been unknown to him. He had also supposed anything of the sort to have been, more or less as a matter of course, enacted at whatever premises Widmerpool provided.

'How does Fiona occupy herself in London?'

'Odd jobs.'

'Has she gone back to her journalism?'

'Not exactly that. She has been doing bits of research. I myself was able to put some of that in her way. She's quite efficient.'

'Her parents always alleged she could work hard if she liked.'

One saw that in a certain sense Fiona had worked hard placating Murtlock. Delavacquerie looked a little embarrassed again.

'It seems that Fiona revealed some of her plans about leaving the cult to Gwinnett, when he was himself in touch with them. Gwinnett suggested that—if she managed to kick free from Murtlock—Fiona should help him in some of the seventeenth-century donkey-work with the Jacobean dramatists. I hadn't quite realized—'

Delavacquerie did not finish the sentence. I suppose he meant he had not grasped the extent to which Gwinnett, too, had been concerned in Fiona's ritual activities. Evidently she herself had softpedalled the Devil's Fingers incident, as such. He ended off a little lamely.

'Living at my place is as convenient as any other for that sort of work.'

I expressed agreement. Delavacquerie thought for a moment.

'I may add that having Fiona in the flat has inevitably buggered up my other arrangements.'

'Polly Duport?'

He laughed rather unhappily, but gave no details.

6

WHEN, IN THE EARLY SPRING of the following year, an invitation arrived for the wedding of our nephew, Sebastian Cutts, to a girl called Clare Akworth, I decided at once to attend. Isobel would almost certainly have gone in any case. Considerations touched on earlier—pressures of work, pressures of indolence—could have kept me away. Negative attitudes were counteracted by an unexpected aspect of the ceremony. The reception was to take place at Stourwater. Several factors combined to explain that choice of setting. Not only had the bride been educated at the girls' school which had occupied the Castle now for more than thirty years, but her grandfather was one of the school's governing body. The church service was to be held in a village not far away, where Clare Akworth's mother, a widow, had settled, when her husband died in his late thirties. Mrs Akworth's cottage had, I believe, been chosen in the first instance with an eye to the daughter's schooling, for which her father-in-law was thought to have assumed responsibility. Anyway, the Stourwater premises had been made available during a holiday period, offering a prospect that Moreland might have regarded as almost alarmingly nostalgic in possibilities.

That was not all, where conjuring up the past was concerned. In this same field of reminiscences, the bride's grandfather—no doubt the main influence in putting Stourwater thus on view—also sustained a personal rôle, even if an infinitely trivial one. In short, I could not pretend freedom from all curiosity as to what Sir Bertram Akworth now looked like. This interest had nothing to do with his being a governor of a well reputed school for girls, nor with the long catalogue of company directorships and committee memberships (ranging from Independent Television to the Diocesan Synod), which followed his name in *Who's Who*. On the contrary, Sir Bertram Akworth was memorable in my mind solely on account of the fact that, as a schoolboy, he had sent a note of an amatory nature to a younger boy (my near contemporary, later friend, Peter Templer), been reported by Widmerpool to the authorities for this unlicensed act; in consequence, sacked.

The incident had aroused a certain amount of rather heartless laughter at the time by the incongruity of a suggestion (Stringham's, I think) that an element of jealousy on Widmerpool's part was not to be ruled out. Templer's Akworth (Widmerpool's Akworth, if you prefer), a boy several years older than myself, was known to me only by sight. I doubt if we ever spoke together. Like Widmerpool himself, unremarkable at work or games, Akworth had a sallow emaciated face, and kept himself to himself on the whole, his most prominent outward characteristic being an unusually raucous voice. These minor traits assumed a sinister significance in my eyes, when, not without horror, I heard of his expulsion. The dispatch of the note, in due course, took on a less diabolical aspect, as sophistication increased, and, during the period when Stringham, Templer, and I used all to mess together, Stringham would sometimes (never in front of Templer) joke about the incident, which shed for me its earlier aura of fiendish depravity.

In later life, as indicated, Akworth (knighted for various

188

public services and benefactions) had atoned for this adolescent lapse by a career of almost sanctified respectability. From where we were sitting, rather far at the back of the church—in a pew with Isobel's eldest sister, Frederica, and her husband, Dicky Umfraville—Sir Bertram Akworth was out of view. One would be able to take a look at him later, during the reception. It was unexpected that Umfraville had turned up. He was close on eighty now, rather deaf, walking with a stick. On occasions like this, if dragged to them by Frederica, he could be irritable. Today he was in the best of spirits, keeping up a running fire of comment before the service began. I had no idea how he had been induced to attend the wedding. Perhaps he himself had insisted on coming. He reported a hangover. Its origins could have had something to do with his presence.

'Rare for me these days. One of those hangovers like sheet lightning. Sudden flashes round the head at irregular intervals. Not at all unpleasant.'

The comparison recalled that morning at The Devil's Fingers, when lightning had raced round the sky. The Government Enquiry had taken place, and, to the satisfaction of those concerned with the preservation of the site, judgment had been against further quarry development in the area of the Stones. Our meeting there was the last time I had seen Gwinnett. He had never got in touch. I left it at that. Delavacquerie spoke of him occasionally, but, for one reason or another—not on account of any shift in relationship—our luncheons together had been less frequent. Fiona was still lodging at his flat when we last met. Without too closely setting limits to what was meant by what Delavacquerie himself called a 'heteroclite verb', my impression was that he could be called in love with her. He never spoke of Fiona unless asked, the situation no less enigmatic than his association with Matilda years before.

Matilda Donners had died. She had told Delavacquerie

that she was not returning to London after the end of the summer. He had assumed her to mean that she had decided to live in the country or abroad. When questioned as to her plans Matilda had been evasive. Only after her death was it clear that she must have known what was going to happen. That was like Matilda. She had always been mistress of her own life. The organ began playing a voluntary. Frederica attempted to check Umfraville's chatter, which was becoming louder.

'Do be quiet, darling. The whole congregation don't want to hear about your hangovers.'

'What?'

'Speak more quietly.'

Umfraville indicated that he could not hear what his wife was talking about, but said no more for the moment. He was not alone in taking part in murmured conversation, the bride's grandmother, a small jolly woman, also conversing animatedly with relations in the pew behind that in which she sat. Umfraville began again.

'Who's the handsome lady next to the one in a funny hat?'

'The one in the hat, who's talking a lot, like you, is Lady Akworth. The one you mean is the bride's mother.'

'What about her?'

'She was called Jamieson—one of the innumerable Ardglass ramifications, not a close relation—her husband was in Shell or BP, and caught a tropical disease in Africa that killed him.'

That seemed to satisfy Umfraville for the moment. He closed his eyes, showing signs of nodding off to sleep. Sebastian Cutts, the bridegroom, tall, sandy-haired like his father, also shared Roddy's now ended political ambitions. He and his brother, Jonathan, resembled their father, too, in delivering a flow of information, and figures, about their respective computers and art sales. Hard work at his computers had not engrossed Sebastian Cutts to the exclusion of what was judged—by his own generation—as a not less than ample succession of love affairs; a backlog of ex-girlfriends Clare Akworth was thought well able to dispose of. An only child, she had been working as typist-secretary in an advertising firm. Her pleasing *beauté de singe*—the phrase Umfraville's—was of a type calculated to raise the ghost of Sir Magnus Donners in the Stourwater corridors. Perhaps it had done so, when she was a school-girl. Her spell at Stourwater had been later than that of the Quiggin twins (recently much publicized in connexion with *Toilet Paper*, a newly founded 'underground' maga-zine), both withdrawn from the school before Clare Akworth's arrival there. Umfraville, coming-to suddenly, showed signs of impatience.

'Buck up. Get cracking. We can't sit here all day. Ah, here she is.'

The congregation rose. Clare Akworth, who had an excellent figure, came gracefully up the aisle on the arm of her uncle, Rupert Akworth, one of her father's several brothers. He was employed in the rival firm of fine arts auctioneers to that of Jonathan Cutts. There were several small children in attendance. I did not know which families they represented. The best-man was Jeremy Warminster, the bridegroom's first-cousin. Junior Research Fellow in Science at my own former college, Jeremy Warminster was a young man of severe good looks, offhand manner, reputation for brilliance at whatever was his own form of biological studies. A throwback to his great-great-uncle, the so-called Chemist-Earl (specialist in marsh gases, though more renowned in family myth for contributions to the deodorization of sewage), Jeremy had always known exactly what he wanted to do. This firmness of purpose, engrained seriousness, allied to an abrupt way of talking, made him rather a daunting young man. His plan, not yet accomplished, was to turn Thrubworth into an institution for scientific research, while he himself continued to occupy the wing of the house converted into a flat by his uncle and predecessor. Jeremy Warminster's mother, stepbrother and stepsister (children of the drunken Lagos businessman, Collins, long deceased), had lived at Thrubworth until his coming of age. Then Veronica Tolland moved to London, which she had always preferred. Her Collins offspring were now married, with children of their own; Angus, a journalist, specializing in industrial relations; Iris, wife of an architect, her husband one of the extensive Vowchurch family.

There was no address at the wedding service, but—an unexpected bonus—Sir Bertram Akworth read the Lesson. This gave an excellent opportunity to study his bearing in later life. White hair, a small moustache, had neither much changed the appearance, so far as remembered from the days when Templer had aroused his passions. In failing to acquire a great deal of outward distinction, he resembled Sir Magnus Donners, a man of wider abilities in the same line. Sir Bertram Akworth showed, anyway at long range, no sign of projecting Sir Magnus's air of being nevertheless a little disturbing. Sir Bertram, still spare, sallow, rather gloomy, looked ordinary enough. Before he began to read he glanced round the church, as if to make sure all was arranged in a manner to be approved. Possibly he himself had decided that his own reading of the Lesson should be alternative to an address. The passage, one often chosen for such occasions, was from Corinthians. As the voice began to rasp through the church, the memory of the schoolboy Akworth (not yet Sir Bertram) came perceptibly back.

'Though I speak with the tongues of men and of angels, and have not charity, I am become as sounding brass, or a tinkling cymbal. And though I have the gift of prophecy, and understand all mysteries, and all knowledge; and though I have all faith, so that I could remove mountains, and have not charity, I am nothing. And though I bestow all my goods to feed the poor, and though I give my body to be burned, and have not charity, it profiteth me nothing.'

The reference to sounding brass was appropriate, recalling a sole personal memory of the reader, the rebuke administered by our housemaster, his nerves always tried by pupils with strident voices.

'Don't shout, Akworth.' Le Bas had said. 'It's a bad habit of yours, especially when answering a question. Try to speak more quietly.'

The habit remained. It seemed to have been no handicap in Sir Bertram's subsequent career. At one of the closing sentences of the Lesson he hardened the pitch of the utterance. It rang through the nave.

'For now we see through a glass, darkly; but then face to face.'

Giving a final glance round the congregation, he returned to his seat. The striking image of seeing through a glass darkly again brought thoughts of The Devil's Fingers. Fiona did not appear to be present in the church. She might well have decided to skip the service, just turn up at the reception. In the light of her newly organized life she was unlikely to forgo altogether her brother's wedding. So far as I knew she was still living at Delavacquerie's flat, their relationship no less undefined. Her parents were united in agreeing that, whatever the situation, it was preferable to the previous one. The impression was that Roddy and Susan Cutts, perhaps deliberately, had known little enough about the Murtlock period too. The handout issued by them now was that their daughter had taken a room in an Islington flat that belonged to a man who worked, respectably enough, in Donners-Brebner. Poets not playing much part in Cutts life, Delavacquerie's business side was more emphasized than the poetic; potential emotional ties with

Fiona not envisaged, more probably ignored. Delavacquerie was after all considerably older than their daughter; though, it had to be admitted, so too had been the handsome married electrician. The Wedding March struck up. For some minutes the congregation was penned in while photographers operated at the church door. Outside, we walked with Veronica Tolland towards the car park.

'Are your kids here? Angus couldn't get away either. He had to cover a strike. Iris will be at the reception. Fancy fetching up at Stourwater again. I used to go on visitors' day when I was a child. The park's open to the public now. My father's job was in the local town. I expect I've often said that—also I was at school with Matilda Donners, when she was a little girl called Betty Updike. Did you hear she'd died?'

'Apparently been ill for some time. I didn't know that. I always liked Matilda.'

'She made quite a career for herself. I don't know half the people here. Who's the good-looking black girl with the young Huntercombes. I know—she's wife of Jocelyn Fettiplace-Jones. His mother was an Akworth. How glad I am I live in London now.'

Like Ted Jeavons, Veronica had taken on the workings of a world rather different from that of her earlier life, without ever in the least wanting to be part. She had always regarded that world, not without a certain enjoyment, from the outside. Now she felt free of it all, except on occasions such as this one, which she liked to attend. In spite of such inherent sentiments, Veronica had come by now to look more than a little like a conventional dowager on the stage.

'See you later.'

The immediate vision of Stourwater, in thin vaporous April sunshine, was altogether unchanged. On the higher ground, in the shadows of huge contorted oaks, sheep still grazed. Down in the hollow lay the Castle; keep; turrets;

moat; narrow causeway across the water, leading to the main gate with double portcullis. All seemed built out of cardboard. Its realities had in any case belonged more to the days of Sir Magnus Donners, rather than to the later Middle Ages, when the Castle's history had been obscure. The anachronistic black swans were gone from the greenish waters of the moat. A large noticeboard directed to a car park. Round about the Castle itself playing fields came into view.

'What games would they be?'

'Net-ball, hockey, I suppose.'

We parked, then crossed the causeway on foot. The reception was taking place in the Great Hall, now the school's Assembly Room. Armoured horsemen no longer guarded the door. Forms had been pushed back against the walls, a long table for refreshments set across the far end. In place of Sir Magnus's Old Masters—several of doubtful authenticity according to Smethyck, and others with a taste for picture attribution—hung reproductions of the better known French Impressionists. We joined the queue, a long one, formed by guests waiting to meet bride and bridegroom. The two families had turned out in force. There must have been a hundred or more guests at least. We took a place far back in the line, working our way up slowly, as Roddy, relic of his parliamentary days, liked to talk for a minute or two to everyone he knew personally. When at last we found ourselves greeting the newly married pair, their closer relations in support, I felt this no moment to remind Sir Bertram Akworth that we had been at school together. There would in any case have been no opportunity. Susan Cutts drew us aside.

'Come away from them all for a moment. There's something I must tell you both.'

Leaving her husband to undertake whatever formalities were required, Susan was evidently impatient to reveal some piece of news, good or ill was not clear, which greatly excited her.

'Have you heard about Fiona?'

'No, what?'

One was prepared for anything. My first thought was that Fiona had returned to Murtlock and the cult.

'She's married.'

I thought I saw how things had at last fallen out.

'To Gibson Delavacquerie?'

Susan looked puzzled by the question. The name did not seem to convey anything to her, certainly not that of their daughter's new husband. Susan's words plainly stated that Fiona possessed a husband.

'You mean her landlord? No, not him. What could have made you think that, Nick?'

So far from Susan considering Delavacquerie to rate as a potential suitor, she was momentarily put off her stride at the very strangeness of such a proposition. Any emotional undercurrents of the Delavacquerie association must have completely passed by the Cutts parents, unless Susan was doing a superb piece of acting, which was most unlikely.

'No—it's an American. I believe you know him, Nick? He's called Russell Gwinnett.'

Roddy, disengaging himself from the last guest for whom he felt any serious responsibility at the moment, was unable to keep away from all share in imparting such news.

'Wasn't there some sort of contretemps years ago about Gwinnett? I believe there was. That fellow Widmerpool was mixed up with it, I have an idea. I used to come across Widmerpool sometimes in the House. Not too bad a fellow, even if he was on the other side. He's sunk without a trace, if ever a man did. I can't remember exactly what happened. Gwinnett seems a nice chap. He's a bit older than Fiona, of course, but I don't see why that should matter.'

Susan agreed heartily.

'In his forties. I always liked older men myself. Anyway they're married, so there it is.'

'When did this happen?'

'Yesterday, actually.'

'No warning?'

'You can imagine what it was like to be told this, with Sebastian's wedding taking place the following day.'

'They just turned up man and wife?'

'Fiona brought Mr Gwinnett—I suppose I should call him Russell now—along to see us the same afternoon. She seems very pleased about it. That's the great thing. They both do. He doesn't talk much, but I never mind that with people.'

'Have they gone off on a honeymoon?'

'They're just going to do a short drive round England, then Russell has to go back to America. He's got a little car he dashes about in all over the country, doing his research. He's a don at an American university, as you probably know. They're coming to the reception. Fiona suggested they should do that herself. Wasn't it sweet of her? They haven't arrived yet. At least I haven't seen them.'

Susan, in spite of determined cheerfulness, was showing signs of nervous strain. That was not to be wondered at. I mentioned—less from snobbish reasons than avoidance of cross-questioning about Gwinnett in other directions—that he was collaterally descended from one of the Signers of the Declaration of Independence. Roddy showed interest. At least he was deflected from closer enquiry into the subject of what exactly had happened to connect his new son-in-law with Widmerpool.

'Is he indeed? I must say I took to Russell at first sight. I'd like to have a talk with him about the coming Presidential election, and a lot of other American matters too.'

'I wish Evangeline were still here,' said Susan. 'She might

know something about the Gwinnetts. We'll talk about it all later. I'll have to go back and do my stuff now. There are some more people arriving ... darling, how sweet of you to come ... lovely to see you both ...'

There was no time to contemplate further Fiona's marriage to Gwinnett, beyond making the reflection that, if he had done some dubious things in his time, so too had she. Leaving the threshold of the reception, we moved in among the crowd that filled the Great Hall. Most of the guests had chosen to wear conventional wedding garments, some of the younger ones letting themselves go, either with variations on these, or trappings that approximated to fancy dress. The children, of whom there was quite a large collection, scuffled about gaily, the whole assemblage making a lively foreground to the mediaeval setting. Hugo, Norah, and Blanche Tolland had all turned up, Norah grumbling about the superabundance of Alford relations present.

'Susie was always very thick with the Alford cousins. I hardly knew any of them. They look a seedy lot, large red faces and snub noses.'

'I find them charming,' said Hugo. 'Look here, what's all this about Fiona marrying an American? The last thing I heard was that she had given up all those odd friends of hers Norah was once so keen on, and was working hard at something or other in Islington.'

Norah was not prepared to be saddled with an admiration for Murtlock.

'I wasn't keen on Fiona's last lot of friends. I've been saying for ages she's hung about much too long doing that sort of thing. If she wants to get married, I'm glad it's an American. It will give her the chance of a new kind of life, if she goes to live there. Somebody said you knew him, Nick?'

'Yes, I know him.'

198

There was no point in trying to explain Gwinnett to Norah. In any case, given the most favourable circumstances, I was not sure I could explain him to anyone, including myself. The attempt was not demanded, because we were joined by Umfraville, carrying his rubber-tipped stick in one hand, a very full glass of champagne in the other. As prelude to an impersonation of some sort, he raised the glass.

> 'Here's to the wings of love,
> May they never lose a feather,
> Till your little shoes, and my big boots,
> Stand outside the door together.'

Hugo held up a hand.

'We don't want a scandal, Dicky, after all these years as brothers-in-law.'

Before Umfraville could further elaborate whatever form of comic turn contemplated, his own attention was taken up by a grey-haired lady touching his arm.

'Hullo, Dicky.'

Umfraville clearly possessed not the least idea who was accosting him. The lady, smartly dressed, though by no means young, might at the same time have been ten years short of Umfraville's age. She was tall, pale, distinguished in appearance, very sad.

'I'm Flavia.'

'Flavia.'

Carefully balancing his stick and champagne, Umfraville embraced her.

'How horrid of you not to recognize me.'

Umfraville swept that aside.

'Flavia, this is an altogether unexpected delight. Does your presence at our nephew's wedding mean that you and I are now related—in consequence of the marriage of these young people? How much I hope that, Flavia.'

The grey-haired lady—Stringham's sister—laughed a rather tinkly laugh.

'Dicky, you haven't changed at all.'

Flavia Wisebite—it was to be assumed she still bore the name of her American second husband, Harrison Wisebite (like Veronica Tolland's first, alcoholic, long departed)— laughed again tremulously. Her own affiliations with Umfraville dated back to infinitely distant days; Kenya, the Happy Valley, surroundings where, according to Umfraville himself—he had emphasized with a certain complacency his own caddishness in revealing the information—he had been the first to seduce her. That possibility was more credible than Umfraville's follow-up, that he (rather than the reprehensible Cosmo Flitton, married to Flavia not long after) could be true father of Flavia's daughter, Pamela. Pamela Flitton, it might be thought, carried all the marks of being Cosmo Flitton's daughter. Age had done little or nothing to impair Umfraville's capacities for routine banter, if he happened to be in the right mood. He continued to press the possibility of a remote family tie emerging from the Cutts/Akworth union that would connect Flavia Wisebite with himself.

'Bride or bridegroom? Come on, Flavia. I want to be able to introduce you as my little cousin.'

'No good, Dicky. I'm not a blood relation. I'm Clare Akworth's godmother. Her mother's a dear friend of mine. We live in cottages almost next door to each other, practically in walking distance of Stourwater.'

Flavia Wisebite began to narrate her past history to Umfraville in her rapid trembling voice; how nervous diseases had prostrated her, she had been in and out of hospital, was now cured. In spite of that assurance she still seemed in a highly nervous state. Umfraville, less tough in certain respects than in his younger days, was beginning to look rather upset himself at all this. No doubt he felt sorry for Flavia, but had reached a time of life when, if he came to a wedding, he hoped not to be harassed by having poured into his ears the troubles of a former mistress. His face became quite drawn as he listened. I should have been willing to escape myself, scarcely knowing her, and feeling in no way responsible. Before withdrawal were possible, Umfraville manoeuvred me into the conversation. Flavia Wisebite at once recalled the sole occasion when we had met in the past.

'It was when Dicky was first engaged to your sister-in-law, Frederica. You drove over from Aldershot to Frederica's house during the war. I was there with poor Robert, just before he was killed. I'm a contemporary of Frederica's, you know. We came out at the same time. I remember you talking about my brother, Charles.'

She began to speak disjointedly of Stringham. She was, I thought, perhaps a little mad now. As one gets older, one gets increasingly used to encountering this development in friends and acquaintances; causing periods of self-examination in a similar connexion. Seeing that Flavia and I had something in common to talk about together, Umfraville slipped away. Out of the corner of my eye I saw him stumping across the room on his stick to have a further word with the bride. Flavia Wisebite rambled on.

'Charles was never sent into the world to make old bones, of course I always knew that, but how sad that he should have died as he did, how sad. He was a hero, of course, but what difference does that make, when you're dead?'

She seemed to require an answer to that question. It was hard to offer one free from sententiousness. I made no attempt to do so.

'I suppose it makes a difference the way a few people remember you.'

That seemed to satisfy her.

'Yes, yes. Like Robert.'

'Yes. Robert too.'

She appeared to have been made quite happy by this justifiable, if unoriginal conclusion. Oddly enough, when at Frederica's, Flavia Wisebite had spoken almost disparagingly of her brother's determination, in face of poor health, to join the army. This canonization of Stringham after death had something of her daughter Pamela's way of remembering dead lovers. Now, in a somewhat similar manner, Flavia began to talk of Umfraville with affection, though she had hardly noticed him at Frederica's. Then, of course, she had been involved with Robert Tolland. Even so, the enthusiasm with which she went on about Kenya, how amusing Umfraville had been there, how much her father had liked him, was an illustration of the way human relationships fluctuate, without any action taking place; Umfraville, from being entirely disregarded, now occupying a prominent place in Flavia Wisebite's personal myth. Without warning, she switched to Pamela.

'Did you ever meet my daughter?'

'Yes. I knew Pamela.'

I was about to say that I knew Pamela well, then saw that, in Pamela Flitton's case, that might imply closer affiliations than had ever in fact existed. It was a needless adjustment of phrase. Her mother had certainly long ceased to worry, if she had ever done so, about her daughter's affairs, with whom she had, or had not, slept. Perhaps, in her own state of health, Flavia had been scarcely aware of all that. In any case something else in relation to Pamela was now on her mind.

'She died too.'

'Yes.'

'She married that dreadful man—Widmerpool.'

For the first time it occurred to me as strange, abnormally strange, that Flavia Wisebite had never, so far as I knew, played anything like an active rôle in her capacity as Widmerpool's mother-in-law. In fact I now saw that, without formulating the idea at all clearly in my mind, I had always supposed Flavia to have died. Whatever the reason—chiefly no doubt the interludes in hospitals and nursing-homes—she seemed to have sidestepped the scandals that had enveloped her daughter's name; not least Pamela's unhappy end. If that had been her mother's deliberate intention, she had been remarkably successful in keeping out of the way.

'Did you know Widmerpool?'

'Yes. I know him. I've known him for years.'

'I said *did* you know him. Nobody could know him now.'

'How do you mean?'

I did not grasp immediately the implication that Widmerpool had become literally impossible to know.

'You can't have heard what's happened to him. He's gone out of his mind. He lives with a crowd of dreadful people, most of them quite young, who wear extraordinary clothes, and do the most horrible, horrible things. They are quite near here.'

It was true that Widmerpool's mother's cottage had been only a mile or two from Stourwater.

'I did know he'd become rather odd. I'd forgotten he was in this neighbourhood.'

'I see them out running quite often.'

In the light of the cult's habits there was nothing particularly extraordinary in Flavia Wisebite catching sight of them at their exercises from time to time. During the period of working for Sir Magnus Donners, Widmerpool had often spoken of his good fortune in having his mother's cottage— later enlarged by himself—so close to the Castle.

'Sometimes they're in blue garments, sometimes hardly any clothes at all. I've been told they do wear absolutely nothing, stark naked, when they go out in the middle of the night in summer. They do all sorts of *revolting* things. I wonder it's allowed. But then everything is allowed now.'

Flavia Wisebite grimaced.

'I try not to look at them, if they come running in off a sideroad. When I see them in the distance I go off up a turning.'

'Is Widmerpool head of the cult?'

'How should I know? I thought he was. Didn't he start it? As soon as Pamela married him, he began his horrible goings-on, though they weren't quite like what he does nowadays. Why did she do it? How could she? Find the most horrible man on earth, and then marry him? She always had to have her own way. It was quite enough that everyone agreed that Widmerpool was awful, hideous, monstrous. She just wanted to show that she didn't care in the least what anyone said. She was the same as a child. Absolutely wilful. Nobody could control her.'

No doubt there was much truth in what her mother said. I remembered Pamela Flitton, as a child bridesmaid, being sick in the font at Stringham's wedding. One of the children had made a good deal of noise at the ceremony just attended, but nothing so drastic as that. Flavia's daughter had always been in a class by herself from her earliest days. A girl like Fiona was no real competitor.

'Because Pam didn't always go for unattractive people. When she was a little girl she fell madly in love with Charles—you know the way children do—at the time he was drinking too much. The amount he drank in those days was terrible. Pam didn't see him often because of that. Still, Charles was always fond of her, very nice to her, whenever he came to see us, which wasn't often. Charles left Pam his things, not much, hardly anything by then. Pam never made a will, of course, so Widmerpool must have got whatever there was. The Modigliani drawing. Pam loved that. I wonder what happened to it. I suppose that awful Widmerpool sold it.'

Flavia Wisebite took a small folded pocket handkerchief

from her bag. She lightly dabbed her eyes. It was the precise gesture her mother had used, another memory of Stringham's marriage to Peggy Stepney; Peggy Klein, as she had been for years now. Mrs Foxe's tears had been more prolonged on that occasion, lasting intermittently throughout the whole service. Flavia's were quickly over. She returned the handkerchief to the bag. I did not know what to say. Where could one begin? Stringham's past? Pamela's past? Flavia's own past? These were extensive and delicate themes to set out on; Widmerpool's present, even less approachable. There was no need to say anything at all. Flavia Wisebite, in the manner of persons of her sort, had suddenly recovered herself. She was perfectly all right again. Now she spoke once more in her tremulous social voice.

'Isn't Clare Akworth a sweet girl?'

'I don't really know her. She looks very attractive.'

'I'm so proud to be her godmother. He's a charming young man too. He told me all about his computers. It was far above my head, I'm afraid. I'm sure they'll be very happy. I never was, but I'm sure they will be. So nice to have met again.'

Smiling goodbye, she disappeared into the crowd. In its own particular way the encounter had been disturbing. I was glad it was over. One of its side effects was a sense of temporary inability to chat with other guests, most of them, unless relations, from their age unknown to me. Flavia Wisebite had diminished exuberance for seeking out members of an older generation, whom one had not seen for some time, hearing their news, listening to their troubles. In that line, Flavia Wisebite herself was enough for one day. She had also in some way infected me with her own sense of disorientation. I required to recover. The idea suggested itself to slip away from the reception for a few minutes, find release in wandering through the corridors and galleries of the Castle. After all, that was really why I had come here. There was the dining-room, for example, draped with the tapestries of the Seven Deadly Sins, the little library or study, drawings and small oils between bookshelves, where Barnby's portrait of the waitress from Casanova's Chinese Restaurant had hung. A side door seemed the most convenient exit from the party. Rupert Akworth, the bride's uncle, who had given her away, saw me about to leave.

'The gents? Down the stairs on the left. Rather classy.'

'Thanks.'

The Stourwater passages had by now acquired the smell common to all schools: furniture polish: disinfectant: fumes of unambitious cooking. I found the little library—now a schoolroom hung with maps—which Sir Magnus had entered with such dramatic effect that he seemed to have been watching for his guests' arrival through a peephole in the far door (concealed with dummy books), the night we had come over with the Morelands to dinner at the Castle. One of the pictures in this room had been another Barnby, an oil sketch of the model Conchita, described by Moreland as 'antithesis of the pavement artist's traditional representation of a loaf of bread, captioned *Easy to Draw but Hard to Get.*'

After striking one or two false trails, I came at last to the dining-room of the Seven Deadly Sins. Rows of tables indicated that its function remained unchanged, though the Sins no longer exemplified their graphic warning to those who ate there. The fine chimneypiece, decorated with nymphs and satyrs—no doubt installed by Sir Magnus to harmonize with the tapestries—had been allowed to remain as adjunct to school meals. Above this hung a large reproduction of an Annigoni portrait of the Queen. Here, scene of the luncheon where I had first met Jean Templer after her marriage to Duport; later, of the great impersonation of the Sins themselves, recorded in the photographs shown by

Matilda, were more pungent memories. I stood for a moment by the door, reconstructing some of these past incidents in the mind. While I was doing so, a man and a girl entered the dining-room from the far end. They were holding hands. Without abandoning this clasp, they advanced up the room. If wedding guests, like quite a few others present at the reception, neither had dressed up much for the occasion.

'Hullo, Fiona—hullo, Russell.'

Gwinnett offered the hand that was not holding Fiona's.

'Hullo, Nicholas.'

'Congratulations.'

'You've heard.'

'Yes.'

Gwinnett gave one of his rare smiles. I kissed Fiona, who accepted with good grace this tribute to her marriage. She, too, looked pleased. Her dress still swept the ground—as on the crayfishing afternoon, the last time I had actually set eyes on her—but her breast no longer bore the legend HARMONY. In her disengaged hand she carried a large straw hat trimmed with multicoloured flowers. A considerable cleaning up, positive remodelling, had taken place in Fiona's general style. No doubt much of that was owed to Delavacquerie. Gwinnett had surmounted the sober suit of the Magnus Donners dinner with a thin strip of bow tie. His head seemed to have been newly shaved.

'Have you both just arrived?'

'A side door outside was open. We thought we might look around before meeting the family. Is the Castle thirteenth or early fourteenth-century? I'd say that was the date. The machicolations might be later. What's its history?'

Gwinnett had shown architectural interests in Venice.

'Not much history, I think. Sir Magnus Donners, who owned it, had some story about a mediaeval lord of Stourwater, whose daughter drowned herself in the moat for love of a monk.'

Halfway through the sentence I saw that tradition was one preferably to have remained unrepeated in the circumstances. Sir Magnus had narrated the tale to Prince Theodoric the day the Walpole-Wilsons had taken me to luncheon here. I added quickly that the room we were in had once contained some remarkable tapestries depicting the Seven Deadly Sins. That seemed scarcely an improvement as a topic. Fiona may have felt the same, as she enquired about the wedding.

'How did Sebastian stand up to it?'

'Very well. Let's return to them, and drink some champagne.'

Fiona looked questioningly at Gwinnett, as she used to look at Murtlock for a decision; perhaps had so looked at Delavacquerie, before relinquishing him.

'Do you want to see them all yet?'

'Whatever you say.'

I supposed they would prefer to remain alone together.

'I'm going to continue my exploration of the Castle for a short time, then I'll see you later at the reception.'

Fiona did not seem anxious to face her relations yet.

'We'll come with you. You can show us round. I'd like to see a bit more of it. Wouldn't you, Rus?'

'I don't know the place at all well. I was here absolutely years ago, and only went into a few rooms then.'

'Never mind.'

The three of us set off together.

'I'm glad I wasn't at school here.'

Stourwater was one of the educational establishments Fiona had never sampled. The new rôle of young married woman seemed to come with complete ease to her. There could be no doubt that she liked exceptional types. Gwinnett's attraction to Fiona was less easy to classify. A faint train of thought was perceptible so far as Pamela Widmerpool was concerned, though Fiona had neither Pamela's looks, nor force of character. The impact of Pamela might even have jolted Gwinnett into an entirely different emotional channel, his former inhibitions cured once and for all. That was not impossible.

'Sir Magnus Donners once took some of his guests down to the so-called dungeons, but I'm not sure I can find them.'

Gwinnett pricked up his ears.

'The dungeons? Let's see them. I'd like to look over the dungeons.'

Fiona agreed.

'Me, too. Do have a try to find them.'

They did not cease to hold hands, while several rooms and passages were traversed. Structural alterations had taken place in the course of adapting the Castle to the needs of a school. The head of the staircase leading to these lower regions, where the alleged dungeons were on view—knowledgable people said they were merely storerooms—could not be found. Several doors were locked. Then a low door, a postern, brought us out into a small courtyard, a side of the Castle unenclosed by moat. Here school outbuildings had been added. Beyond this open space lay playing fields, a wooden pavilion, some seats. Further off were the trees of the park. Gwinnett surveyed the courtyard.

'This near building might have been a brewhouse. The brickwork looks Tudor.'

Fiona turned towards the fields.

'At least I'll never have to play hockey again.'

'Did you hate games?'

'I used to long to die, playing hockey on winter afternoons.'

Gwinnett gave up examining the supposed brewhouse. We moved towards the open.

'In the ball-courts of the Aztecs a game was played of which scarcely anything is known, except that the captain of the winning side is believed to have been made a human sacrifice.'

Gwinnett said that rather pedantically.

'The rule would certainly add to the excitement of a cup-tie or test match.'

'Another feature was that, when a goal was scored—a very rare event—all the clothes and jewellery of the spectators were forfeit to the players.'

'Less good. An incitement to rowdyism.'

'I think they both sound excellent rules,' said Fiona. 'Nothing I'd have liked better than to execute the captain, and I never watched any games, if I could help it, so they wouldn't have got my gear.'

Gwinnett would have liked to remain serious, but gave way to her mood. Marriage seemed already to have loosened up both of them. Further discussion of Aztec sport was brought to an end by something happening on the far side of the hockey-field, which distracted attention. Beyond the field a path led through the park. Along this path, some way off, a party of persons was slowly running. They might well have been the Aztec team, doubling up to play a sacrificial contest. There were about a dozen of them approaching, mostly dressed in blue, trotting in a leisurely way, knees high, across the park. Fiona, naturally enough, grasped at once the identity of this straggling body. I don't know how soon Gwinnett also took that in. Probably at once too. The strange thing was that, before comprehending the meaning of what was taking place, I thought for a second of childhood, of Dr Trelawney and his young disciples.

'Look! Look!'

Fiona was displaying great excitement. By that time I, too, had understood the scene.

'It's them all right.'

Fiona tried to discern something.

'Is *he* there?'

She spoke with a certain apprehension. Obviously she meant Murtlock. No one answered her. Gwinnett seemed interested. He watched the runners. Fiona examined them intently too.

'No—he's not there. I'm sure he's not there. But I can see Barnabas.'

There were at least a dozen of them, perhaps more. Not all wore the robes or tunic of the cult, some almost in rags. Both sexes were represented, the average age appeared to be early twenties. The only two older persons were much older. One of them, Widmerpool, was leading the pack. He wore the blue robe. The other elderly man lacked a robe. Dressed in a red sweater and trousers, greybearded, dishevelled, incredibly filthy in appearance even from far-off, this one was by a long way the last of the runners. Fiona was thrilled.

'He's not there. Let's talk to them. Let's talk to Barnabas.'

'OK.'

Gwinnett said that quite warmly, as if he too would enjoy the encounter.

'You don't mind?'

'Not at all.'

She turned towards the runners, and shouted.

'Barnabas! Barnabas!'

At the sound of Fiona's voice, the pace set by Widmerpool became even more sluggish, some of the party slowing up to the extent of not running at all. These last stood staring in our direction, as if we, rather than they, were the odd figures on the landscape. That may well have seemed so to them. Fiona cried out again.

'Come and talk to us, Barnabas.'

Widmerpool was the last to stop running. He had to walk back some little way to where the rest had drawn up. He was evidently in charge. If the run were to be interrupted, he might have been supposed the correct individual to be hailed by Fiona. I was not sure what her attitude towards him had been when herself a member of the cult. No doubt he was a figure to be taken very much into account, but, if only from his age, having no such grip as Murtlock on her imagination. It was unlikely she would ever have made our presence known had Murtlock been sighted among the runners. Now, behaving like a girl seeing old schoolfriends again, some of the pleasure coming from their being still at a school from which she had herself escaped, Fiona began to walk across the field to meet them. Gwinnett followed. It was not clear whether he was indifferent to the reunion, wanting only to humour his bride, or still felt curiosity as what this encounter might bring forth. The runners, Henderson foremost among them, strayed across the grass towards us, the elderly man with the tangled beard remaining well to the rear.

'How are you, Barnabas?'

Henderson looked as if a far more ascetic life had been imposed on him since crayfishing days. His face was pale and thinner. He had removed the moustache, and taken to wire spectacles. The sight of Fiona greatly cheered him. She began to explain what was happening at Stourwater.

'Sebastian's wedding reception is going on here this afternoon. Chuck told me he was going to come to it. Chuck knows Clare Akworth.'

I did not grasp the significance of that, nor hear Henderson's answer. The sight of Widmerpool at close quarters absorbed all my attention. Although I knew he had by now been more or less entangled with the cult for the best part of two years, was accustomed to take part in its esoteric rites, in all respects identified himself with this new mode of life—as The Devil's Fingers showed—the spectacle of him wearing a blue robe was nevertheless a startling one. Flavia Wisebite had been justified in the account she had given, so far as that went. The image immediately brought to mind was one not thought of for years; the picture, reproduced in colour, that used to hang in the flat Widmerpool shared with his mother in his early London days. It had been called *The Omnipresent*. Three blue-robed figures respectively knelt, stood with bowed head, gazed heavenward with extended hands, all poised on the brink of a precipice. It was a long time ago. I may have remembered the scene incorrectly. Nevertheless it was these figures Widmerpool conjured up, as he advanced towards me.

'Nicholas?'

When he spoke, within a second, that impression was altered. What had momentarily given him something never achieved before, a kind of suitability, almost dignity, dwindled to no more than a man gone into the garden wearing a blue dressing-gown. It was largely the clothes that had outraged Flavia Wisebite, but, in the end, it was not this kind of bathrobe that made the strong impression —any more than with Murtlock—it was the man himself. Widmerpool looked ill, desperate, worn out. The extreme debility of his appearance brought one up short. The low neckband of the garment he wore revealed a scar that ran from somewhere below the neck to the upper part of one cheek; possibly the gash inflicted on the night of The Devil's Fingers ceremony. In this physical state it was surprising that he was able to run at all, even at the slow pace he himself had been setting. No doubt the determination always shown to go through with anything he took up, carry on to the furthest limit of his capacity, was as painfully exercised in the activities to which he had latterly given himself, as in any undertakings of earlier life.

'Hullo.'

His manner was as changed as his costume. He sounded altogether bemused. He stood there limply, haunted in expression, glancing from time to time at Fiona and Gwinnett, though not speaking to either. So far as could be seen, Fiona was introducing her husband to these former associates; Henderson, the young ones, all crowding round. There was a hum of chatter. The filthy grey-beard hung about in the background. Widmerpool seemed to make an effort to pull himself together.

'Why are you wearing a tailcoat?'

'A wedding is taking place. I'm one of the guests.'

'A wedding's taking place in Stourwater?'

'Yes.'

'But—but the Chief's dead, isn't he?'

Sir Magnus Donners, in days when Widmerpool worked for him, had always been referred to by subordinates as the Chief. Widmerpool put the question in an uncertain puzzled voice that seemed to indicate loss of memory more damaging than reasonably to be associated with a man of his age.

'He died some little while ago—close on twenty years.'

'Of course he did, of course. Extraordinary that I should have doubted for a moment that the Chief had passed over. A mistaken term escaped me too. I shall do penance for that. At our age transmutations take place all the time. Yes, yes.'

Widmerpool gazed round again. Perhaps more to steady himself than because he had not already recognized Gwinnett, he suddenly held up a hand in Murtlock's benedictional manner.

'It is Professor Gwinnett—to use an absurd prefix?'

'It is, Lord Widmerpool.'

Gwinnett smiled faintly, without the least friendliness. That was hardly surprising in the circumstances.

'Not Lord, not Lord—Ken, Ken.'

Gwinnett withdrew his smile.

'You came to see us about a year ago?'

'Yes.'

Fiona turned from the group with which she had been talking. Perhaps she wanted to impress on Widmerpool her ownership of Gwinnett; anyway now absolute separation from the cult, whatever her taste for still hobnobbing with its members.

'Russell and I have have just got married, Ken.'

'Married?'

The way Widmerpool spoke the word was hard to define. It might have been horror; it might, on the other hand, have aroused in his mind some infinitely complicated chain of ideas as to what Fiona meant by using such a term. Fiona may also have wished to shock by stating that she had taken so conventional a step. Acceptance of the fact that she gave the word its normal face value seemed to sink into Widmerpool's head only slowly. Not unnaturally, in the light of what he had just been told about a wedding taking place in the Castle, he mistook the implications.

'You've just been married at Stourwater, Fiona?'

He looked more astounded than ever. Fiona laughed derisively. I think she intended to make fun of him, now that she was free from any possible reprisals. Even Gwinnett smiled at the question.

'No, it's my brother's wedding.'

Taking Gwinnett's arm, Fiona turned back to her younger acquaintances. Widmerpool reverted to the subject of Sir Magnus Donners. It seemed to trouble him.

'Extraordinary I should not only have forgotten about Donners, but used that erroneous formula, there being no death, only transition, blending, synthesis, mutation—just as there are no marriages, except mystic marriages. Marriages that transcend the boundaries of awareness, the unmanifest solutions of Harmony, galvanized by meditation and appropriate rites, the source of all Power—rather than the lethal manufacture of tensions as constructed in these very surroundings today.'

Widmerpool's observations on such matters were suddenly interrupted by a burst of singing. The notes, thin and quavering, possessed something of Flavia Wisebite's conversational tones, mysteriously transmuted to music, weird, eerie, not at all unpleasant all the same. They came from the other elderly man, the bearded one, who had still moved no nearer to join the rest of the group.

'Open now the crystal fountain,
Whence the healing stream doth flow:
Let the fire and cloudy pillar
Lead me all my journey through.'

Widmerpool started violently. It was as if someone had touched him with a red-hot iron. Then he recovered himself, was about to go on talking.

'Who is that singing?'

'Take no notice. He's all right, if left alone. He finds Harmony in singing that sort of thing.'

The bearded man stood a little way apart, hands clasped, eyes uplifted. He had hardly more hair on his head than Gwinnett. Something about the singing suggested he had absolutely no teeth. It crossed my mind that the old red high-necked sweater he wore, over torn corduroy trousers, might have been passed on by Widmerpool himself. The beard was matted and grubby, his feet bare and horrible. Entirely self-occupied, he took no notice at all of what was otherwise going on. What he chose to sing altogether distracted my attention from Widmerpool's discourse on death and marriage. The strains brought back the early days of the war. It was the hymn my Regiment used to sing on the line of march. The chant seemed to disturb Widmerpool, irritate, upset him. His expression became more agonized than ever.

'Don't you remember the men singing that on route marches?'

'Singing what?'

Widmerpool, himself on the staff of the Division of which my Battalion had been one of the units, might not have heard the motif so often as I, but the tune could hardly have passed entirely unnoticed, even by someone so uninterested in human behaviour.

'Who is he?'

'One of us.'

Widmerpool had to be pressed for an answer. He was prepared to agree that I might have heard the verse sung before.

'True, true. He's a man I apparently ran across in the army. Somebody brought him along to us. He'd been a dropout for years—before people knew about an alternative lifestyle—and was at the end of his tether. We thought he was going to pass over. When he got better, Scorp took a fancy to him. At the time he came to us, I didn't remember seeing him before. Didn't recognize him at all. Then one day Bith brought it all up himself.'

'Bith?'

'He's named Bithel. I seem to have known him in the army. Through no fault of my own, it seems I had something to do with his leaving the army. Many people would have been grateful for that. Scorp likes Bith. Thinks he contributes to Harmony. I expect he does. Scorp is usually right about that sort of thing.'

Widmerpool sighed.

'But I know Bithel too. I knew all about him in those days. He commanded the Mobile Laundry. Don't you remember?'

Widmerpool looked blank. While he had been speaking these words, his thoughts were evidently far away. He was almost talking to himself. If he had forgotten about the death of Sir Magnus Donners, he could well have forgotten about Bithel; even the fact that he and I had soldiered together. In any case the matter did not interest him so far as Bithel was concerned. He was evidently thinking of himself, overcome now with self-pity.

'When Scorp found out that I'd had to tell Bith he must leave the army—leave the Mobile Laundry, you say—Scorp made me do penance. What happened had been duty—what I then quite wrongly thought duty to be—and wasn't at all my fault. I must have been told by those above me that I'd got to tell Bith he had to go. I tried to explain that to Scorp. He said—he'd got the story from Bith, of course—that I acted without Harmony, and must make amends, mystical amends. He was right, of course. Scorp made me . . . made me . . .'

Widmerpool's voice trailed away. He shuddered violently, at the same time swallowing several times. His eyes filled with tears. Whatever Murtlock had made him do as penance for relieving Bithel of his commission was too horrific to be spoken aloud by Widmerpool himself, even though he had brought the matter up, still brooded on it. I was decidedly glad not to be told. One's capacity for hearing about ghastly doings lessens with age. At least this showed that Murtlock had taken over complete command. Even thinking about the retribution visited on him had brought Widmerpool to near collapse. In fact he looked much as he had described Bithel, when—not at all unjustly so far as the actual sentence went—the alternatives of court martial, or acceptance of a report declaring Bithel unsuitable for retention as an officer were put before him. This was the incident to which Greening had referred. It may well have been true —as Greening had said—that Widmerpool had talked in a callous manner later in the Mess about Bithel breaking down. Certainly he had spoken of it to me.

'Bithel's one of your community?'

'For a year or more now.'

Again Widmerpool answered as if his thoughts were elsewhere. Bithel continued to stand apart, smiling and mutter-

218

ing to himself, apparently quite happy. His demeanour was not unlike what it had been in the army after he had drunk a good deal. Fiona left the group with which she had been talking, and came up to Widmerpool.

'Look, Ken, I want you all to look in on my brother's wedding party for a minute or two. Barnabas's old boyfriend, Chuck, is there, and rows of people Barnabas knows. You must come. Just for a moment. Scorp always said that Harmony, in one form, was to be widely known.'

It looked very much as if marriage had caused Fiona to revert, from the gloom of recent years, to the more carefree style of her rampageous schoolgirl stage. Widmerpool made an attempt to avoid the question by taking a general line of disapproval.

'You went away, Fiona. You left us. You abandoned Harmony.'

The others, uneasy perhaps, but certainly tempted, now began to crowd round. Fiona continued her efforts to persuade Widmerpool, who was plainly uncertain how the suggestion should be correctly handled. It seemed to daze him. Possibly he was not without all curiosity to enter Stourwater again himself. Bithel began to sing once more.

'From every dark nook they press forward to meet me,
I lift up my eyes to the tall leafy dome.
And others are there looking downward to greet me,
The ashgrove, the ashgrove, alone is my home.'

At this, Fiona abandoned Widmerpool, and made for Bithel. Bithel seemed all at once to recognize her for the first time. He held his arms above his head. Fiona said something to him, then taking his hand, led him towards the rest of the group.

'Come along all of you. Bith's coming, if no one else is.'

Widmerpool's powers of decision were finally put out of

action by the inclusion of Bithel in an already apparently insoluble situation. It could well be that one of his responsibilities was to keep an eye on Bithel, probably easy enough out on a run, quite another matter in what was now promised. He made a final effort to impose discipline.

'Remember, no drink.'

'All right,' said Fiona. 'How do we find our way?'

The last question was addressed to myself. It was a disconcerting one. I was not particularly anxious to take on the responsibility of leading this mob into the wedding reception. If Fiona wanted to present them all to her brother and his bride that was her own affair. She must do it herself. Apart from other considerations, such as uncertainty how they would behave, was the very real possibility that I might not be able to find the way back to the Great Hall by the path we came. Some of them might easily get left behind in the Stourwater corridors. This last probability suggested an alternative route to the reception.

'The easiest would be to walk round to the front of the Castle. You follow the banks of the moat, then cross the causeway, and straight ahead.'

Fiona looked uncertain for a moment. Gwinnett, either because he saw the tactical advantages of such an approach, or simply speaking his own wish, gave support to this direction.

'I'd like to do that. We haven't seen the double-portcullised gateway yet.'

Fiona concurred. Her chief desire seemed to be to transfer her former friends of the cult to the party the quickest possible way. This was no doubt intended as a double-edged tease; on the one hand, aimed at her relations; on the other, at Murtlock. That was how things looked.

'All right. This way. Come along, Bith.'

They set off; Fiona, Gwinnett, Henderson, Bithel, all in the first wave. Widmerpool lagged behind. He had been taken by surprise, unable to make up his mind, incapable of a plan. If I did not wish to appear at the head of the column, there was no alternative to walking with him. This also solved for the moment the question of Bithel; whether or not to draw his attention to our former acquaintance. We strolled along side by side, Widmerpool now apparently resigned to looking in on the reception. It could be true, as Fiona had hinted, that Murtlock encouraged his people to show themselves, from time to time, in unlikely places. This might not be Widmerpool's main worry so much as Bithel. Widmerpool's own words now gave some confirmation to that. He was still speaking more or less to himself.

'I daresay it's all right if we don't stay too long. People can see Harmony in action. Bith, in my opinion, has never achieved much Harmony—still slips away and drinks, when he can lay hands on any money—and I must be sure to keep an eye on him where we're going. The others are all right. One glass doesn't matter for Bith—Scorp recognizes that. He says it won't necessarily make bad vibrations in Bith's individual validation. He's a special case. Scorp thinks a lot of Bith. Says he has remarkable mystic powers inherent in him. Still, I mustn't let him out of my sight. I'm in charge of today's mystical exercises, and Scorp will hold me responsible. Who are the couple going through these meaningless formulas today?'

Widmerpool asked the last question in a more coherent tone.

'Fiona's brother, Sebastian Cutts, and a girl called Clare Akworth.'

Widmerpool winced, much as he had done when Bithel had first begun to sing.

'Akworth?'

'Akworth.'

He began to stammer.

'Like . . . like . . .'

He did not finish the question. His face went the dull red colour its skin sometimes took on under stress. I knew, of course, what he meant. At least I thought I knew. As it turned out, I knew less than I supposed. In any case there was no point in pretending ignorance of the essence of the enquiry. The obvious assumption was that, even after half a century, Widmerpool was unwilling to be confronted with Akworth, if there were any danger of such a thing. This was only the second occasion, so far as I could remember, when the Akworth matter had ever cropped up between us. The first had been when we had not long left school, and were both learning French with the Leroy family at La Grenadière.

'The name is spelt like the boy who was at school with us. In fact the bride is that Akworth's granddaughter.'

'Granddaughter of Bertram Akworth?'

'Yes.'

'Is he still—still on this side?'

'Who?'

'Bertram Akworth.'

'If you mean is he still alive, he's actually at the wedding. He read the Lesson in church.'

'He's—at Stourwater?'

'If you're coming to the reception you'll see him.'

Widmerpool stopped abruptly. I had hoped for that. It looked as if he might now decide not to enter the Castle at all. His absence would make one less potentially unwelcome addition to the wedding party; in fact remove what was probably the least assimilable factor. The young people were likely to mix easily enough with their own contemporaries. At worst Bithel would pass out. He could be put in the cloakroom, until time came to take him away. That sort of thing should easily be dealt with on premises as large as Stourwater. Widmerpool was another matter. Not only would his appearance in a blue robe attract—owing to his age—undue attention, but his nervous condition might assume some inconvenient form. With any luck, now he knew Akworth would be present, he would make for home right away. Instead of doing so Widmerpool began to babble disconnectedly.

'I've know Bertram Akworth for years ... years ... We were on the board of the same bank together—until he and Farebrother got me off it, between them. Farebrother always had it in for me. So did Akworth. It was natural enough.'

It was certainly natural enough in Akworth's case; even if surprising that Widmerpool recognized the fact. A moment's thought ought to have made it obvious that Widmerpool and Sir Bertram Akworth were certain to encounter each other in the City. It seemed to have been more than occasional acquaintance, indeed looking as if they had been engaged in a running fight all their lives. This prolonged duel added to the drama of the original story. If I had known about it, I should have been more than ever convinced that this cross-questioning on Widmerpool's part was aimed at avoiding a meeting with his schoolboy victim and commercial rival. That was a dire misjudgment. On the contrary, Widmerpool was filled with an inspired fervour, carried away with delighted agitation, at the prospect of a face-to-face confrontation.

'Bertram Akworth will be there? He will actually be present? It can't be true. This is an opportunity I have been longing for. I behaved to Akworth in a way I now know to be not wrong—so-called right and wrong being illusory concepts—but what must be deplored as transcendentally discordant, mystically in error, in short, contrary to Harmony. In those days I was only a boy—a simple boy at that—who knew nothing of such experiences as cohabiting with the Elements, as a means of training the will. Moreover, I should have encouraged any breaking of the rules, struck a blow for, rather than against, rebellion, aided the subversion of that detestable thing law and order, as commonly understood. In those days—my schoolboy years —I had already dedicated myself to so-called reason, so-called practical affairs. I allowed no—at least very little— unfettered play of those animal forces that free the spirit, though later I began to understand the way, for example, that nakedness removes impediments of all sorts. Besides, if the universe is to be subjected to his will, a man must develop his female nature as well as the male—without lessening his own masculinity—I knew nothing of that...but Akworth...long misunderstood...should make amends ...as with Bith...though not...not...'

Again Widmerpool tailed off, unable to bring himself to mention whatever Murtlock had made him act out in relation to the Bithel penance. What he said about Sir Bertram Akworth was most disturbing. A far more threatening situation than before had now suddenly come into being. It was one thing for Fiona, the bridegroom's sister, to bring into her brother's wedding party a crowd of young persons, curious specimens perhaps, but, not long before, closely associated with herself. It was quite another to allow the occasion to be one for Widmerpool to give rein to an ambition—apparently become obsessive with him—that he should make some sort of an apology to a lifelong business antagonist, grandfather of the bride, the boy he had caused to be sacked from school half a century earlier. In his present mood Widmerpool was capable of exploring in public, in much the same manner that he had been expatiating on them to me, all the mystical implications of Sir Bertram Akworth's youthful desires.

'If the matter of reporting Akworth has never come up in the years you've been meeting him, doesn't it seem wiser to leave things at that now? It might even be preferable not to go to the reception?'

Widmerpool was not listening.

'Amazing how long it took me to understand the ritual

side of sex. Although I never enjoyed sex much myself, I'd always supposed you were meant to enjoy it. Now I know better. I see now that, even when I was young, I was reaching out for the ritual side, to the exclusion of enjoyment. In objecting to Akworth's conduct, I was displaying an attitude I later took up in my own mind in relation to Donners and his irregular practices. He, too, may have had his own instinctive reactions in the same field. In those days I knew nothing of the Dionysiac necessities. They were revealed to me all but too late. If Donners was aware of such needs earlier than myself, he fell altogether short in combining them with transcendental meditation, or mystical exercises of a physical kind, other than sexual.'

Widmerpool, absorbed with the case of Sir Magnus, shook his head. By this time we were crossing the causeway, about to pass under the portcullised gate, through which Fiona's vanguard had already disappeared. Either to catch up with the rest of his company, or from impatience to make contact with Sir Bertram Akworth, Widmerpool pressed forward. This urgency on his part impelled his own entry into the Great Hall well ahead of myself, something I was anxious to manoeuvre, but had seen no way of bringing about. Widmerpool was lost in the crowd by the time I came through the doorway. Caroline Lovell—a niece of ours, married to a soldier called Thwaites—was standing just by. She began some sort of conversation before it was possible to estimate the effect of Fiona's additions to the party. We talked for a minute or two.

'Is Alan here?'

Caroline said her husband, having just been posted to Northern Ireland, had been unable to come to the wedding. She looked worried, but was prevented from saying more of this by Jonathan Cutts, who joined us, and began to speak of the Sleaford Veronese—as it once had been—a favourite subject of Caroline's father, Chips Lovell. The *Iphigenia* had come on the market again, handled by Jonathan's firm, and achieved a record price. Neither Jonathan Cutts nor Caroline seemed to have noticed the incursion of Fiona's friends from the cult; confirming the impression that, once within the lofty dimly lit limits of the Great Hall, they had quickly merged with other less than conventionally clad guests. Certainly there was no clearcut isolation of the group. For a second I caught a glimpse of Bithel; a moment later he disappeared. He had been surrounded by a circle of laughing young men. By this time a fair amount of champagne had been drunk. Widmerpool was nowhere to be seen. No doubt he was searching for Sir Bertram Akworth, but Sir Bertram, too, had disappeared for the moment. I asked Caroline where he had gone.

'There was a hitch about the car to take Sebastian and Clare to the airport. Sir Bertram's making some new arrangement, somebody said.'

Flavia Wisebite appeared again at my elbow.

'Have you seen who's just come in?'

'Do you mean Fiona Cutts and her former crowd?'

'Widmerpool.'

She was overcome with indignation, her face dead white.

'The dreadful man is wandering about the room in his loathsome clothes. What could have made them invite him? Young people will do anything these days. I'm sure it wasn't Clare's choice. She's such a sweet girl. Sebastian seemed a nice young man too. Surely he can't have asked Widmerpool? Do you think his father—who used to be an MP—had to have Widmerpool for political reasons. That's a possibility.'

'Widmerpool and his lot were brought in by Fiona Cutts, Sebastian's sister.'

'Fiona brought them? I see. Now I understand. Do you know who Fiona Cutts has just married—who my goddaughter, little Clare, is going to have for a brother-in-law?

An American called Gwinnett. I don't expect you've even heard of him. I have. I know a great deal about Mr Gwinnett. It's all too dreadful to say. Dreadful. Dreadful.'

Gwinnett, in sight on the far side of the room, was talking in a comparatively animated manner to his new in-laws. Behind them, in a corner, Jeremy Warminster had made contact with one of the prettier girls of the cult, whether or not for the first time was hard to judge. The two of them seemed already on easy terms with each other. A husband and wife, introduced as Colonel and Mrs Alford-Green, came up to speak with Flavia Wisebite. Their friendship seemed to date back to very ancient days, when Flavia had still been married to Cosmo Flitton. Colonel Alford-Green was evidently a retired regular soldier. While they were talking Sir Bertram Akworth reappeared. Hailing the Alford-Greens in his loud harsh voice, he greeted Flavia, too, as one already well known to him.

'How are you, Rosamund, how are you, Gerald? How nice to see old friends like you both, and Flavia here today. The honeymoon car broke down. All is now fixed. I've seen to it. No cause for panic.'

'We thought you read the Lesson very well, Bertram.'

'You did, Rosamund? Thank you very much. I'm glad you thought I did it all right. You know I rather pride myself on my reading. It's a beautiful passage. A great favourite of mine. It was the one on the agenda anyway. A bit of luck. I was very glad. If I'd been asked, I'd certainly have chosen it.'

'When are you coming up to our part of the world again, Bertram?'

'I hope I shall one of these days. I very much hope I shall. You know how hard it is to get away. Is Reggie still joint-master?'

The question prompted a rather complicated account of some quarrel in which the local hunt had been involved for a long time. I was about to move away, when I became aware that Widmerpool was near by. In fact he was very close. He must have been wandering about in the crowd, looking for Sir Bertram. Now at last he had run him to ground. Sir Bertram had not yet seen him. He was much too engrossed with the foxhunting feuds of the Alford-Greens. Widmerpool began muttering to himself. Suddenly he spoke out.

'Bertram.'

Use of the christian name somehow surprised me; though obviously, if the two of them had come across each other as often as Widmerpool indicated, they would be on those sort of terms, however great their mutual dislike.

'Bertram.'

Widmerpool repeated the name. He spoke quite quietly, in an almost beseeching voice. Sir Bertram either did not hear the first appeal, or, more probably, decided that, whoever it was, he wanted to hear the end of the Alford-Greens' story, which treated of one of those rows between foxhunting people, which have a peculiar intensity of virulence. At the second summons, Sir Bertram turned. Plainly not recognizing an old business adversary under the blue robe Widmerpool wore, he did not seem more than a trifle taken aback at what might quite reasonably have been regarded as an extraordinary spectacle of humanity. His face merely assumed an expression of rather self-consciously wry amusement; the tolerant good humour of a man of the world, who is prepared for anything in the circumstances of the moment in which he finds himself; in this case, unexpected guests invited by his granddaughter to her wedding.

Without making excessive claims for Sir Bertram's imperturbability, or good humour, one could see that it took more than an excited elderly man, not too clean and wearing a blue robe, socially to discompose him these days. Sir Bertram had not reached the position he had in his own world without achieving a smattering of what was afoot in an essentially disparate one. This particular instance happened to be considerably more than a sharp contrast, to be neutralized by tactful ingenuity, with his own way of life. In short, Sir Bertram Akworth became suddenly aware that he was contemplating Widmerpool. No doubt he had already heard rumours of Widmerpool's changed ways—probably associated in his mind more with treasonable contacts and equivocal financial dealings—but, a man not given to imaginative reconstructions, Sir Bertram was not altogether prepared for the reality now set before him. Enlightenment caused a series of violent emotions—deep hatred the most definable—to pass swiftly across his sallow cadaverous features; reactions gone in a split second, recovery all but instantaneous.

'Kenneth, what are you up to?'

Sir Bertram spoke calmly. There was no time for him to say more. Instead of answering an undoubtedly rhetorical question—even if some sort of explanation were required, conventionally speaking, for thus arriving unasked at a party—Widmerpool, in terms of ritual of another kind, went straight to the point; if repentance were to be expressed in physical form. While Sir Bertram Akworth stood, eyebrows slightly raised, a rather fixed expression of humorous enquiry imposed on his features, like that of a reasonably talented amateur actor, Widmerpool, without the slightest warning, knelt before him; then bent forward, lowering his face almost to the parquet.

This description of what Widmerpool did suggests, in fact, something much more immediate, more outwardly astounding, than the act seemed at the time. I should myself have been completely at a loss to know what Widmerpool was at, if he had not expressed only a short time before his intention of making some sort of an apology about what had happened at school. Even so, when Widmerpool went down on all fours in utter self-abasement, I supposed at first that he was searching for something he had dropped on the floor. That was almost certainly the explanation that offered itself to those standing round about who witnessed the scene at close quarters. Of these last no one, so far as I knew, had ever heard of the incident from which the action stemmed. Even had they been familiar with it, the complexity of Widmerpool's declared attitude towards social revolt, ritual sex, mystical repentance, was likely to be lost on them, as it was lost, collectively and separately, on Sir Bertram Akworth himself.

If quite other events had not at that moment intervened, Widmerpool's innate perseverance, his unsnubbableness, might at last have made his motives clear to the object of this melodramatic self-condemnation. As things fell out, two happenings diminished the force of the act—in any case for the moment generally misunderstood—to almost nothing, altogether removing possibility of its meaning being driven home. The first of these interpolations, not more than a matter of routine, was the reappearance of bride and bridegroom, who had retired a short time before to put on their going-away clothes. This entry naturally caused a stir among the guests, distracting the attention of those even in the immediate Widmerpool area of the Great Hall. The second occurrence, individual, distressing, even more calculated in its own way to cause concentration on itself, was prefigured by a sort of low gasp from Flavia Wisebite.

'Oh . . . Oh . . .'

She must have moved up quite close to Widmerpool, possibly with the object of making some sort of a contact, in order to express in her own words, personally, the detestation she felt for himself and all his works. If that were the end she had in view, Widmerpool's own unexpected obeisance to Sir Bertram Akworth had taken her completely by surprise. It seemed later that, when Widmerpool went down on his knees, Flavia Wisebite, brought up short in her advance, had fallen almost on top of his crouching body. This caused considerable localized commotion among guests in that part of the room; by this time beginning to empty in preparation for seeing off the newly married pair. Sir Bertram Akworth and Colonel Alford-Green, who were the nearest to the place of her collapse, with help from several others, managed to get Flavia to one of the forms by the wall. Finally, at the suggestion of Sir Bertram, she was borne away to the school's sickroom. Perhaps someone lifted Widmerpool from the floor too. When I next looked in that direction he was gone. Isobel came up.

'Are we going out to see them off? Did somebody faint near where you were standing?'

'Widmerpool's mother-in-law.'

'What do you mean?'

'Flavia Wisebite.'

'Is she here?'

'Her son-in-law is a subject she feels strongly about.'

Outside, farewells were taking place round the bridal car. Whatever the mishap, the vehicle had been repaired or replaced. Sir Bertram Akworth came across the causeway. He looked rather flustered. Somebody asked about Flavia Wisebite.

'Not at all well, I'm afraid.'

'Where is she?'

'Being looked after by the school's skeleton staff. We've rung for a doctor.'

Absurdly, the phrase made me think of the opening inscription of *Death's-head Swordsman*, conjured up a picture of the dead ministering to the dead, which would have appealed to Gwinnett. He and Fiona, once more hand in hand, moved away now that the car had driven off, crossing the drive to continue their examination of the exterior features of the Castle. Having gone to some trouble to bring her former associates to the wedding reception, Fiona seemed now to have lost interest in them. As usual, bride and bridegroom departed, there was a certain sense of anticlimax. Some of the guests continued to stand about in small groups, chatting to friends and relations; others were going off to look for their cars. The members of the cult were, most of them, standing, rather apart from the wedding guests, in a small forlorn circle, which included Widmerpool. Looking somewhat distraught, he was now at least upright, apparently haranguing his young companions; either explaining the significance of his own prostration before Sir Bertram Akworth, or merely taking the first steps in rounding up the crew, preparatory to setting out on the homeward run.

'To hell with all that.'

The voice, shrill, unconsenting, sounded like that of Barnabas Henderson. It appeared that he was arguing with Widmerpool. One of the wedding guests, a long-haired beefy young man in a grey tailcoat, was standing beside Henderson. Both these last two were in a state of some excitement. So was Widmerpool. It was at first not possible to hear what was being said, though Widmerpool was evidently speaking in an admonitory manner. The young man in the tailcoat, whose muscles were bursting from its contours, was becoming angry.

'Barnabas wants to get out. That's all about it.'

Henderson must have been asserting that intention too. Widmerpool was inaudible. His voice was more measured than theirs, possibly advised that things should be thought over before any such step be taken. Henderson almost shrieked.

'Not now I've found Chuck again. I'm going right away. Chuck will put me up at his place.'

Clearly a wrangle of some magnitude was in progress.

The big young man, who spoke in scathing cockney when addressing Widmerpool, snatched Henderson by the arm, walking him across to the side of the drive where Fiona and Gwinnett stood discussing the Castle. I felt no particular interest in the row. It was no affair of mine. Isobel, with Frederica and Norah, were chatting with Alford cousins. They would be some little time dishing up family news. I strolled towards the moat. As I did so, Widmerpool's tones sounded desperately.

'I forbid it.'

Since the days of Sir Magnus, the waterlilies had greatly increased in volume. If not eradicated, they would soon cover the whole surface of the stagnant water. On the far side, placed rather low in the wall near the main gate, was a small window, scarcely more than an arrow-slit, probably sited for observation purposes. A frantic face appeared at this opening for a moment, then was instantly withdrawn. The features could have been Bithel's. There was not time to make sure; only the upper half visible. It was just as likely I was mistaken, though Bithel was not among those standing round Widmerpool, nor, apparently, elsewhere on the drive. He might have decided to make his own way home. Some of the cult, possibly Bithel among them, were straying about in the neighbourhood of the Castle, because a blue robe was visible at some distance from where I stood. Its wearer was crossing one of the playing-fields. This was likely to be a straggler returning to the main body for the homeward journey.

Watching the approaching figure, I was reminded of a remark made by Moreland ages before. It related to one of those childhood memories we sometimes found in common. This particular recollection had referred to an incident in *The Pilgrim's Progress* that had stuck in both our minds. Moreland said that, after his aunt read the book aloud to him as a child, he could never, even after he was grown-up,

233

watch a lone figure draw nearer across a field, without thinking this was Apollyon come to contend with him. From the moment of first hearing that passage read aloud— assisted by a lively portrayal of the fiend in an illustration, realistically depicting his goat's horns, bat's wings, lion's claws, lizard's legs—the terror of that image, bursting out from an otherwise at moments prosy narrative, had embedded itself for all time in the imagination. I, too, as a child, had been riveted by the vividness of Apollyon's advance across the quiet meadow. Now, surveying the personage in the blue robe picking his way slowly, almost delicately, over the grass of the hockey-field, I felt for some reason that, if ever the arrival of Apollyon was imminent, the moment was this one. That had nothing to do with the blue robe, such costume, as I have said before, if it made any difference to Murtlock at all, softened the edge of whatever caused his personality to be a disturbing one. Henderson must have seen Murtlock too. His high squeak became a positive shout.

'Look—he's coming!'

Fiona seemed a little frightened herself. She appeared to be giving Henderson moral support by what she was saying. For the moment, while doing that, she had relinquished Gwinnett's hand. Now she took hold of it again. Murtlock continued his slow relentless progress. As this descent upon them of their leader became known among the cult—such of them as were present on the drive—a sense of trepidation was noticeable, not least in the case of Widmerpool. Abandoning the group he appeared to have been exhorting, he crossed the drive to where Henderson was standing with Fiona and Gwinnett. Widmerpool began a muttered conversation, first with Henderson, then with Fiona.

'So much the better.'

Fiona spoke with what was evidently deliberate loudness. At the same time she turned to glance in the direction of

234

Murtlock. He had somewhat quickened his pace for the last lap, reaching the gravel of the drive. Small pockets of ordinary wedding guests still stood about chatting. Most of these were some distance away from the point where Murtlock would have to decide whether he made for the bulk of his followers, or for the splinter group represented by Widmerpool and Henderson. There was no special reason why the run-of-the-mill guests, having accepted the blue-robed intruders as an integral part of the wedding reception, should suppose Murtlock anything but an offshoot of the original body. Of the two groups—the one huddled together, robed or otherwise; the other, consisting of Widmerpool, Henderson, Fiona, Gwinnett, together with the beefy young man called Chuck—Murtlock made unhesitatingly for the second. He stopped a yard or two away, uttering his greeting gently, the tone not much more than a murmur, well below the pitch of everyday speech. I heard it because I had moved closer. It was possible to ignore squabbles between Widmerpool and Henderson; Murtlock had that about him to fire interest.

'The Essence of the All is the Godhead of the True.'

Only Widmerpool answered, even then very feebly.

'The Visions of Visions heals the Blindness of Sight— and, Scorp, there is—'

Murtlock, disregarding the others, held up a hand towards Widmerpool to command silence. There was a moment's pause. When Murtlock answered, it was sharply, and in an altogether unliturgical manner.

'Why are you here?'

Widmerpool faltered. There was another long pause. Murtlock spoke again.

'You do not know?'

This time Murtlock's question was delivered in an almost amused tone. Widmerpool made great effort to utter. He had gone an awful colour, almost mauve.

'There is an explanation, Scorp. All can be accounted for. We met Fiona. She asked us in. I saw an opportunity to take part in an active rite of penitence, a piece of ritual discipline, painful to myself, of the sort you most recommend. You will approve, Scorp. I'm sure you will approve, when I tell you about it.'

After saying that, Widmerpool began to mumble distractedly. Murtlock turned away from him. Without troubling to give further attention to whatever Widmerpool was attempting to explain, he fixed his eyes on Henderson, who began to tremble violently. Fiona let go of Gwinnett's hand. She stepped forward.

'Barnabas is leaving you. He's staying here with Chuck.'

'He is?'

'Aren't you, Barnabas?'

Henderson, still shaking perceptibly, managed to confirm that.

'I'm going back with Chuck.'

'You are, Barnabas?'

'Yes.'

'I hope you will be happier together than you were before you came to us.'

Murtlock smiled benevolently. He seemed in the best of humours. Only Widmerpool gave the impression of angering him. The defection of Henderson appeared not to worry him in the least. His reply to Fiona, too, had been in the jocular tone he had sometimes used on the crayfishing afternoon; though it was clear that Murtlock had moved a long way, in terms of power, since that period. Perhaps he had learnt something from Widmerpool, while at the same time subduing him.

'A mystical sister has been lost, and gained. You are not alone in abandoning us, Fiona. Rusty, too, has returned to Soho.'

Fiona did not answer. She looked rather angry. Her

236

general air was a shade more grown-up than formerly. Murtlock turned to Gwinnett.

'Was not the Unicorn tamed by a Virgin?'

Gwinnett did not answer either. Had he wished to do so, in itself unlikely, there was no time. At that moment Widmerpool seemed to lose all control. He came tottering forward towards Murtlock.

'Scorp, I'm leaving too. I can't stand it any longer. You and the others need not be disturbed. I'll find somewhere else to live. I won't need much of the money.'

Apparently lacking breath to continue, he stopped, standing there panting. Murtlock's demeanour underwent a complete change. He dropped altogether the sneering bantering manner he had been using intermittently. Now he was angry again; not merely angry, furious, consumed with cold rage. For a second he did not speak, while Widmerpool ran on about Harmony.

'No.'

Murtlock cut Widmerpool short. Chuck, not at all interested in the strangeness of this duel of wills, put a protective arm round Henderson. He may have thought his friend in danger of capitulating, now that Murtlock was so enraged. That passion in Murtlock was not without its own horror.

'Come on, Barnabas. No point in hanging about. Let's be getting back.'

After Henderson had spoken some sort of farewell to Fiona, he went off with Chuck towards the cars. Murtlock took no notice of this withdrawal. His attention was entirely concentrated on Widmerpool, who, avoiding the eyes Murtlock fixed on him, continued to beg for release.

'Where could you go?'

Widmerpool made a gesture to signify that was no problem, but seemed unable to think of a spoken reply.

'No.'

237

'Scorp...'

'No.'

Murtlock repeated the negative in a dead toneless voice. Widmerpool was unable to speak. He stood there stupefied. Murtlock came closer. This conflict—in which Widmerpool, too, was evidently showing a certain amount of passive will power—was brought to an end by the re-entry of an actor forgotten in the course of rapid movement of events. The sound of singing came from the gates of the Castle.

> 'When I tread the verge of Jordan,
> Bid my anxious fears subside,
> Death of Death and hell's destruction,
> Land me safe on Canaan's side.'

Bithel was staggering across the causeway. His voice, high, quavering, much enhanced in volume by champagne, swelled on the spring air. Some sort of echo of the hymn was briefly taken up by another chant, possibly Umfraville's —he had served with the Welsh Guards—on the far side of the drive. Murtlock, as remarked earlier, was not in the least lacking in practical grasp. At a glance he took in the implications of this new situation.

'You allowed Bith to drink?'

'I—'

'What have I always said?'

'It was—'

'Lead the others back. I will manage Bith myself.'

This time Widmerpool made no demur. He accepted defeat. An unforeseen factor had put him in the wrong. He was beaten for the moment. The rest of the cult still stood in a glum group, no doubt contemplating trouble on return to base. Widmerpool beckoned to them. There was some giving of orders. A minute or two later Widmerpool, once more at the head of the pack, was leading the run home; a trot even slower than that employed when we first sighted

238

them. Bithel had stopped half-way across the causeway. He was leaning over the parapet, staring down at the water-lilies of the moat. The possibility that he might be sick was not to be excluded. That idea may have crossed Murtlock's practical mind too, because a slight smile flickered across his face, altering its sternness only for a moment, as he strode towards the Castle. Some words were exchanged. Then they moved off together towards the playing-fields. Bithel could walk; if not very straight. Once he fell down. Murtlock waited until Bithel managed to pick himself up again, but made no effort to help. They disappeared from sight. Fiona came over to where I was standing.

'Will you be seeing Gibson?'

'I expect so.'

'I want you to give him a message from me.'

'Of course.'

'When Russell and I first knew each other, Rus lent me his copy of Middleton's *Plays*. It's got some of his own notes pencilled in. I can't find it, and must have left it at Gibson's flat. Could you get him to send the book on—airmail it—to Russell's college? Just address it to the English Department. We're not going to have any time at all when we get back to London.'

'You're going straight to America?'

'The following day.'

'No other messages for Gibson?'

'No, just the book.'

By the time I next saw Delavacquerie he was aware that Fiona was married to Gwinnett. I don't know whether he heard directly from her, or the news just got round. She appeared to have left the flat without warning, taking her belongings with her. He smiled rather grimly when I passed on the request to send the Middleton book to Gwinnett's college.

'As a matter of fact I read some of the plays myself in

239

consequence—*The Roaring Girle*, which Dekker also had a hand in. I enjoyed the thieves' cant. Listen to this:

> A gage of ben rom-bouse
> In a bousing ken of Rom-vile,
> Is benar than a caster,
> Peck, pennam, lay, or popler,
> Which we mill in deuse a vile.
> O I wud lib all the lightmans,
> O I wud lib all the darkmans
> By the salomon, under the ruffmans,
> By the saloman, in the hartmans,
> And scour the queer cramp ring,
> And couch till a palliard docked my dell,
> So my bousy nab might skew rom-bouse well.
> Avast to the pad, let us bing;
> Avast to the pad, let us bing.

Not bad, is it?'
'It all sounds very contemporary. What does it mean?'
'Roughly, that a quart of good wine in London is better than anything to be stolen in the country, and, as long as wine's to be drunk, it doesn't matter if you're in the stocks, while some heel is stuffing your tart—that's a palliard docking your dell. Owing to Gwinnett, I came across a good couplet in Tourneur too:

> Lust is a spirit, which whosoe'er doth raise,
> The next man that encounters boldly, lays.

There seems a foot too many in the first line. They may have elided those relatives in a different way at that period.'
'How does the thieves' slang poem come into the Middleton play?'
'The Roaring Girl sings it herself, with a character called

Tearcat. The Roaring Girl dresses like a man, smokes, carries a sword, fights duels. A narcissistic type, rather than specifically lesbian, one would say. At least there are no scenes where she dallies with her own sex.'

Delavacquerie's good memory, eye for things that were unusual, had certainly been useful to him as a PR-man; for which he also possessed the requisite toughness. What he said next was a side he much less often revealed. It suggested reflections on Fiona.

'It's odd how one gets acclimatized to other people's sexual experiences. At a younger age, they strike one so differently. For instance, during the war I knew a married woman—a captain's wife—who told me of her first seduction. She was seventeen or eighteen, and on the way to her art-school one morning. Running to catch a bus, she just missed it. Two men, cruising by in a car, laughed at her standing breathless on the pavement. They stopped and offered her a lift. When they dropped her at the art-school door, the one who wasn't driving asked if she'd dine with him later in the week. She agreed. They went to a roadhouse outside London. In the course of dinner—establishing his bonafides as *homme sérieux*—her host remarked that he had lived with one girl for two years. Telling the story to me, she commented that—in those days—she thought love was for ever. Anyway, the chap gave her dinner, they had a good deal to drink—which she wasn't used to—and, afterwards, went into the garden of the roadhouse where he had her in the shrubbery. When she got home, finding her knickers all over blood, she thought to herself: I've been a silly girl. That's what she told me.'

'What's the moral of all that?'

'There isn't one, except that the story used to haunt me. I don't quite know why. It seemed to start so well, and end so badly. Perhaps that's how well constructed stories ought to terminate.'

241

'She never saw the bloke again?'

'No. I don't think it really made a ha'p'orth of difference to her. All I say is that for a while the story haunted me.'

'You were in love with the heroine?'

'Naturally. In a way that wasn't the point, which is that, in due course, you find girls are really perfectly well able to look after themselves, most of them. Even allowing for the fact that *les chiens sont fidèles, mais pas aux chiennes.* To retain the metaphor—bring it up to date—in sexual matters, as in others, the dogs bark, the Caravelle takes off.'

I never knew what Delavacquerie really felt about the Fiona business. Afterwards I wondered whether the heroine of the story he had told was really his dead wife. As Canon Fenneau had observed, we go through life lacking understanding of many things, though I think the Canon inwardly made something of an exception of his own case, where knowledge was concerned. That, at least, was modestly implied in an article I came across later that year, in which he contrasted Chaldean Magic with the worship of Isis and Osiris.

7

BAD WEATHER, OTHER ODD JOBS, mere lack of energy, had all
contributed to allowing the unlit bonfire, projected as a few
hours' clearing and burning, to become an untidy pile of
miscellaneous débris; laurel (cut down months before),
briars, nettles, leaves, unsold rubbish from a jumble sale, on
top of it all several quite large branches of oak and copper
beech snapped off by the gales. In spite of fog, something
calm, peaceful, communicative, about the afternoon suggested the time had come to end this too long survival. A
livid sky could mean snow. That dense muffled feeling
pervaded the air. The day was not cold for the season, but
an autumnal spell of mild weather—short, though notably
warm that year—was now over. It had given place to a
continuous wind blowing from the west, dropped the night
before, after bringing down a lot of leaves and the sizeable
boughs. There was a great stillness everywhere, except for a
monotonous thud-thud from the quarry; a persistent low
rumble, like a faraway train making laborious headway
along a rough stretch of track. White vapour, less thick
over by Gauntlett's farm, where a few ghostly trees penetrated its mists, wholly obscured the quarry's limestone
platforms and Assyrian rampart.

For kindling, I shoved twists of newspaper in at the base
of the heap. At the moment of ignition, the match flared

against capital letters of a headline displayed on the outward surface of one of these scraps of newsprint.

EDWARDIAN SYMBOLIST
SEASCAPE VOTARIES

The enigmatic antithesis topped an article read a week or two before. Even allowing for contemporary changes in art fashions, the critic's enthusiasm had then seemed surprising. After seeing the pictures, remembering the piece, I vaguely thought of glancing through the notice again, to see if I now felt more agreement with the opinions expressed. By then the newspaper had been thrown away, or disappeared among a heap of others; kept for such uses as lighting fires. A search, likely to be unfruitful, seemed scarcely worth the trouble. Now, inclination to read about what had been said of the exhibition—the two exhibitions—was reanimated. In any case the visit to the gallery had been rather an historic occasion; setting something of a seal on all sorts of past matters.

Lighting another screw of newspaper under the stack, I extracted a handful of crumpled up pages, and straightened them out. On the back of one of these was a paragraph reporting Quentin Shuckerly's end in New York (battered to death in Greenwich Village), while on a cultural mission of some kind. I tore out Edwardian Symbolist/Seascape Votaries, committing Shuckerly's obituary lines to their funeral pyre. The paper flared up, dry twigs began to crackle, damp weeds smouldered, smoke rose high into the white mists, merging into grey-blueness. The atmosphere was filled all at once with the heart-searing bonfire smell.

'. . . albeit his roots lie in Continental Symbolism, Deacon's art remains unique in itself. In certain moods he can recall Fernand Khnopff or Max Klinger, the Belgian's near-photographic technique observable in Deacon's semi-naturalistic treatment of more than one of his favourite

244

renderings of Greek or Roman legend. In his genre pictures, the academic compliances of the Secession School of Vienna are given strong homosexual bias—even Deacon's sphinxes and chimaeras possessing solely male attributes—a fearless sexual candour that must have shocked the susceptibilities of his own generation, sadomasochist broodings in paint that grope towards the psychedelic . . .'

The writer of the critique, a young journalist, with already something of a name in art circles, had been less enthralled by the late Victorian seascapes, also on view at the gallery; though he drew attention to the fact that here too, as with the Deacons, an exciting revival had taken place of a type of painting long out of fashion with yesterday's art critics. He expressed his welcome of these aesthetic reinstatements; noting the fact that at least a few connoisseurs, undeterred by the narrow tastes of the day, had followed their own preference for straightforward marine subjects, painted in an unaffectedly naturalistic manner. Most of those on view at the gallery had come from a single collection. He praised the 'virtuosity' and 'tightness of finish' of *Gannets Nesting*, *The Needles: Schooner Aground*, *Angry Seas off Land's End*, all by different hands.

Although a card had arrived for a Private View at this gallery, a new one, these two exhibitions had run for at least a fortnight before I found opportunity to pay a visit. Returning to the newspaper article—having been to the gallery—I felt less surprise at the critic's warm responses, not only to the Deacons, but also to the Victorian seascapes. That was probably due, as much as anything else, to a desire to keep in the swim. There was also a sense of satisfaction in reading praise of Mr Deacon (to me he always remained 'Mr Deacon'), given by a responsible art critic; a young one at that. The last quality would have delighted Mr Deacon himself. He had once remarked that youth was the only valid criterion in any field. He himself never quite achieved a fusion of the physical and intellectual in propagating that view. Certainly the notice marked how far tastes had altered since the period—just after the second war—when I had watched four Deacons knocked down for a few pounds in a shabby saleroom between Euston Road and Camden Town. At the time, I had supposed those to be the last Deacons I should ever set eyes on. In a sense they were; the last of the old dispensation. The pictures on view at the Barnabas Henderson Gallery (the show specifically advertised as the Bosworth Deacon Centenary Exhibition) were not so much a Resurrection as a Second Coming.

If the rehabilitation of Mr Deacon's art had not in itself provided an overriding inducement to visit the exhibition, the name of the gallery—proving all curiosity was not at an end—would have gone a long way as an alternative inducement to do so. A single-page pamphlet, accompanying the Private View card, outlined the aims of this new picture firm, which had just come into being. They seemed admirable ones. The premises were in the neighbourhood of Berkeley Square. It was rather late in the afternoon when I finally reached the place, a newly painted exterior, the street in process of being rebuilt, the road up, several Georgian houses opposite looking as if they had been recently bombed. In the window of the Barnabas Henderson Gallery itself a poster proclaimed Mr Deacon's name in typography of a size, and fount, he would have approved, an aureole of favourable press notices pinned round about.

Within, I found myself surrounded by Deacon canvases assembled on an unprecedented scale; more Deacons than might be supposed even to have been painted, far less survived. The Victorian seascapes were segregated in a room beyond, but an arrow pointed to an extension of the Deacon Centenary Exhibition on the upper floor, which I decided to explore first. The red tag of a sale marked a high proportion of the pictures. Two of those so summarily dismissed at the down-at-heel auction-rooms were immediately recognizable from their black-and-gold Art Nouveau frames, Deacon-designed to form part of the picture itself; a technique Mr Deacon rather precariously supported by quoting two lines from *Pericles:*

In framing an artist, art hath thus decreed:
To make some good, but others to exceed.

In the shabby saleroom this purpose of the frames had been obscured by dirt and tarnished paint, which cleaning and restoration now made clear. Light in pigment, some of the canvases were huge in size, remembered subjects included Hellenic athletes painfully straining in some contest; another (too grimy at the time to be properly appreciated), a boy slave reproved by his toga-enveloped master, whose dignified figure was not without all resemblance to Mr Deacon himself in his palmy days. The show was stylish in presentation. In fact Barnabas Henderson had done a stupendous rescue job from the Valley of Lost Things; Mr Deacon's Astolpho, or perhaps one of the well disposed swans, fishing up his medallion for the Temple of Fame. Henderson clearly knew his business. To have supposed him the dim figure he had seemed, only a few months earlier in the same year, under the Murtlock régime, was an error of judgment. Since his self-manumission at Stourwater the Private View card was the first I had heard of him; nor was there any further news of Murtlock and Widmerpool.

Even Mr Deacon's closest friends were accustomed to smile tolerantly, behind his back, about his painting. The few patrons had all faded away by the later stages of his life, when he had exchanged an artist's career for an antique-dealer's. All the same, in days when Barnby's studio was above the antique shop, Barnby had remarked that, little as he approved himself, Sickert had once put in a good word for Mr Deacon's work. Looking round, more impressed than I should have been prepared to admit, I took heart from Sickert's judgment; at the same time trying to restore self-confidence as to an earlier scepticism by noting something undoubtedly less than satisfactory in the foreshortening of the slave boy's loins.

There was still no one about in the first ground floor room of the gallery when I returned there, the attendant's desk in the corner unoccupied. Through a door at the far end several persons, one of them in a wheel-chair, were to be seen perambulating among the Victorian seascapes. I had not at first noticed that one of the smaller pictures in this first room was *Boyhood of Cyrus*. Moving across to ascertain how closely, if at all, the palace in its background resembled the configurations of the local quarry, I was intercepted by Barnabas Henderson himself, who came hurrying up a flight of stairs leading from the basement. It was instantaneously apparent that he was a new man; no less renovated than the Deacon pictures on the walls. That was clear in a flash, a transformation not in the least due to adjustments in dress and personal appearance, also to be observed. He had slightly shortened his haircut, reverted to a suit, elegant in cut without being humdrum in style, wore a tie of similar mood. These, however different from a blue robe, were trivial modifications in relation to the general air of rebirth. There was a newly acquired briskness, even firmness of manner, sense of self-confidence amply restored.

'Oh, hullo, Nicholas. You received our card all right? I was afraid it might have gone astray, as you hadn't been in.'

'I couldn't get to the Private View.'

'I hope your wife will look in, too, before the Deacon show closes. I always remember how good she was about our turning up once with that awful man. I was quite ashamed at the time. We went crayfishing, do you remember? It was an unusual experience. I can't say I enjoyed it much. Still, I didn't enjoy anything much in the circumstances of what my life was then. I hope you like these pictures—and the ones in the next room too, which are by various painters. Bosworth Deacon is one of my own discoveries.'

'I used to know him.'

'Know whom?'

'Edgar Deacon.'

'Who was Edgar Deacon—a relation of Bosworth Deacon?'

'He was called Edgar. Bosworth was only his middle name.'

'No, no. Bosworth is the painter's name. Are you sure you aren't confusing your other Deacon man? Bosworth Deacon is a most remarkable artist. In his way unique. I can think of no other painter like him.'

Henderson, possibly with reason, was not in the least interested in whether or not I had known Mr Deacon. Perhaps it was not really a relevant subject; or rather seemed relevant only to myself. It was clear that Mr Deacon—born a hundred years before—seemed in Henderson's eyes a personage scarcely less remote in time than the kindly slave-master of the artist's own self-image.

'I saw you were making for *Boyhood of Cyrus*, one of Deacon's best. On the whole I prefer the smaller compositions. He's more at ease with figure relationships. Several of the critics picked out *Cyrus* in their notices. I sold it within an hour of the show opening.'

'The background looks rather like the quarry to be seen from our windows. You may have noticed it on your caravan visit?'

Henderson raised his eyebrows. They could have been plucked. The comparison of Mr Deacon's picture with the quarry landscape struck no chord. Henderson sold pictures, rather than pondered their extraneous imagery.

'Surely the palace in the distance represents Persepolis. It's symbolic.'

'Well Persepolis isn't unlike Battersea Power Station in silhouette. An industrial parallel is not excluded out of hand.'

Henderson did not reply. He pursed his lips a little. We were getting nowhere. The subject was better changed. Eleanor Walpole-Wilson had probably sold *Cyrus* after her parents died. When, in days of frequenting the house, I had once referred to 'their Deacon', she was all but unaware of its existence, hanging over the barometer in the hall.

'When I was young I sometimes dined with the people to whom *Boyhood of Cyrus* used to belong.'

At this information Henderson regarded me with keener interest.

'You knew Lord Aberavon?'

He was not incredulous; merely mildly surprised. One had to be grateful even for surprise.

'Not actually. Aberavon died five or six years before I was born. My hostess was his daughter. She owned the picture. Her husband was a diplomat called Walpole-Wilson.'

Henderson was no more prepared to allow that the Walpole-Wilsons had once possessed *Boyhood of Cyrus* than for Mr Deacon to have been commonly addressed as Edgar.

'The provenance of *Cyrus* has always been recognized as the Aberavon Collection. Several Aberavon pictures—by a variety of artists—have been coming on the market lately. They're usually good sellers. Aberavon was an erratic collector, but not an uninstructed one. Have you looked at *By the Will of Diocletian*? It hasn't found a buyer yet. Owing to being rather large for most people's accommodation these days it is very reasonably priced, if you're thinking of getting a Deacon yourself.'

'The younger of the two torturers is not unlike Scorpio Murtlock.'

This time Henderson reacted more favourably to extension of a picture's imaginative possibilities.

'Canon Fenneau said the same, when he was in here the other day. He's someone who knew Scorp when he was quite young. One of the few who can control him.'

'Where did you come across Fenneau?'

'Scorp once sent me with a message to him. Chuck and I sometimes go to his church. It was Canon Fenneau who told me that *By the Will of Diocletian* was painted during Bosworth Deacon's Roman Catholic period.'

'Do you ever hear of Murtlock now? Or Widmerpool?'

Henderson, facetiously, made the sign to keep off the Evil Eye.

'As a matter of fact I do once in a way. Somebody I knew there comes to see me on the quiet if he's in London. There's a thing I'm still interested in they've got in the house.'

'Would coming to see you not be allowed?'

'Of course not.'

Henderson might perhaps have said more on that subject had not Chuck appeared from the inner room. Chuck (perhaps also of seafaring origins) had some of the same burly working-class geniality—now adapted to the uses of the art world—that had once characterized Hugo Tolland's former partner, Sam.

'Can you come through for a moment, Barney? Mr Duport wants a word.'

Henderson indicated that he would be along in a moment. Towards Chuck, too, his manner had changed. Himself no longer a victim requiring rescue, Henderson had become something not much short of Mr Deacon's benign slave-owner. No doubt mutual relationship was carefully worked out in that connexion, Chuck showing no resentment at the readjustment. On the contrary, they seemed on the best of terms.

'There are some rather interesting people in the further room. The actress, Polly Duport, and her parents. Far the best of the Victorian marine painters show come from the Duport Collection. He's decided to sell now the going's good. He's quite right, I think. I expect you've seen Polly Duport in the Strindberg play. Super, I thought. She's an absolute saint too, the way she looks after her father. Wheels him round all the time in that chair. He's not at all easy. Can be very bad mannered, in fact. He was a businessman —in oil, I'm told—then had to retire on account of whatever's wrong with him. He'd always been interested in these Victorian seascapes, picked them up at one time or another for practically nothing. Now they're quite the thing. He comes in almost every day to see how they're selling.'

'I know Polly Duport—and her father.'

'Do you? But you won't know her mother, who's come with them this afternoon. She's lived most of her life in South America. She must be partly South American, I think. She looks like one of those sad Goya duchesses. She and Robert Duport, the owner of the Collection, have been separated for years, so Polly Duport told me, but have been seeing a good deal of each other lately. He's never brought her along before. She was married to a South American politician, who was killed by urban guerillas. That's why she came back to England.'

Henderson's explanation had taken so long that the people next door, tired of waiting, now moved into the room where we were talking; Duport's wheeled-chair pushed by his daughter. Her mother followed. Norman Chandler, who was directing the Strindberg production to which Henderson referred, was one of this party. Henderson was right about Jean. The metamorphosis, begun when the late Colonel Flores had been his country's military attaché in London at the end of the war, was complete.

She was now altogether transformed into a foreign lady of distinction. The phrase 'sad Goya duchess' did not at all overstate the case. Chandler gave a dramatic cry of satisfaction at seeing someone with whom he could exchange reminiscences of Mr Deacon.

'Nick, so you've come to see Edgar's pictures? Who'd ever have thought it? Do you remember when I sold him that statuette called *Truth unveiled by Time*? Barney and Chuck ought to have that on show here too. I wonder where it is now?'

Duport stirred in the wheel-chair. He looked a rather ghastly sight. All the same he recognized me at once, and let out a hoarse laugh.

'How the hell do you know he hasn't come to see my pictures, Norman, not these naked Roman queers? He probably loves the sea.'

He turned in my direction.

'I can't remember your name, because I can't remember anyone's name these days, including my own most of the time, but we were in Brussels together, looking after different fragments of the Belgian military machine.'

'We were indeed.'

I told Duport my name. Chandler hastened to make additional introductions.

'So you and Bob know each other, Nick, and I'm sure you've met Polly. This is her mother, Madame Flores—'

Jean smiled graciously. She held out the hand of a former near-dictator's lady—Carlos Flores cannot have been much short of dictator at the height of his power—a clasp, brief and light, not without a sense of power about it too. There could have been no doubt in the mind of an onlooker— Henderson, say, or Chuck—that Jean and I had met before. That was about the best you could say for past love. In fact Jean's former husband, whom I had never much liked, was appreciably less distant than she.

253

'I've gone down the drain since those Brussels days. It all started in the Middle East. Gyppy Tummy, then complications. Never got things properly right. Look at me now. Shunted round in a bathchair. Penny for the guy. That's how I feel. One of the things I remember about you is that you knew that château-bottled shit Widmerpool.'

Polly Duport patted her father's head in deprecation of such forcible metaphor. Duport's appearance certainly bore out an assertion that he was not at all well. There seemed scarcely room in the chair for his long legs, the knees thrust up at an uncomfortable angle. Spectacles much altered his appearance. His daughter looked much younger than her forties. Firmly dedicated—somebody said like a nun—to her profession, she was dressed with great simplicity, as if to emphasize an absolute detachment from anything at all like the popular idea of an actress. This was in contrast with Jean, who had acquired a dramatic luxuriousness of turnout, not at all hers as a girl. Polly had always greatly resembled her mother, but, their styles now so different, perhaps only someone like myself, who had known Jean in her young days, would notice much similarity. Duport was not in the least disposed to abandon the theme of Widmerpool, whom he regarded as having at one moment all but ruined him financially.

'Polly once saw Widmerpool knocked out by an American film star. I wish I'd been there to shake him by the hand.'

'He wasn't really knocked out, Papa. Only his specs broken. And Louis Glober wasn't a film star, though he looked like one.'

'It was something to break that bastard's glasses. I'd have castrated him too, if I'd ever had the chance. Not much to remove, I'd guess.'

Jean made a gesture to silence her former husband.

'How are you, Nick? You're looking well. Better than the time you and your wife came to a party we gave, when

254

Carlos was over here. Everybody in London was so utterly tired out at the end of the war. Do you remember our party? How is your wife? I liked her so much.'

'I was sorry to hear—'

Before Jean could answer, Duport, recognizing the imminence of condolences for the death of Colonel Flores, broke in again.

'Oh, don't worry about Carlos. Carlos didn't do too badly. Had the time of his life, when the going was good, then went out instantaneously. Lucky devil. I envy him like hell. Wish I'd met him. He always sounded the sort of bloke I like.'

Jean accepted that view.

'I've often said you'd both of you have got on very well together.'

Polly Duport, possibly lacking her parents' toughness in handling such matters, at the same reminded by them of emotional complications suffered by herself, turned the conversation in the direction of these.

'You know Gibson Delavacquerie, don't you?'

'Of course. I haven't seen him for a month or two. He said he was working very hard.'

'Gibson and I are getting married.'

'You are? How splendid. Best possible wishes.'

'He's got a new book of poems coming out. That's why he's gone into retirement as much as possible.'

She looked very pleased; at the same time a little sad. I wondered whether the poems had anything to do with the sadness. In any case there had been quite a bit of sadness to surmount. She had given this information in an aside, while her parents were laughing, with Chandler and the owners of the gallery, about some incident illustrated in one of the Deacons, to which Chandler was pointing. Now he turned to Polly and myself.

'Goodness, don't these bring Edgar back? Do you

255

remember his last birthday party when he fell down stairs at that awful dive, *The Brass Monkey*?'

'I wasn't there. I knew that was the final disaster.'

Duport stared round disapprovingly.

'I prefer my wind and waves. Smart of me to hang on to them all these years, wasn't it? That took some doing. Do you remember, Jean, how your brother, Peter, used to grumble about looking after my pictures for me, when I was in low water, and hadn't anywhere to put them. He hung them in the dining-room of that house he had at Maidenhead. He'd no pictures of his own to speak of—except that terrible Isbister of his old man—so I can't see what he was grousing at. I might easily have got rid of them, but was spry enough not to sell. They wouldn't have made a cent.'

Jean laughed.

'Poor Peter. Why should he keep your junk? You weren't in low water. You were running round with Bijou Ardglass.'

'Perhaps I was. One forgets these things. Poor Bijou too.'

'Do you remember the pictures in the dining-room, Nick? Peter's Maidenhead house was where we met.'

'And played planchette.'

'Yes—we played planchette.'

Duport, becoming suddenly tired, lay back in his chair. He gave a very faint groan. I felt I liked him better than I used. His daughter made a movement to leave.

'I think we'd better go home now, Papa.'

Duport sat up straight again.

'So we've only got one more to sell?'

Henderson agreed. Jean once more held out her hand. Fashion, decreeing one kissed almost everyone these days, might not unreasonably have brought that about had she kept herself less erect. It was thus avoided without prejudice to good manners.

'So nice to have met.'

'Yes, so nice.'

Polly Duport smiled goodbye. I told her how glad I was to hear about herself and Delavacquerie. She smiled again, but did not say anything. Chandler waved. Taking Henderson and Chuck each by an arm, he led them towards the door, evidently imparting an anecdote about Mr Deacon. Duport gave a nod, as he was wheeled away. I strolled round the marine painters. There was—as Jean had said— a vague memory of sea pictures, hung rather askew, on Templer's dining-room wall. Rather a job lot they had seemed to me that weekend. Even if other things had not been on my mind—that soft laugh of Jean's—Victorian seascapes would have made no great appeal.

'It's the bedroom next to yours. Give it half an hour. Don't be too long.'

The Needles: Schooner Aground was by no means without all merit. The painter had evidently seen the work of Bonington. I was less keen on *Angry Seas off Land's End*. Henderson returned.

'Polly Duport's sweet, isn't she? Don't you find her mother a little alarming? But then you'd met her before. She must have been very handsome when young. Let me show you that last remaining one of the Duport Collection. You might like to consider it yourself.'

He did so. There was no sale. Chuck reappeared.

'Time to close.'

Henderson looked at his watch.

'You were telling me you still had some line on the Murtlock/Widmerpool setup. I'd be most interested to hear more of what went on there.'

Chuck interposed.

'Do you want me to stay?'

Henderson hesitated.

'No thanks, Chuck. I'll deal with everything. Just do the usual, and go home. I'll follow on.'

Henderson seemed divided between wanting to tell his

story, and something else that appeared to weigh on his mind. Then he must have decided that telling the story would be sufficiently gratifying to make up for possible indiscretion in other directions.

'If you've got a moment, we could go down to the office.'

I said goodnight to Chuck, by then making preparations to leave. Henderson led the way down a spiral staircase to the basement. The narrow passages below were cluttered with more pictures, framed and unframed. We entered a small room filled with filing cabinets and presses for drawings. Henderson took up his position behind a desk. I chose an armchair of somewhat exotic design, of which there were two. Henderson now seemed to relish the idea of making a fairly elaborate narration. He had perhaps exhausted the extent of persons of his own age prepared to listen.

'When we all crashed Clare Akworth's wedding, did you notice an old fellow with us. He had a beard and a red sweater. It was him all the trouble was about at the end, so I heard. Chuck and I had gone off by then.'

'You mean Bithel?'

'You know about him? I was told Scorp had almost to carry him home. Bith was a drunk. Somebody sent him along to us when he was just about to freak out. Bith was the only man or woman I've ever seen Scorp behave in a decent way to. He pretty well saved Bith's life. Bith worshipped Scorp in return. When he got better, Bith did odd jobs about the place nobody else wanted to do. That was pretty useful. There was no one who liked household chores. There was another side too. Scorp said an aged man was required for certain rites. Bith didn't mind that. He didn't mind what he did.'

Henderson's face suggested that some of the acts Bithel had been required to perform were less than agreeable, bearing out Widmerpool's reluctance to detail his own experience in that line.

'Could he stand being allowed no alcohol?'

'That's the point. Bith found that a drag. It was just the knowledge he was being kept alive prevented him from packing it in—plus adoration for Scorp. From time to time Bith would get hold of a little money, and have a drink on the quiet. Scorp winked at that. He'd never have stood it from anyone else, unless for strictly ritual purposes. That was permitted, like getting high on whatever Scorp might sometimes decide to produce. I used to give Bith the price of a drink once in a while, so he'd do things for me. I'd got some money hidden away.'

'You weren't allowed money?'

'Scorp controlled all that. Most of them hadn't much anyway. I'd hidden some at the top of the house under the eaves. I'd been thinking about getting away for some time, but it wasn't so easy. Then seeing Chuck gave me the chance. If Chuck hadn't been working in the same firm as Clare Akworth—he's one of their drivers, and gives her lifts to the office—I might not be here. I might not even be alive, if she'd not invited Chuck to the wedding, and he hadn't always wanted to wear a grey tailcoat.'

Henderson looked absolutely serious when he said he might not have been alive. His manner had become even a little disconcerting in its seriousness.

'It's Bith who looks in to see me occasionally. Scorp sends him to London sometimes to do odd jobs. Perhaps with a message to Canon Fenneau, if a respectable link is needed. It is sometimes. Fenneau helped once about getting a girl who was having a baby into hospital. Scorp recognizes that Bith will arrive back drunk, but he just makes him do a small penance. There's a particular thing Widmerpool's got that I hope one of these days to get out of him. That's why I keep in touch with Bith. He isn't very coherent as a rule. That doesn't much matter. Do you ever hear anything of Fiona? She used to use Bith too.'

'Her mother got a letter from her the other day. Fiona seems all right. They're in the Middle West.'

The Cutts parents, 'good' as ever, never complained about hearing rarely from their daughter. Probably they took the view that no news was better than bad news.

'Scorp used to talk a lot about that American Fiona married.'

'In connexion with Fiona?'

'No, not at all. Scorp was angry when Fiona went away, but I don't think he foresaw she would end up with Gwinnett. It was Gwinnett's own potential powers that attracted Scorp.'

'Transcendental ones?'

'Yes.'

'What about Widmerpool? Did Murtlock think he possessed transcendental powers too?'

The question was put lightly, even ironically. Henderson chose to answer it seriously. Having now abandoned the cult, he was prepared to denounce Murtlock as an individual; he had been too long connected with its system and disciplines utterly to reject their foundations. That was the impression his manner suggested.

'Ken's transcendental gifts were not what Scorp valued him for. I doubt if he possessed any. Not like Gwinnett. It was Ken's will-power. Also, of course, the basic fact of being able to live in and around his house. Ken wanted to be head. I see now he never could have been. At first it seemed touch and go. At least I thought so. I was afraid Ken would take over. He picked up the doctrinal part so quickly. I was terrified.'

'Why terrified?'

Henderson looked surprise at being asked that.

'Because I was in love with Scorp. I wanted him at the head.'

'Is Widmerpool in love with Murtlock too?'

This time Henderson did not give a snap answer. He hesitated. When he spoke it was objectively, almost primly.

'I don't know. It was hard for me to judge. I thought everybody was in love with Scorp. I was jealous of them for that. Ken doesn't actively dislike girls. He'd watch them naked, whenever he could. He may like boys better now he's used to them.'

'You mean in sexual rites?'

'Or on runs.'

'You went for naked runs?'

'Not at all often. Very rarely. Sometimes the ritual required it. In spring or autumn we would have to wait for a fairly warm night. Even then it could be dreadful.'

'Before breakfast?'

'Breakfast—you don't suppose we had breakfast? It was usually about half-past four in the morning. Only about once a year.'

'Murtlock himself?'

'Of course.'

'Widmerpool too?'

'Why not?'

'Bithel?'

'No—not Bith. Bith was let off. He'd make up for it by the other things he had to do.'

'And Widmerpool took part in the sexual rites?'

'When he was able.'

'Didn't you meet anyone on your naked runs?'

'Not in the middle of the night. It wasn't often. Scorp took us along paths through the woods.'

'Murtlock had Widmerpool completely under control in the end?'

'Only after the arrival of Bith. That was the turning point. Ken hated Bith. There was no Harmony. No Harmony at all. That made Scorp angry. It made bad vibrations. He was quite right. It did. I won't tell you some of the things Scorp made them do together. I don't like to think of it.'

Henderson shuddered.

'Why didn't Widmerpool leave?'

'Where would he go? If he went, Scorp remained in possession of the house. There's no getting him out. Ken's believed to have bequeathed it to the cult anyway. He could have made it over already.'

'Was thought of the house what caused Widmerpool to change his mind at Stourwater?'

'It was Scorp's will-power. That's stronger than anything. You'd know, if you'd ever had to face it. He came to Chuck's flat, and tried to get me back. There was an awful scene. I don't know how I got through it. I was shaky for a fortnight after. I did somehow—with the help of Chuck.'

Henderson shuddered again.

'But what was the point of it all. What did—what does—Widmerpool expect to get out of it?'

Once more Henderson seemed surprised. He was prepared to accept that he himself might find the ways of Murtlock harsh, horrible, even murderous. The aim of the cult, if impossible to express in words, was to him an altogether understandable one.

'Ken was playing for high stakes, if he really became head. It's hard to explain. Of course I don't believe now, not in the least. But Scorp, for instance, where's he going to end? He might go anywhere. That's what Ken felt. Of course Ken was too old, apart from anything else.'

'A messiah?'

'If you like.'

A bell rang at some length from upstairs. It sounded as if someone was following that up by rattling on the front door. Henderson rose,

'What can that be? It's just possible . . . Wait a moment. I'll go and see.'

When Henderson's voice sounded again, at the top of the spiral staircase, its note suggested unexpected satisfaction. Henderson himself seemed to be doing all the talking. At least no replies were audible from whomever he had let in. There was a crash, a pause, a great scrambling and stumbling on the stairs, several steps missed; then Bithel, closely piloted from behind by Henderson, arrived—almost fell down—in the office. The immediate conclusion seemed to be that, whatever gratified Henderson, was not the fact of Bithel having arrived sober. On the contrary, Bithel was in a state of extreme intoxication. He was clutching a brown-paper parcel. Henderson spoke formally, as if nothing were more natural than Bithel's state.

'Here's Bith. I thought it might be him, but I never guessed what he'd bring with him. He can't speak at present. Wait till he's unwrapped the parcel.'

Henderson made an unsuccessful effort to get hold of this. Bithel clung on. He was, as described, entirely speechless. If Bithel had seemed filthy at Stourwater, out in the open, he looked infinitely filthier enclosed within the narrow confines of the gallery's office. He smelt horrible. In the army he had admitted to an age in the late thirties, so now was at least seventy, if not more. He appeared a great deal older than that; some dreadful ancient, brought in from tramping the roads day in day out. A decaying pushteen, torn and grimy, covered patched corduroy trousers. This time his feet were in sandals.

'Sit down, Bith. When did you get to London? Pretty early I'd guess from your state. Let's have a look at the picture.'

Bithel, deposited in the other exotically designed armchair, evidently wanting desperately to make some statement, was literally unable to speak. What had at first seemed a mere state of drunkenness gave signs of being something more than that. Drink had at least brought no

solace, none of the extreme garrulousness that had characterized Bithel's army toping. He conveyed the air of a man,
whatever his innately broken-down state, who had been
seriously upset. That might be the form Bithel's intoxication now took. Henderson was chiefly interested in the
brown-paper parcel, trying to get it into his own hands,
always failing. Then Bithel got a word out.

'Scotch.'

'Haven't you had enough?'

'Not . . . feeling . . . myself.'

'No, you're not your usual self, Bith, on a day off. All
right. We'll see what can be done.'

Henderson, opening a cupboard, brought back to the desk
a bottle and glasses.

'Now unwrap it. How did you manage? It wasn't theft?
You're sure of that? I'm not going to handle it, if it's
stolen. There must be evidence you were allowed to take it.
That's absolutely definite.'

Bithel made a jerky movement of his shoulders,
apparently indicating that nothing at all nefarious had taken
place in regard to whatever was under discussion.

'All right, but why can't you say more? You're not
usually like this, Bith. You've had much too much. What
will Scorp do to you? Try and tell me about it.'

Bithel took a deep gulp, finishing off the reasonably
generous shot of whisky Henderson had poured for him.
He held out the glass for more. Henderson allowed him an
individual replenishment. I attempted to explain to Bithel
that we had been comrades-in-arms. It was hard to think of
an incident that had not reflected some unhappy moment
in his own military career; any happy ones almost certainly
experienced at times he would have been too drunk to recall.

'Do you remember our Company Commander, Rowland
Gwatkin?'

Bithel's eyes, damp and bleary, suddenly reacted.

'Fol-low, fol-low, we will fol-low Gwatkin—
We will fol-low Gwatkin, everywhere he leads.'

Bithel sang the words gently. Their reference to romping round the Mess on Christmas night, following the Commanding Officer over tables and chairs, sideboards and sofas, must have been entirely lost on Henderson. In any case the Commanding Officer's name had been Davies. Now Colonel was evidently merged as a single entity with Gwatkin in Bithel's mind. Becoming more than ever impatient, Henderson once more tried to get hold of the parcel. Bithel demanded a third round before giving it up.

'Not before I see the picture—know how you got it.'

Bithel made a violent effort to give an explanation.

'Going to . . . be burnt.'

'Scorp wanted to burn it. You rescued it?'

Bithel's twitching face seemed to indicate that solution as near the mark.

'Does Ken know?'

This question threw Bithel into a paroxysm of coughing, followed by an awful dry retching. He seemed about to vomit, something not at all out of the question in experience of him. An alternative possibility was apoplexy. When this violent attack was at an end he got out a sentence.

'Lord Widmerpool's . . . dead.'

'What?'

Both Henderson and I exclaimed simultaneously.

'Murdered.'

Bithel's powers of speech made some sort of recovery now. He had contrived to articulate what was on his mind. This was when it became clear that nervous strain, at least as much as drink, was powerfully affecting him. In fact the whisky he had just drunk had undoubtedly pulled him together. At first his words, dramatically gasped out, aroused a picture of gun, knife, poison, length of lead piping.

Then one saw that Bithel was almost certainly speaking with exaggeration. Even so, some ritual—like the gash at The Devil's Fingers—might have gone too far; for example, misuse of a dangerous drug. Allowing for overstatement, I was not at all sure which was meant. Henderson, with closer knowledge of the circumstances, seemed to regard anything as possible. He had gone white in the face.

'Was he found dead? Has this just happened? Are the police in on it?'

'Scorp was responsible. You can't call it anything but murder. I'm not going back. I've left for good. I'm fond of Scorp—fonder than I've ever been of any boy—but he's gone too far. I'm not going back.'

'But what happened? You don't really mean murder?'

'What Scorp made him do.'

'Say what that was.'

The story came out only by degrees. Even in a slightly improved condition Bithel was not easy to follow. In his—comparatively speaking—less dilapidated days, Bithel's rambling narratives had been far from lucid. The events he had just been through seemed to have been enough to disturb anyone. They had, at the same time, to some degree galvanized him out of the state of brain-softening he had displayed at Stourwater. He kept on muttering to himself, his voice at times entirely dying away.

'Lord Widmerpool ought never to have gone. Wasn't fit. Wasn't in the least fit. It was murder. Nothing short.'

That the old Bithel—with his respect for the 'varsity man'—survived under the tangled beard and foul rags, was shown by dogged adherence to calling Widmerpool by a title he had himself renounced by word and deed; if never by official procedure. After a bout of breathlessness, Bithel now showed signs of falling asleep. Henderson prodded him with a paper-knife.

'What happened?'

266

Bithel opened his eyes. Henderson repeated the question.

'What happened about Ken?'

'We could all see Lord Widmerpool wasn't well. He hadn't been well for weeks. He was bloody ill, in fact. Not himself at all. He could hardly get up from the floor.'

I asked why Widmerpool was on the floor. Henderson explained that the cult did not use beds. Bithel groaned in confirmation of that.

'When Lord Widmerpool did get up he was all shaky. He wasn't fit, even though it was a warmish night last night. It was Scorp who insisted.'

'Was Widmerpool unwilling to go?'

Bithel looked at me as if he did not understand what I was talking about. Even if prepared to accept that we had served in the same regiment, could recognize the same songs or horseplay, he certainly had not the least personal recollection of a common knowledge of Widmerpool.

'Lord Widmerpool didn't object. He wanted to be in Harmony. He always wanted that. He took a moment to get properly awake. At first he could hardly stand, when he got up from the floor. All the same, he took his clothes off.'

'Why did he take his clothes off?'

Henderson explained that was the rite. He seemed to have fallen back into regarding what had gone forward as natural enough in the light of the ritual, a normal piece of ceremonial. Not only did he understand, he seemed a little carried away by the devotional aspects of the story.

'Scorp must have thought it would get too cold if use was not made of that late mild spell we've been having. He was right. The temperature dropped this afternoon. If he'd left it till tonight they'd never have been able to go out.'

'Do you mean they all went out on a naked run in the early hours of this morning?'

'Ken never wanted to be outdone in Harmony by Scorp.'

Henderson and Bithel agreed about that, Bithel almost showing animation.

'Didn't we all? Didn't we all? But I'm through. I'm bloody well through. I swear I am. If I go back, it won't be for long. I swear that. I can't stand it. I'll find somewhere else. I swear I will.'

Bithel rocked himself backwards and forwards.

'What happened on the run?'

'It was through the woods.'

'Scorp was leading of course. Did Ken feel ill when he got outside?'

'Lord Widmerpool seemed recovered at first, they said. There was a warm mist. It was cold enough, they told me, but not as bad as they thought it would be.'

'So they set off?'

'Then Lord Widmerpool shouted they weren't going fast enough.'

Henderson showed amazement at such a thing happening.

'Why should Ken have done that? It was never a race. The slow pace was to give a sense of Harmony. Scorp always made a point of that.'

'When Lord Widmerpool shouted, they said Scorp sounded very angry, and said no. They were going fast enough. To increase the speed would disrupt the Harmony. Lord Widmerpool didn't take any notice of Scorp.'

'That was unlike Ken.'

Bithel lay back, so far as doing so were possible, in the pop-art armchair. The Scotch had greatly revived him, calmed his immediate fears, enabled him to tell the story with a kind of objectivity.

'If Lord Widmerpool disagreed with Scorp he'd always say why. They quite often argued. Lord Widmerpool seemed to enjoy a tussle, then giving in, and being given a penance. Never knew such a man for penances.'

Abandoning his narrative, at the thought of Widmerpool's penances, Bithel sighed.

'Did Widmerpool increase his own speed?'

'Not at first, they told me. Then he began complaining again that they weren't running fast enough. He started to shout "I'm running, I'm running, I've got to keep it up." Everybody thought he was laughing, trying to get himself warm. After shouting out this for a while, he did increase his pace. Some of the others went faster too. Scorp wouldn't allow that. He ordered Lord Widmerpool to slow down, but of course he couldn't stop him. He was way on ahead by then. Somebody heard Lord Widmerpool shout "I'm leading, I'm leading now."'

'How did it end?'

'It was rather a twisty way through the woods. Nobody could see him, especially in the mist. When they came round a corner, out of the trees, he was lying just in the road.'

'Collapsed?'

'Dead.'

Bithel held out his glass for yet another refill. Henderson topped it up. There was quite a long silence.

'How did they carry the body back?'

'They managed somehow.'

'It must have been quite a way.'

'You bet.'

'What did Scorp say?'

Henderson's voice shook a little when he asked that. I felt disturbed myself. Bithel seemed glad to leave the more macabre side of the story, for its administrative elements.

'I was sent to London to ask Canon Fenneau what should be done.'

'That's why you came up?'

'I couldn't find Canon Fenneau till this afternoon. He wasn't too keen on being mixed up with it all. In the end he said he'd do what he could to help.'

'And the drawing?'

'Scorp said the first thing was for all Lord Widmerpool's things to be ritually burned. There wasn't much. You know there was hardly anything, Barnabas, except the picture you told me to try to get hold of, if ever Scorp, in one of his destructive moods, insisted on throwing it out. You said it was between the cupboard and the wall, bring it along, if you've half a chance. It looks like a rough scribble to me, but I'm sure it's the one you said. I hope it's the right picture, and you'll make me a nice bakshee for bringing it along. I got it off the fire without Scorp seeing, just as he was going to set everything alight with the ritual torch. I stuffed it away somewhere, and here it is. God, I'm tired. Bloody well done in. I haven't had any sleep since they got back at five this morning.'

Henderson snatched the parcel, and began to open it. Bithel lay still further back in the pop-art armchair. He closed his eyes. Henderson threw away the brown paper. He held the Modigliani drawing up in front of him. The glass of the frame was cracked in several places; the elongated nude no worse than a little crumpled. It had been executed with a few strokes running diagonally across the paper. The marvellous economy of line would help in making it hard to identify—if anybody bothered—as more than a Modigliani drawing of its own particular period. It was signed. In any case, no one was likely to worry. It had hung in Stringham's London flat in early days; then passed to Stringham's niece, Pamela Flitton; on Pamela's demise, to her husband, Widmerpool. Pictures had never been Widmerpool's strong point. For some reason he must have clung on to this one. It was odd that he had never sold it. Henderson, even at the period of his renunciation of such vanities as art, must have marked it down, as it lay about somewhere in the commune. Now the agent, even at secondhand, of its preservation, he deserved his prize. Bithel gave a terrible groan in his sleep.

He had begun to slip from the exotically shaped armchair; would soon reach the floor.

'I shall have to be going.'

'I'll come and let you out.'

'What will you do about Bithel?'

'I'll ring up Chuck. He'll lend a hand. Chuck won't be too pleased. He doesn't like Bith. This has happened before. We put him on the late train.'

'You'll send him back?'

'Of course. Where else can he go? He'll be all right.'

'Will Fenneau do the clearing up down there?'

'Everything he can. He's very good about that sort of thing. He understands. Now I know about it, I'll get in touch with him too.'

We said goodbye. Henderson was right about the temperature dropping. It was getting dark outside, and much colder. A snowflake fell. At first that seemed a chance descent. Now others followed in a leisurely way. The men taking up the road in front of the gallery were preparing to knock off work. Some of them were gathering round their fire-bucket.

The smell from my bonfire, its smoke perhaps fusing with one of the quarry's metallic odours drifting down through the silvery fog, now brought back that of the workmen's bucket of glowing coke, burning outside their shelter. For some reason one of Robert Burton's torrential passages from *The Anatomy of Melancholy* came to mind:

'I hear new news every day, and those ordinary rumours of war, plagues, fires, inundations, thefts, murders, massacres, meteors, comets, spectrums, prodigies, apparitions, of towns taken, cities besieged, in *France, Germany, Turkey, Persia, Poland, &c.*, daily musters and preparations, and suchlike, which these tempestuous times afford, battles fought, so many men slain, monomachies, shipwrecks, piracies, and sea-fights, peace, leagues, stratagems, and fresh alarms. A vast confusion of vows, wishes, actions, edicts, petitions, lawsuits, pleas, laws, proclamations, complaints, grievances, are daily brought to our ears. New books every day, pamphlets, currantoes, stories, whole catalogues of volumes of all sorts, new paradoxes, opinions, schisms, heresies, controversies in philosophy, religion, &c. Now come tidings of weddings, maskings, mummeries, entertainments, jubilees, embassies, tilts and tournaments, trophies, triumphs, revels, sports, plays: then again, as in a new shifted scene, treasons, cheating tricks, robberies, enormous villainies in all kinds, funerals, burials, deaths of Princes, new discoveries, expeditions; now comical then tragical matters. Today we hear of new Lords and officers created, to-morrow of some great men deposed, and then again of fresh honours conferred; one is let loose, another imprisoned, one purchaseth, another breaketh; he thrives, his neighbour turns bankrupt; now plenty, then again dearth and famine; one runs, another rides, wrangles, laughs, weeps, &c.'

The thudding sound from the quarry had declined now to no more than a gentle reverberation, infinitely remote. It ceased altogether at the long drawn wail of a hooter—the distant pounding of centaurs' hoofs dying away, as the last note of their conch trumpeted out over hyperborean seas. Even the formal measure of the Seasons seemed suspended in the wintry silence.